ON THE BRINK OF TEARS

FIFTH BOOK IN THE BRIGANDSHAW CHRONICLES

PETER RIMMER

ABOUT PETER RIMMER

Peter Rimmer was born in London, England, and grew up in the south of the city where he went to school. After the Second World War, and aged eighteen, he joined the Royal Air Force, reaching the rank of Pilot Officer before he was nineteen. At the end of his National Service, he sailed for Africa to grow tobacco in what was then Rhodesia, now Zimbabwe.

The years went by and Peter found himself in Johannesburg where he established an insurance brokering company. Over 2% of the companies listed on the Johannesburg Stock Exchange were clients of Rimmer Associates. He opened branches in the United States of America, Australia and Hong Kong and travelled extensively between them.

Having lived a reclusive life on his beloved smallholding in Knysna, South Africa, for over 25 years, Peter passed away in July 2018. He has left an enormous legacy of unpublished work for his family to release over the coming years, and not only them but also his readers from around the world will sorely miss him. Peter Rimmer was 81 years old.

ALSO BY PETER RIMMER

∾

STANDALONE NOVELS

All Our Yesterdays

Cry of the Fish Eagle

Just the Memory of Love

Vultures in the Wind

∾

NOVELLA

Second Beach

∾

THE ASIAN SAGAS

Bend with the Wind (Book 1)

Each to His Own (Book 2)

∾

THE BRIGANDSHAW CHRONICLES

(*The Rise and Fall of the Anglo Saxon Empire*)

Echoes from the Past (Book 1)

Elephant Walk (Book 2)

Mad Dogs and Englishmen (Book 3)

To the Manor Born (Book 4)

On the Brink of Tears (Book 5)

Treason If You Lose (Book 6)

Horns of Dilemma (Book 7)

First published in Great Britain in May 2019 by

KAMBA PUBLISHING, United Kingdom

10 9 8 7 6 5 4 3 2 1

PART 1

HOPE SPRINGS ETERNAL — FEBRUARY TO NOVEMBER 1931

1

*D*e Wet Cronjé died of malaria in February 1931, thirty-two lunar months after the crash that had broken his back, paralysing him from the neck down. Finally, Harry Brigandshaw was free to look for a way home.

As captain of the seaplane, he had done his duty. Alone, thin and sick at the age of forty-four, he was going to get to London and England, out of the Belgian Congo forest.

'The Lord,' Harry told himself after burying the flight engineer, 'helps those that help themselves.' He still had a gun and ammunition. After thirty lunar months that Harry had counted out, Iggy Bowes-Lyon and Fred Dwyer, the civil engineer, were dead or they would have come back with enough equipment to transport de Wet Cronjé out of the bush.

THEY HAD FLOWN out of Khartoum on their way down Africa in the seaplane. The port engine had overheated, making Harry land on Lake Victoria close to the shore. The local tribesmen had run away. It was still the dry season.

Two days later de Wet had the engine stripped, repaired and running smoothly. Harry took off across the calm water of the lake. An hour later, the engine overheated bringing them down again. With the malfunctioning engine feathered, Harry had taxied into the shore. Again, the locals ran back into the forest.

With rain clouds building, de Wet stripped and repaired the engine. When they took off and climbed to five thousand feet, Harry could see the cyclone over the lake. Turning the seaplane, Harry flew away from the bad weather deeper into the Belgian Congo, looking for a river.

Both engines were performing normally. Iggy Bowes-Lyon, Harry's co-pilot, had found a river on the map. Ten minutes later, they sighted it, the rain driving hard into the safety glass of the closed cockpit.

The river was wide with enough room between the branches of the tall trees to land the seaplane, but it wound through dense forest. It took Harry half an hour to find a stretch long and straight enough to land. But by now they had lost all sense of direction, with the rain lashing and the light dimming as black clouds filled the sky.

"You can take her down here, Harry," said Iggy Bowes-Lyon, pointing.

"Everyone take their seats. I don't have time to do this twice."

The seaplane came down in a perfect landing, kissing the smooth surface of the river, the floats sending volumes of water out behind its tail. The tall trees to either side kept the wind off the surface. Harry relaxed as the aircraft settled onto the water.

The hippopotamus came up in front of the starboard float, snapping the struts to the starboard wing and pulling it down into the water at forty miles an hour, sending the seaplane straight at the shore.

De Wet Cronjé was still standing up, the impact twisting him violently into the seat he should have been strapped into, breaking a vertebra in his spine.

The safety glass of the cockpit two feet in front of Harry slammed into the boughs of the trees that came down to the water, cushioning the impact. At rest, nothing happened other than the rain. There was silence.

"Everyone okay?"

"I've buggered up my back. I can't move... Where are we?... Shit it hurts."

HAVING BUILT a portable boat from the hull of the aircraft, Iggy and Fred went for help two months after the crash and their first contact with Tutsi tribesmen. The boat was big enough for two men, powered by paddles and light enough to porter around the rapids. There were parts of the river that ran under the trees. Quite impenetrable.

In the months of nursing de Wet, Harry had picked up enough Tutsi to make himself understood. A mile from the river, the Tutsis had cut themselves a clearing in the forest for their village. The villagers had found the crashed aircraft when they came to fish in the river.

The tribesmen had helped carry de Wet to their village in Hutu country. It was built like a fortress with a high log fence round the huts. There were no guns in the village. The tribesmen had never even heard of white men. It took Harry a week to realise the Tutsis thought they were gods. In sign language, Harry had explained how they fell out of the sky.

They were fed and given a hut of their own next to the local priest. Every day the priest threw the bones in front of the four white men, grinning at them toothlessly. The priest was an old man, the oldest black man Harry had ever seen.

When Iggy and Fred left, they went at night. The priest found out in the morning and flew into a rage.

When the Hutu attacked the village at the end of the year that was 1930, Harry had fired his gun in self-defence, the first time the Tutsis had heard a gun. The attack came in the night from all sides. Harry ran round the perimeter of the stockade firing into the forest. The Hutu ran away.

The priest smiled at Harry with deep understanding, now certain Harry was the Great River God, fallen from the sky.

By then Harry was certain Iggy Bowes-Lyon and Fred Dwyer had perished. They knew where the seaplane had crashed. With the on-board compass and the sextant, Harry had pinpointed the crash on the map. They were two hundred miles by air from the shore of Lake Victoria. The river ran into the lake.

Harry Brigandshaw knew every man had his price. The price for the village headman was guns. Ever since Harry had fired indiscriminately into the forest giving the impression of many guns, the village had been left alone by the Hutu.

"I need six men to build rafts as we make our way down the river. We will walk round obstacles cutting a path through the forest. At each part of the journey, we will make a new raft until we reach the big lake where I will make contact with my people. Your man will bring back guns like this one on the backs of horses. Many guns. You will become a powerful king, and you will rid your country of Hutu. Only when I give your men the guns will they let me go. Until then I will remain your prisoner."

Deep in the eyes of the village headman Harry saw the sickening mix of power, greed and lust.

The next day, over two years after he crashed into the forest, Harry Brigandshaw began the long journey home to his family in Rhodesia. The bribe had worked. The priest was told by the headman to mind his own business; the guns were more powerful than the priest.

Harry's price was selling his soul to the devil. He was running guns to save his life. Once more in his life he was going to be instrumental in killing other people. For Harry, wherever he was, it always came to war.

SIX MONTHS later the SS *Corfe Castle* put into the port of Dar es Salaam in British East Africa. Before the war that had ended with the Treaty of Versailles, with unobtainable restitution imposed by the French on the losing Germans, the port and surrounding country inland had belonged to Germany.

The captain of the ship went ashore, the smell of cloves still rich in his nostrils, the wind blowing south from the spice island of Zanzibar. The *Corfe Castle* was part cargo with two hundred passengers on their way round Africa from the Cape of Good Hope. After Dar es Salaam the ship would call at Mombasa in Kenya and Aden before steaming slowly up the Suez Canal into the Mediterranean.

The holds were already open with cranes pulling cargo from the depths of the ship, a task that would take two days while the passengers enjoyed themselves ashore. Dar es Salaam was an old Arab port from far back before the colonisation of Africa by the Europeans and a favourite of Captain Cyrus Craig. He had handed the ship over to the duty officer so he could enjoy some spare time on his own looking over the ancient Arab forts and byzantine buildings.

"Good morning, Cyrus, you look chirpy."

The voice was quite familiar. The face looking at him from the end of the gangway was not. The man had grey hair down to his shoulders, pulled back from his face by a red band an inch in width round his forehead. He was as thin as a rake, with yellow skin and eyes full of mirth. To Cyrus Craig, the man seemed to be thoroughly enjoying himself.

"I've been waiting a month in Dar," said the familiar voice that broke into a hearty laugh as Cyrus took the last step onto the dock.

"If you don't remember, I own that ship you just stepped off. Fact is, I gave you your job. If I look that bad it's not surprising. Three months getting down the bloody river. A month at the river mouth in a Tutsi village waiting for a stray dhow to sail in and take me across the lake to Mwanza and the railhead where I bought some guns for my friends. Before that a prisoner with a paralysed flight engineer, the headman not willing to let us go. They called us the River Gods, falling out of the sky... And I am not dead. Iggy and Fred probably, my co-pilot and the civil engineer, who tried to get out of the village to find help. Couldn't move de Wet, poor sod, died of malaria six months ago... So here I am. Fred Dwyer was going to build a dam across the Mazowe River to irrigate five thousand acres of orange trees next to my farm."

"*Harry?*"

"That's better. However, I hope you can take me to a hotel and buy me lunch after a few civilised drinks. The chief in Mwanza took my cheque for the guns after the British Resident signed the back of it for me. Nice chap. Said the photograph on my passport which I salvaged from the crash looked nothing like me. He was in the trenches near my squadron during the war. After I described a few things, including the insignia of my Royal Flying Corps squadron and my own aircraft in particular, we got drunk together for me to try and kill some of the bugs. Flew over his trench every morning for three months on dawn patrol before he was wounded and sent back to blighty. It's a long story. I don't think he believed a bloody word but he was lonely. Cashed a cheque for me to get on the train and buy food in Dar while I waited for the two-monthly roundtrip of one of my ships. Slept on the beach."

"You don't own the *Corfe Castle*, Harry. Don't own Colonial Shipping. The government with the help of Percy Grainger sold your shares to pay death duty when the court pronounced you dead after you were missing for two years. They took everything."

"What's Percy got to do with it?"

"He now controls Colonial Shipping. While you were missing, the stock markets crashed. We're in a terrible depression that many think will lead us into another war with Germany. For the purposes of death duty, so the story goes, they valued your shares when you went missing, selling them two years later for less than half that price. Grainger made an offer to buy your Colonial Shipping stock at a higher price than quoted on the stock exchange, enough for your estate to pay the government what it was owed in death duty. Since then the stocks have again dropped in half so Grainger and his syndicate aren't laughing. He even offered the captains some of the shares, which a few of them bought, more to keep their jobs than anything... Are you all right, Harry? Of course I will still buy you lunch. We're old friends. I'll give you passage to England even if the purser, who's a skinflint, makes you share my cabin... Why are you laughing hysterically?"

"'Cause I'm not dead. The government will have to give me back my money. Percy will have to give me back my shares at the current price. I'll still have the company and a piss-pot full of money. The captains can keep their shares till they go up again."

"The rest are going to lose half their investment."

Only then did Harry stop laughing.

"Where are my wife and children?"

"In Rhodesia on Elephant Walk. You never registered the farm in your name when your father died. The government took everything you owned in England but couldn't take the farm."

"What's my house in Berkeley Square now worth?"

"About half what the new man paid for it."

"Being dead gets better and better... So no one else heard a word?"

"Nothing until now."

"The Tutsi must have killed Iggy, or the canoe we made turned over. The bloody river was infested with crocodiles... We were in the RFC together. One of the best friends a man ever had. His cousin is married to the Duke of York. If anything happened to the Prince of Wales and King George, York would be King of England... Poor Iggy. All that way through the war to die going down a bloody river in the middle of the African bush. I know if he got through, he would have come back with another aircraft to lift de Wet out of the forest. De Wet was Iggy Bowes-Lyon's ground engineer at the beginning of the war before they joined my squadron. There were a lot of South Africans fighting for the British during the war. Like us Rhodesians. Even some of the Afrikaners fought for the British despite what we did to their women and children in the concentration camps... Don't let me get going on that subject, Cyrus... Come along now, we're going for lunch. Some hotel with good food that doesn't have a dress code at lunchtime or they won't let me in."

VIVIAN MAKEPEACE and Thornton Holmes were having lunch when Cyrus Craig and Harry Brigandshaw walked into the dining room of the Zanzibar Hotel. Colonel Makepeace was the Controller of British East

Africa, the Governor's administrator of the territory that stretched as far north as Uganda. Kenya to the northeast was a colony with its own administration.

District Commissioner Holmes was in charge of the Tanganyika Territory. The two were equal in rank by the rules of the British Colonial Service. Both had been in South House together at Cranleigh, a boarding school in the Surrey countryside. The public schools bred what was considered the right kind of man to administer the empire safely and had done so for centuries.

The two men had first become friends at the age of fifteen when they played rugby for the Colts, the school under-16 side. Later they had gone on to play cricket and rugby for the school. Playing for the school at Cranleigh was just as important as passing any examinations and more difficult, or so it was said in the school of empire.

Vivian saw Harry first, and put down his knife and fork.

"That's the chap I was talking about." Thornton turned in his chair to look in the same direction as his friend. "White man sleeping rough on the beach is a disgrace. We had an askari look at him from a distance. The chap was sleeping under palm fronds. Built the shelter himself, according to the askari, said it kept out the rain. Man couldn't make out what he was, skin the colour of putty. I mean we couldn't really have a white man lying on the beach. Bad show, that kind of thing. Had him followed into town. Bought food with money he'd probably stolen. Funny thing, when he spoke they said he sounded like us so I went to have a look for myself. Didn't get close, of course, the chap stank. Do you know, that chap over there almost had an English public school accent! I was in the bazaar looking to mind my own business but I heard him speaking to the shopkeeper in English. There was a nasal twang in his speech that certainly wasn't British. South African, maybe. Man shouldn't be allowed in a hotel like this. I'll call the manager and have him thrown out. Who's he lunching with?"

"They're having a jolly good time, Viv. Friends, I'd say. Old friends. The other chap looks all right... Waiter! Please call the manager of the hotel to my table. I want a word with him."

They both watched the black waiter go off on his errand.

"Do you know, I rather think I can smell him from here," said Colonel Makepeace.

"Don't be silly. Burns wouldn't allow that," said the District

Commissioner, looking at the unkempt man whose blue eyes fixed on him in return and refused to let go. Thornton was the first to look away.

"That's no bum, old chap. Gave me a look just then. The type that doesn't lose a challenge. Looked straight into me. That chap's used to people doing what he tells them. Gave me the bloody shivers... Here comes Burns."

"Burns," said Vivian Makepeace. "Who's that bum having lunch in your restaurant?"

"Captain Craig won't say other than the man is his guest."

"Who is Captain Craig?"

"Captain of the SS *Corfe Castle* that came into port today. Half my guests to lunch are off his ship. The captain likes oriental food. Recommends the Zanzibar to his passengers whenever his ship comes into port."

"Find out, Burns... Be a good chap."

"Yes, sir."

Colonel Vivian Makepeace went back to eating his lunch, satisfied the man with the shoulder-length hair wearing shorts would be thrown into the street. A ship's captain was one thing; the Controller of British East Africa was quite another kettle of fish. He went on eating, smiling to himself.

Feeling someone standing at his shoulder, the Controller looked up expecting to see Burns and hear his apology for letting the man into the dining room. The man with the long white hair down to his shoulders was looking at him pleasantly. His eyes were bursting with humour, as if he were enjoying a private joke with himself.

"It would please me, sir, if you would not divulge my name before I personally reach England. Your man in Mwanza kindly cashed me a cheque on the same understanding. We were in France together. I flew over his forward trench every morning, weather permitting. Very good man. Didn't believe a word of my story but neither will you... Do I have your word as a gentleman? Captain Craig is an old friend. Fact is, I gave him his present job... Your word, sir, we were lunching without fuss. You are the one making something out of nothing."

Vivian Makepeace got up, staring at Harry Brigandshaw with his mouth open.

"You are dead, sir."

"What Cyrus said... Now do I have your word?"

"Of course... What happened?... We were looking..."

"Ask your man in Mwanza in six weeks' time when I've had a chance to sort out the mess. Colonel Makepeace, Mr Holmes, a very good day to you both. The food is excellent. Something I have not shared in almost three years. The Tutsi are fine fellows but their food is lousy, to my palate... Not a word. I will consider it a favour if you do not so much as mention my name. One day I will return the favour to both of you... Gentlemen, good day."

Harry went back to finish his lunch, not even bothering to look back.

"Fact is, Cyrus, I'm rather enjoying myself. Let's have another bottle of wine... Do I really look that bad?"

AFTER WASHING his hair in the bath, dinner in the captain's cabin and a good night's sleep without having to keep one eye open, Harry looked better to himself in the mirror although he did not feel much better inside. His body was full of parasites. His stomach tumbled every time he had food. He was tired most of the day, nauseous half of the time.

Lucky not to go down with the malaria that had killed de Wet Cronjé, Harry knew he had contracted bilharzia. The disease had started in ancient Egypt with the Pharaohs. Archaeologists had found the destruction caused by the parasite in ancient Egyptian mummies.

Living in freshwater snails, the parasite had spread down the Nile into the Great Lakes and rivers as far as Rhodesia. If left, it ate away the liver, slowly killing a man in twenty years.

Harry's first stop in London would be the Hospital for Tropical Diseases in Bloomsbury. It was not Harry's first dose of bilharzia, which could be caught simply by putting a hand in contaminated water in the shallows of most African rivers; the parasite entered the body through the pores of the skin quite unbeknown to the victim at the time.

Harry knew it was why he felt and looked awful, why his skin had turned yellow. Had his condition been yellow fever he knew he would have been dead.

Even had he not known Tina was on Elephant Walk with his children, he would have gone back to London first to have his body checked out. There were probably diseases in the Congo even London did not know about.

THREE MONTHS before de Wet died they had run out of quinine. Their mosquito nets had fallen apart, rotting in the tropical heat, and the aircraft medical chest was exhausted. For both of them it had then been just a matter of time. The Tutsi had built up immunity to the bilharzia disease over their evolution, like the modern Egyptians who lived on the banks of the Nile. Each race had survived in its own environment where others would have died.

It seemed to Harry that mixing civilisations caused more problems than each absorbing the other's culture, as the Red Indians had found in North America where the common European flu had wiped out most of them. Harry had been saying for years that guns and the Christian Church alone would not conquer Africa the way the civilised world seemed to wish.

One day Africa would take its revenge, spreading sickness across the world; man tampered with his own natural evolution at his peril.

"You'll survive this time," he told the image of himself in the mirror. "Just." He was looking forward to the day he felt well again. The way he had before his aeroplane crashed into the jungle those long three years back in his memory.

BY THE TIME the ship sailed the following day with all the passengers back on board, Harry and Cyrus Craig had agreed on their story. Harry could not hide out in the captain's cabin even had he wished to do so. The stewards would have seen him. As in any small community, the story of a strange man in the captain's cabin would have spread round the ship, to crew and passengers alike.

Better to sit at the captain's table in the first class dining room and face the other passengers with a smile and a good story. A story that began to go wrong from the first night out of Dar es Salaam.

The idea was for Harry to be a big game hunter in the mould of his father, so no one would catch him out. Along with Frederick Courtney Selous and Tinus Oosthuizen, Sebastian Brigandshaw had roamed the bush along the banks of the Zambezi River, shooting elephants for their tusks long before the territory became Rhodesia and a British Crown Colony.

Harry's story was his father's story set in Tanganyika. He was now going home on long leave for the first time in years, a white man who had lived under the African sun for most of his life making him look the way he was.

At the captain's table, Harry was ready to tell a host of good hunting stories to keep the passengers amused. Even if one of them asked any questions about the colour of his skin, the truth of bilharzia would suffice.

HARRY HAD TAKEN his mother's maiden name for the voyage back to England. An Indian tailor in Dar es Salaam had run him up evening clothes in twenty-four hours with Cyrus Craig's money. Harry had filled a cabin trunk with all the trappings of a first class passenger travelling on an English boat.

"We have a new passenger at our table, ladies and gentlemen. An old friend of mine, the celebrated hunter Harry Manderville."

The captain went round his table naming the other nine passengers one by one. It was their first night at sea out of Dar es Salaam. A woman in her seventies looked up from her soup, putting down the spoon with a studied deliberation before staring straight at Harry with a look that turned from interest to amazement.

"Manderville... Did you say Manderville? I knew a Sir Henry Manderville when I was a gal. Went out to Africa. No idea where. There was a scandal with his daughter... No relation, I suppose. We grew up very close to each other. Don't his wife's family own this ship, the Brigandshaws? There was a Harry Brigandshaw who disappeared some years ago. All over the papers. Dead as mutton by now, I'm sure. I wonder what happened to Sir Henry? He was a baronet, very old title. You look like him, Mr Manderville. You must be a relation."

"I have no idea, Lady Gascoigne," said Harry, smiling at the lady opposite to him at the table and thinking looks passed down a family could sometimes be a pain in the neck.

THE WORLD, he told Cyrus Craig when they were alone, was indeed a small place.

"Who is Sir Henry Manderville?" asked Cyrus Craig.

"My grandfather. The old bag probably knows more about my family than I do."

"Bluff it out, Harry. Bluff it out. Some voyages are destined to be boring. This shall not be one of them... Is your bank account still open in London, or should I hold your cheque for the clothes until you regain the right to spend your own money? How strange to be so rich and not be able to spend a penny. You do have relatives in England, in London?"

"Not that I talk to or even know. Granny Brigandshaw died a few years ago. My grandmother Manderville died giving birth to my mother. My sister Madge and her children live on Elephant Walk. As does my mother and the now well-known Sir Henry Manderville, Bart.

"After my grandmother died he never married again. My guess is Lady Gascoigne had her maiden's eye on grandfather. By then that side of my family was broke. Just the old house mortgaged to the hilt. The rich usually marry the rich. She was rich, he was poor. Makes sense.

"Grandfather Brigandshaw, the Pirate, is well known to you, Cyrus. He founded this shipping line and bought Sir Henry's family house for a large unwarranted sum in exchange for his eldest son marrying my mother. Trouble was she was pregnant with me and my father was the youngest son. They ran away eventually to Africa, my mother and father. I'm a bastard, Cyrus. So is Madge. Mother had been forced to marry my uncle. In the eyes of the law I was legitimate, born to my mother when she was married to my uncle.

"Grandfather Brigandshaw wanted to buy himself a title and start a dynasty of his own at Hastings Court, grandfather Manderville's ancestral home, passing the title down through the eldest son. Which brings us back to the old bag at the table... You want another Scotch? I've never travelled in the captain's suite before. Always the owner's suite, which I did away with to make room for more passengers when my ships were always full. What are we now? Half full by the look of it."

"Including the cargo. Break even. Gets worse you'll have to mothball some of the fleet."

"Should have stayed with the Tutsi. Not a bad life until the Hutu attack. Those two tribes really hate each other. I heard a saying once when I was young: there's no pleasure without pain. The pleasure is drinking your whisky. The pain will be saving grandfather's shipping line if this depression carries on... We were going to have the first airline down Africa. The excuse for flying my ill-fated trip with Iggy. We wanted to build a flying boat. We had tried the seaplanes, which failed commercially. There were too many things missing, like a wireless that would always be in range. Room for enough passengers. Friendly natives on the lakes where we would land to refuel. One day we'll fly from England to Africa. Now I am even more determined. I still can't believe

Iggy is dead... We were trying to find any way to make the flying boats work commercially. Iggy was the head of my airline."

"How are you feeling, Harry? You look terrible."

"The bugs like Scotch. Thought it would drown them. No such luck."

"You know you have another child. It was in the papers. The newspapers made a fortune out of your story. The RAF sent a search party. A chap called Howland went looking on horseback, the modern Stanley looking for the modern Livingstone. All splashed in the papers. Some said the papers increased their circulation by ten per cent... The boy was named Kim."

Harry was smiling to himself. They had made up after the birth of Frank, fathered by Barnaby St Clair, a few months before his plane crashlanded on the river.

"She'll like that. I'm happy for her. Did you know I sired our first son Anthony on this boat? It was the SS *Corfe Castle*'s maiden voyage. Tina was travelling out to her brother alone; we had known each other in London. She was Barnaby's girl though he wouldn't marry her, the silly idiot. Lucinda was dead, Barnaby's sister. Strange how Frank is part of my first wife. Lucinda was pregnant with our first child when Fishy Braithwaite shot her. Maybe Frank was meant to have her blood but not mine. He'll never know, of course, we all agreed... Kim, I like the name... Let's drink to Kim Brigandshaw, my youngest son."

"Not for me another drink. I'm the ship's captain."

"Pardon me!... Just a sip."

"Just a sip. Just don't tell the owners."

"Not a word shall pass my lips... To Kim."

"To your son, Harry... It's good to have you back with us."

"Oh, you mean the depression," said Harry, trying to cover up the choke in Cyrus Craig's voice.

"That as well. A company is only as good as the man at the top, especially in adversity. From what I hear, the Germans are building a new fleet. And a new air force."

"Then we'll have to shoot it down again, Captain Craig... Funny, you don't drink hard liquor for years and you get pissed as a fart."

"Blame it on the bugs."

"Those are the little sods I'm after... Thank you, Cyrus. For everything."

2

_____

Three weeks later, when the SS *Corfe Castle* was steaming out of Alexandria Bay into the Mediterranean with Harry Brigandshaw feeling as sick as a dog, Zachariah Aird, the general manager of Cox and King's Bank in the West End of London, was facing a dilemma with his chief clerk.

"Dead men don't write cheques," said Zachariah Aird. "Someone has found his cheque book and forged his signature."

"Look on the back, sir."

"The same someone could know my name."

"We have this second cheque, sir. This one made out to a man that the Tanganyika Bank in Dar es Salaam, to whom the cheque was presented, states is the British Resident in Mwanza. The same signature is on the back of the first cheque under the note to you, sir. Why would a dead man write a cheque to Salaam Gunsmiths in Mwanza, which I looked up with some effort, and found on the shores of Lake Victoria? Who, may I ask, sir, knows you personally in Mwanza? The note on the back is clearly written, 'Please cash this Zach. I'll sort it out later'."

With arms folded in front of him, the chief clerk smugly watched the general manager confront the puzzle, knowing the decision to honour the cheque was now out of his hands.

"Doesn't his brother-in-law bank with us? They were both in the services. Why they started banking with us in the first place when we were paymasters for the army and the Royal Flying Corps. The first Mrs Brigandshaw was St Clair's sister. I'll give him a ring. Meantime, pay the Tanganyika Bank in Dar es Salaam even though Brigandshaw's account was closed a year ago when the court pronounced him dead."

"Whose account shall I debit, sir?" The chief clerk was now enjoying himself.

"Mine for the time being. Goodness gracious, Jones, he was one of our biggest clients."

"But he's dead. And as you said, sir, dead men don't write out cheques."

BARNABY ST CLAIR was bored as usual having nothing to do. Once in a while, he sold the stock market short when the markets bounced. In the old days before the crash, he bought shares on good information which he gleaned on his social round of London, the process that made his considerable fortune taking up much of his time.

At the age of thirty-four, he was bored stiff sitting in his Piccadilly townhouse gazing through the window at Green Park where the leaves were falling, adding to his mood of depression. So far as he could see he had done everything he wanted to do in life too early. The years beckoned with boredom.

Whatever he wanted he bought, and this included people. The wrong kind of women hung on his words because he was rich. The right kind of women wished to marry him, which was even more boring. He had a son in Frank so his biological needs were fulfilled without all the problems of being a father to his son.

The boy was living happily in Rhodesia with his mother, thinking he was Frank Brigandshaw. He had little brothers and a sister to keep him happy as a lark. They even had a family of tame giraffe, something Barnaby was sure every small boy would kill for.

When the telephone rang he let his man Edward do the answering. There was no one he wished to speak to so there was no point getting out of the chair to answer the phone himself. Outside in the park it had begun to rain. Racking his brain, Barnaby tried to think of something to do for the rest of the day which did not include making himself drunk.

"Mr Aird for you, sir."

"What the hell does he want?"

"He didn't say."

"Tell him I'm not here."

For Barnaby, having a conversation with his bank manager was the last idea in the world to spark his excitement.

"Says he wants you to verify a cheque signed by Mr Harry Brigandshaw."

"Harry's dead. Tell him to go to hell."

"Mr Aird says the cheque was dated last month and presented in a place I am unable to pronounce. He asks you to come to his office as a particular favour. He says you were Mr Brigandshaw's brother-in-law."

"Tell him I'm coming. Then order me a taxi."

There was something to do after all... As Barnaby walked into the rain he was grinning his head off.

HAVING VERIFIED Harry's handwriting in Aird's office, Barnaby called on the shipping lines. There was a railway line from Mwanza to Dar es Salaam. Excited for the first time in months, he demanded to see the passenger lists of every vessel out of Dar es Salaam, in particular the names of passengers embarking at the East African port. Most shipping lines wired their London head office of new passengers and cargo picked up *en route* to be certain payment was made correctly. Harry himself had told Barnaby of the practice.

Chuckling at the prospect of other people's pain when Harry rose from the dead, the last call he made was to Colonial Shipping. A sweet girl's voice eventually told him what he wanted to hear.

"You old fox, Harry. Someone has tipped you off. H Manderville. My oh my. On your own ship that was... Of course... The captain. You would know the captains personally..."

"Lady," said Barnaby, putting the mouthpiece where the girl could again hear what he was saying, "when does the SS *Corfe Castle* dock in London?"

"Tilbury Dock on Wednesday in the morning, sir."

BY THE TIME Barnaby St Clair had worked out his one-time brother-in-law was on his way back to England assuming his grandfather's surname, Harry was in the sickbay of the SS *Corfe Castle* being watched over by a concerned ship's doctor.

The problem for Harry was far more than the bilharzia parasite slowly eating his liver... And the doctor had no idea what it was. Harry found the irony at the end of his three-year ordeal amusing. The young doctor had dosed him with quinine and given him three injections of penicillin, but nothing had brought down his temperature of 103. Quite lucid and aware of his predicament, Harry managed a smile.

"I'm a bit run down. Haven't had a proper meal for three years. They live on a type of cornmeal most of the time. They try to catch animals but the animals live high in the canopy out of their reach. They didn't have the right equipment to fish. It was the purest form of hunting and gathering with animals on equal terms competing all the way, something our ancestors developed from thousands of years ago when we lived in caves."

"Where have you been, Mr Manderville? The captain said you were a big game hunter."

"With a tribe of Tutsi. Three years. Deep in the jungle northwest of Lake Victoria. The village was surrounded by thick forest and periodically raided by the Hutu."

"But you are a hunter."

"I was all right. Ammunition was low. Kept the cartridges for the Hutu. We couldn't take much on the plane."

"What plane?"

"I'm raving, don't take any notice. In London they'll find out what's wrong with me. You're doing the best you can, Doctor Nash. Can't expect a man to do more than that."

BY THE TIME the Wednesday came, they carried Harry off the ship at Tilbury Dock on a stretcher, Cyrus Craig leading the way to the waiting ambulance. By then Harry was delirious and unable to recognise Barnaby who had waited all morning for the ship to dock.

They all got in the ambulance that drove to Bloomsbury and the Hospital for Tropical Diseases, where Barnaby signed Harry in. The young ship's doctor who had gone as far as the ambulance reported a temperature of 104. Looking at the delirious man on the stretcher, Barnaby knew he would not have recognised the man without knowing who he was.

"Thank you, Mr Craig. You'll want to go back to your ship. Does anyone else on board know who he is? Harry has a lot to unravel. People to confront. A good lawyer. Once the government has your money it's not that easy to get it back again. When you get a moment phone me at this number and tell me what you know... Where are the others?"

"One died of malaria, the aircraft engineer. The others went for help and never came back. He lived with a local tribe as a prisoner."

WITHIN TEN MINUTES, the blood tests were being sent to the laboratory for analysis. The laboratory assistant found amoebic dysentery in the blood. Now knowing what to look for, the doctor found blood in the patient's stool. Harry had a potentially lethal disease.

Patiently, carefully, the hospital set about bringing Harry back to good health.

For the first time in three years, Harry Brigandshaw found himself in the right place at the right time, blissfully unaware of his luck.

DOCTOR ANDREW NASH had watched the ambulance go off with his patient until it was out of sight around the corner of a long shed before turning back to his ship and climbing up the gangplank. There was a lot more going on than met his eye. He had never heard of a ship's captain going off with a sick passenger, however important the man.

Captain Craig and the big game hunter had to be friends. Very good friends. The other man who seemed to be waiting for them at the dockside had fallen into the crisis as if both he and the captain knew what was at stake. Big game hunters, so far as Andrew Nash knew, did not ply their trade from aeroplanes, or live with tribes who hunted meat and picked their food from the forest. There was something wrong with the story of patient H Manderville.

Packing his small suitcase to go on two weeks' leave before his ship sailed again for Africa, he found himself thinking about the nature of the man's true identity. It was then that the chance of making some extra money first came to his mind.

As usual, he would give his mother most of his pay, which would leave him broke. His mother had used every penny of his late father's legacy to put him through medical school. Andrew's salary kept up the small house in Wimbledon, opposite the common. He had six bottles of good Cape wine in the case, wine he had bought cheap in Cape Town, which he would enjoy with his mother who spent each of his long voyages waiting for him to come home.

What she would do if he met a nice girl and decided to get married Andrew had no idea. For five years, since his father had died of cancer after a four-year illness, Andrew's mother had barely been out of the house except to go to the shops, wallowing in her own self-pity. What he needed was money to take her up to the West End and the theatre to prise her out of her self-imposed rut.

"Oh my goodness," he said aloud to the cabin with its roof just high enough not to bump his head.

The scene at the ambulance began to run through his mind. The other man called him Harry. "How's Harry?" the man had said to Captain Craig as Andrew Nash helped put the stretcher into the ambulance.

The story had broken in the *Daily Mail*, that much he clearly remembered. Everyone at the hospital was talking about the famous fighter pilot who had disappeared on his way down Africa flying a seaplane designed to land on the big lakes and rivers of the continent.

Searching his memory for the story he had intermittently read in the papers, Andrew worked out that the man had disappeared with his crew three years ago, the same time his patient said he'd lived with a tribe of black people. Covered it up by saying he was rambling. The other man had asked Captain Craig what happened to the others.

The patient he had just kept alive was not H Manderville but H Brigandshaw, the owner of the shipping line, pronounced dead by a London court after a two-year waiting period, finally closing out all the hullabaloo in the papers.

Half running down the gangplank leaving the suitcase behind, Andrew found himself a telephone kiosk in the docks. All fingers and thumbs, he found the number of the *Daily Mail* in the phone book and dialled it, pressing button B when told by the operator to dislodge the coins he had slotted into the metal box beside the telephone.

"The *Daily Mail*, can I help you?" came a distant voice down the line.

"Put me through to the reporter on the Harry Brigandshaw story. The one about Africa. Stanley looking for Doctor Livingstone three years ago, if you remember?"

"Hold on."

Andrew Nash had to wait less than a minute before a male voice came on the line.

"Horatio Wakefield. What do you know about Harry Brigandshaw?"

"Do you pay for a story?"

"Of course."

"How much will you pay me if I tell you where to find Harry Brigandshaw?"

"He's dead, sir."

"My name is Doctor Andrew Nash. A medical doctor. I have just put my patient in an ambulance."

"Please, old chap, I'm busy."

"I am now certain my patient was Harry Brigandshaw whose aircraft went down in Africa three years ago."

"Where are you?"

"At Tilbury Docks."

"Don't bloody move, Doctor Nash. Fifty quid. How does that sound?"

"Just fine. My mother will be so pleased."

"What's your mother got to do with it... Which ship?"

"The SS *Corfe Castle*."

"Now that makes sense, so you're not talking shit. The shipping line once owned by Harry Brigandshaw before it was sold after his death owns the SS *Corfe Castle*. So you are the SS *Corfe Castle*'s ship's doctor?"

PUTTING DOWN THE PHONE, Horatio Wakefield could not believe his luck. The biggest story of his life was back on track. He had liked being the pin-up boy of the *Daily Mail*. He had also liked Mrs Brigandshaw, a good-looking woman much younger than her husband with a body Horatio could still see in his mind.

He had put the poor girl through hell with his story, chasing it right to the end. His reports in the paper had sent the Royal Air Force searching the path flown by the ill-fated plane, keeping up Mrs Brigandshaw's hopes.

More than once, she had slammed the front door of her townhouse in his face; a big four-storey townhouse in Berkeley Square where she lived with servants and a pack of kids all under ten who, though Horatio tried hard to keep the story afloat for as long as possible, would never see their father again.

THE UNMAPPED JUNGLE in the heart of Africa was vast. The only reason for the first search party was public relations. Both dead pilots of the ill-fated seaplane had fought with the Royal Flying Corps during the war.

Harry Brigandshaw had shot down twenty-three enemy aircraft and been decorated by the King.

The second search party under Keppel Howland that went out on the ground by horseback had been financed by an American newspaper with the same motive as himself: the circulation of a newspaper.

Now Saturday's edition of the *Daily Mail* blazing the headline under his byline would sell out across London.

FAME WAS AGAIN BECKONING Horatio Wakefield as he fell into the taxi. This time he was going to write a book. To hell with Keppel Howland and his lost cause. His cause was no longer lost. He had found him. The man was alive. The story he was about to hear of the man who had disappeared in darkest Africa for three years was going to be far bigger than the story of Stanley finding Livingstone, or Howland's modern version.

The ramifications went tumbling through his mind: an uncompromising government forcing the estate to pay an exorbitant amount of death duty that, when paid, wiped out the deceased's estate, beggaring the widow and children of a war hero, a country's memory so quickly lost.

A rapacious manager of the shipping line forcing the estate to sell him the shipping line to pay the government's bill, 'we all have to pay our tax' an excuse for extortion.

The widow and her children fleeing to sanctuary in the colonies. Afterwards no one giving a damn.

As THE TAXI flew through the streets of London, the stories flooded through his mind, whole, ready to print.

"Fifty quid for you, Doctor Nash, if it's true. If Brigandshaw is alive," he mused.

Leaning forward and opening the partition between himself and the taxi driver he was more excited than he'd been in a long time.

"That's him," he pointed, "the lone young man on the dockside. Here's a quid."

"Thanks, guv."

"Just wait."

As he got out of the taxi and walked to the man, it began to spit with rain. Neither of them seemed to notice.

"Doctor Nash?" The man nodded. "Where is he?"

"Bloomsbury. Hospital for Tropical Diseases. The captain and another man took him through in an ambulance five hours ago. My goodness you were quick."

"Fleet Street isn't that far away... What's wrong with him?"

"We don't know."

"How sick is he?"

"Very."

"Can he talk?"

"He couldn't when I helped put him in the ambulance."

"Tell me what you know."

With Horatio Wakefield taking notes in shorthand, the taxi driver steered the cab out of the docks. No one took any notice of them speeding parallel with the wet rails of the railway line that ran the length of Tilbury Dock.

LYING IN BED, Harry Brigandshaw wondered if he was going to leave the hospital alive. Everything ached. His head was splitting. His bowels were red hot. Every bone in his body ached at touching the bedclothes. Sweat was pouring out of him. Nothing worked normally except his brain, which registered every movement of the pain as it coursed through his body.

Cyrus Craig and Barnaby St Clair had left half an hour ago. By then he was wide awake.

"The last thing I want is a couple of idiots staring at me. You've got a ship to run, Cyrus, off you go. Barnaby, thanks for the bridging finance. They know what's wrong with me, so you say, time will tell. If I could stop my brain I could get some sleep."

The hospital was quiet; with so many things to undo, Harry willed his body to get better. Someone had said to him life was mind over matter. Strangely, he was not even frightened of death. Like during the war when aerial combat commenced, he cleared his brain to crystal clarity.

WHEN HORATIO WAKEFIELD was shown into his private ward, there was a faint smile on his face. Harry knew the best mental strength a man could play on was revenge.

"Are you Harry Brigandshaw?"

"Who the hell are you?"

"Wakefield. *Daily Mail*. I ran your story that forced the RAF to go and have a look. What was your mother's maiden name?"

"Manderville. Now piss off."

"Her name?"

"Emily."

"What is your degree?"

"Geology."

"Which you never practised."

"Yes I did. Once. In South West Africa when I found diamonds on the Skeleton Coast. Not like the pipe stones washed ashore. If you go to my farm in Rhodesia, you'll find what looks like a chunk of quartz embedded in the mantelpiece over the fire in the lounge that no one but me knows about. An insurance for the future of my family. The stone is a fifty carat diamond, safe as the Bank of England."

"Welcome back, Mr Brigandshaw."

"When I get out of here, we'll talk. You can help me."

"They said you couldn't speak in the ambulance."

"I was thinking about my family, or dreaming. They must have given me shots."

"She's very beautiful. Your company tried to roll her over."

"If you have something in life, something of value, there are always people trying to take it away from you. That is a fact of life that will never change. No one cares a damn about poor people however much they say to the contrary... Leave your card on the bedside table. When I'm up I'll call you."

"I'm going to report you alive in my paper."

"I'm sure you are. Didn't I just say everything was about money?"

"What's wrong with you?"

"Amoebic dysentery, bilharzia, among others. They are still doing tests. Ask them. You are from the press. Why should they lie? Barnaby St Clair's footing the bill so the longer they keep me alive, the more money they make."

"You've become a cynic, Mr Brigandshaw."

"A realist, Mr Wakefield... How was Tina?"

"As good as any woman with five kids and no husband. You don't know they sold your estate to pay death duty. She's in Rhodesia. You have another son. She called him Kim."

"Did anyone try and help her?"

"Not a soul, in London."

"Not even Barnaby St Clair?"

"Not that I heard."

"They didn't get back together? They were lovers before I married Tina. My first wife was his sister. I rather hoped he would have taken up with her again. In the first few months, I was jealous of the idea. When Iggy didn't come back and de Wet was still alive, I thought the idea was a good one. All women need a man. All men need a good woman."

WHEN THE REPORTER left the hospital having agreed not to say where the man actually was, to give Harry Brigandshaw time to recover his strength to be able to fight to regain what was his, Horatio was amazed by people. There was the man who had fathered Harry Brigandshaw's fourth child paying for his hospital bed.

From the man's look when he spoke of Barnaby St Clair, the two of them were friends. Underneath the façade of social rightness, they shared the same woman. Harry knew Frank was not his son, a fact which Horatio had established three years earlier. Harry Brigandshaw had accepted his wife's infidelity.

No, he told himself, people never failed to amaze him. There was always the tide of true emotion flowing beneath the surface designed to confuse the issue. All the habits of man's self-styled civilisation were only skin deep, a way to get through life without tearing each other to pieces, physically and emotionally.

By the time he reached his rundown flat that evening, having promised Doctor Andrew Nash fifty pounds from his paper, his flatmate William Smythe was already home and Andrew Nash, who had waited downstairs at the hospital so as not to seem a Judas Iscariot to the sick Harry Brigandshaw, was presumably back at his ship.

Horatio had walked a mile back towards Fleet Street in the rain before flagging down an empty taxi. All the way while plodding through the wet from the hospital he had contemplated the vagaries of life, oblivious to his physical discomfort... By the beginning of November the rain was cold, an east wind blowing down the empty road as dusk folded into night. The airman had seemed disoriented when he left, making Horatio question in his mind how long he had to live.

"Poor Tina Brigandshaw," he said, opening the door to his small flat. He knew that once it was in the paper, she would hear soon enough. To have her happiness soar to the heavens, or crash if he died.

"Harry Brigandshaw's alive, William. Just spoke to him. Remember the pilot lost in darkest Africa three years ago?"

"You've got to be kidding... Are we going to the club Saturday?"

"Why not? It's cheap and full of warm bodies. This flat is freezing."

WILLIAM SMYTHE WAS twenty-eight years old, the same age as his friend Horatio Wakefield. When he worked for the *Manchester Guardian* before losing his money, he told the girls he was the paper's political correspondent. It sounded better than plain reporter.

He had found out from an early age women liked more than the look of a man, especially if they were going to bed with him.

Despite Kidderminster Grammar, three years at left-leaning Manchester University after his brief stint at the *Mail* with Horatio as a cub reporter, joining the British Communist Party, then the British Labour Party in his third year, even despite all his espoused philosophy of socialism, William knew in his true heart that the biggest aphrodisiac for women was money.

When the stock market crashed he owed the bank twelve thousand pounds, backed by fifteen thousand pounds' worth of shares as espoused by Jack Shephard, the financial analyst at his own paper. William sold his proud portfolio three days too late for less than he paid for them.

Were it not for Horatio giving him a home when they fired him from the *Guardian*, he would have been out in a very cold street, not even the Communist Party wanting him back again now he couldn't pay his dues.

He had, as he realised, made a second mistake. He had blamed Jack Shephard and, by implication, his own paper in an unpublished article he submitted to his editor.

They had waited three months to let him go, using the drop in circulation as a valid excuse. Not for the first time, William Smythe found out telling the truth was not the best story; that one way or the other, whatever financial system was in place, the unsuspecting citizen was going to lose his proverbial shirt, manipulated by the few who knew what they were doing.

Like all the rest that had lost their money in the feeding frenzy of getting rich, there was nothing he could do except look for another job. Fortunately for William, the system could take away his money but not take away his brains. He was still a good writer. Educated. His brain was clear. Freelance journalism for some papers was better than paying a salary. From a freelancer they only had to pay for what they printed, saving them money.

By the time Horatio burst into the flat with the story of Harry Brigandshaw's resurrection, William was back into the system, paying off his bank, trying to get back on top before it was all too late. Before he was too old to attract the women to even be interested in him.

For half an hour, William listened to the story of Harry Brigandshaw and Barnaby St Clair, something he had gone through at length when the aircraft went down three years earlier, helping Horatio Wakefield make a name for himself in the newspaper world.

William could also remember Tina Brigandshaw and what she looked like at the opening night of a Christopher Marlowe musical financed by her husband before he disappeared on his flight down Africa. Horatio had written the human side of the story, which centred on the wife who was probably a widow.

They had broken open a bottle of whisky and William had put a match to the fire, the old flat's only redeeming feature. First the kindling wood caught and then the coal. Soon the small room was warm, the curtains drawn against the October wind howling down the street outside, slanting the rain at the windowpanes.

There were two rooms in the flat apart from the small kitchen. William slept on the couch near the fireplace, which he had done since coming down from Manchester after the wreck of his journalistic career, or so it seemed at the time.

What they enjoyed most was their conversations. Sitting around the fire in the winter. Sitting on a park bench in Holland Park in the summer under the lime-green leaves of the elm trees with the birds singing at dusk, away from the traffic noise down the Bayswater Road.

Both of them had read extensively through twenty of their twenty-eight years on every subject under the sun. Delving into new books and newsworthy magazines like good eaters enjoyed their food, always giving the food time to digest afterwards in good conversation. Sometimes colleagues joined their dialogue but mostly it was just them, never arguing, dissecting the facts of life and the troubled progress of the human condition in its brief moment of existence.

"I'm going to press on Saturday," said Horatio, taking a lump of coal out of the coal scuttle and putting it carefully on the fire so as not to douse the flames. "Did you fill the coal scuttle, old chap? All the way up three flights of stairs?... Listen to it... It's a stinker outside. Why is the English climate so utterly appalling?... No wonder Brigandshaw went to live in Africa where the sun shines all the year round."

"No, you are not."

"What am I not, Will?"

"Writing the story."

"*You* don't think it's news?"

"Of course it is, idiot. It's enormous. Why I'm going to write the story... You did say no one at the *Mail* knew where you were going when you went to find your Doctor Nash?"

"I didn't breathe a word. Some other desperate soul would have jumped on the story."

"Exactly. I'm going to offer the resurrection to half a dozen papers and sell it to the highest bidder. I'm a freelancer. You are a hack. However good the story, you won't add one penny to your miserable salary. What was the name of the American paper that sent Keppel Howland out to Africa? It wasn't the *New York Herald* that sent Stanley to look for Doctor Livingstone?... What a headline! 'Doctor Livingstone, I presume.'"

"The *Denver Telegraph*. Editor's a chap called Glen Hamilton. He met Harry Brigandshaw in France during the war when the Americans joined, in 1917."

"Having let the British Empire bleed to death. There's outside influence behind Gandhi which no one admits. Isn't he originally from South Africa? What's he doing stirring anti-British sentiment? The Americans are jealous of us. Always have been. They'll do it again, mark my word. There's going to be another war. This time we'll be on our own."

"Sometimes you talk nonsense, Will. The Americans are our cousins. Our friends."

"Not when it comes to trade. Then no one is a friend. Business is competition. We still make the rules in the empire. The Americans want the empire to fall. They say colonialism is bad. What utter rot, without honest British administration half our colonies will collapse. We are good for world order. Bad for American business. When Germany seeks revenge, the Americans will watch from across the Atlantic while we haemorrhage again."

"What about the French?"

"The French bled to death at Verdun, poor bastards. They're finished as a military power. Strange when you think about it: apart from the last war, we and the Germans were on the same side against the French. Without the Prussians, Wellington would have lost the Battle of Waterloo. You and I would be speaking French instead of my brilliant English... Of course we'll write the Brigandshaw story together. We'll split the fee in half."

"My paper will fire me. They know you live in my flat."

"Not if you offer the story to the *Mail* first. As an exclusive for a week. The lucky chap who shared a flat with the freelance journalist who unearthed Harry Brigandshaw from the dead. The whole idea is absolutely lovely."

"You are still talking rot about the Americans. If they had not come to help us in 1917, we would have lost the war."

"The Americans knew that. What they wanted was a depleted Britain. Not a rampant Germany. They want to take over running the world."

The two men drifted into the comfortable silence of old friends.

WILLIAM SMYTHE CAME from a military family. As far back as they could remember. His father had been the regimental sergeant major of the Lancashire Fusiliers when war broke out. By 1916, he was dead along with the rest of the regular British Army.

It was said in the family that a Smythe ancestor had fought with King Henry at the Battle of Agincourt. Another at Crécy. In America against the Colonial rebellion. At Waterloo with Wellington. At Spion Kop. In 1916, RSM Smythe died standing to attention with his swagger stick in exact place under his left arm, his boots shining, his battledress immaculate. His mouth was open letting out the power of his commands in the face of the German enemy.

Only when the first battle of the Somme was over did the remnants of the regiment find the body of their RSM. Buried him with full military honours, the man's life fulfilled.

By April 1917, William's two older brothers were dead. William's mother walked into the river not far from their home in Nantwich and drowned herself; spring flowers were blooming along the banks. William was still at school. Polly was nineteen, the only girl in the family.

The regiment continued to pay for William's schooling at Kidderminster Grammar. He was a boarder. Later the regiment paid for him to go to Manchester University when the war was finally over. Polly went to America with a GI. She never wrote.

William was proud of his father and brothers. War was part of the family heritage, what they were paid for as soldiers. Dying in battle was the highest honour any of them could find in mortal life. His mother should have understood that before walking into the river feeling sorry for herself. William had shut the memory of his mother right out of his mind.

Through school, he had always been top of his class, as befitted the youngest son of an RSM of a British regiment whose history went back with the Smythes, the Smythes who faced life with squared shoulders and a straight back.

They had lived all over the world, wherever the British stationed a garrison. India, Ceylon, Hong Kong, Nigeria, Borneo, Malta. Of the years when the family were together, only two had been spent in England, home leaves being translated into money to send the boys to England and school. To give them a chance to get on in the world, only the eldest destined for the regular army.

For centuries, the family had been non-commissioned officers. It was William's father's great ambition that his eldest son receive a King's commission, would become an officer and a gentleman. To live in the officers' mess, hobnobbing with the best.

Writing had long been part of William's imagination. He wanted to write down and keep the multitude of flavours he had smelt and tasted as a child. So many strange sights and cultures. So much more than the other boys at school had ever seen.

At Manchester University, instead of taking English as his main subject, a dead-end, he had entered the faculty nearest to what he needed for journalism. PPE they called it: Philosophy, Politics and Economics. A grand grounding, William thought, to pepper the world with his brilliant articles that would change the direction of modern civilisation. Change it to a caring, softer place that better understood the needs of man without so many barked commands.

"I was an idealist until my second year, Horatio. A genuine, one hundred per cent idealist... You'd better put some more coal on the fire...

I soaked up Plato and the words of Socrates. The Romans. The French. The Russians. I read them all. Believed in all their high philosophies of right over wrong, of good over bad. That, as Socrates said, it was always better to do that which was right, not that which was wrong... Back then it was so easy. So obvious. So right... Except, of course, like all the rest of us I did not know the difference between right and wrong. It's all very well wanting to do the right things in life but only if you know what you are doing. When I met Lily Gray, she was the only member of our class who had not joined the Communist Party. She was also the prettiest, with a sex appeal that could break a man's balls..."

"Are you going to be rich, William?" she asked.

"Of course not. I'm going to do good!"

"Then get out of my way. You are a fool, William. I never waste my time on fools. You need money to go through life. Not ideals. You can't eat bright ideas. Communism is just another bright idea dreamed up by a few in search of power to enslave the rest of the people. When they tell you it's for the good of mankind you should know it's for their own good. Plato had his philosopher king who would always know when to do right, which is poppycock except for the king and his sycophants. The power-hungry dreamed up theocracies so the church could rule. Oligarchies for the rich. Aristocracies. And the one I like best, democracies that let every idiot in the country vote for bigger idiots to govern them. Idiots who only have to make promises to get the other idiots to vote for them... Five years later, they all change horses and vote for another pie in the sky. Give me a full-blooded dictator any day. At least you know where you stand. You are either with him or against him."

"So you won't go for a cup of coffee in town?"

"Or anywhere else, William. I only go out with men who want to be rich..."

"So there I was, Horatio. From idealist to my present state of cynic in one brief exchange. The frightening part is, the lady was right. She married a man who went through the war supplying the army with tinned food at inflated prices. Said he had a gammy leg, which kept him from the fighting. Rich as Croesus by the end of the war.

"Now she's fat, going on ugly with five kids. But Lily's laughing. Her husband's rich. Saw her four years ago which set me on the path of buying the shares that crashed all around me. But I understood she was right. A man has to be rich to get through this world. All my father got from the war was his head blown off. Now tell me which of the two was right. If all those Smythes in history had just made money instead of being heroes, I wouldn't be where I am now, owing money I never even spent. But things are now going to change, thanks to the resurrection of Mr Harry Brigandshaw."

"I'm going to get fired. Then we won't have this flat or that bottle of whisky you are clutching... But is Lily happy?"

"Of course she's happy. Her husband is rich. The house is big enough to get away from him when she wants. To get away from screaming kids. She can buy her solitude in the country. He's away half the time. Probably has a mistress. She doesn't care. If she wants a lover, she takes one who's impressed with her wealth. She was only going to be pretty for a short time of her life. She's going to be rich until the day she dies. What she sees in the mirror doesn't matter anymore... Ask your friend Brigandshaw when he's up and well, money counts. He's going to want his money back. You and I are going to write the story and this time get paid... I give you Lily, who taught me more at university in five minutes than the rest of them in three years. She had learnt a lot for a nineteen-year-old."

Horatio gave his friend a queer look before attending to the fire.

They had been born not far from each other, William in Nantwich, Horatio in Chester. The same class. Men of men. Military on the one hand, sailors on the other. That's why Horatio had the name that had plagued him throughout his life, a name that, however hard they tried, no one could make smaller or sound less, as William put it, like a twit... And even the cross given him at his christening was a lie, something Horatio only found out when he went into journalism as a cub reporter with the *Daily Mail*... When he first met William Smythe.

"He fought on the *Victory* at Trafalgar. Only a cabin boy of fourteen. The greatest battle in our naval history."

"Who, Father?"

"The man you are named for. Your ancestor."

"Nelson! We are not related to Lord Nelson, Father. Wish we were. The kids at school wouldn't laugh at my name. Why did you call me Horatio? Jim would have been much better. Like my Uncle Jim."

"Your grandfather, two greats back, was a cabin boy on HMS *Victory*."

His father had said the words with such reverence, Horatio thought his father was going to cry from the thought of such an illustrious ancestor. A man going from admiral to cabin boy didn't seem to matter a bit. From that day on, Horatio looked at his father in a different light.

The first mate of a cargo ship that plied the China route had fallen off his pedestal. Even at the age of ten, Horatio thought there was more to life than being a cabin boy on Nelson's *Victory*. A story that wasn't even the truth. Uncle Jim, drunk, told him the real story in a pub off the Waterloo Bridge many years later, Uncle Jim at the end of shore leave and broke as usual just before going back to sea.

"The old bugger lived to ninety-seven. Kept him in free drinks 'til the week before he died. He was a cabin boy all right. Conscripted off a coal boat that sailed round Wales to and from the Port of Liverpool. He was at the Battle of Trafalgar, that much was fact. On another ship. The Nelson bit came later when he came ashore as tough as old teak, after fifty years at sea. Got to bosun, did great-grandfather. Just don't tell your father. Split my bloody side when he called you Horatio. Now run along with that first pay packet and buy your uncle another drink. How much you've got left?"

"One shilling and eleven pence three farthings."

"Then make it a big one."

"Can I change my name?"

"Not once you're christened. Church of England don't allow that. You're stuck with it, Horatio."

"You sure?... When do you go back to sea?"

"Tomorrow, thank God. Train to Liverpool then off to South America. My money was gone last week."

"Why didn't you marry?"

"Whatever for? Enough trouble finding drinking money without having a wife. Now off you go to the bar. I'm still thirsty. Why didn't you go to sea like the rest of us Wakefields?"

Horatio, on his way to the bar, had chosen to ignore his uncle, the answer was so obvious. He wanted to get on in his life. Like Lily Gray, he said to himself as he thought back on his evening in the pub with Uncle Jim. The old scoundrel now dead at the bottom of the sea in a storm off Argentina. When Horatio had left that pub the last time he saw Uncle Jim he was down to sixpence to last him the rest of the month.

"It was worth it."

"What was?" said William, coming out of his own reverie as he stared at the flickering fire.

"Buying Uncle Jim those drinks. They don't make characters like that nowadays. He worked for months in harsh conditions just to get drunk when he came on shore. Never heard him say a nasty word about anyone in his life. Except about my great-great-grandfather who, as you know, turned out to be something of a fraud."

"He got free drinks. Told a good story. That's not fraud. That's entertainment... Stop hogging the bottle, Horatio. Remember, I'm soon to be rich. Then I will be buying the bottles of whisky."

3

The bidding began the next day much to Horatio's amusement, tinged with fear for his job at the *Daily Mail*.

"The strangest thing, Mr Glass, a friend of mine claims he knows Harry Brigandshaw is alive and back in England. Has talked to him. William Smythe is offering the story to one paper as an exclusive. He's a freelance journalist."

"Don't talk rubbish, Wakefield. If anyone has found a dead man still breathing, it's you. Smythe, remember, worked for me before going all highfalutin' at the *Guardian*. Even Smythe can't bring back the dead."

"Oh, he's alive all right. My friend took me to see him to vouch for the story. He has three independent witnesses. He asked me to ask you as my editor if the *Mail* is still interested in the story. He's over at the *Telegraph* right now. The *Denver Telegraph* is being offered an American exclusive."

"They won't swallow rubbish like this."

"They will, sir. Mr Brigandshaw and the editor of the *Denver Telegraph* met during the war. Brigandshaw has told Smythe a wartime story that involved both men that no one else could possibly have known about. Mr Hamilton is very excited his old friend is still alive."

"How much is he paying?"

"Five hundred dollars at the moment."

"Take me to Brigandshaw."

"He's sick. Wants time to get well. Amoebic dysentery and something called bilharzia he picked up in the Congo when his plane went down and paralysed the flight engineer. Bowes-Lyon and another man left to find help and never came back. When de Wet Cronjé died from malaria, Brigandshaw made his escape from a tribe of Tutsis, bartering his freedom for guns. Smythe's agreement with Brigandshaw is to let him get well before he faces anyone. He wants his money back."

"Is he going to die?"

"There's a chance."

"You are behind this, Wakefield, aren't you? But who gives a damn. What are the *Telegraph* offering?"

"I'll let you know."

"We'll match Hamilton if I find the war story is true when my call gets through to Denver. Not a penny more or you are fired. If any other paper gets the exclusive you are fired."

"You believe me?"

"Some of it, Wakefield. Some of it. Particularly your friend's extortion."

HALF AN HOUR later Horatio was back in the editor's office. The editor looked agitated. By lunchtime, with William Smythe going from newspaper to newspaper, up and down Fleet Street and phoning Horatio the bids, the *Mail* topped the *Times* and secured the exclusive.

By then, the editor was jaded and sweating. Horatio was trying not to smile. The bidding had taken itself to two hundred pounds for five articles. Anything over five was negotiable.

"Mr Smythe wishes to have our cheque, sir."

"It's Mr Smythe now."

"Mr Hamilton has gone to three thousand dollars."

"Where's the first article?"

"In my pocket. My instructions are to give it to you when I have the cheque, which please make out to cash. Bank of England pound notes will also be acceptable."

"You're enjoying this, Wakefield."

"I'm afraid I am, sir. If we go to press now the story will headline the morning edition."

With the dollar at fourteen to the pound, Horatio had never heard of so much money coming his way. When the clerk from the accounts department returned from the bank, Horatio found his hands trembling as he stuffed the notes into his wallet, pushing the overflow into his jacket pocket.

Dutifully he waited for his editor to finish reading the thousand-word article that described Harry Brigandshaw's ordeal when the seaplane lost a float coming down on a hippopotamus in the river, smashing up the aircraft as it veered into the trees. Harry Brigandshaw had given them half an hour at the hospital. He looked terrible. The tests were still going on to find out if anything else was wrong with him.

William Smythe had taken flash photographs of Harry in bed, which were being developed by the *Mail*.

The editor finished reading the typed article and sighed.

"You wrote this, Wakefield, didn't you?"

"Some of it, sir. Just wait till you see the photograph."

"Go away, Wakefield."

THE NEXT MORNING every other newspaper in London said the photograph was a hoax. The *Mail* had hit the newsstands with an early morning edition. The late editions of their competitors called foul. With lank hair all around the pillow, the photograph on the front page of the *Daily Mail* was claimed by old friends not to be that of Harry Brigandshaw... One had gone so far as to swear an affidavit.

Only Percy Grainger, the chairman and controlling shareholder of Colonial Shipping, recognised his worst fears. The eyes with the penetrating stare looking out at him from the paper spread on his desk were the same eyes that had looked deep into his soul before offering him the job of managing director so many years earlier.

Going into a funk, his body began to shake uncontrollably.

When the later papers were brought to him by his secretary in complete silence, quoting the story as a lie, it made no difference. It was only a matter of time before they would ask him for an interview. He had even bought what he thought was a dead man's house in Berkeley Square. A house now worth half of what he had paid when he bought it from the deceased's estate.

At that moment, Percy Grainger knew what it felt like to want to die. Even his arms were too weak to bring his hands up to the latch on the tall sash window to push it open. To make it worse, he was crying silently in self-pity. He could hear them talking outside the door. The door he had locked hoping he had the courage to kill himself.

. . .

THAT NIGHT, while Mrs Grainger was trying to convince her husband he had done nothing wrong – she liked the house in Berkeley Square and everything that went with it – Horatio and William were having a celebration. It was the first time Janet Bray was being entertained in a restaurant by Horatio, her friend Pippa from the Hall making up the foursome at Simpson's in the Strand.

Soon after they sat down a man two tables away put a monocle in his right eye and rudely turned to look at their table. Horatio thought the middle-aged man was looking at William Smythe. He obviously did not like what he saw. Then the man took the monocle from his eye, giving William a final look of dislike. Like someone who had been unfortunate to see something distasteful where it did not belong.

Vaguely, Horatio's instinct from too many years in journalism saw the iris of the man's eyes were distinctly different in colour. The one that had been covered up by the monocle was pitch black, the other sky blue. Horatio thought the stare at William was probably due to William's picture in two of the *Mail's* competitors' late editions. Both papers had found William and interviewed him, taking photographs. Over a photograph of William Smythe, both newspapers had headlined 'The Hoaxer'. When Horatio had pointed out the slur to his reputation as a journalist, William had only smiled.

"I encouraged them. Said only God knew the final truth of life. The one man gave me a knowing look when he took my photograph, as if I was seeking publicity. The reason for the hoax... The moment newspapers start arguing with each other over a story, the readership jumps. Human nature. The public don't like newspapers, so one of them now has to be wrong... It was like leading a lamb to the slaughter, got him hook, line and sinker... You have to think when building a story, Horatio. Sometimes, old friend, you are beautifully naive. Like giving Andrew Nash his fifty pounds, half of which, I might add, was my hard-earned money and belonged to me."

EARLIER IN THE evening Horatio had had a rush of conscience. He had taken the Tube to Wimbledon Station and walked two blocks to the mother's house where Andrew Nash was staying. The look of thankful surprise on the mother's face had been worth every one of the spent pounds.

"So few people are honest, Mr Wakefield. Andrew said you had promised him fifty pounds for your very successful story. It's so wonderful the man is alive after such an ordeal. Andrew wants to take me to the theatre, don't you, darling? Since his father died, we've been rather poor. I was brought up to be married to a good man, not to train for a job like some of the women these days. A woman's true job is to her family. Giving them a good home. Bringing up the children. If you try to do two things in life at the same time, you do two bad jobs. Either have a career or have a family. That was what my mother and father taught me. We were seven children. The happiest of childhoods a girl ever had. It was the war. The war tore us apart literally and now they say there is going to be another one. As if England hasn't suffered enough... You are a good man, Mr Wakefield. I always say the papers are out for themselves but I was wrong. Andrew thought you would forget him once the story was safely in your paper, but you didn't."

"Why is the byline William Smythe?"

"So you could get your fifty pounds, Nash. William is my flatmate. A freelance journalist. A very old friend. My editor would never have forked out fifty pounds, no matter what I said about promises."

"God goes in strange ways," the mother had said, slipping her hand into the crook of her son's elbow and making him turn his face to beam at her.

"Noël Coward is doing a revue at Drury Lane. Mostly his own songs about the empire. We'll go tomorrow if I can get tickets. The *Corfe Castle* sails on Tuesday, earlier than usual. They're trying to turn the ship around faster, to get in an extra voyage as business is so bad. After the show, I'll take mother out to dinner."

GIVING AWAY some of the money Horatio had forced from his editor made him feel less guilty. Like Mrs Nash, he had hoped he had been brought up the right way. There was nothing wrong with sharing the happiness, even tarnished happiness.

When his mind came back to the restaurant and the present, Horatio found William staring at the pretty girl sitting at the table opposite the middle-aged man with the monocle hanging from a cord onto his chest. William was sitting square to the man and must have felt the stare, causing him to turn his head. Horatio was sure staring at a person brought up the eighth instinct.

Nine times out of ten, if he concentrated a stare on the back of a man's head, soon enough the man would turn around. When William had turned round, he must have seen the girl not the man. The girl was exquisite with flawless skin and a soft red blush high up on her cheeks. From years of watching pretty girls, Horatio knew she would be tall and slim if she stood up from the table.

"I know that girl," said Janet Bray, following the direction of the men's looks. "Pippa, isn't that Genevieve from the Hall? The future glamour girl of stage and screen?"

"Must be the dirty old man she says is her father. Yes, that's Genevieve."

Pippa's nose was out of joint, Horatio had noticed. Ever since she and William were introduced, William's eyes kept straying round the room full of well-dressed people. A big story had always made William distracted, as if it were constantly playing in his head looking for angles.

"She says she's nineteen. I think she's younger. Do you know she doesn't have a surname? Just Genevieve."

"Can't she do better than a dirty old man?" It was clear to Horatio Pippa hated to be ignored; the girl was being catty.

Horatio, not wishing to hear the undercurrent going on at the table, now studied the girl. As he would a painting, without lust in his eyes, unconscious of Janet smiling at him as he looked; they were far too comfortable with each other to be jealous.

"It's her father," said Horatio, taking his eyes off the girl.

"How can you tell?" said Pippa. "She's a young girl. He's an old man. Maybe the mother…"

"Look at their eyes," said Horatio, stopping Pippa's one-track mind.

"You're right," said William, laughing. "Both their eyes are of distinctly different colours."

"I suggest you stop staring at the daughter, William, or the father will come over and box your ears."

"He's coming," said Pippa, happily thinking she was about to get her own back as the man put the monocle into his right eye and strode towards their table. In self-defence, Horatio and William stood up as the man reached them.

"You have no right to make a fool out of my brother-in-law's memory."

The tables around them went quiet, watching the drama, everyone trying not to look as if they were enjoying the sudden confrontation in so civilised a place.

"It's a hoax," said a man from the table behind William, suggesting to Horatio their story was causing more havoc than he had hoped.

"Who are you, sir?" said William.

"You are Smythe, a disreputable freelance reporter! I am Merlin St Clair of Purbeck."

"Pleased to meet you, Mr St Clair."

"The Honourable Merlin St Clair. My father is Lord St Clair of Purbeck."

"I'm very pleased to hear it, Mr St Clair."

"What do you have to say for yourself?"

"Only what I say in the paper. May I compliment you on the beauty of your daughter?"

Horatio, watching, almost burst out laughing. The crafty fox that was William Smythe had turned his eyes away from the fuming father to smile at the daughter. The problem as it turned out was not the daughter. The problem was the price of fame. Horatio turned to the man with the monocle and smiled gently. Then he whispered softly into the man's ear so no one else could hear.

Janet, attuned to Horatio's voice, heard the one word, Barnaby. The man's tirade came to an abrupt end as he snapped round and walked back to his daughter at their table. William sat down and started a conversation with Pippa.

As Horatio sank back into his chair to resume eating his supper the tension went out of the room. People picked up on their own conversations. For the moment, the drama of Harry Brigandshaw was over.

"We're going to get a lot more than five articles," he said to his plate.

"I know," said William sweetly. "How's the food, Horatio?"

"Lovely... If Janet doesn't mind me saying so, that girl is utterly beautiful. Not my type, but utterly beautiful. What's she studying at the Hall, Janet? Speech therapy or drama?"

"Drama, darling. That one is headed straight for the stage."

Later in the evening, when the girl got up to dance with her father, Horatio found out he was right. The girl was unusually tall, and slim... As he watched them dance he hoped a daughter of his would one day dance with him and look at him in just such a way. To anyone looking, father and daughter loved each other with the pureness of driven snow.

"If we have a daughter, can we have one who will look at me like that after she's grown up?"

"After all these years are you proposing to me, Horatio?"

"One swallow doesn't make a summer. I'm still a hack reporter on a pittance of a salary. Tonight is a windfall. How's the new practice going? With all the personal drama going around I haven't had the chance to ask."

"Would you like a working wife?"

"Not according to Mrs Nash."

"Who is Mrs Nash?... Did I tell you I have that appointment to Harrow School in writing? They have a whole flock of stutterers to be cured... Who's Barnaby?"

"His brother, the Honourable Barnaby St Clair."

"Why don't you go freelance?"

"Not pushy enough. Anyway, I like a monthly salary, however small... Writers are not meant to make money. It's meant to be a vocation."

"Talk some sense into him, Janet," said William. "My friend has too many morals. Do you know he just gave fifty pounds to Doctor Nash for tipping him off about Harry Brigandshaw?"

"Was Mrs Nash his wife?"

"His mother."

"She sounds a nice woman."

"Doesn't believe in working wives. I'll tell you the whole story later. It's still a sore point with William. Half the fifty quid was his."

When they had finished arguing about the fifty pounds and looked up, Merlin St Clair and Genevieve had gone. For the first time William Smythe asked Pippa for a dance. Janet and Horatio watched them from the table. Under the double damask pure white tablecloth they held each other's hands.

On the dance floor, Pippa was now smiling. The three-piece band was playing a love song from Christopher Marlowe's West End hit musical *Happy Times*. Only then did Horatio remember where he had seen the girl before.

It was at the final night of the show three years ago. As an occasional theatre critic he had been given the *Daily Mail's* invitation to the after-show party. That same night he had picked up on a rumour. Merlin St Clair had never been married to the girl's mother. The mother, according to the rumour, was a barmaid at the Running Horses at Mickleham. Something Horatio was never going to tell William Smythe or he would read the story as part of the Brigandshaw saga in his employer's paper, a family titbit too choice for the public not to want to hear. The very beautiful skeleton in the family closet... The poor girl had a lot ahead of her to learn about life and its penchant for cruelty... Even the best of fatherly love came at a price.

As William sat down after his dance with Pippa, still wearing the earlier smirk, Horatio knew he was going to see more of the tall, slim girl who called herself just Genevieve. The idea made him excited.

WATCHING ALL the interplay had given Janet Bray a sinking feeling, even with the smiling exchanges and holding hands under the table. Girls like Genevieve had the power to turn men's heads. To control them. To make them yearn for something they would never be able to have. Even make fools of themselves trying to be something they were not.

After four years attending the Central School of Speech and Drama at the Royal Albert Hall and in the process of becoming a qualified speech therapist, she had learnt more about life than stutters and cleft palates. She had learnt about people. The inside of people. What went on in their heads.

Janet knew her opinions would likely change over the years. She rather hoped they would. To be too sure of anything at the age of twenty-three was a trap. Especially taking an opinion about minds that could never be seen in daylight. Never exposed. Never comparable to something already known.

Cleft palates were a physical impediment to speech she could see. Stutters, like Genevieve's power over men, were in the mind. Janet had seen a hundred girls in the drama section of her school prettier than Genevieve but without real power over men. Genevieve's power was deep behind the penetrating eyes that sucked sexual want out of men into the light of day where the need was exposed.

To cure a stutter she liked to go behind the voice, to convince the person's mind to tell the tongue to execute its work properly from the tip to the palate. To make words whole and crisply understandable to one single person or an audience in a large auditorium.

In order to cure the stutter she liked to think of it as kidding the mind to behave properly. She had even given it a word, kidology. It had taken just six weeks to send her first patient home without his stutter to his parents' delight and astonishment. The boy's father was a politician. His family had been politicians for three centuries, something the boy would have been unable to be with the impediment of a stutter.

He attended Harrow School, which had brought Janet's name to the notice of the board of governors. Speech therapy was a new vocation for a girl, a new form of therapy for a modernising world of medicine.

At Harrow, with so many pupils, they had found seventeen boys who required her help, putting them all into one class for Janet to attend weekly at the school, to become the only woman on the staff, as far as she knew, at Harrow School.

As THEY ALL went their separate ways that night, Janet to her small flat close to the rooms where she practised her speech therapy, she was not sure whether the thought of Genevieve frightened her more than the seventeen boys she was going to confront on Monday.

It was the first time in two years Horatio had even looked at another woman, let alone with the blood draining out of his face, his eyes seeing something Janet was sure he had never seen before.

When the taxi dropped off Pippa with another mile for her to go to her flat, she began to shiver with fright, the thought of losing Horatio the worst catastrophe in her young life. She had spent so many hours imagining them together with a family. Three children. A small house. Holidays once a year by the sea. Growing old gracefully together in harmony.

Now it was not even the lack of money that stood in the way of her happiness. She felt it in her mind. In her bones. Suddenly her life looked dark. Black. No end to the tunnel she had spent twenty-three years going through, looking for the light.

When she closed her front door on the October night, she knew there was only one answer to her problem. She would give up one of her principles. She would seduce Horatio. Do what he wanted. Take him to bed and hope that sensual love would drive thoughts of the other woman right out of his mind.

THE NEXT DAY, with neither of them aware of Janet Bray's insight, to William Smythe's delight the *Daily Mirror* picked up on the Brigandshaw story. Someone at Simpson's on the Strand had told the paper about the brief contretemps with Merlin St Clair.

"Probably the staff. The patrons would have phoned a better newspaper. Some waiters with long ears have contacts at the tabloids so the plebs can get an insight into the seamy side of the rich."

"You are being a snob, William, but you are probably right. How does a man from Kidderminster Grammar and a socialist university end up with his nose in the air?"

"That girl was quite something."

"Yes she was. You'll find she likes rich men with titles. Her grandfather is a baron."

"There's something fishy there. What's a baron's granddaughter doing on the stage?"

"She hasn't got there yet."

"We'll both go to her first night in the West End. She'll probably go into repertory in the provinces before hitting the big time... Do you know the *Mirror* has more readers than the *Times*? Now we have the brother-in-law quoted as saying I'm a fraud. That Brigandshaw is still dead. Now the game is really on. When you get to work, show Glass the *Mirror* and tell him I need an office. You have to keep on top of these things and I need a phone and secretary. He'll understand. Likely piddling in his pants with excitement."

"My editor does not pee in his pants but I'll ask him... Like old times. Do you want a job?"

"I have one. A well-paid job. After Brigandshaw fades, I'm going to look for high-class scandal. You'll be amazed what a freelancer can do once he has a reputation. I'll set up my own office. When I have enough to do you can join me, but I'm changing your name."

"What to?"

"Jim. You always wanted to be your Uncle Jim."

"Equal partners. Thanks, I'll stick with Horatio."

"I suppose so."

"Just remember who picks up the breaking stories... Did you think Janet was a bit funny at the end of the evening?"

"I was looking at Pippa. On the dance floor she pushed her crotch hard into my loins."

"I thought you were dreaming of Genevieve?"

"Not at all, old boy. First secret of women, always take what's offered. They all look like sisters when you stand on their heads."

"You are vulgar. I'm going to work."

"Don't forget what I said about Glass."

· · ·

THE FIRST CALL Barnaby St Clair made that morning was the easy one. Edward had made him his breakfast while Barnaby built up courage for the second call to Tina Brigandshaw. The telephone exchange put him through to his brother Robert in less than half an hour. The line to his family home in Dorset was surprisingly clear.

With the rain slanting down outside his window, the wind lashing the rapidly defoliating trees in Green Park the other side of Piccadilly, he had somehow expected the line to crackle as the wind whipped all that wire to Purbeck Manor, where Robert and his wife Freya lived with Lord and Lady St Clair.

To stop being questioned by his mother on why he was calling home out of the blue, Barnaby had placed a person to person call with the local telephone exchange. With all the rumours flying around in the press, he did not wish for Tina's mother to read about Harry's return to England in a newspaper.

Barnaby had known Mrs P since he was a boy, as he had her husband, now the stationmaster at Corfe Castle railway station where Pringle had worked all his life just a few miles from Purbeck Manor.

WHEN THE EXCHANGE finally rang back with the call, Robert was on the line wondering what on earth was going on.

As a successful novelist, Robert was suspicious of unexpected phone calls, especially from his brother Barnaby who rarely appeared on the scene without a crisis in hand.

"What's gone wrong this time, Barnaby?" he asked into the mouthpiece of the phone that stood in the hall of the old manor house not far from the big, gothic front door. "It's bloody cold standing in the hall. There's a draught coming at me right under the door. A howling draught, Barnaby."

"Have you read a newspaper for the last few days?"

"I hate newspapers, despite Freya."

"How are Freya and Richard?"

"The boy is fine. Freya is miserable. The opening of her play has been delayed, as you well know. It's the slump."

"There's a depression... We've found Harry."

"How do you mean 'we'? You haven't been to Africa in years. Freya was relying on you, Barnaby. A good opening in the West End will give her a very nice career. You may not think so but women also need something to do other than having babies."

"In London."

"Don't be absurd."

"He's in a Bloomsbury hospital, sick as a dog. It's in all the papers. Only the *Mail* has the right story. Merlin's in the *Mirror* shouting his mouth off, having confronted the journalist in Simpson's last night. Chap called William Smythe."

"What was Merlin doing there?"

"With Genevieve. The *Mirror* printed a picture of Genevieve and Merlin. That paper really is a scandal sheet. Someone had taken a photograph of them while they were on the dance floor looking like lovers. Our niece is not only beautiful but also photogenic. She'll end up in the films."

"Can't you convince Oscar Fleming to put on my wife's play? Most of it is your money on the line. You made enough out of Marlowe's second hit. Please, Barnaby. It's the girl's pride."

"Be patient."

"Have you ever met a patient woman? Now, if you've finished talking rot about Harry and you don't want to put on my wife's play after all, I have work to do. My books are not selling as well as before the crash but they are still selling as I have a publisher. Unlike my poor wife who doesn't have a backer to put on her plays... Now she wants to go back to America and work again for Glen Hamilton at the *Denver Telegraph*."

"Glen is also running the story of Harry coming back from the dead. Ask Freya. She knows Glen would never knowingly print a lie."

"Now I really am cold."

"Shut up and listen. Afterwards I want you to go and see Mrs P at the cottage, before the bloody papers knock on her door."

"Does Tina know?"

"Not yet. Getting a phone call through to Rhodesia is going to take me all day... I've given Harry *Holy Knight* to read when he's well enough. Said he liked your picture on the back of the cover. He brought bugs in his body from Africa even the doctors don't know about."

"What kind of bugs?"

"Just listen."

.   .   .

FOUR HOURS LATER, while Barnaby St Clair was making another call to the telephone exchange to find out what was happening to his call to Rhodesia, not far away at the Department of Inland Revenue, Milton Landan was having a good chuckle with his civil service friends.

"Unbelievable, my boy. Unbelievable... Did you read this, Pimm? What people do in this world to try and make money."

"Don't you read the papers? It's been headline news for days."

"I assessed that estate for payment of death duty. Wasn't my fault they demanded to fix the share price when the plane went down. I thought I was doing them a favour. The market was going up. Not the slightest idea of the crash to come. Now three years later some con-artist says he is Harry Brigandshaw."

"What happens to the money if the man is found alive?"

"He'd get his money back, of course. You can't charge a man death duty when he's still alive. That's the beauty of death duty tax. You can do what you like to a dead man when he can't argue."

"Do you know how much it is?"

"To the penny."

"And interest?"

"If a chap doesn't pay his tax on time and we catch up with him we charge him compound interest and then add a fine. This has never happened before. He'd get compound interest I suppose but we don't get a fine."

"Did a smart thing going dead for three years. With the stock markets still on the way down, he'll be worth far more now than if the courts hadn't pronounced him dead. You must have taxed the estate for more than the assets would now be worth and he still gets three years' interest."

"They've still got to prove the right man is still alive, Pimm. What do the other papers say?"

"That it's a hoax, even his brother-in-law. There's a picture of the brother-in-law's so-called daughter that made me drool. Now there's a girl to meet. My wife looks like a sack of potatoes. With everything going down, the budget is going to be terribly short this year. What happens if the government can't borrow more money?"

"We're off the gold standard. They print it... Where was the picture of the brother-in-law's daughter? If it was his daughter of course. Rich men keep together so the chap's likely rich. Lucky bloke. Wish I could keep a mistress the age of my daughter... If Brigandshaw is alive, I wonder what he'll do with that chap at Colonial Shipping who had the bright idea to ask us to fix the share price at the time of the plane crash? Wouldn't like to be in his boots when his old boss comes back from the dead and asks him what the bloody hell he was doing. I wouldn't like to be in his shoes, oh no... I never thought I'd say it, Pimm, but you and I are lucky to have passed the civil service exams when we did and work for the government. At least we have a job."

"You may not have if you give Brigandshaw back his money."

"That's not my problem. That's the law. Anyway, it's all a question of whether he's alive. A man like that with so much money wouldn't want to hide himself away for three years. Why on earth would he do that?"

"Maybe you'll find out. He'll have to come and see you. Then you will be a celebrity if you let the papers know what's going on. You'll be the talk of the town. Never does a career any harm being talked about when you are in the right."

"Do you know, sometimes I like you, Pimm."

WHEN MILTON LANDAN went home that night still convinced the *Daily Mail* had started a hoax, Barnaby St Clair was putting down his telephone having spoken to the supervisor. There were only three lines to Rhodesia through Cape Town, but it appeared that was not his only problem.

In the farming areas outside Salisbury, the farmers shared a party line, which had a small handle next to the phone set fixed to a wall inside the house. Each of them had a combination of rings different to their neighbours. The original idea to save money was to let the farmer only answer his own rings when set off by the Post Office. After the call, a single long ring told the other farmers on the party line the call was finished and the line was clear.

The idea had been that of a man not thinking properly at the time: bored wives stuck out in the bush could chat to their neighbours three miles away without moving out of the farmhouse or paying the Post Office a penny. Frustrated operators broke into these hen parties asking the women to put down their phones when an outside call was on its way.

The trouble for Barnaby was, by the time Salisbury had connected to Cape Town, another pair of bored women were on the party line chatting away.

"How do you ever get a call to the right person?" he had asked the supervisor.

"Patience, sir. Patience. At least those people far away in Africa can talk to you in England."

"Keep trying."

"We will, sir... Now, what was that number again?"

ROBERT WAS NOW on his way up to London to see Harry, bringing Freya and leaving Richard with his grandmother. Barnaby smiled at the thought of his mother having her grandson all to herself. She and Mrs Mason, the old cook at the Manor, would be having the time of their lives.

Freya coming to London had more to do with her play than visiting Harry in hospital. That much Barnaby knew about playwrights. If he had his own way, the show would go on even if the small audiences made the play run at a loss.

Earlier Barnaby had received a lecture from Oscar Fleming on people and the theatre.

Only Christopher Marlowe's show was making any money, a whimsical musical that took people's minds off their problems. A straight-shooting play on the stupidity of war was not what the public wanted on its mind, however brilliant the writing or the story.

After the Great War, the crash in the stock market and the worldwide depression, London audiences wanted cheering up, according to Oscar Fleming. Plays with a strong message went down better with affluent audiences who were better equipped to enjoy and smile at other people's affliction.

When Freya arrived, Barnaby was going to suggest his new sister-in-law write something fantastical. In his own mind what he thought of as a nice mindless piece where no one in the audience was required to think, a pleasant message for raw nerves.

As usual when Barnaby thought back on the conversation, Oscar Fleming was right. The real art was not theatre but making money.

"Never tell an audience what they don't want to hear, Barnaby. Never tell anybody for that matter, certainly not if you want to make money or a friend. And never ever overrate the cerebral capacity of the human mind unless it reflects well on themselves. It doesn't matter if they don't have a clue what you are talking about if you convince them first only a clever person like themselves would understand. Then they feel superior. A truly good play has a splendid, easy to understand story, like *Romeo and Juliet*, and slips the knife into the audience with the truth without them knowing. Making them think and understand later when they get home."

WHEN THE CALL was finally picked up on Elephant Walk in the hottest month of their year, the old Mrs Brigandshaw, Harry's mother, answered. By then the other wives of the white men in Africa had gone to bed, their phones at last on the hooks, their tongues relaxed in sleep.

"Harry's alive, Mrs Brigandshaw," said Barnaby, all the way from London clear as a bell.

PART 2

ONE MAN'S FISH IS ANOTHER MAN'S
POISON — NOVEMBER 1931

1

There were five houses on the family compound on Elephant Walk. Tina Brigandshaw and her five children were asleep in the newly renovated house that had been built by Martinus Oosthuizen back before the British raised the Union Jack at Fort Salisbury and declared the land of the Shona a British colony. Then, he and Sebastian Brigandshaw, Harry Brigandshaw's father, owned the property they loosely called a farm.

The old house had fallen derelict from lack of attention for many years and again after Barend, the son, had died instead of Harry Brigandshaw. Barend was the dead father of Martinus junior, named for his grandfather hanged by the British in the Anglo-Boer War for going out with his fellow Boers.

By the time the phone call came through in the middle of the night, Martinus junior, or plain Tinus as he preferred to be called, Harry's nephew (Madge, his sister, had married Barend despite her being British) was away at school at the Diocesan College in Cape Town known to the boys and masters as Bishops. Paula and Doris, the sisters of Tinus, were also away at boarding school.

Tina, fast asleep, failed to wake up to the two long and one short ring that said the incoming call was for her. Neither Sir Henry Manderville in his one-bedroom house on the compound, Ralph Madgwick in the manager's house, or the children's nurses, Molly and

Ivy in the rondavel, had heard the call, their brains attuned to wake only to their own call rings, each having one of the thirty-six houses that made up the party line Barnaby had been battling to break into all day.

The dogs had heard and were wide awake. A lion roared. Emily, Harry Brigandshaw's mother, now trying to wake up properly, could hear splashes from the direction of the river down below the houses.

In the old days, at the time of the Shona rebellion, Tinus senior and Sebastian had built a stockade around the houses in case they were attacked, something the rebels of the first Chimurenga knew to be inadvisable as such white hunters had shot their way through elephant halfway up Africa, collecting the ivory and shipping it back to England.

For years there had been peace and tranquillity in the self-governing colony of Southern Rhodesia. The stockade had now been taken down, letting the lawns sweep through the msasa trees to the river at the bottom of the long slope.

Emily Brigandshaw, Sebastian's widow and daughter of Sir Henry Manderville, had not been sleeping well for years, dozing only on and off through the heat of the African nights, listening for long hours to the wild animals and the night birds that called to each other in the dark. Emily was not sure if the lion or the ringing phone had woken her from her dreams. Lying awake in the house she now only shared with Madge in the term-time, she had waited for Tina to pick up the phone. Only when the exchange rang for the third time did she pick it up. In the night, in the dark, her dreams more relevant than reality, she had no idea who was speaking on the other end of the line. She was getting old and tired and no longer very interested in what was going on in her life where nothing seemed to matter anymore. With Harry dead, she had given up worrying about her children.

"Please, I'm sorry, who is that? Would you start all over again? I only got out of bed to go and answer the phone."

When Emily shouted for Madge asleep in her bedroom next door, the dogs began to bark, making the lion give out a full-blooded roar from the river where it had gone to drink. The family compound came alive, making the dogs in the nearby native compound bark in reply. Emily now realised there was more than a lion drinking at the river. Wild animals were crashing away into the bush, setting off the alarm calls from a flock of guinea fowl.

After Tina finally picked up her phone and spoke to Barnaby a voice from the exchange said the six minutes were up. By then they all understood. Harry Brigandshaw was alive.

PRINCESS, Tembo's seventeen-year-old fourth wife, had no idea what the fuss was all about. If the man had been dead and was now alive, he had not been dead in the first place. The people who had died in her father's village had never come out of the ground however many dreams people had in their sleep.

Ever since Tembo had paid her father twenty cows, he had talked about the owner of Elephant Walk he saw nearly every night in his dreams. So far as Princess was concerned, old people were stupid. They imagined the ancestors telling them all sorts of silly things. Tembo had ranted on about a great sea of water with Harry Brigandshaw far away on the other side no one could see, living with an old wizened man who threw the bones.

Like so many old people who told her the same old story time and time again, she had stopped listening. If she had ever seen Harry Brigandshaw, it might have been different. Now it was plain boring. Worst of all she was being ignored; the girl whose father had received more cows as *lobola* than any other father in the history of her village. Such an expensive bride who was pregnant, unlike the first wife who was too old, deserved the undivided attention of a man ten years older than her father.

Sulking as she looked at her husband playing the drums in the middle of the night, she had a good mind to go back to her village and tell her father to give back the cows. Her father, like all other men up to that moment in her life, did whatever she wanted.

Next to her husband, with another drum tucked in between his knees, was Chirow, the man on the farm who built all the funny brick buildings. Both of them were beating the drums in perfect rhythm, each melding their sound into the other. Chirow was looking her way as he drummed in a trance, the light from the nearby fire playing in the whites of his eyes. Her husband's eyes were glazed over from the power of the rhythm. Two of Tembo's wives were shuffling barefoot in the red dust, swaying to the beat of the drums. The rhythmic sound swept far out into the heat of the night.

For the first time Chirow ignored her look of invitation. The situation was out of hand. In a circle round the dancers and the drums the men were drinking bottles of the white man's beer sent down from the big house with the news this Harry Brigandshaw was still alive. For Princess, it was a terrible feeling. For the first time in her life, she was powerless over men. In the blink of an eye, she was just like the other three old wives. Silently, Princess, with the big child in her belly, began to cry.

LATER THAT DAY, when Tina was packing up the children to go to England, sixteen hundred miles away in Cape Town young Tinus was lounging under the oaks with his best friend Andre Cloete. Their cricket match had taken place earlier that day against Rondebosch High. Bishops had won by two wickets with Tinus batting through their innings scoring forty-six runs, his best opening score for Bishops that season. Andre had gone on to take three wickets. For five minutes the two friends had been diminishing their achievements with practised downplay, both silently bursting with pride for what they had done on the pitch. In case they spooked their chances, neither mentioned their burning hope to play for the senior eleven in the following season.

Tinus was going on fifteen, a year younger than his friend and the youngest player in the under-16 side. Tinus had two secret hopes in his life: to fly an aeroplane, and play cricket first for Rhodesia and then for South Africa; the international side fielded by South Africa to play England included players from Rhodesia. In the winter, Tinus had played rugby with a similar but not quite equal passion. The whole game of cricket appealed to his English heritage, from Granny Ford to his mother. Cricket to Tinus Oosthuizen was a game for gentlemen, something Tinus wished to be most of all in his life. After Bishops, he was going up to Oxford, to New College where his Uncle Harry had studied geology. With the same geology degree and hopefully a blue at cricket, Tinus was going to join Anglo-American and rise to the top of Africa's largest mining house. He was going to live in Johannesburg with a summerhouse in the Cape. At the age of fourteen Tinus had fired a clean arrow into the future of his life. He knew where he was going, the life he had in his mind one long beautiful summer.

Both boys were deliberately ignoring Tomkins Minor walking towards them across the well-cut grass of the school lawn. The boy with the round glasses halfway down his nose was holding a book in one hand, what looked to Tinus like a newspaper in the other. Tomkins Minor never played sport and always came top of the class, the same class attended by Tinus who had tried unsuccessfully for two years to beat him.

"Spiffing show, Oosthuizen," Tomkins Minor said, pushing his glasses back up the bridge of his nose.

"Did you watch?" asked Tinus, hoping the other boy had seen him bat.

"Of course not. Just heard the score. I hate any form of exercise, even watching it. Wasn't that flying type who disappeared three years ago your uncle? They've found him according to the London *Daily Mail*. It's all in the *Cape Times*, including a photograph of Brigandshaw lying in hospital. The other British papers say it's a hoax to boost their circulation. Have a look. The photograph isn't very good but if he is your uncle you should know... Here, have a look for yourself. I thought you would have heard all about it by now... Twenty-three kills in the war, I'm impressed. You can keep the paper, I've read it right through. You'll probably want to look at the sports page after you've read about your uncle... Spiffing show, both of you. See you in class on Monday, Oosthuizen. I'm off to read Plato."

Grabbing the newspaper out of the boy's hand, Tinus looked at the front-page photograph and promptly began to feel sick, forgetting where he was. The face with the sunken cheeks surrounded by long hair on the pillow was not that of Uncle Harry.

Embarrassed, Andre had turned away. Thankfully, Tomkins Minor had his back to them. Andre had never before seen his friend blubbing, not even after the housemaster had beaten Tinus with a cane for smoking behind the lats. That day, Tinus had come jauntily out of the housemaster's study with a sore bottom and a big grin on his face.

Realising what he was doing, Tinus took out his big handkerchief, wiped his eyes and blew hard on his nose.

"Sorry, Andre. After my father was shot dead standing next to him at the railway station, Uncle Harry was like a father. Some said my father stood in front deliberately. That Braithwaite was aiming at Uncle Harry. My father and Uncle Harry were like brothers. For a moment I had some hope, but look at the photograph. This man looks seventy."

"People look older when they've been sick. Have another look. If you ask me those eyes have the steady look of a fighter pilot. Why would they put it in the paper if it wasn't true? They'd just make fools of themselves. I'll leave you to read the paper, Tinus. To be alone. Why don't you try and phone your farm in Rhodesia?"

"It's a party line. You can never get through."

"You can try."

For the first time in their friendship, Andre put an arm round his friend's shoulder. Then he walked towards the school buildings a hundred yards behind Tomkins Minor. Suddenly his three wickets were not so important for Andre Cloete. Tinus watched them go before reading the paper.

And there it was. The great lake, the largest of them all, Lake Victoria. Tembo's dream playing out in the story as Tinus read. The plane going down in a storm. Blown off course from the route they had searched on horseback. The river feeding Lake Victoria, the Great Lake impossible to see across, had harboured the man the paper claimed was Harry Brigandshaw. All those long weeks in the heat and rain with Keppel Howland, Ralph Madgwick and Tembo had almost not been in vain.

Tembo's dream was right. The ancestors' message was right. The search party had not gone far enough, if what he read was true and not, as some in England claimed, a newspaper hoax.

Looking again at the photograph, Tinus tried his best. The eyes, yes, the eyes did stare at him. But so did the man on page three. However much he wanted to believe, he was still not sure. He wanted it so much he still had to see with his own eyes to truly know his Uncle Harry was back from the dead. That the magical life he pictured for himself would really come true. Could people be that cruel to make money out of a newspaper article, he asked himself.

As he rose to follow the path of Andre across the school lawn, tears pricked the back of his eyes.

2

When William Smythe came down from his flat on the Monday morning, Bruno Kannberg of the *Mirror* was waiting with his camera. The fog was swirling in Notting Hill Gate, the street grey, colourless, the leaves of autumn from the plane trees that flanked the side road long swept away. Even the pigeons were silent on the rooftops, their small heads sunk into their grey chests. Bruno had never met the man he had been following for three days, only knowing his quarry from a photograph shown to him by the editor of his paper who had told him to follow the man to Harry Brigandshaw just in case the story of the dead man rising was true.

"If you find him, Kannberg, get an interview or another job."

"But you said he was dead. The *Daily Mail*'s story a hoax."

"Nothing like building up reader interest. Find him. Even the *Daily Mail* doesn't print such a lie and expect to get away with it."

"Why should the man be in London?"

"He's sick. If Smythe goes anywhere near the Tropical Diseases Hospital, we've got him."

"Have you asked the hospital, sir?"

"Don't be so naive."

With the fog swirling it was not the best day to sleuth. With Smythe was a shorter man wearing glasses. The man with the glasses had come back the previous night with a woman. The woman had furtively come out into the dank street ten minutes earlier before being swallowed up in the fog. Bruno had been twenty yards from the girl in a doorway. When she passed, she was smiling to herself, making Bruno jealous of the shorter man with the glasses. The girl's face looked like the face of the cat that had swallowed the cream. Both men as they passed him deep in his doorway were older than himself. Men of the world he would expect to find with women leaving their flats early in the morning. At twenty-three, Bruno hoped one day a girl would leave his room early in the morning with the fog swirling down the street to stop the landlady seeing what was going on.

"If I find girls in your room after eight o'clock at night, you are out."

Mrs Portman, his landlady, was an aristocrat fallen on hard times. Rumour had it her maternal grandfather was an Earl. Now she lived in the basement at the bottom of the house in Holland Park and rented out the rooms above to young men.

Whenever Bruno saw Mrs Portman, she was wearing red rubber gloves that came halfway to her elbows. She was either washing up or peeling potatoes when he paid his three shillings every week for the room at the top of three flights of stairs that creaked loud enough to bring the old woman out of her basement with her hands on her hips if she heard shenanigans in the early hours of the night. Theodore Wells, the out of work actor who shared the top floor and the cupboard of a bathroom, had had to use all his charm not to be thrown out on the street. Especially having not paid his rent for six weeks... Mrs Portman was full of contradictions.

With the idea of illicit sex foremost in his mind, Bruno broke cover behind William Smythe and the man with the glasses, following them down the street into the London fog. It was drizzling and Bruno pulled down the brim of his trilby hat to keep the rain out of his eyes, like the man in the picture he had seen at the Odeon cinema the previous Friday night before his editor made him into a sleuth. Usually he lost his quarry early on in the pursuit, which was why he was again waiting for his man in the street outside the place where William Smythe had gone to ground late on Saturday night.

To Bruno's surprise, despite the swirling fog, today seemed to be much easier. Instead of calling a cab which always gave Bruno problems, his quarry walked up the main street to Notting Hill Tube station and bought himself a ticket on the underground train.

Quietly, Bruno went through the same procedure and followed his man onto the down escalator, all three of them going underground in the morning rush-hour crowd as thousands of men and women wearing wet raincoats down to their ankles made their way to work. Even the faces of the young girls looked pinched and unattractive. Bruno's only consolation was his father saying that where the family had come from in Riga, running away from the Russians when the communists invaded Latvia, the weather was worse than London. His father had fought in the White Russian Army until 1920. Like all optimists, Bruno only remembered the summers by the sea in Riga. In winter, the big family house had been full of warmth from big fires in every room tended by a host of servants, memories all lost in the panic and running that came in the aftermath of war.

When Bruno came out of his private thoughts, hanging from a strap by his right hand, he could still see the back of William Smythe's head and the face of the man with the glasses. The man in the glasses looked very pleased with himself, which came as no surprise to Bruno.

BY THE TIME they arrived at the offices of the *Daily Mail* in Fleet Street with the man still following them, William Smythe was thoroughly enjoying himself, the jealousy from Horatio's conquest of Janet Bray having temporarily evaporated.

"That Russian émigré from the *Mirror* is a twit. Look at him down there standing in the rain with the brim of his hat pulled down like some cheap private detective."

"If you want to see the editor about an office you'd better stop looking out of the window."

"How was she?"

"I've no idea what you are talking about. Come on."

In his hand, William held the next instalment of the Brigandshaw saga. The two pages were hidden in a large brown envelope. Earlier on the Sunday, hungover and still slightly drunk, he had typed the thousand words on Horatio's typewriter in the flat.

It was nice to be on the winning side for once in his life.

The editor seemed pleased to see him.

"You can share Wakefield's office. The typing pool will give you a stenographer... Is that the next one?"

"Yes, sir. We have an interview with Brigandshaw this afternoon. The matron says he looks much better... If you look out of the window, you'll see a chap in a trilby hat standing in the street in the rain. He looks very wet. It's Bruno Kannberg of the *Mirror*. Was waiting outside the flat when we came to work."

"You are not employed by this paper, Smythe, strictly piecemeal, one article at a time."

"As it should be, sir. That way each time we can discuss the price. You'll like what you read inside the envelope."

"Won't he follow you to the hospital?"

"He had trouble following us to Fleet Street."

"Are there any other newspapers on your tail?"

"He's the only one still standing in the street."

"Report to me after you see Brigandshaw."

"Yes, sir."

"And don't call me sir. It makes me nervous."

"Of course, Mr Editor."

WHEN HE SAW them come out into the rain that afternoon, a wet and hungry Bruno Kannberg followed as far as the taxi rank. By the time his own taxi had pulled out into the street he had lost them. For some reason the man in the glasses had taken a separate taxi.

Three hundred yards down the road, Bruno paid the cab driver the minimum fare. Across the road was a Lyons Corner House.

"Those buggers had me on a piece of string all day," he said to himself.

The cup of hot, sweet tea was delicious, making his empty stomach talk back as the hot liquid went down inside. After a big plate of bacon and eggs with two plump Wall's sausages smothered in tomato sauce, Bruno went outside. He had an idea and was smiling as he crossed the road heading for the taxi rank.

"The Tropical Diseases Hospital in Bloomsbury," he told the driver.

"Why didn't you say that the first time?" The man had a thick accent.

He had found the same cab driver who must have turned round and gone back to the rank. With a strong feeling his luck had changed, Bruno began to enjoy himself. His mother said a good meal was like a blood transfusion. His mother was right. Looking at his watch, Bruno saw the time was half past four in the afternoon. With luck he'd have his proof before the pubs opened again at six o'clock, in time for a celebration even if he had to drink on his own... He began whistling out of tune.

. . .

THE CAB DRIVER quickly shut the window that separated him from the fare. He was an opera buff and hated anything out of tune.

The cab driver was a Russian Count in better times, a second cousin of Leo Tolstoy who had gone over to the peasants at the end of his life, throwing away his land and title. The first revolution in 1905 had been brutally put down by the Cossacks at the order of the Tsar. As was his habit, the cab driver always lived in his head, ignoring his body driving the car. He found living in the past was better than living in the present. The communists had killed his family, which had made him bitter. He had been away fighting Trotsky's Red Army with the brief help of the United States and Britain, which was how he came to be driving in the London rain.

He dropped the young man at the hospital after taking one unintentional wrong turn. His upbringing had made him honest for life. Foolishly, he had expected others to behave the same way. With his mind in a muddle the Count drove off, hoping someone would flag him down on his way back to the Fleet Street taxi rank. Business was bad. Men took the Tube or walked in the rain. He was so cold his body was numb, something he had grown used to after the revolution that had destroyed his world.

WILLIAM SMYTHE HAD ARRIVED at the hospital at two-thirty, two hours earlier. A different-looking Harry Brigandshaw was sitting up in bed; someone had come in and given him a haircut. The matron of the ward had been right on the telephone. His man looked much better. The skin was still the colour of yellow parchment but the short hair looked less grey, making Brigandshaw ten years younger. There were now laughter lines at the corners of his eyes.

"Come in, Smythe. You know one of my brothers-in-law. This one is the writer, Robert St Clair. His wife is out shopping. Barnaby, ask that pretty nurse for another chair so I can give our friend some more to write about."

"You look much better, Mr Brigandshaw."

"Barnaby made his barber come all the way from Regent Street. How do you like my haircut? They injected me right into the stomach to kill the bilharzia worm. That chap on the boat did his best but you need a laboratory to find out what is wrong. They gave me some new-fangled drug to kill the rest of the bugs in my body that the Tutsi tribe is immune to. Each race builds up its own immunity, so the doctor explained."

"When are they letting you out?"

"In a week or so. They want to monitor the new drug. If you keep my whereabouts to yourself until I get out of here, I'll give you more story than you can ever write. You and your readers will be sick of Brigandshaw. Now, where was I in the story, Mr Smythe? Barnaby, why don't you take your brother home and give him some lunch?

"Robert's up from Dorset where he's writing a new book. He's let his flat in London to an old friend of mine but we won't go into my past on that one. Robert's wife has written a play I intend financing if the Receiver of Revenue gives me back my money. Why is it when we feel well, problems are so much smaller? I had a message from the managing director of my old company saying he wants to visit. Poor chap must be feeling rotten... Visiting hours finish at half past four. Good to see you again, Robert. All those years ago at Oxford. Your friendship has meant a lot to me. All of you St Clairs. I still think of Lucinda at least once a day. She was my first wife, Mr Smythe. Yes, she was my first wife. Still wonderfully alive in my mind...

"Barnaby finally got a call through to Rhodesia. My wife is bringing the children home. Though what is home these days I'm never sure. Home with the Tutsis was a very long time. I owe them my life. I just hope they don't kill too many Hutus with the guns I sent them in exchange for my freedom. There is always a price to pay, Mr Smythe. Often paid by someone else. One man's good fortune is often another man's disaster... Adele, my dear, we don't need the chair after all but thank you for showing your pretty face. Two of these gentlemen are just leaving... Mr William Smythe, I would like you to meet Miss Adele Cornfelt... Are you married, Mr Smythe?"

"No, sir, I'm not."

"Every man should have a wife don't you think, Adele?"

UNABLE TO SPEAK, Adele Cornfelt left Harry Brigandshaw's private room, her face as red as a beetroot, something that only happened to her when she looked into the eyes of a man and saw what she was looking for. As she closed the door with her back to them, she was certain the young man was still looking her way.

. . .

WHEN WILLIAM LOOKED BACK after the door shut, he saw Harry Brigandshaw was having a good chuckle.

"That's one thing that hasn't changed while I was away."

It was William Smythe's turn to feel hot flushes on his cheeks, something he thought was long past in his nefarious life.

"Was I that obvious?"

"Both of you... Now I do feel better. Remind me again where I left off the story. Then I want to hear about you. To me my own story is boring. Yours will be more interesting. How old are you?"

"Twenty-eight."

"The prime of life, so they say, which of course is wrong. So long as we live it is always the prime of life. We just look at life from a different angle."

"Does she know who you are?"

"That's a tricky question. Probably. All men are the same when they look at a pretty girl. An open book of hope and desire. Here my name is Harry Manderville. Until I get out... Take the girl for a coffee in the hospital canteen when you finish your work. My bet is she'll accept. What do you think, William?"

"I hope so. If you don't mind me asking, what is the name of your old friend living in Robert St Clair's flat? I love Robert's books. Every one of them."

"Brett Kentrich. Mrs Christopher Marlowe. I financed his musicals while Brett played the lead."

"She must be happy you are alive?"

"I hope so. I hope they are happy together."

"Are you happy, Mr Brigandshaw? I'm sorry, that's very impertinent."

"For the moment. That's the most we can hope for. Little bits of happiness down the journey of life. Why is it the old clichés are so damnably true?... Bush happy, they call it in Africa. White men go funny after a while in the African bush. It's different to being happy but quite all right. Something to do with the sun and the teeming wild animals. We find our roots as animals again. Part of the food chain... Those Tutsi were more civilised than we are, what we call civilisation is bricks and mortar, cars, aeroplanes, material comfort, a false belief we have arrived at our destination... What are you writing down?"

"The human side of the story. Something about man's conceit that he doesn't consider himself an animal."

"Oh, he's an animal all right. The only difference is, when we kill each other in modern, civilised society we don't eat what we kill... The war made me cynical. The Tutsi only kill what they are going to eat... Except the Hutus, which makes them human like the rest of us."

WHEN ADELE CAME to tell them visiting hours were over, it was five o'clock. Many pages of his notebook were covered with meticulous shorthand. Having recovered his poise, William asked Adele to show him the hospital canteen.

"Not for visitors, Mr Smythe." Adele also had a grip on herself.

"It will be six o'clock fairly soon. Could you show me the whereabouts of the nearest public house?" He was smiling. Harry had told him earlier Adele went off duty when the visitors left.

"On my way home, I pass the Crown on the way to the Tube."

"Lovely. I'll be able to stand in the rain until it opens."

In his desire to get to know Adele Cornfelt, William had forgotten all about Bruno Kannberg. He had given him the slip by climbing out of a ground floor window and shinning over the high wall that dropped him in the back street on the other side to the busy Fleet Street and the entrance to the *Daily Mail* offices. So far as he knew, had he thought of it, the man would still be standing in the rain.

Harry, using all his charm from a propped-up position in bed, had suggested breaking hospital rules by another ten minutes while Adele went off to change out of her uniform. Half an hour later, she came back. A civilian overcoat covered her clothes. There was a touch of red on her lips and her eyes looked bigger.

"Goodnight, Mr Brigandshaw. You really do look much better."

"So do you, Miss Cornfelt. See you in the morning." Harry was smiling.

This time Adele managed not to blush.

Five minutes later, when Bruno saw his quarry leaving the hospital, it was to see William Smythe in the company of a young girl. They were talking animatedly and looking into each other's eyes. The hunch had been right; where else would a man from Africa go for medicine? The girl had to be a nurse going off duty. Why would Smythe have brought a girlfriend to an interview with Harry Brigandshaw? The hospital porter dressed in a long coat and purple top hat was holding open the door for the girl to go out into the street. Outside it was darkness and a wet street. The gaslight had come on across the road and cars with their lights on were passing in the opposite directions down the busy street. Earlier Bruno had deliberately made a friend of the porter.

"Who was the girl, Johnson?"

"Nurse Cornfelt. Don't know the man."

"Do you know her ward?"

"She looks after a private ward with one patient. The man came back sick from Africa."

When Harry opened his eyes from a short snooze, a man was standing at the foot of his bed.

"Who are you?"

"Bruno Kannberg from the *Mirror*, Mr Brigandshaw. Welcome back to England."

"You want an interview?"

Harry began to pull himself up in the bed. The man came round the bed and put the pillows up behind Harry's back. He was still physically weak but mentally alert to the intruder.

"That would soothe my editor. I've been standing in the rain all day waiting for William Smythe to leave the *Mail* in Fleet Street. Chap must have gone out somehow without my seeing."

"Ah! He was with the nurse."

'Someone must have given this man the name of the nurse and the number of her ward,' Harry thought to himself.

"How is it we men are always tripped up by women? You've ten minutes before the night nurse walks in and throws you out. She's a lot bigger than Adele Cornfelt and not so accommodating. In exchange, I want another week of privacy. Then I will give a press conference and face the world once again... Kannberg. Never heard that name before. Where are your family from?"

Harry always liked to make friends with people he had just met. Getting them to talk about themselves usually worked.

"Riga. In Latvia. We fled the communists with the clothes on our back. Father fought with the British against the Reds. Why the British let us into the country. The communists confiscated three blocks of flats on the waterfront and took away our house. All to house the people. I hope they are comfortable."

"Anyone with a gun can take away your property, Mr Kannberg. No one can take away your brains... Unless they kill you. With your brains and your obvious tenacity, I am sure your new life will be good. The excitement in life is building success, not inheriting money. I was lucky enough to do both. I built Elephant Walk out of the bush. Colonial Shipping was my paternal grandfather's company. I still have a lot to do on the farm. The shipping company has gone."

"But they'll have to give it back."

"Maybe."

Pulling up a chair, Bruno sat down next to the man in the bed. He liked the man which always made doing interviews a lot easier.

ON THE FOLLOWING WEDNESDAY, when Percy Grainger was facing his worst nightmare after reading the confirmation in the *Daily Mirror*, the news vendors' billboards screaming out, *He's alive – the Mirror*, all over London, and knowing he must now go into the lion's den, Janet Bray was facing her first class of stutterers at Harrow School, an experience that was proving worse than anything she had imagined.

It seemed every boy in the class, ranging in age from fourteen to eighteen, her class of stutterers coming from all ages attending the school, was eating cherries from paper bags and spitting out the pips at each other, only giving sidelong looks at the young girl now standing in front of the blackboard trying to take control.

After her blissful few days with Horatio Wakefield who had made her feel all woman, she had been in a good mood despite the warning of the matron at the school sanitarium. For some reason her appointment to try and cure the children's stutters fell under the senior matron.

Janet's first job was to cure their stutters, not to teach them how to speak good English, something the establishment at Harrow assumed they were taught at home. Back when Winston Churchill was at Harrow the school had never presumed to teach him how to pronounce his words.

A boy six feet tall in a black tailcoat stood up and tried to speak, his mouth moving, not a word coming up from his throat. Someone hit him on the cheek with a cherry pip and made him turn round angrily.

"Who the hell did that?"

"What is your name?" asked Janet, smiling with the sudden silence. The boy tried his best to speak again but nothing came out.

"It's in the mind, gentlemen, not in the mouth. This young man, who I hope was trying to make you behave yourselves in the presence of a lady, spoke perfectly when his temper stopped him thinking before he spoke. By the time I am finished with you everyone will speak without a pronounced stutter. My name is Janet Bray, your speech therapist. I'm probably not a lot older than some of you men, but I have spent four years at the Royal Albert Hall being taught how to cure your impediment. To win for each one of you I need your help. First, always speak using the tip of the tongue. Think of clouds in a beautiful blue sky before you speak. Think of the sea rolling on the shore. Anything but how you are about to speak. You all want to ask out a girl and have her say yes on the first request. Forget about public speaking and what you may have to do in your chosen careers. Think of the girl in your life and what she will want to hear you say."

Janet was smiling at the boy still standing. The bags of cherries disappeared into the desks. Somewhere from outside in the quadrangle a pigeon began to call. The sound of a pin dropping would have been heard in her classroom of seventeen boys mostly from the British aristocracy.

"Tell me now, what is your name?"

"Willis. Willis....." The surname stayed deep in his throat.

"Willis is just fine, and thank you, Willis. We're all going to get along as all of us are on exactly the same side. Even the Duke of York has problems when speaking which he has learnt to overcome slowly but surely."

"Can you really cure my stutter?" the boy said slowly.

"I just did, Willis. Now we have to work to make the cure permanent."

When Janet reached home that night, she was glowing. All the hard work at the Central School of Speech and Drama had been worth every minute. The look on Willis Phillips's face when he realised his tongue was not tied for the rest of his life was wonderful.

When she told Horatio much later that night he just held her hand, pressing his fingers softly into her palm, Janet felt sure he understood the deepness of her satisfaction.

"I'm going to rent a room, furnish it nicely and open my own practice. It's not so much science but what I call kidology. Harrow takes up one afternoon of my week... What do you think of a woman going into business on her own?"

"I think it's wonderful... What are you going to do when we have children?"

"Make sure they don't stutter and teach them how to speak properly. Are we going to have children?"

"William wants me to go freelance with him. On my present salary I can't afford to keep myself properly let alone a family, and there's no point to life without a family of our own. Otherwise, we'll have to wait until I make assistant editor or write a book like Robert St Clair. William met him with Brigandshaw at the hospital when the *Mirror* caught William off guard. He's like a butterfly, flits from one girl to the next. He was talking endlessly about Genevieve we saw in the restaurant. Now it's some girl called Adele."

"I can wait. We want to be secure financially before we have a family. Children are very expensive... Do you know how much it costs to send a boy to Harrow School?"

"I dread to think."

"Not necessarily Harrow. That's for the toffs. The old English families. But a public school, yes. With a good English public school education, a boy can go anywhere in life."

"How many children?"

"At least eleven."

"I'd better start writing my book first thing in the morning. Now we have to sneak you down the creaking stairs and out the front door without waking Mrs Caversham."

"My landlady is worse."

"That's why you are here and not in Holland Park."

PERCY GRAINGER, the managing director and now controlling shareholder of Colonial Shipping, had made his appointment to see Harry Brigandshaw through the intermediary of Barnaby St Clair. He had made the phone call after searching his soul; facing the problem now, rather than later, seemed the best course of action to calm his nerves. His whole body was strung like piano wire.

"I presume you know where he is?" he had asked Barnaby. They had used the same stockbroker, CE Porter, before the crash, and so had obtained Barnaby's number through CE.

"Of course."

"Will Harry see me?"

"Why ever not? He's much better after the treatment. Sitting up in bed with his hair cut. My barber did a first class job... You did see the pictures in the *Mirror*?"

"Why I am calling, Mr St Clair, the first photograph in the *Mail* left a small shadow of doubt... I did everything with her best interests at heart."

"Explain that to Harry. Tina was not so sure. She and I go back to our childhoods."

"Rumours do abound, Mr St Clair. All of us are selfish. The share market could have gone the other way. Hindsight is an exact calculation. I have nothing to be ashamed of."

Which was the same thing he said the following afternoon to Harry Brigandshaw in the Hospital for Tropical Diseases.

"Of course you haven't, Percy. Remember, I gave you the top job. When I came from Rhodesia to take over the company that dropped into my lap and frightened the hell out of me. Friends don't have to explain to each other. Your coming to see me is proof of your good intentions now and in the past."

"Do you want the company back? You will get the share at half the price the government got to pay your death duties. They are going to give it all back with compound interest. The man I negotiated with is still the man in charge. You'll own your same percentage of the public company and still have a large sum of money in the bank. Since you went away the world has entered a terrible depression. Of course I will sell you back your Berkeley Square house at current market value, which is less than half what I paid for it."

"*You* are living in my house?" Harry was enjoying himself. He knew from Barnaby perfectly well what had happened to his house.

"Yes, I am... Why are you laughing, Harry? This is no laughing matter."

"Oh, but it is. I hated that house. Tina was the one who wanted to live in London and go to the theatre once a week... Did they sell Hastings Court, the house that belonged to both my grandfathers in turn?"

"But I thought the house wasn't yours. Didn't you give it to the Royal Air Force Association as a rehabilitation centre for wounded airmen after the war? I wondered why the old house hadn't been sold, but there again the sale of your shares covered death duties. The RAF Association would love to get rid of it. Upkeep and rates are enormous. There are just three blind airmen still at the home. The aftermath of wars are soon forgotten by those who did not suffer."

"I had agreed to pay the overheads and the rates. My maternal grandfather is still alive. The house had been in his family for centuries. I'm even booked in here under his surname. For grandfather's sake, I could not sell the house so I lent it to the RAF Association. That was after the National Trust not wanting it."

"But you'll want the company back?"

"Of course not, Percy. The whole idea of taking it public in the '20s was to get out from under some of my responsibilities. Make the board responsible, not just me. I'm a Rhodesian farmer now growing tobacco thanks to grandfather Manderville's cousin in Virginia. If my wife still wishes to live in England after all she has been through, we will live in Hastings Court half of the year. I only ask you one question: when I disappeared, was what you did in utmost good faith?"

"Of course it was, Harry. Back then it looked like the stock market was going all the way up to heaven."

"Give your wife my regards and thank you for coming to see me."

"So that's it?"

"That and the man at the Department of Inland Revenue, ask him for my cheque as soon as possible. I'll talk to the RAF Association. Pay them the rates and overheads they lost after I disappeared."

"You are a good person, Harry."

"So are you. Don't forget it. We all give advice and most of it is not very good, though in the end it turned out just fine. For all of us, we all got what we wanted! Now that doesn't happen often in life."

"You don't even want to be on the board?"

"Not in a fit, Percy Grainger. Not in a fit."

"Your wife and children sailed from Cape Town to Southampton yesterday. It will be the company's honour to pay for their trip."

"I believe they're on the *King Emperor*. The children will rip it apart, bless them. I'm getting out of here tomorrow and going down to Dorset. The children's grandparents will be happy to hear they are coming home."

"You'll be staying with them?"

"With the St Clairs. And not for any reason of snobbery. Robert and I were up at Oxford together. My first wife grew up at Purbeck Manor."

"Life is complicated."

"And then we die."

"Welcome back, Harry."

$\mathcal{H}$arry Brigandshaw was discharged from the Tropical Diseases Hospital the following week when Tina, the children and the nurses, Ivy and Molly, had been on the water for six days on their way back to England; Percy Grainger had advised the captain on behalf of Harry to say Harry was leaving hospital for Dorset to recuperate.

Harry was still shaky when he walked out of the lift to reception with Robert and Freya St Clair, to find Barnaby St Clair had paid his bill in full making Harry, with his back to the others, smile wryly; the circle had again turned since he knocked Barnaby into the Thames for chasing after Tina.

"Nice to see you walk again, Mr Brigandshaw," said the doorman smiling.

"Ah, the man who blew my cover."

"I didn't realise at the time, sir."

"Robert, give the man a quid. That chap Landan has yet to send me my cheque, though Percy says we'll have it next week. Like all government departments, they need ten men to authorise the payment before they draw the cheque. I'll pay you back, I promise. It really feels funny standing up straight after lying in bed so long."

"The air will do you good in Dorset," said Freya. She had him firmly by the left elbow.

The American lady was not going to let him go now he had read her play and agreed to finance the production. The previous day, Oscar Fleming had visited him in hospital to go over the details. When Harry had made a decision, he hated beating around the bush. Oscar Fleming had made a fortune with him out of *Happy Times*, the Christopher Marlowe musical that had run for over three years in the West End.

"I'm not asking you, Oscar. I'm telling you. It's my money."

"And my time. My word, you have recovered. Good to see you back, Harry. All right, as a favour. Straight plays don't make money. We'll start in Bristol and see if it works."

"How's Brett?" He was smiling to himself. Harry liked the idea of convincing Oscar Fleming after Barnaby had failed.

"She's fine. A mother. She's not going back on the stage. Can I give her your love?"

"Why ever not? She was an important part of my life. You can't change that. All our lives are made up of different parts. Lots of them... Are they happy, she and Christopher?"

"No one is ever happy, Harry. We just say we are. I've known Brett even longer than you, but that's enough detail."

Harry knew perfectly well Brett the up-and-coming actress had once been Oscar's mistress. The theatre was incestuous. Always had been.

"You're a cynic, Oscar."

"A sceptic. When you come back from Dorset we'll have lunch at my club. I always enjoy lunch at the Garrick..."

"Do you think the Freya St Clair play any good?"

"You never can be certain without an audience. Why so many people lose money in the theatre. Let's hope we don't lose too much."

Johnson, the doorman, had taken the pound note and put it in his overcoat pocket. Then he opened the door and let them out into the December cold where Robert St Clair's car was waiting in the parking lot. The cold air gripped the back of Harry's throat. He was a long way from the Belgian Congo.

Wrapped up in rugs they began the long journey down the coast. Freya had packed two large Thermos flasks into a picnic basket, she told him smiling, still warm from the good news about her play. Harry could smell the hot pork pies inside the basket that sat with him on the back seat. Robert's wife was organised. Like all other Americans Harry had met through his life. Harry huddled back in the seat and was soon fast asleep.

. . .

"W‌ELL?" said Robert an hour later as they motored through the cold Surrey countryside on the Kingston bypass. There had been little or no traffic on the road in the middle of the week. Harry had woken up when they left the built-up sprawl of London. The trees were leafless but there was no ice on the road he was glad to see. A watery sun had only lifted the temperature outside the car a few degrees, as he found out when he misguidedly wound down an inch of the back window for a brief moment.

To Harry, watching everything outside as it went by, England looked beautiful. His Tutsi friends were another life away. It was difficult for Harry to contemplate he was the same person.

"When are we going to eat the pies?" he said, ignoring Robert's question, only too aware of what it meant.

"At lunchtime," said Freya, her voice on edge. Harry guessed right they had been talking about his reading of *Holy Knight*, given to him in hospital by Barnaby.

Harry, back with the living, was enjoying himself again. For days now, he had not said a word about the book, teasing his old friend.

"Well, did you read my book?" snapped Robert.

"Why don't we wait until lunch? Or we could stop under that oak tree on the side of the road."

The car came to an abrupt halt, with Robert reversing towards the tree where he pulled the car off the road. They had left the Kingston bypass and were driving down a country lane. The big tree was next to a four-bar gate that opened onto a farmer's field where sheep with thick dirty coats were grazing the dark green winter grass taking no notice of the noisy intrusion.

There were still signs of the previous night's white frost where the watery sun had been unable to have any effect through the leafless boughs of the old tree. Harry could still smell the pork pies in their greaseproof packets. After hospital food, they were going to eat well.

"Now out with it. You hated the damn book despite my selling millions of copies here and in America."

"May I open the picnic basket, Freya? I can pass you both what I am sure by the delicious smell is a pork pie."

"Didn't they give you breakfast?" said Robert. "Look, Harry... What you think means more to me than the bloody critics or the bloody sales figures. Does the book work, Harry?"

"Perfectly. Now may I have a pork pie? I'm starving. They cleaned out my stomach so well I feel there is nothing left but a hollow."

"Are you serious?"

"Even better than *Keeper of the Legend*... Oh, you are clever, Freya. She's wrapped the pies in the greaseproof packets in the tea cloth. They are still warm. No wonder they were enticing my nostrils."

"You were playing with me."

"Don't you know me by now, old friend? I was waiting to sit by the fire with your family and tell everyone in detail, as I know what it means to you. The reader, the other side of the page, the mirror without which your story can never come alive... But teasing you has been fun... Now, can I pass you one of these delicious-smelling pies? Then we can have a nice cup of tea. After that, the farmer in me says I have to climb over that gate and look at the sheep. Do blowflies lay eggs in the wool in England? Leaves a dark patch. If you don't cut out that bit of the wool in Africa, when the eggs hatch the worms eat the sheep alive, horrible... I'm going to take back Hastings Court from the RAF Association."

WHEN THEY REACHED Corfe Castle seven miles from Purbeck Manor, the ancient family home of the St Clairs, dusk was falling with the snow. Small, pure white snow, whirling down in the headlights, melting on the ground. It was early for snow in Dorset. Up on its hill, they could see the ruins of the castle, the first home of the St Clairs before Oliver Cromwell knocked it down after the army of Parliament defeated the king, cut off his head and punished the royalist aristocracy.

Harry looked up at the ruins and thought of his first wife, Lucinda St Clair. Tina was coming over from Africa on the SS *King Emperor*, the same ship that had taken him out with Lucinda on the ill-fated journey at the end of the war when Lucinda was shot dead by a madman. There were tears in his eyes. For everyone. For Tina's pain. The unborn child in the belly of his first wife, dying. Hutus killing Tutsis. Tutsis with his guns killing the Hutu. So many German pilots killed by the press of his forefinger on the firing button of his Vickers machine gun... They were driving past the railway station when Harry saw old Pringle, the station master at Corfe Castle who carried bags and gave out the train tickets through the round hold in the glass of the station ticket office.

To Harry looking past the swirling snow, his father-in-law looked as old as the hills. As old as the castle on the hill. Like the St Clairs, his second wife's family had been in the surrounding parts all through the centuries. From before the French St Clairs landed at Hastings with Harry's maternal ancestors to wrestle England from the Saxon King Harold; the French under the command of William the Conqueror, the first William of England. The Pringles were Saxon. Before that they had been Celt, part of the Dorset soil for all eternity.

"Stop the car, Robert. That's Tina's father."

Harry got out of the car, standing with one hand on the door to give himself support. He still felt as weak as a kitten. The pies had rumbled in his stomach all the way down in the car. The old man saw him and turned away, moving quickly for an old man. Harry understood the last train for the day had left the station and old Pringle was going home to the railway cottage by the small stream where Tina was born. To his old wife in the kitchen, the grandmother of Harry's children without whom they would never have been born.

"Mr P. It's me, Harry," he called.

The old man began to run, the snow falling, the falling light taking him away.

"What's the matter?" Harry asked Robert who had wound down the driver's window and was leaning out of the car.

"They don't read the papers. Fact is, he can't read well enough. The inspector does the bookwork once a month up from Swanage. He thinks you are a ghost, Harry. You put the fear of God in him by calling out. The old people are fey in these parts and not just the old of age. They believe in things much further back than Jesus Christ. They are as much druid as Christian. Lucinda was murdered. You died in a plane crash. Of course your spirit would come back to her roots. To old Pringle seeing you here in the gloaming was perfectly natural, even if it did scare the wits out of him."

"We should give him a lift home."

"No, Harry. Leave him alone. Any more and you'll kill him. His heart will be racing enough for one afternoon. Another afternoon when the sun is shining we'll visit Mrs P and eat some of her plum pie, the best in the world. She bottles their own plums off their trees in the autumn that gives them fruit right through to spring. Get back in the car before you fall over. It's cold. We don't want you going down with something after what you have been through. When he gets home to Mrs P, she'll give him a cup of tea and a plate of kippers and his heart will beat normally. He won't even mention a word to his wife. People have always seen ghosts in this neck of the woods. Let it go, Harry. Think of Tina and your five children, including the one born after you disappeared. I presume Barnaby told you?"

"She called him Kim. I love the name. Rudyard Kipling... After so long we are all so close again. I can see their ship in my mind's eye drawing nearer and nearer to England... All right then. Home, James, and don't spare the horses... Your own mother and father do know I am alive?"

"And well they love you, Harry. You know that from your first visit when I brought you down from Oxford so many years ago so Lucinda could fall in love. She was fifteen. You first met in the garden. Lucinda said her heart melted at first sight... Home it is. I wonder what Mrs Mason is cooking for supper? I'm starving."

In the car next to him, Freya was smiling. Her husband was always hungry and always thin, never putting on a pound. It was the one thing she hated about Robert St Clair... Then she was thinking of her two-year-old Richard left in the care of Lady St Clair while they went up to London.

"I've missed him terribly."

"Me too," said Robert. There was no need for either of them to explain.

Behind them, Harry was climbing back into the car, snowflakes in his hair. Robert smiled at him through the rear-view mirror.

"You're covered in snow."

Robert took his left hand from his wife's knee, put the car into gear and they continued their journey. He was happy. There had never been a time in his life when he was not pleased to be going home. There was something more to life, having solid roots.

GOING OUT OF CORFE CASTLE, they took the high road that would bring them round to the old manor house. When Robert walked the seven miles home from the railway station he took the low road, the path that wound along the river, the one taken by old Pringle on his way to the tea and kippers, away from what he thought was the ghost of his son-in-law.

When the car and the three of them reached Purbeck Manor, it was dark. In one bottom corner of the big house, they could see the lights from the family.

As Harry walked through the side door built into the tall gothic entrance, he could feel Lucinda's presence, a welcoming presence that made him sad to be alive. So many memories.

Lady St Clair was older than he remembered. Lord St Clair was somewhere out the back of the house with old Warren as usual. Mrs Mason was holding her hands together in front of her apron, standing just behind Lady St Clair.

"Welcome back, Harry," said Lady St Clair. "It's a miracle."

"I saw Mr P near the station but he ran away."

"Yes, there's that too... We're in the cosy room with the fire. That sounds like my husband banging the kitchen door. Come and drink a glass of sherry. We have roasted suckling pig on the spit in the banquet hall if we don't all freeze to death. This house is cold as charity in the winter. Not quite the fatted calf but it will have to do... Come and tell me what happened."

She had taken Harry by the arm.

A small boy came running and jumped straight into his father's arms, mentally kicking Harry in the stomach at the thought of his own children. Then Freya was kissing the child, the boy's grandmother looking on happily, nostalgia written all over her face. The child was screaming and laughing, sending sweet notes up into the rafters of the old house, peace and happiness mingling high up with the dark. The dogs were everywhere for a moment then went, satisfied with the intruders. The old tug between England and Africa was pulling Harry apart, bringing Elephant Walk into the house making him homesick. He was carrying a small overnight bag. No one dressed for dinner anymore at the Manor.

With all the mingled thoughts from his life playing through his mind, the St Clairs led Harry into the one warm room in the house. Lord St Clair was already waiting with Harry's glass of sherry in his hand.

"One of the pigs is sick but you're a farmer and know all about that. Have a sherry, warm the cockles of your heart."

Nothing for Harry had changed at Purbeck Manor. Nothing ever did. His world was once more back in place. By the fire, with dry logs giving out a good heat, Harry was glad to sit down and warm himself at the family hearth. Only then did he remember his manners.

"I'm sorry. I sat down before you, Lady St Clair."

"You've been in hospital."

Mrs Mason had taken his small bag away. Robert would tell him which room to go to when the time was right. Harry hoped he would get through the sherry and the wine with the suckling pig before falling asleep. Since being taken off the boat, he had slept most of the time. The drugs they had given him were still playing through his system.

"Mrs Mason is lighting the fire in your room," said Lady St Clair. "Are you eating all right?"

"Like a horse."

"We'll eat early and soon have you tucked up in bed. You can tell us everything when you feel stronger, Harry. You're here to get your strength back."

The dogs had got into the room and were sitting round the fire, the flames dancing in their eyes. A ginger cat, just like the one on Elephant Walk, was sitting on the back of the settee fast asleep where it had been when they came into the room. One of the dogs was looking at the cat from a safe distance.

After a second glass of sherry, they all trooped into the old dining hall with the high vaulted ceiling. At both ends of the long room, fires were burning in tall alcoves. On the side of one of the walls in the fireplaces was a spit with the suckling pig. Mrs Mason was sitting comfortably inside the fireplace with a glass of wine, turning the spit occasionally to cook the meat all over.

The family sat at the top of the table as close to the fire as possible. Someone had opened the bottles of red wine earlier to let them breathe. There was no first course, only the pig and large serving dishes of vegetables. The smell of the food made Harry's mouth water. He had never had a bad meal at Purbeck Manor... Then Robert gave him a glass of French red wine. They all stood up and drank a toast to the King, Mrs Mason standing up in the fireplace next to the pig.

Mrs Mason had a reputation for falling asleep on the bench in the alcove of the fire.

When Harry readied for his bed he was full of good food and slightly tipsy. Robert had turned out the light. Then Harry fell asleep and dreamed all night of so many strange things, he could remember none of them in the dawn.

The room was cold; the bed warm, the world outside the long window that came to within a foot of the wooden floor was white and beautiful. Throughout the old house there was not a sound. Rolling over, Harry went back to sleep again. When he woke, Mrs Mason was standing in the room pouring him tea into a large breakfast cup from a round brown teapot.

"It's eleven o'clock," she said.

"My goodness."

They smiled at each other as Mrs Mason put the cup down on the side table beside his bed, then left the room without another word. Harry managed to drink half the cup of tea before falling back into the deep sleep of late morning. Outside the window the snow was still falling.

4

*I*n London, one hundred miles away, the snow had stopped falling earlier when Oscar Fleming was having his breakfast. The small flat he had lived in for most of his life looked out onto a small private garden of grass and trees that belonged to the flats. A key to the garden gate was given to each of the tenants. The hundred-year lease to his flat expired in twenty-two years, by which time Oscar Fleming hoped he would be dead. At sixty-five, despite planning the last tryst of his life while having his breakfast, he was feeling his age. The ponytail that dropped to the height of his shoulders was white, the white goatee beard barely flecked with grey. From vigorous exercise, only his body was still in shape, which gave him the confidence to indulge his life-long fascination, the pursuit of young girls who needed his help to further their careers in their mindless pursuit of stardom.

The very idea of what he was going to be up to made him chuckle long after the snow had stopped falling. By then he was sitting in front of his fire still in the red silk dressing gown some said was his trademark; the same people who erroneously claimed he was the leading impresario in the London theatre, something he was careful never to claim for himself.

Like many people in the theatre, Oscar Fleming was superstitious. Plays and musicals were more often a disaster. Money made was just as easily lost, something he never forgot. Putting on Robert St Clair's

American wife's play was going to be just one of those disasters unless something electric could be added to the play to make it explode on the stage. Which was when the thought of Genevieve, the by-blow of lower echelon aristocracy, the daughter of Merlin St Clair and the barmaid of the Running Horses at Mickleham, entered his mind.

Twirling his cigarette holder designed especially for his flat-shaped Turkish cigarettes, Oscar played the picture of Genevieve through his mind, something he had found himself doing often, checking up on the progress of what was going to be his protégée.

Barnaby St Clair had asked him to get the girl into the Central School of Speech and Drama as a favour. They had all attended the aftershow party at the last night of *Happy Times*, the Christopher Marlowe musical he had put on with Harry Brigandshaw's money and Brett Kentrich in the lead. Brett at that point was Harry's mistress, and the show had launched her career into stardom.

That night, late in 1928, was when he first set eyes on Genevieve. Her father had said she was fourteen. Even then he knew what he was going to do. She was perfect. Full of the power that made men fools. The school thought she was nineteen. Oscar thought her two years younger, the perfect age of attraction; all the heroic loves in the history of theatre-depicted girls the age of Genevieve.

Mulling over taking her from school one year short of the end of a three-year drama course, Oscar let the rich oriental flavour of his cigarette drift up to the ceiling.

"What the hell," he said. "It's now or never. Another year may be too long for me. One last brilliant affair and then I'll retire from everything and go down into the country to breed dogs. After all, I'm her only chance for stardom. Even the finest talent in the world has to be sponsored. In a few years, she'll look like the rest of them... Oh, what a good idea, you old rogue. Even if it doesn't work it will be fun trying... Nothing ventured nothing gained."

Throwing the mostly unburnt cigarette in the fire, putting the holder in the pocket of his red dressing gown and feeling a good ten years younger, Oscar Fleming got up from his fireside chair to put his plan into operation.

"We'll keep it all in the family," he said, smiling broadly to himself. "Great talent has to be nurtured, haven't I said that a thousand times to myself... Now where on earth would Brett Kentrich have been without me?"

. . .

WHILE OSCAR FLEMING was plotting the start of her career, not far from Oscar Fleming's flat in Chelsea Genevieve was enjoying the luxury of solitude in her own flat in St John's Wood. Living with her mother had become a pain in the neck. Somewhere definitely not to take her friends. Her mother Esther was a mess, drinking gin from lunchtime with not the slightest interest in anything. Esther had a flat and a pension for life from an affair with a toff twenty years ago.

"Look, luv. I've got what I want in life. A nice little flat, money to drink, a lovely little daughter and no one giving me shit. What else can a girl like me ever want? I'm in heaven even if it is all a bit hazy most of the time. Cheer up, Genevieve. If you have my luck you'll be all right."

"I want a place of my own."

"That's fine by me, ducks. Ask your father. You always could twist him round your little finger. He dotes on you. What's another flat to Merlin? I'll ask him if you want."

"Leave him to me, Mother."

"I'm your mum not your mother. All this highfalutin' stuff they teach you at the Hall makes me sick. Move out. See if I care. You're old enough. Just don't get yourself up the pole without working it all out beforehand like I did. You've got to be calculating to get through this life and that means money."

"Are you coming to the year-end show?"

"Of course not. I look a mess. Think of your father. He'll be there, you can bet your socks on that."

"Why are you crying, Mum?"

"'Cause I love you… Just come and visit your old mum sometimes. Merlin says you are going to be a star."

"My father is ever so slightly biased… You've been a good mum to me. Did I ever tell you that?"

"No. Now bugger off before I really start to cry. Just remember, keep your chin up."

"I'll stay in the flat if you want."

"I just told you to bugger off didn't I?"

THE YEAR-END SHOW took place on the Saturday when Harry Brigandshaw had walked the woods and fields around Purbeck Manor building up his strength for the arrival of his wife and family at Southampton on the SS *King Emperor* the following week.

The show was a collage of bits and pieces to showcase the individual talent of the students. Only the drama students took part in the show, the students studying speech therapy sitting in the great auditorium of the Albert Hall as guests. Any past student was entitled to a seat in the theatre to fill the place up as much as possible; even the most doting family and friends of the young performers were not enough.

Janet Bray had arrived in time to see the curtain go up on the first sketch, the balcony scene of Shakespeare's *Romeo and Juliet*. After the young girl's performance, the rest of the evening went flat. It was said that only two per cent of the drama students found lifelong work in their chosen profession; Janet was glad she was a qualified speech therapist and not an actress.

Since the cherry pip-blowing in her first class at Harrow, two new patients had come her way. She thought her interplay with Willis Phillips and the aristocratic background of the two new patients was not a coincidence. The search for rooms was now urgent. Finding the right furnished accommodation for a practice at the price she could afford was difficult, the right address in London being as important as the right qualifications.

They had held hands throughout the evening, comfortable with each other, ignoring most of what was going on up on the stage. Horatio Wakefield had been quiet all evening, something on his mind.

"That's Oscar Fleming the impresario with Juliet," he said at the bar during the interval. "So that's why he is here. That old bastard has seduced every one of his leading ladies for thirty years. If Genevieve wants to be a star, she's found the right man. All she has to do is close her eyes and think of England."

"You are being catty. What's been irritating you?"

"The fickleness of newspapers. The short attention span of the public. Once the *Mirror* confirmed our story, everyone lost interest in Harry Brigandshaw. He's yesterday's news."

"I'm sure he'll be glad."

"It's William. He's a bear with a sore head. My editor is only paying him for three articles as first agreed, just enough to pay the interest on William's overdraft. Just glad I still have a job. Even the Brigandshaw family back from Africa isn't going to make the papers. Harry is yesterday's hero. I don't think people give a damn really. They only call on people like Harry Brigandshaw when they are in trouble. In war. When they want something. They don't want to remember for too long after they have got what they want as it makes them feel guilty... Can we go? This year's show is an anti-climax after Genevieve playing Juliet... Look, she's going off with Fleming. He's old enough to be her grandfather, for God's sake."

"He wouldn't take advantage of a young girl," said Janet, not believing what she saw.

"Only if she wants him to. Some people will do anything to get on in this world. See, over there is her father. The one with the monocle and the stare at Fleming's back that would kill if he had a gun. Genevieve must have her father under her thumb like the rest of them to get away with that right in front of him."

"Don't you mean like the rest of us? You've been besotted ever since you saw her in Simpson's on the Strand."

"Are you jealous, Janet?"

"Damn right I am. Every man in this room is watching her right now and not because she just played Juliet. And just look at that. She's put her hand on the crook of the old man's arm as if she belongs to him already... Why doesn't her father do something?"

"Maybe he will... We'd better stay for the second half of the show. It would be rude to the rest of the cast. Maybe there's a new star to be born in the second half I can write about."

"What about Genevieve? Aren't you going to write about her?"

"I don't think that would be wise," said Horatio, giving his lady a smile.

GETTING what she wanted out of men was the biggest art in her life. Acting for Genevieve was only part of the process, the window display for what she was really after. Looking back over her shoulder with her right hand gently resting in the crook of the old man's elbow, she sweet-smiled her father standing alone and about to explode, changing his angry expression into pleasure... It was always so easy she told herself, turning back to the task in question.

"Where are we going, Mr Fleming?"

"Where would you like to go, Genevieve? I have a proposition for you that entails leaving school."

"Then it doesn't matter where we go." This time she gave Fleming the sweet smile.

The horny old goat returned her smile with a flash of raw lust, more revealing than taking off his clothes, which she intended to keep on him for as long as possible. The trick was to give them hope, never exactly what they wanted. Just enough of a taste to keep their hormones screaming for more. In her short experience of life, a satisfied man was a bored man, no longer pliable in a woman's hands. With luck he would now be jealous, the most devilish form of jealousy, that of a father, especially when the man in question was older than himself.

Genevieve, graciously handed into the back of a taxi outside the Albert Hall, knew her life was going to go exactly the way she wanted. No matter as she snuggled into the old man's shoulder that even the smell of him was quite repulsive.

"What have you got for me, Mr Fleming?"

"You were very good tonight."

"I hope so. So you have a part for me?"

"I think so."

"Don't think, Mr Fleming, just give it to me. I promise you won't be disappointed. Take me to a nice place for supper and tell me what you want me to do. I learn very quickly. Another year at school would have been boring. You either have it or you don't, Mr Fleming. Do you have friends in film?"

"Have you had a screen test?"

"I would love one. I love tests. Tonight was a test, don't you think? And haven't I come through with flying colours?"

"Yes," said Oscar Fleming.

"My Juliet was perfect. So sad she had to die... Is it a big part, Mr Fleming?"

"The juvenile lead. A young soldier comes back from the war blind, no longer able to see the love of his life. You will be the love of his life."

"How beautiful. How lovely. So to him she stays beautiful for the rest of his life. Now that's a happy ending. The girl could end up an old bag and still get away with it."

"He dies at the end of the play."

"What a horrible ending. You'll have to make them re-write. Now, where are we going?"

"To the Savoy."

"Don't worry about Daddy. He loves me so much. I've just moved into my own flat in St John's Wood thanks to my father. He'll be so thrilled to hear I have the lead in the new Oscar Fleming play at one of London's top theatres."

"We were thinking of Bristol."

"Whatever for! Didn't you see them looking at me tonight? No, Bristol would be a waste of our time don't you think? I believe in going head first, don't you? Right in, straight away."

When the taxi reached the Savoy, Genevieve could see the old man was positively drooling. 'Why,' she asked herself, 'were men always so stupid?'

The dress her father had bought for her the previous day was perfect for the Savoy. As she got out of the taxi after Oscar Fleming had walked round to help her out onto the pavement she flashed him an inch of her ankle, followed by a glimpse of her breasts. Then they were walking arm in arm into the grillroom of the Savoy Hotel. It was the power over the old man she found so intoxicating, not the thought of the part in his play.

"How old are you really, Genevieve?"

"Isn't that rude to ask a girl?" she said smiling. "I'm seventeen. I turned seventeen at the end of last month... Am I too old for you, Oscar?"

"Just right."

"I meant for the play."

"I know."

For the first time she tried her schoolgirl giggle on the man. Just a little one. Like the rest of them, it worked as intended. The final thrust into the old goat's groin. After that, Bristol was never mentioned again the whole evening.

THERE WAS ALWAYS a price to pay, that much Merlin St Clair had known all his life. He could give her money but never his class. She would marry some man in the lower class or become a rich man's mistress like her mother. The fact her grandfather was a peer of the realm meant nothing in England. She was born out of wedlock. Beyond the pale. Something to be used, never cherished.

As Hughes, the doorman of his block of flats on Park Lane, pressed the lift button for him he gave the man a smile.

"Smithers is out, sir."

"I gave him the night off, Hughes." Smithers was his man. The gentleman's gentleman who ran his flat.

Upstairs he let himself in, not sure what to do. It was her life. Ever since she was a child, she had known what she was doing. The thought of Oscar Fleming touching his daughter made his mind twist and turn with physical pain... But what right had he to interfere? What was the difference between Brett Kentrich, star of the stage, who had used Fleming the same way to make her career? A career that ended in a brilliant marriage to Christopher Marlowe, a man of Merlin's own class.

"It's happened before, actresses marrying into the aristocracy. For some reason they don't ask famous actresses about the legitimacy of *their* parents."

Miserable, Merlin poured himself a stiff whisky, conscious that Smithers had also been at the bottle. Probably with Hughes before Hughes went on duty. The man's breath had smelt of whisky.

"Poor sod standing at a cold door all night. Who's to blame him?... The world has always been bloody unfair."

Trying not to let his imagination run riot, Merlin took his drink to the fire and sat down in his armchair. Smithers had damped down the fire. Opening the vent to let in the draught, Merlin poked the fire and watched the hot coals break into a blue flame... She was now on her own. A grown woman of seventeen. In a less civilised world, he would have gone and shot the old bastard for even thinking of seducing his daughter... There was always a price to pay, which in that case would be hanging by his neck from a rope... And where would that get Genevieve?

"It's all my fault," he said miserably as he stared at the fire.

He had never married. Too selfish, of that much he was certain. He was forty-six years old and alone staring at the fire. At least Harry Brigandshaw had his wife and children coming back to him, according to the morning paper he had read with his breakfast. All he had was Genevieve. There was no point in talking to her mother Esther, who had never read a book in her life. It seemed ironical that Esther was happy with his money and he was miserable. She had never wanted very much. Enough to put a roof over her head and keep her in gin. Knowing too much in life was a curse. The ignorant were more blessed. They could think as far as the next meal and the next glass of gin. She had not even seemed worried at Genevieve moving out on her own. They looked at their child with different eyes. What was abhorrent to him was the start of a success story to Esther. The road to fame and fortune.

Pouring himself another stiff drink, he hoped Harry would be happy back with Tina and the children. Sitting back, Merlin sighed at the ceiling. Harry had always been the better man. Then he thought of Genevieve somewhere with Oscar Fleming and his mind began to seethe all over again.

By the time he went to bed, he knew he was tight as a tick. At least his mind had floated off in all its tangents... It was her life after all like everyone else's.

WHEN SMITHERS CAME BACK JUST after midnight the flat was quiet as a tomb. The fire had gone out. A second bottle of whisky was open on the table and half empty. Merlin St Clair's evening at the theatre had not been a success, that much was obvious to Smithers.

Pouring himself a drink, Smithers sat down in Merlin's chair and drank with appreciation. Shortly afterwards he fell fast asleep. When he woke he was stiff and cold in the dark of the night. Yawning, he took himself off to his bed, washing the whisky glasses in the kitchen.

PART 3

BERLIN — DECEMBER 1933

1

Berlin was bitterly cold. The room William Smythe rented above the bicycle shop was less than a mile from the burned-out Reichstag. The only way to keep warm was to stay in bed fully clothed under a pile of blankets wearing two pairs of socks. The gas heater had little effect even when there was any gas. The paraffin heater he had installed was no better.

It was his thirtieth birthday. No one had wished him a happy birthday. Letters never reached him from London, ever since the National Socialist Party had warred with the communists on the streets, forcing President von Hindenburg to appoint Hitler Chancellor of Germany.

Will's reports to Reuters were smuggled out of the country by hand. If he wasn't making so much money he would have packed his bags. Two men followed him wherever he went, twice beating up Germans who had given him information.

The bang on the door made Will get out of bed and hurriedly put on his shoes. The door burst open. Brownshirts pushed past each other screaming German Will could not understand. They quickly had his hands behind his back and frogmarched him out of the room. He was lucky to be properly clothed with his passport and British money in his jacket pocket. Expecting the worst was the way he survived.

"I'm British," he kept shouting as they pushed him out onto the street.

Passers-by took no notice, crossing the road or averting their eyes, every man for himself. In the street, they beat him up, kicking him on the ground with hobnailed boots. The road on his cheek was ice cold, his blood quickly freezing. Four of them threw him into a van and took him to the railway station, his money and passport still in his pocket.

"Happy Birthday, Will."

One of the men hit him across the face for talking. In the train, the men pushed him onto the floor of the compartment. When the train moved out of the station, they were still in the compartment with Will on the floor.

At Hamburg, the four men took Will from the train and put him on a Danish freighter. The men stayed on the dockside until the boat sailed. The Danish captain spoke good English.

"You, my friend, are one of the lucky ones. Best you keep out of Germany. What did you do?"

"I'm a journalist."

"Then you are very lucky."

"It's my birthday."

"Consider the trip my birthday present. Come down to my cabin for schnapps. Your face looks terrible. My name is Captain Preisler, welcome aboard... Did you leave much behind?"

"Very little."

A TWIN-ENGINE AIRCRAFT flew Will from Copenhagen to Croydon Airport south of London where he filed a report the next day, only just able to see out of his eyes. The story was syndicated across the world. Freelance journalism had made him rich. The byline William Smythe was worth money in America where Glen Hamilton of the *Denver Telegraph* had syndicated Will's work ever since Will broke the story of Harry Brigandshaw.

Now safely out of Germany after six months hiding away in the room over the bicycle shop, Will could tell the truth without fear for his life. Only when everything had gone out on the wire did Will begin to shake with fear. His temper writing the story had kept his body in check.

From Croydon, Will took the train up to London. People avoided looking at his face. From Waterloo Station he took a taxi to the flat he had once shared with Horatio Wakefield.

When Horatio opened the door to his flat, Will stepped inside. Janet Bray took one look and telephoned her doctor.

THE NEXT MORNING, while Will was still asleep on his old pull-out couch, Horatio read what had happened to his friend in the *Sunday Times*. Only then did Horatio begin to shiver, his teacup rattling on the saucer, his hand unable to bring the cup to his lips.

"You never appreciate what you have until you lose it," said Will from the couch bed. "You have no idea how good it is to be back in England. Where's Janet?"

"She doesn't live here. Anyway, she'll be at work. The doctor said you have a cracked rib and dislocated jaw."

"My teeth wouldn't close together."

"He pulled your jaw straight last night... Is it really as bad as you write in the paper, Will?"

"The communists tried to take over. German industrialists paid the Nazis to fight the communists in the streets. Faust. Pure Faust. The Jews with the money are now the target, too few of them to give Hitler trouble. It's always been popular to steal from the rich and give it to the poor. What German industry was trying to avoid. Russia is worse, so they say."

"And the rest of Europe?"

"We'll have to fight. Re-arm. Why Hitler needs the likes of Krupp, who are making him guns. They want to conquer the world. The people of Germany want revenge and their pride back. That man can talk a mob into a frenzy."

"Which is worse, Stalin or Hitler? How are you feeling?"

"Bruised. My pride mostly. When the law doesn't work for you it's scary."

"Are you going back?"

"Later. Under a different passport."

"They'll kill you without British protection."

"Means nothing in Berlin. You are either on Hitler's side or his thugs will bash your head in for you. The Danish captain said I was lucky."

"Then don't go back."

"I'm pissed off. If we appease him, turn a blind eye, he'll swallow the whole British Empire which will please the Americans. They want to throw the empire on the garbage heap so they can trade with our colonies."

"Let someone else get their heads bashed in."

"That's what they all say."

"Did I wish you a happy birthday?"

"No, you didn't. Why are you not at work?"

"It's Sunday."

"I'm not sure even which year it is."

"1933. December. Two years since you wrote about Harry Brigandshaw and went freelance. Will, I'm becoming the poor relation. Janet expects to make a thousand pounds next year. You've paid off your overdraft from the '29 crash and I'm still getting exactly the same piddling salary."

"I told you to go freelance."

"Maybe I will."

"Go back to Germany with me. We can watch each other's backs."

"Even the idea makes me break into a cold sweat."

"I'll split the fees with you right down the line. Being alone in Berlin for six months was unpleasant. Only Fritz Wendel spoke English."

"Who's Fritz Wendel?"

"One of my sources. He's a Jew."

"Why doesn't he get out?"

"No money. Only the rich Jews are going to America. Hitler wants the houses and factories of the rich. A poor man is of no interest to a thief."

"How do you see it ending?"

"We'll have to blow his bollocks off... Hitler's, not Fritz Wendel's." Will was trying to smile through his broken face.

"When will war break out?"

"When Hitler's ready with a new navy and air force. When he's made sure America will sit on the fence again. When he's sure the Russians have enough problems of their own... If it's Sunday, why is Janet working?"

"Some of her patients can only get away on weekends. Having a stutter is not like seeing the doctor. Her rooms are down the road from her flat. The receptionist works for three of them, on the fringe of the medical profession, only she doesn't come in on a Sunday."

"No wonder your lady is getting rich."

"When do you want to go back to Germany?"

"When the bruises are gone. When I've seen Genevieve. When you and I have got drunk together."

"If I want to marry Janet I've got to do something about money."

"Just don't tell her first. Women are funny."

"She thinks we have enough money as we are."

"I've always wanted to marry a rich woman."

"Maybe for a while. After that I'd feel an idiot. A man has to provide for his family or he isn't a man."

"Well said, partner."

WHILE WILL WAS TRYING to drink a hot cup of tea through swollen lips, twenty miles away Tinus Oosthuizen was reading the same article in the *Sunday Times* just read by Horatio Wakefield. He was standing in front of the fire in the morning room of Hastings Court, the front of his body boiling hot, his back cold from the east wind rattling the French doors.

Outside the day was bleak, not a leaf on the trees, the wind howling from the direction of Headley Common where Tinus had taken an early morning walk with his Uncle Harry, both muffled up against the winter cold. No one else was down, even the children preferring to stay in their warm beds, which for Tinus was a blessing.

Halfway through the story of the reporter himself being beaten up by thugs, Tinus lost interest and turned to the sports page. Coming from Elephant Walk deep in the African bush, Tinus had never heard of Hitler. Berlin he knew from his geography lessons. There was nothing in the paper about South African cricket and English football bored him to tears.

Turning seventeen in six weeks, what was going on in the streets of Germany or the football pitches of England was of little interest. Throwing the paper on the sofa, Tinus went to the window and looked out over the windswept lawns; it was a bad day for flying, the other passion in his life after cricket.

Tinus heard his friend Andre Cloete come into the morning room without turning round.

"There you are. Looking all over the house. Did you go outside or something with your Uncle Harry? Saw two bent figures earlier from my bedroom window. This old house is freezing... Anything in the paper?"

Tinus turned from the window and smiled at Andre Cloete. Andre was down from Oxford for the Christmas holiday, staying at Hastings Court for the first time.

"Nothing. Uncle Harry has promised to teach me how to fly. When I come up next year, I am going to join the University Air Squadron. I need a private pilot's licence to get into the squadron. Do you know anything about the Oxford University Air Squadron?"

"Not a thing. Where's your Uncle Harry?"

"Up in the bedroom. His wife's got a cold. Luckily, the monsters are still in bed."

"They are terrible. What's on the menu for today?"

"I didn't think you would want to go for a walk. Uncle Harry wanted to know all about Elephant Walk. Poor chap really hates the English weather. Today's pretty much as you see it half the year. Saturday he's taking the two of us to the theatre. We'll spend the night in the West End at a hotel. A friend of Uncle Harry's daughter is an actress. Apparently, it's a new show and needs all the support it can get. Going up to London will be fun. Uncle Harry financed the show. Her last play flopped after three months. This one is a comedy and we get to go backstage."

"Did you read this, Tinus? The reporter himself got beaten up. That's a turn-up for the books."

Andre Cloete had retrieved the paper from the sofa and was reading standing up next to the fire.

"Some of it."

"Is the girl pretty?"

"A real smasher, according to Uncle Harry... Do you think there is going to be another war?"

"Who the hell cares? We're Afrikaans."

"My mother was English."

"Your mother is Rhodesian."

"Uncle Harry says we can take the guns out and shoot rabbits."

Andre Cloete began to laugh, throwing the paper back onto the sofa; he too did not relate to William Smythe's article in the *Sunday Times*. To Andre, Berlin was too far away from his house in South Africa.

"What's so funny?"

"The last thing I shot on the family farm was a male lion."

"Why did you shoot it? You can't eat a lion. Uncle Harry says you should never kill anything you are not going to eat."

"The lion was eating the cattle so it made sense. And one of the workers' legs."

"Poor sod... I'm starving. Let's go and find some breakfast... I didn't tell you yesterday when you came down into the country but it's come through."

"What has, Tinus?... What are we getting for breakfast?"

"My Rhodes Scholarship. Just as well as the farm isn't making much money. Since the war ended, the price of tobacco has dropped by half, according to grandfather. Did you know this house was once his? It's belonged to the Mandervilles for hundreds of years."

"So has Venterskraal. Ten generations of Cloetes. Oh, and jolly well done. They treat us Rhodes Scholars at Oxford rather specially. Cecil Rhodes would have been proud of you, you being Rhodesian. Did you get the one allocated to Bishops? Thought you would. Cricket and rugby teams. The top three in class. Makes sense. All-rounders, that's what Rhodes said in his will... What are you going to read?"

"I was going to read geology, like Uncle Harry. The headmaster says I should read PPE, philosophy, politics and economics, if I want to join Anglo-American. Geologists are too specialist and never get into management where it counts."

"Have you told your Uncle Harry?"

"Not yet. It's a whole year before I go up. Anything can happen in a year. According to that chap in the paper, there's going to be another war in Europe."

"Doesn't affect us, Tinus."

"But it might affect Oxford if the Germans win."

"Then you tell them your grandfather was a Boer general, hanged by the British for being a Cape Boer and going out with G J Scheepers. The Germans were on our side during the Anglo-Boer war."

"Both my mother and grandmother were English."

"It's the male line that counts. You're an Afrikaner, Tinus Oosthuizen. The Germans will love you. Just don't say so when you come up to Oxford next year... That's bacon I smell. And coffee."

They had both walked together to the breakfast room where another fire was burning in the grate. On the sideboard, the servants had placed a silver dish on top of two small methylated spirit burners to keep the food hot. Tinus lifted the heavy silver lid and smiled at what he saw inside.

"Bacon, sausage, tomatoes from the greenhouse, scrambled eggs and sheep's kidney. We make our own toast in the electric toaster a chap in Denver, Colorado sent Uncle Harry. Uncle Harry and the American were in the war together. Bloody clever thing, really. Everyone gets hot toast."

"You can leave out the sheep's kidneys. Had enough of those at Venterskraal."

"Help yourself. Just look at all this. Orange juice, fresh fruit salad; cream from Uncle Harry's cows, now he's buying up the surrounding land."

"He was jolly lucky to get all his money back from the government. Once they have their hands on your money, it's difficult to get it back, so my father says. Can't live properly without a lot of money. Do you want to be rich?"

"I have no idea."

"I think you had better be rich."

"Coffee or tea, Andre?"

"Don't be silly. I've had to drink enough tea since I've been in England to drown myself."

"You've only been here four months, but I know what you mean. Grandfather has started growing coffee on Elephant Walk. Just a few bushes to see if it grows. He's always up to something."

"How old is your grandfather?"

"As old as the hills."

"Do you know what? These English sheep kidneys taste different to ours at home. The cook's done something with them."

"She calls them devilled kidneys, whatever that means... I could eat a horse. The weather outside may be lousy but it makes you hungry. I expect Uncle Harry had something sent up to their room. All those bugs he picked up in the Congo haven't affected his appetite."

"How is he? Any after effects?"

"None at all."

"He was lucky to come out alive."

"He never talks about it. His friend Iggy Bowes-Lyon was on the plane that went down. Went off for help and never seen again. I think Uncle Harry feels guilty. They flew in the war together. I want to be a fighter pilot, like Uncle Harry."

Andre smiled to himself. Once Tinus got on the subject of Uncle Harry, it was difficult to get him off. Andre put it all down to Tinus losing his father when he was a boy; the thought of losing his own father was too horrible to bear.

"Your toast is burning, Tinus."

"I haven't quite mastered the toaster... Look out. Here they come."

"Who?"

"The monsters. My cousins."

"How old are they?"

"Anthony is ten, the youngest Kim, four. Then there's Beth, Frank and Dorian in between. No wonder the cook put so much food on the burner."

"Do they make their own toast?"

"Don't be silly. That's my job... Or yours, if you want to help. Why do young kids have to make so much noise?"

"It's a way of expressing themselves. I have eleven siblings and I'm the eldest. Kind of makes me feel homesick. Sounds as if one of them fell down the stairs."

"Or was pushed."

"I'm going to have a big family of my own one day."

"Never even thought of it."

"You will, Tinus. You will. That's what life is all about, a family. According to father and father is always right."

"A bit like Uncle Harry."

The breakfast room door burst open admitting the five children. Frank was dressed like a Red Indian and was hollering at the top of his voice.

"No wonder their mother and father take breakfast in their room," said Andre, getting up from the table to help the children as the dogs burst in, barking at the chaos.

"Get those dogs out of here," shouted Mrs Craddock bringing up the rear.

MRS CRADDOCK WAS the cook and looked to Andre at the end of her wits. She had fat bare arms and fingers the size of sausages, and a dishcloth in her right hand which she was using to swipe at the pack of dogs. The dogs were spaniels, reddish in colour with big long ears that brushed the ground. They all went to the fireplace and sat down looking at the flames while they ignored Mrs Craddock and her dishcloth.

Mrs Craddock gave up with the dogs and went to the sideboard to fill small dishes with fruit for the children. The children had a small wooden table of their own with short wooden chairs in the corner of the breakfast room away from the fire and the dogs. They never complained they felt the cold. On the back of the dwarf chairs were painted giant toadstools and fairies; some of the fairies were sitting on the toadstools.

The tablecloth designed to soak up the spills was covered with fairy-tale pictures. Each of the children had a glass of milk waiting on the table.

Andre Cloete smiled while making the toast in the toaster sent over from America by Glen Hamilton. With food in their mouths, the noise had abated as spoons shovelled food into gaping mouths. There was juice dribbling down every one of the chins.

Mrs Craddock was trying to tie bibs round the necks of the two youngest, the white bibs getting in the way of the spoons feeding the mouths. To Andre's surprise, Anthony looked up from his empty fruit dish and winked. The clatter of feet on the wooden floor started up again when the bowls were all empty. No one had touched the milk.

"Drink your milk! Now. Back you go." Mrs Craddock had her hand on her hips protecting the sideboard, her ample bosom heaving, her dishcloth ready for a clout.

"Andre, now it's you burning the toast," said Tinus.

"If they were speaking Afrikaans, this place could just as well be Venterskraal," Andre said, burning his fingers.

"What's Afrikaans?" asked Anthony after swallowing down his milk without sitting back at the table.

"Didn't you live in Africa? Afrikaans is my home language."

"Only English on Elephant Walk. And Shona... Princess and Tembo were teaching me Shona. But you speak English like cousin Tinus... Is that burned toast for me? What we do is scrape the burned bits out of the window."

"Don't you dare open the window!" screamed Mrs Craddock.

"Do it in the fire," said Tinus. "Just don't wake the dogs."

BY THE TIME breakfast was over for the children the top of the tablecloth looked like a battleground to Andre. Outside the window the children, now warmly dressed by the children's nurse he had only heard and not seen, were screaming at the dogs, children and dogs running all over the frozen lawn.

A maid came into the breakfast room to clear the mess off the table.

"I want to show you the library built up by my Manderville ancestors," said Tinus. "It was locked when the RAF took over the house as a rehabilitation centre after the war. The family furniture was locked in the basement. It cost Uncle Harry a small fortune to restore the house. The place was falling down from old age. Why my Manderville grandfather sold it to my Brigandshaw grandfather in the first place. By then the Mandervilles were broke. They were really my great-grandfathers but grandfather Manderville says that's too complicated when I'm on the farm in Rhodesia."

"Let's go and have a look at the books. My tutor says all the knowledge of the world is locked inside books. All you have to do is open them... Have you read Plato?"

"Of course."

At the ages of eighteen and going on seventeen, they had the world at their feet without a cloud in the sky. In the morning room as they passed, the newspaper shouting William Smythe's article was still lying on the sofa. Someone had left the door open, which Tinus closed as they went by, hoping the fire in the grate would heat up the rest of the room.

Having his friend and cricket mentor in the house was a great joy to Tinus. As the years passed, the difference in their age meant less and less. Tinus hoped they would stay friends for the rest of their lives.

In the library, two coal fires were burning at either end of the long room. Uncle Harry had been told the fires would drive the mildew out of the room. The mildew had crept in through the damp walls while the library was locked up. Uncle Harry had said there was always a price to pay for everything; but at least now the books were still on the shelves instead of being borrowed and never returned by the chaps in the air force.

"Wow! Now this is something," said Andre Cloete in awe.

"I thought you would like it... Over there is every word Plato ever wrote more than two thousand years ago... Older than the New Testament... The whole meaning of government, the whole meaning of democracy."

"Now you're going over my head, old chap. I'm a mathematician. I only asked you if you'd read Plato. Didn't say I'd read it all."

"I'll give you the *Republic* to read while you are staying at Hastings Court. It's very rewarding."

"Now I know why you've changed your degree to PPE... I say, that fire does look inviting. How did that cat get in?"

"They are all over the house. Why we don't have rats and mice."

"Sensible. I much prefer cats to rats."

THE NEXT DAY Tinus left his friend in front of the fire in the library and went off with Uncle Harry on the motorcycle. The weather had changed for the better. The wind had dropped.

"Perfect day for flying," Uncle Harry had said, handing Tinus a flying coat that dropped below his knees. "Flew in that one during the war. I was thinner in those days. It'll be cold in the air and on the back of the bike."

"Where are we going?"

"Redhill Aerodrome. A few miles south. Tina is staying in bed nursing her cold. Doesn't want to give it to everyone... Borrowed one of the new dual-control Tiger Moths. My promise to teach you to fly was made years ago but I never forget a promise... We've been over the theory so many times we won't do that again... Some people are naturals. Let's go and see! The bike is more fun than the car. John Woodall knows we are coming... Hell, those children of mine make a lot of noise. Afterwards we'll get a bite of lunch together and drink a pint of beer. Andre says he doesn't even like the idea of flying or we would have taken the car."

"He's scared of heights. Brave enough to shoot a man-eating lion, but scared of heights."

"Just the two of us then."

TINUS WAS SWEPT through the English country lanes clinging to the back of his Uncle Harry, the powerful engine throbbing through his loins. He had never felt so happy. Most of the time in the short straights the bike was at full throttle, the rider confident they would not hit the leafless boughs of the trees. Both of them were wearing flying goggles, their long flying jackets cracking in the wind, the winter fields of Surrey passing them at speed.

The small biplane, with two round open cockpits in line along the top of the fuselage, was waiting at the end of the runway. They all strolled out to it. John Woodall had flown with his Uncle Harry during the war. Tinus, despite his excitement, managed to keep quiet while the two older men reminisced. Even before he flew up into the clear blue sky, it was heaven on earth for Tinus, his dream unfolding in front of his eyes.

John Woodall had explained the dual controls when they were both seated in the aircraft. Then the man swung the propeller three times and the aircraft came to life with Uncle Harry in control. In short time they were running down the runway and lifting into the air, the fields quickly becoming smaller.

At two thousand feet, Uncle Harry signalled he was handing Tinus control. The stick came alive along with the rudder bar. He was flying the plane, his heart in his mouth. Then Tinus explored the rudder bar, tipping the wings. Uncle Harry tapped him on the shoulder from the rear cockpit. Up came the gloved hand with the thumbs up.

Twenty minutes later, they were down on the ground with Uncle Harry back in control of the aircraft. When Uncle Harry took off his goggles, he was grinning. Neither of them had to say a word. By then Tinus knew instinctively he was born to be a flyer.

There was no sign of John Woodall as they left the plane where they found it and walked back to the bike. Soon again the fields and hedgerows were rushing by them.

When they pulled off the road, crunching the wheels of the motorcycle on loose gravel, they came to a stop outside the Running Horses at Mickleham, not far from Hastings Court. Both of them were cold and glad of the promise of the fire in the bar.

"How are you liking England, Tinus?"

"It's different. Very different."

"Homesick for Elephant Walk? Me too. Tina won't hear of going back and the children are happy in England... Maybe one day... I am going to tell the landlord you are eighteen and up at Oxford or he won't give you a beer. You look eighteen. Are you hungry?"

"Starving."

"Just rounds off the morning, you and I having lunch together. Two men talking without the clutter of women and kids, bless them all."

Uncle Harry seemed to know the landlord well, which to Tinus was not surprising; Uncle Harry knew everyone well. Tinus shook the publican's hand and followed his uncle into the empty bar where they found the promised fire. The small room smelt of beer.

"This is where it all began for Merlin," said Uncle Harry.

"*King Arthur's Merlin*?"

"No, no. My brother-in-law, Merlin. Esther was the barmaid during the war when they fell in love. Your aunt Lucinda was Merlin's sister. Well, you know that terrible story when your father died instead of me... I'm sorry. Not the subject for a day like today."

Tinus found tears coming to his eyes. The same man who had killed Aunt Lucinda on Salisbury Station had killed his father years later in the same place. Tembo had shot dead Mervyn Braithwaite on the platform with Tinus's father lying dead on the ground, changing Tinus's life forever.

Uncle Harry went to the bar to order the drinks. When he came back with two pints of draught beer, Tinus had gained control of himself; poor Uncle Harry had lost his pregnant wife so why should he feel sorry for himself?

"Esther is Genevieve's mother. Merlin St Clair her father, though she does not carry his name. She's the actress we are going to see on Saturday. I'm making sure she is going to be a big star. When you see her onstage, you will understand. I have a present for her on Saturday when we go backstage. A man I knew in the war that now runs a film studio in Elstree... A good friend of mine... Cheers, Tinus. Glad to have you in England."

"Cheers, Uncle Harry."

They both drank, Tinus pulling a face.

"What's the matter?"

"It's warm!"

"My nephew's from Africa," Uncle Harry said to the barmaid who was giving Tinus the eye.

"We drink it ice-cold in Rhodesia," Tinus said to the girl. The girl looked not much older than himself.

"Expect you do, luv... When in Rome... Where's Rhodesia?"

With Uncle Harry smiling, Tinus went up to the bar to explain... His day just couldn't stop getting better.

THERE WERE MORE people in the dining room when they went through to lunch. Back in the bar, Tinus had been torn between telling the barmaid all about Rhodesia and going back to Uncle Harry standing at the fire with a knowing smile on his face drinking his pint. The girl had seen his dilemma and gone off to wash glasses in the kitchen behind the bar. There was an open hatch through which she could see any new customers. She gave Tinus a last lascivious smile, which sent feelings rushing through his body he had only dreamed about in his sleep. His lifelong pursuit of women had just begun.

"Just as I hoped," said Uncle Harry when the landlord handed him the menu at the table. "This place is renowned for its jugged hare."

"How do they make it?" asked Tinus, happy to keep the conversation away from the girl in the bar.

"Better I tell you when we've eaten... We'll have a small bottle of red wine to go with the hare."

When the food came in large brown bowls, the smell made his mouth water. The waiter had taken off the lids. Inside was a rich sauce covering pieces of meat with round balls of something floating in the gravy. Uncle Harry never had a starter. He had told Tinus more than once it ruined his appetite for the main treat. On a side dish came the Brussels sprouts and boiled new potatoes, the potatoes sprinkled with fresh parsley. Two glasses of wine were poured, a toast drunk to their mutual health and then they tucked in.

The taste of the food was as good as the smell. In deference, they ate in silence, both accepting a second helping from the earthen serving bowl brought to the table by the publican. By the time Tinus finished his lunch the beer and wine had gone to his head, another feeling that was going to stay with him through his life.

"All right. How do they make it, Uncle Harry?"

"First they shoot themselves a wild hare somewhere out in the fields. Then they bring it back and hang it up in the larder by its back legs with a silver cup at its mouth to catch the blood. They then close the door of the larder for a week or two until they find white maggots in the hare's dead eyes. Then they cut it down, careful not to spill the congealed blood in the silver cup. With forced meatballs they cook the meat in red wine with a mix of herbs and spices for hour after hour, just keeping the pot bubbling. Right at the end, they throw in the congealed blood and stir to make the gravy. By the time they cook the hare the meat is basically rotten. The term is gamey, the most appetising taste on earth."

"I'm glad you told me when I'd finished."

"Thought you would be."

THE THREE OF them drove up to London on the Saturday morning. Aunty Tina was still bunged up with her cold and stayed behind with the children. It was to be the first time Tinus had been to the theatre. The day before, Tinus had landed the Tiger Moth without Uncle Harry touching the controls. John Woodall had been on the field to watch the perfect landing. Next week, with luck, Tinus was going solo, his pilot licence now within reach.

"It's coordination, young man. Some have it, some don't. Are you by any chance good at sport?"

"Not bad," Tinus had said, grinning at John Woodall.

The second lunch at the Running Horses would take place when John Woodall, the owner of the flying school, handed him his licence. The thought of going back to Cape Town on the boat after Christmas was far from Tinus's mind.

To test the theory of the jugged hare, he and Andre had shot themselves a brace of hare in the twenty-acre field behind Hastings Court. Mrs Craddock had hung them in the larder each with a silver cup strapped to their heads to catch the drips.

They were to stay at the Savoy Hotel on the River Thames, an old haunt of Uncle Harry's. By then Tinus was quite sure he was in love with the barmaid at the Running Horses who had given him his first sexually insinuating smile. Her name was Minnie, the most beautiful name for Tinus in the world.

2

When William Smythe arrived at the theatre that night, he was struck by the normalcy. After what he had been through for six months in Berlin, London reminded him of Rome before it burned to the ground while Nero played his fiddle.

As they passed through the foyer, no one in the crowd had a care in the world. All Will overheard was trivia.

It had taken some persuasion for Janet Bray to come along with Horatio Wakefield. The girl had some absurd idea Genevieve was a threat.

Will's face had recovered enough from the beating for him to go out in public; the swelling had gone, leaving the area around his eyes discoloured.

It was the first time he was going to see Genevieve since his Berlin assignment. To Will's surprise, there to the right of him was Harry Brigandshaw looking the man-about-town, not the yellow-faced half-dead corpse he had been two years earlier when Will found him in the hospital.

With Harry Brigandshaw were two tall young men, equally confident with themselves. One of them had the same look as Harry and had to be a relative but not a son. The last interview with Brigandshaw had been a year earlier at Hastings Court with a pack of children screaming round the house, none of them old enough to be standing in the foyer of the theatre dressed in a dinner jacket. The young man talking animatedly to Harry Brigandshaw had to be the nephew from Rhodesia, the one whose father had been killed by Brigandshaw's commanding officer in the Royal Flying Corps after the war; the one who had gone mad and kept on killing, the man they had put into an institution, the state blaming the war for his mental condition. The thin difference between hero and killer made Will shudder.

Just as Will was turning to follow Horatio and Janet into the auditorium, Harry Brigandshaw recognised him through the crowd, mouthing a big hello followed by what looked like the words 'after the show' repeated twice and pointing with his hand where to go. Will mouthed the word 'backstage', getting back a smile. Of course, Brigandshaw had financed the show.

Feeling his stomach flip, Will followed the others through the open doors into the lighted auditorium. The second bell had gone. As they found their seats and sat down the house lights dimmed and the audience went quiet with anticipation. Not only was Will going to see Genevieve up on the stage, he now had an excuse to see her face to face. A face that had stayed in his mind all the long months in the cold room over the bicycle shop, watching and writing his story of Adolf Hitler's rise to power alongside the rise of militant Germany. To want a woman so much, he told himself hugging his sides with pent-up expectation, had to be called an obsession. The one thing he coveted as much as money in his life was the girl who called herself Genevieve. Just Genevieve.

SITTING BETWEEN THE TWO FRIENDS, Janet Bray's reluctance had nothing to do with the girl on the stage. Janet had enough confidence in herself to know Genevieve was not a threat. What was churning up her stomach was a conversation she had overheard between Horatio and Will while she was making the supper earlier that evening in the small flat the two men were again sharing in Notting Hill Gate.

Will wanted Horatio to go with him back to Germany so Horatio could make some money. Some real money, so she and Horatio could afford to get married. Up to that point, Will's smashed-up face had had nothing to do with her.

"I've talked to Reuters and they agree, Horatio. Two of us will have a better chance of looking out for each other. Anyway, I was out there six months and only got bashed up once. They are going to get me an

American passport and I'm going to talk American, an accent even easier to fall into than the Irish. No one will suspect Brad Sikorski to be William Smythe. They don't have a photograph of me."

"You hope."

"Even then they'll be looking for one man on his own answering to my description. You'll make more money than Janet in a year and make yourself famous."

"That's the point, Will, you made yourself famous and now look at your face."

"The byline will be Horatio Wakefield. By the time we get out you'll be a famous foreign correspondent writing your own ticket wherever you go."

"You want to use my name because you can't use your own."

"I want to make you famous, Horatio. As a hack, you've gone nowhere. Glass treats you like a lackey. You'd eat his shit if he told you to."

"That's vulgar. I do what my editor tells me because that is my job."

"Then get another one. That pays better. That gives you a chance to get on in life. You're in a rut, my old friend. And it's getting deeper."

"I have a secure job. Many people in this depression don't have jobs. By the way, while you're here you're paying half the rent like in the old days. I can't afford to be an altruist."

"That's my point. For God's sake, you have to take risks in this life or you get nowhere. Do you want to spend the rest of your life in this flat hiring out the couch? Just think about it."

"I'll think about it. Don't tell Janet."

"Don't tell me what?" she had said brightly, bringing in the pot of stew having heard every word of the conversation.

AFTER THAT, the last thing she had wished to do was go to the theatre and watch some trite comedy. There was nothing worth seeing in the theatre anyway. She had read all the critics. The current plays were either medieval and miserable or light and fluffy. Anything to keep people's minds off what was going on to the east of them in Russia, where they had shot all the aristocrats and intellectuals, or in Germany, where they hated the Jews and anyone else who did not look Aryan. And poor Horatio thought her reluctance was not wishing him to see Genevieve, the least serious problem she had in the world.

Sitting back in her seat, not hearing the words spoken in the play, a world full of darkness began passing through her mind, a world where once again the human race was gone mad, the evil that men did living after them, not interred with their bones; Janet went on thinking of Shakespeare, of Brutus, Mark Antony and Julius Caesar.

After ten minutes, she sniffed and blew her nose, getting a funny sideways look from Horatio.

'The man still thinks it's Genevieve,' she said to herself.

The audience laughed brightly and brought Janet's mind back into the theatre. Soon she laughed herself. Then the play took hold; not as bad as she thought. By the time the lights came up for the intermission she was enjoying herself, Horatio's hand firmly held in her own; in life Janet knew it was always better to laugh than cry. If there was going to be a war, Horatio at thirty would be too old to go into the army to fight.

OSCAR FLEMING, sitting by invitation between Harry Brigandshaw and Louis Casimir from the Elstree Studio, decided he felt nothing anymore. Even the last lust of his life up on the stage was having no effect. He was old, jaded and bored. It was time to give up the theatre, go live in the country and breed dogs. Maybe write his memoirs. Maybe not. The girl was good, carrying the play as she had done the first one written by Freya St Clair. No one was making money in the theatre. Well, he smiled to himself, she had got her way without having to seduce him in bed. She was a rising star who had stepped on his head.

Oscar yawned, quickly putting his hand over his face, hoping the film man had not seen his boredom. This was his last favour for Harry Brigandshaw, then it was over, the thought passing through his mind: 'what did I see in all those giggling girls in pursuit of worthless fame?' He had never married which was probably just as well. It was better to keep his cynicism all to himself.

Only when the final curtain had fallen and the house lights came up did his mood lighten.

"You'll love her," he said to Louis Casimir. "She'll make a great star of the silver screen, Louis. Now, let's go meet her. Are the young men coming with us, Harry?"

"Of course. Then I am taking everyone out to a supper club. The chap who was beaten up by Hitler's Brownshirts is in the audience. He's joining us with his party backstage."

"It can't be as bad as it sounds," said Louis Casimir.

"Better ask him."

WHEN TINUS TROOPED in behind the others the dressing room was full of flowers and people. Their various scents mingled with the stage make-up the star was wiping with a towel from her face, a face that Tinus watched in the mirror with the same fascination he had watched on the stage. For a brief flash, their eyes met as they recognised each other, two teenagers trying to be grown-ups.

Everyone was in evening dress, including Genevieve from her part in the play. For the first time that night Tinus felt awkward and gauche; standing at the back not knowing what to do, he felt like the farm boy from the African bush he was, not the flyer who ate in restaurants. With everyone concentrated on the star, he and Andre were left out of it. Tinus's new dinner jacket made him feel ridiculous.

Uncle Harry had been swallowed up by the crowd along with the two sophisticates who had sat with them in the theatre. Searching through the gaps in the moving backs of people, Tinus occasionally saw Uncle Harry talking animatedly with the man who looked as though his face had recently taken a severe beating, something Tinus had seen before at Bishops when one of the boys was beaten badly in the boxing ring for being a queer.

"She's much younger than she looks, Andre. About our age," he said.

"Can't be, old boy. The woman was married in the play. Anyway, how would you know?"

"She looked at me in the mirror. How long will this go on? I'm starving. The film man's met her now. Isn't that enough?"

"This is the way to live. Theatre. Backstage. Supper clubs. London is the centre of the world. Be patient, Tinus. You'll eat soon enough. Your uncle wants to invite her to join us. Now this is going to be a party. Film directors, impresarios, famous men from the newspapers, actresses. It won't get better than this, Tinus."

TALENT SCOUTING WAS NOT his job. It was not even Harry Brigandshaw's money that had persuaded Louis Casimir to take a look at Genevieve; there were rich men right across London trying to impress young girls with their connections so they could take the poor creatures to bed. The approach, as Louis put it, had come from Oscar Fleming, which made better sense; the man had a reputation with young girls.

"She's ambitious, Louis. I'll give her that."

"Oscar, she's not one of yours?"

"Of course not. I'm sixty years old."

"But you tried?"

"A reflex action."

"In *Who's Who*, they say you're a bit older than sixty."

"Who on earth reads *Who's Who*! Vulgar. I never gave them an interview. Just do it for Harry. You two fought in the war together. Doesn't all this nonsense in Germany get you frightened?"

"What do you mean?"

"Oh. I'm sorry. You're hiding being Jewish like I'm hiding my age."

"There's going to be another war or Hitler will exterminate the world's Jews."

To each other, they both looked scared.

"Will you come to the theatre and see her on Saturday, Louis? Frankly, I think she's worth looking at but make up your own mind. She has that something which if it comes across on the screen will have the male population howling for more."

"So you did have something more in mind for this Genevieve?"

"There's no fool like an old fool, Louis. She ran rings round me."

"How is Harry after his ordeal in the Congo?"

"Knocked the stuffing out of him, if you want my opinion. Either that or we are all getting old."

"Speak for yourself."

"You chaps will never have any trouble in England."

"I know that. Why grandfather came to England from Hungary. I'm going to America. Did I tell you that? Hollywood is the place to be."

"To live?"

"Maybe."

"So you are frightened of Hitler?"

"So would you be if you were Jewish... Now what's the matter?"

"We all have our secrets. My ancestors came from Russia."

"How far back?"

"Far enough to change our surname to Fleming. You should think of that, Louis. You can never be too careful in this world. When in Rome be like the Romans. Did you know surgeons can change the shape of your nose?"

Only at the Mayfair did Louis Casimir realise what Genevieve was all about. It was the girl's eyes. One was chocolate brown, the other as blue as the sky. For the first time, when they sat down at the table in the supper club, the girl looked at him directly, unflinchingly, goading him to see the difference between the eyes. The blue one was beautiful, the girl behind the eye as light as a feather, full of laughter and joy. Inside the chocolate eye was the devil, the promise of wicked passion, the promise of hell; instantly, his genitals came alive.

"Why are you shuddering, Mr Casimir?" she said sweetly.

"I just looked through into your soul."

"Welcome aboard. Be careful not to drown."

"Would you like a film test, Miss Genevieve?"

"Of course. Isn't that what all this is about?"

All Genevieve had done was smile at him. Men were so stupid. So easy to manipulate. When the man from Drake Films was firmly on her hook, she left him dangling and turned her attention to Will sitting on her other side; the poor man was besotted with her. Then she smiled at Tinus across the table, meeting a solid stare; to Genevieve's surprise, the boy was not intimidated. His eyes were mocking her. Like his Uncle Harry, she knew then Tinus would never dance to her tune like the rest of them.

"How old are you, Tinus?"

"I'll be seventeen in February. Just don't tell the waiter or I won't get my one glass of wine. Uncle Harry's teaching me to fly an aeroplane."

"Is that wise? William here says we're going to be in another war."

"That's our job, Genevieve. Keeping the world safe so when they let loose the dogs of war there will be someone to stop them. In a year I'm going up to Oxford."

"So you'll be over here for three years."

"Yes I will. Maybe we can meet again."

"I'd like that. What's it like in Africa?"

"Wild. And very beautiful."

Smiling, she turned her attention back to the film director. The band was playing. Couples were making their way to the dance floor.

"Why don't you ask me to dance, Mr Casimir?"

"Call me Louis."

"Oh, I couldn't. We barely know each other." Then she let her smile jolt him once again, bringing him to his feet.

When she looked over his shoulder from the small dance floor, she caught Tinus looking at her with a smile on his face. William was leaving the table. For the rest of the supper she watched Tinus locked in animated conversation with his Uncle Harry. William did not come back to the table. Horatio said William's face was hurting before Janet took Horatio off to the dance floor.

"This is the life," said Andre Cloete to no one in particular.

The supper club was now so full the waiters were having difficulty moving between the tables. To Genevieve looking around the smoke-filled room, buzzing with the noise of happy people, no one seemed to have a care in the world.

WHEN THEY ALL WENT HOME, Harry Brigandshaw helped her into the taxi, giving the driver the address of her flat in St John's Wood.

"Did it work out all right, Genevieve?"

"Perfectly, Uncle Harry."

"Just be careful. Give my love to your father. When are you going down to Purbeck Manor again?"

"Not for some time. Aunty Freya is still sore her play was not the grand success we all hoped."

"We did our best. They are talking about going to live in America again so she can take up where she left off writing her column for the *Denver Telegraph*. Robert doesn't seem to mind where he writes his books. I'll miss my old friend if they go."

"Uncle Robert is a darling."

"Good luck with the film test."

He was still watching her when she looked through the back window of the taxi. Tinus and the other young man from Africa were trying to hail another one. There was a slight flurry of snow in the air caught by the gas streetlights. With no one looking at her anymore, Genevieve slumped in her seat. She was tired but knew she would have difficulty sleeping. It took her hours after a show finished to come out of her part. She could still see the smile on the face of the young boy whose full name was Martinus; she had asked him how he came by the name Tinus.

When she got out into the cold night at St John's Wood, the taxi driver told her the man who gave him the address had paid the fare.

"Goodnight."

"Goodnight, Miss Genevieve."

Even the cab driver knew her name. With her coat collar pulled up over her ears, she hurried across the pavement and through the entrance to her block of flats. The doorman was sitting inside on a chair.

"It's cold outside, Miss Genevieve."

Genevieve gave the old man a peck on the cheek before getting into the lift. The operator was half asleep and neither of them spoke; the lift operator was even older than the doorman.

Alone in her flat she put a record on the gramophone. Brahms's *Third Symphony* began to play softly into the silence of her flat. By the time she had turned over two records from the set of ten she went to bed, the music having pushed her character in the play out of her head.

When she lay down to sleep in her bedroom with the lights off she thought of Tinus, christened Martinus, and not the man who she knew wanted to make her a film star. If they all knew the nearest she had been in her life to a man was holding his hand they would probably laugh in disbelief. She was sure Janet and Horatio were lovers. Poor William, he did so much want to take her out.

As she dozed into sleep, she was wondering what it would be like to be someone's lover. Poor old Oscar Fleming; she had driven him up and down the proverbial wall so many times without him getting anywhere, the words of her mother always ringing in her ear: 'Never give 'em what they want, luv. Once they get what they want they don't need you no more.' The reality of her thoughts fed into a dream as she fell fast asleep, folded in the warmth of her own bed.

THE PHONE RINGING by the side of the bed woke her in the morning. The alarm clock on the bedside table told her it was just gone eleven o'clock. Genevieve had slept right through the night. She could not remember any of her dreams.

"Hello."

"Louis Casimir. Ten o'clock on Wednesday. A driver will pick you up at your flat and bring you to the studio. This Wednesday coming, Genevieve."

"This Wednesday at ten o'clock in the morning. Thank you."

"Thank you, Genevieve."

The man's voice was loaded with innuendo.

Within seconds, she was fast asleep again, only waking when her alarm clock went off at noon, the start of her day. She remembered to write the ten o'clock collection time from St John's Wood on the notepad beside the phone. Then she went and ran the bath.

THEY MADE HER READ SHAKESPEARE. The lights were hot in the studio. Genevieve spoke with the slightly husky voice they had taught her to use at the Central School of Speech and Drama. She knew the part by heart even though they gave her the script. When she had played a part she never forgot the words. They made her read the part of Juliet on her own. They didn't have a Romeo on call in the studio. There were four cameras set up taking pictures from different angles. She read her part twice before it was all over.

Louis Casimir invited her to lunch. There was a small executive dining room in the studio. Genevieve refused the proffered wine. They were lunching alone.

"I have to go onstage tonight, Louis. This is all so nice just the two of us."

She had dressed provocatively, spending an hour on making sure everything looked right before the driver rang for her from downstairs in the foyer of her block of flats. The man's look had told her all she needed to know.

"Will you dine with me after the show on Saturday night?"

"We can have a lovely long evening. I don't work on Sundays."

"I know, Genevieve."

"I must go now, Louis. I have an appointment with my hairdresser."

"The driver will take you wherever you want to go."

"I know he will."

"The board will have looked at your film test by Saturday."

"I said there's no rush, Louis. Where are you going to take me? Somewhere nice?"

"Somewhere very nice."

"That will be wonderful."

In the company car, the driver smiled at her in the rear-view mirror.

"Where do you want to go?"

"Home. Don't tell your boss. I said I had a hair appointment."

The man winked at her in the mirror.

BY FRIDAY AFTERNOON when Paul Dexter barged into his office, Louis

Casimir had removed Genevieve from his mind; he had not thought of her all morning.

"You'd better come and see the rushes, Mr Casimir. They are back from the lab."

"Are they any good?"

"See for yourself. I've sent out calls to the rest of the board. I told them three o'clock."

The man was visibly excited. Louis went back to the paperwork on his desk to hide his own trepidation.

All the blood had drained from his face. He was frightened, not sure if he wanted Genevieve in his life. Ever since their lunch for two she had taken over part of his mind, the part his wife would not want to know about.

At five minutes to three, Louis got up from his desk and made his feet walk to the small cinema at the end of the offices, the tension gripping his chest. Most of the people who counted to make a decision were waiting. They all sat down in the rows of seats in front of the big screen when he made his entrance. Everyone knew something abnormal was about to happen. Word, good or bad, spread like bush fire in a film studio.

The house lights went down reducing the audience to silence. The projector whirred from the small room high up at the back of the theatre. Then Genevieve was in front of them up on the big screen larger than life, her sensuality screaming before she opened her mouth. Louis had never seen so much sex appeal up on a screen, the girl's slightly husky voice adding to her attack on the senses of every male in the room. The camera had taken the meaning behind Genevieve's eyes and thrown it in their faces.

"Are we all agreed then?" he said when the house lights came up. "Fine. Paul, draw up the contract."

Back in his office, Louis poured himself a drink from the whisky bottle. The last thing he wanted to do was go home to his wife. She was far too perceptive. He wanted to go somewhere and get drunk on his own in a place no one would ask him questions.

"See you on Monday," he told his secretary.

"Don't you want them to send up the car from the garage?"

"Tell the driver to go home. I'll come back later and drive myself."

In the dark street outside, Louis had no idea where he was going. He put his hat firmly on his head, hunched his shoulders into the overcoat and began to walk, quickening his pace in an attempt to relieve the tension gripping his body. Everything he wanted from her was physical, none of it mental. By the time he found a public house, snow had gathered on the shoulders of his overcoat.

"Give me a large whisky."

"Aren't you a bit out of your way?"

A big man with rough hands pushed through the working class drinkers. In his left hand he carried a sheaf of flyers he was handing out. Louis sensed the big man did not like him dressed in an expensive overcoat with fur trim round the collar.

"You need one of these, my china. Read it and get out. This is working men. Englishmen. You ain't English. Not with a nozzle like that. You're Jewish, my china."

The man had bad breath. The barman had yet to pass Louis his drink.

"Thank you," he said taking the leaflet.

They jostled him on his way out to the door. Someone kicked the door shut behind him after they'd pushed him back onto the street.

He had forgotten which way he came, looking both ways up the street. He was shaking with fear. He began to run up the street to where traffic was crossing. At the intersection, he flagged down a taxi, giving the man his home address in Hampstead.

Half an hour later he stumbled into his own home, the leaflet still clutched in his hand.

"What's the matter, Louis?"

He put the leaflet in his wife's hand and went to pour himself a drink.

"It's here in England," said his wife from the hallway.

"We're going to America."

Earlier that week Louis had joined thirty thousand of his fellow Jews demonstrating against the Nazis. The pamphlet was retaliation from the British fascists led by Oswald Mosley telling the Jews they were not wanted in England.

When he and his wife looked into each other's eyes, all they saw was fear. They were Jews. Nobody wanted them. Even in England where both of them were born.

THE NEXT DAY, when the curtain went down on the evening performance of *Lady Come Home*, Genevieve expected to see Louis Casimir in her dressing room. She was thinking of Christmas and where she was going to be. Her father was spending a week at his ancestral home, which was too far to travel with a performance of the play on Christmas Eve. The previous year, Genevieve had been out of work and had spent the day with her father and grandparents at Purbeck Manor, despite the sour looks of Mrs Mason who frowned on the circumstances of her birth. Harry Brigandshaw had eaten Christmas lunch with them without his family who were staying with the Pringles in the railway cottage. No one had even mentioned Mrs Brigandshaw during Christmas lunch.

She found her dressing room full of flowers and people but no sign of Louis Casimir. In a corner by himself was William Smythe, his face better than the last time she had seen him at the Mayfair. He was grinning his head off, which made her annoyed now she was not going to be a film star. Obviously her screen test had been a disaster. Oscar Fleming had made her prepared the day after the test.

"Film tests can have strange results, Genevieve. What comes across on a stage doesn't always work on the big screen. Don't get your hopes up. Wait and see."

Oscar Fleming as usual was right. He too had heard not a word when she spoke to him at the start of the show. She sat down to take off her make-up, ignoring William Smythe and the rest of the people in her dressing room. It was a let-down that was not expected, despite Oscar Fleming's warning.

By the time the greasepaint was wiped and washed from her face, she had forgotten William Smythe. There was still no sign of Louis Casimir and the promised supper. Even if the screen test had been lousy, there was no reason for him to doubt her personal charm. It seemed to Genevieve at the age of nineteen she was losing her grip on men. Looking at herself in the mirror, she wondered what had gone wrong. Behind her, still grinning like a Cheshire cat, stood William Smythe having come out of his corner.

"What do you want?" she said without turning round.

"What I want and what I will get are two different things."

"Why are you here? Where's Janet?"

"Janet belongs to Horatio. Or, more exactly, my friend Horatio belongs to Janet. Aren't you pleased about the screen test?"

"It was a disaster."

"What gave you that indication?"

"Mr Casimir was meant to be here to take me out."

"Then his wife got him first. I have a source at the studio. They've already drawn up a three-picture contract to start when this play closes."

"Are you sure?"

"Have dinner with me and I'll show you a copy of the contract my friend filched this morning. I told him I was your agent."

"You are at least persistent, William Smythe."

"In my line of work it pays to be persistent."

"Your face looks better."

"You didn't know he was married?"

"In my line of work it doesn't really matter. Where are we going?"

JANET BRAY HAD NEVER BEEN jealous in her life. So far as she knew, no one from the Hall had become a film star. When William came back with a copy of the three-picture contract he had obtained under false pretences posing as a freelance journalist, she was happy for Genevieve.

"She needs an agent. They tell that to the drama students at the Hall. Why don't you act as her agent?"

"I know nothing about the theatre."

"Of course you do. You've reported on its ups and downs long enough. The girl isn't even twenty. They'll take what they want and throw her out."

"She's twenty-one."

"As a matter of fact she isn't. You're freelance. Make this another string to your bow."

"You don't want me to go back to Germany?"

"Of course I don't, silly. Just look at your face all bashed up. Why get yourself killed?"

Janet almost said 'and get Horatio killed in the process', but held her tongue. She wasn't meant to know William wanted Horatio to go with him back to Germany. The man was besotted with Genevieve, the only person Janet knew who could stop William putting his life in danger.

"An agent takes ten per cent of the contract," she went on. "I can get someone from the Hall who teaches the law of contract to see you. The Central School of Speech and Drama gave us all a general education as well as our specialisation."

"What about Oscar Fleming?"

"All he wants to do is bed the poor girl."

"You don't think he hasn't? Don't all actresses get where they want to go from the casting couch?"

"Not all of them. Not ones with talent."

"What about her father?"

"I don't think the Honourable Merlin St Clair would know one end of a contract from another. He bought shares in Vickers Armstrong at the start of the war and made a fortune; they made the machine guns that killed half the German army. He's lived off the money ever since."

"Harry Brigandshaw, he put up the money for *Lady Come Home*. He was once a big businessman. I'm sure he would like to look after her."

"Tina his wife won't let him anywhere near such a girl. She went through it with Brett Kentrich. What's the matter, William? Don't you have the girl's best interests at heart? If you are very clever, which I know you to be, you can kill two birds with one stone."

"You have a dirty mind."

"A practical one. Keep your mind on what's important. The wellbeing of your own life. I don't want my friend killed by Hitler's thugs any more than Horatio wants you in harm's way. You two have been friends a long time."

"I don't need to see a legal expert to read a contract."

"Good. There's a firm of solicitors in the City who specialises in the laws of contract. When you've made it what you want, ask them to legalise the terms."

"That sounds better. I'll go see Genevieve tonight after her show. Are you sure she's not even twenty?"

"Positive. Just avoid asking a woman her age. We all lie one way or the other depending on what age we want to be. At fifteen you want to be grown up."

"*She's fifteen, for goodness sake?*"

To stop William seeing the smirk welling up on her face, Janet quickly turned her back and buried her hands in the soapsuds in the sink. 'There's more than one way to skin a cat,' she told herself smugly.

WHEN WILLIAM finally went off with the contract to see Genevieve in her dressing room, Berlin with its hatred again seemed a long way away. Why people always thought making more money made them happier was beyond her comprehension. She and Horatio had each other to go through life. With the two of them earning money, they had enough. The next thing she had to do for William was suggest a bachelor on the prowl needed a flat of his own. There was always Adele Cornfelt to bring back from the past if Genevieve was unable to keep William's mind off Adolf Hitler. The girl was still a nurse at the Tropical Diseases Hospital. She was humming to herself when Horatio came back from a late-night assignment for his newspaper.

"Was the show worth a good review?" she asked.

"It was lousy. I thought you were going home?"

"Not tonight. Tomorrow's Sunday."

"Where's Will?"

"He's gone out to see Genevieve. To take her the contract and ask to be her agent. We have the place to ourselves for once in a while. Oh, and William says he's looking for his own flat."

"Thought he was going back to Germany as Brad Sikorski, American."

"Not anymore he isn't."

"Did you make him change his mind?"

"Why would he take any notice of me?"

THE FOLLOWING DAY, Bruno Kannberg was sent by his newspaper, the *Daily Mirror*, to Hyde Park.

Sleet was falling on the cold afternoon as the crowd continued to swell. Bowler hats mingled with cloth caps. Uniformed policemen on horseback watched and waited. Bruno stamped his feet on the hard frost-bitten ground to keep warm. When he puffed warm air into his cupped hands, he could see his breath. The leaflets had said three o'clock at Speakers' Corner where a row of soap boxes were being kept clear by young men wearing brown shirts over layers of vests both to keep them warm and, Bruno suspected, to give them protection in a brawl. The similarity to Germany's National Socialists was meant to be obvious. It was only two o'clock in the afternoon and thousands of people were milling around waiting for Sir Oswald Mosley. Groups of Jews were watching the imitation Brownshirts. A senior policeman in uniform standing close to Bruno was clearly worried.

"I'm from the *Daily Mirror*. Can you tell me what's going on?"

"If you didn't know, sonny, you wouldn't be here."

"Is there going to be trouble?"

"Not if I can help it."

"May I quote you?"

"It's a free country."

"May I have your name, sir?"

"No you may not, now bugger off."

Both of them continued to stand next to each other in silence, stamping their feet. Bruno's curiosity was turning to fear. Fascists ran Germany. Large numbers of Spaniards and Italians were leaning the same way. Now Bruno was looking at the same thing in England.

"Ask me," said a man on his left, "they're better than the communists. You gotter have discipline or the commies will take over."

"England's a democracy," snapped Bruno without thinking.

"You a commie, mate?"

"My father fought in the White Russian army."

"Then piss off where you belong. This is England. It's all you foreigners what crept in gives us English problems. England for the English, I say. Mosley's an English baronet who knows best for England. Don't want no commies or a French blood revolution. Some say the Prince of Wales is a supporter of Mosley, that they're friends."

"Don't you start trouble," said the senior policeman.

"Sorry, guv. Like you said. It's a free country."

"Not if this bloody lot get their way. And you," he said pointing at Bruno, "keep your trap shut. It's words what makes trouble. Just you see when Sir Oswald opens his big mouth."

The senior policeman glared at the other man, staring him into silence. Bruno wished he had bought a packet of cigarettes despite giving up smoking, the morning coughs too much for his chest. Taking the policeman's flick of the head as a warning he moved off into the crowd.

BY THE TIME Oswald Mosley's oratory had gone on for ten minutes, the crowd was beginning to punch each other and the horsemen moved in to stop a riot; the groups of Jews were standing toe to toe with the Brownshirts. For moments, Bruno found himself agreeing with the man ranting from the soap box, demanding the people protect their England against the conspiracy of the Jews to take over the world; the rich Jews who controlled the banks and most of England's wealth, stolen from Englishmen by cunning and deceit. Then Mosley was ranting against communism, the crowd swelling with indignation, Bruno having no idea what the Jews now had to do with communism.

"Give us the power to protect you," the man from the box shouted, punching his words, pulling Bruno's brain back to sanity.

The indignant noise from the crowd rose, from what Bruno now saw as a rabble, drowning out the speaker. Bruno found a gap in the crowd and pushed his way out, sweating despite the cold, his notebook and pen clutched in his right hand. Looking back, he saw the crowd was fighting, the policemen on the horses struggling to gain control. There was no sign of the senior policeman as Bruno looked around.

Standing with his back to the safety of a tree, Bruno watched as the police brought the melee under control, bullhorns telling them to go home, Mosley no longer on his soap box. Then it was over, litter all over Speakers' Corner, the ugliness evaporating as fast as it had come, ordinary people going home. One of the Brownshirts was stuffing his brown shirt into his trouser pocket, showing his layers of white vests, the man going off to mingle with the melting crowd like the rest of them. Then it was all over.

WHEN BRUNO REACHED his home in Holland Park, having written his piece on Mosley, he waved at Mrs Portman who was watching him from her vantage point at the basement window. Then he let himself into the house with his key and walked up to the top of the stairs to his room.

In the next room, Theodore Wells was playing his gramophone. There were other voices in the room. Female voices.

"Ah, there you are, Bruno. What took you so long?" Theo had put his head round the door of Bruno's room.

"A riot. There's a man called Mosley after power. Can that man raise a crowd? Had me going for a moment. Mostly hate talk appealing to our rotten instincts. They say Hitler's ten times better at raising a rabble but what I saw just now gave me enough of the shivers."

"We've got some wine. Two of the girls from the show. Pippa wants to meet you, though don't inflate your ego. Pippa wants to meet as many men in her life as possible. We have a record HMV made of the show. In one bit you can even hear me sing. Are you all right, Bruno?"

"I'm not sure."

"That bad?"

"Bloody frightening. The world's going to the dogs."

"It always is. Come and have some wine."

"It really is, Theo."

"It always is, Bruno. The best thing is to enjoy life while you can. Pippa is blonde and you like blondes. All you have to do is give her a rave review when she's a star. That's better. Now you are smiling."

How the world could be so different, so normal, was beyond Bruno's comprehension. Inside Theo's room with the record playing and a glass of wine in his hand, a chorus girl with legs so long they went all the way up to heaven giving him the eye, he was unable to imagine the earlier riot not so far up the Bayswater Road, the piece he had written for the *Daily Mirror* hot on the press.

"Why didn't you take a camera, Kannberg?" his editor had said.

"I don't have one."

"Get one. The paper will pay. This piece is good. What I wanted was a picture of the riot for the front page. Don't you think calling Mosley 'Britain's Hitler' a bit much? The man's a hereditary knight of the realm."

"Churchill is right. England needs to re-arm, and quickly. Unless Mosley takes over the government. Like Hitler, he wants to get rid of the Jews. Then his brand of nationalism, the same brand as Hitler's, can fight communism."

"I don't understand you, Kannberg. Wasn't your father a White Russian fighting communism?"

"They both want uncontrolled power. Both as bad as each other. In those regimes there is no loyal opposition. One party. One power. Their power, with everyone else doing what they are told. We take our parliamentary system far too much for granted."

"All right. Write about it. Briefly in a few words, we're a tabloid. Maybe you're right... You didn't find out the name of the policeman?"

"Not yet. If I'm going to go on covering Mosley, we'll meet again."

"Enjoy what's left of your Sunday."

The editor had a frown on his face when Bruno had left the offices of the *Daily Mirror*.

"You're miles away," said Pippa.

"Not that far. Just up the road."

"Theo says you sometimes do reviews of the shows."

Bruno smiled at her. There was always a trade in life. It seemed they both had what the other wanted. The room was warm and comfortable, the wine having reached his brain making everything much better. Then they were dancing together without a care in the world.

3

*H*oratio and William set sail across the English Channel on the Wednesday. Both had witnessed the riot in Hyde Park. Both had vowed to do something about it. The American passport in the name of Brad Sikorski had been forged by an expert. The forger specialised in passports for rich Jews fleeing Europe for America. Part of the consortium smuggled Jews out of Germany into England to send them on to America as legitimate citizens with a set of forged papers, English or American.

Will suspected the Americans knew what was going on and turned a blind eye. Even if the governments of Europe refused to face the reality in Germany, the Jews knew what was happening; in their history they had been through pogroms for centuries. The only right action was to get out of the way with their families before it was too late.

The forger, when Will found him, was a Jew from the East End of London whose family had lived peacefully in England for five hundred years, never forsaking their religion.

"I don't understand. You want to go back to Germany after the Nazis threw you out? My, my, that is not so good. They find my passport a forgery they kill you, Mr Smythe. Those are not good people."

"If the press stays silent, the Nazis will conquer Europe with the help of the fascists in Spain and Italy."

"But not England. They will not cross the Channel. America will not let them. There are many powerful Jews in America, I am told."

"There are Americans who also hate Jews. I'm a reporter. It's my job and I don't like my face kicked in by a jackboot."

"You are foolishly brave. Remember the words of old Isaac. The passport will cost you nothing, Mr Smythe. May God go with you. May God bring you home safely. I read your pieces, like all other Jews in England. Is your ancestral name Smythe or Cohen?"

"Smythe as far as I know. Thank you for your help. How soon, Isaac?"

"Tomorrow. Friends of ours send authentic blank passports from America. Thank you for the photographs."

"There's a boat from Dover on Wednesday."

"No problem."

Janet Bray's tantrum had gone from pleading to hysteria in ten minutes in front of both of them.

"*What about me, Horatio?*"

"What about all of us, Janet? If what happened yesterday in Hyde Park can happen in England, the world we like to think of as free will be destroyed, probably for centuries. This has nothing to do with money anymore. If the newspapers don't do something to warn the public, the politicians will appease Hitler, hoping he will leave them alone. William says Hitler rouses rabbles in the tens of thousands, sending them rampaging through the streets. Mosley is only a minor irritant to democracy in comparison. No, I'm going with Will on Wednesday, and don't worry, I have a British passport."

"But you'll be with Will as Brad Sikorski and what happened to his protection as a British citizen? They won't care about your passport. And Will, don't you want to be with Genevieve now you are her agent?" By that stage, the tone of Janet's voice was wheedling.

"Genevieve is not interested in me. However much I would like her to be. She's got much bigger plans in her life and none of them include William Smythe. Anyway, she likes men her own age. Didn't you see the way she looked at that schoolboy nephew of Harry Brigandshaw? She even mentioned he's coming back to England to go up to Oxford."

THE STORM HAD COME up soon after they left the shelter of Dover harbour *en route* for Calais. The wind was strong, pitching and rolling the cross-Channel steamer at the same time. The American, Brad

Sikorski, previously of the *Denver Telegraph*, now on the great tour of Europe, and the English freelance journalist Horatio Wakefield, had headed for the bar to drink beer, which the barman found amusing.

Will had checked the other drinkers looking for Germans, his Midwestern accent hopefully good enough. They were good sailors, planting their feet firmly on the deck as the old vessel heaved, their pints of beer riding the roll in their hands. Will liked speaking in an American accent, as it was so easy to imitate with enough variations from coast to coast to fool any Englishman, or German, who might be listening.

Will was brimming with confidence, in contrast to Horatio who was frightened at what could happen if something went wrong.

"Don't you Americans drink rye whisky?" asked the barman.

"Call me Brad. I was over during the war and liked your beer."

"You don't look old enough to have been in the war."

"Well, thanks buddy. Fact is, I lied about my age. My family came across the pond from Poland. Cavalry family, Sikorski, Brad Sikorski. My, but this tub of yours is rolling around."

"Going to be a long crossing."

"Give us another beer."

Horatio, listening to all the bonhomie, thought William had overshot the mark but they were still safe on an English boat. As the storm rose, the other drinkers in the bar left. A young girl was sick down the plate glass window of the door before she could open it and make the side of the rail. The door was heavy to open, the wind pummelling it closed. She began to cry before the vomit came up from her stomach a second time.

"You'll feel better now," said Horatio, ten feet away from the girl.

"I'm dying," she said.

"Of course you are not."

Horatio helped the girl lie down on a leather couch beneath the window that ran the length of the long bar at one end. He had never seen a face go so green before.

"She'll be all right," said the barman.

"How long can this go on?"

"Once we were at sea for five hours trying to get into Calais."

"The poor girl. Give us another beer, me and my American friend."

"Are you sure? Getting drunk in a storm can make the seasickness worse."

"My first name is Horatio. One of my ancestors sailed with Nelson at Trafalgar. We've been at sea for as long as England has had a navy."

"How come the Polish American isn't sick?"

"Genetics, buddy. Just put up the beers."

When they landed in France four hours after leaving the White Cliffs of Dover behind, both of them were drunk, as well as the barman. Will had lost his American accent. No one seemed to care.

The girl had recovered and was sitting at one of the tables drinking tea. She smiled at Horatio as he left the bar to go on shore.

When they reached the German border the next day, the grip of fear was back in Horatio's stomach. Will was full of bravado.

"This is it, Will," whispered Horatio. "No draft beer and no losing your accent. How do I stop my hands shaking?"

In Berlin, Fritz Wendel was waiting for them at the railway station with enough material to fill a small book. They all spoke briefly and parted.

When William had picked up his passport, Isaac had given him a draft for ten thousand American dollars on a Berlin bank.

"American dollars. American passport. More authentic, Mr Smythe."

"Why?"

"You are helping us. We Jews need all the help we can get. Behave like a rich American tourist. The bank account you will open with this draft, Mr Smythe, will have the same amount deposited in it every month. Money transferred from America. Even in Nazi Germany people are impressed with money. Rub shoulders with the rich and you will find out more."

"The reports will be under the Horatio Wakefield byline."

"Good. Take separate apartments. See each other sparingly once you reach Berlin. As an American, Germans will speak to you freely, knowing how much America dislikes the British Empire. The Americans only came into the last war at the end. The Germans don't forget. There are nearly as many Americans with German ancestors as there are English in America. Among themselves, the Germans think they nearly won the war. That with America on their side and Russia neutral they will win the next one and have their revenge on the French and the British. If you play your American part well they will make your friend the scapegoat for giving them bad press and never imagine the information came from you."

"I will put Horatio in danger!"

"Everyone who is against Hitler in Germany is at risk. Don't let them find out who you are or likely they'll kill you, Mr Smythe. Your friend they will put on a train. Go to the opera. Go to the concerts. Mingle with the rich and make friends. Have a good time, Mr Smythe. Look as if you are enjoying yourself."

William and Horatio parted company at the station after the brief meeting with Fritz Wendel and Horatio's introduction.

"Now you have a good visit, Chuck," William shouted at his back for everyone to hear. "Meet again on a train one day. You go enjoy yourself."

Then Horatio was swallowed up in the crowd. On his own. Lonelier than he had ever been in his life. The loud imitation American voice of his friend only for the benefit of unseen ears; ships passing in the night for anyone following Fritz Wendel, the package slipped into Horatio's coat pocket that he pulled close outside in the street, the afternoon sun having no effect on the cold air.

HORATIO CLIMBED into the back of the first taxi and told the driver "Cheap hotel," picked out from the phrasebook he had found in the Portobello Road with Janet. The driver smiled and dropped him off with his suitcase in a side alley not far from the station.

William had given him German money he had collected from his bank in London the day they left on the train down to Dover. Fritz Wendel was following the taxi in another cab as they had arranged at the station; William knew where to contact Fritz Wendel to keep them all in touch.

Horatio explained to the woman who owned the hotel he was English, which had no effect. They smiled at each other then she took him on a short tour, his suitcase left in front of the reception desk. Apparently no one stole suitcases in Germany.

There was a room off the entrance hall with a coal fire that looked like the lounge to Horatio. Another was the dining room. The woman found who she was looking for, an old man sitting next to the fire with a rug over his knees. The man was older than any man Horatio had met before. He spoke English with an Oxford accent after the woman spoke to him in German.

"Three meals are included, young man. Welcome to Germany. Even in front of the fire, it is cold in winter. Come and talk to me when Mrs Schneider has shown you your room. I like a little company every now and again."

"Your English is very good."

"In the old days educated German people spoke French and English. Do you speak French, Mr...?"

"Wakefield. Horatio Wakefield. Thank you, sir, for the information in English."

"It's indeed my pleasure. Hillier. My name is Hillier. Not to be confused with Hitler. At the Battle of Waterloo, you British and us Prussians were on the same side defeating Napoleon. We are cousins. Now off with you and Mrs Schneider. I have a mind for a short sleep in front of the fire."

As Horatio followed Mrs Schneider up the narrow stairs to be shown his room, he told himself the gods were on his side. He could hear the old man whose name was Hillier snoring. Horatio had picked up his suitcase. He didn't think there was anyone else staying in the small hotel. The landing was dark, his room small when the woman pushed open the door. A fire with kindling wood was laid in the grate with coal in the scuttle next to the hearth. They smiled at each other after Mrs Schneider put a match to the paper under the kindling. Then the door was closed behind the woman.

Horatio was alone in Berlin, everything looking quite normal. His watch said it was three o'clock in the afternoon. Outside the small window it was getting dark. The fire was burning well. Janet was right: he would have done a lot better staying in England with the *Daily Mail*. If he had stayed at home and not gone to Hyde Park to listen to Mosley speak he would still be in his flat in London. He had paid three months' rent in advance after Janet put her foot down. The thought of the flat and Janet waiting for him was comforting.

When Horatio went downstairs at four o'clock to look for a cup of tea or whatever they drank at teatime in Germany, the old man was still asleep by the side of the fire. The rug had fallen from his knees onto the old threadbare carpet. He was no longer snoring. There was no sign of Mrs Schneider.

Through the lounge window, it was now dark outside. No one had drawn the curtains. Before sitting down in front of the fire, Horatio went across and drew the curtains against the outside. He felt safer. Then he sat down in the other armchair and warmed his hands at the fire where the coals were burning a deep red. Little blue flames were dancing on top of the burning coals.

Then he took Fritz Wendel's notebook from his pocket and began to read. English translations of articles from old German newspapers. The old man was still asleep as Horatio furtively read his material.

When he finished three pages of the notes, the colour had drained out of his face. The old man was awake and looking at him.

"You don't like what you read, Mr Wakefield?"

"No, I don't, Mr Hillier. Do you think it possible to get a cup of tea?"

"You make me nostalgic. For my long-lost youth. That long and beautiful summer in England. Her name was Agatha. I don't remember the last part of her name. We were young, Mr Wakefield. Young and in love. Can you even imagine a man as old as me being ever in love? Such memories make the rest of life worth living, or so I tell myself. Tea? No, not here. Supper is served in the dining room at six o'clock. Will you dine with me tonight, Mr Wakefield? Maybe you would be good enough to ask Lord Nelson to join us, with Lady Hamilton."

There was a twinkle in the old man's eyes; he was pulling Horatio's proverbial leg, tickled, Horatio thought, by the Christian name.

"It will be my pleasure," Horatio said formally to the old man as he picked up the rug from the carpet and put it back over the thin legs.

"Thank you. Thank you very much. Did you know Lady Hamilton was Lord Nelson's love?"

They talked quietly together by the fire until it was time to go into the dining room for supper where they sat alone through the meal. They spoke of literature, of history, but never of themselves. For the other person, Horatio had found talking about himself and the smallness of his life boring.

Across town, in contrast to Mrs Schneider's residential hotel, the Continental was bustling with people. It was the cocktail hour for Vince Engelbrecht, sitting on his own drinking a Manhattan and eating peanuts out of the palm of his hand, his belly almost touching the top of the bar. He was smiling to himself as he munched his way through the second bowl of peanuts while he waited for the man from Krupp to keep his appointment for dinner.

"Meet me in the bar, Herr Vogel, I'll be waiting. You just got to try an American cocktail. The Continental Hotel is American. How do you say in Germany, seven-thirty for eight?"

Vince liked a drink or two in his belly before doing business. It made him relax. Less impatient. His need for the deal as a salesman less obvious to the customer. He liked his sales pitch to look as if he was doing the other fellow a favour, which in the current circumstances in Germany he probably was.

They had spent the previous day on a shooting range somewhere in Saxony. The Germans had driven him out of Berlin for three hours. By the time the big chauffeur-driven car arrived, Vince had no idea where he was, which was probably Herr Vogel's intention.

The armour plate had been shipped from Mobile in Alabama under cover of night with equal secrecy, arriving in Germany the week before Vince booked himself into the Continental Hotel. The test fire had gone as Vince expected; machine gun bullets, high-velocity rifle bullets, a twelve-inch artillery shell had failed to penetrate the sheets of armour plating surrounding a prototype German tank and secured in place for the trial by a small team of Americans from Alabama.

All Vince needed now was a written contract and payment for enough armour plate to cover a hundred tanks; his personal five per cent commission enough to make him rich. Business was business he told himself, pouring nuts into the palm of his left hand from the bowl on the bar, who was he to judge. His German ancestors had fled Prussia in the seventeenth century and ended up in America, at that time Lutherans and Catholics persecuting each other in the name of religion.

Back in Europe, it just depended on which part you lived in whether you were the oppressed or the oppressor, whether you were Catholic or Protestant. Mostly, Vince concluded from his cynical view of human life, it was a struggle for power and privilege; in the end, it was all about money.

DOWN THE BAR, a man was putting on a bad imitation of an American accent. Vince guessed the man was in Germany like himself selling something someone else would not like him to sell. Over the man's shoulder, Vince saw his man walking into the bar with two other men, one on either side of him. They were the same bodyguards who had been in the car, no one trusting anyone in Germany. The two burly men stood back as Herr Vogel reached the bar and Vince stood up to shake his hand.

"We wish to buy the formula, Herr Engelbrecht."

"Impossible."

"Five million American dollars."

"Will you have a drink, Herr Vogel?"

"No, we require an answer by tomorrow."

The bar was now filling up with fellow Americans. Herr Vogel had been speaking directly into his ear. The German turned his back and left the bar, the bodyguards falling in behind. In Vince's private opinion, all three men were German soldiers. Krupp had been the front who would now be given the formula. Vince had known all along that in all probability he was doing business with the government of Adolf Hitler, the man von Hindenburg had recently appointed Chancellor of Germany.

When Vince ordered his third Manhattan from the barman, he was chuckling inside while he worked out his own commission on the way the deal had finally gone down.

THE MAN at the other end of the bar with a big belly stuffing himself with peanuts had twice caught William Smythe's eye and both times raised his eyebrows as he chucked the nuts down his throat. William knew he was playing the part of a loud-mouthed American badly, and that the fat man knew. The reality of the brief encounter of the two men down the bar was obvious to William after his earlier stint in Berlin; a German officer did not have to wear uniform to be recognised, his civilian attire as regulated as everything else in his life. The two military police also in mufti led William to speculate on the brief words spoken into the fat man's ear, that soon after, when the German officer had left the bar, turned the fat man's expression to a smirk.

The German, to William's trained eye, was a senior officer, the business with the fat man important and lucrative. Catching the man's eye for the third time, William smiled, the confidential smile of two expatriates in someone else's country. As William hoped, the fat man began to walk down the bar.

"You ain't American, buddy," the man said loudly for all the bar to hear. The man, to William, was slightly drunk, which made what William wished to do easier.

Before leaving London, and at the instigation of Harry Brigandshaw, William had phoned Freya St Clair in Dorset to make up a cover for his story. To have some answers for German questions and now American. He had first phoned Harry Brigandshaw at Hastings Court to tell him of Genevieve's film contract and to ask Harry to look after the girl while

William was away. The story had quickly come out along with Harry Brigandshaw's advice.

"The passport sounds good. The story worries me. You have never even been to the States. Get hold of Freya and build yourself some background. Commit it to memory. You'll need it. As a member of the British Communist Party when you were at Manchester University, I thought you would dislike the fascists. Communism is the stumbling block to fascist domination of Europe. Along with Anglo-Saxon democracy."

"I forgot I told you my history while you were telling me yours. We are all going to change the world at university; youth thinks it has all the answers. After Berlin, the two are as bad as each other. Thugs in different clothing."

"Be careful, William. And phone Freya. While you're building your story, imagine your toenails being pulled out slowly. It will give you urgency. Concentrate your mind."

"How are you?"

"Not as good as I used to be. My wife says the bilharzia ate away some of my brain."

"I don't believe it."

"Just tired. Getting old. Call me when you're back."

The fat American had come to a stop a foot behind his belly, grinning crookedly all over his face, a face that suggested the man was well pleased with himself.

"Sure I am. Just not born and bred like you. My name's Bradley Sikorski from Denver, Colorado."

"You here on business, buddy? Name's Vince Engelbrecht. Family been Americans for centuries. Before that we were Prussians."

"Can I buy you a drink, Vince?"

"'Course you can, why I came over. We can practise teaching you to speak proper American. How long you lived in the States?"

"Ten years. Once you get past eighteen they say you always keep part of your native accent which, despite a Polish father, is English. Born in Nantwich, Cheshire. What are you having, Vince?"

"A Manhattan. Glad to clear that up. Now it all makes sense. I like to know what I'm dealing with, Brad."

"Don't we all, Vince."

For the first time that day, William had his perfect cover. Later, they went into dinner arm in arm, two Americans away from home.

Like all drunks, the man liked to boast. William had ordered two bottles of wine to go on top of the Manhattans, nodding to the attentive German waiter who couldn't speak English when Vince's wine glass needed filling.

WILLIAM WAITED two long days after Vince Engelbrecht went back to the States before giving Horatio Wakefield the story, chapter and verse, Fritz Wendel delivering his notes to the small residential hotel near the railway station.

Whether the Germans received the alloy formula for the armour plating, William never knew. But after that, anything with the Horatio Wakefield byline was easy to sell in England and America. As foreign correspondents, they were well on their way under the single byline, splitting fees down the middle. For the first time in his life, Horatio Wakefield began to build up a bank account in England.

When they met, they met in a public area surrounded by other people, walking through the crowd as if they did not know each other, speaking out of the side of their mouths.

Horatio was having trouble with the icy rain wetting the lenses of his glasses, distorting his vision.

"There was more to that story than meets the eye or the police would have paid me a visit," he said, wiping his glasses with his handkerchief. "My guess is America is happy to do business. That either side making a song and dance about our story would make them partisan to the politics. German nationalism is far enough away from America to not be a threat. They want to dump our empire and take over the world after communism and German nationalism have destroyed each other. A shift in the centre of gravity of world power from London to Washington, or more rightly New York and the money. What the American people think right and what their government think right are two different things. Democracy only goes as far as electing a government, not telling it what to do. For Britain, it's the son challenging the father. Most Americans forget that not long ago America was a British colony. There was Rome and Constantinople. Now there's New York trying for hegemony over the English-speaking world. For heaven's sake, Churchill is half American. In years to come historians will look at it as the same empire. The Anglo-Saxon Empire, not the British."

"Just be careful, Horatio. How's the hotel?"

"I have a friend. An old man called Hillier. Hillier, not Hitler."

"Make sure he is a friend and never trust anyone. It's getting worse by the day, everyone in the world jockeying for position. Looking after their own positions. The American government may not be so wrong after all. I'll tell you when to make a run for it."

"How comforting."

"The bigger the risk, the bigger the profit. I just doubled our fees. None of the papers running your stories blinked an eyelid."

"So when do we get out?"

"When we have enough money... Think of Janet."

"I do. Money becomes less important when your life is on the line."

"Some people stay clerks all their lives."

"And live to a ripe old age."

"How boring."

When Horatio turned round to make an irritated comment, his friend had disappeared into the crowd. The loneliness and fear flooded back into his mind. As he crossed the road dodging the traffic, Horatio felt physically ill. Was a future he was never sure about worth so much mental turmoil, he kept asking himself. Could they not just be happy with each other in a garret?

PART 4

RITES OF PASSAGE — APRIL 1935

1

$\mathcal{T}$inus Oosthuizen stood at the rail of the ship, listening to his memories.

THE RAINS HAD BEEN over for six months. All day white clouds stood motionless in a clear blue sky. He had checked every strut and bolt on the old Handley Page, thinking of his Uncle Harry and all they would have to talk about in a month's time when he sailed into Southampton on the SS *Corfe Castle*. The wartime bomber, converted to private use by his uncle after the war, was more a relic from the past than an aeroplane but it was all Tinus had to fly on Elephant Walk. New tyres had been bought in Salisbury, fitted and pumped up with a hand pump by Tembo with Princess watching.

"Don't worry, Princess. Everything will be fine."

"What about my children? What about me? I was the most expensive wife ever to come to Elephant Walk. You two try to fly in a machine, you will kill my husband. What then for Princess? Stop it. The ancestors will rise from their graves. They have already spoken to me. A man flying in the air, they said, is against the laws of God. No man can fly in the air."

"I can, Princess. I am a qualified pilot. With a British licence."

"What's that?"

"A piece of paper that lets me fly aeroplanes."

"How can a piece of paper let you fly aeroplanes?"

"Maybe best you stay on the ground, Tembo," he said to his assistant; they were all speaking Shona, the aircraft terms difficult to translate into the African language.

"I come up. My first wife says it won't work; no questions. My second wife laughs in my face. My third wife says I will die which is all right by her. Ever since I bought Princess from her father for twenty cows, my third wife has sulked and become difficult to make pregnant. We fly and you write the boss in England. When Boss Harry come back?"

"Not for a long while. His wife doesn't like living in Africa."

"Tell him when you write to buy another wife. He has something called 'pots of money', your sisters say."

"We don't buy our wives, Tembo."

"Then how you get them?"

Down by the river, far away from the airstrip, black children were swimming bare-arse in the Mazowe in great excitement. At the family compound of houses, Tinus could hear the pack of dogs barking and chasing each other round the flowerbeds and being yelled at by his mother. All work had stopped on the farm with everyone lined up to watch Tembo fly up into the air.

The small school started by Paula, Tinus's older sister, was empty of children. Even Paula did not think the old plane would fly and had taken the precaution of sending the children to stand at the top of the runway.

After everything had been checked, the wooden chocks were put in place in front of the wheels. The end of the lengths of rope from the chocks were given to Princess to hold. Tembo went to stand in front of the engine ready to turn the propeller. Tinus got into the rear cockpit.

"Contact," he shouted imperiously. The crowd fell silent while nothing happened.

"Contact," Tinus shouted again.

The engine let out a single loud bang, which bounced round the valley making the impala buck, and the buffalo leave the runway in a stampede. Again, silence.

"Contact!"

The engine fired properly. Tembo jumped back from the whirling propeller and clambered up into the front cockpit. The aircraft strained against the chocks.

"Let go, Princess," shouted Tinus.

Princess, now totally in command of the situation, yanked on the ropes freeing the wheels, sending the plane lurching forward down the airstrip, Tinus shouting with excitement at the top of his voice as he pushed down on the throttle. Then they lifted quickly, up over the river, the naked children standing in the shallows looking up in awe. Then the aircraft climbed to join the white fluffy clouds still motionless up in the African sky.

"A PENNY FOR YOUR THOUGHTS." The girl had come to stand behind Tinus as he looked out at the rolling sea as the SS *Corfe Castle* sailed nearer England.

"Sweet memories, Vera. When will I go back again, I wonder?"

"Come for a swim. You didn't come down to breakfast."

"Overslept. Have you ever flown in an aeroplane?"

"Are you going to fly at Oxford?"

"University Air Squadron. Andre Cloete put down my name six months ago with a copy of my pilot's licence. This year he'll be in the Oxford first eleven. Do you think school friends can last a lifetime?"

"I hope so for your sake. You always talk of Andre Cloete."

"After the swim we run round the deck ten times."

"You can run round the deck, young ladies walk. Are you excited?"

"Of course. A whole new life. The start of my real life with so much to do."

"Aunty Janice says she'll introduce me to people in the theatre. To start my career. There was no point in making a stage career in Cape Town. Dead end."

"I know a famous film star."

"You don't. There are no famous film stars in Cape Town or Rhodesia."

"Have you heard of Genevieve?"

"Of course. Everyone has. She's going to America."

"She's a friend of mine. Fact is, in a roundabout way, she's my Uncle Harry's niece."

"You're just dropping names."

"Maybe. I can still see her in my mind's eye."

"What's her surname?"

"She doesn't have one. Her mother and father were never married."

"You mentioned before that you have a Rhodes Scholarship. What's that?"

"An educational endowment set up by Cecil Rhodes who was up at Oxford after he made his fortune in Africa in the Kimberley diamond fields."

"So you're a Rhodes Scholar?"

"That's right. And I do know Genevieve."

"Then introduce me when we get to England."

"Of course."

"That's a promise?"

"Of course. We flew right up the Zambezi River to the Victoria Falls where we landed to refuel at the new airfield."

"Who?"

"Me and Tembo."

"I never quite know what you are talking about, Tinus."

"Memories. Sweet memories that never die."

"Why don't you write them down?"

"I'm going into business. A man has to be rich to get on in the world. Very rich."

"How are you going into business?"

"By joining Anglo-American."

"Then you'll be an employee."

"Not when I am right at the top. Right at the top, I will be a director of the company. And rich."

"You're boasting."

"I never boast. Vain boasting is a waste of time. Ever since I went to Bishops, I set myself goals. To fly. To play cricket and rugby for the school. To go up to Oxford on a Rhodes Scholarship. To be a director of Africa's largest mining house. My Uncle Harry says you always have to set yourself difficult goals."

Vera took him by the hand. She liked him but not when he went off about Uncle Harry. The boy was too young for her, but there was no one else on the boat. In a week they would arrive in England and go their separate ways. The idea of a boy out of school knowing Genevieve was too far-fetched. Everyone had a second name. Bastards – if the poor girl *was* a bastard – generally took their mother's family name if the father had not stayed around to get married. The boy had a vivid imagination though; what with the sea air and constant closeness, she had a good mind to seduce him before the ship reached England. He was an athlete with a perfect body. Seducing people would be part of her job in London if she was to get anywhere with a career on the stage. Even Genevieve was said by the newspapers in South Africa to have slept her way to the top, which had to be true; the girl had not sued the newspapers for libel. Then again, she thought, she only read the occasional newspaper when a scandalous headline caught her eye.

When they reached the small swimming pool on the top deck, King Neptune was sitting in his throne in full regalia. The crew had erected a small dais next to the pool. Vera had forgotten the ceremony of crossing the line. Passengers who had not before crossed the equator were given parchment scrolls by King Neptune. Vera had crossed twice before and received a scroll with her name on when she was ten years old and travelling to England with her parents. Now being alone made the idea of seducing Tinus possible.

"Do you have your own cabin, Tinus?"

"No. Share it with a chap from school who's going up to Cambridge."

"What a pity. Are they going to throw anyone in the pool?"

"They always do. Part of the ceremony."

"Why don't you volunteer to be thrown in? I know you are a good swimmer. Didn't you say your great-grandfather started this shipping line?"

"We don't own it anymore."

"Why ever not?"

"My Uncle Harry disappeared in the Congo while trying to fly from England to Rhodesia. He was legally presumed dead. When he came back, the family shares in the company had been sold."

"Why didn't Uncle Harry demand his shares back?"

"It's a long story."

"I'm sure it is."

Vera was giving Tinus a knowing look, which told him she did not believe a word he said. She almost had her tongue in her cheek. Behind King Neptune hung a row of lifeboats on davits that caught her eye. The open boats were covered in tarpaulins tied on by ropes to their sides and easy to release in an emergency. There was a walkway at the level of the hanging lifeboats with iron steps leading up to them from the deck behind King Neptune. In five days' time, she would be in the safest part of her monthly cycle, which made her speculate.

"Could you climb up to that walkway behind his majesty?"

"Of course."

"At night?"

"Why ever not?"

"With me?"

"What for? Look, they are throwing my friend from school into the pool. It's his first time over the equator... Well done, Roberts! Well done! Jolly good show." Then he turned to Vera. "Have you got your costume on under your clothes?"

"Yes. My dress comes off in a flash."

"Come on then. Once the victim has been thrown in, the ceremony is over."

Vera smiled, a little less sure of herself. The boy was completely innocent. A virgin. The best excitement a girl of twenty-three could have; an eighteen-year-old virgin straight out of school; wicked, plain wicked.

2

_S_even days later Andre Cloete met the boat at Southampton. He was driving an open two-seater Morgan sports car, its three wheels glittering with aluminium trim. The two friends had not seen each other since Christmas 1933 at Hastings Court. Instead of paying for a trip home to Cape Town in 1934, Andre's father had bought him the Morgan.

When the friends shook hands it was brief and casual, befitting two undergraduates. Andre was wearing his Oxford second eleven blazer. On his head at an angle was a boater, and on the back of the car was strapped the cabin trunk Tinus had packed on Elephant Walk.

Tinus had said goodbye to his cabin-mate Roberts after breakfast. It had taken an hour to clear customs with the rest of the passengers. Vera had waved goodbye from the other side of the customs shed. With her was an older man who had met her when the ship docked. Vera had said the day before she was being met by her theatrical agent. She had on a wide-brimmed hat with blue ribbons. The white dress made her tiny waist look even smaller than Tinus remembered from the lifeboat when he had almost got both of his hands to touch around her middle as he hoisted her up the vertical metal ladder that had taken them to the lifeboat in the dark of the night, both of them sneaking out of their cabins on the night of the farewell ball.

After days of clear skies and millions of stars in the tropical heavens, layer upon layer of stars going deeper into space than Tinus could imagine, the night sky was overcast and getting her up the ladder was more difficult than he had first imagined it would be. Tinus had unlaced one side of the tarpaulin, the side facing the sea. There was a heavy swell rolling the ship. Thankfully for what they were about to do, both of them were good sailors. In the bottom of the lifeboat on top of three cork life jackets Tinus found Vera had already taken off her panties in her cabin. It was all over in ten seconds without Tinus feeling her as he went inside the excited girl. After that, she did something to herself in the dark under the tarpaulin before they went back to their cabins.

As Tinus waved to her in the customs shed, he doubted he would see her again. After the event in the lifeboat they had barely spoken. Genevieve and the introduction were no longer mentioned; Tinus just hoped the girl was not going to be pregnant.

"Have a good trip?" asked Andre Cloete, straightening up from putting his boater under the dashboard.

"Very good, Andre. I like the car. How fast does it go?"

"They say it can do eighty on a straight road. Present from the pater. Spring in England is the best time of year, don't you think? Lots of flowers and that sort of thing. Start of the cricket season. You been playing?"

"A little bit."

"Mater wrote you were captain at school."

"Waiting for a place at Oxford kept me at school for an extra term. Just the oldest pupil, Andre."

"You're modest. Who was the girl in the picture hat waving to you in the customs shed?"

"Just a girl I met on the boat."

"Well, you have a surprise waiting for you at Hastings Court. Genevieve is staying with your Uncle Harry. Sorry to hear about your great-grandfather."

"Thanks, old chap. I always called him grandfather. Thought him indestructible... What is Genevieve doing at Hastings Court?"

"She and her father are visiting. Did you know they have the same mismatched eyes?"

"You called in on your way down, I suppose?"

"Spent last night with them to be in time for the boat. Bit out of the way. Your Uncle Harry said it would save me the cost of a hotel room. Anyway, I like staying at Hastings Court."

"Hear you're playing first eleven for Oxford this summer."

"Never count your chickens before they hatch."

"You are too modest."

"Put your hat under the dashboard. There's a piece of straight road up ahead. What was her name?"

"Vera."

THEY ARRIVED at the old house with the façade of turrets and battlements in time for tea and straight into a commotion. The pack of spaniels had met Anthony and Beth at the bottom of the driveway as the Morgan turned into the grand entrance to the home that had belonged to his Manderville ancestors for centuries. Uncle Harry had inherited the house from his Brigandshaw grandfather who had bought the house from Sir Henry Manderville under dubious circumstances, circumstances Tinus had yet to fully understand; his grandmother Emily said some skeletons were best left in the cupboard, whatever that was meant to mean.

Since eloping with his grandfather Sebastian, Uncle Harry's father, grandmother Emily had never been home to England until she brought her father back to Hastings Court to be buried in the Manderville family mausoleum. To everyone's surprise she had returned to Rhodesia on the next boat saying Madge, Tinus's mother, could not run Elephant Walk on her own, which to Tinus had seemed at the time strange. Ralph Madgwick ran Elephant Walk as the manager, his mother ran the houses in the family compound while Paula his sister ran the school for the children of the black workers. There was even talk of offering Ralph Madgwick a share in the farm to keep him on as manager until Uncle Harry came home and Ralph could go off on his own farm with substantial capital from the sale of his share in Elephant Walk.

The first thing Tinus saw of his English family was cousin Beth careering into the rhododendron bushes on her bicycle, the dogs yapping with delight at her ankles as she pedalled to get away. Cousin Anthony, back from his prep school for the night, was leaning on the handlebars of his bicycle smiling at the ruckus as Andre Cloete slowly turned the Morgan into the drive.

"Why don't you do something, Anthony?"

"Hello, Tinus. Heard you were coming. Hello, Andre. I like your car. What is it?"

"A Morgan. Don't you think you should help your sister?"

"Why? She kicked Gunner who gave her a nip."

"Now she's stuck in the bushes. Be a good chap. I've got a cricket bat for you. Are you all right, Beth?" Tinus called.

"No. Gunner wants to bite me."

"No he doesn't, silly. It's all a game," said her brother.

"See you both up at the house for tea," said Tinus.

"Can I go for a ride?"

"Only if you help your sister. Gunner! Come here."

The dogs broke away from the bushes to rush back to the car, barking with excitement at something new. Tinus understood; the dogs, like the dogs on Elephant Walk, were bored.

"I told you they were only playing. Do you want some help, old girl?" called Anthony, his face on his hands on the handlebars.

"How old are they?" said Andre as they drove up the tree-lined driveway away from the gatehouse.

"Twelve and ten, or round about."

"And he calls his sister old girl! What's it all coming to?"

"There's Uncle Harry coming down the steps."

By the time they got out of the car, the boater was back on Andre Cloete's head.

"Beth rode her bike into the bushes. Nice to see you again, sir."

"What's all this 'sir'? Is she all right?"

"Gunner tried to nip her heels."

"Come up. Your aunt is somewhere. She likes houseguests now we live in the country. You'll have lots of good company. Tomorrow you and I will go for a walk on our own. I want to hear everything without a rush. You're just in time for tea. Thank you for picking him up, Andre. The tea's laid out on the lawn at the back of the house. Mrs Craddock has baked you some fresh scones. It's such a beautiful day we can all take tea outside for once. I never get used to not having a dry season when you know for certain there won't be any rain for months and months. You remember Genevieve, Tinus? She's staying with us for a few days with her father and agent. I think you met William Smythe. They are both famous now. As a foreign correspondent and a film star, will you believe it? My first wife, Genevieve's aunt Lucinda, would have been so proud. I can still hear the shot that killed her but there's no point in feeling sorry for myself. Then we have Jesse from Kentucky, an acquaintance of Cousin George in America."

"Jesse? Why is he visiting?" said Tinus.

"To quiz us about our farming methods. Jesse's twenty-nine years old and can't keep his eyes off Genevieve... Good. Mrs Craddock must have sent them."

Tinus looked back to where his uncle was looking. At the bottom of the steps that led up to the terrace of the big house two young men were lifting his cabin trunk from the bracket at the back of the Morgan.

"Always surprised they don't fall off a perch like that," said his Uncle Harry.

"The leather straps attached to the sides of the boot hold it down," said Andre.

"Ah, there she is with a basket of cut flowers. Go and say hello to your Aunt Tina."

"Why didn't you warn me about this Jesse from Kentucky?" said Tinus in a whisper to Andre as they watched the trunk being brought up the stairs. His aunt had seen them and disappeared into the house through the French doors. Tinus waved but his aunt had already gone inside.

"Thought he'd make a pleasant surprise. Oh, and he's anti the empire. Anything to do with British colonialism. He'll tell you all about that I'm sure. Mind you, as Afrikaners we also don't think much of British imperialism, Mr Oosthuizen."

"So why the interest in our farming methods?"

"He's a tobacco farmer. Wanted to meet you and your Uncle Harry and learn about your farming methods in Rhodesia."

"I look forward to meeting him! When are we driving up to Oxford?"

"Genevieve makes up for him. She's even better looking than I last remembered. She talks a lot about you, Tinus. What did you do to her?"

"We understand each other. Do you know, my legs are still a bit wobbly from the rolls and swells of the boat."

"Were you seasick?"

"With a man they called the Pirate as a great-grandfather, not likely. Vera wasn't seasick either."

"Ah, Vera. Do those chaps know where they are taking your trunk?"

"I have absolutely no idea, Mr Cloete."

Uncle Harry was looking at them both with avuncular approval.

"Come on then," he said. "You'll be in the same room as last time, where the under-gardeners are taking your trunk. Even with a motor mower it takes five gardeners to keep the grounds under control. I was lucky to get my money back from the government or we would not be able to afford any of this. Tina has opened up all the spare bedrooms so she can invite lots of people from London to stay. Kind of a compromise. I don't want a London townhouse anymore and Tina won't go back to Rhodesia. So London comes to us in the country. There's always a bit of give and take in life. You'll both find that out. You can't have five children running around a townhouse but they can run around here. It's not the African bush but they can't have everything."

"Do they want to live on Elephant Walk?" asked Tinus.

"I've never dared ask them."

That night at dinner in the dining hall, where family legend had the Pirate dying all on his own at the long table, Tinus found himself sitting down to his supper in a dinner jacket, thankfully without the requirement from his Aunt Tina to wear tails and white tie.

When Tinus first saw Jesse, he giggled and Andre gave his shin a kick under the table. The man was sitting down in a maroon-coloured tuxedo with what looked like a bootlace strung round his neck in place of a tie. They had said few words but already disliked each other intensely, the giggle causing Jesse to glare at Tinus openly for a full five seconds after the man had sat down.

Taking a sip of wine, Jesse gave Genevieve the once-over and winked at Tinus knowing it would not help their relationship. Tinus blanched and for the first time Uncle Harry looked uncomfortable. Aunt Tina in a dress Tinus knew had cost his uncle a fortune, missed the exchange. William Smythe, the now famous foreign correspondent, was smiling at the interplay. Genevieve, looking gorgeous, gave Tinus just the hint of a smile while her father screwed a monocle in his left eye, the one the colour of coal, and gave Tinus a quizzical stare.

Then the waiter Aunt Tina had managed to dress in Manderville livery started to place the first course in front of the seated guests, making Tinus glad his great-grandfather, the man who had installed the first pull-and-let-go flush toilet in Rhodesia, was in the cedar trees at the back of the house and well out of the way. Never, ever, as far as Tinus knew, had anyone dressed for dinner on Elephant Walk where they sat down most nights on the stoep of the main house, the long veranda guarded by windows of mosquito-gauze against the flying bugs, dressed in shorts and open shirts, bush hats left on the rack standing at the end of the table, men, women and children, with the dogs under the white painted table hoping for some luck to fall their way.

Looking at the minute amount of food sitting in front of him on an enormous porcelain plate with the Manderville family crest emblazoned on the side, only the second time he had seen the crest, Tinus now knew why his grandmother had caught the first available boat back to Africa after delivering her father to the cedar trees, a place Tinus had visited after tea to say a last farewell to the lovely man he had always called grandfather.

At least the wine began to flow in Uncle Harry's direction, which soon took the edge off the tension of the evening as Tinus proceeded to get himself tight on South African wine, the one line, he found out later, drawn by his Uncle Harry in the sand.

By the sixth course, everyone but Aunt Tina was as tight as a tick, Jesse looking better and better, the string tie and maroon coat no longer an affront to anyone. By the time the port was passed, everyone was having a good time except Aunt Tina, who constantly looked at the waiters whose main job had been topping up the glasses.

Apparently, getting drunk in front of the help was not to his aunt's liking. When Jesse told a plainly vulgar joke, sending a guffaw of laughter up into the old rafters of the vaulted hall, Tinus got up from his chair, went around the table and slapped Jesse from America on the back, all animosity gone.

"Better sit down, Tinus, before you fall down," said Uncle Harry approvingly; Uncle Harry never liked bad blood between anyone.

"Best joke I heard since we won the inter-schools cricket," said Tinus, his teeth getting in the way of his words.

"Maybe the ladies would like to powder their noses," proposed his Uncle Harry, coming to the defence of his wife who for some reason didn't seem to like the joke.

"What for?" said Genevieve. "I don't see any cameras."

Tinus, using the backs of the chairs to steady himself, made it back to his seat and sat down. Only then did his aunt get up and leave the room, followed by his Uncle Harry.

"You lot carry on," he said over his shoulder.

Everyone watched the host and hostess leave the room before restarting their conversations.

Five minutes later Uncle Harry came back alone.

"I'm afraid my wife disapproves of over-drinking, a taste she has only recently acquired."

There was no doubt for Tinus; his Uncle Harry was fuming.

By the time Tinus woke in the morning, he hoped he had learnt another truism of life; the best way to make a man a friend was to get drunk with him and talk a lot of rubbish. At breakfast, the man's colourful attire was still dreadful but no longer jarred.

"Good morning, Tinus."

"Good morning, Jesse."

There was no sign of Aunt Tina or Uncle Harry or the uncle with the two-coloured eyes. William Smythe, they learnt from Mrs Craddock, had been up early and gone for a walk over Headley Heath.

In better mental shape than they had been the night before, they continued their discussion about farming, both men having grown up on tobacco farms.

"We have more in common than tobacco, Tinus. Like your grandfather, one of my ancestors was killed by the British. Your grandfather was your Uncle Harry's father's partner and best friend but they still hanged him for high treason; he was still a Boer despite being born in the British Cape of Good Hope. It was Oliver Cromwell who said after he cut off the head of his king that it was only treason if you lost. We won our war of independence, the Boers lost, more's the pity. Did you know I had read about General Tinus Oosthuizen who went out with the Cape rebel Scheepers? Many of my ancestors survived to bring America to where it is today, a free, democratic country where every man has the same opportunity without let or hindrance. Come to America, Tinus."

"I'm an African."

"With the wrong colour of skin. They'll roll you over in Rhodesia in the end. How many whites are there in Southern Rhodesia?"

"Thirty thousand. Maybe more. People come and go."

"And blacks?"

"A million, but most of them live in the bush."

"Are we friends?"

"Of course."

"Remember what I said, Tinus. You're always welcome in America. Free from any dark clouds. Like the clouds building up over Germany that will likely plunge the rest of Europe into chaos."

"Thank you."

"I've enjoyed visiting with your Uncle Harry. He's a good man. You're lucky. He told me how your own father was killed. He's trying his best to make up for your loss... Isn't that girl Genevieve something? She's coming to America with her producer."

"When's she going?" said Tinus, suddenly feeling lonely.

"Soon. Very soon. She's going to make her next movie in Hollywood. Why she's here saying goodbye to your Uncle Harry. He was some kind of mentor to the girl; your Uncle Harry got her into the drama college, but you know that. They are sort of related. What's the matter, Tinus?"

"I'm not quite sure... So it's only treason if you lose?"

"Always has been. Right through history. In another scenario, some of the most famous and best loved men in history would have been hung before anyone heard of them. This chap Hitler is a hero in Germany. He's introducing conscription and all the young men are answering the call to the colours. If the last Tsar had put down his own rebellion no one would have heard of Lenin or Stalin. Both would have been shot. The world's changing. Some call it evolution. Some call it the pursuit of personal power in the name of the people. Funny how they all say it's in the name of the people... You want to walk on the heath after breakfast? Clear our heads. The kids and the dogs are out of the house on such a beautiful day. Maybe I shouldn't be so rude about England; without England could there ever have been an America?"

"I rather think, Jesse, we are all subjects of the British Empire. Let's have a second cup of coffee and then go for a walk. Are you going to see Genevieve in America?"

"I hope so."

Only outside, walking across the freshly cut lawns of the Hastings estate, did Tinus understand; he was jealous. Jealous of Jesse seeing Genevieve in America. Then he smiled and strode on with the American by his side. He was only eighteen. There was still plenty of time. Jesse would likely see Genevieve in America but there it would stop. The look she had given him told him she knew he was no longer a virgin, her look far away. Tinus quickened his pace looking ahead, hoping to find her walking on the heath.

William Smythe watched them from a distance, striding side by side, talking with great animation, and smiled to himself. Neither young Tinus or the American had seen him sitting quietly on his bench under the spreading oak tree, the new spring leaves the colour of lime. The old bench was in the perfect position to look out from the grounds of Hastings Court to the rising hills of Headley Heath. The bench, William thought, had been in the same place for many years, the good English oak from which it was made not rotting in the rain.

William was glad the animosity caused by the American's strange ways had fallen into friendship. The man was a Southerner, where the ways of life were much different to Hastings Court and all the frippery of crests and men dressed in strange coats that would be more at home in a Shakespeare play. Poor Tina was trying to make up for her lack of family background by taking everything to an extreme. William was sure she and her children would be better off living in the British Crown Colony of Southern Rhodesia on the farm Harry Brigandshaw's family had called Elephant Walk, the place Harry had told him where the elephants walked on their ten-year migrations to the hinterland of central Africa.

Even for William the thought of giving up his job and the horror he knew was soon to unfold in Europe and going to live alone in the African bush was appealing... If it were not for Horatio.

"There's a hermit in every one of us," he said to himself as he stood up to stretch and walk out into the sweet yellow of the morning sun, making sure not to tread on the crocuses, the two men now a couple of hundred yards ahead of him still walking fast. He was feeling tired and mentally weary. Janet, of course, had been right. They should never have gone to Berlin in the first place. Despite all the subterfuge, they must have stood out like pork chops in a synagogue, the phrase Fritz Wendel used when warning him to get out, too late for Horatio. The taxi driver who took Horatio Wakefield to Mrs Schneider's residential hotel had been working for the new Nationalist government to curry favour in a society where knowing the right people could mean the difference between life and death, poverty and riches.

The sweet old man, Hillier, was trying to regain the riches lost by his family in the war, or so he said, William suspecting from his subsequent research in his bid to find Horatio Wakefield that Hillier's family had lost their estate in Prussia from living beyond their means, a common cause of bankruptcy for many aristocratic families throughout history. Hillier, so Fritz Wendel had warned him, was working not for the German government but for the Nazi Party.

Horatio had disappeared on the Night of the Long Knives, when Hitler killed off his opposition in the Nazi Party along with any prominent German who questioned his power, including the former Chancellor Kurt von Schleicher. From obscurity in the Schneider residential hotel, the mild-mannered, well-educated Hillier, who had fascinated Horatio night after night and wormed his way into his confidence and the reality of what William and Horatio were up to, was given a senior post in the Party: the post of propaganda officer directed at the English-speaking world, Hillier being fluent in English as Horatio had found out to his cost.

They had been in Berlin for over a year while Hillier reported the name of every person they met, every article they wrote before it was published in the British and American press. The story of the Americans selling the formula for high-grade armour plating had been countered by a false story of an American firm selling Britain armour-piercing shells that went through the new armour plating like a hot knife through butter, causing many Americans to have a good laugh at the ingenuity of their free enterprise system. The press hadn't bothered to check the validity of the planted story, leaving the German Tiger tanks with an outer skin that nothing the British or French armies had in their armouries could ever penetrate.

By the time the British and the French found out and asked the Americans to supply them with the new armour-piercing shells, so prominently vaunted in the press, they were given the runaround by an American administration who had no idea what was going on and little incentive to interfere with their own free market system, which was making America the richest nation on earth.

Hillier had played Horatio right up to the end, when German police in civilian clothes took him away to what William feared was one of the new camps for undesirables. Ever since, William had been trying to find his friend. Janet Bray was beside herself. Even the British government did nothing to help.

"You say he disappeared in Berlin, old man. What was he doing there?... Well, if he's the famous correspondent you say he is why did the Germans, as you put it, make him disappear after reporting from Berlin for a year? Who were the men you say took him away? Where's this Fritz Wendel man you tell me is a Jew? You admit the men were in ordinary clothes. You chaps in the press should watch it. You make enemies. You make up these stories to sell your papers and then come to us for help when something goes wrong. Sorry, old man. Nothing the Foreign Office can do. As you say, the fellow disappeared. How should we at the Foreign Office in London know why or where?"

The only thing to be said for it was both of them had grown rich, which did not help Horatio wherever he was. Having chased fruitlessly around the halls of London for weeks, William decided to go back again under a second disguise.

"All you'll do is get yourself killed."

"It was my fault, Janet."

"I know, but getting yourself killed won't help anyone."

"I have contacts. Fritz Wendel said he was going to make himself disappear. Isaac has given me a list of people to contact in Germany, which I will commit to memory. Would they just kill Horatio out of hand? These are the people of Goethe and Beethoven. They're civilised."

"There's evil in every civilisation that mostly only cares about power. Hitler doesn't care about Beethoven, or this man Hillier who hoodwinked the pair of you for over a year. My love is dead, William. Go away. Leave me alone."

"I'm going to find him."

Coming down to Hastings Court had been William's last resort. To ask Harry Brigandshaw for his help.

"I have friends in the army and air force from the war. Why didn't you come down earlier, William? It's important to know the right people. At the least, we must find out if Horatio is alive. When my American cousin goes back to Virginia, I'll come up to London with my wife. She'll be delighted, which will be my excuse for being in town. In the meantime, try to relax at Hastings Court. If you are going back to Berlin, you'll need all the strength you can muster. And what about Genevieve? Don't you like her anymore? You are meant to be her agent. I always thought you were sweet on the girl."

The one thing William was certain about was that Germany calling up its young men meant there was going to be another war in Europe. Despite whatever Baldwin said. There was going to be war. And soon. And before war broke out he was going to find his friend and bring him home.

Somewhere far away, William could hear the children calling to each other, the happy sound of treble voices bringing him back to the present moment, to where he was standing next to the bench. Then he began the walk he had told Mrs Craddock about after she gave him an early breakfast. Tinus and Jesse had disappeared but far away on the heath, silhouetted in the yellow morning sun, William could see a girl with long hair blowing in the wind. Putting his best foot forward while he made his mind think positively, he strode out to see if the girl on the hill was Genevieve.

Before William had gone another hundred yards, the girl on the hill disappeared and William felt a tap on his shoulder, making him swing around in fright.

"Sorry. Thought you'd heard me. I missed breakfast. Overslept."

"Not surprised, Andre. We all drank a lot last night."

"Was that Genevieve on the hill?"

"I thought so."

"Have you seen Tinus?"

"Up ahead, passing through those trees with his American friend. Thick as thieves. When do you two drive up to Oxford?"

"Monday. Monday morning. You're right, there they are. Come on, let's run."

"You run, Andre. I'm too old to run."

"How old are you, for goodness sake?"

"Thirty-three at the end of the year."

"That is a bit old, I suppose. See you later."

Feeling more like fifty than thirty-two, William watched the young man run to catch up with his friend, envying his youth and the joy of his friendship that lay just up the slope between the trees.

The phone call came into Hastings Court from Germany at the moment William found Genevieve on the heath. She was looking at the young Tinus in a way she had never looked at William, even in the beginning before she was famous. William, walking up the last of the hill-climb, felt a stab of jealousy in the pit of his stomach. The look reminded him of lovers happy in the present, not wanting anything more from their lives than the moment. A look of complete fulfilment. Jesse and Andre were out on a limb talking to each other about nothing in particular, both aware of what was going on between Genevieve and Tinus. William thought women went for men older than themselves but this seemed the exception to the rule. Despite what Harry Brigandshaw had said, he was not the girl's agent despite checking for her the first contract with Louis Casimir, who was also besotted with the girl. Instead of joining her, William went and joined the conversation of Andre Cloete and the American. The hard walk had done him good, strengthening his resolve to go to Germany. Like most things in William's life, he found it necessary to get a job done himself and not rely on other people.

The spring day was perfect. Larks singing high in the sky. Trees in the pale green leaves of youth. The sun warming with the day. The most beautiful woman he had ever seen standing not twenty feet away. And he was miserable. A hard, aching misery of the kind that never went away. He had killed his best friend. There was nothing in life worse than that... Down the hill in the trees, a pheasant called stridently, demanding attention. Tinus was telling Genevieve about flying an aeroplane up the Zambezi River.

"Are you all right, William?" asked Andre Cloete, breaking off his conversation with the American.

"No, Andre, I am not. There is nothing you can do, but thank you for asking."

"I heard about Horatio. I'm sorry."

"So am I... I think she loves that boy."

"Don't be ridiculous. He's eighteen years old. Genevieve is famous, whatever could she see in Tinus other than a friend with their Uncle Harry as the glue?... Wow, it really is a beautiful day. Did you hear that pheasant? When does the shooting season open for pheasant? The grouse season opens on the twelfth of August. There's something about the English countryside with a shotgun in the crook of your arm. Something very solid."

Harry Brigandshaw put down the phone and let his mind's eye range back to the spring of 1917. He had shot down the German Fokker triplane, a long line of black smoke trailing from the German's engine. The propeller had stopped but the aircraft was still under the pilot's control.

Harry had flown alongside his victim, saluting the falling pilot. The plane crash-landed at the end of a small field, ten miles behind the French lines Harry's squadron had been patrolling that morning. The triplane tipped into the ditch, the tail coming up, the pilot slumping forward, the engine catching fire.

Harry had landed his Sopwith Camel and taxied to the end of the field. The pilot was either dead or unconscious. The flames were dying down. The dog-fight with the German squadron had lasted half an hour. All the aircraft were light on fuel, including Harry's own plane. The rest of his squadron had flown back to their airfield, the ones that could still fly. Looking up, Harry could see the Germans had also left the sky.

Harry had managed to get the young German pilot out of the crashed plane and lay him flat on his back on the grass of the farmer's field. At the corner of the field, a flock of sheep were watching, having run as far away as possible from the commotion, stopped by the ditch and the thorn hedge. The pilot came round looking up at the sky.

The man sat up at the noise of his aircraft exploding, the small engine fire finding the last of the fuel. Two French soldiers with rifles at the ready were running towards them across the field making the flock of sheep make a run at the hedge. Most of the sheep floundered in the ditch as Harry stood up, the French soldiers pointing their guns at his belly.

In their flying clothes, the pilots looked much the same, the leather coat of the Royal Flying Corps brown, the German's coat black. Harry pointed at the roundels of his own aircraft thirty yards away and smiled. The French soldiers lowered their guns. Having never studied French growing up in the African bush, all Harry could do was make signals and grin.

"Klaus von Lieberman. Your name, sir?" The German pilot had spoken perfect English.

"Harry Brigandshaw. Royal Flying Corps."

The German spoke in French to the soldiers.

"I told them I would like to be your prisoner."

Scratching the back of his head, standing in the drawing room at Hastings Court where Harry had taken the call from Germany, with the sun flooding the room and picking out his wife's beautifully arranged bowls of flowers, he was smiling. The voice from Germany despite the bad line had sounded the same as the voice in the French field back then in 1917.

When William Smythe returned alone from his walk, he was met on the lawn by Harry. The servants were laying out the white tablecloths over trestle tables preparing for lunch under the shade of the trees, the spring day surprisingly warm.

"If he's alive, Klaus will find him for me. The man gave me his word as a gentleman."

"I don't understand."

"Klaus von Lieberman. The von Liebermans have been powerful in Germany for centuries. I shot him down in 1917. Somehow we got my aircraft up from the field with the two of us crammed into my cockpit. We were thinner in those days. Both of us left our long flying coats for the sheep and I flew us both back to my squadron. He spent the rest of the war in Scotland as a prisoner, the only one of his pilots to come out of the war alive. We kept in touch. After the war, we made visits to each other. Once he visited Elephant Walk with the intention of hunting big game. When he saw the beauty of the animals in the bush, he couldn't pull the trigger. Now I have asked him a favour. To find Horatio Wakefield. You can smile, William. Not all Germans are sadists who hate Jews. Most of them came from the same stock as ourselves. We British are Angles and Saxons, Danes and Normans, Celts and Swedes. The

Germanic, Norse and Celt tribes. Underneath we are all the same. Just the few of us are different. The few that spoil everything. One rotten apple in the barrel, so to speak... Did you see Genevieve on your walk?"

"Yes I did. Deep in conversation with Tinus."

"They are two of my favourite young people. How about you and me going into my study for a cup of tea? I'll tell you about my friend Klaus and the crass stupidity of war. If you ever meet him he'll tell you the identical story."

Catching the eye of the servant laying the lunch table, Harry ordered a pot of tea sent to his study.

Later, from a canvas chair under the trees while he waited for lunch, Harry watched them come back together, the backs of their hands brushing occasionally as they walked side by side, and only then understood what William Smythe had been trying to say. He was even a little jealous of the intimacy that had once been his; they had still not had their walk together for Harry to hear all about Elephant Walk. Nothing ever stayed the same in relationships. The boy had become a man. It was more interesting to walk the heath with a girl than an uncle trying his best to take the place of a father.

Whether the two beautiful young people understood what was going on themselves, Harry doubted. Good-looking men and women took their power for granted, especially when they were young.

For lunch there was a large salmon from the lochs of Scotland, sent down by express train to London and delivered the last few miles in a small truck to Hastings Court, Harry not even daring to ask Tina how much it had cost. She imagined his money to be endless, something he hoped a new war in Europe would not prove wrong.

In Harry's experience, it was more difficult to hold on to money than make it in the first place. Even Elephant Walk gave him qualms, with a few Englishmen controlling the whole country lived in by so many blacks, most of whom were living the same way their ancestors had lived for centuries, happily oblivious to civilisation's trappings, the trappings that for Harry only gave the appearance of making life happier. A thatched hut next to an African river teeming with fish surrounded by game, was to Harry the perfect setting; a Zambezi bream fresh from the river onto the fire as good to eat as any salmon shipped down from Scotland.

Once, he had drawn the mental picture for Tina and seen her

physically shudder, the idea of living in harmony only with nature repulsive.

The children arrived with the food, the pink fish splendid on a long silver tray, the children scrubbed and cleaned by their respective nannies.

One by one, the rest of the guests assembled on the lawn. Then they sat down at the long table to eat their lunch.

"Straight after lunch, Uncle Harry."

"What, Tinus?"

"Our walk. You and me. Elephant Walk. Tembo and Princess. The last tobacco crop. I was telling Genevieve of my flight up the Zambezi to the Victoria Falls with Tembo in the front cockpit."

"You made it fly again?"

"Perfectly... After lunch. In the woods I'll tell you everything."

"Can I come too, Father?" asked Anthony across the table.

"Of course... Beth, do you want to come? You, Merlin?"

"Why did you teach him to fly, Harry?" asked Merlin sitting next to Genevieve, father and daughter enjoying each other's company.

"What do you mean?"

"There's going to be another war."

"Nonsense. I just spoke to Klaus von Lieberman on his estate in Bavaria. He says the German establishment are still in control. They don't want war."

"For how long can they control the situation? Hitler wants war. He's re-arming. He wants back what they lost in the war. Don't you agree, Mr Smythe? You were there... This salmon is wonderful, Tina. Hastings Court reminds me of my own family home at Purbeck Manor. What do you think, Mr Smythe? Is there going to be war?"

"Yes."

"We're coming up to town on Monday," said Harry into the silence. "We can all drive up together in the big car while the boys drive to Oxford. I have a surprise for you, Tinus. Something to show you before we go on our walk after this wonderful lunch. It's in the driveway. Came down from London while you were out walking over the heath."

The dogs had a better lunch than the three youngest children, being fed Scottish salmon under the table while the children waited to eat their pudding. No one except Harry seemed to notice. The tablecloth fell almost to the grass, hiding the dogs. He smiled to his youngest son, to tell him to stop feeding the dogs. The boy feigned innocence, bringing his pudgy hands back from under the cloth.

Harry wondered whether later in life his son would regret wasting good food. Nine-year-old Frank, as usual, was the ringleader. Seven-year-old Dorian, always thoughtful, had his thumb in his mouth at the lunch table, a faraway look on his face. Ever since Harry came back, he found it difficult to make them understand; that children had to be trained, to give them good and fruitful lives.

After lunch, with the dogs gone and the cats under the long table seeing what they could find, Harry took the guests and his family through the front of the house and let them range out along the terrace to look down on the gravel courtyard at the cars.

Standing next to Andre Cloete's black Morgan was an identical model painted in English racing green. Both of the hoods were down, the man from London standing next to it holding the keys.

"Go and get your keys, Tinus. Congratulations on winning a Rhodes Scholarship. Why don't you take Genevieve for a spin? There'll be lots of time for you and me to talk. Enjoy the car. You earned it. Barend, your father, would have done the same thing for you. Anthony and I will go for the walk in the woods."

"Tinus, you're blubbing," said Andre.

"I'm afraid I am," said Tinus. "Shall we try her out, Genevieve?"

"Maybe I can come up to Oxford on Monday? We only leave for America at the end of the month."

"We can follow each other, Andre," said Tinus... "Where will you stay?"

"Don't they have hotels? I can walk beneath the spires with a lovely man on each arm. You can show me off. How does that sound?"

"Perfect," said Andre.

3

On Monday afternoon, Harry Brigandshaw called on Air Commodore Arthur Tedder at the Air Ministry in Whitehall. Harry was a man who never gave up a job before it was finished, or so he liked to believe in conversations with himself.

After seeing the three off to Oxford in the green and black sports cars, they had driven up to London, dropping William at the flat rented by Horatio Wakefield in Notting Hill Gate. Merlin St Clair, who had gone down by train to Hastings Court for the weekend, was dropped outside his block of flats in Park Lane overlooking Hyde Park.

After leaving the luggage at the Savoy Hotel, where Harry made his appointment with the air commodore with surprising ease, Harry had driven his wife to Harrods to begin her shopping. The five children had been left behind at Hastings Court in the hands of Mrs Craddock; the children's schools were within bicycle distance for Anthony and Beth, the three younger children still being schooled at home by a governess who came in from the village.

Harry was shown into the airman's office. Tedder had risen rapidly through the ranks of the Royal Flying Corps during the war, and Harry had commanded one of his fighter squadrons.

"Good to see you again, Harry."

"I appreciate your seeing me now, sir."

"You never did anything without a damn good reason. What's up?"

"Is there going to be another war?"

"Churchill thinks so. Luckily he's in charge of supplying the air force. We have a new fighter on the way that is better than anything the Germans have. The Schneider Trophy has been won recently by an amphibious Supermarine model. We are building a fighter plane from that model."

"Do you have a name?"

"Not yet. The designer says it will break the sound barrier in a dive, which is ridiculous. That's over seven hundred miles an hour. The aircraft in current service can't fly faster than a hundred miles an hour before the wings break off. The aircraft's designer wants the new plane to fly at three hundred miles an hour in level flight, something this latest design achieved. Of course, as a racing seaplane it wasn't armed."

"How many cannon?"

"Two that will shoot anything out of the sky."

"When will it be ready?"

"Not for years, despite Churchill saying it may be too late. The new aircraft will be made completely out of metal. Hawkers have a fighter on the drawing board they call the Hurricane. Not as fast but more manoeuvrable, so they claim."

"In a dog-fight the turning is as important as the speed."

"You didn't come here to talk about aircraft, Harry."

"A young friend of mine. One of the reporters who pressured the RAF to go look for me has disappeared in Germany."

"We didn't need any pressure, Harry. Just sorry we didn't find you. Are you well again? Like anyone else, here in the RAF we followed your plight in the newspapers. Tell me how I can help this young man. Are you sure he's alive?"

"If they'd killed him the papers would have been told. As a warning. I just don't know, sir..."

"Go on."

THE MEETING WAS over in ten minutes, with Harry making the drive from Whitehall to the Royal Air Force Club at the corner of Piccadilly and Park Lane, down the road from Merlin St Clair's flat.

Harry wanted to be alone. He knew what it was like to be alone and lost, not knowing if anyone was trying to help. Iggy Bowes-Lyon, his co-pilot on the ill-fated amphibious flight down Africa, had been a member of the club. As Harry walked up the steps to the Piccadilly entrance, that only allowed men to walk through its portal, the memories of Iggy came back.

Tina had arranged to go back to the hotel by taxi, Harry having no idea how long he would have to wait to see the air commodore. In the club, he recognised not one soul other than the doorman. The men at the long bar were so young, deferring to Harry as if he were a senior officer in civvies as he walked up to the bar and ordered himself a pint of beer.

Tinus would have been more at home with the present company, which brought back to Harry the words spoken earlier by his brother-in-law.

"Why did you teach him to fly, Harry?"

No one in the bar wore glasses. All were younger than thirty. By their brief faraway stares, Harry guessed they were all pilots, even the ones out of uniform. If war broke out with Germany, how many of the young men in the bar would live to tell the tale? 'Less than one out of ten,' Harry thought to himself.

In the last war in France, only one pilot in ten had come back alive. It made Harry quite miserable looking at all their enthusiasm at youth's belief that every man was immortal.

Raising the glass mentally to Iggy Bowes-Lyon, Harry drank the one beer, unable to face another one among so many young men who had no idea what they were in for.

"Are you a pilot, sir?"

"No. I was in admin during the war. Eyes not good enough to fly."

"They look all right to me, sir."

"Please don't call me 'sir'. If I was back in my old RFC uniform, likely I'd be calling *you* sir as the senior officer."

"Attention!" called the same young man in the uniform of a flight lieutenant; the wings on his chest were dulled by being up for two or three years, Harry thought, as he turned to face the intrusion.

"Hoped you'd come here, Harry," said Tedder. The man was in civvies as he had been earlier in the afternoon. "Let me buy you a drink. Had two more people to see after you. Nice to talk to an old comrade... Gentlemen, may I have your attention. This is Colonel Harry Brigandshaw, Royal Flying Corps, with twenty-three kills to his name. Barman, please give everyone a drink on my card... Harry, we'll sit at that table where we can talk alone... At ease, gentlemen."

In complete silence, Harry walked to the table and sat down. Only when Harry looked up at them did they all stop staring. Tedder was a born leader, knowing when to give a problem his personal attention. Harry suspected the doorman had been given instructions to telephone the air commodore the moment Harry stepped over the threshold of the club. The drive from Whitehall up The Mall and Constitution Hill took just a few minutes, the time it had taken Harry to order and drink his first beer.

NOT FAR AWAY AS the crow flies, Janet Bray had given up hope. She had left her rooms where she practised speech therapy and walked to her nearby flat in Holland Park. All the praise from the success of her practice was nothing compared to the joy of family life. Before William Smythe had persuaded Horatio to put his head in a noose, the life she had wanted was just ahead, the happiness there to be taken with both hands. Then money had stepped in the way.

She was now twenty-seven, on the shelf, with nothing to look forward to for the rest of her life. The man she wanted was dead and the other men had passed her by. All the success and money in the world would never bring her happiness. The picture in her mind of a little old lady all on her own made Janet want to scream out loud.

At the front door of her flat, waiting, was the man who had caused her pain.

"I miss him as much as you," said William Smythe.

"No, you don't. You weren't going to marry him and have his kids. By the look of you, it isn't good news. What do you want, Will? Has the Foreign Office decided to do something?"

"I went down to Hastings Court to see Harry Brigandshaw who is right on top of Horatio's case. He's up in London now. During the weekend, he phoned an old friend in Germany. Harry says the German has real clout."

"Why would Mr Brigandshaw care about Horatio?"

"He thinks we are part of his coming back. His survival in the hospital. Our success in getting the RAF to make a search down his flight plan in Africa, even though they never found a sign of him or the others. Through three long years he didn't think anyone cared a damn what had happened to him outside of his family. He wants to say thank you, I expect."

"What can he do except talk?"

"I don't know. His friend in Bavaria has promised to find out what happened. Old money. Old power in Germany. Harry shot him down during the war."

Janet laughed bitterly before putting the key in the door to her flat.

"You'd better come in, Will. I'm exhausted. Just an hour ago I was trying to get a rich man's son to utter a word. Clammed up on me and quite frankly I didn't care. What's the point? I suppose Genevieve was there and you had a good time?"

"How did you know?"

"Actually, it was in the paper. In the gossip column of the *Mail*. The girl's famous. Are you going out with her?"

"She won't look at me."

"At least that's some retribution for ruining my life."

"Harry has a number of people to see in London."

"He can go and see the King of England for all I care. It won't bring back Horatio. Put on the kettle and make yourself useful. I'm sick of being on my own. Over a year waiting patiently for nothing... We were going to have eleven children."

Putting a small carry-all on the kitchen table, William unzipped the top and pulled out a bottle of whisky.

"Better than tea, Janet. I gave Harry your phone number if he finds where he is."

"All right. You know where the glasses are. I might as well get tight. Everything is over. My whole life is over. Do you know what it means to a girl of my age?... People only talk, William. They never do anything. They just talk."

Janet Bray was still crying when William handed her a tumbler half full of neat whisky. The girl was right; it was all his fault.

WHILE JANET WAS CRYING into her drink, Genevieve was having the time of her life. With no formal education outside of drama school, Oxford was a revelation. The old spires and courtyards shouted history to Genevieve and she watched the new generation of young men take it all for granted, their birthright passed down for them to enjoy from all the centuries past, the cornerstone of the empire. The cornerstone of British power that stretched round the globe and seemingly to the young men in flowing black robes walking intently between lectures to be theirs forever, a fact of life that would never change.

Genevieve knew she was a romantic, knew the romance of life was the best part of her acting, why she looked so longingly into the lens of the camera, seeing the world full of love and hope. Her confidence reflected in her eyes, the young men's in their stride as they took hold of life in all its young glory.

Left alone by the boys during the day as they attended their own classes, she wondered what her life would have been had she come into the world legitimate, her parents married, a brother certain to inherit a title as old as Oxford itself. A future husband born to the aristocracy, a place at Somerville College instead of drama classes at the Albert Hall, where she was no more than a woman destined to prostitute her looks to find fame and fortune in a world where she had no protection other than her wits.

Tinus found her by the River Thames, in the shade of a willow tree, white swans on the water, young men rowing long boats in short white sleeves, the oars dipping to the water, pulling the boats over the smooth surface of the river, not a care in their world.

"How was your first day at university?" she asked, looking up from her shaded patch of grass.

"Probably like your first day on a film set. I had no idea what I was meant to be doing. Unlike school, you are expected to find out for yourself. Has anyone bothered you? There was something about you in the press along with a photograph."

"No. Here each person is as important as the next one. I only made one film."

"It won't always be like this. Do you like people loving you? This is all so far from Africa I have to pinch myself it's me."

"It mostly depends on who is doing the loving. So far so good. It's the older lechers who put me off sometimes."

"I'm definitely in the University Air Squadron. To them, Uncle Harry is God."

"Isn't he your God too?"

Tinus sat down quietly on the grass next to her, pulling gently at a wand from the weeping willow tree.

"My father had gone away to find himself. Bitter his own father had been killed by the British, grandfather's only sin was being born a Boer in the Cape ruled by the British. My father was on his way home having found God when Braithwaite shot him the same way he shot Uncle Harry's first wife, your Aunt Lucinda... What do you think of Aunt Tina?"

"Like me, she is out of her depth. Unlike me, she is not an actress able to hide her birth. Class is powerful in England, unlike Africa where if you are white, they tell me, the rest doesn't really matter. In England, they don't like people getting above themselves however much money they have to spend. It's breeding they think more important than self-made wealth, old money. Everyone wants to come from old money."

"You are from old money."

"Only half. A by-blow, Tinus. Very much frowned upon... Can you find a boat and take me for a row on the river? Tina is a fool, she should take her children to Rhodesia. Where her father, a one-time railway porter, a stationmaster, won't make any difference to what people think of her. And that's the St Clair part of me talking. The snob in me I suppose. Where having the one-time Tina Pringle to Christmas lunch at Purbeck Manor was impossible. Mrs Mason nearly threw a fit at the very idea of the Lord of the Manor entertaining someone from the working class. And Tina's mother was just as opposed to the whole idea. Poor Uncle Harry. If Aunt Lucinda had lived he would not be in his present mess."

"Is he in a mess?"

"Oil and water. They don't mix. The classes in England don't mix. They probably don't mix anywhere for all I know. Just ask my mother. Would you like to meet my mother, Tinus?"

"Of course, if you want me to."

"You're a liar... You can row a boat?"

"We do have rivers in Africa, even if they are infested with hippo and crocodiles. A hippo can cut a boat in half with one bite of its colossal jaws."

"There are no hippos in the Thames."

"Good. Here comes Andre. He'll know where to find us a boat. I'm going to enjoy Oxford. Are you going to enjoy America?"

"I'll leave just a little of me in Oxford just for you."

"Genevieve, you do know I am only eighteen?"

"What's the difference? I'm only twenty-one."

"The papers say you are twenty-three."

"I lied about my age to get into drama school... Andre, darling. Can you find us a boat? I want you both to take me out on the river. Tomorrow I have to go. Early. I spoke to Mr Casimir, my boss, on the phone. I'll never forget my days at Oxford. In many years' time we'll all remember this, when we three are old and not having so much fun."

THE TELEGRAM REACHED Harry from Germany the next day, redirected from Hastings Court.

'What is the size of his suit?' which made Harry think. There was nothing else on the Post Office form except the name Klaus.

Harry telephoned William at the office the reporter rented in Fleet Street close to the newspapers that bought his stories. Business was brisk with his fellow newspapermen concerned about one of their own. William called Janet in her rooms.

"What's the size of Horatio's suits?" he asked her over the phone.

By evening, a cable went back to Bavaria with the measurements obtained from Horatio Wakefield's tailor. Not buying his suit off the peg was the one luxury in his life, even though the last suit had been bought three years earlier.

"No," said Janet to William, "he had not put on weight."

None of them had any idea what was going on but something happening, however strange, was better than nothing. Janet, for the first time since William's hasty return from Berlin, had hope.

TWO DAYS LATER, a second telegram made its way up from Hastings Court to the Savoy Hotel, the last day of Tina's shopping that had taken her from one end of Regent Street to the other. This telegram was also signed Klaus: 'What is the prescription of his eye glasses?'

BY THE TIME the cable reached Hastings Court, Horatio had no idea where he was. They had smashed his glasses the night Hillier gave him up to the Brownshirts, the last thing Horatio had expected from the nice old man he had talked to night after night in front of the fire in the lounge of Mrs Schneider's hotel, the smashed glasses turning his world into a blur.

There was commotion all around him as he was manhandled through the dark streets but without his glasses, Horatio had been unable to see what was going on. Five men in trench coats had picked him up at the hotel.

"Is this the man, Herr Hillier?" they had asked in German, something after a year in Berlin Horatio was able to understand.

"Yes, it is."

Without a word, one man took off Horatio's glasses and ground them under his boot on Mr Schneider's carpet, leaving nothing but broken glass and a twisted frame. Horatio, about to open his mouth in protest, was hit hard across the mouth and marched out of the hotel surrounded by the five men. Horatio managed to stare back at Hillier who was still sitting beside the fire, now looking to Horatio like a smudge.

Then he was out in the cold street without his coat. As always his wallet and his passport were in the pockets of his jacket, a precaution he had taken from the time Fritz Wendel met them at the station where he had taken the first taxi that had then directed him to Mrs Schneider's hotel. If Fritz Wendel was also working for the Nazis, William was not going to be any help; he had no faith in anyone.

A gunshot went off down the street in the direction they were walking him. His mouth was swollen and bleeding. The cold had entered the marrow of his bones.

An hour later he was bundled into a room, the door slammed shut and locked. Horatio could hear the sound of boots going away down the stairs. He knew he was somewhere in Berlin, even though everything was a short-sighted haze. His watch read eleven o'clock, which was how he had reckoned the hour. At ten o'clock he and Hillier had been about to go up to their rooms as usual when the five men marched him out of the lounge. Peering close at everything, Horatio walked round the room. There was a fire burning in the grate, coal in the coalscuttle, and one light burning in the middle of the room.

Getting warm took him five minutes. The one window looked down onto a blurred dark street but it was too high to jump from, which maybe they hoped he was going to try to do, killing himself by accident. Sitting silently in the chair by the fire, Horatio tried to think what they were going to do to him now they had him locked up in a room.

In his mind there was no doubt; the men who had marched him out of the hotel were Brownshirts, the storm troopers of Hitler's Nazi Party.

For the rest of the night no one came near him. Without pen or paper Horatio had written his betrayed article in his head, every word locked in his memory. Somewhere he had read that all men were evil given the right opportunity. Horatio hoped his Judas choked on the spoils of betrayal; a man could get away with murder but still have to live with himself.

In the first light of the morning, as Horatio emptied the last of the coal out of the scuttle, the same thought came back to him with little comfort. He had not slept a wink all night. As the day progressed in his blurry world, fear took hold. Poor Janet, he thought. Their children were never going to be born. They were going to kill him. Let him starve to death in the cold of the room. Even if he smashed down the heavy door he would not be able to find his way, half-blind, looking for a friendly stranger; there was no chance of salvation.

Quietly, on his knees, Horatio had begun to pray.

At twenty-five minutes past twelve by his wristwatch, they took him out of the room to a waiting car and drove out of Berlin into the countryside. They drove all day and half the night, Horatio too frightened to ask for food. When they reached what seemed in his out-of-focus world to be an isolated farmhouse, they gave him food in silence before locking him in one of the upstairs bedrooms. Exhausted, Horatio fell into bed and slept well into the next day.

For week after week, the routine was the same with precise German punctuality. They walked him in the surrounding woods, even in the rain. He was taken to the toilet once a day. He was fed three times a day on the hour. No one, even once, said a word to him.

When a German army staff car drove up to the farmhouse, Horatio thought he had been captive for well over a month, time, like his eyesight, blurring. The three men in the car were in uniform, two of them so far as he could see were armed. As he was put in the car, one of the five men who had taken him from Berlin saw him off.

Horatio was sure they were taking him into the woods this time to be shot. By then it was late spring, the sun warm on the car. Horatio was sat in the back with the officer who for ten minutes said not a word as the car drove. Then the man handed him a pair of glasses. When Horatio put them on, his eyesight was perfect. On the fold-down seat in front of Horatio, he could now see a leather suitcase, not a blurred shape.

"In the suitcase is the uniform of a German officer," said the man next to him in perfect English. "Put it on please."

When Horatio struggled into the uniform, it fitted perfectly.

"That's better, there's a village coming up."

"Where are we going, sir?"

"You are going to France. And Mr Wakefield, please don't come back to Germany or write one word of what has happened since you were taken from your hotel, or about Hillier. I want your word as a gentleman. Our mutual friend has also given me his word as a gentleman that you will keep quiet, Mr Wakefield. You will say you went to Moscow. Your reason for disappearing was that you had no wish to report your presence in Russia."

"Who is our mutual friend?"

"Harry Brigandshaw. He shot my plane down during the war."

TWO DAYS later Harry sent a thank-you cable to Bavaria from Hastings Court inviting his friend to pay them a visit. A reply was delivered by the village Post Office the following day.

"Not anymore, Harry. Not anymore."

Reading the telegram in the drawing room of Hastings Court, Mrs Craddock having brought him the brown envelope on a silver tray, Harry had the same fear in his stomach he had had walking out to his aircraft for the dawn patrol; there was going to be another war.

When Tina came into the drawing room to find out what Mrs Craddock had brought her husband on the tray, Harry was standing stock still in the middle of the room, white as a sheet.

"What's the matter, Harry?"

"You'd better get used to it, Tina. Sooner or later we are all going back to Elephant Walk. One war was enough for me. I want my family as far away from the next one as possible. And that includes Tinus."

"Don't be silly, the government says there won't be a war."

"Oh yes there will be. Appeasement never works."

FROM THE DISTANCE and comfort of his own flat which he had reached the day Harry Brigandshaw sent his thank-you telegraph, Horatio understood more clearly what had happened; the Nazis wanted the two of them out of the way on the Night of the Long Knives, when, Horatio now knew, Hitler had murdered his opposition. His captives never intended killing him. Even Klaus von Lieberman might have been part of a larger plan to keep Horatio's mouth shut while Hitler consolidated his power. Germany after the war had seen its currency rendered worthless, and riots in the streets with German communists wanting to make their country take the same path as Russia who had shot their intellectuals, industrialists and landowners. To a man like von Lieberman, who had fought for his country, Hitler was the better of two evils; or so Horatio surmised. Hitler needed the German aristocracy to command the army and stop a proletariat revolution. The aristocrats needed Hitler to protect their property. The fact the money-lending Jews were eliminated from the Germany economy benefited many in the German aristocracy who had borrowed money from the Jewish banks. Dead Jews did not ask for their money back.

Throughout history, no one had liked the Jews. Time and time again, history had made them the scapegoat. Horatio shuddered at history repeating itself right in front of him.

Klaus von Lieberman had given Horatio back his civilian clothes at the German border. The man had said little on the journey except to remark that a civilian in the back of the car would have been conspicuous in a German army staff car. When they stopped for lunch at a hotel, it was important for Horatio to be properly dressed; an ill-fitting uniform would never have been worn by an officer, especially an officer driving in a car with a full colonel. Where the driver and staff car came from, Horatio never found out. At lunch, befitting a colonel lunching with a junior officer, not a word was spoken between the pair of them.

"They are the problem over there," von Lieberman had said quietly in English at the border post two hours after lunch. "The Versailles agreement was designed by the French to make Germany subservient for centuries. Don't blame Hitler, Mr Wakefield. Blame the greed of the French. Give my regards to Mr Brigandshaw. Tell him if we ever meet again, it will be in Africa."

"I can't thank you enough, sir."

"Probably not."

With his passport and money in his pocket, Horatio had left Germany. When he looked back from the French border post, up the road into Germany, the staff car and its occupant were gone. Horatio was then wondering how the man had known the prescription of his glasses or the size of his clothes. At the end, just before getting back into the comfort of his car, the man dressed as a German army colonel had given Horatio a last enigmatic smile, making Horatio question whether the man was friend or foe. Perhaps, looking back safely from London, he was both.

4

William had already found himself a flat of his own. The rent for Horatio's flat in Notting Hill Gate had been kept up to date from Germany. Isaac, the Jew who had given William his false identity documents, had stopped the monthly payments when William had left Berlin in a hurry. The rest of their earnings from selling their stories was still in the bank.

In the new office they were both meant to share in Fleet Street, William showed Horatio his bank balance. The sum was enough to buy himself and Janet a house.

"Was it worth it, Horatio?" asked William.

"Of course, sitting here. Over there at the end I thought I was dead."

"Are you going to write more about Germany?"

"No."

"Don't you think it too much of a coincidence the way in which von Lieberman drove you out of Germany? How did he know you had broken your glasses? Do you keep your word to thugs? Don't you want your own back on that nice old man, Hillier, now you know how he took you for a ride?"

"Is there any word of Fritz Wendel?"

"None. They are making camps for Jews. He knew the risk. If you want to keep your mouth shut, what about Fritz? Doesn't he deserve a memorial?"

"Harry Brigandshaw gave his word."

"Ask him?"

"I did. He said he would never speak a word to me if I wrote one sentence in the press. He said that once a man breaks his word he might as well be dead. He said a lot more, Will, but I won't go on. About trust, honour, loyalty and duty. Words most modern people think of as a joke. No, I'm not saying anything. Anyway, are we sure about Fritz being our friend? Everything blurs at a certain point when you don't know what happened."

"I'm going to Moscow next week."

"Who as? By the way, that's my cover story for disappearing. I went to Russia."

"William Smythe. Anyway, I didn't like being an American."

"Then you won't need my byline to write under. First, I am going to marry Janet in St Martin-in-the-Fields. Then I am going back to my old job. Thanks to you, William, we will have a house without a mortgage for the rest of our lives. A large house by the look of that balance in my bank statement."

"Good. I'd better postpone Moscow for after the wedding. I have one last good idea. Why don't we all invite ourselves down to Hastings Court for next weekend? You can thank Harry in person. His wife likes company now she's buried in the countryside. Just don't tell him what you think of von Lieberman or your suspicions. Harry Brigandshaw never thinks badly of anyone. Oh, and before you ask, Genevieve is on her way to America. Making her second film."

"So you didn't get anywhere?"

"Not even to first base, an expression I learnt posing as an American in Berlin. She thinks I'm far too old, more's the pity. Welcome home, Horatio. You frightened the shit out of me disappearing. Have you spoken to Mr Glass at the *Mail*?"

"He's made me foreign correspondent."

"You'll be after his job if he isn't careful."

"I do have a short story in my head. Fiction, of course. I've called it *Betrayal*. I'll have to use a pseudonym, as journalists we are not meant to write fiction. Anyway, the story is set in the lounge of a German residential hotel and I gave my word that Horatio Wakefield would keep quiet."

"They pay well for good fiction. I have a friend who publishes magazines."

"Did I tell you Janet wants eleven kids?"

"She'll tone that down after the first one. Mark my words... You're a lucky man. I wish I could find someone to love me."

Looking at the man he had known since their days together as cub reporters on the *Daily Mail*, before William joined the *Manchester Guardian*, Horatio was not sure if William was being serious or pulling his leg. Over the years there had been a number of girls happy to call themselves Mrs Smythe.

"We're getting old and sentimental," he said to William.

"Funny how we always want what we can't have."

"You're talking of Genevieve?"

"She just keeps me on the very end of the hook. As if she doesn't quite want to let me go, or that's what I think. You never really know what's in the mind of a woman."

"Or anyone else... Are you really going to Moscow? Haven't you had enough frights for one lifetime?"

"I want to know what Stalin will do if Hitler offers him a non-aggression pact. I have heard a rumour of something in the wind. The last thing Hitler wants is to fight a war on two fronts."

"Do you ever regret being a member of the British Communist Party when you were up at Manchester University?" asked Horatio.

"Of course not. The basic ideals of communism are the best way for man to live in harmony."

"Bad people have an ability to create an idea that looks good to remove the incumbent establishment who mostly stole their power the same way. Stealing from those who have and giving to those who haven't is good politics."

"You're a cynic, Horatio."

"We all are, William, underneath. Come back safely. Are you really going to wait for my wedding?"

"That depends on Janet."

"Why?"

"Women take a long time to put on their own wedding. It's the one moment in their lives when they are the sole centre of attention."

"You really are a cynic. All we have to do is call the banns of marriage at St Martin-in-the-Fields and that takes just three weeks."

"We'll see. So you won't be sharing this office?"

"Not after the end of the month. So you think Fritz Wendel is dead? And not a traitor to us?"

"I thought you were dead, old boy. Now look at you. Foreign correspondent for the *Daily Mail* and about to walk up the aisle. I hope he survives. I hope we all do. He was a good man. Now, before we get morbid, let us go across the road for a pint or two and forget the problems of the world. Janet won't mind you getting drunk this once. I asked her."

"Are we really going down to Hastings Court for the weekend?"

"Let's get drunk first."

"Is it Harry you want to see or Tina?"

"Both. She's still a damnably good-looking woman for a gal with five children. No, don't be silly. She's married. To a man for whom I have the greatest respect. It's just the way Tina looks at a man that makes him think."

THE DAY GENEVIEVE finally sailed out of Liverpool on the RMS *Aquitania* with Louis Casimir on her way to America, Klaus von Lieberman arrived home at his estate in southern Bavaria twenty miles from Lake Constance and the Swiss border. Far away, he could see the snowcaps of the Swiss mountains strangely shimmering in the warm spring air. Bergit was waiting for him; Bergit had always been waiting for him.

After returning the uniform to Uncle Werner in Berlin, he had driven his own car alone across Germany, knowing what it felt like to sell his soul to the devil. Within weeks of joining the Nazi Party Uncle Werner, the second brother of three next to Klaus's father, had been promoted to general, which was why Uncle Werner had been the man Klaus went to in order to solve Harry Brigandshaw's problem. Neither uncle nor nephew had mentioned the Party. No one ever did; silence and a stony stare were more convenient. A man had to be pragmatic he told himself, trying to believe.

When Harry Brigandshaw made contact after so many years, the family estate was almost bankrupt. What with the war and the aftermath, many old families were insolvent. The prices paid for farm goods was so low his tenants, most of them, were unable to pay their rent. Trying to extract rent from a tenant without money was as hopeless as throwing him off his rented land, there being no one in Germany with money and skill to take his place.

The savings many of them had had in the bank were rendered worthless by inflation that at one point, before Hitler took control, required a wheelbarrow to carry the number of notes needed to buy the morning newspaper.

At the estate that had been in the von Lieberman family for centuries, they were all living off homegrown food. Provided nothing was wanted from outside the farms, the people survived. Ploughing had come down to horses; there was no money for fuel or tractor parts. To keep the family estate afloat financially when Klaus came back from Scotland after the war, he had pledged his family land to a Jewish banker in exchange for a dollar loan. There had been no point in the banker lending him German money to have its value halved the next day.

"In dollars, Herr von Lieberman. Dollars backed by an equal amount in gold by the American government, or pounds sterling backed by gold in the Bank of England. That I will lend you against your estate. That you must return to me in kind."

In 1921, when Klaus had mortgaged the estate, the German mark had gone into freefall when Germany was forced to accept an unpayable war reparations bill, and after Britain and France threatened military force to implement the Versailles agreement. Whichever way Klaus turned he was beaten.

Soon after borrowing the money to pay his father's bills, the tenants stopped paying for reasons Klaus understood only too well: they were all in the same predicament. None of them had any money. The war had bled Germany dry. And as he said to Bergit, "Now the French and British want to suck the stone for blood. Can't they see they are doing more harm to themselves than good?"

What was left of the dollars was banked in America to pay the interest on the loan to the bank, Klaus hoping that once Germany had recovered from the war, the estate would again pay its own way and, with frugal living, Klaus would be able to pay back the banker his money.

The thought of losing his ancestral home had never been allowed to enter his head. Like so many generations before him, Klaus considered his job in life to protect the family estate and hand it down to his eldest son. By the time he decided to take a few of the dollars to marry Bergit and take her on honeymoon, he thought his father lucky to be dead, killed in the war that was also now killing the family estate.

With an open invitation to visit Harry Brigandshaw and free passage on a Brigandshaw family boat, the Brigandshaws owning Colonial Shipping, he had taken his wife into the bush of Rhodesia for the best three months of his life. For the first time since 1914 when he had gone off to war, Klaus von Lieberman was able to leave his problems behind. It was summer in Germany, mid-winter and the dry season in Africa, the best time to roam the bush with his beautiful wife, a girl he had known most of his life.

When they returned to Germany, Bergit was pregnant with their first child. The financial situation on the estate was worse. Germany was in its worst state since Bismarck cobbled the principalities of Germany into one state.

By the time the wheels of his car crunched the driveway in front of the old house with its spires and steep roof, Klaus was sickened by what he had done to save Horatio Wakefield. Trying to keep a bright smile on his face, he strode towards his wife who came forward gently into his arms. She was crying. Tears of happiness. Foolishly the girl thought he was the only person able to solve their problems.

"It may sound silly and trite, Klaus, but nothing else matters if we have each other. Did you get him out of the country?"

"At a price. Uncle Werner made me join the Nazi Party without actually saying so. He even said he will stop the Jews taking the estate. Where are the children?"

"At school."

"I had forgotten the time of the week."

"How can Uncle Werner stop the bank taking the estate and the house?"

"I asked him. He smiled. He said in an emergency we had to be practical. That it wasn't the first time the von Liebermans had changed sides to save the estate. That the preservation of a man's family was his first duty."

"Harry suggested on the phone, when he asked you his favour, you should go to Africa. He knows we're in trouble. Everyone in the world knows we're in trouble and all they want is war reparations. Maybe Adolf Hitler is right. Uncle Werner is right. What else can we do?"

The sickening feeling was back in Klaus's stomach as he looked out over the family estate.

"That old car's on its last legs," he said, trying to focus on reality.

"Good. I always preferred riding horses."

Inside and outside the house the servants went about their jobs. None of them had been paid for over a year except in board and lodging. The dollars had run out in the German bank's American branch. Further afield the tenants were going about their work, though none of them had less than three years net in arrears and some of their houses were falling down in disrepair; repairing houses was the landlord's job. Klaus understood it did not matter on the estate who owned what, which class they came from; they all had to rely upon each other to survive. They were all part of the same complexity of life. They were part of a single process that gave them existence. Had done for centuries. The same families in the same place. All doing their jobs.

On the table in the hall, Klaus picked up the letter from the Rosenzweig Bank in Berlin. He did not have to open the letter to know what was inside.

"Maybe we should take the children to Rhodesia. They'll pick up English soon enough. Get away from all this," said Klaus.

They were both speaking in English after Bergit pointed to the letter sitting ominously on the silver tray; so the servants were unable to understand.

"We can't. We are not free to go. What about them? What about the tenants? There is more to owning an estate than having comfort without giving in return. We are responsible for them. The same way my father is responsible for his people whether he likes it or not. We were born to responsibility. Maybe Hitler is the only way out for everyone."

"The French won't let us. Neither will the British. In the end it's just another war to be fought. More treasure to be blown to pieces. The idea of living in a thatched house in the African bush, miles away from anyone, with a gun to shoot supper, is very appealing. When we are tossed out of here by the bank, what happens to the children? Don't we owe our first allegiance to our children?"

"They are no different to the other children on the estate. We can't take everyone to Africa to run away even if we wanted. Many of the people talk about Hitler behind my back, as if I shouldn't hear, even though they know I do. They all know the problem, a problem you can't solve, Klaus. Hitler is stopping war reparations. Stabling the mark. Giving men jobs in the cities. Giving them back their pride. The only people he hurts are the people who want to stop him. We can't have it both ways. We can't run Germany like the rest of the world. Losing the war stopped that. If they get rid of Hitler, the communists will take over and then where will we be? And when I say we I mean everyone on this estate. You can't run an estate this size without trained management. There's more to successful farming than ploughing and planting seeds. An estate, like a country, has to make a profit to succeed. The bank won't know what to do with the estate. Ask them. They'll try and sell it for whatever pittance they can get and still come after you as no one in his right mind will pay good money for a bankrupt business, which is what a big estate is today. A business. With everyone working for the business. Including you and me. However many *vons* we have in front of our aristocratic name. We all need each other, including the bank. If Hitler can make the bank understand calling up the loan is self-destructive, then like your Uncle Werner I am all for Hitler. Desperate times require desperate measures however much that sounds like a cliché, Klaus. We can't go to Africa. We can't run away. We are responsible for these people. The responsibility is of your ancestral inheritance. Ask my father. He'll tell you the same. Now, get your shotgun. We still have game in Germany even if they are not the size of an elephant... Now what are you laughing at?"

"You. You are wonderful. Come on then. Let's go and shoot everyone's supper, though likely it will only be our own. Do we have any wine left in the back of the cellar?"

"Right at the back."

"Good. We'll have a bottle together with supper. The two of us. If Wakefield could see me now out of my borrowed uniform, he'd likely think me a different man. Keeping in the part of his colonel, I managed to go through a whole lunch without saying one word. What do you think of that, Bergit?"

"Did you really join the Nazi Party?"

"I had to."

"Do you know what it entails?"

"I have no idea."

"The wine sounds lovely. If we wait until eight o'clock, the children will be in the nursery. Rabbit stew. Lots of rabbit stew. That's what we'll all have for supper."

FOUR DAYS later the RMS *Aquitania* sailed into New York harbour giving Genevieve her first sight of America. The voyage for Genevieve had been unpleasant. Throughout she could feel Louis Casimir staring at her. When she looked at him the unveiled lust made her put up her hands to hide her face. He never did anything. Never smiled. Never acknowledged her embarrassment.

As they docked in all the excitement at the end of the voyage, she asked him when his wife was coming to America.

"Deirdre won't leave the children."

"How long are we going to be in America?"

"That depends. Did I tell you I am changing my name by deed poll? In America I am Gerry Hollingsworth."

"Why, Louis?"

"Gerry, Genevieve... I don't like being a Jew anymore. Not an obvious Jew. Better for the children and for Deirdre."

"Is your wife Jewish?"

"Of course. We rarely marry out of our faith."

"Affairs don't count I suppose, Louis?"

"Really, Genevieve."

"I've seen the way you look at me. I'm an actress who will make you money. So please don't look at my face all the time. It gives me the creeps."

"I can't stop. You are safe. I promised my wife."

"I'm so glad to hear it. Well, how long?"

"I need to raise money. Making a film of Robin Hood is expensive. I want Errol Flynn to play the outlaw opposite your Maid Marian."

"He's American!"

"Actually, he's Australian. We have a lot of publicity work to do. To build you up on this side of the Atlantic. You'll see in a few minutes. My co-producer in America has a welcome ready for you... Probably six months."

"And all the time your wife stays in England?"

"Don't you find me attractive?"

"Frankly, no. I don't go for old men. The only man I have any time for is eighteen."

"I did not know you have a lover. Please keep that to yourself. The public like their stars to be unattached."

"He's not my lover. I never even kissed him. He shied away."

"Ah, the boy up at Oxford. Now I remember. Is he not Harry Brigandshaw's nephew? Harry does get around, introducing you to men... There they are on the docks. A whole gaggle of them with cameras at the ready. The American press. Smile at them. Be nice to them. Flirt with them. Give them a little flash of leg and bust you are so good at."

"Have you asked Errol Flynn?"

"Of course not. I want him to ask me."

"Why would he want to do that?"

"You, darling. Don't you know that expression 'in like Flynn'?"

"Don't be vulgar."

"Whatever it takes."

"It will take more than me flashing my breasts at the cameras to get Errol Flynn to play opposite me."

"I'm not so sure."

"There's that look again. You're mentally stripping me."

"Exactly... Are you ready for the gentlemen of the press? The gangplank is going down. I want you to pose at the top. Good luck. Good luck to both of us. If we play our cards right, we'll leave all the nonsense in Europe behind forever. Gerry Hollingsworth. Have you got the name?"

When Genevieve walked down the last few yards of her journey to America, she was met by a frenzy. The American producer had done a good job. Beside her, holding her arm, Louis Casimir, the about to be Gerry Hollingsworth, was making the most of her. In a moment of inspiration, Genevieve bent to whisper in his ear.

"At drama school they told us it was one per cent inspiration and ninety-nine per cent perspiration and they were wrong. It's ninety-nine per cent tit and bum. The rest is luck."

Down below, the press thought she was whispering sweet nothings in his ear and went into a renewed frenzy.

An hour later, they were in a yellow taxi on their way to the Waldorf Astoria Hotel.

"You are wonderful, Genevieve."

"Why thank you, kind sir... But if you don't take your hand off my knee I'll give you a clout, Mr Hollingsworth."

"We're going to win."

"I hope so."

"All our worries left behind us. Tomorrow your picture will be plastered over half the newspapers in New York."

"All of them, Mr Hollingsworth."

PART 5

THE AGE OF INNOCENCE — JUNE TO DECEMBER 1936

1

$\mathcal{A}$ndre Cloete was convinced every butterfly in England was fluttering in his stomach as he walked down the steps from the Lord's Pavilion. Murray had just been bowled round his legs by the Cambridge spinner leaving Oxford in trouble at fifty-six for three. In his panic, the pitch seemed a mile away while his legs felt they were made of lead.

On the other side of the rail, halfway down the imposing flight of steps, Tinus Oosthuizen was holding up a South African flag for his friend. Briefly they smiled, which stopped the butterflies fluttering and gave Andre back control of his legs.

"Good luck," Andre heard Tinus call as he put his right boot on the grass of the field and strode to the crease.

Four hours later, he was walking back to the pavilion. Everyone in the Oxford team was waiting for him at the top of the steps. All were politely clapping, Tinus nowhere to be seen.

"Where were you?" he asked after the game.

"In the toilet. I couldn't watch the last few runs for your hundred. You know of course you're a bloody hero."

"It'll be your turn next year."

"Hope so."

"The chaps are going to the Mitre. Would you like to join us?"

"Not today. This is your day, Andre."

"You'll score a ton next year."

"I'll be happy to get in the side. That was the best century I ever saw. Not one chance. Next, you'll be playing for South Africa on the same field against England. Proud of you. Your father will be proud of you when he reads tomorrow's newspaper in Cape Town. It'll be plastered on the front page of the *Cape Times*. 'South African wins game for Oxford.' They'll have a whole piece on you including your Rhodes Scholarship. Bishops will declare a holiday."

"Now you're being ridiculous."

"Go and get drunk with them, you deserve it. See you on Monday. I want to go and phone Uncle Harry. I'd phone Genevieve in America if I knew her number. I'll just have to write. Ever since we rowed together on the river she thinks us a team."

"You don't want to come?"

"Not today. I'm going to drive the green peril straight back to Oxford after I've made my call to Hastings Court. Anthony will be tickled pink. He's playing in his prep school first eleven this year. Before he goes to boarding school next term, poor chap."

"Didn't we enjoy boarding school?"

"Of course we did. Now run along like a good chap and join the rest of them. I don't think they'll be letting you buy any drinks tonight."

WITH WIND in his face and his friend having scored one hundred and twelve runs in the annual inter-varsity cricket match, Tinus thought life could never get any better. The fields were green, the trees bursting with life, his scarf trailing out behind the Morgan as he roared his way through the evening air, twilight yet to fold over the English countryside.

"He got a hundred and twelve, Uncle Harry. You will tell Anthony the ripping news?"

Good old Uncle Harry was always enthusiastic. It made a chap feel good. All Tinus needed to make the day the best day in his life was to tell Genevieve the good news to her face.

Then at the top of his voice, Tinus began to sing, his first year up at Oxford having been a happy time for everyone.

BY THE TIME Genevieve had read Tinus's letter on the set of *Robin Hood and his Merry Men*, all was well in the England of yore. The bad King

John gone; the good King Richard back from his Crusade in the Holy Land; Robin of Loxley restored to his family estate; the Sheriff of Nottingham out on his neck; the rich fleeced, their money given to the poor. Love had prevailed.

Genevieve, as Maid Marian, dressed in green tights, a tight green jacket, a jaunty green felt pointed hat with a hawk's feather, her eyes shining on Robin Hood, strode through Sherwood Forest for the last time, elated as the rest of them, months of hard work over, in the can.

"Well done, everyone," called out Gerry Hollingsworth the producer as the cameras stopped filming.

"My lord is generous," mocked Genevieve, bowing and sweeping off her feathered hat.

Then they were shouting and hugging each other in the knowledge of a job well done. The fact that Sherwood Forest had moved to the state of Washington USA seemed lost on everyone except Genevieve.

The letter from Tinus had been a breath of fresh air after the material world of Hollywood, where nothing else seemed to matter other than wealth and fame. Scoring a hundred runs in an amateur cricket match would have meant nothing to the people milling around Genevieve in their excitement.

After Errol Flynn turned down the part, not even acknowledging her existence, the newly christened Gerry Hollingsworth had pursued another rising star for the part, despite Genevieve being a head taller than her prospective leading man.

"Why should his height matter, stand him on an orange box and film down to his knees. It's what appears on the screen that counts. As long as the public believe he is strong and tall the reality doesn't matter. This is Hollywood, Genevieve. The land of make believe. They want to believe in love. They want good to win over evil. They want the sun to shine. Anything to contrast their own miserable lives working in a factory. Our job is to take them out of their misery for two hours of time, to transport them into the world they want but can never get. Who cares whether the actor playing him is only five feet tall when Robin Hood appears on screen as the man of their dreams? It's all illusion. The only time in life when they get what they want. They don't even realise they are stuffing their face with popcorn, they are drawn so deeply into the film up on the screen. We give them what they want, Genevieve. We show them their dream, sitting in the dark in a cinema."

"Will he take the part, Mr Hollingsworth?"

"Who knows? And please don't call me Mr Hollingsworth."

They had told her the money had come from the Jews. Both the writer and the American producer were Jews.

"You see, Genevieve, it's how we run away from our misery by living our lives through films. Our world becomes the world of Robin Hood, a beautiful smiling world where the rich are robbed for the poor. We make people smile. We smile ourselves. No one cares whether we are Jews. They can't see us, only you as the beautiful Maid Marian trumpeting the triumph of good over evil. They don't see you as Genevieve up there on the screen. Yes, it's a Jewish business but no one cares. Sir Jacob Rosenzweig, an English Jew in New York, lent us the money. Not out of charity. He'll get twenty per cent of the gross if the film is a success."

"And if it flops, Mr Hollingsworth?"

"With your beautiful face, how could it flop? They were German and French bankers before they came to London and New York."

"How does he still use his title?"

"He's not yet an American citizen, something we all will be someday soon."

In the end, Gregory L'Amour had taken the part of Robin Hood. They were made for each other, so it seemed for a while, on and off the screen. Now the film, like Genevieve's affair with Gregory L'Amour, was over.

Putting the letter back in the small pocket of her green hunting jacket after reading it again, Genevieve felt homesick. She could hear the sound of the chock as the bat hit the ball and flew to the boundary.

"Well played," she said.

"I know, I was good."

"Not you, Gregory. A friend of mine. Scored a century at Lord's."

"What are you talking about, Genevieve?"

"What are you going to do?" asked another voice as she watched her American co-star walk away.

"Go home, I suppose. I've been in America over a year... Oh, you mean him? Nothing. Why should I? For a brief few weeks, I was infatuated with Robin Hood. It helps the chemistry on film. He's just another predator."

"The newspapers say you are going to marry him."

"That's publicity. To get the film talked about. All part of the business."

"Was having an affair with him part of the business?"

"No... You are very perceptive."

"I'm a writer. We have to be perceptive. Even *Robin Hood* has to be true. You are very beautiful, Genevieve."

"That's what they all say."

"Do you mind?"

"Not if it makes you happy. I can't see what you are all looking at even when I look in the mirror, something I do as little as possible."

"Don't you watch what we put of you on film?"

"That's narcissism."

"Gregory L'Amour likes watching the rushes."

"That's why I'm going home. He's in love with himself."

"Will you make another film with him?"

"Not if I can help it. Did you know his real name is Joseph Pott? Will you excuse me? I'm going to change. I want to be myself again."

"Don't go back to England. There's going to be a war."

"More reason for going home. My father's family have been in the same part of England for a very long time."

"How do you know?"

"My grandfather is the seventeenth Baron St Clair of Purbeck."

"You're kidding."

"As a matter of fact I am not. We'll defend England, all right. The last conqueror was William of Normandy. The same man who brought my ancestor from France to England. And that's real history and not *Robin Hood*."

"Does Gerry Hollingsworth know?"

"Probably. I'm a bastard. My mother was a barmaid at the Running Horses at Mickleham."

"What happened to her?"

"She had me and lived happily ever after. My father still supports her. He's a gentleman."

"Do you see him?"

"Of course. I love him very much. I've been the apple of his eye ever since I can remember. That kind of love is genuine... When it's all over I feel flat. Don't you? All that expectation and then it's over. Just another film. A film that now belongs to everyone else."

The next day they all went their separate ways, the last of the work left to the editors. Genevieve went up to Canada, catching a boat from Vancouver that would take her to England. She wanted to be alone. To think. To try to see where life might take her. The boat was a freighter carrying timber from British Columbia to Europe. There were four passengers on the Canadian boat who ate their meals with the officers.

By the time the ship reached the English port of Bristol they were all friends. No one on board had seen her first film. No one had gawped at her.

As Genevieve put her luggage into a taxi to go to the railway station, she wondered if such anonymity would ever happen to her again once *Robin Hood* was the success they all expected. The film was due to have its first night at the Odeon in Leicester Square where many of the actors would be together again for the premiere at the start of November.

As the taxi moved through the streets of Bristol, Genevieve was inordinately happy. She was going to surprise him by going straight to Oxford. There would be less time in her future for rowing anonymously on the Thames.

By the time she stepped onto the train, her luggage back in the luggage van, her mind was full of the ominous words on the billboards she had seen on every newsstand on every street corner: *Tensions grow over Hitler's invasion of the Rhineland*

Instead of changing trains at Reading for Oxford, Genevieve went through to London, paying the ticket inspector the extra fare on the train. At Paddington Station, she phoned her father at his flat in Hyde Park.

"Where are you?"

"Paddington Station, platform ten."

"Stay where you are. What's the matter, Genevieve?"

"I'm frightened. What's going on in Germany? The American papers don't say much about England."

"I'm going down to Dorset this afternoon. We can go together. Did you finish the film?"

"It's all over."

"So will England be if we don't do something about Hitler. Will your luggage fit in the car?"

"No. I'll leave most of it at the left luggage office until I decide where I am going to live."

Half an hour later they were on their way out of the station, in her father's Bentley 3 Litre.

"Aren't you going the wrong way if we want to drive down to Dorset?"

"First I want you to see your mother. You've been away a long time. She's lonely, Genevieve."

"Aren't we all? Sometimes on the set with people all around me was the worst. Even though everyone in America calls each other by their Christian name, on a film set we were all strangers. People thrown together by the film for a few months, everything disjointed. In the theatre, I could get into a part and stay there for hours, long after the curtain came down. In film you take shots of everything. The editors put it together, give it continuity. I never felt I was inside the part, playing another person. It was just me dressed up. They don't even take all the shots in sequence."

"Did you write to her?"

"For a while. Mother doesn't write letters."

"She can't, or not without difficulty. Give her a hug and have a cup of tea."

"When did you last make a call?"

"With you, before you left for America."

"Do all love affairs fizzle out? Come to nothing?"

"You must find out for yourself."

"What does she do all day? It's one thing to have money but if you don't have to work, what do you do all day?"

"Are you asking about your mother or about me? I have a routine that includes the club, a walk in the park in good weather, seeing friends, your Uncle Barnaby, who is only down the road. Once a week I sit down at my desk and pay the bills. My money is safe in the Bank of England so I don't have to think about that since I sold my Vickers shares at the end of the war."

"Don't you get bored?"

"I'm long past being bored. Once or twice I've found myself missing my days in the trenches. In the trenches with Jerry shooting at you there was no time to think of yourself. In wartime, people are closer to each other. What they talk about is real. Men get bored too easily in peacetime and end up wanting to fight each other. Women have the children to bring up and stop them thinking of themselves. When we get to your mother's flat I will stay in the car so as not to distract her and make it all uncomfortable."

"What are we going to do with her?"

"Why don't you ask your mother? She'll tell you. She'll never tell me. Why doesn't she find herself a man?"

"Don't be silly, Daddy, and lose your support? My mother may well be bored but she does have money. She likes not having to work. It can't be worse doing nothing than serving drinks in a bar to drunks all day. She had her time. She had you. A handsome officer fighting for his country. What else could a barmaid want?"

"I just thought there was more to life than temporary happiness."

Her mother was still in her dressing gown after lunch, her hair in disarray; she was not wearing make-up. When Genevieve kissed her, she could smell the booze on her mother's breath. Genevieve looked around the small Chelsea flat for the bottle.

"I put it away before I answered the door."

"Did you expect me?"

"Thought you were in America, luv. How've you been?"

"Do you ever go out?"

"Not much. What's the point? Tarted up I look like an old dragon. I got nothing no one wants except this nice flat and an income. I'm not stupid. Don't want no bum living off Esther. What would your father say?"

"He's downstairs in the car. We're driving down to Dorset. Want me to bring him up?"

"Looking like this! Don't be daft. He's a good man. Bet he was the one what made you come and see your old mother."

"You're not old."

"Might as well be... Want a drink? It's gin. Drink it with a drop of orange cordial. Just a bit at a time. You don't get your looks from me, more's the pity. Just look at you, Genevieve... What have you been doing with yourself?"

"Making a film."

"I asked what you been doing?"

"Making a fool of myself with a man called Gregory. Once they've had you they don't care."

"Told you. Who's Gregory?"

"My leading man."

"Good. He's not important. It's the men with the money you got to keep on the hook. How's Mr Casimir?"

"Still on the hook. He's now Mr Hollingsworth, no longer a Jew."

"Good for you. Good for him. No point in sticking your neck out. Mind if I help myself? Where you going to live?"

"The flat's been sublet in St John's Wood for another year."

"No, which country? You can always move back here if you stay in

London. Go on, bugger off. You're fidgeting, Genevieve. You don't want to drink with your mother?"

"It's three o'clock in the afternoon."

"So bloody what?... You do look lovely, but they all tell you that. Enjoy it. One day when you're old you'll remember all the attention. Wasn't that bad a looker in my day. Most of us have a few years when the men come calling. Cheers. Lovely to see my daughter. Now bugger off."

The road through the countryside was beautiful in July. It had taken her father an hour to drive out of London. Neither of them had spoken a word since Genevieve got back in the car. While waiting, her father had taken down the hood, the big windscreen giving them enough protection in the front seats of the car. Unlike Tinus and Uncle Harry, her father drove sedately through the country lanes, the road sunk deep between the hedgerows and the fields.

"Is she all right? I should have come up."

"No you shouldn't. When are you going to buy a new car?"

"Whatever for? I only use the car to drive into the country. In town I catch a taxi. Last week I caught a bus. Why ever should I want to buy another car? The old Bentley is still the best on the road. We'll arrive at the Manor in time for dinner. You know I inherit the title and the Manor when father dies? I say this to warn you. He's not been well. Mother doesn't think he'll get through next winter."

"What will your mother do?"

"What we all do. The best we can. She has Robert and young Richard, though Freya wants to go back to America. Dying is part of life."

"Will you live at the Manor?"

"Of course."

"If you had married my mother and I had been a boy, I would also inherit the title."

"Only after I am dead."

"But I'm a girl."

"I thank God and Esther for you every day. You are all I have really got from my life. Everything else is material... Genevieve! Why on earth are you crying?"

Somewhere down an English lane Genevieve had fallen asleep. Talking with the wind whipping over the windscreen was difficult. When she woke, she could only remember the shadow of her dream where nothing had been real, the place or the people. The car slowing down had brought her awake.

"Where are we?"

"Corfe Castle. You know we lived up there in the castle before Cromwell knocked it down in retaliation for the St Clairs going out with the King? Cromwell cut off his head. We were lucky and survived to build Purbeck Manor down the road when the monarchy was restored. Deep under the rubble is the St Clairs' secret cavern. Only the Baron and his immediate heir are meant to know how to get in. I went down with father."

"There's nothing up there but old stones. If there were, why hasn't someone found it? Will you show me?"

"Of course not. You are not my heir. First, there is Robert. After him young Richard. If everyone knew, it would have been found and looted."

"What's down there, Daddy?"

"Plaques. Pictures depicting the story of the old St Clairs."

"Grandfather would have sold them when he was short of money. When Uncle Barnaby fixed the roof of the Manor and you bought grandfather a herd of pedigree cows from your war profiteering."

"I wasn't war profiteering. I merely invested in shares."

"At the start of the war in a company that happened to make machine guns. Or did you fix the roof and Uncle Barnaby buy the cows? There are so many family stories I can't remember. No, there's no hidden family treasure. That one is a tall story."

"Have it your own way. It was the first time I brought you down to the Manor, but we never told anyone what we were doing."

"Are we in time for dinner?"

"Even time for a glass of my father's sherry if he's up and about. Your Uncles Robert and Barnaby were with me when father showed us the priest's bolthole. In those days we were Catholics in Protestant England."

"Now it's a priest's bolthole. How old is grandfather?"

"Seventy-four."

"That is old."

"Not to him. You can go back to sleep for another ten minutes. You were talking in your sleep."

"What did I say?"

"I couldn't make it out. Do you know we dream for one tenth of our lives and mostly don't remember a thing? The one book I read on the subject said we dream everything that happened to our ancestors. Do you dream in colour or black and white?"

"I don't know."

"That's my point. Some people say they dream in colour but how can we be sure? No one ever sees into another man's dreams... My goodness it is a clear day. I can just see the chimney pots of the Manor behind the tops of the trees. We're almost home. Better stay awake and watch your family home grow bigger and bigger."

Slowly, Merlin St Clair drove home the last few miles where everything around him was familiar.

"What are all the cars doing in the driveway?" said her father as they came out onto the gravel courtyard in front of the old house.

Two of them, side by side, were Morgan sports cars, one black and one English racing green. Her stomach gave a sharp flip of excitement. There was no one around, only the cars. Her father parked the Bentley next to a motorcycle; the rider had left his goggles hanging from the handlebars. The goggles were big, of the type used by pilots flying in aircraft with open cockpits.

"That's your Uncle Barnaby's Rolls next to the motorcycle. Mother didn't say anything about visitors. Why look, here comes your Uncle Harry. What's he doing here? Hello, Harry! Has something happened to my father?"

"He's having a glass of sherry on the lawn. Tina said she'd take the opportunity to visit her parents with the children. The chauffeur brought them down. That's my motorcycle. Outside of flying, roaring down the English lanes on a powerful bike is the next best thing. My word Genevieve, you look gorgeous. Why didn't you tell Tinus you were coming?"

"I was on my way to Oxford from the boat. I decided to go to Daddy first."

"Do you know Andre scored a century for Oxford?" said Harry Brigandshaw. "To celebrate I persuaded your grandmother to invite them down to the country for the weekend. Well, come on in. We can get someone to take up your luggage. How are you, Merlin? I've got a job at the Air Ministry, I'll tell you all about it. So *Robin Hood* is in the can, as they say in America?"

"How is my father?" asked Merlin St Clair.

"He's old, Merlin. We all get old. Your mother asked me to come down for the weekend. Tina's now with her parents who love seeing the children. Well, you know the rest. Never the twain shall meet. One day all that nonsense won't matter. My grandfather Brigandshaw said we all look the same under a bus. Why do people so often complicate their lives with petty rules that separate them?... Where are you going in a hurry, Genevieve?"

"To find Tinus. It's over a year. He wrote to me about Andre. At Oxford that time we called ourselves the three musketeers."

Before Merlin could follow, Harry gave him a look that said the girl should go alone.

"I'll help you with the luggage, Merlin old boy. Why not? Those servants have enough to do. You two brothers really like your cars. How's the old car going?"

"What's going on, Harry?"

"The boys drove down with their girlfriends."

"What's that got to do with Genevieve?"

"You don't know?"

"Nobody tells me anything."

"Ask her, these things have nothing to do with me."

"Is he very sick?"

"Your father has cancer. He had a lump on his leg they tried to cut out. Now they want to cut off his leg. They didn't get all the cancer growth the first time."

"Will it save him?"

"Probably not. Likely he won't let them cut it off anyway."

"How's mother?"

"Practical as ever... You carry that one. Mrs Mason has put you in your old room with your dressing room next door for Genevieve. How did the filming go in America?"

"I don't know."

THE LAST PERSON Tinus expected to see walking across the lawn was Genevieve. So far as he knew she was still in America. The four of them were standing on the lawn in the shade of a tree at the back of the house. Lord St Clair was sitting on a chair in front of them drinking a glass of sherry. Next to him, Barnaby was talking to his father.

"I say, isn't that Genevieve?" said Lord St Clair brightening up. "This little party is getting better and better."

GENEVIEVE STOPPED DEAD. In between the two boys were two young girls. The girls had their arms linked with the boys'. They were obviously together, more than casual visitors who had come down to the country for a weekend. One of the girls was smiling up at Tinus from the level of his shoulder. Even at the distance across the lawn, Genevieve could see the girl's eyes were shining. Tinus was looking embarrassed, the tableau frozen. Then Genevieve moved forward easily, smiling her enigmatic smile that was about to sweep the world. When she reached them under the shade of the tree, she bent to kiss her grandfather.

"Hello, Tinus and Andre," she said as an afterthought as if she had just seen them in the dappled shade of the tree for the first time. "What a lovely surprise."

"Do you drink sherry, Genevieve?" asked Lord St Clair.

"Only with you, grandfather. What are all the cars in the driveway?"

"They think I'm dying."

"You look wonderful."

"I don't but thank you just the same. May I introduce you to the two young ladies from the Royal College of Music? They have promised to play after supper in the dining hall. A medley from Beethoven's late quartets arranged by their music teacher for two violins, or so they tell me. Quite frankly I don't know what a Beethoven quartet looks like, early or late."

Genevieve gave the girls the same smile she gave everyone when she did not want them to know what she was thinking. The same smile she gave to the newspapers.

"Andre, what a century. Congratulations."

"Thank you, Genevieve. This is Celia Larson and her friend Fleur Brooks."

"How nice to meet you."

"Aren't you an actress?" said Celia Larson.

"I believe so. I have just finished making a film in America."

"How jolly exciting. What's it called?"

"*Robin Hood and his Merry Men*. I played the part of Maid Marian. The premiere is in November at the Leicester Square cinema. Why don't you all come? I'm sure Tinus would love to bring you. So Tinus, how are tricks?"

"Did you get my letter?"

"Of course. How would I have known about Andre's proliferation of runs? Will you excuse me while I go and look for my grandmother?"

"She's in the dining hall," said her grandfather. "Arranging the flowers. Your grandmother has always been a stickler for her fresh flowers on the dining table."

Even as she walked away she wondered what her grandfather thought of his illegitimate granddaughter he had first seen when she was fifteen, taken down to Purbeck Manor by her father. Thinking back to the conversation with her father earlier in the car when they drove past the ruins of Corfe Castle up on its hill, she remembered all the male members of the family leaving her alone with her grandmother while they went off together; it must have been the time her grandfather showed her father the family secrets.

Looking back over her shoulder, she could see Tinus still looking in her direction. She smiled at him. Her real smile, the one they shared together without having to say a word. Happy again, she walked into the house to find her grandmother in the dining hall.

"Hello, Grandmother."

"Hello, darling. What a lovely surprise. You want to help me arrange these flowers?"

"That's why I'm here," said Genevieve smiling.

"Now, tell me everything you've been doing this last year."

"Are you and grandfather coming to the premiere in London?"

"Don't be silly. We never leave Dorset. That's your world, Genevieve. This is ours. What's left of it. We are having a cold supper without any fuss. There are two young girls visiting who are going to play some lovely music... Did you hear that boy scored one hundred runs for Oxford?"

"One hundred and twelve."

"As a young girl I watched my brothers play cricket with the villagers on the village green. There is nothing more soothing for the nerves than watching a game of cricket. It was on one of those late afternoons that I met your grandfather... Enough of me. I want to hear all about you. You look radiant. Are you in love? Who did you meet in America? Oh dear, does this mean you are going to live in the States? I lost one daughter to the colonies when Lucinda married Harry and went off to Rhodesia. Did you know he's got a job at the Air Ministry? All very hush-hush. There's going to be another terrible war. Harry says so and he should know. The Germans have walked into the Rhineland. I suppose it was theirs before they lost the war. You can't just take someone else's country and expect to keep it."

"It was plastered over every newsstand. I was first going to Oxford and changed my mind to visit father, which was just as well."

"What do you mean?"

"Tinus has a girlfriend out there on the lawn."

"He's only a boy... What a strange coincidence for you to come down to Dorset now."

"Are things like that truly a coincidence? Uncle Harry said during the war he never stared at the back of the head of a German pilot he was stalking or the man would feel his presence and turn around."

"Don't be silly. He would have heard Harry's engine."

"Not over the sound of his own propeller; Tinus told me you can't hear another thing. No, there are more senses than we give ourselves credit for."

"That kind of idea is too complicated... Bring me that bunch of freesias with some of those ferns. The green of the fern brings out the yellow of the flower. And why haven't you given me a kiss?"

For Celia Larson back on the lawn there were more important things than playing the violin or Tinus Oosthuizen. She was twenty-one years old and far too old for him anyway. Despite winning a Rhodes Scholarship, the boy had to prove he could get on in the world and make money. Celia had never banked her life on prospects. She wanted certainty in her future, not a hope and a prayer. The two boys from Oxford were, in Celia's opinion of life, still wet behind the ears. Fun for the moment, a vehicle for better things to come.

Looking up at Tinus with the hope of love in her eyes had been a ploy to attract the other man on the lawn, the rich one talking to his grandfather. Celia's whole idea of playing Beethoven later in the evening was to make herself more aware to Barnaby, the bachelor who she had heard only liked young girls.

When Andre and Tinus mentioned a weekend in the country at the St Clair manor house, she had first asked questions, never a girl to waste her time. Anyone in London with an eye to the future had heard of Barnaby St Clair. Celia had even heard a rumour about a bastard son foisted on the man's friend when the friend wasn't looking. That the father of one of Harry Brigandshaw's children was the Honourable Barnaby St Clair.

"They want you both to play the violin. Lord St Clair is sick. It's a gathering of family and old friends with the four of us to lighten the mood. Tinus's Uncle Harry suggested we bring you down in the

Morgans. Nice run through the countryside. We can detour to London and pick you both up on the way."

"Will all the family be there?" she had asked Andre Cloete down the phone.

"So far as I know, Celia."

"Will Barnaby St Clair?"

"What do you know about the Honourable Barnaby?"

"That he's rich. Very rich. Charming."

"You'll be going down with Tinus, Celia. The Honourable is old enough to be your father. They want you both to bring your violins. It'll be a hoot."

"Of course we'll come. When do you want us?"

"This weekend. We can strap the violin cases on the back. Just don't bring too big a suitcase. We'll be just staying the one night. Is there anything you two can play together?"

"A medley from Beethoven's late quartets. It's part of our curriculum."

"I thought a quartet was for four instruments?"

"It is. I can get the music teacher to write some pieces just for two violins. He's a darling. Do anything for me and Fleur."

"I'll bet he would."

"What does that mean, Andre?"

"The next thing, you'll be thinking both of us are virgins."

"Aren't you?"

"How old do you think we are?"

"Tinus is nineteen. Never mind. Come to our flat on Saturday morning. We'll be ready."

"Don't you want to ask Fleur first?"

"The only thing Fleur thinks about is playing the violin."

"Doesn't she even like me?"

"Of course she likes you. We all do. Jolly good show about the runs. Fleur's daddy pointed it out to her in the *Telegraph*. Toodle-oo."

2

Long before the half-hour recital due after dinner in the dining hall, when the notes of Beethoven would be playing up high into the old vaulted ceiling, Genevieve understood what was going on. The little bitch with Tinus was making a play for the old reprobate, her Uncle Barnaby, the very idea giving Genevieve a giggle.

Mildly curious, she wondered if her uncle had made off with a fiddler before. Maybe, with luck, Celia would find herself on Barnaby's list of conquests, some of which Genevieve tried not to think about. Like everyone else in the family, despite all his bad habits, she liked her Uncle Barnaby the best of all her uncles, even her Uncle Harry whose sweet head Uncle Barnaby adorned with horns, meaning the fact that Aunt Tina was staying with her parents in the railway cottage a few miles down the road made as much sense as not mixing the classes. Now she knew what to do, she was back in full control, the brief hiccup on the lawn a misunderstanding of what was really going on in the other girl's head. Playing the violin was one thing, playing the field of men quite another. The girl was an amateur.

When they all trooped into the long vaulted dining room, Genevieve had to smile. Her grandmother's idea of a cold supper looked more like a medieval banquet. The long oak table, the wood black with age and three inches thick, was covered from one end to the other with silver dishes of food; a haunch of venison, legs of lamb, a side of beef, ducks, chickens and what looked like to Genevieve a whole suckling pig including the apple stuck in its mouth.

There were silver boats with fresh mint sauce from the Manor's boxed-in herb garden that always smelt of lavender in the summer, the box hedges retaining the smell; Mrs Mason's bread sauce with onions and fresh herbs; homemade red currant jelly to go with the venison; plates of Mrs Mason's cold stuffing; green salads in crystal bowls; open bottles of red wine that Genevieve knew had been opened for the wine to breathe from early in the morning. As Genevieve told her mother afterwards, there was enough food on the table to feed a small army, and enough wine to get them drunk.

When everyone was seated, family, old friends, the two boys and two young girls who were going to play the violins, Lord St Clair said grace from his place at the head of the table, holding his wife's hand on the one side, his eldest living son and heir on the other. Then one after the other down the table her uncles stood up, pushing back the old, carved, high-backed wooden chairs to give themselves room to carve the joints. Up and down the long table under the high roof of the hall there was banter and conversation, a scene perpetuated by the same family in the same hall for centuries. Plates were passed by the guests and each was filled by the carvers with not a servant in the hall.

Lord St Clair poured his wife the first glass of wine, then filled his own crystal glass with the rich red liquid before giving the bottle to his son on his right. Everyone waited for the glasses to be filled up and down the table, the bottles passed using only the right hand like Genevieve had once seen in a film of army officers dining at night in India amidst the splendour of the British Raj.

Unable to get up, her grandfather raised his glass, moving it to acknowledge everyone sitting at the table. The room fell silent except for the dogs that had slunk in under the table looking for a chance of pickings.

"Ladies and gentlemen. The King."

Everyone in the room stood up, the full plates of food left waiting in front of them on the ancient table.

"The King. God bless him." The chorus of words rang out in perfect unison before everyone sat down and tucked into their food, smiling around in happy appreciation.

"So what do you think of that?" said Genevieve to Tinus sitting next to her.

"Perfect. But I want to cry. It's his last supper isn't it?"

"Probably." When she looked up the table, she found her grandfather smiling at her. From her seat, Genevieve made him a bow before lifting her glass in his direction.

On the other side of Tinus, Celia was flirting with Genevieve's Uncle Barnaby.

"The food's good," said Tinus.

"So is the company."

"You can say that again. Thank goodness this family does not make speeches."

"Probably why we have lasted so long."

In earlier days, Merlin had told his daughter, the family sat at a separate table on a raised dais. The smaller table, making the shape of a T, cut across the top of the longer table that extended the length of the hall. Everyone on the estate sat down to eat with the Lord of the Manor, those of lesser status sitting below the salt, then a precious commodity reserved for the family and important people visiting the estate. Somewhere in the family history, servants ate in the servants' hall, the tenants in their own homes, the family and their guests at one long table. The raised dais was kept where it was for visiting minstrels and performers, the minstrels' gallery high above the table left unused and forgotten up in the darkness, the brackets that once held the lighted faggots never lighted.

The two young women, dressed in long black skirts and white shirts with short puffed sleeves, took their violins to the dais before the red wine took its full effects on the gathering. Everyone turned in their chairs to look in the girls' direction. Silence fell, the dogs under the table looking out to see what was happening, ignored by the family and guests as they waited for the violins to play. Only Lord St Clair did not turn round until Merlin moved his chair to face the dais, his leg too painful to move. Mrs Mason, who was more family and friend than housekeeper, filled her glass.

"Ludwig van Beethoven," said Celia putting the bow to her strings, smiling at Fleur. "A medley of his late quartets arranged for two violins."

For ten minutes, the girls played while their audience tried to look wise and knowledgeable, the strange last works of Beethoven nothing like the grand sound of his concertos and symphonies. Surreptitiously some of the guests went back to sipping their wine, their stomachs so full their eyes were closing as their bodies fought to digest so much food.

Celia raised her right hand, the bow pointing up at the ceiling, letting the last notes of Beethoven fade through the stone of the old house. Then again she smiled at Fleur and gave her a wink. Instantly their demure stances changed; the girls planted their feet apart, each stamping a foot as the bows joined the strings and an old English jig danced its notes down the hall, breaking the sombre mood in a second. With the sad last works of Beethoven gone, the smile came back to Lord St Clair's face despite the pain of cancer breeding in his rotting leg. The music rollicked, the guests clapped, the atmosphere spun around with joy as the dogs came out barking from under the long table. At the end, Lord St Clair raised his right hand for silence.

"In our midst is someone some of us know as my granddaughter, Merlin's daughter, the story of which is not for tonight. She is recently back from America, from making a film she imagines we know little about, a fact that I tell her now is plainly wrong. Like all good fathers, Merlin had his spy who let us know what was going on through the year of her stay in America. You see, I have an American daughter-in-law, Freya, married to Robert, mother of Richard and, after Merlin, my heir. In America, Freya has many friends in the world of newspapers where she worked before marrying my son. One of those friends, Genevieve, told Freya in a letter that once in the film, deep in the glades of Sherwood Forest you sang 'Greensleeves' to Robin Hood and his Merry Men, a tune by some reports composed by King Henry the Eighth. Please rise, Maid Marian, and sing that song in the ancient hall of your ancestors. Then this old man must find his bed while the revelry goes on. Thank you, my family and friends. Thank you for a wonderful life. Both Miss Larson and Miss Brooks, I am told, were warned to learn a tune so old it is part of Merry England. Let the sounds of old England be heard again in my hall. If by some silly nonsense I should cry, believe them to be the sentimental tears of an old man among his friends."

"No one told me you could sing," said Tinus.

"No one told me either. The tune doesn't go up and down the scales which made it easier."

As Genevieve walked half the length of the table to the dais, she wondered how much else was written to Aunt Freya in the letters. There would come a day when Tinus found out she was not the innocent girl he thought. She had a crooked smile on her face as she stepped up, the irony of her jealousy at Celia's look at Tinus on the lawn so small in comparison to her blistering affair with Gregory L'Amour.

As she sang the sweet words of 'Greensleeves' she watched both her grandfather and grandmother cry, both of them leaving the hall soon after she finished her song, not before her grandfather ordered everyone to stay, to drink and be merry, to dance the night away.

As her grandparents left, the guests had stood and applauded the meal, the night, the life of a man. Then it was Genevieve's turn to cry and look away.

"Don't be sad, Genevieve. My father has had a good life and that is what counts. We all have to die. Come dance a jig with your father. You have no idea how proud you have made me tonight."

"My sadness is just as much for not knowing him better. Why do some of the best parts of life slip through our fingers? Why do we only miss something so much when it is gone?"

"I have found it is better not to think too much. In the trenches, we lived for the moment. The can of bully beef we were eating from the can with a spoon. A trench rat with sad, speculative eyes. A friend. You were part of his life, Genevieve. What else could you have given him? The only thing we can hold forever are our memories... They are very good violin players."

"If young girls in America looking like those two girls played jigs like that, they would make a fortune. There's no money in playing classical music."

"Why don't you tell them?"

"We'd have to dress them better."

"How do you mean?"

"You have to show it off in America when you are on the stage."

"There is a spare room in the flat if you don't wish to live with your mother."

"Father, are you suggesting I live with you for the first time in my life?"

"Until you decide your next step in life. Now, go and dance with your friend from Rhodesia. He's been watching you while we danced."

"Are you sure he wasn't looking at Celia?"

"Quite sure."

"Dad, you are naive. You can never be sure of anything. You can only hope. What will you do with the Manor when you inherit?"

"Leave it exactly as it is, unless the Germans have something else to say. Your Uncle Harry, as you like to call him, which he was when he married your Aunt Lucinda, is in charge of building eyes that can see further than the horizon. All along the south coast. Harry says the German bombers will fly across France and bomb our cities."

"Won't the French have something to say to the Germans?"

They had stopped dancing and moved to the safety of the old walls of the hall; an old Indian Army colonel who had been to school with her grandfather was showing the youngsters how a jig was performed in his day. The colonel was half drunk and a little dangerous, the others giving him space as they clapped his wild performance.

"Not if Germany overruns France like the Rhineland."

"No one fought back in the Rhineland. I read the paper. They were all Germans in the Rhineland happy to reunite with Germany."

"Churchill says the French exhausted themselves at Verdun."

"How can an eye see over a horizon?"

"Radar can, according to Harry. They are building a tower at Poling, just in from the coast from Littlehampton. The tower sends radar signals that bounce off metal aircraft telling the operator on a screen underground in a bunker how many aircraft are coming and where they are. The bunkers are to be connected to a Fighter Command communication centre with phone lines to the RAF squadrons at their stations around England. When every aircraft has been identified by radar units, the squadrons will be scrambled with full tanks of petrol to intercept enemy aircraft. Harry said in the war, during a dawn patrol, he often had to break off an engagement and return to his base for lack of fuel. Very often, they only intercepted Jerry at the end of the patrol. This way, if the Air Ministry get their way to build a string of radar stations up and down the south coast, the RAF can sit on the ground waiting for a German raid. The aircraft won't be using up petrol and the pilots can rest. Harry says our problem won't be building aircraft but training pilots. That the aircraft will be replaceable but not the pilots. During the last war, only one out of ten pilots came out alive... What's the matter, Genevieve? You've gone white as a sheet."

"Tinus. He's a pilot. Uncle Harry taught him to fly. He's a member of the Oxford University Air Squadron. If there's a war, Tinus will be in the thick of it. Why the hell did Uncle Harry teach him to fly?"

"You'd better ask him. I too had asked Harry the same thing... Tinus is coming over to ask you to dance. Just look out for Colonel Jones. How can a man that old have so much energy? There won't be a war, Genevieve."

"Then why is Uncle Harry building his eyes in the sky, which make no sense to me... Hello, Tinus. You want to dance? Your girlfriend plays a mean violin."

"She's not my girlfriend. She's Fleur's best friend and Fleur goes out with Andre. Celia thinks I'm a kid. Let's show them, Genevieve. Why are you looking at me like that? Your grandfather has a soft spot for you, do you know that? Will you excuse us, sir, if I dance with your daughter?"

"Enjoy yourselves. Always enjoy yourselves while you can."

When they finished dancing, they went back to sit at their table places. Tinus pulled back the chair for Genevieve to sit down, pushing it in for her as she sat. She had a half-finished glass of wine she had toyed with all evening. Getting drunk or even tipsy in public was something Genevieve disliked; it was different for two people together on their own.

"What's the matter, Genevieve? You're not saying a word."

"If there was another war in Europe you would stay in Africa, wouldn't you?"

"Whatever for? All the fun would be over here. Andre says he's going to learn to fly so we can both join the RAF... Where are you going, Genevieve!"

"To bed. Say goodnight for me, I'm tired."

"We're leaving tomorrow after breakfast."

She kissed him on the cheek before fleeing the room. Only when she was safe inside the small dressing room next to her father's bedroom did she cry, her imagination too strong to control herself anymore. First, the damn newsstands had told her. Now Uncle Harry.

Later, she heard her father go to bed. Outside the open window the owls were hooting from the woods. In the middle of the night, Genevieve heard something bark, not knowing what it was; the sound was different from a dog. When the morning sun came up, she fell asleep exhausted. When she woke, it was after breakfast. Down on the driveway when she looked out of the window the black and green Morgans had gone. There was a note under her door.

WELCOME HOME. LOVE FROM TINUS.

With a broad smile on her face, Genevieve washed her face in the round bowl on the wooden stand having sloshed in water from the silver jug. Then she dressed and walked downstairs to see what was going on. In his note, Tinus had said he loved her even if he had not meant what he said. The boys and the two girls were coming to the premiere. She could wait. Only when she walked out onto the grass into a beautiful June morning did she remember Gregory L'Amour would be her partner at the premiere.

"You look radiant," said her grandfather, back on his wicker chair under the tree.

She pecked him on the cheek before sitting down on the grass at his feet.

"There isn't going to be another war is there, Grandfather?"

"Of course not. It's what they call sabre-rattling to get what they want. Nobody ever wants war... We've changed our minds. Your grandmother and I are coming up to London for your premiere. We are staying with Barnaby, who is the closest to Leicester Square. My word, I haven't been to London for more years than I can count. Do you see what you've done to me, Genevieve?"

"That will be wonderful. Where is grandmother?"

"In the kitchen, I expect. Supervising lunch with Mrs Mason. We're having it out on the lawn on such a lovely day. Most of my guests did not come down to breakfast so they'll be hungry by now. Whatever did you all do last night after I went to bed to stop people having their breakfast?"

"Well, Colonel Jones did a jig on his own."

"Poor Larry. He still hasn't come down from his room. When will he realise we aren't young anymore? Oh, there he is. Do you know we went to school together? Larry, old chap. Come over here and talk with me and my granddaughter. She tells me you were up to tricks last night once my back was turned. Just as well those two girls with the violins have gone back to London. Genevieve will go and find a chair for you, Larry. I love talking about old times. I'm going to Genevieve's film premiere in London."

By teatime, most of the weekend guests had left. Uncle Harry had roared off on his motorcycle, half his face hidden by the goggles. He had told them he was going straight back to London to be at the Air Ministry first thing in the morning. There was no doubt her Uncle Harry took his job seriously. He was briefly to visit his wife on the low road to Corfe

Castle where she was staying in the railway cottage where she was born. The chauffeur was to bring the children back in time for school.

No one except Genevieve found it strange that Mrs Brigandshaw, not five miles away, had not made an appearance at Purbeck Manor with her children. Except from Uncle Harry, not once had Genevieve heard Tina's name even mentioned.

"Is Mrs Pringle as common as my mother?" she asked her father in the car when the Bentley, its hood down, was halfway to London, the slipstream surging over the windscreen, the car going faster than usual.

"I can't hear, Genevieve," shouted her father over the noise of the rushing wind. Genevieve shouted her question again on the top of her voice.

"I don't know what you are talking about."

"Tina. Why wasn't she at the supper?"

"She was staying with her mother and father with the children. Harry said they would have wrecked the Manor had he let them loose."

"Was that the real reason?"

"Probably not. Do we have to shout at each other anymore? Let sleeping dogs lie."

"Can I bring my mother down to the Manor to meet my grandparents?"

"Don't be ridiculous."

"Why not?"

"Because your mother would be embarrassed, uncomfortable, if not downright miserable, that's why."

Even at speed on a short stretch of road, the two identical pairs of mismatched eyes glared at each other before Genevieve burst out laughing; with all the wine laid out, her mother would have fallen under the table. Even then the idea of her mother not being welcomed at the Manor rankled. There had been a bitter echo in her laughter that left her with a bad taste.

When they reached the built-up area on the outskirts of London, dusk was falling. By the time they reached her father's flat in Park Lane, it was dark. Smithers, her father's long-time manservant, showed her the spare bedroom. When she had finished putting her few things from her travelling case in the drawers, she went down the hallway. Smithers had made them sandwiches and hot chocolate. After the previous sleepless night, Genevieve was half-asleep, barely able to keep her eyes open.

"Go to bed, Genevieve, before you fall down. See you in the morning.

We'll get you some more clothes from the left-luggage office tomorrow. Do you have anything to do this week?"

"Press interviews most probably. I was to report at Elstree when I arrived in England. My mail will be at the studio. Publicity is all the rage after making a film. It's part of my contract. Sleep tight."

*B*runo Kannberg of the *Daily Mirror* was the first to phone; the studio had given him the number in Park Lane. Paul Dexter had contacted every newspaper in London on instructions from Gerry Hollingsworth once Elstree knew the star of the film was in town. Bruno knew the connection between Harry Brigandshaw and Genevieve. He intended bringing the two stories together, the lost and found war hero and the beautiful film star who had once been his niece by marriage, to give the article more reader interest, connecting the fear of a new war in Europe to give a separate layer to his story.

Earlier in the morning Bruno had been called into his new editor's office, a grim weather-beaten man who had worked his way through every aspect of journalism and went by the unfortunate name of Arthur Bumley.

"Why me, Mr Bumley? I don't do the arts anymore."

"You'll want to do this one, Kannberg. Saw her once in the flesh at a theatre function. She wasn't the star then but the only one worth looking at. She has that rare magnetism that makes some women stand out. Unless she marries a rich man, she'll go far in film. Don't you remember the Harry Brigandshaw saga that hooked readers for weeks? Brigandshaw's first wife, who was shot by his old CO from the Royal Flying Corps when he flipped his lid after getting out of the loony bin, was Genevieve's aunt. And it gets better. Her father is heir to the St Clair

Barony, the next Lord St Clair. She was born to a barmaid from the Running Horses at Mickleham during the war, according to the feed from Dexter at Elstree Studio. I'm giving this one to you and not Featherstone. He can do the film crit if you don't want to go any further. The premiere's in November in Leicester Square. Enjoy yourself. She's staying with the father in Park Lane, the rotten cad, getting barmaids pregnant. I wish I was so unlucky. The last barmaid I made a pass at threw a drink in my face."

"Where's the mother?"

"She's a drunk."

"Might be a story. By the way, Sir Oswald bloody Mosley is stirring shit again. He's organising a fascist march through the East End. The locals are building barricades in the streets to stop them. The police think over one hundred thousand are coming out for it. Some people are far more scared of the commies than the fascists. Mosley thinks he's going to make himself Chancellor of England and kiss Hitler's arse. He's a damn good rabble-rouser. Watched him once at Hyde Park Corner. Had the mob tearing each other apart in less than an hour. What makes some men such powerful orators?"

"When's the march?"

"We don't know. This week, next week or the month after next. Mosley keeps his cards close to his chest. He came back from Germany last week, that much we do know."

"Did he see Hitler?"

"Who knows?"

"All these politicians ever want is power and don't care how they get it, once they find an axe to grind. People out of jobs and hungry make easy prey, poor sods. Can you imagine being put out of a job and seeing your kids go hungry? Hitler's put the Germans back to work, we can't deny that. One day people are fascists, next day they are screaming democracy if it suits their purpose. Churchill's changed parties more than once to suit his political career. One day he'll be prime minister. Sometimes you don't know who is right and who is wrong. In Russia under communism everyone has a job, that's the law, whether they have any work to do or not, according to William Smythe of the *Daily Mail*; but then who can believe the newspapers? We all feed off each other, including the church when it gets a chance. They say the King is pro-Hitler after what the commies did to his cousin Tsar Nicholas. It's inclined to tighten a man's bottom sphincter when they shoot members of your family in the name of some bright new way to run society that in the end won't work any better than the rest of them."

"May I go, Mr Bumley?"

"Bugger off. You can have another go at Mosely later. I don't trust that bastard."

THEY HAD ARRANGED to meet in Hyde Park under the trees opposite her father's block of flats so Bruno's photographer could get some shots, the *Daily Mirror* preferring to use photographs to attract readers rather than words. When they met face to face the girl to Bruno was far more attractive than her photographs. Featherstone, the paper's entertainment editor, had said the extra quality was more visible on a moving film where it was easier for the camera to penetrate the eyes to see what was going on behind. "You can see it in the eyes, Bruno, she's telling everyone she wants to fuck them."

"Your eyes are different," he said to Genevieve, realising again what Featherstone had meant.

"So are my father's. Identical, in fact. Daddy's one eye has gone much darker over the years. Almost coal black. There's a flaw in the family genes passed down the generations. Anyway, at least I'm sure that way he really is my father. Mother was a barmaid."

"Do you see your mother?"

"Of course. She'd love to give you an interview if you thought your readers would be interested. But I ask you not to."

"Where does she live?"

"Chelsea. In a flat. My father pays for everything. Always has."

"Can I interview your father?"

"Don't be silly, Mr Kannberg. He's next in line to be the eighteenth Baron St Clair of Purbeck. Aristocrats don't give interviews to the press, let alone the *Daily Mirror*."

"But you are of aristocratic descent and you are giving me an interview. Do you mind if Stanley over there takes some shots?"

"I'm a bastard, Mr Kannberg. You can quote me. Just keep my grandfather, as well as the St Clairs, out of your story. He's the sweetest man alive and he's dying of cancer. With God's help, he'll be alive to come to the premiere of *Robin Hood*. He's promised me he'll come but he doesn't know about you chaps. So I want your word of honour. When he's dead you can say what you like about me and my mother... Okay, Stanley, fire away. How does this look?"

When Genevieve returned to the flat, hopeful she had not let down her father's family, there were eleven messages on the silver tray taken by Smithers, his bad handwriting barely legible. Most of the callers wanted interviews. Paul Dexter and his public relations team had been working harder than she expected. Her father was out somewhere when she looked around the flat, finding only Smithers in his upstairs room.

"How am I going to see all these people, Smithers? The last interview took me two hours; a nice young man from the *Mirror* whose father hailed from Latvia, wherever that may be. Did you know there were White Russians as well as the Reds? The Whites lost so that probably explains why I never heard of them."

"Why don't you invite them all to the flat, Miss Genevieve? Then you can kill all the birds with one stone. Excuse me, there goes the phone again. I tried referring them to Elstree Studio but that apparently isn't good enough. There are, I am now told, a number of film producers who work out of Elstree Studios and they all have different phone numbers. Mr Dexter and his staff are just one of many."

"My father will have a heart attack if I brought them here."

"Let me talk to him after I answer the phone. Or you can have them all running around the Park."

"Are you enjoying this, Smithers?"

"I rather think I am. I made a fresh pot of tea when I saw you cross the road."

"Were you watching through the window?"

"You can never be too careful with young men these days, Miss Genevieve. Especially from the press, particularly the *Daily Mirror*. I rather think the *Daily Mirror* has never crossed this threshold and never will."

"You're a snob, Smithers."

"Of course... The Honourable Merlin St Clair residence, may I help you?... Yes, sir. She is in the flat... I'll tell her. Good afternoon."

"What will you tell me?"

"That Mr William Smythe is on his way. He only just heard you are in London. Something about a delayed message from your Mr Dexter."

"He's a famous foreign correspondent. What does he want with me and *Robin Hood*?"

"Probably your company. He seemed excited you were back in London."

In the pile of other messages there was one from Horatio Wakefield and one from Paul Dexter saying Gregory L'Amour had called from America four times. She put the sheaf of messages back on the silver tray.

"If Mr L'Amour should ever get this number, Smithers, tell him I am on my way back to America."

"You're leaving us!"

"No, I'm leaving Gregory L'Amour."

WILLIAM SMYTHE HAD NOT RECEIVED the message direct from Paul Dexter. He had gone round to the new, three-storey house in Chelsea where Janet Bray, now Janet Wakefield, had her speech therapy practice on the ground floor. Horatio had bought the house for cash with the money he had made in Berlin.

It was young Harry's christening the next day and William was to be one of the godfathers along with Harry Brigandshaw, after whom the boy was to be named. Pippa Tucker, who had attended the Central School of Speech and Drama with Janet, was to be the only godmother. William had brought a pair of ivory hairbrushes on loan from Harrods for Janet's approval before having the boy's initials carved into the ivory and inlaid in black.

"If you don't like them I'll take them back. Silver spoons and rattles are all very well but they outlast their usefulness for the recipient."

"His name is Harry."

"With luck the hairbrushes will go with Harry through his life long after I am dead."

"Thoughtful of you, William. They'll do just fine. So nice of you to come to the christening since you missed your best friend's wedding."

"I was in Moscow interviewing Stalin."

"Nonsense, you didn't get within a mile of Stalin. Nobody does. More people have tried to kill him than tried to kill the Tsar, and we all know what happened to the Tsar."

"He was shot, not assassinated, with his family."

"He is still dead."

"You are still mad with me for taking Horatio to Berlin to make some money. How do you like the house? When's your next appointment?

Must be more convenient having your practice at the bottom of your house. You can be a wife, mother and woman of business all at the same time."

"In half an hour."

"That is my point. Under your old arrangement you would have stayed down the road at your practice doing nothing, waiting for the patient. You should thank me more often for putting good order into your life. Now you can have your cake and eat it. So the initials to go on the brushes?"

"The hairbrushes look very nice. I'd better go. That's Harry bawling his head off upstairs. The nurse can do everything but she can't feed him with mother's milk."

"There you go again. Now run upstairs and feed the brat before your patient arrives."

"He's not a brat. He's your godson. Did you know Genevieve is back in town? Horatio had a message in his office from her studio. He phones me every hour to find out if the baby is still all right."

"Is there something wrong with Harry?"

"Why should there be? Genevieve is staying with her father in Park Lane. The phone number is in the book under Merlin St Clair. You can use the phone if you want to. If she's at home you can order a taxi. I saw that look in your eye, William, when I brought up her name. What you need is a wife, and that doesn't mean a film actress half your age."

"She's not half my age."

"Give or take ten years. I worked it out using Genevieve's real age. That's cradle snatching for an old man like you."

"I can't get her out of my mind."

"So you always tell us. Let yourself out. If the patient arrives, let him in and put him in the waiting room. Give my love to Genevieve, you poor besotted fool. I want an invite to the premiere. Horatio says it's November at Leicester Square. He's going to interview her for the *Mail* when she returns his call. Oh hell, there goes the phone again. That'll be Horatio. Pick up the call and talk some sense into him. He's obsessed something is going to happen to his baby. Can you imagine what he'll be like when we have eleven of them?"

"There's going to be a war."

"There always is. Right through history. Now answer the bloody phone."

. . .

HALF AN HOUR LATER, and with the certainty that there was no fool like an old fool, William rang the doorbell of Merlin St Clair's flat having navigated Hughes the doorman downstairs in the foyer before being allowed into the lift. Smithers opened the door with a smirk on his face; in his experience servants, like mothers, always knew what was going on. The look told William clearly he was going nowhere with Genevieve.

For a moment, he thought of turning away from the open front door and going off with his tail between his legs. Then she appeared just behind Smithers's shoulder looking more radiant than ever and sent his mind into panic. He had been right after all; she was the most exciting woman he had ever seen.

"Hello, Will. Won't you come in? What's the matter?"

"Janet had a baby. I'm the godfather with Harry Brigandshaw. They called him Harry, of course," said William to cover his nerves.

"Good for her. How's Horatio taking it? Are you here to give me an interview so you can syndicate it round the world? You could if you wanted to. Why is it famous people never realise they are famous? Come in and stop dithering. You remind me of Louis Casimir my esteemed producer, now known by the Anglican name of Gerry Hollingsworth. The only thing he didn't do was have himself christened. Are you up to the job of godfather with your reputation? You will be expected to put the poor child on the straight and narrow."

"I'd love to try an interview if it would help your career. I go to Warsaw on Thursday. The Poles are worried Hitler wants to annex Poland with its large German population."

"I'm sure you can fit in a teeny-weeny story about Genevieve before you go. Why don't we go out to dinner tonight? Just the two of us. Seeing old friends after America is special."

"Didn't you like America?"

"Of course. I just like England better. Have a cup of tea. Do you know in America they make tea straight into the cup? Disgusting. Tastes revolting. William! What on earth is the matter with you, are you coming in or not? My father isn't here if that's what you're worried about."

THE INVITATION for William to visit Warsaw had come through old Isaac, the Jew who had forged his American passport in the name of Brad Sikorski and sent him back to Berlin on the ill-fated mission that saw Horatio beaten up and imprisoned in the farmhouse by Hitler's

Brownshirts. The message was from the same Fritz Wendel William had presumed dead, having received no further contact from his Jewish informant who had given him so much story on both his visits to Berlin in 1933.

According to old Isaac, the Jewish network that stretched across Europe from Moscow to London wanted William to make the world aware of Germany's intent to incorporate the ethnic Germans living in Poland into a greater Germany, the way Bismarck had forged the Principalities of Germany into one state during the previous century. Everything Hitler did, according to old Isaac, was aimed at building up German patriotism to give the Germans back their pride after their defeat in 1918. German East and West Africa had been ceded to Britain by the League of Nations, the first conquests of Germany in an attempt to compete with the British Empire in the previous century. William said more than once in his syndicated articles that empire was the real reason for the Great War, not some Austro-Hungarian being assassinated by a Serb in Bosnia that finally set the Great War in terrible motion.

William thought he was being used by the Jews but that did not matter to him when he knew it produced good copy; like most writers, a journalist was only as good as his last story. Everyone, wherever he looked in the world, had their own hidden agenda, their own reasons for outwitting someone else if the someone else was vulnerable; the British government called it diplomacy.

"Everyone is plain selfish, Genevieve, something they always try to hide. No one ever does anything for the good of the other person however much they make it look like they are doing him a favour. The Jews have a lot of money and want to keep it. The rest are trying to take it away from them. Some fools think we human animals have principles which sadly, like so many of the other things we were taught as kids, is a lie. I'm boring you. I'm sorry."

"You're not. I got sick of small talk over dinner."

"You're not interested in me as a man, are you?"

"No I'm not."

"And you never were?"

"No."

"Now you're going to talk about staying friends."

"I need a good mind to make sense of life. Most people tell me what they think I want to hear."

"You could have said you loved me."

"And wasted your time. Why does sex always get in the way?"

"I won't answer an obvious question, only to say without it none of us would be here in this restaurant. Do you want some more coffee?"

"I'd like to go home. My father said he would wait up. He's never played father before. Never really had a life and now never will. Sometimes too much money can be a curse as it stops a person doing something with their life. I'd much rather go to Warsaw, to the real problem, than make believe in a film."

"We all want what we can't have. Just my problem. I can't have you."

"If you had me you'd get bored like Gregory L'Amour."

"You slept with your leading man?"

"Makes a better film. Then I ditched him when he'd had enough. Now he can't get me he wants me back again. What do you make of that?"

"I'm jealous. I will take you home."

"Come and meet father."

"Do you know, Genevieve, I've never been turned down like this before."

"About time. William, I like men my own age. I thought we all married a few years either way of our age. You are in Uncle Barnaby's generation, though it doesn't stop him chasing the young girls. His latest is a violin player. Sadly for you, William, I am not like Celia."

"Are you going to marry Tinus?"

"Of course I am. You were there the first night we met. We're the same person."

"And live in Africa?"

"That's the bit he doesn't know yet. I want to be a farmer's wife. Live on Elephant Walk until Harry's children are old enough to take over the farm. Then we'll buy our own. I'm saving lots of money at the moment."

"Be careful. Africa has its problems. Like the defeated Germans, the black man has his pride. Another war will likely shatter the empire if we ask the colonies to help us. The Indians may help but they'll want their independence afterwards. The population explosion in Africa will drown the white man in a sea of black. All our good medicine and doctors are letting families have ten to fifteen surviving kids with the girls bearing children from the age of fourteen. You start multiplying a life from the age of fourteen a dozen times and a country drowns in people within fifty years. When they haven't enough land to go round and feed themselves all hell breaks loose. No, not Africa, Genevieve."

"Or Europe?"

"Go to America. There's still lots of room in America and they all speak English, or most of them. And America is far enough away from all this nonsense."

Later in his flat he had taken the year before on the Bayswater Road, William tried to take stock of his life and found it wanting. All the other women in his life had come and gone without him looking back at any of them with the slightest regret; the one for him was always still to come. Now the one for him was gone. Going back to his old habits had no appeal, the satisfaction too temporary, never fulfilment. He had even forgotten many of the girls' names. Some had lasted a night, a few had trailed away into months with neither of them able to put a date on when the affair had ended.

The likelihood was he would end up his life without a family, without himself through his seed going on through the generations, whatever the future would bring. Without children he, William Smythe, would be dead forever, decomposed matter fertilising the ground, not living matter in the generations to come.

He was slightly drunk and morbid while sitting with a glass of whisky in his hand wondering whether any of it mattered; thirty-three years old, on his own in the middle of the night at the end of the road of life so far as he could see. The more he thought of her, the more it made him sick. He hoped the job in Warsaw would keep him out of London until she went back to America. If the film was a success they would want her back in Hollywood for another film.

WILLIAM WENT to bed when the sun came up and the whisky bottle was empty. He had drunk himself sober. By then he had convinced himself he was going to spend the rest of his life on his own.

"Shut up!" he snarled at the pigeon outside the window on the ledge that was calling happily in the first light of the day. The bird ignored him and carried on calling over the slate rooftops to its mate.

"Maybe another war won't be so bad after all," he said to the bird. He put his head down again, intending to sleep through the day; being his own employer was always an advantage. There was not a soul in the world who cared a damn anyway whether he slept or cried. His small office in Fleet Street could do without him for a day, his motive for making money having drowned in rejection.

"Maybe," he said to himself, "you did too much too soon, too early in life."

THAT DAY the calls still came into the Park Lane flat, Smithers always answering the phone. By lunchtime Genevieve knew a mass interview in the park was out of the question. One of the callers was from the BBC looking to interview her on air. Others were now magazines, the people at her studio spreading their wings. The one call Genevieve did take was from Paul Dexter, Gerry Hollingsworth's chief of publicity.

"Why aren't you giving interviews, Genevieve? They're driving me nuts. Do you know someone has let out of the bag your family ancestry? In the past the aristocracy married actresses, they did not breed them. Quite a turn-up for the book."

"I can only wonder who opened the bag. My poor grandfather, and he wanted to come up from Dorset to the premiere."

"That's just wonderful. The papers will lap it up. I'll tell them."

"Haven't you told them enough?"

"You think it was me?"

"Of course it was you, Paul. It's your job. Didn't you say ticket sales are in direct proportion to the number of times the film is mentioned in the media? The BBC for goodness sake told Smithers they want me to sing."

"Who's Smithers?"

"A gentleman's gentleman. The only sane man I know on earth."

"What does a gentleman's gentleman do?"

"Looks after my father."

"I don't know what you are talking about but come into the studio. We are going to schedule interviews in Elstree before the whole damn thing spins out of control. My secretary can handle everything."

"Not as well as Smithers. I'll get myself a taxi."

"That's a good girl. Dress sexily. *Robin Hood* cost a fortune to make and the banker is breathing down Hollingsworth's neck. You know, I still only think of him as Louis Casimir. The world's a mess."

BY THE TIME William met Fritz Wendel in the Jewish quarter of Warsaw, both William and Genevieve had better things to think about than their love-lives, which for both of them had come to a halt. Tinus was studying hard for his degree at Oxford. Gregory L'Amour was still in America. Neither of them were aware that Paul Dexter was about to announce their love affair to the world in much the same way he had headlined the sordid affair of a Lord's son and a barmaid, leaving the girl with a bastard daughter without a name. Paul Dexter had flogged every last drop of publicity out of the aristocrat's illegitimate granddaughter.

"Did you have to go this far, Mr Dexter?"

"It's in your contract to give every help to our publicity campaign. How did your grandfather take it?" The man was positively gloating when Genevieve marched into his office demanding an explanation.

"He doesn't know. They don't get the papers at Purbeck Manor. My grandmother stopped them being delivered at the start of the Great War. My father's the problem now I've had to move out of his flat. They were waiting for him in Park Lane and all of them rude. They even joked about his monocle. Being embarrassed in public is my father's worst nightmare. The papers have rubbed his nose in the dirt. Every one of them. Some old woman came by and hit him with her handbag for being a cad. Recognised his face from the papers. They literally push the camera in his face to make him react and look foolish. He won't go out of the flat. Then they interviewed my mother who was drunk as usual. They can mangle anything to make a good story and sell newspapers. They act like rabid dogs some of them... Stop laughing. This is my family being torn to pieces. If Gerry Hollingsworth were here, I'd slap his damn face. He put you up to all of this. Just because I wouldn't sleep with him, and that you can quote to the press. I wouldn't fuck that bastard in a fit."

"Calm down, Genevieve. There's a price to everything. If you hadn't agreed in writing the price with us for your next three pictures you could have made a fortune. Everyone in England wants to see Genevieve. You're splashed all over the provincial papers as well. My word, what a job we have done. Even two of the New York papers have picked up on the story."

"That was William Smythe."

"Not the bastard story. That wasn't in America. I've never seen Smythe so tame. Was he your lover?"

"No, but he loves me."

"Poor fool."

"We are all fools, Mr Dexter. I was a fool to trust you and Louis Casimir. One day the press will pick up on his pathetic story and give me a good laugh. Then his family can suffer like mine."

"It's all just part of the business. Publicity is our life-blood. Calm down! You have a long career ahead, Genevieve. This is just the beginning."

"You own me, don't you?"

"Yes we do. Let it run off like water from a duck's back."

"What about my father holed up in his flat?"

"It'll blow over."

"For the public, probably. For my father, never. We were just getting to really know each other. Now he wishes the Germans had killed him in the trenches before he dishonoured the family name... Where are you going?"

"To lunch. You are boring me. Like all women you are never satisfied. I suggest you grow up and look at the world. The world is about money. Never forget. Nothing else. Just money."

"You're a pathetic fool."

"Don't talk like that or I'll get your contract cancelled."

"Please do and when you've cancelled it, shove it up your arse."

"You really can be a rude little bitch."

"I get that from my mother. According to half the papers, she's a whore and whores don't behave like ladies. So if I had fucked Louis none of this would have happened?"

"None of it, Genevieve. He'd have dumped you after half a dozen fucks. Like the rest of them. Good-looking women are two a penny. The businessmen create the money. We make the star. We made you. So get off your high little horse while I'm having my lunch. Go home." To Genevieve's surprise Paul Dexter slammed his own door behind him as he went out.

"I don't have a home," she said to herself when the room was empty.

WHEN SHE REACHED her mother's flat in Chelsea there was no one waiting at the door. Not one single reporter. All stories had a short life. For the rest of London the excitement was already over.

"Come on in, ducky. Have a drink. Never seen such a right royal song and dance. So after all I'm coming to the premiere. A nice young man from your studio is having a dress made up for me. They're going to tart me up good and proper. You see, my daughter, everything will turn out for the best. Life always does. A few years from now you and I will laugh our heads off at all the palaver."

It was, as she told her mother later when she had recovered her sense of humour, a dirty business making films.

"Why don't you sell the real inside story to one of the magazines? Say a friend leaked the story, ducks, if Mr bloody Dexter asks. Never get mad, get even and always put your money under the pillow for a rainy day. Make hay while the sun shines... Do you want me to go on? Have another bloody drink and drown your sorrows. Tomorrow's another day."

"You're a good woman, Mum."

"That's better. One day the world will come to an end. Until then enjoy yourself and always make sure you've got money. What my mother said. You come out of this with money like I did with your father and you'll be laughing all the way to the bank. It's money what gives us what we want. Freedom. Love. A daughter dressed up and looking like a million dollars. As I always say, it's better to be miserable and rich than miserable and poor. Better to be pissed off than pissed on."

"Good grief, Mum. Where do you get them all from?"

"Get what?"

"The little sayings that always make sense."

"I've no idea what you are talking about. The bloke in the boozer sent up a new case of gin. From his off sales. It's under the kitchen table. Be a dear. The orange cordial's in the bottle on the shelf."

4

The Royal Air Force had taught Andre Cloete to fly an aeroplane in a week. Every evening after lectures Tinus and Andre had raced their Morgan sports cars to RAF Abingdon, an RAF aerodrome a few miles south of Oxford.

"It's the same eye-hand coordination," explained Squadron Leader Cunningham. "A chap who scores a hundred against Cambridge is likely to be a natural. You'll make a good fighter pilot, Cloete. Congratulations on your first solo flight. Talk has it we're getting some new aircraft in Fighter Command. You'll have to go down south for that. Tangmere on the south coast will be the first station to get the Hurricane, according to rumour. Some say as soon as the end of the year. They did the test flights at Redhill where Oosthuizen learnt to fly with Colonel Brigandshaw. Now there was a fighter pilot. Twenty-three kills and not a scratch. Where do you chaps get your funny names from, by the way?"

"We're both Afrikaners," said Tinus.

"You speak all right. Where do Afrikaners come from? Never heard of them."

"South Africa," said Andre Cloete. "They also call us Boers. My friend here's grandfather was hung by you British for going out with the Boer army. He was from the Cape which was British. The British hanged him for treason."

"But young Tinus here is English! His uncle is Harry Brigandshaw."

"I'm a Boer, sir, like Andre. My mother was English. Uncle Harry's sister."

"Don't you hate us?"

"My father did. Life in Africa can be very complicated."

"And if war breaks out with Germany, which side are you on? From my memory at school, the Germans were on the side of the Boers in the Boer War, where the Boers got their Mauser rifles from, the best long-range gun of its time. If I'd known you might be on the other side... Did you two tell the University Air Squadron?"

"The Union of South Africa is now part of the British Empire," said Andre smiling. "Botha and Smuts buried the hatchet. Largely we Boers now have control of the whole country, not just the Transvaal and the Free State. Ironically, we lost the war and won the peace. Natal and the Cape are part of the Union with the old Boer republics. We came out for the British in the Great War and will do again. Don't worry, sir."

"Actually, I'm Rhodesian," said Tinus.

"Where's that?"

"A British Crown colony to the north of the old Transvaal. Across the Limpopo."

"That's right," said Squadron Leader Cunningham as they walked away from the dual-control Tiger Moth they had been flying. "I read somewhere Harry Brigandshaw was a Rhodesian."

"And a great admirer of Cecil John Rhodes, who implemented the Trust that pays for our Rhodes Scholarships at Oxford."

"It's a big empire. Chap I know was in Sarawak. Place called Kuching, it's the capital. Colonial Service. Bet you've never heard of either of them. Don't know how long it will last. Jolly good show, Cloete. You're going to be a fine pilot. Congratulations again on your century. Maybe one day you'll play for South Africa against England."

As they walked side by side towards their cars, feeling pleased with themselves, Andre put a hand on his friend's shoulder.

"Thanks for bringing me to flying, Tinus. What an experience up there all on my own, even though I do throw up before every flight. I felt the whole world down below was mine. I have a suggestion. It's Friday. Why don't we tootle on south down to London and visit the girls? I told Fleur I might come down. Celia can make up the four. See a show. Have some fun. After flying by myself for the first time, I want to do something to celebrate. Fleur's a great girl. I'll race you down to London. No traffic at this time of day. Any cars will be coming the other way into the country."

"You don't think they'll mind?"

"Of course they won't... I'm a pilot. Isn't that spiffing, old boy?"

"I hate that word, spiffing."

"Fleur says topping."

"That's worse... Come on. Last at the door of the flat buys theatre tickets for tomorrow. It's too late for tonight by the time we get there. We can find a cheap hotel once we've seen the girls. Can't believe that squadron leader didn't know where to find Rhodesia."

"Comes of having too much of an empire when you don't know where half of it is. You ever heard of Kuching?"

HALF AN HOUR LATER, Fleur Brooks opened the door to the flat she shared with Celia Larson in Paddington hoping to find Andre Cloete in the doorway waiting for a response to ringing the doorbell. Instead, she found an overexcited Celia Larson. Behind Celia, grinning like a Cheshire cat, as she complained later to Celia, stood the Honourable Barnaby St Clair. To Fleur there was no doubt who had eaten the cat's cream, both of them were very pleased with themselves.

"We had to come straight over. You remember Barnaby, Fleur? We're going to be famous and not just playing for the London Philharmonic. Come on in, Barnaby. In my excitement I've left my keys at Barnaby's house. You'll never believe what's happened. Never. Where's the drink? We all need a drink to celebrate. Oh my goodness, it all happened so quickly. Out of the blue."

"Slow down, Celia." Fleur was looking at her friend, hoping she did not understand. "Hello, Mr St Clair. We met in Dorset, you remember, when you met Celia, which now all makes sense. When are you two getting married?"

"Don't be silly. Whatever gave you that idea? Barnaby is putting on a revue at the Windmill. He puts on West End shows, silly. He's an impresario. You and I and two other girls are going to play together. Like we did at Purbeck Manor. He wants us dressed in very smart clothes with oomph. Lots of oomph. He's got a man who is going to rearrange the popular classics for two fiddles, a flute and a cello. We can make oodles of money and still attend classes at the college during the day. Oh, I'm so excited I could die. This is far better than playing second fiddle in an orchestra. You'll have all the men running after you, Fleur. Think of it. *The Three Strings and a Flute.* That's what we are going to call ourselves. Just think, your father won't have to pay our rent anymore. We'll both be quite independent long before we leave college."

"When does all this happen, Celia?"

"Soon. Very soon. Barnaby promised. Give me a hug."

"Andre said he'd drive down for the weekend."

"Oh, Andre. He's lovely but a student. You can't make any money out of playing cricket. Anyway he lives somewhere in Africa. You should see Barnaby's town house overlooking Green Park in Piccadilly. Three storeys. Enormous. Edward is a gem. Barnaby's valet. So what do you think of it all?"

"I'm not quite sure but someone should close the front door before the neighbour's cat gets in. Isn't the Windmill where they show all the leg? Are you sure what kind of clothes we are meant to wear?"

"I've no idea except it's off Shaftesbury Avenue, right in the West End. Isn't Barnaby a dear?... I'm sure we have a bottle of wine somewhere at the back of the kitchen cupboard to celebrate. Then we're going out to dinner."

"The three of us?"

"No, darling. Myself and Barnaby. You just said you were waiting for Andre."

"I HAVE A BETTER IDEA," said Tinus when they found Fleur alone in the flat not sure when her flatmate was coming home. "You two go out and celebrate Andre flying solo. I'll make a surprise call on Genevieve at her father's flat. It's only round the corner, so to speak."

"Haven't you been reading the papers?"

"I never have time at Oxford. What's wrong?"

"The papers found out about her grandfather. I asked my tutor, who said it was all about publicity."

"Genevieve would never embarrass him or her father," said Tinus.

"The studio. The people who put up the money for her film. Mr Strachan says they do things like that. Mr Strachan is my tutor."

"How awful. They'd never get away with that in Rhodesia. No one would ever talk to them again."

"In London that would not worry the newspapers one bit, or the film company."

"Will Celia be here tomorrow morning?" asked Tinus.

"I don't think so. Fact is, she said she might go down to the country and visit her parents. Why she hasn't been back from college this afternoon."

"Just as well we brought two cars, Andre. You never know what's going to happen. I was looking forward to a show with the four of us tomorrow. Andre flew a Tiger Moth solo this afternoon. Going to be a fighter pilot. The chaps are getting Hurricanes at Tangmere. See you back at Oxford, Andre."

"Where are you going to stay?"

"No idea. Fleur will know where to find you a bed. It was all fine being three of us with Genevieve when I first arrived in England. We're too old for that now. If Genevieve isn't there I'll drive straight back. That's probably a better idea. Famous film stars don't just sit around waiting for the likes of me. Pity if she isn't home. I could really do with a good natter. She and I get on so well together... Or I could drive down and surprise Uncle Harry if I stay in town tonight. You two have a good time whatever you get up to. Strange, Celia said she rarely spoke to her mother. I thought they lived in Wapping, which isn't exactly the country. Please tell her I called."

"The Honourable Merlin St Clair is not receiving tonight, sir," said Smithers frostily when the door to the Park Lane flat was answered to Tinus; even the man downstairs had been rude before he even got into the lift.

"Actually, I came to see Genevieve. She told me she lives here with her father."

"Not anymore."

"Where has she gone?"

"I do not divulge information about the family to the press. Goodnight to you, sir. And at this time of night! Vultures the lot of you. Disgusting profession."

"My name is Tinus Oosthuizen. I'm from Rhodesia, not the press. Genevieve and I are close friends. If she is in trouble I want to help."

"She's probably with her mother if they've even left her mother alone. I'll write down the address. Miss Genevieve mentioned your name. Mentioned it more than once. Everything is in a pickle."

Back in the Morgan, which Tinus had parked on the other side of

Park Lane to the flat under a tree, Tinus sat thinking what he should do. Were it not for the man telling him to call at the Chelsea flat as soon as possible, he would have driven in the dark straight back to his digs in Oxford. In the glove compartment were two bars of chocolate, in his room some stale bread and a lump of Cheddar cheese. She was, as he told himself for the umpteenth time, a film star with many friends. He was in his second year at Oxford with no plans in his life other than the week ahead and Saturday's game of cricket. On the piece of paper the man at the door of the flat had written a phone number. One dead-end for the night was probably enough for one day. He did not need another girl to tell him by her absence he was only nineteen. Celia and Genevieve had better things to do, so to hell with it.

Pressing the starter button on the wooden dashboard with a jab he made the car fire first time. Putting the car into gear, Tinus let out the clutch and pulled out onto the road. At Marble Arch he turned the car in the direction of Oxford and home.

Feeling the joy of driving a car given to him by Uncle Harry, Tinus began to sing to himself. The late July sky was mostly clear of cloud. Once he drove out of London he would be able to see the stars when he looked up at the night air, the breeze warm in his face. Tinus began the long comfortable drive, alone with his thoughts.

When Tinus reached his Oxford room it was well past midnight; stale bread and old cheese eaten along with a jar of onion pickles had never tasted better in his life. When he went to bed, Tinus lay back without a care in the world, waiting to fall asleep.

Next he knew it was morning. Putting on his shorts and gym shoes, Tinus went for his morning run. At the willow tree where Genevieve had sat the day the three of them went rowing on the River Thames before the Thames met the River Cherwell, Tinus sat down to catch his breath. When he got home the landlady had his breakfast almost ready.

"Lots of toast, Mrs Witherspoon. I'm starving. It's a lovely morning down by the river. Hope I didn't wake you last night. Bacon and eggs! My favourite. You look after me just like my mother."

"Don't you miss Rhodesia, Tinus?"

"All the time. Do you know I once flew my uncle's aeroplane up the Zambezi River with Tembo and flew over the Victoria Falls? We all thought Princess was going to have a heart attack."

"Who was Princess?" asked Mrs Witherspoon to keep the conversation going; Mrs Witherspoon was a widow of many years and lonely for company.

"Tembo's wife. His fourth wife to be exact. The most expensive bride in Mashonaland, if not the whole of Rhodesia. When Tembo came back from looking for Uncle Harry's crashed aeroplane in the Congo he had lots of money. Paid twenty cows for Princess. Unheard of. Tembo's older wives are as jealous as snakes."

"Are snakes jealous?"

"Probably. If Princess runs away her father has to give back the twenty cows. Now that's a system that needs more looking into."

"In England, buying a woman is called prostitution."

"In Africa it is called *lobola*. Do you want me to go on, Mrs Witherspoon?"

"Eat your bacon and eggs first while I make you some more toast."

"Yesterday all I had after breakfast was bread and cheese. Andre flew solo and we went down to London to see the girls."

"Where is Andre? His bed wasn't slept in."

"With Fleur, I expect."

"What is the world coming to? In Africa, it seems they buy their wives. In London they don't even marry them before staying the night. Now in my day we would never have got away with such behaviour."

"Neither would Andre with Fleur, Mrs Witherspoon. Whatever he says, I'll bet he stayed in a cheap hotel. These eggs are done just right."

Feeling he had scored at least one point for Andre, Tinus finished his breakfast without saying another word. When he looked up from his cleaned plate Mrs Witherspoon had left the room.

IN LONDON, Bruno Kannberg was not enjoying his breakfast, the meeting with Arthur Bumley later in the day weighing on his mind. To add to it all, Gillian West had told him to go to hell the previous night after a courtship that had lasted a year. When the phone rang in his one-roomed flat on the Edgware Road he was not sure which one he feared most; the meeting or losing Gillian.

"Tomorrow, ten o'clock sharp I want you in my office, Kannberg," the editor had told him belligerently.

"What's it about, Mr Bumley?"

"You'll find out soon enough."

Before Bruno had been able to say another word the man was four desks away striding through the newsroom where Bruno sat at his small desk; the fact that Mr Bumley always sounded belligerent did not help. Everyone else on the paper had told him he was a fool for not being the first to headline *Genevieve The Illegitimate, Granddaughter of a Lord*, seeing the *Daily Mirror* had been the only one to take what had turned out to be a beautiful photograph which two of the opposition papers had tried to buy. Saying he had given his word of honour had made them laugh. Something else must have happened to add to a story he had failed to make the most of. Now Bumley was going to give him the sack. Then had come the argument with his girlfriend.

"A whole damn year you wasted, Bruno, and you still live in a one-roomed flat," she had said.

"It does have a separate bathroom and kitchen."

"The bathroom is a shower on the top of a toilet, the kitchen you have to walk in sideways to get at the sink. Now I've finished at Pitman's Secretarial College I'll likely earn more than you."

"Good. We'll share the flat."

"Are you asking me to live with you?"

"Of course I am. We have an understanding, Gillian."

"My understanding was you earning enough money so we can get married and have kids. I'm twenty-one, Bruno. My biological clock is ticking. It's bad to have the first kid past the age of twenty-one."

"With two incomes we'll be fine, even if they do tax us together."

"So you want to get married. It sounded like you wanted to live in sin."

"How could you think of such a thing?"

"Tell you what. Ten o'clock tomorrow with Arthur Bumley, you ask for a raise, I tell you. A raise, Bruno. Two quid a week raise or I'm looking for another husband before my looks go. A girl can't just sit around."

"He's going to sack me for messing up the Genevieve story and I wasn't even meant to do the films."

"The sack will put the kibosh on everything between us."

"Gillian, can't you just be patient?"

"You've had a year, damn it. Two quid. Not a penny less. The sack it's the kibosh, understand, Bruno Kannberg? And by the way, Kannberg sounds Jewish."

"I'm not Jewish."

"I know that but change your name to something that sounds English."

"Maybe you better find another man."

"Are you threatening me?"

"Of course not."

"Then make some proper money. I want a proper house. A proper family. A proper name."

"I barely earn four quid a week now."

"That's my point if you want to marry me, Bruno. You're twenty-eight years old. Most men of your age have at least three kids. Now get a move on or it's all over. He might not have got the smut but you were still first with the Genevieve story and that photograph was lovely."

"She's a beautiful woman."

"Oh, so that's it. Mixing work and play."

"Darling, you really can go off at a tangent. And as for changing my name, I would never insult my ancestors."

"They were Russians. You're English."

"Latvian Russians. White Russians who fought the Reds. With more help from the West in 1919 there wouldn't be any communism. Hitler would not have frightened the Germans into being fascists. The world would be a far better place and not the time bomb it is at the moment."

"I don't care about that. Two quid, Bruno or it's the kibosh for us."

"Mr Bumley will laugh at me."

"Ask him."

"Yes, dear... Now where are you going?"

"Home. On my own. The next time we speak you'd better have that increase or don't bother calling me. I have my own life to think of."

Reflecting that life was cruel, that he was now likely to spend his life all alone in one small room, Bruno got up from the small round table where he ate the meals he cooked in the small corridor that served for a kitchen and went to answer the phone that was ringing on top of his writing bureau beside his unmade bed.

Only the people at the office and Gillian had his phone number in what he liked to call his hideaway; his parents and friends and informants with news called him at the office, the only way to get an undisturbed night's sleep. He had tried leaving the phone off the hook when he was first given a number but the telephone exchange objected for some reason. It turned out some people in an emergency made the telephone operator interrupt the call when the number was unavailable and would not listen when the girl explained the line was open but no one was answering her call. The telephone department had threatened to remove the phone, instead giving him a new number for his flat.

"Hello, Jane," he said. "What's up?" Jane was the telephone operator at the *Daily Mirror*.

"It's Genevieve, Bruno. Have you ever written a book?"

"Of course. Every journalist has an unpublished novel in his bottom drawer. Most of us are frustrated novelists."

"I want you to write a book for me. Ghostwrite a book, they call it. My name will appear as the author. We'll split the royalty in half. You were the only one to keep his word. Now I'm going to tell the truth about my life and make some money for me this time."

"Why don't you write it yourself? Anyone can edit out grammatical mistakes."

"Fact is, apart from the Hall, I never went to school. I still have difficulty reading the scripts, though that is getting better. My mother was a barmaid. They don't take bastards at good schools. My father tried. The next idea was a tutor but mother wouldn't have one in the house when I was growing up. Do you think publishers would be interested in the inside story now my family have been dropped in the shit?"

"They'll fight over it."

"Then start them fighting by announcing what we are up to."

"Won't you change your mind about the ghostwriter and give it to someone else?"

"You kept your word. Now I'll keep mine. Meet me in Chelsea at my mother's tonight. It was her idea. I want to put some money in the bank before they kick me out on the street where the papers say I came from."

"So do I."

"Perfect. Got a pen?"

"Go ahead... Well, this was a nice surprise. Where'd you get my number?"

"From Jane. She was a bit overawed for some reason when I told her who it was."

"You're famous, Genevieve."

"I hope so. For the sake of the book."

"Doesn't your film contract have something to say about writing your memoirs?"

"William Smythe helped me with the contract. There's no preclusion for telling my own story. He had them take it out when he sent them his own typed up draft of the contract. Probably they missed what William had deliberately left out."

"Why not ask William to write your book?"

"He's in Warsaw. There's another reason I won't tell you. Six o'clock tonight at 10 The Royal Crescent, Maple Road, Chelsea."

"Very grand."

"It is, actually. My dad's paid for it ever since I was born."

"How's your grandfather taking it?"

"He's dead... Died last night full of morphine to control the pain. He never knew what they were saying as Gran stopped the paper being delivered to the Manor House at the start of the war. My father is the one to worry about. Life can be cruel."

"Tell me about it. I am sorry about your grandfather... Gillian wants to give me the kibosh."

"Why?"

"I don't have any money."

"You will if we handle this one right. Do you know any publishers?"

"All of them. They all rejected my novel. I'll get the more likely non-fiction publishers on the phone in the office after Bumley gives me my grilling for not telling him about your family."

"Give me a ring when you have something."

"Goodbye, Genevieve," he said wearily.

AT TEN O'CLOCK, Bruno knocked on the door of his editor's office to find the room full of people.

"Come in, Bruno. You're heading this one up. Mosley is planning a march through the East End. He thinks the workers will come out for him like they did for Hitler. Our information is the Londoners are going to barricade the roads and disrupt the march. We may have a class system in England that many of us hate, but none of us are communists or fascists. That's what you are going to tell Hitler in your articles, Bruno. Short and sharp. England is not for buying. Why they don't throw Mosley in jail I just don't know."

"Because if we did we would also be fascists, Mr Bumley."

"Perhaps you are right, Bruno... Right, I want you all out on the streets the moment Mosley's mob appears. Is that clear?"

Feeling a little relieved, Bruno hung back. "Can I have a word in your ear, sir?"

"What do you want, Kannberg?"

"An extra two quid a week."

"You getting married?"

"How did you know? We haven't announced anything."

"Only women have the guts to ask for a raise. If you get this story right, as I know you will, the raise is yours. Now bugger off."

"Genevieve's grandfather died of cancer last night."

"I'm sorry to hear that. I hope the press didn't hound him to his grave."

"He didn't read any of the papers. She wants me to ghostwrite a book of her life. The true story of her family and how we the press treated them."

"That'll make the publishers start a bidding war."

"You don't mind?"

"You write a novel in your spare time, why should I care? Nothing like a fellow journalist shitting on his peers. I know all the publishers if you want help. Did I tell you how many novels they rejected of mine? Stick to the facts. Story telling is for romantic idiots who themselves live miserable lives. And I should know after nine books. The *Mirror* crapping on the snooty press. I love it."

"Have you stopped writing then?"

"Of course not."

"If the Genevieve story is a great success we might have some leverage with a publisher."

"Kannberg, are you exhorting a raise?"

"Of course not, sir. When I walked in here today I thought you were going to fire me. The idea came from my gladdened heart at still having a job. Now her father is the Eighteenth Baron St Clair of Purbeck. At least he's getting out of London and away from the press. Purbeck Manor is in the middle of nowhere."

"Why does he want to bury himself in the country?"

"According to his daughter when I interviewed her at the start, the Lord of the Manor always lives in the Manor House. It's part of the job. Part of her family history."

IN WARSAW, while Bruno was marshalling his troops for the arrival of Sir Oswald Mosley in London, William Smythe was watching an air display by the Polish air force through a pair of Zeiss binoculars, the irony of using German lenses not lost on him. What he saw was superb airmanship in aircraft of a type that had gone out of squadron service in the RAF just after the Great War. The Poles, in the face of Stalin on one border and Hitler on the other, were flying obsolete aircraft, no match for the Germans or the Russians, both of whom according to Fritz Wendel had designs on the great farmlands of ancient Poland, the most productive agricultural areas in Europe.

"Now you see what I'm saying. Unless the British re-arm the Poles with modern aircraft those poor fellows up there will be shot out of the sky in a day, the most skilful pilot unable to fight superior machinery. Write it up, William. The bravery and skill of young pilots about to commit suicide. To add to it, the Polish cavalry still go to war on horses. It's a land of land and more land, not of factories to make modern aircraft and guns. They need help. If Poland falls, the Germans will only have one flank to fight on and all that Polish food to feed the masses of industrialised Germany living in their cities. Come on. They're landing. I want to introduce you to a young Polish Count of impeccable lineage; Count Janusz Kowalski. His father is a judge, young Janusz is a lawyer in training at the university. The pilot bit is part-time as a reserve officer. Both of them hate communists and fascists, communists most. The family have an estate that goes for miles and miles I'm told. He'll confirm the antiquity of the Polish aircraft. Don't you have a friend that flew in the last war? A British ace. Take down every detail of what the Polish air force is flying and ask your friend what chance they will have if the Germans or Russians attack."

Five minutes later the pilots were walking away from their aircraft wearing heavy clothing and boots; open cockpits were freezing cold up in the air.

"There he is... Janusz, may I present the famous journalist Mr William Smythe from England?"

"How do you do, sir," said the young man in perfect English; to William's amusement the pilot looked more like a boy than a man.

"How old are you, flying those things?"

"Nineteen, sir. Nineteen last Wednesday."

"You don't have to call me sir. Do I really look that old?"

"About the same age as my father, sir, who I also address as sir with the same respect. Mr Wendel told me he was bringing you to our air show. Your reputation as a courageous journalist goes before you."

"Could those aircraft shoot down a Sopwith Camel?"

"Probably not. They are good for aerobatics and not much else. Mr Wendel tells me you know Colonel Brigandshaw, the British fighter ace. He's one of my boyhood heroes. I've read everything they wrote about the war in the air over France. Colonel Brigandshaw flew Sopwith Camels, the best in his day. Why don't we go to the officers' mess and have a drink together? I can tell you the statistics of our sadly ill-equipped air force. You can tell me all you know about Harry Brigandshaw, sir."

"No wonder Genevieve thinks I'm too old."

"I don't understand, sir."

"I do. Lead on, Macduff."

"Again, I don't understand."

"I need a drink, for more reasons than the antiquity of your aeroplanes."

Feeling ten years older than his thirty-three years, William increased the pace of his walking to keep up with the young man headed for a wooden building among trees at the edge of the airfield, Fritz Wendel his old friend and informant from his days in Berlin puffing away alongside him in the warmth of the afternoon sun.

The next morning Bruno Kannberg was out on the streets of London as the first light of day showed him the barricades. He was smiling, not so much at the thought of the imminent arrival of Mosley's marchers, but at Gillian West, who the night before had totally changed her tune; it was no longer the kibosh.

"He's promised me another two quid a week but that's not the best of it. Ghostwriting the true story of Genevieve is going to make me a small fortune. Macmillan and Longman are both after the rights already. They want the book in a hurry while the story of the Lord's bastard granddaughter is still on everyone's mind. I'm going to be burning the midnight oil to put down two hundred pages in time to coincide with the premiere of the film. Five hours sleep a night is more than enough when the adrenaline is pumping. Three thousand words a day for a month should do the trick. She's going to sit with me while I listen to her story and type at the same time. The listening part will give my fingers a chance to rest from the typewriter while you bring us black coffee. A book's in the timing and time is short. If Mosley gets his comeuppance from the East Enders tomorrow, I'll have my piece in the *Mirror* down and out of the way to let me concentrate on the book."

"And if Mosley starts a revolution like General Franco in Spain you won't be thinking of movie stars as they call them now. You'll be worrying about your own skin. Fascists like Franco and Hitler eliminate newspaper reporters who disagree with them, according to an article I read in the *Manchester Guardian*. But two quid a week extra is just wonderful, darling. Give me a big hug."

Give a girl security and she purrs like a pussycat, he told himself. But such contentment seemed far from the minds of the residents now coming out of their council houses to stand behind their dustbins, carts and bits of rusty corrugated iron. The mob was due from the north by some reports, from the east by others. Whichever way, it would have to climb over the barricade to pass down the Waterloo Road. According to a police release, similar barricades were blocking the routes into the borough of Lambeth down Blackfriars, Westminster Bridge and Lambeth Roads, most of them flimsy constructions easily pushed out of the way.

By eight o'clock nothing had happened, the people in the street with Bruno getting bored. By eleven o'clock Bruno saw the same senior policeman he had met at the Hyde Park Corner riot. The uniformed man with the peaked hat was sauntering towards him beating a thin, leather-bound swagger stick against his right leg, keeping time with the leisurely pace of his walk; even from a distance Bruno sensed the man was not going to stand any nonsense. Waiting, Bruno remembered a day at school watching the approach of his headmaster who thought Bruno was the boy who had broken the window in the Physics laboratory.

"You again! They said you were here, Kannberg. *Daily Mirror*. Not a good omen, Kannberg. Last time we spoke I had a riot on my hands within minutes."

"What's happening?"

"Nothing much. Mosely's mob has met resistance he didn't expect. He thought London would welcome him in the working class boroughs. The Germans and Italians sent Franco help to maintain his civil war. Can't get across the English Channel that easy."

"Can I have your name?"

"Why?"

"To give credence to my article."

"Bugger off, Kannberg. I know you but you don't know me and that's how it stays. In half an hour we're clearing the streets for traffic. Mosley got the message he's not welcome. Big mouths are usually cowards. People like him hide behind mobs to do their dirty work. Seen the type throughout my life. They stir up shit but when the work has to be done they are nowhere to be found."

"So there isn't going to be a revolution?"

"Probably not this week, my china. We're British, remember. Last time we had a go at each other was Oliver Cromwell and that fizzled out when he died. Sir Oswald is history. This was his go for power. It didn't work... Lads, you can all go home."

Bruno waited for the barricades to come down before walking all the way back to Fleet Street to write the story that some had thought would be plunging England into civil war. He had the headline in his head: *Bugger off Mosley*. Whether swearing on the front page of the *Daily Mirror* was allowed was up to Arthur Bumley.

With his mind concentrating on writing a book in a hurry, Bruno went home at six o'clock to tell Gillian his good news, that Arthur Bumley had confirmed his raise in writing. What the previous day had looked like the biggest story of his life had largely come to nothing. Once again he had still not found out the name of the senior policeman and doubted he ever would. In most countries in Europe the man would have been carrying a gun, not a swagger stick, something Bruno found comforting.

Later in the day, the number that had come into the streets of the East End of London to protect what was theirs was estimated by the police to exceed one hundred thousand, too much for Mosley's much smaller mob who, by all reports, had faded away in the face of the Londoners. The ways of war were always interesting to Bruno, the ways of men rarely predictable.

With a bottle of beer on the table next to his typewriter, Bruno began his opening chapter, his mind concentrated on the page in front of him. Most of her story was in his head. The rest she would tell him in the days to come. When the book was finally written, Bruno had made up his mind to propose to Gillian West. He was going to have a family and live to a ripe old age in the best country in the world without fear of war or revolution.

For his story, Horatio Wakefield had watched the protestors marching down the road, banners waving, determined men shoulder to shoulder, chins up, believing in their cause. Marshals on the side of the mob kept the lines in order but no one on the streets was cheering. Some of the locals were pouring dirty water from their windows onto the marchers.

By the time the mob passed Horatio with his photographer waiting by his side at their third vantage point, the marshals on the sides of the mob were raising fists at the upper windows of the houses. One of the bucketloads, by the smell, was full of human excrement. The front banners calling for jobs and the rights of the working class passed away down the road, followed by what was now a disintegrating rabble.

"Must be more lines of marchers on other streets," Horatio said to Gordon Stark by his side. "No sign of Mosley here."

"Or he's done a bunk. He must have been told about the barricades up ahead where he expected a wild welcome from the workers in the East End."

"I don't think the French revolutionaries knew where they were going until the mob stormed the Bastille. That was shit someone dumped."

"Tell me."

"The blokes coming past now don't look as cocky as the blokes up front. There's not a policeman in sight except the one man with the swagger stick. By the amount of scrambled egg on the peak of his cap he must be the bloody commissioner of police."

"Not likely. The side-kick likely. The top brass never stick their necks out. He's just watching with a cynical smirk on his face. That one knows Mosley's failed. Why don't we try and get his name and a photograph?"

"I heard that, sonny. You try to take my picture and that thing in your hand will end up in pieces in a terrible accident with bits of it stuck up your arse."

"What's your name?" asked Horatio.

"Bugger off."

They both watched the man in uniform walk away, peering into the crowd as if he was looking for someone.

"The ringleaders," said Horatio. "He's picking out the ringleaders to remember their faces. I'll bet that bastard has a better memory than your camera. Come on. It's coming to nothing, they're breaking up on their own. That bucket of shit stinks. The pubs are open," he added, looking at his watch.

"Now you're talking."

"Nothing for me to write about here."

. . .

ALFIE HANSHAW WAS in the Crown and Anchor when the two men walked in, one of them carrying a large camera of the type used by the press. The buckets of shit had told Alfie all he needed to know about their chances. As he stood hesitating, not sure whether to drink what was left of his money, the man wearing the glasses wrinkled his nose.

"You caught some shit too?"

"What's it to you? You looking for trouble?"

"Were you part of the march?"

"What do you know about it? You got a job. I been on the bloody road for days. Now I got to walk home halfway up Britain sleeping in hedgerows and catching the odd rabbit."

"I'll buy you drinks if you tell me your story. I work for the *Daily Mail*. This is Gordon Stark from just over the border, north of Newcastle. By the sound of it, that's where you come from. Do you have money for the train home or a place to stay?"

"I come all the way down from Jarrow specially. Been out of work since '33. Riveter I was, on the ships. After the war the navy stopped building ships. With the depression, half the merchant fleet sits in port. We're all out of work up at Jarrow. I heard talk up there they was organising some kind of procession, to deliver a petition to Downing Street. But I come down early because I thought this Mosley toff had the right idea. Proper action, not just words and peaceful protest."

"What's your name?"

"Alfie Hanshaw... You got any kids? Ever see them hungry? Mosley said Hitler put the workers back to work. Promised *us* work. Now look at us."

"If I buy you your train ticket home, will you tell us your story with a photograph for Gordon? Papers like photographs. Makes the story more human so the reader can relate it to himself."

"I'll kiss your arse if you get me back to Nel and the kids. On the way down I was sleeping in hedgerows and nicking farmers' vegetables. Now I got nothing except the price of a pint. What's going to happen to us?"

"Go home. Soon the Royal Navy will be laying down hulls and riveters will be at a premium."

"I done my apprenticeship. I'm good at my work. Mosley's lot said he'd see us right. What's going on?"

"Mosley wants to be Chancellor of England. Someone's giving him money to further his ambition. You're just a pawn in the bigger game. Revolutions need angry mobs that can't be controlled."

"All I wanted was a job."

"Why don't you go into the washroom and clean that shit off your jacket? When you come back we'll talk. Tonight you stay with me and my wife."

"You're a Good Samaritan. When I lost my job the parish church were all what helped me and Nel."

"No I am not. I'm using you. Like Mosley. Only all I want is a story."

"The rich stay rich. Always do. What happens to the sheep?"

"That's what we're going to ask them in the article I am going to write in my paper. When you come back not smelling so much of someone else's shit."

"You'll piss off once I go."

"No I won't. I need you for a story."

"You'll buy me a train ticket?"

"Right to your door."

"Do I really smell that bad? Who would throw shit out of their bloody window?"

"You're lucky it was only shit. In Berlin they take you away to be shot if you don't do what they tell you. Were it not for a man called Klaus Lieberman I would not be here talking to you."

"How old are your kids?"

"Harry's a few weeks old."

"The older ones?"

"Harry's the only child."

"Aren't you a bit old to start a family?"

"You can ask Janet tonight. I didn't have enough money to get married. He's evil, Alfie, is Mosley. If we go to war with Germany, they'll lock him up for the duration of the war."

"He sounded like he knew we were suffering and was going to do something."

"So did Hitler. Now be a good chap and go and have a wash or my wife will throw a fit when I take you home stinking of shit."

A week later, after the British newspapers claimed Sir Oswald Mosley and his fascists were history, William Smythe walked into the office of Harry Brigandshaw at the Air Ministry to tell him the plight of the Polish air force, the plea of Janusz Kowalski still ringing in his ears.

"Are you all right, sir?" The man behind the desk looked terrible.

"Tired mentally and physically, William. How nice to see you again. If you move those books from the chair you can sit down. I've been reading history. If we had built up Germany after the war, instead of rubbing their noses in the dirt so they didn't have an economy, we wouldn't be facing them now as an enemy. My wife has another house party this weekend. Quite the socialite. Why don't you come down and help keep my sanity? Genevieve will be there with her ghostwriter. She's writing a book, or rather Bruno Kannberg, your old nemesis, is writing a book. He was the chap from the *Daily Mirror* who ran me down at the Bloomsbury hospital. I don't understand why Tina always wants people at Hastings Court. During the week I stay at the club, going home on the train each Friday. This job is nerve-wracking. Everyone agrees with Churchill we have to build the air force but nobody does anything. They all have their own pet projects for spending what's left of the money. No one gets their priorities right. Without radar we need twice as many aircraft to keep patrols up in the air even while the Germans are sitting on the ground having their breakfast.

"Everyone says the problem belongs to France and not England. The French have built redoubts all along their border with Germany which they say can never be breached. A line of interconnected impregnable forts, so they claim. But what happens if a German armoured division goes round the flank through Belgium? All the French guns will be pointing the same way and all into Germany. After that all we have to stop them is the English Channel and the RAF. That damn bilharzia did more damage to my body than I thought. Why I'm always tired. Now, what have you got for me, William?"

"Another problem. The Polish air force."

"Yes, I know. They are flying kites of the type I flew in the war."

"I've written it all down with photographs. The pilots are first class. They need modern aircraft."

"Who are they thinking of fighting? The Russian communists or the German fascists? As much as I'd like to help, we have enough equipment problems of our own."

"I met one of their young pilots."

"Good. Give him a message from me. If the Germans or Russians overrun Poland, tell him to get out of Poland and join the Royal Air Force. We'll need every trained pilot we can get, whatever language they speak. How do you know the pilots are any good?"

"I was invited to an air display by a Jewish friend of mine. The Polish pilots are just as good as ours by the look of their aerobatics. They are all well trained, so they tell me."

"Now you have my attention. You are coming down to Hastings Court to help keep my sanity this weekend. Of course you are. Your eyes lit up like a beacon at the mention of Genevieve. Did you know her grandfather died? I'm still trying to persuade Merlin to come to the premiere. You chaps of the fourth estate made my first wife's family look terrible. They are good people, William. The St Clairs did not deserve the ridicule. What the papers didn't say in their aristocrat-bashing was Esther being married to Corporal Ray Owen. With Merlin in the trenches she thought the corporal could give her unborn child a home. The corporal knew nothing of the child being Merlin's; was blown to pieces a few weeks later after their marriage. Merlin only found out about Genevieve being born after the war. It's all going in Kannberg's book he wants ready for the premiere of *Robin Hood*. Longman are processing each chapter as he writes them. Being a newsman like you he's used to deadlines. He's bringing his girlfriend who doesn't trust him with Genevieve on his own."

"Will Tinus be at Hastings Court?"

"I don't think so. You never know. Probably studying furiously. Young Tinus is taking Oxford seriously. They've taught Andre Cloete how to fly, now they are both in the University Air Squadron. Just leave your Polish report on the pile of books. I heard from Klaus von Lieberman the other day. He was my contact that got Horatio Wakefield out of Germany. His son Erwin has just turned sixteen and learnt to fly, which makes me shiver. I just hope Tinus or Andre doesn't have to shoot down Erwin. The boy was named after a German general friend of Lieberman named Rommel. Rommel and Klaus went to school together."

"What a mess. How did Europe get into this mess again? Well, not again after reading those books. Europe's been a mess ever since the collapse of the Roman Empire, everyone trying to gain the upper hand. A good honest empire is what people need. Can you imagine what will happen in India if the British get out, Muslim killing Hindu, Hindu slaughtering Muslim, in a frenzy of religious hatred? For two hundred years we British have kept them apart from each other, away from each other's throats, impartial policemen respected by both sides if not damn well needed. That chap Gandhi should read his own history before he lands his people in a bloodbath that will go on for centuries like Europe, everyone wanting to be the top dog. Often the only answer is a status quo whatever the moral implications. Once you disturb the status quo all hell breaks loose. RDF radar, that's what they call it and it works. Likely it will save this little island from invasion. You know what I miss most, William?"

"Matter of fact I do. Elephant Walk. Your farm in Rhodesia."

"Peace and quiet and everyone getting on with each other."

"How long will that last?"

"Who knows? The population is exploding with modern medicine. The average life span of a black man has doubled since Mashonaland became a British colony. Birth mortality is now ten per cent not eighty or ninety, and the mothers don't die in childbirth. The children now get inoculated against a host of diseases that killed them off before they were five. One day they'll hate us. But you were right. I miss the farm but Tina won't hear of it."

"Maybe if your war breaks out?"

"It'll be yours as well as mine, William. The next war is going to affect everyone. German bombers will bring the war right over our heads. You remember the Zeppelins, those flying balloons that dropped bombs on England in the last war? They were pinpricks and had the public in a screaming panic. They'll fly the new bombers at us looking like locusts in the sky there will be so many of them. I sometimes wonder why we even bother going through our lives."

"Because we believe in God."

"Some people don't think there is a god. That we evolved in a chemical process out of the primal slime, not as a result of God's creation. If man ever found proof that he is just a result of a chemical reaction the world would give up trying to solve its problems. There has to be a God. Radar, William. That's what we need. Right down the south coast."

KLAUS VON LIEBERMAN had written Harry Brigandshaw only part of the story, but enough, he hoped, to send the man who had saved his life out of England and back to Rhodesia with his wife and family, far away from what Klaus knew for certain was going to happen in Europe: war for the second time in the century. Erwin, his eldest son, had not only been taught how to fly an aeroplane by the new German air force, the boy had joined the Hitler Youth Movement while still at school; Uncle Werner had been adamant.

"He'll meet the kind of people who will help him in the new Germany. The now Third Reich. You know it's family connections that count going through life. The British have a silly saying and like so many silly sayings it's true: 'it's not what you know but who you know'. How is the estate running? So you agree, Klaus? I can tell them young Erwin, the next owner of the great von Lieberman estate, will join the Youth Movement of our Party?"

"With people going back to work, the produce market has picked up. More than half the tenants are paying rent with a smile now the worst is over. I'll never recover the back rent but at least the estate is solvent again. Do you know, I haven't had a demand from the Rosenzweig Bank for over a year?"

"As a matter of fact, I do know."

"I thought it was you, Werner! What did you do? They just stopped sending bank statements. Not a word from New York or Berlin after I joined the Nazi Party."

"What did I just say about knowing the right people? Sometimes people value their lives more than they value their money. Not everyone, of course. After the Wall Street crash in '29 bankers who had lost all their money were jumping out of windows; a man took his life into his own hands just walking down Wall Street. Your problem was much more simple, as were many others in the Party. In exchange for certain favours, including the cancellation of the bond covering the family estate, Jews with money have been allowed to leave the Fatherland. You can all thank Adolf Hitler. The Jews are now in America and out of our way. You have an estate no longer mortgaged to the Jews. I think when they look back they will say they had the best of the bargain, which is what doing business is all about. Young Erwin will be proud of the Fatherland in his new uniform with our big black swastika emblazoned on his right arm. A young man must have passion for his country. Believe in his country. Believe he is part of God's chosen race, a young, blue-eyed blond boy proud of his Aryan heritage, obliged to no other race, master of his destiny, conqueror of the world."

"Do you really mean all that, Uncle Werner?" Klaus by then was looking at his uncle in horror.

"Be careful, nephew, I am now a very powerful man. More powerful than your old school friend General Rommel. You see, I am higher up in the Nazi Party, which is all that counts. Attend the Party rallies, Klaus. That is an order. As is Erwin joining the Hitler Youth Movement. For the good of your health."

"Is there going to be war, Uncle?"

"Of course there is going to be war. Haven't you been listening? The last one was never finished. The war will only finish when Germany is master of Europe and all the European colonies. The Third Reich will last a thousand years, Herr Hitler the most revered leader in our history."

"What about America? America is no longer a European colony."

"America will sit on the fence again. They trade happily with us now, even in guns despite American government laws that are meant to prevent the sale of arms to Germany. America will be thankful to see the end of the British Empire, for historical reasons of hate and modern reasons of trade. Germany and America will trade with each other and grow rich. We will do business. After all, many Americans are of good German Aryan descent. America will not get in our way once we have conquered the whole of Europe. It will be the Roman Empire all over again, except the capital of Europe will be in Berlin, not Rome. A united Europe will be strong, powerful in guns and treasure, never to be challenged from any part of the globe. We will give Europe peace and stability, stop the squabbles once and for all. An Aryan Europe free of the Jews and other tainted blood. Germany will be magnificent. Tell your son. Make him proud to be a German. Heil Hitler!"

Right at the end, before Klaus left his uncle's office in Berlin feeling more frightened for his family than at any time before, Uncle Werner had stood up behind his desk and given the room a stiff-armed Nazi salute, his eyes blazing.

"HE'S MAD, OF COURSE," Klaus said to his wife Bergit two days later when he arrived home from his trip to the capital, a cold fear still tearing at his chest.

"Maybe but it doesn't make him less dangerous. Can Germany win such a war?"

"I don't know. War and rumours of war. It never stops."

"And Erwin?"

"I asked him at school the next day. His eyes shone like I was offering him the world. He's sixteen. Young men believe in ideals that make their nation powerful. It was Werner who had the Jews cancel our mortgage. Why they stopped writing."

"That's good or we would have lost the estate and all these people would have starved. Now everyone here can stop being frightened about their future. You were in uniform. Now Erwin will put on a uniform. One is much the same as another. He'll be all right. Better to be part of it than on the outside running away. He can celebrate learning to fly with putting on a German uniform. There's nothing you or I can do about it. Your Uncle Werner made that quite clear by the sound of it. You joined the party, Klaus, and reaped the benefit. Now you have to live with it. Isn't one political party in today's world much the same as another?"

"I'm going to write to Harry Brigandshaw. Tell him about Erwin's flying. Tell him how nice it would be for both our families to visit Elephant Walk together. Once in the African bush he and I can go for a walk without the wrong people listening. I can tell him the truth. Tell him to stay in Africa. One war was enough for both of us. Bergit, I'll ask again, would you like to live in Africa?"

"You can't run away even if you wanted. You have too many responsibilities here. Write to Harry, yes. A holiday, yes. Write him a letter but be very careful. They read what they want going through the post."

"You think they read my letters?"

"They've done a lot worse than reading a man's mail when it comes to the best interest of the Party. Would another form of government be better for Germany after what we went through after the war? Would communism be better for us, Klaus? Think of our children. Once again the world is in a financial mess and Chancellor Hitler is doing the best job possible. It's easy to criticise but what is the alternative?"

"It's a nightmare in the making and there is nothing we can do."

"That's better, Klaus. Just calm down. Now tell me, how is our big son, apart from his euphoria at the chance of wearing a uniform?"

"I think the Party controls his teachers. They are brainwashing him. The boy has no mind of his own. Only the future glory of Germany. How do they twist a mind so easily?"

"He's still our boy."

"I'm not so sure anymore."

"Let us go for a walk across our fields and you will feel better. We are not going to lose the estate. Isn't that more important for us all than anything else?"

"I suppose so. Maybe one day I can pay back the Rosenzweigs after all this is over."

"There you are. It isn't as bad as you thought."

"If I don't pay my debt it will haunt my mind for the rest of my life."

"I don't think we have enough money to go on a long holiday. Just write a chatty letter to Harry and keep away from politics."

"You're right. You are always right. Harry will have to read between the lines to understand my fears for our futures."

"Come on. We're going to walk. By the look of the sky there isn't going to be any rain. Did you know some of the swallows have gone on their migration across Europe and down Africa? Even if we can't go, the swallows have left for Elephant Walk. Harry told me the birds we saw on the farm came all the way from Europe. It's going to be a cold winter. We need to tell everyone to fill their barns to the rafters with hay. Don't look so miserable. Life is never as bad as it seems. Can you imagine all those tiny wings flying all the way to Africa? It's a miracle every year when they come back to exactly the same spot... Here come the dogs. They've seen your walking stick. Oh, I do love this place. It feels so permanent. Your family have been here so long. Down all the centuries. What can possibly go wrong with Germany after all these years? What looks like disaster brewing one minute turns out very nicely in the end. If it didn't, the human race would never have got this far. Like our own little lives, nations have their ups and downs."

"You make it all sound so simple."

"Of course I do. Because it is. Life is a lot more simple than we think. All you have to do is believe in God."

"I love you, Bergit."

"I know you do. That's why everything is going to turn out all right."

Taking his wife's hand, the dogs coursing out and around them, Klaus walked across the field towards the far gate that led to a path in the woods; through the woods beyond that, they would be able to see the snow-capped Alps far away in Switzerland.

They had stayed at Hastings Court for two weeks, Gillian West typing and editing the copy bashed out on the Remington typewriter by Bruno Kannberg, Genevieve reading and approving the final copy. Three heads, as Bruno said, were better than one. Each weekday evening the chauffeur took the day's work to one of the girls that commuted to the London office of the Longman's publishing house from her parents' home in nearby Leatherhead.

Harry Brigandshaw had phoned Arthur Bumley at his home suggesting Bruno take his two weeks' annual leave, offering Hastings Court as the perfect place to write a book without interruptions. Harry was smiling to himself when he told Bruno about the call.

"You don't have to go to the office tomorrow. Without all the weekend guests the house will be as quiet as a church. My wife is coming with me to London to do her shopping. Tell the children to keep out of your wing of the house. The staff know what to do with the children in the summer hols. Mostly they scream around outside. Two of them are away with friends. Make yourselves at home. I have an interest in setting the record straight which I owe to Genevieve's grandfather. When I explained that to Arthur after tracking him down to his home he agreed to two weeks' leave. The papers made the family out to be snobs who despised the common folk. Took what they wanted giving nothing in return. I will also have a word with Longman asking him not to change the story you give him in any way. We don't want fancy publishers editing to make the book a cover-up for the newspapers. Gillian hasn't got a job yet and Genevieve is best out of the way until the premiere of the film and the launch of her book. I'll see you all next weekend. Good luck. I'm looking forward to reading the book, as will a lot of people who like the truth once in a while. It doesn't look as if William Smythe is coming down despite my telling him Genevieve would be here. Anything you want, ask the staff."

In these favourable circumstances the book had been finished ahead of schedule with Genevieve saying her reading ability was a lot better at the end of it. On the third Sunday at Hastings Court the Brigandshaw family chauffeur drove them up to London with the final pages in Bruno's suitcase, giving him enough time to read the publisher's galleys before the book went to press. The premiere of *Robin Hood* was scheduled for the coming Saturday. All three of them in the back of the car had self-satisfied smiles, Bruno's eyes mingling his smirk with a look of relief.

Once he reached home he planned to sleep straight through a night and a day without lifting his head off the pillow; his mind and body were exhausted. Genevieve was to accompany Gillian West back to her parents' house where she lived to answer any awkward questions about the two weeks spent at Hastings Court.

Bruno had proposed to her the night before the book was finished, when they took their half hour walk at the end of the working day. Gillian was hopeful her mother would be so excited she would not be able to talk of anything else once she told her the good news. They planned to get married in the following spring, when the book had made them enough money to buy themselves a house of their own.

Genevieve, silent in the car, was consumed with what she was going to say to Gregory L'Amour who was due by boat from America on the Thursday in time to walk her up the long red carpet into the cinema and the first public showing of *Robin Hood and his Merry Men*; not once had she replied to any of his messages.

WHILE GENEVIEVE WAS STILL in the car, brooding, Gerry Hollingsworth was back in his old London house confronting the wife he had not seen in over a year. Largely, his three children had ignored him ever since he arrived home from America.

"My name is Carmel Casimir. My children are Rachel, David and Ephraim, who all have the surname of Casimir. Who is this Gerry Hollingsworth?"

Looking at his wife properly for the first time, Gerry Hollingsworth became aware the time for small talk was over. Looking defiant, he kept his mouth shut and waited for the worst.

"You've been having a year-long affair with her like all your other tarts you call film stars. Where has the bond between us gone we found again when they chased you out of that working men's pub?"

"I was frightened."

"And you aren't anymore now you have a mistress?"

"I'm not frightened anymore now I am Gerry Hollingsworth of Los Angeles. Why won't you bring the kids to America?"

"Because they don't want to go. Because we are English, no matter what our religion or where our parents were born. The children have friends here. Like me. This is our home. What if this film doesn't make any money?"

"It will, Carmel."

"Of course. Your mistress is the leading lady."

"She isn't my mistress. She wouldn't look at me."

"There you are, you see, you did try, you bastard! Now you want us all to live as a nice new family with a nice new name halfway across the world."

"I didn't mean it that way."

"Oh yes you did. I've been married to you for twenty-six years. David has joined the Territorial Army so he can't leave England anyway. Ephraim has another two years at Manchester University. Rachel is going to get married, not that you ever asked in your weekly duty letter home."

"Is she marrying a Jew?"

"As a matter of fact she isn't. He's in the Royal Navy. A lieutenant. Dartmouth after Pangbourne College. So nice of you to ask."

"Carmel, stop being a bitch."

"What do you want me to do? Take you to bed after you've slept with all those women in America?"

"Are you coming to the premiere?"

"And have her laugh in my face!"

"I thought you fancied Gregory L'Amour, who by the way is Genevieve's lover. It will be all over the papers tomorrow in time to give the film a good boost. Lovers on screen. Lovers in life. The audience will love it."

"You'd use anyone to make you money. Was it your idea to make fun of her grandfather? You killed him, Louis, or whatever you want to call yourself. The poor old man is dead. You didn't even let an old man who never harmed you die in peace."

"It's all part of the film industry."

"Then the film industry stinks. Why did you change your name?"

"I don't want to be Jewish anymore. It's too exhausting."

"Well I do. You want to live with your wife and family, Louis, come back here with the right name or you can go to hell with all the others who deny their God... Shame on you."

"There's going to be a war, Carmel. From what I hear in America, if Hitler gets his way he's going to exterminate all the Jews."

"Chase them out of Germany maybe. We've been changing countries for centuries. What else can he do?"

"He's going to kill us."

"You can't just go out and kill thousands of people. What would everyone say?"

"Not much. They've always hated the children of Israel."

"You are saying this to frighten me."

"Don't you remember what was in that pamphlet of Mosley's? And that's England. Germany and half of Europe are far more anti-semitic."

"Mosley's a spent force. This is England. The Jews have been here hundreds of years without a problem."

"And if Germany defeats England?"

"Don't be daft. He'd have to beat the whole British Empire."

"There are a few in that glorious empire who would dearly like to see the back of the British. Gandhi wants independence for India. No one likes to be ruled by foreigners."

"The whole subcontinent would implode. Russia would invade from one side and China from the other. Then where would Gandhi be? People like that like the limelight."

"The Japs have invaded China. Russia is still in turmoil. India would survive on its own without the British."

"I'm not going to stand here arguing with you, Louis. I'm not going to America."

"My name is Gerry Hollingsworth."

"Then go to hell."

"I want to talk to the children."

"They will also tell you to go to hell. Their friends think you are a skunk. They all know what you have been up to in America. It goes with the film industry. It goes with being a film producer. You said so yourself. You made your bed in America. Leave us alone. Didn't you know your children are ashamed of you? Probably the best thing you did was change your name."

THE CHEAP HOTEL in Hackney cost them each two shillings and sixpence which included a good English breakfast. The students who patronised the Williams Hotel knew a bargain when they saw one. Tinus and Andre shared a small room with twin beds against each wall and a bathroom down the corridor that served all the rooms on the third floor. Before breakfast there was a lot of banging on the bathroom door to hurry people up. On the first Saturday in November the hotel was half full. Andre and Tinus had taken the train down to London leaving the Morgans in Oxford; there was no parking for smart cars outside the Williams, which had decided them to go down by train.

Having stood in line for their morning shower, an African habit that had stayed with them, whereas in England people bathed once a week, they had gone down to the dining room to eat as much breakfast as possible to prepare themselves for the big day. At eleven o'clock, Tinus and Andre were going to the bookshop at Harrods store where Genevieve was signing her book. At eight o'clock in the evening they were going to Leicester Square for the premiere of *Robin Hood and his Merry Men* dressed in their best dinner jackets with red roses in their button holes, a touch suggested by Andre in the train coming down.

"The three musketeers, don't forget. Got to look spiffing, Tinus. I suggest a small rose bud in each of our lapels. I've never before been to a film premiere. What's all this about a book?"

"Publicity I suppose. Oxford doesn't teach you much about real life and how people make money. The tickets she sent us are right at the back of the cinema according to her note, but beggars can't be choosers. What a time in her life to think of us. Most people I'm told, when they get up in the world, forget their friends.

"Isn't she more than just a friend to you, Tinus?"

"How could she be? Well, maybe. There's something behind those different-coloured eyes that call to me. Not in her beautiful face but deep in the recesses of her mind, as if we know there's more to come in our lives together. Maybe she does it to everyone. Why Genevieve is a film star. Her charisma that calls to every male on the planet."

"All I see is the beautiful face and her sexuality. There's nothing else calling me or the rest of us. I think you two have something going together that is very special. Far away from anything to do with films or you being up at Oxford."

"Like you and Fleur?"

"We're chums more than lovers."

"So you are lovers!"

"Don't look so shocked. I seem to remember a story about a lifeboat. Did you ever hear from her again?"

"Not a word. Ships in the night except on that night we were both in the same ship. Was I drunk when I told you, Andre?"

"Yes you were."

"You do know the worst thing in life is a drinking companion with a memory?"

"Sorry, old chap. I'll forget it right away. Well, you can now read her book to find out everything you don't want to know. You think she's spilt the spicy bits in her life?"

"I asked her if she had had a lover. She said it was a question I would not like answered, whatever that meant."

"In the film business, it's inevitable, or so I read somewhere in one of those magazines."

"I think she's as pure as the driven snow."

"I say, Tinus, you're in love with the girl. You know, I like travelling by train. Gives you a chance to look at the countryside. Barely another month and I'm going home for good. I like England but my home is in Africa."

"What are you going to do with your degree in History?"

"Absolutely nothing. Oxford is an experience to enjoy, a place to learn how to think. The subject matter learnt doesn't matter. It's all about training the mind to think clearly, to be able to see what is going on in life. Anyway, that is what Plato had to say. Practical knowledge comes after university."

"So it was all an excuse to play cricket and rugby?"

"Something like that. At our age, who knows what the future will bring? The trick is to enjoy what you are doing at the time. Right up to the hilt."

"Are you going to see Fleur this trip?"

"Not this time. Tomorrow is all about Genevieve."

From the railway station they had caught the Tube and walked half a mile to their hotel. By then it was dark, both were tired and went up to the room, each with a box given them by Mrs Witherspoon containing their supper. After eating their sandwiches they both got into their beds, falling asleep before either of them had a chance to say goodnight.

On the table next to the cornflakes and milk was a section of the morning newspapers being ignored by most of the guests; students found newspapers boring. Having filled a plate with cornflakes, Tinus picked up the jug of milk, glancing at the newspapers. As he did so, his whole stomach flipped over as he read, his eye first drawn to the *Daily Mirror*'s widely published picture of Genevieve. Next to the picture of her was the picture of a man; a very good-looking man, Tinus thought, as his whole body tensed, making him put down the jug without pouring milk into his plate of cornflakes. The headline was simple:

LOVERS OFF AND ON THE SCREEN. WHEN'S THE WEDDING?

Quietly Andre, who had read the headline, picked up the milk jug and poured for Tinus.

"Bad luck, old chap."

"I've been in a stupid dream ever since I saw her the first time at the Mayfair party with Uncle Harry."

"There are plenty of fish in the sea."

"Not like Genevieve."

"You can congratulate her at the book signing."

"Of course I can. Whatever was I thinking? Lucky I haven't made a damn fool of myself."

"It could just be publicity."

"You're a good friend, Andre. Let's just go sit down and eat our breakfast. The memory will never go. That's something I will always have for the rest of my life. Thanks for the milk. My right arm locked for some reason."

"My pleasure, old friend. Just remember next year you'll be playing cricket for Oxford while I'm looking for some kind of job in Cape Town."

. . .

LATER, when she looked up from the desk where she was signing copies of her book and saw him standing at the back of the crowd, Tinus saw pain flicker in Genevieve's eyes followed by a resigned smile and a mouthed hello. Neither of them had ever said to each other what they were thinking. Andre was thumbing through a copy of *Genevieve* he had picked off the pile at a long table on the side of the Harrods bookshop. Tinus thought his friend understood the embarrassment caused by the story in all the morning newspapers and needed something to do with his hands. The request for the both of them to attend the signing, in Genevieve's note with the cinema tickets, had said *lunch with me afterwards.*

So they waited, in Tinus's words, 'like spare parts', until a literary-looking Harrods flunky announced the signing was over. Half the people with books in their hands yet to be paid for put them back on the pile. Genevieve gave Tinus a wry smile and again mouthed a word over the noise of the disgruntled customers that Tinus thought was, 'wait'. Very soon the side of the room set aside for the signing was empty. Genevieve, looking more gorgeous to Tinus than ever before, stood up and walked round the desk. Someone turned back from the door, one of those who had put her unsigned book back on the table.

"Where's Gregory L'Amour? Where's the lover?"

Genevieve gave the middle-aged woman a stare that was anything but friendly. Tinus, nearer the woman, gaped at the rudeness of the remark, said in a way that implied the woman had been cheated out of something rightfully hers. When he turned back Genevieve was standing next to him. Andre was still thumbing through the book, not reading a word so far as Tinus could see.

"Buying a cinema ticket or a book, they think they own part of you. Half of these people won't even read the book I just signed. They just want a piece of me."

"Where is Mr L'Amour?"

"He'll be at the premiere. We are not getting married. We are no longer lovers."

"But you were?"

"Things get complicated on film sets. He's actually a narcissistic twit. Does that make you feel better?"

"Much better. I had no right to ask."

"How are you, Andre? You can put it down now. I knew when you both walked in you'd seen the papers. Mr Hollingsworth's revenge, I rather think. His wife wants to kick him out of the house now he's back in England for God only knows how long. She doesn't like me. Uncle Harry is giving us lunch at Simpson's on the Strand. Believe it or not, his wife will be with him and the only other guests, other than my Uncle Barnaby and Merlin, are you two. No, I'm wrong. Uncle Barnaby will have his new girlfriend on his arm."

"Celia Larson," said Tinus.

"How did you know? Oh, of course. You brought her down to Purbeck Manor the night grandfather made me sing 'Greensleeves'."

"I'm sorry. He seemed a nice old man."

"He was much more than that to me, Tinus... The only thing that stays the same for Uncle Barnaby is the age of his girlfriends. I wonder what he'll think of Aunty Tina after all these years? They were inseparable as children despite the difference in their family class, but we won't go into that. Uncle Barnaby, when he was a bit drunk once, said seeing an old girlfriend from the past was a miserable way of ruining a good memory. With luck after tonight's premiere I won't have to clap eyes on Gregory L'Amour again. The only person he will ever marry is himself. The lunch is as much to remember my grandfather as it is for the book, which tells the truth about my mother and father, who is now the Eighteenth Baron St Clair of Purbeck, for what the hell that is worth in a modern England. He's going to live at the Manor from tomorrow. Bury himself in the country. We'll see how long that lasts, if I have anything to say about it. Well, there's grandmother so maybe he'll have to stay for the time being. Come on now, one on each arm. The three musketeers. I'll never forget that day on the Thames when you two rowed me in a boat. Cheer up, Tinus. The war hasn't broken out yet, though Uncle Harry thinks it won't be long."

"So does Squadron Leader Cunningham."

"I thought it was just Uncle Harry?"

With a firm, almost claw-like grip on his arm, Tinus was led out of Harrods and finally into a taxi downstairs in the street.

"You're hurting my arm."

"Sorry."

"There's not going to be a war."

Smiling happily in a way that Andre later described as a smirk, Tinus finally relaxed and the taxi took them to the restaurant where the family were going to have lunch.

. . .

To ADD to their day's consternation, when they stood at the desk inside the door of Simpson's waiting for the *maître d'hôtel* to show them to Uncle Harry's table, across the room, smiling happily and sitting between his uncles Barnaby and Merlin, was Celia Larson showing not the least surprise at finding Andre in London. Giving the gathering a full appraisal as they walked between the crowded tables behind the obsequious *maître d'hôtel*, Tinus noticed Aunt Tina looking sour while Uncle Barnaby was holding everyone's attention.

"There they are," said Uncle Harry standing up, followed by the rest of the men as Genevieve took her seat at the long table. "How did the signing go?"

Conversation over lunch was continuous but inconsequential as no one ever seemed to get a reply, much to Tinus's amusement as he watched the social swirl; Celia Larson was the only one showing interest in anything, so absorbed was she in Uncle Barnaby. Quite quickly it became apparent to Tinus that everyone at the table had tickets to the night's premiere, obtained somehow by his Uncle Harry.

"Had a letter from mother, Uncle Harry, who asked when are you coming back to the farm."

"Is everything all right?"

"Of course. The big news is Tembo taking a surname that he's given to all his children. Princess says her boy can't just have one name. Apparently the chief's name of the Matabele village Tembo came from was Makoni. Four-year-old Josiah is now Josiah Makoni. Mother says it sounds very classy. There wasn't much more news of any excitement. I brought you mother's letter to read... How did you get them all tickets for tonight?"

"Gerry Hollingsworth flew with me during the war. How Genevieve got her break. He was then Louis Casimir and proud to be Jewish. His people are having a bad time. Seeing I found him Genevieve, he couldn't very well refuse me tickets for my friends. Barnaby's launching the girls in some kind of a band at the Windmill. Place has a terrible reputation but Celia doesn't seem to mind. Just hope she knows what she's doing, but that's show business if that's what she wants. Robert and Freya are staying at Purbeck Manor to look after Genevieve's grandmother. She's taken Lord St Clair's death very badly. I don't know what to do for her except pray.

"The *filet mignon* is good but ask for it rare. There's nothing worse than overcooked beef or underdone wild boar. Anthony came down with the mumps staying with his friend while Genevieve and Bruno Kannberg were writing her book at Hastings Court. Now all the children are in quarantine and no children allowed in the house. Tina never had mumps as a child and has to stay away. Grownup mumps can be serious, according to the doctor. You never know what's going to happen next with five children. Miss Dixon the new governess is nearly beside herself but I'm sure she can cope. She's fifty and a real dragon, just what the children needed to stop them running wild. Tina and I are no good at punishing our own children. We both have a bad habit of laughing when they do something positively awful. You'll find out yourself one day, Tinus, when you have your own children.

"You'd better order your lunch as that chap isn't going to stand at your elbow all day. Doesn't Genevieve look smashing, or is it spiffing? I never know what the right words are anymore. There's definitely going to be a war but it won't come before you finish university and then you'll go back to Elephant Walk."

"I'd want to stay and join the RAF."

"No you wouldn't. I promised your mother when she phoned last Christmas from Meikles Hotel. The telephone exchange in Salisbury gave us exactly three minutes. Not enough cables. Andre, how's the cricket? Tina, what's the matter? Oh no, you're not coming down with mumps?"

"It has nothing to do with mumps."

"Then what's the matter?"

"I'm getting old."

"Aren't we all? I'm nearly fifty."

Tinus, watching the last exchange, took in the man he called Uncle Barnaby. As with all the older men in his extended family, he used the title as a sign of respect. Despite the look from Aunty Tina, a look of panic as if she had lost something very important, Uncle Barnaby carried on his conversation with Celia Larson as if nothing was happening. When Uncle Harry seemed to mentally sigh, catching the glance his wife cast towards Uncle Barnaby, Tinus felt a new pang of understanding; it was not only nineteen-year-olds who had their love lives tied up in knots. When he turned away from the triangle he found Genevieve regarding him across the table with a sad faraway expression on her face. Their eyes locked on each other, neither having to say what the other one was thinking. At the end, Tinus could have sworn Genevieve blew him the lightest kiss in the world.

*B*y seven-thirty that evening Gerry Hollingsworth knew the film was going to be a winner and the money would make his wife change her mind whatever he called himself. Across the British Isles every theatre was sold out, his publicity campaign, as he put it to Paul Dexter, 'a howling success'.

"The best advertising for any product is free publicity," he told Paul Dexter in the limousine on the way to Leicester Square. "There's nothing like a scandal to grab everyone's attention."

"All we now need is a good film to make them tell their friends."

"The film is all right. Any film about Robin Hood will be all right. You'll see, Paul. I feel good despite Carmel."

"Women always come round when there's lots of money to be had."

"Just what I was thinking. If you have money the world sits at your feet. Even Genevieve's book will work to our advantage, whatever she has to say. How on earth didn't we own the rights to her story in our contract, Paul? It's standard practice. Anything anyone makes after we make them a star belongs to us. Without me she wouldn't have anyone interested in how she was born or where she damn well came from. She'd be just another pretty woman who happened to be a by-blow of the defunct aristocracy. What's with the public about a title?"

"That chap Smythe who first helped her as an agent took the

biography rights out of her contract when he gave us back what he said was an acceptable draft. We missed it."

"You missed it, Paul. I never miss anything. That was your job."

"You can't think of everything."

"You should. I did. Every paper in England ran the Genevieve and Gregory L'Amour story."

"They are very photogenic."

"Of course they are."

"When are you going back to America?"

"Monday, if your telephoned reports about tonight from the rest of Britain are correct. I need to sell the film into more American cinemas so we can open them all on the same night with *Robin Hood and his Merry Men*. My goodness, what a crass title."

"Do you have a next film for Genevieve? Do you know, Gerry, I heard you never laid the girl?"

"Patience, Paul. It's all timing. All women get insecure at one time or the other in their lives and then they're easy to manipulate. The best things in life take time. It's the chase that is all the fun. Just look at her now walking up the red carpet. Makes more than your mouth water. Look at her looking into his eyes and look at all the cameramen looking at the pair of them. You'd think she loved that bastard instead of despising him. You know something, Paul, inside that man's head is absolutely nothing. He's just a pretty face. It's the camera for some reason that makes him look sincere. The public will love him."

"So you're not going to use him again?"

"Of course I am. With Genevieve. I'm looking for a script to bring them together again. We'll milk them both dry."

"Aren't you jealous of him?"

"I'm never jealous of anyone who makes me money, Paul. You should know that. We'd better go in. The red carpet calls. The next two hours will tell us what the public think of our film. Robin Hood, I wonder if he ever did exist? Lucky for us the legend lives on."

"Who the hell cares, if he makes us money? Sorry about the book rights, Gerry Hollingsworth."

"So you should be. Longman printed twenty thousand copies. They'll be the ones to make real money not Genevieve and her ghost-writer friend. What a terrible thing to call the person who does all the real work writing the book. Genevieve can barely write her own name."

"Life isn't fair."

"Oh, I think it is. It's the businessman who should make the money. The rest of them just provide the product. The best product in the world won't make a penny if it isn't sold properly. They've got to excite the press. People have to be told what to buy. To the winner the spoils. Tonight we win, Paul Dexter, whatever Carmel has to say about me. Do you know she even tried to throw me out of my house? Can you believe these women? She'd have spent her life being a nothing without me. They forget what they do in life. Any one of them can do the job of bringing up kids if the husband has money. I often wonder why we marry the one we did."

"Isn't it because of love?"

"Don't be daft. Lust, maybe. Love is something we sell them in a cinema. Why I encouraged their affair. At one stage during the filming they were looking at each other so dopily it made me want to laugh. But I didn't laugh once I saw those rushes. That dopey look looks like real love up there on the screen. You'll see. Wow, what a crowd. Not a drop of rain. The gods are with us tonight, I feel it in my bones. Poor Carmel. She doesn't know what she is missing, or the kids. Even the kids will stop hating me once they see how much money their father is making. Some idiot said money was the root of all evil. I say money is the route to go for any successful life. Do you know, not one newspaper has mentioned I was once Louis Casimir?"

Slowly, majestically, like some king wanting the manage of unruly jades, as Gerry Hollingsworth put it the next day to Paul Dexter, mincing up the words of Shakespeare's Richard II, the two film executives stepped from the inside safety of the tinted-window limousine onto the pavement outside the cinema.

As they walked up the red carpet into the theatre both of them had big smiles on their faces to show the crowd. Then they were inside in their seats. The lights went down. The show began. Everyone in the cinema found themselves transported into another world, a better world where good always transcended evil, where women were always beautiful and good men always strong. The world of fantasy where people always fell deeply in love forever.

In the weeks after, Genevieve went back to America to make a new film, this time travelling by aeroplane across the pond. Her film played to packed houses the length and breadth of England while the country moved closer to war, and Harry Brigandshaw tried again to persuade his wife to go back to Rhodesia and leave Europe's problems behind them.

Genevieve had said goodbye to Tinus on the night of the premiere in Leicester Square before she was again swallowed up in the euphoria that poured out of the cinema with the people transported even for a brief while from their imminent problems. She had no idea if she would ever see him again, a feeling of loss she likened to death when she said goodbye to her mother at the beginning of November.

After he found out about her affair with Gregory L'Amour, she never heard another word from him; her only hope was he was working so hard on his PPE degree he had no time for distractions.

"Calf love, ducky," her mother assured her. "We all go through it, like losing our virginity. What do you want to be, a farmer's wife in the middle of Africa with darkies all around you? Enough to give anyone the creeps. You go back to America and find yourself a rich man. My friend Joan from Lambeth says that in America when you marry a man he has to give you half his money which you keep when he wants a divorce if the divorce is his fault. Good-looking women in America have got it made. The husband either has to put up with their nagging or pay through the neck; why women in America have so much power over their men."

"Would you come and live with me if I was rich and divorced?"

"Don't be daft. I've already got my bum in the butter."

"What about Hitler?"

"What's he got to do with me? Your father may have gone to live in the country but he still pays my bills. You know what, Genevieve, had Merlin married me and I hadn't married Corporal Ray Owen, poor sod who never got a life, I'd be Lady Muck. Not that your father had any idea of marrying Esther despite all the rubbish you wrote in your book. Had a good laugh, me and Joan, when she read out the parts of the book. Proper little romantic, my daughter. How's the book selling? Remember it was my idea. Put the money in a safe place where no one can get at it. You go and have a nice time in America and forget your young man at Oxford. I'm going to put in a phone so we can at least talk to each other every now and again."

"Will you be all right, Mum?"

"'Course I will. Why ever not? It's your father you should worry about, buried in the country at his age. At least in London there were places for him to go. What's he done with poor Smithers?"

"Left him to look after the flat in Park Lane."

"Good. Then Merlin will come back again. Sometimes we get together for a good natter about old times. The best memories we make are when we are young. Your father was quite a card in his day. They all were during the war, trying to get the best out of life before it was too late... So it's an aeroplane this time? Wouldn't catch me dead on one of them things. Now off you go. You're fidgeting. What's the new film called?"

"They haven't got one yet. My first job is the premiere of *Robin Hood* in New York. He says the good returns in Britain have made the Americans more interested. He's been letting it build up before releasing the film in the cinemas."

"Who's he?"

"Mr Hollingsworth."

"Watch out for him. Never trust a man who changes his name. You mark my words. What's he doing with his wife and family?"

"They're staying in England for the moment."

"Poor bloody wife. In America she'd have got half his money. Here she can't get a divorce unless she can prove he's been with another woman. The men laugh at us women in England, according to my friend Joan. What you doing with all them clothes you bought yourself?"

"Sending them over by boat. You can only take so much luggage on the aircraft. Sent a trunk off two weeks ago to New York. They are going to meet me at the airport and take me to the hotel where they've put my trunk."

"It's all go isn't it?"

"Never stops."

"Give your mother a kiss and bugger off before I start to cry."

THE SECOND YEAR OF PHILOSOPHY, Politics and Economics was more interesting to Tinus than the first. The philosophy had really made him think; to be a good politician, a man had to be devious. While in economics, to make money for yourself required twisting the rules and riding with the swings of an economic market that never stayed the same. Tinus had even asked his tutor if being a crook was a pre-requisite for making money after the professor had explained what went wrong in America that led to the depression. The men who came out of the crash smiling had all used knowledge only possessed by a few insiders to manipulate the price of the share.

"Can a man make money from an honest day's work?"

"Maybe in Africa, Oosthuizen. By making the fallow land bring forth new fruit."

"But it's easier to crook people if the law lets you get away with it?"

"I wouldn't put it so bluntly."

"Isn't Joseph Kennedy, in a Socratic society of good, what Plato would have called an evil man where now he's a very rich man in America with political pretensions for his children? One of the richest, I read in the paper."

"I'm glad you came to my rooms to ask these questions. Society is very complex in its diversification. What Kennedy is alleged to have done, bootlegging liquor, is now an honest occupation without the legal restrictions of Prohibition."

"But not as profitable. They've locked up Al Capone for tax evasion and a good part of his money came from selling illegal liquor."

"Kennedy has political connections. Trading shares with inside information and selling the market short will one day be against the law, in my opinion."

"You wouldn't then call him a gentleman?"

"Not in the British sense of the word."

"I'm glad I'm reading PPE and not geology as was my first intention, and go on to join the Anglo-American corporation in Johannesburg. Instead of wasting my life making a salary, the amount of which is determined by how nice you are to someone senior, I'm going to become a politician."

"An honest one I hope, Oosthuizen."

"Is there such a thing, Mr Bowden? Was there ever a truly good man who became a politician, who in Plato's philosophy only attempted to do that which was right and not what was politically expedient?"

"In a perfect world. Why in England under Queen Victoria they didn't pay the members of parliament for all intents and purposes. A man had to be rich first before going into politics. Rich and a gentleman."

"Did it help?"

"We created the biggest empire the world has ever known."

"I'm not sure if that answers the question."

"Like the Romans, every British administration was honest. It's a privilege, Oosthuizen, to be born into a society that has a culture of not stealing from each other. Culprits were ostracised by their own society for breaking the rules of a gentleman. It's worked as well as the Roman Empire. Corrupt government is man's worst evil. History is littered with it, as you suggest. When history judges the British Empire it will have something to say about our snobbery, our class system that keeps the rulers away from social contact with the common people. I don't think it will say we were dishonest. Some of the colonial people talk of being oppressed, though the thought comes from some of their own people looking for power. Plato says a good government is one that maintains law and order and moves the economy forward to the best benefit of all the governed people. Are your people in Rhodesia not being offered schooling in missions, medical attention, help when they run out of food? I know some of your history. Isn't British rule better than being raided by a Matabele *impi* every second year to steal your cattle and women?"

"Tembo says that doesn't matter if a man loses his pride under a foreign ruler."

"Who is Tembo?"

"Tembo Makoni. He's the boss boy on our farm."

"Maybe if you called him farm manager it would help. How old is this boy?"

"Fifty or sixty."

"That's my point. Plato, I rather think, would have given him a nicer title to call himself."

"He'd still be the boss boy."

"Think about it, Oosthuizen, if you want to become a successful politician. A good politician has to make a man feel important whatever his status in life. That is if he wants the man to vote for him."

"The blacks don't vote in Rhodesia."

"Don't or can't?"

"Can't. They'd throw us out of the country if they did, despite all our good and honest government."

"Are you laughing at me, Oosthuizen?"

"Of course not, sir. Whatever gave you that impression? I'm just trying to learn what's going on in the world."

"And you shall at Oxford."

After the private discussion with his tutor, a man Tinus wanted to admire, Tinus found himself thinking in circles.

Back in his room, for the first time since he was a small boy, Tinus felt lonely. Andre was going back to South Africa. Since his last visit to London in August, when they had stayed at the Williams Hotel and he had first read about Genevieve's affair with Gregory L'Amour, there had been no contact with Genevieve after the brief goodbye at the premiere of her film. By the time Tinus returned to Oxford he was convinced it was all over with their lives together. By now, he told himself as he walked across the cold quadrangle, she would be long back in America and back in the arms of her lover. To make his life more miserable, he had been to see *Robin Hood* three more times at the local cinema, the very sight of the two of them together up on the screen churning his stomach for weeks afterwards.

"You see that damn film again and you and I are going to fight."

"Andre, it's none of your business. You've been down to London three times to see Fleur at the Windmill."

"That's different. She's my girlfriend."

"And how many others? The Windmill is a girlie show for jaded old men to look at young girls kicking up their legs. Don't tell me Celia isn't being bedded by my Uncle Barnaby for all his trouble."

"He's not your real uncle."

"You're right. He isn't. I thoroughly despise the man. He'll dump her when he's had enough. They were both fools to give up their music studies at the Royal College and I feel responsible as I introduced Celia to Barnaby St Clair who promptly twisted her mind."

"Fleur seems happy. There's not much scope for a violin player in an orchestra even if they got into one at the end of four years' hard study. Fleur said they were tired of waiting for their lives to begin."

"And you're going home in January."

"You make it sound as if I have been using her."

"Let's go get a beer, Andre. It's the thought of that smooth bastard in bed with my girl."

"We all have to move on. If you think of her as your girl, why haven't you come down to London with me at the weekends?"

"She was going back to America with him. The only thing I won't do is make a fool of myself."

"I have a better idea. Let's go down to the Mitre and get tight."

For a moment the two friends looked at each other. Tinus knew that to tell his male friend he was going to miss him when Andre went back to Africa would have been worse than making a fool of himself in public.

Tinus knew and Tinus knew Andre knew; they were at the parting of their ways. They had grown up, no longer schoolboys but adults going out into a hostile world.

"If there is a war, are you coming back to join the RAF?"

"Of course I am... You'll see her again. Mark my words. We're the three musketeers."

WHILE TINUS WAS TRYING to come to terms with his love life and education, in Tyneside a thick fog was rolling up the river from the North Sea. Above the shipyard a dark sky was looking like snow to Alfie Hanshaw. Over his shoulder was a canvas sack containing the tools of his trade as a riveter. The sign said *wanted* and underneath a list of trades, the third on the list reading riveter. The rumour was right. The yard was about to lay the keel to a new ship for the British navy. Horatio Wakefield had been right, even if he did refer to a keel as a hull. All Alfie wanted now was a job to retrieve his long-lost self-respect. If war meant work, he had told Nel, then roll out the guns. She had listened to him ranting on as she always did, the only solid part left in his life.

"How it works for the likes of you and me is a bloody mystery. We have a damn big war which we win to save the world, next minute we're starving. Some bugger in Germany shouts off his mouth, frightens the shit out of all them toffs in London, and now Fred Corbit says they're hiring. If we have a war the Huns will sink our merchant ships which the yard will have to replace putting me, Alfie Hanshaw, back to work for the rest of his life. Can you tell me what's going on, Nel? It's daft. People got to threaten to blow off each other's bollocks for the working man to get a job. You'd think it would be the other way round. The likes of me would help build ships to trade with the world, not end up on the bottom of the sea."

"I don't care so long you got work. Neither Chris nor Megan got a pair of shoes and winter's coming. We ain't got no coal and weren't it not for your cousin Paul on the council we'd been kicked out of this council house more likely."

"First I got to get one of them jobs."

By the time he stood in the shed after showing the geezer his apprenticeship papers he was blowing warm breath into his hands with a broad grin on his face. Everyone, it seemed, was being offered a job sweeping up the floors if they didn't have a trade. All round the shipyard it was a hive of activity that came and went from Alfie's view as the fog swirled around from the sea.

"Riveter," he said again with pride.

"Sign here."

"How much?"

"Two bob an hour."

"Thanks, guv."

"Tomorrow with your sack. Seven o'clock sharp until six when the whistle blows, six days a week."

"Blimey."

"What's the matter, cock?"

"I can't add up enough of them two bobs."

"You get paid once a week. Can you last that long?"

"Just... What's it going to be?"

"An aircraft carrier. We're going to blow Jerry back into the sea. Swordfish. Them's the aircraft. Carry a bloody big torpedo under their belly, according to the man from the Ministry. You were too young to be in the last war. Least this time I'm too old to go to sea... Next! What you done before, cock?"

As he told Nel when he got home, being ignored at the end was a right royal pleasure; he had a job. By then the thick fog had swallowed up their semi-detached house.

Three weeks later, when Horatio Wakefield opened a registered letter that had been delivered to his door, a postal order for the exact amount of a third class train ticket from London to Newcastle-upon-Tyne fell into his hand. With the money order was a note in two handwritings: 'Thank you from Alfie, Nel, Chris and Megan'. They had all signed the laboriously written note, the children with different coloured crosses made with crayons. On the note was an address which Horatio put aside to add to his Christmas card list.

Later that day in the evening, when William Smythe came round for supper, the postal order was on the dining room table next to the uncorked bottle of red wine.

"It restores my faith in humanity, William. Why is it the ordinary people are honest in kind and word while the rest of the world rob their grandmother to get on in the world? Must have got himself a job. I told you about that night Alfie Hanshaw came to stay with us after Mosley's march fizzled out leaving hundreds of poor sods without the means of getting home. You think Mosley with all his upper-class crap worried about the workers? Sod them. He wanted power."

"They're laying a keel for a new aircraft carrier on Tyneside," said William.

"Must be the job. He's a riveter. What's the matter with you, Will? You don't want to have a drink. You look miserable."

"I am. At London airport at the beginning of the month she gave me a peck on the cheek. That chap Paul Dexter was with her, his hands all over the place. Hate the bastard. At the other end Hollingsworth and L'Amour were waiting to greet the big star, both of them panting, I have no doubt. Since then not a word, but what could I expect?"

"Sounds like you are jealous," said Janet Wakefield from the couch where she was feeding young Harry from a bottle, her milk having dried up after five months. "You should find a young girl and impress her with your worldliness. That can work. Then you can settle down and become an ordinary family man like the rest of us."

"Sarcasm will get you nowhere, Janet."

"I'm being realistic, William. Look at us; we're happy. Look at you; you're miserable."

"Not sure I can settle down to married life. I'm off and away too often."

"But you'd marry Genevieve if she let you."

"That's different."

"Not at all. Just proves if you find a nice girl you'll settle down."

"And if war breaks out?"

"We're all in the same boat," said Horatio.

"At least Genevieve is far from the brewing trouble. Europe's getting out of hand. They are flocking to Spain. Can you imagine getting yourself killed for some stupid ideal you know nothing about? They call it the International Brigade and half of them idealistic young Frenchmen fighting the Republican cause against Franco. They should mind their own damn business. The governments are giving lip service to telling the young men of Europe to leave Spain alone to fight its own battles. My guess is they are testing men and weapons for the bigger war to come. Germany has sent squadrons of its air force to help the fascist Franco; dive-bombers. Italy is supporting Franco. Even a few stupid Americans are waving self-righteous flags for the Republicans and getting themselves killed fighting Franco's fascists. What is it with young men? They all think they know best and all want to go to war."

"Fools rush in where angels fear to tread," said Janet primly, taking the bottle out of Harry's small mouth; the baby had fallen fast asleep.

"Does anyone ever know what they are doing?" asked William.

"I do. I want ten more children."

"So the boys will grow up and go to war?"

"I'll box their ears."

"To add to the mix of crass stupidity," William went on to keep his mind off Genevieve, "Italy has conquered Ethiopia for a reason that quite escapes me, using mustard gas on Ethiopian troops and civilians, weapons banned by the Geneva Convention."

"They're jealous of us," said Horatio. "Want their own empire. Mussolini likes to strut around. He's a bully and the Italians love him now he's restoring their pride."

"Everyone thinks they can change the world for the better," said Janet getting up from the couch, "but they can't. They just keep stirring the same old mess. We will now have supper. Both of you can go and wash your hands in the downstairs closet."

The two men sheepishly went off to wash their hands in the small basin before sitting down to supper.

"Your poor children are going to have a hard time growing up in this house," said William half under his breath to Horatio.

"I heard that," said Janet.

"They'll love their mother like I do," said Horatio, taking his place at the head of the table after dutifully washing his clean hands.

Then they all grinned at each other and tucked into the food Janet had laid out on the table, Harry safely in his cot next to her chair. When Horatio stopped eating to pour the wine they raised their glasses to each other.

"To friendship," said William, the word echoed by Janet and Horatio.

"This food is delicious, Janet," said William. "At least young Harry and his siblings won't starve. My father said the second most important thing after being born is to be born to a mother who is a damn good cook. That the way to any man's heart is through his stomach."

PART 6

THE ALL AMERICAN MAN — MARCH TO
JUNE 1937

1

The children were growing up. Watching his youngest son Kim screaming down the narrow path between the elm trees, Harry Brigandshaw remembered it was the boy's seventh birthday at the end of the month. The red tricycle was under full control as it careered over the bumps and through the piles of last year's wet leaves. Some of the other children were further into the small wood at the end of the path; Harry could hear them calling to each other, the perfect sound of happiness.

Ever since the spring flowers had come out on the banks of the lawns, Harry had begun to lose his mental and physical lethargy as his body finally threw off the effects of his forced stay in the Tutsi village after his seaplane had crashed into the river. The bugs, as his local doctor liked to call them, had finally worked their way through his system, even the bilharzia parasite leaving no permanent scars in the way the London doctors had expected.

By the time he watched Kim hurtle down the slope and disappear through the trees into the wood, Harry had convinced himself he was as right as rain, the work at the Air Ministry during the week a daily pleasure, no longer a burden. Best of all he again had the joy for life, a hope for the future and with it the energy to do something about it for his children.

Anthony, the eldest boy, was turning fourteen in just over a month, already pestering Harry to teach him to fly an aeroplane, something with a war brewing Harry had no intention of doing; the lad's voice was breaking, the boy turning into a man in front of Harry's eyes. The younger boys, Frank and Dorian, were two years apart from each other. For Beth it would not be so long before the boys began calling to do more than scream around the wood on a bright March morning, the first truly warm day Harry remembered in the year.

To add to everyone's consternation among the older generation who knew, young Frank, eleven years old, looked more and more like Barnaby St Clair. On a visit to Dorset to see Tina's parents with the children they had all gone out walking along the small river that led from the railway cottage of his in-laws towards the ancestral home of his late first wife when they had bumped into Lady St Clair walking the dogs.

The embarrassing coincidence had taken place a mile from Purbeck Manor three weeks earlier, everyone coming upon each other through the trees before they had a chance of doing anything to avoid the meeting. Lady St Clair looked ten years older to Harry after the death of Lord St Clair that had been followed a week later by Old Warren who had turned his face to the wall; the two old men had been inseparable for years in their common love of Lord St Clair's prize pigs and pedigree herd of cows. The master and servant divide was long lost in the true friendship some men were lucky to find, reminding Harry at the time when he heard about Old Warren of how much he missed young Tinus's father.

Young Frank had almost barged into Lady St Clair deep in her own thoughts and memories, the spaniel dogs off the leash and sniffing at anything they could find as they looked for the scent of rabbits.

"Barnaby, please look where you are going!" Lady St Clair had snapped before she came out of her reverie to see the rest of them looking at her in stony silence, acute embarrassment on the faces of Harry and his wife Tina who had not seen Lady St Clair for years.

"My name is Frank, who are you?" said Frank rudely, soliciting a clip round the ear from his father.

Having never before been hit by his father, Frank burst into tears, holding his boxed ear that Harry knew by the pain in his hand would be ringing for a while to come. The happy walk along the familiar river with his young family had turned to frowns of not understanding what was going on.

"Frank, apologise to Lady St Clair for being rude."

"I'm sorry," said the little boy sulkily, still nursing his ear while keeping his eye on his father, the burst of tears quickly drying up.

"So you're Frank. I'm sorry. It was my fault. All young boys look so much alike, Harry. My goodness, I was just remembering when Barnaby threw your Lucinda in the river when they were children which is how I made that mistake. Memories are all I have left. Tina and Harry, how nice to see you. Now tell me, which is which among the rest of the children? Why don't you all come back to the Manor for a glass of lemonade? Merlin would so love to see you, Harry. We had no idea you were in Dorset. Robert has started a new book. You two were such good friends when you were up at Oxford together. My grandson Richard would so like to meet your children. It's been too many years, Tina, since you visited the Manor. How is Mr Pringle? How is Mrs Pringle? Yes, I suppose they are getting old like the rest of us. Please give them both my best regards."

Forgetting all about the lemonade and her grandson Richard, they had watched the old woman whistle politely for the dogs and put the one old bitch on a leash, apparently having forgotten she had met anyone.

"Come along, dogs. Dinner time. Now don't you go pulling on the leash, Pinta."

They had all watched Lady St Clair walk back in the direction from which she had come, the old dog called Pinta straining on the leash trying to get back at the rabbits. Just before the old woman disappeared into the trees she bent down and let Pinta off the leash.

"She's losing her memory," said Harry sadly.

"Who is she?" asked Frank.

"Uncle Barnaby's mother. She mistook you for her son."

"*Does she have a son my age?*"

Over the top of the boy they both called their son, Harry had exchanged glances with Tina before they all trooped home to the railway cottage. Only when Tina's parents were in sight with the children already running into the old cottage built many years earlier by the Southern Railway Company, did Harry's wife Tina utter a word.

"That was a quick cover-up back there. She knows, Harry."

"Probably. Leave it alone, Tina. What's done is done. Nothing any of us can do about Barnaby being Frank's father can ever be changed."

"That's about the first time you have said that out loud."

"What difference does it make? I just hope the boy doesn't turn out as devious as Barnaby with a penchant for young girls. By the way, he's still going out with Celia, if that doesn't make you jealous."

"Please, Harry. We've been through all that a dozen times before, even if we never spoke of it in so many words."

"Do you ever wish you had been born into the same class as Lady St Clair? That he had married you?"

"What do you want me to say, Harry? We have the children to think about. You knew all about Barnaby and me before you seduced me on the SS *Corfe Castle*."

"I rather thought it was you seducing me."

"Successful seduction takes two people, Harry. Would it help if I said I loved you?"

"Not much."

TINA, now walking across the lawn towards him, brought Harry back to the present. At thirty-eight she was still a good-looking woman. As marriages went, theirs was as good as many of the others Harry had watched during his life. They both loved the children despite all their nonsense, if not because of all the mayhem caused by youth and pent-up energy. She was smiling at him, no idea he had played back through his mind the recent embarrassment in Dorset, the rare exchange of truth about their own feelings for each other.

"What are we going to do for the birthday?" she asked, still some way off.

"A few children from school. A cake. The usual. What are we going to give Anthony for his birthday?"

"Your birthday, Harry. It's your birthday next month two weeks before Anthony's. Whilst it won't be your fiftieth until next year, I was thinking of a big party."

"Really, why?"

"Well, we never really celebrated you coming home after being lost in Africa, so why not combine the two? Make it a big celebration. Lots of people. Everyone we know. A marquee on the lawn. A band, of course. I thought we'd cook an ox over an open fire the way we did with the sheep on Elephant Walk. There'll be so many people we'll need an ox. Have you ever cooked a whole ox, Harry?"

"As a matter of fact, I have. It was the time of Tembo's first wife when we all welcomed her on the farm. I told him then I would only do it for his first wife. The party went on all night and half the next day. You have to dig a pit and fill it with dry trees and make some very hot coals before wheeling the *ox-braai*, as we call it in Africa, over the open pit of the fire. Takes a day to cook, turning the ox and feeding more hot coals from a second fire into the pit. Best food in the world. I can't believe Anthony is turning fourteen. I'm sorry what I said the other day."

"So am I. Life is never perfect. My mother says if it was, it would be very boring."

"Does she know about Frank?"

"I tell my mother everything. Don't you?"

"Most of that kind of thing would go over the top of my mother's head. Do you want me to help work out the guest list? What do we have for Anthony's birthday?"

"A set for making a large model aeroplane that flies."

"Isn't he too old for model aeroplanes?"

"You'll never have to help him, Harry, if that's some consolation. Can we go for a walk together? The sound of happy children on a spring day is one of the true joys of life. Did you see the first daffodils and crocuses on the banks of the lawn?"

"I just watched Kim coming to join them, hurtling down the path on his tricycle, his small legs peddling like mad."

"Maybe we'll find our children in the woods and give them a surprise."

"Come on. I think it's going to be a good summer for once in my life in England. Don't know about roasting an ox in April. Never thought anyone would try such a thing in England."

"No, Harry. We are not going back to Elephant Walk."

"Always worth a try."

"Are we going up to London tomorrow?"

"First thing in the morning as usual on a Monday. Did I tell you? The factory has a new fighter for the RAF in production. According to our intelligence from Germany it's better than anything they even have on the drawing board. This war is going to be won or lost in the air, not in the trenches. Why are you crying, Tina?"

"Anthony. If the war started now and went on as long as the last one, they'd have him in the fighting. He's always saying he's going to be a pilot like his father."

"Maybe Baldwin will come to terms with Hitler. Often things turn out better than they are... Use my handkerchief to blow your nose or the children will ask why their mother's been crying."

"It's every mother's nightmare."

"And every father's."

"You are too old to fly in the war, Harry, aren't you?"

"Much too old. The advantage you have over your contemporaries for marrying an older man. They wouldn't let me anywhere near the cockpit of a trainer let alone a fighter plane, though I don't see why not. My reactions won't be as fast as they were in France, but experience counts more than a quick turn or sharp eyesight and there's nothing wrong with my eyes. Maybe they'll let me train the youngsters, pass on what I learnt in the war. There's a chap my age who is a test pilot. All this office work is driving me nuts. No, if there is a war they might let me fly, Tina. I had a sixth sense at where they were coming from by the end of the war. Just ask Klaus von Lieberman. How I got him in my sights. That last letter of his was quite adamant suggesting we go back to Africa out of harm's way. Maybe he's trying to tell us something. That he knows far more than he is allowed to say in a letter. Our chaps think the Nazi police read all the letters going in and out of the country, which is why I am so careful what I say to Klaus. They also listen in to all the telephone conversations. There's a good boys' school near Umtali, perfect for Anthony where he'd be right out of harm's way. Once we are out there and war broke out we'd never be able to get back to England even if we wanted. The Germans have submarines that our chaps think will target civilian liners. We'd be all stuck on Elephant Walk for the duration, right out of harm's way as Klaus is suggesting."

"Nice try, Harry."

"If war breaks out, it would be too late to make our escape."

"War isn't going to break out, Harry. Politicians say these things to frighten us and the people making guns encourage them. In Africa, we'd have a much better chance of being massacred by the blacks. There are hordes of them and just a few of us English right in the middle of nowhere. I like to get my priorities right. Whatever happens we are safe in England where we belong... Oh my God, there's Kim right up the top of that tree. Harry! Do something! He's going to fall."

"One minute you don't want an old man to fly an aeroplane, now you want him to climb a tree... Kim, son, what are you doing up there?"

"Looking for bird nests."

"You'll find those in the hedgerows. Now come down slowly or your mother is going to have a heart attack."

"I'm stuck."

"I'll go and get him, Dad," said Anthony, "he's such a baby."

"No I'm not."

"Then get your own self down. Climbing trees is for kids."

"Go up and get him!" screamed Tina.

"Yes, Mother. Why is it always me? What's wrong with Frank?"

"You are the eldest."

"Dad, when are you going to teach me to fly like Tinus?"

"Never. It's too dangerous with the war coming."

"The sooner I learn, the better I'll be as a pilot. You always say only the good pilots come through the war. I want to be a good pilot like you."

"He's slipping!" shouted Tina.

"Let him slip," said Frank. "When the brat falls and hurts himself he won't do it again... Why did that old woman call me Barnaby?" he said, looking at his mother with a sly, malicious stare.

Harry, standing next to him, was again tempted to box his son's ear.

LOOKING BACK at the ill-fated walk along the river, Tina could see why the old lady was so easily mistaken; Frank was the spitting image of Barnaby when Barnaby was eleven years old and the two of them were thick as thieves. Tina had been ten years old, a frequent visitor to the Manor house, still too young to pose a threat, Lady St Clair treating her the same as any small child. She was a woman Tina had grown to love over the five years she had played with Barnaby, roaming the length of the stream the grown-ups liked to call a river, exploring the whole of the Purbeck Manor estate always with the dogs following. Two children happy with each other, not a care in the world, never the slightest trouble to the grown-ups they kept away from until they were hungry or cold or when the rain pelted down and they had to go inside.

Barnaby said then the best food in the world was made in the old railway cottage by Mrs Pringle, all the children fighting for second helpings, Barnaby no different from the rest of them. Soon after that they had been forced to meet secretly, neither of them knowing why their parents made them stop their friendship.

Even the nasty edge on Frank's voice that wanted his brother to hurt himself made her see the young Barnaby and bring back her loss of their innocence. They had both been banned from seeing each other ever again, neither of them having any understanding of the truth, the cruelty of the grownup world, that ever since Tina had looked at with cynical understanding, taking what she could get including Harry Brigandshaw. After she seduced him in the owner's cabin of the SS *Corfe Castle*, named after Harry's first wife's family, she'd got herself pregnant hoping the rich Rhodesian would marry her, as he did, not being part of the English class system.

Even at the start of the voyage to Africa Tina had realised there was no class distinction between the settlers; in Africa white people were all the same and all in need of each other's protection against the black hordes that surrounded them.

Harry had been out in Africa on an extended visit to Elephant Walk when Barnaby seduced her again, making her pregnant with Frank. For years, before she married Harry, Barnaby had been using her, making her his mistress, laughing at the very idea of marrying a girl from the lower classes. Until Barnaby made his money manipulating the stock market, the two of them had lived off their wits; the aristocrat and the girl so beautiful no man could refuse.

From Africa to London, Barnaby had borrowed money he had no intention of ever paying back, laughing at how easy it was to separate a fool from his money. Even thinking about him as she watched Kim climb down the tree made her wet with excitement, the thought of Celia Larson at half his age in Barnaby's bed making her mind scream with jealousy.

Even now, lady of her own ancient manor, she still felt inferior for a reason she could never understand, still seeing Barnaby with his clipped, upper-class accent she had tried so hard to imitate mocking her, putting her down.

One day, she said to herself, looking from Kim safely on the ground to the same mocking face that was Frank, she'd use Frank to get her own back, when Barnaby was old, without children, a rich old man on his own without a real friend in the world. Then it would be her turn to take revenge on the whole St Clair family, Lady St Clair included. Someone, long ago, had told her that he who laughed last laughed the loudest. She wanted a laugh so loud it would blow the shackles of class to oblivion.

With the image of the old woman scuttling away with her dogs in disarray in her mind, Tina tasted the first sweetness of revenge for being slighted all her life by people who thought themselves better than the rest.

"Are you all right, Tina?" asked Harry.

"I will be. Oh yes, I will be."

Then she walked across and hugged her youngest son. When she looked up, Frank's eyes were mocking her. Not only had the boy inherited Barnaby's good looks, but his mind. A mind that liked to watch people in pain, tear wings off butterflies, a self-centred mind that only thought of himself. This time Tina wanted to box his ears, knowing that she would have no more of Frank than she had of Barnaby.

When Kim ran off with the dogs to help them hunt for rabbits she shuddered with the feeling of premonition, at how much hurt Frank was going to cause in the world just like his father. She had given birth to the evil that lurked in all of them, the very evil himself, the sin of the parents visited on the son.

She sighed remembering some grown-up's words from her past: 'there was a price to pay for everything'. Maybe for Harry, killing all those Germans in what people called a war had killed his first wife and brought him to the woods with his second wife's illegitimate son. A woman he was bound to by the conventions of the same society that had separated her from Barnaby when she was a youngster.

For years now, the power she had once had over men had gone. She didn't even bother with her weight. She dressed in expensive clothes whenever people were visiting to show off the wealth of her husband in the hope of causing envy. Her turn to show she had more than the others, many of whom had suffered financially with the '29 crash.

Somehow it made her feel better, making some other woman jealous. The days of men's hungry eyes searching her out in a crowded room had vanished with her youth. She was a matron, mother of five children, no longer a player in the field of men, the demise of her power the worst loss after Barnaby to happen in her life.

"We have to make the best of them, Tina," said Harry. "Channel the boy's aggression into something that will profit his life." Harry had seen the boy's mocking eyes looking at his mother.

The children had all followed the dogs, even Frank had gone to see what mischief he could cause. She took Harry's hand, feeling sorry for herself.

"Maybe he knows deep down he's different to the rest. He can be so nasty."

"So you won't even consider going back to Elephant Walk?"

"Of course not, Harry. Why leave all this? Here are your real roots. Hastings Court has been in your family for centuries."

"Maybe. But Africa is in my blood."

"I hate all those black people watching me silently. Not understanding but wanting what the whites have. You've made them discontented. Shown them what they think is an easier life with machinery. Some way unknown to them made them well when they were sick. When jealousy explodes inside of them, they'll want to destroy you and everything you have so they won't have to look at it anymore. People hate someone else being better than themselves. Only when it isn't there anymore will they once again be happy with what they have got."

"Don't you think they want to progress?"

"They do but they shouldn't."

"Where have those *damn* dogs gone again? If one of them ever caught a rabbit he'd drop dead with fright."

"It's the chase, Harry. That's the fun. Eating supper afterwards doesn't take very long and is usually an anti-climax until the hunger comes back again. Those dogs are lucky. They never find what they are looking for. Why don't you sell Elephant Walk and bring your mother back to the house where she was born? Your sister and her children will be better off in England. Look at Tinus up at Oxford, happy as a sandboy."

"Our family will never sell Elephant Walk. Mark my words."

"One day those blacks will take it off you, Harry. Mark my words. There are too many of them already."

"Everything in life comes and goes. Are we all right, Tina?"

"Probably."

At Purbeck Manor in Dorset, while Tina Brigandshaw was trying to come to terms with her midlife crisis, Robert St Clair was enjoying writing his new book. The idea for the book had come from his mother without her even knowing. With his brother Merlin permanently back at the Manor House as the Eighteenth Baron St Clair of Purbeck following the death of their father, while Robert had been out walking with his mother and the spaniels, Pinta on the leash as his mother considered the dog too old to chase phantoms with the rest of the dogs, he had asked her a question he had wanted to ask her most of his life.

"Why did you call him Merlin? It can't have been after King Arthur's magician."

"Oh but it was. Don't you remember? You children gave him the nickname when he was ten years old having terrified the cat. Yet, what is more interesting is that your father found somewhere in a book that Merlin the Magician had mismatched eyes just like our Merlin, though they weren't so pronounced as a child as they are now. Your father had even thought Merlin was reincarnated. Only later did I find out from him there was more to the story as in fact his maternal grandfather came from an ancient Saxon family that stretched back further than the Saxon invasions of England, according to the family legend. To the time of the Ancient Britons when our islands were inhabited by Celts. The family name was Pendrogan, a name that went back into the ancient past. Your great-grandfather thought his name should have been Pendragon, that the family did not only go back to the Saxon King Ethelred, some called the Unready, but to Arthur Pendragon, the king who only lives on through the legend of the Knights of the Round Table. The very sight of the mismatched eyes convinced your father one of his ancestors was Merlin, Arthur's mentor, and lover, by some accounts, of Queen Guinevere, which is how the strange eyes found themselves in the descendants of the Pendragons.

"Your father's mother said that though the family name was Pendrogan, that should have been Pendragon with an A, that she was related to the magician with the mismatched eyes, not Arthur, that even in those days people in high places misbehaved themselves. Somewhere in the Manor are the rambling writings of your great-grandfather on the subject. The trouble with inheriting money and an estate is not having much to work for in life. Not much to do. What Harold Pendrogan did with his life was prove he was a descendent of Merlin the Magician, something your father referred to as poppycock until you children renamed Merlin. Genevieve has the same birth trait. She was going to be Guinevere but apparently her mother got it wrong at the christening."

AFTER READING the rambling notes of Harold Pendrogan, Robert was convinced his great-grandfather on the maternal side of the family was quite potty, if not stark raving mad towards the end of his long and fruitless life, a life that Robert determined might not be so fruitless after all. In among all the nonsense, as Robert called it at the start of his reading, were the seeds of a damn good book, a book Robert hoped would keep him out of mischief for over a year. He had called it *The Mark of the Eyes* and writing what by then he had convinced himself to be the truth was giving him the time of his life, despite his wife's pestering him to go back to America before war broke out in Europe.

To save him having his leg pulled by mother and brother, Robert had kept the theme of his new book to himself, only letting Freya into the secret as he worked away in the old room he had lived in as a boy growing up and since turned into his study. A quiet room looking out from the second floor of the Manor House over the tops of the trees as far as the Purbeck Hills that spined the Isle of Purbeck, an island now connected to the rest of Dorset, an island only in name. Like so many things at the Manor, not everyone knew what was really going on. Soon after he started the book his mother had created another crisis by coming home from a walk saying Barnaby was out in the woods.

"What's he doing there?" Merlin had asked before he knew they were in trouble.

"Walking with his family. I asked them to come and have lemonade. No, not our Barnaby. Just the spitting image of Barnaby when he was eleven years old. I was miles away when he bumped into me which made me call him Barnaby. One of Harry Brigandshaw's brood. I always thought the Pringles and St Clairs were related though not officially. You can't have two families living close to each other for centuries without something going wrong. Obviously the boy was a throwback to previous generations. One of the St Clair boys must have been sowing his wild oats, I think is the vulgar term. You never know what went on in the old days in the countryside. Now everyone moves around much more. Rather a rude boy I think. Harry gave him a whack for rudely asking my name. He looks a lot better. His skin isn't so yellow. I would never have recognised Tina after all these years. As a child she was always at the Manor."

Later, when Merlin came to the writing study, they both agreed their mother had no idea what was going on.

"That was bad luck the boy bumping into her like that in the woods. I suppose one day we'll have to tell her, Robert. Can't imagine Barnaby doing the right thing. She took Genevieve quite well, though Esther wasn't married when she conceived her."

"But she was married when your daughter was born."

"I suppose so. I wish Genevieve would write more often. Next thing she'll be married and I'll be all on my own."

"You need a wife, Merlin."

"I'm far too old. Do you know anything about pigs and cows?"

"Not a thing."

"The new chap doesn't either. Old Warren was old but he knew what he was doing."

At the end of the month, when the invitation arrived for the whole family to attend the homecoming and birthday celebration of Harry Brigandshaw in April, the two brothers had another meeting.

"Should we tell mother?"

"If we don't and she finds out what do we do then? She'll know we're hiding something. Barnaby should be there. For once in his life he should take responsibility for his mistakes."

"Then what do you tell the boy? That he's got two fathers? Let sleeping dogs lie. Lots of people look like lots of people and they aren't all related. How's the new book going? You still haven't told me what it's all about."

"Wait till it's finished then you can read all about it. Mother gave me the idea."

"You're hiding something from me."

"Of course I am. It adds to the fun. So we're all going to spend a few days at Hastings Court?"

"Looks like it. Afterwards I'll run up to London and see how Smithers is getting on."

"You don't really like living at the Manor do you, Merlin?"

"Not enough to do. Not enough, anyway, of what I know anything about. I miss the London theatre."

"And all the show girls."

"How did you know?"

"I'm your brother. Freya wants us to pack up and go to America and then you're stuck."

"Mother will be all right with Mrs Mason. I find mother and I have nothing to talk about except Genevieve. I'll miss you, brother, if you go to America. Since I came to live back at the Manor we've got to know each other much better. So we take mother to Harry's party and hope for the best?"

"I always hope for the best, Merlin. You should try it."

When Merlin had gone, Robert immersed himself again in the perfect world of Merlin and Arthur where the knights used words like honour, duty, loyalty, trust, love and knew what they meant. A better world from the mists of time that probably, if Robert was honest with himself, only existed in the hopes of man and the words of fiction.

WHILE HIS BROTHER was painting his perfect world with words, Barnaby was looking for new ways to slake his hedonistic thirst. The show at the Windmill had become boring. Not only had he seduced every girl he fancied – some before they got their jobs, some after – the show he had financed had shown a handsome profit and made him even more money. The only snag was getting rid of Celia Larson, who had given up her classical career to play in a group with Fleur Brooks, whose boyfriend had gone back to South Africa. Barnaby, for some reason that worried him, was feeling a tinge of conscience.

The notion of popular classics played by long-legged girls on two fiddles, a flute and a cello had run its course, the novelty for the public having worn off. By the time Barnaby received his invitation to Harry Brigandshaw's weekend celebration, the last girl he thought of taking was Celia Larson. Not only was he about to hear from the producer of the Windmill revue that the strings and the flute were out of the proverbial window, he had to tell the girl she was no longer a number in his life, and that she never really had been.

The good news, Barnaby convinced himself, when he rationalised his position, was the girls were still young. Fortunately for Barnaby London was a big city, an easy place to hide when he no longer wished to see a girl that had come to bore him, his hormones calling out for something new to bring out the spark of lust. The fact that at thirty-nine the sparks were waning, never entered his head. The pursuit of selfish pleasure had been with Barnaby all his life. Being stuck with one girl for too long was on the top of Barnaby's list of horrors. Not for him a wife and children who only wanted to make him do what he was told.

Picking up Harry's invitation from the table that sat next to the window, looking out into Green Park where the spring had broken out in lime-green leaves while the call of birds carried across the traffic down Piccadilly, Barnaby tried to think who he would take, not for a minute thinking of Tina who had passed out of his lustful mind soon after his childhood friend turned thirty.

Any thought of seeing his son Frank never entered his head. So far as Barnaby ever thought of him, the boy belonged to Harry, the product of a brief ejection of lust he could barely remember, now the mother had lost her charm. Tapping the table with his index finger, Barnaby tried to think of something to do with the rest of the day that would give him pleasure.

SHOWING their legs had never been part of the girls' ambition so when Charlie Fox intimated the quartet were being taken off the bill at the Windmill, they had already made plans to play at a supper club. Celia was having an affair behind Barnaby's back so that did not matter either.

Once they left the show at the Windmill she was going to dump him anyway, his usefulness something of the past; right from the start at Purbeck Manor Celia had used Barnaby to get herself on in life. Playing Beethoven was one thing to Celia Larson; making money something much more important. The months playing at the Windmill had made Fleur and Celia independent of their parents, paying their own rent in the Paddington flat. Celia's conversations with her mother having blissfully come to an end, the financial cord to her sanctimonious parents was severed forever.

In future, no one was going to tell Celia what to do and certainly not the Honourable Barnaby St Clair, as she made plain to Fleur who was still in a state of permanent unhappiness without Andre Cloete.

"He was never going to marry you, Fleur. Anyway who wants to live in South Africa? He was up at Oxford on a fully paid scholarship reading History, a subject as much use as the Pope's balls. You don't know if the family had money or where Andre fits in the picture. Don't the family have a sheep farm or something horrible? It was nice while it lasted. A good-looking boy. A good athlete. You have to get on with your life. We have to get on with our lives. I want to call the group *Dancing Girls*, bring in a piano player. Play nightclubs and make them dance the way you and I did at the old man's last party. I liked him. Dear old soul. Glad we did something to cheer him up at the end. These days bands are being recorded and their songs sold on records. And that's something else: you and I have got to sing. People like good-looking singers in bands, not violinists with a bow stuck up their nose."

"You're going to turn us into a band! We're classical musicians."

"Not anymore. We're good at playing our instruments but that is only part of it. We all four are lucky to be good-looking in very different ways. Sophia is half Italian. Wanda thinks a gypsy got into the family tree somewhere which gives her that slit-eyed sly look the men all fall for. If I could find a girl that plays the drums I'd bring us up to six. We're on our way. Playing the Windmill has given us cachet. Now we move on. Forget Andre, Fleur. He's history. What counts in life is the future, like what's going to happen tonight."

"Have you told Barnaby?"

"Why do I have to tell Barnaby? I'm sick of old men. I want a young, firm, strong man with muscle. Someone to really give me a go. Often Barnaby is too drunk at the end of the evening. Back we go to his posh flat and the bugger falls asleep. Before we do it! Now what's the use of that, I ask you? Men have no idea how to treat a woman, the selfish bastards. It's all over when they are finished. Never think of us."

"Andre did."

"I did leave myself open for that one. Has he written lately? Nothing I've seen in the mail at the flat."

"No, he hasn't."

"Then forget him like he's obviously forgotten you."

"You're cruel, Celia."

"You have to be cruel sometimes to be kind."

"What a terrible cliché. We love each other."

"Then why doesn't he write?"

"I don't know. Life is so horrible. When are you telling Mr Fox we are quitting?"

"When he tells us to bugger off, which he's going to. That way I can force Barnaby to give us a month's salary for doing nothing. You've got to be canny in this world when it comes to men and money."

"Why not ask him for three months? He was the one that took us out of the college. He can find out what we're doing after we have the money."

"That's my girl. After tonight's show we'll talk to Sophia and Wanda."

"What can they lose unless they want to go back to the Royal College of Music? If they can get in again. I can't wait to see Barnaby's face when he walks into our nightclub and sees us playing... So you were using him all the time?"

"What else do you think I was doing with him? If he'd asked me to marry him it might have been different. He's very rich and I don't want to be poor when I am old. You either make your money or marry it. We're going to be famous and independently rich so when we are old and not so good-looking we can hook young men, the way I hooked Barnaby."

"Some people might call you a conniving bitch."

"I'd consider it a compliment, Fleur. Better than some poor man treating you like a skivvy in your own house, cooking and cleaning for the rest of your life with a bunch of screaming brats to add to your worries, old before thirty. Now let's go and catch the bus to Soho. The show must go on, as they say in the classics."

NOT FAR AWAY, in Bruno Kannberg's flat on the Edgware Road, Gillian West, a week younger than Celia Larson, was planning for the biggest day of her life the following month. The royalty cheques for Bruno's half share in *Genevieve* were coming in nicely much to her satisfaction, giving them a good chance if the money continued to buy a small house in Wimbledon by the end of the year.

Robin Hood and his Merry Men was showing to good houses in America, the book having gone on sale in New York the night the film opened at cinemas across the States. A brief note from Genevieve to Bruno said even the Americans wanted to escape into a world where good always triumphed in the end, what with a war brewing across the pond in Europe.

With the nice increase given to Bruno by Arthur Bumley, Gillian was sure the family she was going to make with Bruno would have sufficient money to maintain proper standards, even sending the children to public school, even a third-rate public school like Dulwich College where most of the pupils were day boys, giving them the same education as a boarding school at half the cost. Gillian had yet to make up her mind on the names of the children or where to send them for preparatory school.

She herself had taken a job with a firm of solicitors in Holborn where she intended to work until the first child was born, saving every penny of her salary. Were it not for her father paying for the wedding, she would have taken them both to the Registry Office to save money. The reception, provided the guests brought proper wedding presents, was a good investment that, according to her school friends who were married, reaped a good profit above the cost of the catering. In her mind she had chosen the curtains for the lounge of the Wimbledon house and the wallpaper for the children's nursery.

AT NOT QUITE TWENTY-TWO years old, Bruno had to admit his wife to be was the most organised and practical woman he had met in his life, just the kind of girl to look after him for the rest of his life. With mutual satisfaction they had sent out the wedding invitations to their spring wedding the previous week, by which time Gillian had planned their lives together in detail. Even Arthur Bumley was impressed when Bruno explained some of the detail.

"It's better than having a scatterbrain," Arthur Bumley said, looking at Bruno with sympathy. "While you still can, let's drink some beer together, Kannberg. Before she locks the ball and chain."

"Why are you laughing, Mr Bumley?"

"You'll be able to answer that in a couple of years' time, provided Mosley hasn't teamed up with Hitler, eliminating all freethinking journalists who disagree with them. What a lovely world we live in. Can I give you a little advice from an old married man who's a Catholic, and whose religion doesn't allow divorce?"

"Of course you can. I owe my coming marriage to you and your generous new salary."

"Don't let her henpeck you. Stand up for your rights as a man. Remember who wears the trousers, or you'll look back on my salary increase and curse me to my grave."

"Don't you like being married?"

"Why don't you ask my wife when she comes to your wedding?"

"I'd never be so presumptuous. I can't go to the pub tonight. Gillian is waiting in my small flat with the final details of our wedding."

"May the bells ring out, Kannberg. How's the book selling?"

"Gillian says we can buy a house in Wimbledon by the end of the year. She's going to work until she has our first baby. The sales in America will be important. People have fickle minds. They forget. Depends, I suppose, if Genevieve ever becomes a big star. Gillian says if Genevieve becomes a big star we will buy a bigger house for the children. What's the matter, Mr Bumley? Why are you looking at me in that funny way? And why would I ever want to curse you to your grave?"

IN HORATIO WAKEFIELD's knowledge of human life there was always a war going on somewhere in the world, but why two of them should affect his short life was beyond his comprehension. As foreign correspondent for the *Daily Mail* the information that came to his desk, some of it published, some kept secret for reasons of Britain's security, left him in no doubt appeasement never worked.

A thug was a thug. The means by which they got what they wanted never troubled their minds. The trick, it seemed to Horatio, was first to gain power, then kill off the opposition while telling the mob what they wanted to hear, pandering to envy, jealousy, their feeling of oppression, telling them in simple words their plight was all the fault of someone else, like the Jews, while making them ridiculous promises. And now the Saarland was back under German control following a popular vote the Allies were unable to do anything about, and German troops were marching into the Rhineland in defiance of the Versailles Treaty.

In Horatio's opinion the next in line was Austria with its German-speaking people watching the new euphoria of pride erupting among their fellow Germans just across the border. The tribes of Germany were on the march, the hordes of the Huns massing again in Europe, looking for hegemony, the domination of Europe by an organised Aryan race that would make the world a better place to live in when everyone did what they were told.

To add to the irony was a marriage to Janet that was made in heaven; Horatio knew that at home he was happier than at any time in his life. Only when he reached his office and read the daily reports did he understand what it meant to live in a fool's paradise. In Spain the biggest birds that flew were men in aeroplanes dropping bombs on civilians that had never caused the pilots the slightest harm in their lives.

William Smythe had called into Horatio's office in Fleet Street before he flew to America to find out what English-speaking people thought on the other side of the Atlantic.

"To take the temperature, so to speak," he said to Horatio when the tray of tea was put on Horatio's desk.

"The perks of the job," explained Horatio smugly, picking up the teapot and pouring their cups of tea. "Darjeeling. Only the best for the senior foreign correspondent of the *Mail*. Help yourself to sugar and milk. When are you going?"

"First to New York for a few days. I fly on Monday. Then to Denver, Colorado to see Glen Hamilton of the *Denver Telegraph*."

"Is he still syndicating your articles?"

"I hope so. Especially after what I think I am going to say. I'm doing a series, *Will Americans go to war again?*. Many of my informants in the States are sick of the way we Europeans behave ourselves. Another lot are smugly hoping a war in Europe will loosen our financial bond to the British colonies around the world, giving big American corporations the chance to get in on the business. When America calls for the British Empire to be free and democratic they are not thinking of the poor sods running around putting crosses on bits of paper they know nothing about, or, fortunately, the wonderful people who are going to steal what's left of the taxes instead of uplifting the people."

"You've become a cynic, William."

"A pragmatist. What the hell does the average American care about someone in Kenya or Rhodesia? The people with money want to control the export of coffee and tobacco to prevent competition at home. They want to buy the coffee and tobacco cheap straight from the natives and sell it for a fortune in a smart package. They want access to the raw materials we British dig deep out of the ground. Calling it freedom and democracy makes their plundering all the easier. And best of all, they don't have to run democratic countries, put in roads, build schools, hospitals and maintain law and order. It's much easier to buy what you want cheap and let the natives do what they like, running their own affairs in the good name of democracy. They even come up with nice new words like *indigenous peoples* to show how equal they are to everyone else in the world, ha ha."

"You'll get lynched, William. Don't be a fool. We need the Americans."

"It's all about money."

"So tell me what's new," said Horatio wearily.

"I had a letter at last from Genevieve. She's in New York."

"Now I know why you are going to America. But don't stir up shit."

"In 1929 communism and national socialism, as the fascists like to call it, didn't look so bad. Now in Russia and Germany everyone has a job for the moment. In the end it doesn't matter which system the rich and powerful put into place. The people in the street end up where they started if they are lucky. It's which group of rich and powerful get into power that makes the rest of us go to war with all that lovely patriotism ringing in our ears. We're all puppets of the rich or want to be rich, Horatio."

"You've gone bonkers. Go and interview Adolf Hitler. He'll understand exactly what you are trying to say."

"Of course he will. That's why he's in power and about to plunge the whole damn world into a war. He's gone so far with his rhetoric, his words of rage at the way the world treated Germany at the end of the war, he can't go back now. He's on the proverbial roll. He either wins everything for Germany or loses it all, including his own life. If you go around killing the opposition it's imperative to stay in power for the sake of your own skin."

"Janet's having another baby."

"Won't she have to give up work?"

"Not with her work being at the bottom of the house. With two of us earning solid incomes we're saving good money. Paying Blanche to look after young Harry when Janet's seeing patients makes sense. It also gives Janet a break from the boy who demands attention all the time. Janet's so happy and over the moon she's pregnant again. We match each other so well, William. We have something to say to each other at the end of the day. Her patients are not all schoolboys at Harrow. She teaches people how to speak properly in public. How to make each word carry to the back of an audience. She meets interesting people who are doing something with their lives. Janet says so many people swallow their words which, once they are taught how to change, makes their presentations easier to listen to. Men in big business address meetings. She gives them confidence."

"Who pay Janet well. Who earns most, Horatio?"

"Oh, she does. By about double. She's only limited by the number of hours in the day."

"Tell her from me to put up her price. It's all about supply and demand."

"I'll tell her. If you write too much inflammatory nonsense about America the papers won't publish your articles anyway. Certainly not in America, just ask Glen Hamilton. They hate criticism. Especially from the old colonial power we still like to call Great Britain."

"It's not nonsense, Horatio. Plain business. Competition. Making money. No one ever made money being polite to the competition and that's what we are to the Americans. In 1917 it was in their interest to back the Allies as by then we owed them colossal amounts of money they would have lost had Germany won the war. At the end, we owed them more than the Germans thanks largely to the Royal Navy being able to cut off American supplies to Germany."

"They were on our side long before they came into the war."

"American big business was on any side that paid them money. There are many ways of disguising the origin of a shipment. Send the boat down to a neutral country in South America and change all the shipping documents."

"If you know all this why are you going to America? Oh, I forgot. Genevieve. Would you like another cup of tea?"

"We are so polite. At least you and I are too old to fight in another war. We were born at the right time. Too old for this one that's coming. Too young for the last. Did you get your invitation to Harry Brigandshaw's celebration bash? I don't wish to puncture your ego when you are pouring tea from so nice a china pot but Harry warned me on the phone he had a row with his wife about asking us to the shindig. We're beneath her now, Horatio. Just a couple of hacks, one with a working wife. Just not good enough for her new friends. Harry phoned me to make sure we are coming. He says he doesn't like changing friends. What is it with people? They get rich by making or marrying it and have to show off to the rich they want to call their friends, most of which, according to Harry, are a bunch of freaks. You're lucky to have a good marriage. A bad one is hell. Harry wants to go back to Africa. Says he's done all he can do for the radar units going up along the south coast. He's terribly homesick for Africa. That place has some kind of a draw on people which I don't quite understand. Hastings Court is beautiful with far more of his family history than Elephant Walk."

"But not of himself. A man likes to build his own castle, William. Give my love and Janet's to Genevieve and have a safe flight. For myself I'd catch the boat."

"Flying is wonderful. You feel above it all somehow, away from all the infighting going on in the world down below. I'll send Mr Glass the articles when I come back. You can ask him if he wants to buy them, or you can come to America and see for yourself. How is your editor by the way?"

"Mr Glass is just the same. He still treats me like I wrote my first newspaper article yesterday."

"He's a damn good editor. Why I'd like him to read my stuff, even if he doesn't want to publish. When you know where a person or country is coming from it's easier to know how to react. Right through life people say one thing and mean another."

"You have a tortured mind, William."

"Thank you for the lovely tea."

"Entirely my pleasure. So you don't believe anyone is intrinsically good?"

"No, I don't. There's evil in everyone waiting for the greed to bring it out."

"I feel sorry for you, old friend."

"So do I. It's why one day when we have the power to do it we'll destroy ourselves and our planet. There are many people out there who would rather have nothing than watching his neighbour live in comfort. If they can't have what the other's got they'd rather kill the both of them, or reduce the two of them to abject poverty so they both look the same.

People are funny. They don't like another bloke having more than themselves. It's human nature that some call the evil within mankind."

Only when Horatio returned to his house in Chelsea that evening did the heavy weight lift from his heart; his old friend from the days of his cub reporting had grown depressing. Even after he had sat thinking it through in silence behind his desk did he dare think what William had said was true, as if they were all living in hell and not just one being created by Adolf Hitler and his band of merry men.

Taking his mind away from the talk with William, Horatio smiled at his wife. Janet looked so happy now she knew she was pregnant, her own smile infectious.

"We're going out for dinner tonight to celebrate," she said after Horatio hung his overcoat on the hallstand; despite being spring, the day was cold.

"Of course we are. Just the two of us."

"Just the three of us, Horatio. You and me and our daughter. I won't drink though. The doctor says it's bad for the baby to drink when you are pregnant and we don't want anything to go wrong."

"When I came home I was miserable. Gathering news these days is not a happy experience. Now I'm happy. William thinks the world is only full of evil people. That evil lurks in everyone when they stop kidding each other."

"What nonsense. What William needs is a good wife. Is he still mooning over Genevieve?"

"Going to America on Monday to see her."

"At least he's persistent."

"We had a party invite from Harry Brigandshaw. Tina had a row with Harry according to William. She thinks we are beneath her as she's Lady of the Manor."

"The poor girl has an inferiority complex. They behave that way. We don't have to go."

"Harry wants us to. He wants to see his namesake young Harry."

"Good. Then we'll go if we can take the baby. How was your day, really?"

"All right before William made me miserable."

"You can't spend time worrying about what may never happen. All that is important is our family. What is near and dear to us. The rest of the world has to live with itself, sort out its own problems. So what if William's certain there's going to be another war?"

"So am I certain."

"Then we'll get through it, Horatio. You'll see. All of us here will get through and appreciate each other even more, if that seems possible. Now go up and see your son in the nursery while I change for dinner. I've booked us a table at the Trocadero. I have a craving for fish which is how I know this baby is going to be a girl. Stop worrying. We have each other. Nothing else matters in the world."

3

On the Tuesday, when William Smythe was looking for Genevieve's hotel in Manhattan, not far away Gerry Hollingsworth was on his way in a yellow cab to visit his banker, the man who made the final decision on whether his new film script was going into production. Because of the risk involved, Gerry had been forced to offer Sir Jacob Rosenzweig, late of Rosenzweigs London, a percentage of *Robin Hood*'s gross income rather than a fixed interest rate on the amount of the loan.

Most of the money to make a film came from private banks or backers. *Robin Hood* had already paid back the capital sum from the gross proceeds in Britain and the money was still pouring in making, Gerry hoped, the film's banker a very happy man.

"I do all the bloody work and the bank makes the money," he had complained to Genevieve earlier when he obtained her signature on the new contract, part of Gerry's ammunition for the meeting with the bank.

"But they put up the money. They took the risk of the film being a box office disaster. Without their money, Mr Hollingsworth, you could never have made your film in the first place. It's money that makes money, not hard work. Haven't you heard the expression, 'putting your money to work'? Far better than putting yourself to work."

"I wish you would not call me Mr Hollingsworth."

"Mr Casimir is quite all right with me."

"I meant you calling me Gerry, Genevieve."

"We're not off on that old chestnut again? I'm going to have my time cut out keeping Gregory's hands off my body without you looking at me like that. I don't *have* to sign this contract do I? You forget, my father is now a peer of the realm."

"We've worked together so long, Gerry would be nice once in a while."

"Yes, Gerry. Now give me the bloody contract. How's your wife enjoying New York?"

"Thankfully, she's loving it."

"All women like spending money. When do I get my signing fee?"

"When Sir Jacob Rosenzweig, now plain Jacob in America, has himself signed on to the film."

"Won't he think it odd you bought the film rights to my uncle's book? After the launch of *Genevieve* in America everyone knows where I came from."

"That had nothing to do with it. *Keeper of the Legend* at this time in the world's affairs will take the people's minds off their problems. It's a medieval story. A world of fantasy, even if your uncle claims his novels are based on family history."

"Well they are."

"Poppycock. That was Max Pearl's touch of genius with *Holy Knight*. In the contract Max wants Robert St Clair in America as a consultant on the film in case we say anything untoward about your precious family. His wife will like that. She's American according to Max. Something in his eyes said he knew more about the good wife than he was telling. If you were to ask me straight in the face I'd say Max and Freya St Clair were lovers back before your uncle came into the picture."

"Max tried and failed. He wined and dined her at the 21 Club. She told me."

"We are a close family, aren't we?"

"Which is more than you can say for yours."

"Don't be catty. I think they are coming to terms with the name change."

"But not living in America."

"My children are grown up."

"I wish you would remember that when you look at me in that way. I'm the same age as your daughter. And it was me that made Max Pearl put in the clause about my uncle. He's a good writer and we don't want a phalanx of scriptwriters putting their own interpretation on the book."

"Being a bastard I would have thought the male side of your family would be of no interest. You don't even carry your father's name."

"Now who's being catty, Mr Hollingsworth? Go off and get Mr Rosenzweig to lend us the money. Did you know my Aunt Lucinda's husband Harry Brigandshaw has a roundabout connection with the man they call Sir Jacob Rosenzweig in England?"

"You're writing books again."

"No, I am not. Uncle Harry as I like to call him has a farm in Rhodesia. A very big farm. The manager of Elephant Walk is Sir Jacob's son-in-law, though don't mention it when you see him. My family helped Rebecca run away from New York and marry Ralph Madgwick before the lucky couple went to Africa to live happily ever after. I understand Sir Jacob has not seen his favourite daughter's children, so keep off the subject. So off you go Mr Hollingsworth, and bring back the bacon, an expression you may not have liked before you changed your name and religion. They say seven moves away, everyone knows everyone else in the world, that we all have a connection. Something I rather like as an idea that someone should put into use to stop everyone squabbling with each other."

DOWN THE ROAD in his office Jacob Rosenzweig was waiting for the film producer who was making him so much money. After more than ten years in New York, Jacob thought of himself as an American, having studiously acquired the trappings of an American accent in a bid to fit in. Everything in America, apart from Rebecca, had gone better than he ever could have hoped in the long years since he sailed into New York Harbour with his daughter on the MV *Glasmerden*.

The fact that the Berlin office where the bank first started business in a previous century had closed down leaving the bank with colossal unpaid debts, no longer seemed so important. Profits in America were now larger than in London, where Jacob had first started his career in the family bank. He had learnt to cut his losses, to put his family out of his mind except to hope that whatever they were doing, wherever they were, they were happy.

Minutes before Gerry Hollingsworth arrived for his appointment, Jacob had sat daydreaming behind his desk, wondering what Rebecca and his three grandchildren were doing on Elephant Walk. He was not even sure of the season on the farm in April. Didn't it rain in April? Was it hot? They had agreed in letters soon after she married Ralph Madgwick to leave it at that, to let their worlds stay apart. She had said she was happy. He hoped so. The birth of the children had come to him on simple cards announcing the dates of their christenings. None of their Christian names sounded Jewish, but that did not matter once the two had married, the damage done.

In the tight Jewish community of London and New York it was best not to mention a daughter married out of the faith. It was bad for business. Bad for the bank. Almost as bad as Gerry Hollingsworth changing his name and changing his faith, never once acknowledging to Jacob he had once been a Jew. Like Rebecca, it was better not to talk about what once had been in the current state of the world.

He was now an American, he kept telling himself. An old bachelor of seventy living in a flat overlooking Central Park all on his own, with a servant. All said and done he had had a good life even if he did miss Rebecca, the apple of his eye, the one person in the world he truly loved. What could a man do, he asked himself as his secretary let an obsequious Gerry Hollingsworth into his office. For a moment Jacob wanted to laugh out loud, the man looked so Jewish. But it was business. It always was business.

Slowly, with effort, Jacob brought his mind to the job on hand as he listened, elbows on his desk, his hands touching at the top in what he liked to think of as a steeple as the man on the other side of the table made his pitch, Gerry Hollingsworth's confidence growing as he got into his stride. None of which made any difference to Jacob, who had made up his mind to lend the money long before Gerry Hollingsworth walked into his office washing his hands like a supplicant. It was just nice to let the man sweat a little.

Since the first loan for *Robin Hood* the man had acquired an appalling American accent. With twinkling old eyes behind the long beak of his nose, Jacob waited for the story to come to a close.

"Don't you think you've missed something?" he said into the silence, letting Gerry Hollingsworth squirm in his chair. "The girl will be playing the part of one of her ancestors. The Americans will love that. It blends the fantasy into the real. It makes the character and the actress even more part of the same person. Didn't Max Pearl point it out?"

"You know Max Pearl, Sir Jacob?"

"Rosenzweig, please. We don't use titles in America since the revolution. Mr Pearl is a customer of the bank. Different to yourself, Mr Hollingsworth, he lends us money. Points out customers like yourself. We like to know who we are dealing with. Often the person is more important than the task for which he asks the money. We have to trust each other, Mr Hollingsworth."

"I trust you, Mr Rosenzweig."

"Of course you do. I am the one lending the money. You are the one who has to pay it back."

"*Robin Hood* is hugely successful."

"The public are fickle. Just be a good chap and make a good film. You have your money, Mr Hollingsworth. Have a nice day. My secretary will show you out."

Only when Gerry Hollingsworth left the office did Jacob realise that at the end they had both been speaking in the clipped accents of the English public schools. However hard either of them tried to be otherwise, they were Englishmen, of whatever religion. It made Jacob nostalgic. Not for his children living in England but for the country where he was born and raised. Then he thought of Rebecca in Rhodesia and wondered where his grandchildren would give their allegiance: to the British Empire, or the government of Southern Rhodesia? He even wondered if anyone would tell them they were half Jewish.

Feeling old, Jacob stood up stiffly from behind his desk where he had been sitting still for too long, went downstairs into the street, and caught a cab to Abercrombie Place and his lonely flat. He had once shared it with Rebecca when he brought her to America away from her love for Ralph Madgwick, the boy who was now father to three of his grandchildren, their blood and history mingled forever.

"You all have a good life," he said to his silent flat as he lifted his glass of whisky, wondering not for the first time what life was all about. So there they were, the Jews. Doing business together. Jacob Rosenzweig, Max Pearl and Louis Casimir.

"He could chop wood with that pecker," Gerry Hollingsworth had mumbled when he got into the cab outside the building that housed the bank.

"Where you going?"

"I have no bloody idea."

"You English?"

"No, American."

"Don't sound it."

"Do you know a nice place to get drunk?" he had said, adjusting his speech to sound more American.

"Of course I do. Despite popular opinion, the bars don't pay us cab drivers commission. What is it? A celebration or drowning your sorrows?"

"I think it's drowning my sorrows. Getting money out of that old man is worse than getting your teeth pulled. Makes you suffer right to the end. The old bastard enjoyed every minute of it watching me squirm."

"Why'd you need money?" asked the driver, pulling the cab neatly out into the flow of traffic where people were driving home at the end of their day.

"To make a film."

"Now I heard everything."

"I produced *Robin Hood and his Merry Men*."

"You kidding? Saw it last night. That Genevieve is quite something."

"She's going to be in the one I just borrowed money for. You ever read a book by Robert St Clair called *Keeper of the Legend*?"

"Cab drivers have times we just sit and wait. Then I read books to pass the time. I read that one and *Holy Knight*. Buddy, I'm already looking forward to your film. Here we are. No point in driving you ten times round the block. They call it Harry B's. Harry was a baseball legend, someone led me to believe. Never met Harry nor has anyone else. Nice pretty girls behind the bar serving customers. Nice class of girl. What's she like?"

"Who?"

"Genevieve."

"The most beautiful woman I ever saw. Keep the change."

"This is a fifty!"

"Just borrowed two million. It sounded you meant it about my new film."

"Better still with Genevieve. She's every man's dream when the lights go out and we're all on our own feeling lonely. After seeing her film you feel you know her. Have a nice day."

BY THE TIME Jacob Rosenzweig lifted his first glass of whisky, Gerry

Hollingsworth had drunk three beers in Harry B's and had ordered himself a Scotch. The girls serving drinks in the bar were pretty but little to write home about when compared to Genevieve. They were all good-looking girls that would find a young man so they could stop showing their tits and legs to drunken old men like himself.

What Gerry wanted more than anything was to go round to the Independence Hotel and see Genevieve. It was good for the business to have Carmel in New York when people who made decisions had old wives like himself. At the smart society dinners that went with promoting his films, a wife dripping in diamonds gave his business a solid look, disguising, he hoped, the gamble inherent in every new film.

Max Pearl had been at more than one of the dinners. Now Gerry's apparent wealth and stability had paid off. Looking rich made people doing business with you comfortable, something Gerry had known all his working life. It was appearances that counted, what they could see in front of their nose, even if every nose was not the size of Jacob Rosenzweig's pecker, which was why he could not visit Genevieve for anything other than business; with a wife in tow it was all about appearances and not, as Gerry liked to say, pissing in his own rice bowl.

This time when he thought of the hooked nose and the hawk eyes he smiled instead of frowning, the beers and whisky softening his mood. Soon the girls would look real pretty, he told himself, the thought of going home to Carmel far from his mind. After twenty-seven years of marriage they had grown bored with each other, having nothing left to say now the children were out of the house, off on their own with more important things to think of than their parents. And with no other option, Carmel had decided to join Gerry in America.

When he and Carmel reached Hollywood to make the new film he was going to rent a big house with a swimming pool and throw parties to impress the local people. A big house so he could get away from Carmel when the guests went home.

When he reached the hotel off Fifth Avenue where they were staying, he was drunk and his wife was asleep. Deliberately, Gerry had made a lot of noise opening their room with the key. Likely his wife was feigning sleep. His last thought as he sank into oblivion next to her but separate in the twin bed was, 'who cares'. So far as they were concerned they had had their lives together breeding and bringing up three children, finding they were strangers to each other after so much effort.

· · ·

GERRY HAD PHONED her the next day at the Independence with the good news but it made no difference to her mood. She was homesick. Gerry Hollingsworth's phoney American accent had made her irritated.

"You don't have to be American with me, Mr Hollingsworth. When do we leave for Hollywood?"

"Tomorrow at noon. I'm going to rent a large house. You are welcome to stay."

"No thank you, even though socially Carmel is more fun than you. She doesn't stare at me like some old dog with sad eyes that its master doesn't love anymore."

"Oh, I love you, Genevieve."

"Of course you do. The papers say half of America loves me but it doesn't help."

"Are you all right, Genevieve? I was going to come round last night."

"You stay away. I'll meet you at the airport. Leave the flight details at reception."

"What's the matter?"

"I'm homesick. I'm lonely. I don't know a bloody soul in this great big city. Big cities make me lonely, they are so impersonal."

The phone had clicked off, and her world was once more reduced to the confines of the hotel room where she now ate her meals. Everyone used to stare at her when she ate alone in the dining room, and a constant flow of notes, all wanting the same, would arrive with the head waiter from men sitting at other tables; her face was all over New York, from the billboards for her film to the back jacket of her book. All she had was strangers asking her out, wanting to talk, wanting to boast to their friends they knew Genevieve. At least now, she told herself, they were going to make a film, giving her something to do other than being seen.

She had eaten supper alone on Tuesday night, hoping to get some sleep now she knew she was flying the next day which always kept her awake, when a knock came at the door to her room. Expecting the waiter who collected the meal trolley, she called for the man to come in. Nothing happened other than another knock on her door. If it was some fan looking for an autograph there was no way she was going to be polite, as she flung open the door to find a sheepish William Smythe standing in the corridor. Impulsively, overjoyed with happiness, Genevieve flung her arms round his neck, pushing the man behind him who had come for the trolley out of the way.

"They were reluctant to give me your room number. What's going on?"

"It's so wonderful to see someone from home."

"That's it?"

"Of course not, William. Why didn't you phone? Why are you here? When did you get in? I'm so damn lonely I could scream."

"But you're famous, Genevieve. You're all over the place. I was frightened some big bodyguard would throw me out on my neck."

"Have you eaten?"

"Not a morsel. Are we going out?"

"Bring another supper, like the one I just had," she said to the man still standing behind William. "What do you drink, William?"

"Scotch. Any Scotch."

"What is your name?" she said to the waiter.

"Simon."

"There you have it, Simon. A bottle of Scotch and a meal fit for a king. William, have you booked into a hotel?"

"Not yet."

"Forget it. This suite has two rooms. Simon, don't look like that. We are very old friends. Out you go for the whisky and bring that first. Soda siphon. Ice in a bucket and two glasses. I can never sleep the night before I fly unless I drink and a girl can't drink on her own... William! This is just so wonderful you have no idea. How's Janet? How's Horatio? How's young Harry?"

"Slow down or you are going to burst. It's only me."

"Come in, you old reprobate, and tell me again just how much you love me."

BY THE TIME his supper came on a fresh trolley, William would have sworn the girl was coming on to him. They were both tiddly from the whisky and something else that had never been between them before, putting William on his guard. Genevieve had rejected his advances so many times before, he was wary of again being put in his place; him, a man, as she had once said, old enough to be her father, which William knew was not quite true. To add to his consternation, on the trolley with his food came an open bottle of good Californian red wine with two inviting glasses which Genevieve swooped upon before the waiter was out of the door. No one asked him for money; there was not even the intimation that a tip was in order.

She looked ravishing in simple clothes. In William's mind the girl could wear a sackcloth and still have sex appeal to spare. As always, the power was in her eyes. As always, William felt like a lovesick fool in the presence of a woman he would never know; one-sided love from a distance.

"Now look at that, William. The hotel manager's put a bottle of wine on the trolley for the two of us. Well, I have been here a while and never entertained in my room, but this is beyond the call of looking after guests. Maybe for once a little fame is on my side. You will have a glass of wine with me, William? We'll finish these whiskies and while you eat I'll join you with your glass of wine. It's so marvellous to see a real friend. What are you doing here, William? No, don't tell me if it's boring old work. It's just the two of us cut adrift. We can be ourselves. No need to show off and impress each other. Did you know the new film is based on Uncle Robert's second book? The story of the St Clairs at the time they arrived in England with William the Conqueror. Just one generation, of course. The knights of old treated their women with such chivalry. Putting them on a pedestal would be putting it mildly. Wouldn't you like to put me on a pedestal, William? Even just for this one wonderful night. You can be my knight in shining armour who has come to rescue his love from a den of heathens."

"You don't think Americans are heathens!"

"Of course not. Just men in general the way they look at me. They all make me feel naked the way they stare. Carnal. No love. No beauty. Lust with a capital L. All they want is to take me to bed and as soon as possible as if they own me already, just because they've seen my film and paid money at the little window going into the cinema. For a few shillings they think they own me. You've always looked at me in a way that says I'm too precious to touch."

"You are," said William huskily, taking from her his glass of wine which she had filled right up to the top.

"Oh, William, I'm not a virgin. Everyone knows that. You can't get where I've got without passing out favours. Well, not always favours. A girl likes sex just as much as a man. Do you like sex, William? Looking at you now I think you'd be very good to a lonely girl in bed. In my position it's so difficult to find someone who is genuine like you, William. Finish your food and sit with me on the couch. They are going to swallow me up tomorrow. Once they get you on a film that's it. You belong to the film. One gulp and you're gone, but that's not till tomorrow when I get on that horrible plane. I'm frightened of flying so you'll have to hold my hand on the couch. Would it matter to our friendship if we make love? Tonight I want to be close to someone. Being alone is horrible. You will look after me won't you? We don't have to tell anyone. It'll be something wonderful between the two of us that only we know. Something to remember with a smile when we are old."

"Are you being serious, Genevieve?"

"Never more serious in my life. It's not just the booze, William. Just promise me one thing forever; you never tell Tinus. Now promise me that and we'll stop all this drinking and go next door to my bedroom."

"I promise."

"Come along then. I want you to make love to me and hold me in your arms all night. Tonight, I want to feel safe. Please, William. It's not very much to ask from an old friend."

A WEEK LATER, when William Smythe arrived in Denver, Colorado to see Glen Hamilton of the *Denver Telegraph*, the man who over the years had syndicated his articles across America, he felt so sad he did not care what Glen thought of the three articles he had written in New York. Even the title of the first one, *Why America wants to end the British Empire*, meant nothing anymore. William had experienced the most life-changing one night stand in his life; never again could he ever be the same. For one-night he had owned the world the way he wanted.

JUST BEFORE THEY had met the obnoxious Gerry Hollingsworth with his put-on American accent at the airport the following morning, where William had gone in the taxi with Genevieve and her piles of luggage to see her off, she had put her right index finger on his mouth, the last time he knew she was ever going to touch him. Then she had flowed towards her entourage, the consummate actress, the smile flashing at the people waiting for her to arrive before they all flew off to California. Waiting, hoping, she never looked back as the film crew and hangers-on flowed through the gate to board the aircraft.

It was William's turn to feel more lonely than ever in his life. His turn to feel suicidal. Miserable. They were lovers but only for the once, his promise never to tell Tinus Oosthuizen clear in his mind. If, he thought, standing rooted to the spot as passengers milled around him, she had just used him he might have shrugged and walked off happy with his luck, another conquest under his belt, another day searching for enjoyment. William didn't even feel sorry for himself or sorry for his loss, just miserable with an intensity he had never experienced. Then he had picked up his one small suitcase and gone back to Manhattan in a cab to find his own hotel and to try and forget the only woman he would ever love in his life.

GLEN HAMILTON, across the desk at the newspaper with the three unread articles in front of him, looked a picture of good humour which William suspected would evaporate the moment he read the articles.

"Had an invitation to Harry Brigandshaw's party. Very expensive invitation card like something you'd expect from a king."

"It's his wife," said William, trying to concentrate on Glen Hamilton and forget his problems. "She likes to think of herself as a society lady."

"Did you know I met Harry and the new Lord St Clair at British military headquarters in France back in 1917? In those days I was a war correspondent with the honorary rank of captain in the American army. We'd gone over to save your empire, not to end it." William smiled wryly; Glen had at least read the first heading.

"Save reading the articles for later. You went to make sure the Allies were able to pay back America what we owed you. You're not going to like these articles. They tell the truth. Are you going to Hastings Court?"

"To travel that far to a party is insane. I have to clean out a log cabin this weekend an hour's drive from Denver. Why don't you drive with me?"

"You want *me* to clean out someone else's mess?"

"She was my personal assistant for ten years before she married Robert St Clair. Robert wrote most of *Holy Knight* at the cabin that overlooks the ski slopes. They are coming back for Robert to keep an eye on the filming of the *Legend*. They bought the cabin and three hundred surrounding acres of pine trees with the money Robert made in America from the book. Thought it nice to put back into America what he took out in royalty payments. Freya's mother has a key. So do I. Most weekends one of us or our friends stay at the cabin. It's good for a man after the rough and tumble of city life. You look terrible, William, but I won't ask why."

"Is the cabin empty during the week?"

"Nearly always except in the ski season which is over."

"If I help clean, may I stay a few days on my own? I have some things to think about. If you don't like those articles throw them in the bin."

"We'll go after work on Friday. Why are you in America, William?"

"To assess the mood. See what you are going to do. Try and give the British a better perspective of America. In England we have the silly idea we are cousins, the same family with the same interests at heart. After a week in New York I find we British are very wrong about America. America is a competitor with very different interests. Once America breaks up the British Empire they'll move in on our traditional markets. The mighty dollar as an alternative to the mighty empire which for all intents and purposes amounts to the same thing; hegemony, control, colonisation, call it what you will. I think America is only dictated to by money, the moral claptrap about equality for everyone their way to muscle in on our markets. That all the rhetoric is governed by greed with little to do with freedom. 'Freedom from what?', I ask in those articles. Freedom from colonisation? Freedom from poverty? Freedom to live an average of thirty-six years, which was the lifespan in Africa before British colonialism? None of us are moral, Glen. It's not in human nature. The next three articles will be a rebuttal. The American point of view. Why American-style democracy and freedom is right and empire is wrong. I want to make people argue with each other. To try and understand what we are all up to and realise America and the British Empire have the same imperative in common; stopping the spread of communism and fascism before the whole damn world goes up in flames."

"Sounds like the stuff of good journalism. A provocative title, this first one. I shall read with interest. Always nice to visit with you, William Smythe. Just you and me at the weekend with a couple of bottles of Scotch round the log fire. In April it's still cold on the slopes. There may even be snow. Can you ski?"

"Never tried. Won't your wife want to come?"

"Not if I tell her the subject. Samantha hates arguments. Why we have the perfect marriage and perfect children. We never argue with each other. If we don't agree we shut up. Fortunately we share the same opinions. The two boys are growing up in a happy family. Why haven't you got married?"

"She won't marry me."

GENEVIEVE ONLY REALISED she had ripped the soul out of a man and thrown it in his face when Gregory L'Amour walked onto the set the first day of shooting; they were equally self-centred and selfish, concerned with themselves, caring nothing of what they did to other people. Robbing a good man of his pride and soul just because she felt lonely was worse than stealing his money.

"You're a bitch, Genevieve."

"My word, we are getting somewhere. Are you apologising?"

"Not to you, Genevieve. And don't pretend you lost something. You've only ever loved yourself in your entire life."

"We are edgy."

For the next weeks they never said anything to each other apart from snide remarks and the lines of the dialogue that came between them in the film.

Despite living close to Gerry Hollingsworth, Genevieve had succumbed to his invitation to move into the house. The thought of spending months alone in a hotel suite was worse than putting up with lecherous stares, that largely never came, and when they did, far from the prying eyes of Carmel. Carmel reminded Genevieve of her mum. Genevieve reminded Carmel of her children. Neither said so to each other at first but both were homesick despite the sprawling house they lived in on the perfect stretch of Pacific coast, south of Los Angeles, a mile south of Long Beach, some hundred miles from the Mexican border no one ever seemed to visit.

By the time King Harold looked up at the sky, taking the Norman arrow in his eye just to the side of his nose armour, Uncle Robert and Aunt Freya had arrived from England to watch the scene on the south coast of England play itself out in the surf of the Pacific Ocean, no one remembering what the shores of England looked like back in 1066. By the time the Battle of Hastings was over, the last Saxon king dead in his grave, Robert and Freya had moved into the house on the beach with its superfluous swimming pool.

Gregory L'Amour had rented his own house not far down the beach and surrounded himself with a harem. He made a splendid sight storming ashore from the Norman fleet, cutting up Saxons with a sword the size of himself. His bride, Genevieve, waiting patiently on board for the all-clear, frightened for the life of her knight as she watched the mayhem of battle from a gently undulating spot on the poop deck of the leading boat, looked perfect, the Héloïse of the book in her *bliaut* and veil, the most beautiful woman in France.

Even Uncle Robert was pleased with the rushes and the way the film was panning out, even if there wasn't much resemblance to the story in his book, a story Robert still claimed to be factual, his only proof the word of mouth passed down by his ancestors. Filtered stories even Robert conceded were better than the dirt, filth and lice the knights of old put up with under their suits of anything but shining armour. Fighting the good war, even when it led to a castle on some foreign land, was right; William of Normandy was the rightful King of England, not King Harold.

The trick, according to Denzel Hurst the film's director, was to make the battle scenes happen so fast that no one saw the flaws or doubted the veracity of the story, the whole playing out in the end to so much noise and surging, martial music the audience was saturated.

"By the time we're finished," he said to Robert, "we'll blast their minds into submission."

"I believe you, Denzel."

"Wonderful story."

"Which one?"

"It's all about making money, Robert."

"Of course it is. How foolish of me. Whatever was I thinking."

"They want to live in a more exciting world."

"Who, Denzel?"

"The audience, silly."

"Yes, of course. Our job is to entertain, not inform."

"Now you've got it. Gerry's throwing a party to celebrate the successful end of the battle scenes."

"How nice of him."

"Smile at them all, Robert. Publicity. The press will be there. We start now hyping the movie. Making a film is much easier than selling it. Having the public waiting with anticipation, their money at the ready. That's Gerry's business. Like your publisher. Max Pearl is flying in from New York for the party. He's launching a new edition of your book to whet the audience's appetite. You should be thrilled."

"Oh but I am. How nice it will be to see Max again."

"He's invited the newspapers from right across the country."

"You think they'll come?"

"To a Hollywood bash on the beach? Are you kidding? They'll kill each other to get that invitation in the press rooms. Makes journalism worthwhile. All the starlets get invited. If they don't lay the press boys they don't get invited again."

"You do do things differently in America."

"Bigger and better."

"Will the sun shine for the party?"

"Hey, buddy. This is California."

Poor Uncle Robert, Genevieve thought, watching the exchange. From the backwater of rural England to the go-go of America where money was the only thing, where hype ruled over reason and telling the truth in business was a mortal sin if it was going to cost money. The cold stare in her uncle's eyes said the opposite of his cheerful words; he knew exactly what they were doing with his book. When the director moved away to tell someone else what they were doing wrong she walked across to her uncle standing on his own, an oasis of sanity in a fictional world.

"Are you all right, Uncle Robert?"

"I'm glad your father did not come over as I suggested. He would have taken umbrage at all the commercialisation. To him the understanding from a book is more important than the pace of the story. Here, I'm out of my depth, but you would know that, Genevieve. You are part of them. The smile into the camera the audience see as a smile at your husband is all you have to do to tell the story. Let me just say what we are getting was not in my mind's eye when I wrote the book. Everyone reading the book has a different mind's eye interpretation of what they read. My words just spark their imagination. No two people see the same thing that's right in front of them let alone a picture painted in words. Your father would have been miserable among all the noise and strange conversations. We use the same words most of the time but America speaks a different language. Maybe they understand better what they are saying to each other. We English are a little more reserved. We don't shout our opinion from the rooftops. We don't get quite so up close to each other. I'm too old for all this. Freya says it was easier to take when she was younger."

"Are you going to live in America?"

"Probably, so I'll have to adjust. It's all a trifle too brash for a staid old Englishman. Richard is having fun. Freya wants the new baby to be born in America. She's thirty-eight so we won't have any more children. She wants to be near her mother this time to share the joy with her own parents which I quite understand. We have a cottage with a few acres near Denver where we intend to live until the new baby is born.

"Richard is the problem. He should be in a good prep school by now. His mother has been giving him lessons. Your friend William Smythe was staying in the cottage when we arrived. We were staying with her parents and went to check the cottage during the week. Glen Hamilton had given him the key for helping clean up the place while the two of them talked British-American politics. When I mentioned your name to remind him of our connection he nearly bit my head off. What did you say to him, Genevieve? Never mind, it's none of my business. You youngsters have your own way of doing things. He was as happy as a sandboy until I foolishly mentioned your name.

"Between them they have published a series of articles on transatlantic relations which has caused a furore in American papers, everyone writing rude letters. William thinks America wants to move into our markets when the empire comes to its end, like every other empire in history. That underneath all the nice cousin talk there is a nasty undercurrent of greed. That America siding with what they call the oppressed people of the British colonies is a ruse to get us out and their big corporations into our markets. William told Glen later he learnt more from the letters written in response to his articles than any research could have given him. Glen Hamilton was thrilled. Nothing better than controversy to sell newspapers, though that side of life I don't even try and understand. He also missed Harry Brigandshaw's celebration bash. Freya and I were in America by then."

"Did it go all right? I wrote him a letter in response to my invitation."

"Tina brought in a band. Two of the girls played for my father at his last party. Tina used the inglenooks at the ends of the old banqueting hall to turn sides of carcasses to feed the hordes of guests for the weekend. Hastings Court was a madhouse. Everyone was given a dagger to carry around with them in case they got hungry. The theme was a medieval banquet that became formal on the Saturday evening when everyone sat at the long tables in the old hall while the carved meat was brought to them on silver platters held shoulder high. For the rest of the time food was laid out as a buffet with every kind of drink you can imagine. The guests took their daggers into the inglenooks and cut bits off the carcasses and stuffed their faces with fat dripping down their chins.

"Harry's ancestors looking down from heaven must have thought it was all like old times. Merlin said it took him a week back at Purbeck Manor to recover from the party. Great success. Had another letter from mother. She had gone up to Hastings Court for the shindig with your father. On the Saturday night with Harry's birthday on the Sunday, your grandmother stayed awake until midnight, drank the toast to Harry and only then went off to bed. Every hotel for ten miles was full for the weekend along with every room in the old mansion. That young chap Tinus came down from Oxford."

"Was he on his own?"

"I don't think so, Genevieve. His other friend had gone back to South Africa. Merlin wanted to know what had happened to the other Morgan sports car. The girl with Tinus said he was going to play cricket for Oxford University. Round about now, I suppose. Something about the first week in July. It was all in the letters I received giving me chapter and verse on the party it was such a big event."

"Was she pretty?"

"Who?"

"The girl. The girl with Tinus?"

"Merlin never mentions pretty girls anymore."

"Has William Smythe gone back to England?"

"I imagine so. Here comes your boyfriend, Genevieve. I'd better not monopolise any more of your time. I forget you are a famous actress."

"He's not my boyfriend, despite what they write in the newspapers."

"William thinks in his articles there's going to be another war with Germany. That if England and America don't join forces we're all going to be for the high jump, that if Hitler wins he'll take revenge on the whole lot of us who forced Germany to sign the peace agreement at Versailles. According to William, Hitler's war reparations against the Allies will make the Germans look like a walk in the park. The British Empire will then become part of the Third Reich with American business right out of the picture and Gandhi not even allowed to mention Indian independence. William's good at stirring up controversy. Some of it makes sense. Some of it, in my humble opinion, is a load of rubbish. Except the bit about another war, that's coming. Why Freya wants to live in America. She thinks if Germany were to conquer Europe, America would make peace with Germany. She was a journalist before we married, worked for Glen Hamilton at the *Denver Telegraph* for ten years. She thinks America should fear Russian communism more than fascist Germany. That fascists still do business whichever way they run the country. For me, I'm just a country bumpkin writing a book on Merlin the Magician... I'll leave you two alone. I'm her uncle, Mr L'Amour."

"Pleased to meet you again, Mr St Clair. What do you think of the film so far?"

"I think it's wonderful. Just wonderful. My ancestor would be proud of you."

"Why thank you, kind sir." Gregory L'Amour was smiling comfortably. "Did they really talk that way in the good old days?"

"I have no idea. I wasn't there."

Giving them both a polite laugh, Robert St Clair went to look for his wife who had joined him from the Hollingsworth beach house, young Richard in tow. Despite what William Smythe said, America to Robert was a breath of fresh air. He could go for days without one word about the mess brewing in Europe. For Robert, living in his fictional world was the best place to be. *The Mark of the Eyes* was going well despite all the travel and the other interruptions. Max Pearl had wanted him in America more to boost the sales of his books, flogging, as Robert said to Freya, the relationships of the living with the characters in the new film as the newspapers and magazines picked up on the human side of the story.

"It's just business, Robert," Max Pearl had said, "for us and Hollingsworth. You authors can write your books anywhere. It's all in your head. All you have to carry is a pen or a typewriter."

Thinking back to the simplicity of his publisher's naivety about writing books, Robert caught sight of his pregnant wife standing next to his son.

"Why are you grinning like a Cheshire cat, Daddy?"

"You've never even met a Cheshire cat so how would you know?"

"Making a film looks like permanent chaos," said Freya. "How do they all know what's going on?"

"Ask Denzel Hurst, the director. I just wrote the book. Why don't we all go home and have a swim in the sea?"

"I want to swim in the swimming pool," said Richard, grabbing his father's hand as they all went off to find the car.

"He gets more American every day," said Robert.

. . .

Watching Robert St Clair go off with his wife and son gave Gregory L'Amour a pang of envy; the three of them together looked so happy. The moment her uncle walked away, Genevieve had left him standing. One of the camera crew was visibly sniggering.

Like Genevieve, Gregory had lied about his age when he went into acting, giving himself another five years to impress his first producer. His voice had broken when he was eleven years old. At sixteen he stood six feet in his socks. By the time he was twenty-three and arguing with Genevieve on the set of *Keeper of the Legend* his shoulders were broad from pumping iron every morning in his room. His jaw was square with a dimple right in the middle. He was six feet two inches tall with hands the size of hams. His face, the papers told him, was beautiful, his voice rich in timbre, his eyes sparkling clear, his belly as flat as a board. But best of all, the camera liked him, even the shots of his broad back and tight arse when taken from the rear, walking, running or riding a horse.

The papers called him *The all American man*; strong, silent, bursting with action, a man of few words as he rode through the old American West, the Forest of Nottingham, the battlefields of the knights of old. For America, he was their hero, always their hero, always there when the poor and downtrodden needed him.

Even Gregory knew he was starting to believe in what they said of him, striding off and on the stage to be what people wanted, trying to make himself into what they said, never once himself. For now he was a knight, a giant striding the world. Even Gregory knew he had fallen foul of all the nasty, falling headfirst into the picture of what they told him was himself.

"Gregory! You're on," shouted Denzel Hurst. "Pull your finger out."

"Right with you, Denzel."

"Forget her except when you are together in a scene. How are the girls at your beach house?"

"Fabulous. Wonderful. Everything a man can want."

"That's the spirit. Now go out there and ripple those muscles."

Annoyed at his one vulnerable moment being noticed, Gregory strode onto the set, once again the man they wanted him to be, the beautiful man he saw every day in the mirror. All he had to do was give it to Genevieve one more time, laugh out loud and dump her in the trashcan with the rest of his discarded girls.

PART 7

PARTING OF THE WAYS — JULY 1937

1

---

*H*arry Brigandshaw pushed the Rolls-Royce Merlin engine to full throttle and sent the aircraft into a dive straight for Redhill Aerodrome far down below the clouds, feeling the wings of the new fighter vibrating dangerously, his whole body shaking in the cockpit.

"I'm too bloody old for this," he yelled out in excitement, adrenaline pumping up his brain, the speedometer hovering at three hundred miles an hour. "Bloody thing's stuffed," he said looking at his instruments before pulling back on the stick, sending the Supermarine prototype back up at the patch of blue sky between the white summer clouds, forcing the metal airframe to try and break apart. To add to the pain, Harry barrel rolled the plane and sent it down and up again. In the middle of this loop Harry fired the twin Vickers machine guns, spitting fire at the clouds and the heavens from the aircraft's wings.

For twenty minutes, Harry tested every part of the new plane before pulling back on the speed and making a perfect three-point landing on the field. He taxied the aircraft to the hangars at the other end of the Surrey field where all the VIPs were waiting. By the time Harry climbed out and dropped to the ground he had the same excitement pumping through his body that he had felt the first time he flew solo in 1915.

"We need four guns in each wing, and as for the speedometer, it can't be working properly. Damn thing registered three hundred miles an hour. Surely that can't be right, can it? If we have enough of them we can defend the island against anything. Thirty squadrons of Spitfires flown by well-trained pilots will stop the entire German air force. They have nothing like this, according to our intelligence, nothing on the drawing board. We can win a war with this machine. However hard I tried to rip them off, the wings took the pressure. Let the other test pilots have a go and see what they say, but that's my opinion. Pilot training, that's our next problem. Next time I'm bringing down my nephew to let a youngster fly the plane. Taught him to fly in Rhodesia when he was a kid. He's a good pilot and a damn good cricketer. Pilots, we need pilots. The Ministry of Munitions can lay out workshops to build as many aircraft as we want. It's the pilots. Like the last war. You can build a new aircraft in three weeks. A pilot with three weeks' training will make a sitting duck for the Germans whatever aircraft they are flying. You can tell Air Vice Marshal Tedder and Mr Churchill from me; this aircraft flies. Not even the Americans have anything to compare, let alone the Japanese. The Japanese aircraft fighting in China are ten years behind this plane. Now if you'll excuse me, gentlemen, I have to drive up to London. There's a cricket match I have no intention of missing."

TINUS WAS out for a duck before his Uncle Harry reached the Oval where Oxford University were playing the Surrey Second Eleven in a three-day match during the week; the game was to finish on the Wednesday to give the main county side time to prepare for their match against Yorkshire due to start on the Friday. Harry found Tinus in the players' pavilion having looked at the scoreboard soon after arriving on his motorcycle from Redhill. He was still wearing his flying coat. Tinus was wearing a white sweater with its Oxford dark blue V. Harry gave his nephew a sympathetic smile. Tinus was sitting alone in a deckchair, his pads still on. The rest of his team had left him alone.

"You on the motorcycle? A long way for nothing. Second ball. The swing caught the edge and straight to the wicket keeper."

"There's always the second innings."

"Andre's arriving from Cape Town tomorrow. Jumped the first boat to England. Luckily the boat didn't arrive on time. They'll never put me in the team again. Isn't that a new RAF flying coat? What have you been up to, Uncle harry? There was a rumour in the University Air Squadron about you test flying."

"No. Borrowed this from a grounded pilot working in my office. Chap landed a bomber with its wheels up. My old jacket fell apart."

"What was it like?"

"Walls have ears, Tinus."

"I'm sorry. Have you recovered from your party? I thought Fleur and Celia splendid, despite the sour looks from the Honourable Barnaby St Clair."

"The party was weeks ago. Never again."

"Some party."

"I have some things to do at the office now you aren't batting. Keep in touch. I'll try and make it for your second innings."

"It's late for you to arrive on a Monday if you haven't been to the office."

"I had some things to do."

"I bet you did."

"Why's Andre Cloete coming to England?"

"He's bored, Uncle Harry. Being bored at our age is a sin. He tried teaching History at a school for two terms. Coaching rugby and cricket. Not enough to keep him occupied. If you ask me he missed Fleur. My debut for Oxford was just his excuse but never mind. I have a lot more friends at Oxford but none like Andre. Do you know he's still frightened of heights and flying an aeroplane despite being a good pilot?"

"Why doesn't he join the RAF? They have a good rugby and cricket team. With an Oxford degree and the University Air Squadron they'll make him a pilot officer straight away. He doesn't have to go to Cranwell to get a commission."

"Are you recruiting for the Air Force?"

"He won't be bored in the RAF and the new blue uniforms look splendid."

"He's a South African."

"Still part of the Commonwealth."

"I'll talk to him."

"Better luck next time, Tinus. Merlin phoned me the other day. Letter from Genevieve. Film's going fine though Robert and Freya got bored and went to their cottage outside Denver, wherever that is. Robert writes in his letter that a book's finished when they put it in a cover. He's not interested in the film which bears no resemblance to the book. He's writing a new one. Don't know how he does it... Do you know, I feel ten years younger."

"Not surprised in that flying coat... Sounds like one of the chaps has scored a four. Better go and watch from the balcony and stop moping."

"Have you heard from Genevieve?"

"Not a word. Should I?"

"The way you look at each other I should think so."

"She thinks I'm a kid. Thanks for coming, Uncle Harry. I really appreciate your support."

As they parted company to go their separate ways, both were thinking of Tinus's dead father, the ghost that always stood over them.

ANDRE CLOETE REALISED he had fallen off the pedestal the day he left Oxford University and caught the boat back to his home in South Africa. His boyhood friends from Bishops had gone their separate ways to make a living in life, the need to support themselves more important than hero-worshipping the school captain of cricket. A Rhodes Scholarship to Oxford received more applause at the start than the finish, getting a Blue for cricket and rugby was just another team to play for on the journey through life.

For the first time to Andre's recollection he found money more important to people than sporting or academic achievement. By becoming a school master at Rondebosch Boys' High he was no longer important, no longer the man to look up to for boys to try and emulate. He was Cloete the history teacher who made them practise cricket after school when most of them would have preferred to go home or sit around with their friends doing nothing. Cricket coaching other than for the dedicated few was boring. Talking to girls was much more fun. None of them ever wanted to be the history teacher or even pay a visit once they had left school.

When the letter came from Tinus Oosthuizen announcing his selection for the Oxford first eleven, Andre jumped at the chance to go back to his place of glory. In England, at the Oval match against the Surrey Second Eleven, Andre would be remembered as the man who scored a century against Cambridge. He would be a part of the camaraderie. He would have like-minded friends to talk to about cricket and rugby, rowing on the Cherwell, or their good old days at school when they strode the world head and shoulders above the rest of them, school prefects, school captains of cricket, winners of scholarships to the most prestigious university on earth.

If he could get back to England to watch the cricket, Andre knew he would be among friends, not the History master who bored his pupils and left them yawning in his face, looking longingly out of the window. Looking at their watches to see when the period would be over and they could escape from the boring man standing with his back to the blackboard covered in chalked names, dates and places they would all much prefer to forget.

Resigning his post two days before the end of term, Andre booked his third class passage on the first liner out of Cape Town for England, not one protest from the senior masters at the school. He had been a teacher for two terms. It was over. There had to be something more for him, he told himself sadly. Something, hopefully, that made him a little money, more to live in than a square box of a room, even the chance of dating a girl like Fleur who once he had thought just a little beneath him.

By the time he reached England, the third class section of the ship all he could afford now he was a man no longer supported by his father, Andre knew he was made of the same old stuff as the rest of them; just flesh and bones. When he reached the pavilion in plenty of time to watch Tinus go out to bat for the second time he was a chastened man, no longer expecting the world to give him a living or to listen in awe to his every word. No one had even mentioned his century the previous year; there were new heroes to clap.

'I'm history,' he breathed to himself, feeling that much better for understanding where he now stood in the world.

Then he concentrated on his old friend playing cricket, letting the rest of his life take care of itself.

"Andre! My goodness. Am I too late? Is he out yet? Tinus said you were coming over. Second ball in the first innings. Not quite that magnificent century of yours against Cambridge last year."

"He's taking guard, Mr Brigandshaw."

"Where are you staying?"

"The cheapest hotel. Father isn't financing this one."

"Come and stay at Hastings Court. I've got an idea for you. Why don't you join the RAF? They're looking for pilots. Are you still frightened of flying?"

"I throw up every time before I go up."

"Tinus is coming down after the match. Just like old times."

"Wonderful. I don't have any plans."

With the innings progressing out in the middle, both of them watching Tinus from the balcony of the players' pavilion, old friend and uncle respectively, Andre's worst nightmare of farming sheep began to recede from his mind as the idea of joining the British air force took hold, something he imagined his many Boer relations back home would consider treason. Going over to the enemy, spitting in the faces of his ancestors who had fought two wars against the British to retain their identity and freedom as a nation of Afrikaners, as nationalist as any German who believed in Hitler's National Socialist Party that was restoring the pride of the German people after their humiliation at the hands of the French and British. He could hear his pro-German great-uncle Koos ranting and raving.

"Ten generations of Cloetes on Venterskraal and you join up with the *rooineks*. You are a disgrace to your people who have struggled so long against all the odds to maintain our place in Africa. You have shamed us, Andre."

Smiling to himself as he played through his mind the Afrikaans words of his Uncle Koos, Andre politely clapped with the rest as Tinus cover-drove the ball to the boundary completing his fifty. Tinus acknowledged the players' pavilion by raising his bat as the umpire signalled the four, while the Surrey fielder stepped over the boundary rope to retrieve the ball and throw it back to the wicket keeper. Next to him Harry Brigandshaw, smiling broadly, stood up and added his clapping to the polite applause. Around the ground a sprinkling of Oxford supporters were watching the cricket. Just before the tea break Tinus went out to a good catch in the slips.

"That's it for me, Andre. I told them at the Air Ministry where they have me back again that I'd only watch Nephew bat. Tell Tinus I was here. Do you still have your Morgan?"

"No, sir."

"Then Tinus can bring you down tomorrow. I won't ask what you've been doing since coming down from Oxford as I know. Teaching apathetic teenagers history must be a pain in the arse. I like farming but it isn't for everyone. The bush with all its wild animals around Elephant Walk is what I love most of all. The Karoo is beautiful but flat. You can count the springbok from a mile away and that takes away the excitement. My father started his life in Africa as a big-game hunter with Tinus's grandfather. I can't shoot the animals myself except for the pot but I love to watch them when they come out of the trees. When the lions stand up from the long grass to show themselves not ten yards in front of you having hopefully had their lunch."

"I have too many siblings to allow us all to farm successfully, even if I wanted to farm. There are twelve of us in the family. My mistake was not taking a worthwhile degree instead of only thinking about sport, which all comes to an end sooner than I expected. An economics degree like Tinus has will get him a good job in industry anywhere in the world."

"The RAF can be a career. Not the best paying but a happy lifestyle with many friends."

"Is there going to be a war?"

"Probably, why you'll easily get into the Air Force. Do you want me to ask around? Find out what you have to do? If there's a war your generation will be fighting anyway, like my generation in the last war that killed my brother and brought me from Rhodesia to England looking for revenge. There's great danger, Andre. Think about it carefully. You are a Boer who owes England nothing."

"What else can I do with my life?"

"That's for you to decide... Well played, Tinus. Look who's here all the way from Africa. I've suggested you bring Andre with you to Hastings Court after the game finishes tomorrow."

With a twinkle in his eye, Harry watched the two old friends shake hands formally.

When Andre turned round to say goodbye and thank him for the invitation Harry was on his way out of the door.

"I got a duck in the first innings. Second ball."

"So your uncle was telling me."

"It's almost tea time. Let's go and find ourselves a cup of tea so you can fill me in on everything. How long are you staying in England?"

"Probably forever if your uncle has his way."

"Trying to persuade you to join the RAF? You'll have some fun again. The RAF have quite a good cricket side. Are you still throwing up before you fly?"

"Afraid so."

"Concentrates the mind."

"Is there going to be a war?"

"According to William Smythe it's a certainty. He does a weekly current affairs spot on the BBC Empire Service, 'Smythe in America', 'Smythe in Moscow', 'Smythe in Poland'. He's taken to the airwaves like a duck to water. He says if we don't get the Americans behind us from the start, Hitler will take it as a weakness and do what he likes. The common opinion in America according to Smythe is that Europe should take care of its own problems. That German, Italian and Spanish nationalism, now called fascism, is nothing to do with America. That America is made up of more German, Italians and Spanish than British despite the English language most of them now speak. Did you have any lunch? I'm staying at the Williams Hotel again tonight. You'd better bunk in my room just like old times. Jolly good to see you, old chap."

"Likewise, Tinus."

"They'll have some cucumber sandwiches with the crusts cut off."

"I'm surprised the English haven't starved themselves to death."

"So am I. At least we will get fed properly by Uncle Harry. From what I gather on the grapevine they've made him a test pilot but he won't say a word. Why he's back at the Air Ministry."

"Isn't Smythe the chap who's sweet on Genevieve?"

"I don't know. Is he? Have you heard from Fleur?"

"Have you heard from Genevieve?"

"Only in a roundabout way. She's making a new film in America."

"The three musketeers. Do you remember that time we all went rowing on the Cherwell?"

"It was on the Thames. We were south of Oxford."

"I suppose it was the Thames. You'd better write and tell her you're playing for Oxford. One day you're going to marry her."

"Don't be ridiculous. She's famous. I'm just another chap up at Oxford. Why don't we go round and see Fleur tonight? She and Celia are still in the same flat. She'll love to see you. They have a band now that plays the nightclubs. They're very good and making lots of money."

"What does Barnaby St Clair say about that?"

"He's right out of the picture."

"About time. She was far too young to waste herself on an old man."

"Tell that to Uncle Barnaby. The one he's got right now hasn't turned twenty-one."

"How does he do it?"

"He's rich. How was the trip? Any pretty girls?"

"Pretty girls are not interested in impecunious ex-history teachers who once played cricket, a game most of them have never heard of let alone seen."

"That explains Uncle Barnaby's success; he buys them one way or another... Uncle Harry has a German man and his wife staying at

Hastings Court this weekend. Out of the blue the chap invited himself over from Germany. Uncle Harry shot him down in the war and then saved his life. A bit bizarre if you ask me, making a friend of a man who was doing his best to kill you. Big landowner in Germany. I met him first when he came to Elephant Walk on his honeymoon. If I'm not wrong his wife's name was Bergit. That was years ago. I was something like four years old. Remember more from what my mother said about them afterwards. When Uncle Harry told me about the visit on the phone he sounded puzzled as to why Klaus von Lieberman wanted to pay a visit to England now. Uncle Harry said it was all very well being friends, but if their countries were going to war with each other again they would have split loyalties to each other, despite what Klaus might personally think of Hitler's politics and methods to achieve them. That when push came to shove von Lieberman was firstly a German and secondly a friend. Uncle Harry told me twice on the phone not to talk about his work at the Air Ministry. Sounds to me as if he doesn't trust his friend.

"He's invited William Smythe for the weekend to stop the German talking politics, knowing William will spout his mouth off on the BBC. Bit of a cat and mouse game if you ask me, though who's the cat and who's the mouse is beyond me. Uncle Harry doesn't remember telling me Herr von Lieberman refused an invitation to Hastings Court after he helped that chap Horatio Wakefield escape from Germany after Uncle Harry phoned von Lieberman. At the time the German said the two friends should only meet in Rhodesia and advised Uncle Harry to go home. Neutral territory so to speak. You can't be disloyal to your country just because you don't like the government of the day. Where on earth would democracy be if that happened, the loser hating the winner, though according to Mr Bowden it does happen.

"You remember Bowden? Teaches philosophy and talks more sense than any man I know; Plato didn't think much of a democracy where Mr Average made the decisions. He wanted a philosopher king who knew right from wrong. My guess is friend Klaus is over here to spy. It should be fun over the weekend watching them spar with each other.

"If I know William he'll bring Horatio Wakefield to the party unannounced, ostensibly for Horatio to thank the German for getting him out of Nazi clutches and saving his life. William always felt guilty for taking Horatio to Berlin in the first place, putting his life in jeopardy to sell a few articles just to make money... I'm right. There they are. Cucumber sandwiches in neat little triangles with the crusts cut off nicely and sprinkled with nourishing watercress. Whatever happened to a *braai* at a cricket match and a pile of lamb chops to munch on? *Bon appétit.*

"Welcome back to England, Andre. It's been too long. Just don't eat the whole bloody lot before the others get off the field. If you'd come over two months ago you would have been in time for King George the Sixth's coronation. Poor chap stutters. Edward's gone into exile after abdicating. Edward the Eighth. They never even crowned him."

"What was all that about?"

"We don't talk about such things in England. It's considered impolite. There was a woman involved. American. Divorced twice. Now she's going to be the Duchess of Windsor... Any good?"

"They're delicious, Tinus."

"Of course they are."

"What did your Uncle Harry put in your blazer pocket just as he left?"

"Did he? I say, it's a fiver, what was that for?"

"Your first fifty for Oxford. I haven't seen one of those big white folded pieces of paper for a long time. Why did the Bank of England make the five pound note look like the promissory note my father gave me from his bank when I first went up to Oxford?"

"No, it wasn't that. Fifty is all right but not enough for Uncle Harry. I have no idea about the note."

By the time play finished at six o'clock, Andre was on top of his world again. Two other people had mentioned his hundred by pointing him out to their friends as 'that chap who scored a hundred and twelve against Cambridge'. Each time Andre had made it look as if he had not heard. Each time the old thrill of recognition raced through his body. By the time they reached Fleur Brooks's flat in Paddington he was quite his own self even though he only had two and six in his pocket, the last of his pay from the school. Their luck was in; both girls were at home.

"Well I never. Come here, darling," said Fleur taking Andre firmly by the elbow.

"Fleur, how are you?" He was going to kiss her but Celia and Tinus were watching.

"Better for seeing you. What a sight for sore eyes."

"We want to take you both out to dinner," said Tinus. "You remember that time we all drove down to Purbeck Manor for the old man's last party?"

"Enough said about that night," said Celia. "How are you, Tinus?"

"My Uncle Harry gave me some money so we can do a slap-up dinner. All Andre has eaten all day is a plate of cucumber sandwiches daintily sprinkled with watercress. We are both starving. You must know a place around here we can get a good meal without dressing up. I've been playing cricket."

"So I can see. Fleur, isn't that an Oxford Blue's blazer? Come in. We have one of those new-fangled refrigerators from America where we store bottles of beer in summer. How does that sound while we get ready? Did you score any runs, I think they call it? You're lucky, we don't play in the midweek, yet anyway."

"A few," said Tinus, not wishing to boast to Celia.

"Just do me a favour, Tinus. Don't mention Barnaby St Clair. His latest girlfriend hasn't even turned twenty-one."

"So you're not at the Windmill, I gather?"

"Not anymore. We have our own band that has nothing to do with Barnaby St Clair. What are you doing back in England, Andre? Fleur thought you had gone home to farm sheep. Merino sheep if my memory is correct. You said something then about lots of wool."

"I'm joining the Royal Air Force. Fighters I hope. Tinus's Uncle Harry has promised to put in a good word for me. I tried teaching for a while but it did not work."

"The fridge is in the kitchen. Help yourself. The Americans say within ten years every house will have a fridge so we don't have to throw food away. Whatever are they going to think up next to make us spend our money on? This is a nice surprise, Tinus. You've filled out in the shoulders. Suits you. I was right, that is an Oxford cricket blazer."

"Yes it is, Celia."

"Congratulations. How are the studies?"

"Even more absorbing than cricket."

"Come and hear us play on Friday at the Mayfair."

"You have come up in the world. Not this Friday. Going down to Hastings Court."

"We played at your Uncle Harry's big bash at Hastings Court you remember. Now that was a shindig. Your Aunt Tina knows how to throw a party. Give the two of us half an hour and we'll be ready. There's a Greek restaurant in Soho that is just the best. When they get excited they throw plates on the floor. Can you believe it? The Greek restaurant is in Greek Street."

"I never would have guessed," said Tinus, sitting himself down comfortably in the lounge while the girls went into their bedrooms to change. "They cook lamb and serve it off a spike," he said to Andre. "You'll get enough food. Sometimes those fancy French restaurants are all display and no substance. You don't want a beer either?"

"Not for me without Fleur. They'll have a bottle of wine in the restaurant."

*B*runo Kannberg recognised Tinus Oosthuizen when the four young people came into the Greek restaurant where he was celebrating with his wife of three months. He thought he also recognised the two girls from somewhere. In case Tinus remembered him he made a vague sign of recognition immediately picked up by his wife.

"Do you know those two girls, Bruno?" There was an edge to his wife's voice which suggested it would be better if he did not know the pretty girls. Arthur Bumley, his editor at the *Daily Mirror*, had been right about women; they changed once they became wives, and protected their territory. One of the girls gave Bruno a faint smile of recognition as if she was used to being recognised in public. "That girl knows you, Bruno!"

"I don't think so, darling. One of the chaps is Tinus Oosthuizen. Harry Brigandshaw's nephew. I met him a couple of times with his uncle though I don't think he recognises me. I just nodded my head in his direction. The girl's an entertainer. Now I remember. At the Mayfair."

"Of course, and the other girl? Genevieve talked to me about this Tinus when I was typing her book at Hastings Court. That's a cricket blazer isn't it?"

"Oxford University. They are playing the Surrey Second Eleven at the Oval."

Once the threat disappeared his wife was all smiles again. Ever since the big wedding paid for by her father, Bruno had been on his guard not to look at other women in the presence of Mrs Kannberg let alone, he found, talking to them.

"You look henpecked already, Kannberg," Art Bumley had said that morning in the office of the *Daily Mirror* where Art gave him the good news.

"Everything has to be done her way. I'm permanently on the defensive."

"Are you getting enough nooky?"

"Not as much as before we were married. She uses it as a weapon in case I won't do what she wants."

"Clever girl. Even the perfect girl becomes boring in bed if you get what you want. It's called satisfaction. Once you are satisfied you don't want any more. The clever ones ration it out in a marriage. Give it to you as if they are doing you a big favour. As if sex to them is a chore."

"You are a cynic, Mr Bumley."

"You have to weigh the good with the bad. How is she at cooking?"

"Brilliant."

"There you are, Bruno. Your new book is also brilliant. Read it right through last night. Genevieve's publishers won't touch it. Far too conservative. I'll ask around."

"If you say it's good someone will buy the publishing rights?"

"I'll do my best. Take Gillian out to dinner."

"You mean I can celebrate?"

"Something like that. What you are saying is Edward was forced to abdicate the throne because he sympathises with Hitler after the communists shot his cousin and his cousin's family in Russia. That the Mitford girls, one of whom is married to Mosley, were part of the entourage of Edward when he was Prince of Wales, that Edward, arguably the most popular Prince of Wales in history, would be able to sway the people. A man able, if he so wished, to take England the Mosley fascist route, which is all very well if you had any proof. Conspiracy theories are all very well but they have to stand up in the court of libel. You can't just say the Americans encouraged their own twice-divorced Mrs Simpson in the hope she would jeopardise the future King of England and Emperor of India and help bring down the British Empire in a scandal. That's Smythe's blast at the moment; American determination to see the end of our empire. If you ask me, Edward abdicated because Mrs Simpson has got him by the balls. Some women have that kind of power over men. Poor sod didn't stand a chance once she decided she wanted him as her husband, even if they didn't let her be queen. A twice-divorced American making herself into the Duchess of Windsor is pretty smart social climbing to me. I don't think Prime Minister Neville Chamberlain has the brains to think Edward is pro-German despite Edward's German ancestry, despite the German surname of the royal family being changed to Windsor during the last war. It makes good reading, your book, but whether a publisher will risk a court case to sell a million copies, I'm not so sure. People have been ostracised for less in England, for less of a tilt at the establishment."

"You think my book will sell a million copies, wow! That's a lot of books."

"A million copies across the empire. Then there's America. The Americans will lap it up with an American at the centre of your conspiracy."

"Then I'll go to America."

"Don't forget you work for me, Kannberg. On a new exorbitant salary since you got yourself married."

"Of course."

"Chasing publishers in America where no one knows you will be difficult in any case, however good the book. The public think Genevieve wrote her book, not you. There's nothing about a ghostwriter on the cover. Don't change horses mid-stream. It's good, Kannberg. You're a good writer whose talents are probably wasted on a tabloid like the *Mirror*. But you have a good job. Books are one-off, mostly fame rather than fortune. They don't pay the bills year after year like a good salary. Count your blessings and take your wife out to dinner, tell her from me you are a genius. That should help tonight when you get home."

"But you will have a go for me?"

"Of course."

"Your nodding acquaintance is coming over," said his wife, the previous part of her conversation having gone in one ear and out the other as Bruno thought about his new book, the fear of rejection still gnawing at his stomach.

"I say, aren't you the chap who wrote Genevieve's book for her? We were just talking about Genevieve when you caught my eye. My name is

Tinus Oosthuizen. Harry Brigandshaw is my uncle. How is the book selling we want to know?"

"The print run has gone over the hundred thousand in America."

"Is that good or bad? I don't know much about writing books. Myself and Andre back there and Genevieve are the three musketeers."

"My wife Gillian."

"You helped write the book at Hastings Court."

"Give Mr Brigandshaw my regards," said Gillian formally.

"You won't come and join us?"

"We're having a private celebration," said Gillian.

"I'm so sorry to interrupt. If your husband hadn't..."

"I've written a new book on the abdication," said Bruno to get over the awkward moment.

"I'll look forward to reading it, Kannberg. So nice to meet you both. Enjoy your celebration. Who's publishing?"

"Longman, probably."

"Good for you, Kannberg. When you next write to Genevieve give her my love. She's a very special lady. The world is a small place."

"Isn't it so?"

"You'd better get a publisher," said his wife when Tinus was back at his own table.

"Art Bumley's doing his best. The fact he likes my book means everything."

"Such praise won't buy us a house. If we're going to have a family we need a house, something your portion of the *Genevieve* biography won't buy."

"Of course, dear."

"So long as you understand the house is more important than Arthur Bumley's praise."

"I was hoping for a little praise from you, dear."

"I've told you what I think of the book. More than once. But that doesn't help. *The Abdication of King Edward* will only be worthwhile if it makes money. Otherwise what was the point of writing it?"

After that, as Bruno ate through his meal in small talk, he thought his chances later in the evening rather poor.

AT THE OTHER table Harry Brigandshaw's five pounds was going a long way to get all four of them drunk, the low price of wine in the Greek restaurant something of an incentive. No one felt guilty as new bottles were put on the table at regular intervals.

"I can't bowl to save my life," said Tinus. "I only have to concentrate when I bat. They'll put me out on the boundary when I field tomorrow, out of the way. So let's celebrate. My word, it is good to see you, Andre. Old friends mean so much in life."

"When next are you going home to Rhodesia?" asked Andre.

"Not for some time. It's too expensive. Ralph Madgwick is doing a sterling job as manager of the farm after my great-grandfather's death but tobacco just isn't fetching big prices anymore. American leaf from Virginia is flooding the market. Tucked away inland in Africa and Elephant Walk far from the railhead, we can't compete on price with the American growers, despite the good leaf we produce on the farm. Everyone lives well on Elephant Walk but we don't generate much cash. The cattle and maize are for local Rhodesian consumption, why food at home is so cheap and the grub's good on the farm. Grandfather Manderville started us growing tobacco during the war when the troops were smoking so much to calm themselves down in the trenches. It was easier to get Rhodesian tobacco to England through the Suez Canal from Beira than it was for the American ships to dodge the German submarines crossing the Atlantic. There was a heavy war premium according to grandfather that made Rhodesian tobacco competitive. Then the price went up with the demand."

"Why don't you ask your Uncle Harry?" said Andre.

"He's done far more than an uncle should do already. Including tonight. I'll go home when I finish university to finally decide what to do with my career."

"The price of tobacco will go through the roof if war breaks out," said Celia as she rested her hand on Tinus's knee, the wine having made her amorous. "That man William Smythe is predicting German underwater boats will be able to shut down Europe's trade with America despite the Royal Navy. The Atlantic is so large our surface navy will never be able to find all those German submarines under the sea. We'll be able to keep the Germans out of the Med by blockading the Straits of Gibraltar. You'll make a fortune, Tinus. Tell this Ralph Madgwick to sow lots of tobacco. What a hoot."

"I'll suggest it to mother in my next letter home. Actually we plant out tobacco in the lands as seedlings from just a few seed beds near the family compound. We can store tobacco for up to five years letting it mature. According to grandfather the more mature the tobacco, the better the smoke. Rather like old wine in barrels, we store cured tobacco leaf in wooden hogsheads."

"When you're rich you can give me some," said Celia stroking his leg under the table, making her words perfectly clear to Tinus.

"Ralph's married to a Jewess," said Tinus trying to ignore the hand steadily creeping up the inside of his leg. "There was a rumpus about them getting married which was why they landed on Elephant Walk."

"I'll bet she's glad to be out of Europe," said Andre.

"Like all new Rhodesians they are having lots of kids. Her father's in America but I don't think they communicate. Something about marrying out of their religion. He's a banker. Stinking rich."

"You mean she gave up all that lovely money for love?" said Celia removing her hand from his knee.

"So did he. Ralph had a first class job in New York working for his family company as their American branch manager."

"Must be mad."

"My mother writes they are blissfully happy. They love Africa. Love the life on a big African farm away from all the nonsense, whatever mother means by that."

"People," said Fleur. "Away from people. When Tinus goes to Rhodesia, Celia, we'll have to go visit him and find out what has made the Madgwicks so happy. In London everyone says they are happy. They try hard to look happy."

"Princess says it's Africa. Africans are always happy with each other in the villages. The harmony only gets broken when outsiders interfere."

"Who's Princess?"

"Tembo's fourth wife. Tembo Makoni. They have a first son they called Josiah. Tembo really runs the place. He and Uncle Harry go back to when they were boys together. Everyone listens to what Tembo has to say."

"Sounds like it, with four wives to keep under control," said Fleur.

"Why don't we finish the wine and go back to the flat?" said Celia. "We don't just have beer in the new refrigerator from America. It's party time. We must hope tomorrow they don't hit a ball up in the air for you to catch, Tinus. I don't think you can come to any harm standing on the boundary with a hangover. We'd come with you both to Hastings Court after the game if we weren't playing at the Mayfair. All work and no play. That's Celia and Fleur. Are they all really happy in Africa? No wonder they didn't bother to so-called civilise themselves."

"Tinus loves Elephant Walk," said Andre. "Everything on Elephant Walk is perfect. My father says the same about Venterskraal, our farm in the Karoo."

When the taxi dropped the four of them in the street outside the girls' flat in Paddington the green two-seater Morgan was still parked where Tinus had left it. Everything looked safe including the suitcase Andre had brought from the boat and train to the cricket. For a man on a long journey it was a remarkably small suitcase, Tinus thought, as he pulled it out from behind the seats of his car.

"Better to be safe," said Tinus. "Someone may try and walk off with it."

"What about the car?"

"I have the key and it's heavy."

Upstairs, Fleur took Andre straight into her bedroom shutting the door, leaving Celia and Tinus alone in the sitting room.

"Shall we dance?" said Celia, as she took his hand and led him into the second bedroom, closing the door with the back of her foot after pushing Tinus back onto the bed. "You've had quite enough wine."

Mildly wondering what Barnaby St Clair would think of his predicament, Tinus held out his arms for the girl gently swaying on her stockinged feet, the shoes kicked off around the room.

"What would we do without wine?" she said, folding herself one knee at a time onto the double bed. Then she stretched over Tinus and turned out the small bedside lamp she had left on before they went to the restaurant.

REMARKABLY, when Tinus woke in the morning it was without the trace of a hangover.

"Pick you up after the match," he called to Andre through the still closed door of Fleur's bedroom. "Luckily I can shower and change at the Oval."

"Make sure you win," called Andre.

"If we're gone to the Mayfair, have a nice time at Hastings Court," called Fleur, who still sounded to Tinus to be half asleep. Then he let himself out of the flat, leaving Celia fast asleep in the big bed with his note on the bedside table.

Downstairs, the Morgan started at the first press of the starter button. He was in good time for the eleven o'clock re-start of the match. As he drove through the streets of London Tinus knew he had never felt happier in his life.

THEY ARRIVED that evening at Hastings Court in the glow of the twilight, the countryside passing by gently on their slow drive out of London, both of them savouring this moment in their lives. Both of them satiated from their women, the thoughts of the girls still playing pleasantly through their minds. It was nine o'clock when Tinus took the Morgan up the long drive towards the ancient home of the Mandervilles.

"Which is more your home?" asked Andre. The red glow of the twilight was playing tricks with the small turrets and battlements silhouetted against the last light in the evening sky. On either side birds were calling to each other from the trees to let their friends and lovers know where they were roosting once they were shrouded in night.

Tinus did not answer at first. He could see a clutter of cars parked below the house on the forecourt, the last light playing on the glass of the windscreens. Some of himself came from the Mandervilles. Some of himself came from the old Pirate his great-grandfather Brigandshaw, who had bought for himself both the house and bloodline of the Mandervilles. But all of that beckoning as he slowly drove the last yards up to the old house was no stronger than the pull of Africa in his veins, of the Oosthuizens who had given him his name.

"I don't know, Andre. Come on. Some of them are still up by the looks of it."

"There you are," called Harry Brigandshaw, coming down the steps between the balustrades that marched along the terrace overlooking the forecourt. "Hello, Andre. Who won, Tinus?"

"They did I'm afraid."

"Better luck next time. Come and meet my old friends from Germany. We're having a nightcap on the lawn at the back of the house; Tina has put candles out on the table in paper cups. The owls have been calling, a sound that reminds me of Africa. Bring up your cases. You both have the same rooms you had before so you know where to go. Leave them for the moment in the hall and come and have a snifter of brandy. The servants have all gone to bed. Did you eat on the way? Good. Breakfast is served in the conservatory between eight and ten. Tina has taken to eating her breakfast among the potted plants. What a beautiful evening. What did you two do last night?

"The RAF is most likely on, Andre, if you want to join. Rhodes Scholar and double blue coupled with the Oxford University Air Squadron should do the trick. You'll have to go through an officer cadet training unit for six months. I don't know what you would fly after that. Depends if they put you in bombers or fighters; there's also Coastal Command. But that's enough of business."

"When could I start?"

"The next intake is the first of next month. You can stay with us until then. Tina and the children will love such illustrious sporting company. I'll bring you down a rail pass so you can come up to the Air Ministry for an interview. Pure formality, but you have to go through the hoops with the rest of them... William Smythe is coming down tomorrow. Says he's bringing his old friend, which will be nice for all of us. Tina just loves company at Hastings Court. So do the children. They've all been sent to bed by now, even Anthony. He's fourteen now but likes his sleep. You two can teach him some tricks with a cricket bat and ball tomorrow after you've had your breakfast. There we are," said Harry, shaking both their hands formally when they put their suitcases down in the hall. Then they all walked through the old, high-ceilinged house to the well-cut lawn where beneath the trees the candles were sending up light from the table where the rest of the guests were seated.

"It's been such a joy seeing Klaus and Bergit again after so many years. Such a pity they did not bring their children. I was looking forward to Anthony meeting Erwin. Despite the two-year age gap they would have a lot in common. Erwin's already a pilot but he's older than Anthony. We have so much in common with the Germans, our backgrounds are so similar. I imagined Erwin coming out to Africa. Anthony going for visits to Bavaria. The boys learning to ski together and pick up each other's languages. It's all part of a boy's education. Makes his life much fuller. You two would know what I mean, living both in Africa and Europe. Gives us all a better perspective on life... Bergit and Klaus, I'd like you to meet my nephew. Tinus and his friend Andre. Mr and Mrs von Lieberman, may I present Tinus Oosthuizen and Andre Cloete? Tinus is my sister Madge's son who was a very small boy when you visited Elephant Walk on your honeymoon."

. . .

SEEING the man he had last met as a small boy made Klaus even more sick in the stomach for what he was doing, abusing an old friend's hospitality. The two confident young men reminded him of himself and his younger brothers before the war, when life in Europe was more pleasant for everyone, the rich and the poor.

Uncle Werner had called him to Berlin the previous month to give him the Party's instructions.

"This is an order, Klaus, so I don't want any argument. You said you had refused the invitation to your friend's birthday party. Now we want you to go to England. Your friend works for the British Air Ministry, close to Tedder, the chief of staff of the British air force. We know about the radar on the south coast of England. We even know how it works, bouncing a signal from a metal object to determine its position. What we don't know is the sites of the radar masts or how the British will feed the information to their fighter squadrons. You will go with your wife to Hastings Court, old friends renewing a friendship.

"The Party has information you spent your honeymoon on the man's farm in Rhodesia, something I don't remember. Back then your father was alive and would have known what you were doing, not your uncle.

"Walking through the woods, riding horses, playing tennis and drinking together I want you to find out what the RAF are up to. Old friends talk about what they have been doing. Over days it will all come out if you listen carefully. The Party's information has Hastings Court full of people at the weekends as Brigandshaw's wife likes entertaining. The guests will talk to each other and Brigandshaw. All you have to do is overhear their conversations."

"Are you asking me to spy on a friend? He saved my life, for God's sake."

"I am not asking you, Klaus, I am giving you an order from the Party which you ignore at your family's peril. You seem to forget that before the man saved your life, he had just shot you down. That the two of you were trying to kill each other, not playing a polite game in the sky like gentlemen at a fox hunt. You were enemies. You still are enemies. There is no chivalry in war, only death for one or the other."

"And if I refuse to do something dishonourable?"

"You and your family will be sent to our camp at Dachau where we sent people who disagreed with us in the purge of 1933. I am told it is not a nice place. You will be most uncomfortable. Of course, I will keep young Erwin under my wing. He has dedicated his life with the best of our young boys to the Hitler Youth Movement, which of course is the Party of the Fuehrer."

"You are my uncle!"

"Then do what I tell you. Do what I know is good for the family. Didn't I save the family estate for you once already from the Jews? You are behaving like an ungrateful fool, Klaus. I am told on good authority that anyone sent to Dachau never goes home again."

"And you think that is the place to send a disobedient member of your own family?"

"In such difficult times it is unwise to think. We Germans are good at taking orders. Please take yours. There are many unpleasant tasks we have to do in our lives for the overall good. The world was never a perfect place. Weak people die. The von Liebermans are strong. And don't open your mouth again as I might just lose my temper. When you return from England you will report to me here. Wars are won with the right information. Knowing what to destroy is as important as having the means of its destruction."

"So there's going to be a war?"

"Of course there's going to be a bloody war."

"YOUR UNCLE HARRY tells me you are also a pilot, Tinus. Of course I remember you. You and that pack of dogs on the farm were inseparable. Rhodesian Ridgebacks I think your uncle called them. I asked Erwin to come with me and his mother but he has a summer camp to attend. He's also a pilot."

"So is Andre, here. How do you do, sir? It's an honour to meet you again. I remember your visit to Elephant Walk but more from my mother who often mentions your visit. We don't have too many visitors to Rhodesia to talk about afterwards so mother is inclined to go on a bit. But I do remember then your English was impeccable, as was that of Frau von Lieberman. My mother always said it was wonderful for one-time enemies to become such good friends."

"French cognac in a balloon glass, Tinus. What could be better?" said Harry Brigandshaw, enjoying the conversation.

"Thank you, Uncle Harry. Something of the hair of the dog. After I'd finished batting we went to see Fleur and Celia and did a little celebrating. They were here for your party, playing in the band. Fleur hadn't seen Andre since he went home to Africa so we all went out to dinner at a little Greek restaurant."

"So you did a night out on the tiles?"

"Something like that. I didn't drop a catch, if that's what you're thinking."

"Youth doesn't last for long, Tinus. Enjoy it. You lost the cricket anyway... There goes that owl again in the birch tree. It's either the male calling to the female or the other way round. Their calls are the same. Listen to that. She's calling him back. Give it ten seconds and he'll answer her again. Nature is wonderful."

Klaus, following the conversation, felt like the hypocrite he knew he was, the fake smile on his face belying the gnawing pain in his stomach. Even in the half day that had gone so peacefully at Hastings Court he had found out more than he expected from the entire three-day visit; it was clear to him that Harry Brigandshaw had no idea what was going on and why his German friend had suddenly come to England. He even knew the site of the mast at Poling on the south coast of England, a mast the Luftwaffe would target when war broke out, making one blind spot in the British radar.

There had been one good part of the trip; his wife Bergit knew nothing of the truth, which made finding out what they wanted so much easier when everyone around him was totally relaxed. It was also the first time he had lied to his wife by not telling her the real purpose of their visit.

"A game of tennis after breakfast," his friend was saying, the shadows turning to dark on the lawn that spread among the occasional trees. "To bed, to sleep, perchance to dream."

"Poor old Shakespeare going through it again," said Tina, who liked to show off how well read she was, making Harry Brigandshaw grind his teeth sometimes unbeknown to anyone else on the darkening lawn.

Only when Klaus reached his bedroom and the lights went out did he relax. At least one of the days was over.

"What's the matter, darling?" his wife asked in German.

"Why? There's nothing the matter."

"I'm your wife. I know your moods inside out."

"Then don't ask. We'll be going home on Monday."

"Harry says more houseguests are arriving tomorrow."

"That should be fun. Harry's right. Those owls are calling to each other."

In the dark they both lay awake for a long time before finally going off to sleep. During the night Klaus dreamed he was being shot down in flames, waking in a fright just before his aircraft hit the ground. He was still awake on his back when the sun came up with the birds' dawn chorus, a sound so beautiful in contrast with how he felt. Then he went back to sleep, waking in time to wash his face in the basin on the washstand before dressing and going down to breakfast with his wife, his face drawn from lack of sleep.

"It's never easy to sleep in a strange bed," said Harry, looking at his friend. "Tea or coffee? Coffee will wake you up. I thought a horse ride for all of us before we play tennis. My wife has gone to the village with the chauffeur. She doesn't ride or play tennis, despite my trying to put her on a horse in Rhodesia when we were first married. Then she had Anthony and we never got around to it again. None of the children ride horses. They prefer riding their bikes. Anthony wants a motorbike which he can't have until he turns eighteen and can apply for a licence."

"Coffee, Harry. Thank you. Your owls were calling to each other most of the night."

"Better than listening to the London traffic. I could hear the hum all night from our house in Berkeley Square. In Africa as a boy I lay awake all night listening to the lions. They don't exactly roar but the sound at night is so menacing it makes you think your blood has gone cold. Then you get used to it. Then it's beautiful. The most beautiful sound in the world for a small boy growing up."

"If you miss Africa so much you should go home, Harry. I would if we had a place like Elephant Walk. We both say those memories are precious. Go home, Harry. Take the advice of an old friend who has your best interests at heart." The undertone of misery in Klaus von Lieberman's voice was palpable.

"I haven't heard you talk like that before, Klaus. What's the matter?"

"The whole world."

"You're among friends. Relax. Let the world take care of itself. A friend of mine once said it was pointless worrying. That ninety-nine per cent of what he worried about never happened. The trick, he said, was knowing which one per cent to worry about... Good morning, Tinus. You look bright and breezy. Did you sleep well?

"Like a log. Last night's sleep was the best sleep I had in my whole life. Now I could eat a horse. Andre's on his way down. I beat him to the bathroom where I soaked for half an hour."

"Bacon and eggs, sausages, kidneys, fried tomato. No horse, Tinus. Instead we are going to ride them before tennis... Good morning, Andre. My nephew was telling us how he hogged the bathroom."

"No wonder the door was locked when I went past," said Klaus, taking his cup of coffee from Harry.

"Everyone help themselves. You make your own toast in the electric toaster. Another product from America to make us spend our money. The food is on the sideboard. I don't like to make the servants stand around once they've done the cooking. Under the silver dishes are small spirit lamps to keep the food hot. It's a trick we learnt in Africa where we don't have electricity on the farm. Bergit, I'm so sorry. Klaus has his coffee before you. One look at him when he came down to breakfast said he needed perking up. I'm sorry. What can I give you?"

"Sit down, Harry. I'll help myself. That bacon smells good." In contrast to Klaus, his wife looked perfectly relaxed.

3

*T*he taxi left them standing with their luggage at the foot of the steps that led up to the terrace and the front door to the old house. Except for the taxi going off down the drive, there was no other sound. William Smythe had met Horatio and Janet Wakefield with one-year-old Harry in the pram at Waterloo Station where they all took the train to Leatherhead. The taxi had taken ten minutes from the station. They waited but no one came out to greet them. A little away stood the green Morgan sports car looking lonely by itself, small against the backdrop of the great house.

"At least Tinus and Andre are here. We'd better go up," said William. "Hello! Anyone home?"

The big double door was wide open. They walked through into the old house, Janet pushing the pram the two men had lifted up the steps to the terrace. Harry was wide awake but not making a sound.

"A bloody great house and not a soul," said William as they walked on through the familiar house and out to the lawn at the back. Having been told to bring their tennis rackets, they walked through the trees that sprinkled the large lawn to the tennis courts William had played on before. No one was there. A bridle path along the side of the tennis courts led into the woods and hills beyond.

"Horses. I smell horse dung. They've all gone off riding on the heath."

"Tina doesn't ride."

"Gone to the village to get something. She does her own shopping," said Horatio. "Doesn't trust the staff with money. Says she saved Harry twenty pounds a week running the house herself."

"And then spends two hundred quid in Selfridges, or with her favourite dress designer. The place is set up for tennis. Someone has put up the nets on both courts and the grass has been cut this morning."

"It's going to rain," said Janet. "Those dark clouds just behind the house look menacing. Let's go back to the house. We'll go to the kitchen and make some tea. Why is it everything about this place looks old? From the big gnarled trees to that Greek statue."

"Because it is old, darling. Does he need feeding? How do you know it's Greek?"

"Not yet. I'm hungry," said Janet. "Every time I go into the country it makes me hungry. There's a similar statue on the front lawn of the chemistry lab at Harrow school; I was told it was Greek. How much do you think it costs to run a place like this?"

"We'll never have to find out unless I write a book like Bruno Kannberg at the *Mirror*," said Horatio. "Word has it they'll sell millions of copies in America."

"They won't sell one copy from what I hear," said William. "The British establishment clam up in the face of scandal. Kannberg will find himself in trouble, trying to rock the boat. They don't like washing upper-crust dirty linen in public. Edward forsaking the throne for the woman he loves is one thing the British public can swallow and leave the Royals intact. All that nonsense about the Mitford girls who some say visited Hitler with a message from Edward won't wash in public even if it is true. An English gentleman excuses himself politely when he's in a mess and buggers off."

"William! Harry can't speak properly but he can hear perfectly well. Don't swear. It doesn't sound nice."

"Sorry, Janet. A slip of an old scribe's tongue. You really think young Harry can understand at one year old? We've got a genius in the making."

"How do you know what's in it, Will?"

"He's sent ten copies to various publishers. Chap at Longman gave me a ring. He knew I had my eye on Genevieve's welfare and didn't want to hurt her sales with her ghostwriter making an ass of himself. Told me to have a quiet word with Kannberg, who of course isn't English and wouldn't understand. He's Russian or Latvian or something. How can a man be both Russian and Latvian for God's sake?"

"There are ethnic Russians living in Latvia where his father comes from. His father fought for the White Russian army against the communists, and when they lost he brought his family to England."

"Even more reason to be grateful."

"Have you had a word with Kannberg?"

"Not yet. Cranthorpe only phoned last night. His editor had had a call from someone important. That someone Cranthorpe wouldn't name, wants the book stopped. The *Mirror* thinks I can help. They must get information from the man they can publish or they wouldn't bother."

"Why not help Kannberg write the book and make a fortune together? There are many ways of saying something without being obvious. The reader picks it up. Makes the book more intriguing if it's a bit mysterious. So you haven't actually read the book, Will?"

"Not yet... Here comes someone."

"And here comes the rain," said Janet. "We'd better run for the house. Just look at Harry. He's laughing his head off."

"Probably at Kannberg's book... You did say he could hear, just not speak properly. It's raining cats and dogs. We really do have a lousy climate. Must have been a servant. Bolted back into the old house. We're going to get soaking wet and our cases are still in the courtyard or whatever they call the acre of gravel in front of the house. Run for it! Push, Janet! Harry's the only one not getting wet with the hood up."

"Why, he's laughing."

"Here comes the rest of them. I hear galloping horses."

Laughing hysterically, they all ran towards the shelter of the house. Then the horses broke out of the woods and everyone was waving, Horatio recognising the man who had saved his life in Germany, the man Janet wanted to thank to his face for making her family possible, her happiness, what she liked to call the whole purpose of her life.

THEY FOUND their suitcases in the hall. On top of Janet's was a picture hat with a small bunch of imitation grapes on the side. Everything was dry. Their raincoats and William's rolled umbrella were also on top of the cases.

"Servants must have brought them into the house," said Horatio.

"Sorry you also got wet," said Harry Brigandshaw striding down the hall, his hand held out to William who was nearest. "Welcome to Hastings Court. The others have gone up to their rooms to change. You can dry your clothes out in the hot cupboard that houses the hot water tank. The boiler in the basement keeps the water hot all day... More like an April shower. I never get used to the unpredictability of the English weather. Where are your tennis rackets? No matter, the grass court is soaked and unplayable for today and tomorrow.

"Let me have a look at my namesake. He has grown. Look at those big eyes. He's going to bowl the girls over when he's older. Janet, you look wonderful despite being wet. There are towels in your rooms. Come on, I'll take you up. The hot cupboard, which is really a small room, is next to the second floor bathroom. Do you know there are only three bathrooms in this entire house, all with baths, not one shower. Two for the family and guests, one for the servants. No wonder the English only bath once a week. In Africa I took a shower every day. Sometimes two when I came in from the lands. Mostly my thirst took me straight to a cold beer. You take your cases and I'll carry Janet's. What a lovely summer hat.

"Later, you two can take Klaus aside and thank him. It's so nice to see my old friends again. They spent part of their honeymoon on Elephant Walk where we got to know each other as friends and not enemies. By 1921 the war had been over for three years. Being in Africa helped. Believe it or not, Tinus my nephew says he remembers Klaus and Bergit. He couldn't have been more than four years old. Remembers the Germans spoke perfect English. The things children take in when they are young. The Catholics say give them a child up to the age of ten and the child will always remain a Catholic.

"I hoped young Erwin would have come over with his parents but he's attending a summer camp with his school friends arranged by the government. All young friends together, so Klaus and Bergit came alone. Andre and Tinus have hit it off with Klaus like a house on fire, all being pilots. All they talk about is aeroplanes. Civilian aeroplanes. The Imperial Airways flying boats that fly passengers from London to the Cape landing on the Nile, the African Great Lakes and the Zambezi above the Victoria Falls. My idea of course. Nearly cost me my life. I still think sadly of Iggy Bowes-Lyon; his cousin Elizabeth is now Queen of England since the abdication. They went for help after we hit a submerged hippo coming into land. Never found a trace of them. I had to stay with the other chap who was paralysed, only able to get myself out when he died. But you all remember that. It was how we all met, you two journalists on my story with that chap Kannberg from the *Mirror*. They tell me the book he wrote for Genevieve is selling like hot cakes. I thought I'd ask cook to make up some packed lunches now we can't play tennis. Go up on the heath. The children have haversacks we can borrow to carry our lunch and the flasks of tea."

"Where are the children?" asked Janet.

"With their mother in the village, I expect. There's a teashop where Tina likes to natter. She knows everyone in the village. The children get bored here on their own without friends. In the village they find things to do. Listening to me and Klaus talking about old times bored them to tears I should think. If you want to come, Janet, you can leave young Harry with cook. She'll love it. Mrs Craddock loves children and I'd trust her with my life. Just remember, no politics. We don't want the von Liebermans to feel uncomfortable, despite your strong feelings about the German government. I listen every week to your talk on the BBC Empire Service, William. Do you really think the Americans want us out of the colonies? Who's going to run the countries? Stop them scratching each other's eyes out? It's either the Matabele wanting to dominate the Shona in Rhodesia or the Hindus arguing with the Muslims in India. If the British get out, who's going to keep the peace, build the railway lines and maintain the rule of law? Anyway, I'm not a politician or journalist. I always thought the Americans were our cousins, despite a few spats in the past. If King George the Second had spoken English and not German, America would likely still be part of the Commonwealth like Canada, Australia, New Zealand and South Africa. We're all English-speaking. All have Anglo-Saxon roots... There you are. That room is for Janet, Horatio and my namesake. That one is yours, William. Get out of those wet clothes before you catch a cold. You know where to hang the wet clothes. You can leave the pram where it is downstairs. Tina put all the paraphernalia for young Harry in your room, Janet. Cot, playpen, that sort of thing that we leave to the women. I'm off to change into dry clothes though I'm used to getting wet; in the Congo during my captivity we didn't have much to change into, though it was a lot warmer I suppose. Amazing how the past fades from the mind. My Tutsi friends seem a lifetime ago. I hope they are all all right and not started a war with the Hutu tribe with the guns I sent them in exchange for my freedom."

. . .

AN HOUR later Harry and his houseguests assembled in the drawing room. Everyone was wearing dry clothes, with Andre dressed in an old hacking jacket Tinus had left behind on a previous visit, giving Harry no surprise when he remembered the small size of Andre's suitcase. Tina and the children had not come back from the village. Young Harry, back in his pram, was the centre of attention while Harry went around serving his favourite South African sherry, something he knew would please Andre Cloete. Bergit had been formally introduced to the Wakefields after Horatio emotionally shook Klaus's hand.

"We were in two minds whether to call him Klaus or Harry," said Janet to Bergit, whose finger was being held firmly by young Harry as he glugged with pleasure at all the attention. "If this one is a boy," said Janet putting her hands on her extended belly, "we will call him Klaus, with your permission, Herr von Lieberman. If the child is a girl, Bergit, in honour of the wonderful help your husband gave my husband in those terrible circumstances to remind us all how lucky we are when we look back on life. I told him at the time to stay in England. People can do a lot of harm meddling in other people's business, though journalists never take that kind of advice. I am so happy to meet you both, you have no idea."

"Either way, Klaus or Bergit will be a great honour," said Klaus von Lieberman, bowing formally to Janet. "I propose a toast to the arrival of a healthy boy or a healthy girl. Harry was telling me you are a speech therapist specialising in curing the stutter. That you have an appointment to Harrow School. I have a cousin with a terrible stammer when he has to speak in public. He is General Werner von Lieberman's eldest son. Could you cure him, Mrs Wakefield?"

"Of course I can try. Stutters are in the mind as much as the cleft palate, which is mostly the cause of speech impediment. It is important to enunciate from the tip of the tongue. Can he speak English?"

"All well-educated Germans speak English. Henning spent a year at the London School of Economics after Heidelberg. Many an Englishman has attended our university at Heidelberg as a postgraduate. Germany and England have been leaders in education for centuries. I will speak to my cousin."

Watching the interchange of polite conversation, Harry was puzzled by the look that had hovered for a brief second in the eyes of his old friend when Klaus had suggested sending his cousin to England; the look was a mixture of cunning and relief. As if Klaus had found a way out of a corner. The look put Harry on his guard for the first time in the visit. 'There's always more than meets the eye,' he told himself wearily as he walked back to the small cocktail cabinet to pick up the bottle of sherry and fill up the glasses. If only Tina would live in Africa!... Outside on the gravel he heard the car coming back, followed by slammed car doors that made him grit his teeth. The children were shouting excitedly at each other, something they did most of the time; slamming car doors and yelling as loud as possible was at the top of their pleasures, however much he complained. Then he heard Tina's voice and smiled. Despite their problems it was always nice to have her home, to hear her voice; Harry liked being a family man.

"My wife's back," said Harry cheerfully, offering them the new bottle of sherry.

"One's enough for me if we're going for a hike," said Bergit, who still had her index finger gripped by the baby; the sight of the small child in the pram had made her broody for grandchildren, the sound of happy children outside music to her ears. Dogs were barking at the children. The cat on the sofa woke up and narrowed its eyes at the sound of the dogs. An elderly woman wearing an apron came into the room.

"I've put the lunch in three of the children's haversacks in the hall. Those who want must add sugar to the tea. Will that be all, Mr Brigandshaw? Mrs Brigandshaw is back with the children."

"Thank you, Mrs Craddock. Is it going to rain?"

"Not this afternoon. Mrs Brigandshaw says she will stay with the children and Beth will look after young Harry."

IT WAS MORE of a stroll than a hike with Tinus, Andre and William carrying the packs. On the surface everything looked normal to William, but underneath something was wrong. After years of finding out what was going on, it seemed to William that Herr von Lieberman had something to hide. In contrast to his wife the man was tense and uncomfortable, not the relaxed friend he was trying to portray to Harry Brigandshaw. Horatio, in William's opinion, had made an ass of himself grovelling to the man who had got him out of Germany as a favour to Harry Brigandshaw. The German's wife was relaxed but had William written a story of the two enemies becoming friends, he would have described the two men as walking on glass, as if both of them knew something was going to break; Germany and England were far too close to war for all the frivolous banter going on between the two men.

Mentally shrugging his shoulders, William trudged along next to Janet.

"Why would a German want to come to England to cure a stammer?" William said quietly in her ear.

"Polite conversation, William. Herr von Lieberman's way of putting me at ease."

"The man's a wolf in sheep's clothing."

"How can you say that after what he did for Horatio?"

"The uncle, General Werner von Lieberman, is a Nazi. His son is also in the party."

"You journalists always see the worst in people. Without that man up ahead my son would never have been born. You think Harry will be all right with Beth?"

"She's twelve years old and likes playing mother. Tina and Mrs Craddock will keep an eye on her. You worry too much, Janet. You shouldn't worry so much. What I find strange is those two men up ahead once chased each other round the sky firing machine guns at each other. Can bitter enemies ever be friends? If I were you, Janet, I'd think up other names for your baby than Klaus and Bergit. Once the child is christened it's stuck with the name for the rest of its life. My question is simple: why's he come to England all of a sudden? Or, more importantly, who told him to come?"

Harry Brigandshaw held back to give himself distance. Klaus was talking to Horatio. Nearer, Andre was telling Bergit all about South Africa where she had visited on her way through to Rhodesia on her honeymoon. William had been giving him queer looks which he ignored; all the man ever wanted to talk about was Genevieve. Tinus was out on a limb, not wishing or able to join Andre in his conversation with Bergit. Ever since his mother's letter from Elephant Walk, Harry had wanted to talk to his nephew at a time when they found themselves alone. The dogs were far out on the flanks, coursing the gentle slope of Headley Heath. Mrs Craddock had been right about the weather; the sun came in and out of the clouds. Far away towards Epsom Downs Harry could see the slant of a rain shower onto the race course. Then he watched Tinus break from the side of Andre, walking back down the hill towards him with a smile on his face.

"It's just so great to have Andre back in England," said Tinus as he turned in step with his uncle, the two of them walking slowly side by side away from the others.

"You're both lucky. I had a letter last week from my mother. Your grandmother says you have no plans to go home before you finish Oxford, that the farm is short of money with the slump in the price of tobacco, which is why I want you to go to Elephant Walk on your next vacation to write me a report. By now you should know what you are talking about. Good farming is one part of the equation; making a profit from the farm quite another. Tina won't let me go or I would do it myself. I will write to Ralph Madgwick and explain you are my envoy and that all of us are on the same side. For years I have thought of placing a major dam across the Mazoe River to give us irrigation water right across the farm and stop the risk of bad rains ruining the crops once and for all. I have an idea to grow thousands of acres of citrus, extracting the fruit juice for export back to England. Somewhere I read that people who make perfume use the oil in the peel of an orange as a base for some of their perfumes.

"I want a case study, Tinus. A feasibility study on whether we can make money out of oranges which will let us diversify out of tobacco, maize and cattle. You will have to look at both ends of the equation, there on the farm and here in England. You will have to price everything from what we will get for the exported crop to the cost of machinery imported from England and landed on the farm, the entire range of machinery and equipment to crush the oranges and extract the oil from the peel. I think what's left over in pulp can still be used by feeding it to the cattle, the beef frozen and the meat sent back to England; nothing must be wasted.

"In exchange for your hard work I will pay your return passage and your living expenses. Six weeks should be enough to get you out and back if you start your inquiries in England before you get on the boat. I want you to be my eyes. Tembo will help as much as Ralph Madgwick. If the dam is going to work financially I want to start as soon as possible. It will have to be a concrete and steel dam on the site Tembo will show you as an earth dam would break in the small gorge in the hills. It will have to be a narrow, high dam not a low long one where the river winds round the hills... Are you up to it, Tinus?"

"Sometimes I get so homesick for Africa it actually hurts."

"Don't I know the feeling. That's settled... Those dogs are enjoying themselves."

4

———

$\mathcal{W}$hile Tinus Oosthuizen was trying to work out how two years of economics equipped him to write the financial evaluation of a major project, concluding his Uncle Harry was using the dam project as an excuse to give him a holiday at home without having to appear magnanimous, twelve miles away at Redhill Aerodrome John Woodall, who had tested Tinus for his pilot's licence, was as excited as a small boy with his first cricket bat. They could hear the aircraft coming long before it came into sight, flying five hundred feet above the ground in level flight, the Rolls-Royce Merlin engine screaming.

Before the test flight every instrument in the cockpit had been double-checked with emphasis on the speedometer Harry Brigandshaw thought was faulty earlier in the week. The machine guns in the wings had been taken out, the portals closed while the armourers worked on the drawings for their replacements. At either end of the grass field a man stood next to a flagpole, the first with a stopwatch in his hands, while they waited for the plane to fly over the flagged poles.

John Woodall pointed as the man at the first flagpole started his stopwatch when the prototype Spitfire passed exactly overhead. The man at the top of the field stood next to his pole looking vertically at the sky where the plane would fly at maximum speed over his head. In his right hand held above his shoulder was a red flag he dropped at exactly the moment the Spitfire flew over his pole, while at the start of the measured half mile the first man stopped his watch with a sharp press on the button before jumping on a motorcycle which he raced up the grass runway towards the engineers waiting with John Woodall for the news; the man was riding the bike with one hand, waving the other over his head.

"It's got to be over three hundred," said John Woodall. "I must go and tell Harry the instruments were right after all."

"Taking the guns out helped," said the man next to him. "He's coming back again and lower. He's going to buzz the shed. The phones are out of order again, John. If you want to give Harry Brigandshaw the good news you'll have to use that lunatic's motorcycle. If he hits a bump he'll fall off and kill himself."

"Three hundred and twelve," the man was yelling as he skidded the BSA Blue Star motorcycle to a halt. "It's the fastest fighter in the world. Here he comes again."

"Can I borrow your motorcycle to go to Hastings Court?"

"You can take it to the moon, John. Those instruments were right. Even with four guns in each of the wings. Rolls-Royce can improve on the engine to get the same speed. The airframe is strong enough. Wouldn't the Germans like to know about this?"

Around them, everyone on the team was shaking hands as the Spitfire with the factory test pilot in the cockpit was coming round, this time to land.

"How soon can they get them into mass production?... I'll bring the bike back tomorrow, Tom."

"When you like. I'm going to get drunk in the bar with the rest of them. Say hello to Harry for me. The tank's full of petrol. Put on your flying jacket. It gets cold on the bike at high speed."

"When is the phone going to work again?"

"They promised to send someone out to the aerodrome on Monday."

WHEN JOHN WOODALL rode up the long driveway at Hastings Court half an hour later the only person to come out of the house to meet him was Anthony.

"When are you going to teach me to fly, Mr Woodall? Dad and the rest of the guests are up on the heath having a picnic. The grass is too wet to play tennis."

"When is your father coming back?"

"Not for ages. Cousin Tinus is with him and they talk. Only time Dad has a chance to talk about Africa. My mother hates Africa, though I don't mind. Did you know Tinus's father shot his first leopard when he was eleven? Or was it my grandfather? Can I ride your bike, Mr Woodall?"

"How old are you, Anthony?"

"Fourteen. I'll only ride on the estate where I don't need a licence."

"You fall off and burn your leg on the hot exhaust, your father will never speak to me again."

"Then can I have a ride on the pillion? Doesn't a bike like that go cross country? I'll take you up on the heath to find Dad."

"Do you know where they've gone?"

"Probably. You'll have hours to wait otherwise. Mother's in the house somewhere and Beth is looking after a baby. Why do girls like babies, Mr Woodall?"

"It's built into their maternal make-up."

"My sister must have a strong maternal make-up. She's been pushing the pram round the garden for hours talking to the baby who doesn't say a word."

"Hop on, which way do we go?"

"Down the path behind the house and through the trees. Do you want to tell mother you're here?"

"I have something very important to tell your father."

"You can drive round that side of the house," Anthony said, pointing his finger, "and past the sheds to pick up the path to the heath. Frank has rabbits in one of the sheds if you want to have a look. The buck rabbit is enormous. Frank breeds them for their meat. He likes dangling them headfirst by their hind legs and chopping them behind their ears with the side of his hand. One blow and the rabbit's dead. I can't even look when he does it with that look in his eye, let alone kill the poor things. They have beautiful big eyes and their noses twitch. The rabbits come from Belgium for some reason. English rabbits don't like to live in cages. They prefer burrows in the banks of the ten-acre field. I like the wild rabbits much better. Why do people like to kill rabbits?"

"We'll skip the rabbits, Anthony. Find your father for me quickly and next time you come to Redhill I'll take you up in the Tiger Moth."

"Is that a promise?"

"That's a promise, Anthony. Grab me round the waist and hold tight. I don't want you falling off if we have to ride some rough ground."

"What do you want to tell Dad?"

"It's a secret. A big secret."

"You can't tell me?"

"No I can't. Even the new King doesn't know."

"Why can't he speak properly over the radio?"

"He has a stammer, Anthony. An impediment in his speech. No one ever thought the Duke of York was going to be king so they did nothing about it."

With the boy pointing a finger in front of his nose, John Woodall rode the heavy motorbike round the house to the path that would lead them through the trees. The path was wet from the earlier rain, the big trees dripping occasional drops of water as they rode in under the canopy of green leaves.

THEY WERE SITTING on their raincoats, the warmth of the sun having made the party take them off to carry soon after they came out onto the heath, up the long bridle path from the old house. Someone in an earlier year had placed logs from fallen trees round in a witches' circle; with the raincoats on top, the big logs were more comfortable to sit on and drink tea than sitting on the wet grass.

Everyone had come together for the tea. The rain over the Epsom Downs racecourse had moved further away. There was a ring of strange stones inside the circle of tree trunks with a big flat stone in the middle for one person to sit on; the big stone was polished from years of people's bottoms like a river stone washed by the stream of water over centuries.

"There were druids in England long before the Christians," explained Harry. "I've never seen the coven as they come here on the full moon, according to Mrs Craddock. When I ask her about the stones she goes into a faraway look. I think the stones are courting stones and nothing to do with warlocks or witches. Mrs Craddock grew up around here. It's difficult now to see her as a pretty young girl full of sap, but she was once upon a time like everyone else.

"I like this spot. It speaks of happiness and friends to me from thousands of years ago. In those days the families stayed in the same spot for century after century, living in harmony with each other, the young ones coming here for trysts; or so I like to imagine. My grandfather told me stories of Hastings Court when I was growing up in Rhodesia; where he came after selling the Court to my grandfather Brigandshaw some people called the Pirate. England with the English Channel had been safe from invasion for centuries. The last time England was successfully invaded was when my Manderville ancestors came over with William the Conqueror in 1066, quickly blending into medieval England as they settled down. We never even tried to go back to Normandy, any one of us according to family history. I always feel at peace sitting here as if I am at home with myself, which I suppose I am as without those ancestors I wouldn't be sitting with you drinking this tea… Help yourselves to the sandwiches, if you would like. Mrs Craddock has made enough for an army."

At the sound of man, Harry stood up and cocked his ear to the wind.

"Can any of you hear a motorcycle?… It's coming our way. As my mother said, who was born right here, there's no peace for the wicked."

"It's Anthony," said Tinus. "And Mr Woodall from Redhill Aerodrome."

"What does he want here?" said Harry immediately on his guard. "Please stay where you are, everyone, and enjoy the peace. I'll go and find out what they want. Janet, pass round Mrs Craddock's sandwiches even if it is a bit early for lunch."

The motorbike was making steady progress up the slope towards the circle of fallen trees as Harry moved down towards them, walking fast. Fifty yards away the bike stalled after hitting a clump of grass that hid a small hillock the size of a football; Harry, from hours of walking on his own, knew every hillock on the heath.

"Mr Woodall has a secret for you, Dad, even the King doesn't know about," shouted his eldest son so loud Harry thought they would hear the news on Epsom Downs.

"Then he'd better whisper it in my ear, Anthony, or it won't be a secret. John knows how important good secrets can be. Have you come for a picnic lunch? There's enough for two more. I'll come and help you prop up the bike so it doesn't fall over and leak oil. How are you, John? Lovely surprise, I have my old friends here from Germany but we couldn't play tennis because of this morning's rain and here we are on the heath. Anthony must have known I'd bring them to the magic circle, as the children like to call it."

Harry had seen John Woodall's mouth open ready to shout the news Harry had been expecting on the telephone.

The mouth was closed tight as Harry reached the motorcycle, the announcement of friends from Germany having clouded John Woodall's face.

"What's the matter, Harry?"

"I don't trust him. William Smythe says his uncle and nephew are with the Nazis. I'm going to have a word with him. Just whisper to me, John, and then come and have lunch."

"I won't even whisper, Harry. But I'll tell you this: there's nothing wrong with the instruments."

"I don't even think his wife knows what he is up to. It's bad times a-coming, old friend. We'll need everything we can muster if the Americans don't help. William even thinks the Japs are in on the act now they've invaded China, attacking Peking and Shanghai. After the Japs sort out Chiang Kai-shek and his new reluctant communist allies, William thinks they'll turn on Hong Kong and Singapore. It's going to be even bigger than the last one."

"You really know how to take the wind out of a man's sail. I should have stayed and got drunk with the rest of them."

"That good, was it?"

"Rather, Harry. Even better. We'll be all right now, mark my words."

"Anthony, I want you to be a good chap and go and tell Mrs Craddock Mr Woodall is staying the night with us and to make up a room."

"Mr Woodall's going to take me up in the Tiger Moth for finding you so soon on the heath."

"Thank you, John. Anthony will enjoy the flight. Now be a good lad and run home with my message before Mrs Craddock takes her afternoon nap... Come and meet Herr von Lieberman, John."

"*The chap you shot down?*"

"The same one."

"I was about to shout my mouth off."

"I know you were."

There were never opportunities when he wanted them and Harry had to wait until the Sunday. His friend was going back to Germany the next day. Likely, Harry thought, there would never be another chance. Bergit and Tina were talking servants and children, a conversation Klaus and Harry both tried to avoid.

"Let's make a duck," said Harry quietly, making a face that Klaus understood; women talking women talk were best left alone. "There's not a child to be seen or heard. Why don't you and I walk to the Running Horses at Mickleham and have a pint of beer? Take us half an hour or so and it doesn't look like rain. The pub opens for two hours at lunchtime and Tina has nothing planned now the others have gone back to London and Tinus has taken a run in the Morgan with Andre."

"Was that Woodall man in the Flying Corps with you, Harry?"

"Not with me, Klaus," lied Harry. "He runs a flying school at Redhill Aerodrome where he's taken Anthony for a flip in his Tiger Moth. Tinus is going to pick him up after the flight. Now Anthony is a big lad it's going to be a tight squeeze, three in the Morgan."

Klaus von Lieberman looked around him as if seeking help.

"It's not going to rain, Klaus, if that's what you think. I have Mrs Craddock's word on it. You remember them talking about Genevieve last night; the famous actress? Her mother was once the barmaid at the Running Horses where she met my brother-in-law, Merlin St Clair. He's Lord St Clair now after his father died last year. Every time I've ever been there I found a pretty barmaid."

"Don't talk so loud, Harry. Bergit will hear."

"I'm whispering. Come on. Before those two natterers realise we've gone."

Like two small boys intent on playing truant they sidled away until they were out of sight round the house where they quickened their pace.

"Like sneaking out of Bishop's in Cape Town for a pint at the Foresters Arms, the oldest pub in South Africa. Let's get going before they find out they're on their own on the lawn. Do you remember those long walks we had alone in Rhodesia when we agreed how stupid it was to go to war? When we asked ourselves what all the slaughter in France had been about?"

"You want to talk, don't you, Harry?"

"Yes, I do. But not just now. There's a bench in the woods the Mandervilles have been sitting on for centuries. Not exactly the *same* wooden bench as they rot and have to be replaced, but always under the same oak tree. That's important. It's the kind of place good people should talk to each other. Do you know in the Congo the Tutsis had such a place? Some say man came out of Africa, which is why underneath it all we are exactly the same, however hard we try to be different. Every generation or so the Tutsis made peace with the Hutus at the very same spot. Every generation or so they forgot about peace and slaughtered each other. There's always someone in the pack who sees a way of making himself powerful by going to war. Among men he can always find a grievance to play upon. Right through the history of mankind evil men have found it easier to destroy than build. In Africa they have a saying: follow or lead or get the hell out of the way. You've been telling me to take my family and get out of the way. I will if you and your family come with me to Elephant Walk."

"I can't, Harry."

"Then tell me what the hell's going on. Why you suddenly wanted to pay me a visit."

"Let's first find that bench in the woods."

They walked in silence side by side through the trees until they reached the old oak tree with the largest girth in the county of Surrey. Underneath the spreading oak was an old wooden bench without a back. Around the bench, strewn on the green moss between half emerged gnarled roots, were old, dark brown acorns. The foliage of the tree was dense above the bench without any sign of dead branches. Harry suspected the owls had been asleep inside, waiting to come out and hunt in the dark of the night, and they were now wide awake and listening to intruders.

"Legend has it the first English Manderville planted the acorn that made this magnificent oak. A chap from Kew Gardens told me the tree was older than that, from the previous millennium. I asked him if the tree would live forever and he said it wouldn't, like everything else; one day it would die. I like the acorn from Normandy story better. We'd best sit down... Why did you come to England, Klaus? You have my word that whatever is said under this tree will never be repeated."

"When I went back to Bavaria after the war the family estate was bankrupt. No one had tilled the ground and when we did, there was no money in Germany to buy the crops we produced. You're a farmer, Harry, you'd know all about that. The tenants couldn't pay rent, and I couldn't pay the servants and tradesmen, and Germany was broke with France shouting for more reparations. Everyone who came back from the war was unable to find good jobs. Money became worthless. You needed a wheelbarrow full of Marks to buy a newspaper.

"It was about then I first heard of Adolf Hitler and his National Socialist Party. He was promising to put Germans back to work if the people put him in power; seductive words for a man with no job and no money to feed his family. The Allies were grinding Germany into the dust. I had thought when I came back from the war we would be all right in the country, but taxes had to be paid as well as salaries and tradesmen. No German bank would lend me money however crazy the interest rate, the inflation was so rampant; when the bank got back their Marks they would be worthless.

"My only hope was to borrow from an American bank in American dollars. I borrowed from a Jewish bank, Rosenzweigs if you have ever heard of them. By the time I had exhausted my dollar loan, Rosenzweigs owned the estate by default. Germany was worse off then than before and I went to see Uncle Werner, my dead father's younger brother who had been in the German army most of his life. After that visit I never again heard from Rosenzweigs. By way of thanks, my uncle, a staunch member of the Party, intimated I join the Nazi Party, what he called the only salvation for Germany. Well, we Germans hadn't been going anywhere under von Hindenburg.

"At that point you just hope the new is better than the old and turn a blind eye when the new government does things you don't like. The Nazis say the Jews were to blame, and any of them who could were getting out of Germany, despite being Germans for centuries. Young boys like my son Erwin have been taught the Jews are evil money lenders, and a blight on society that needs eradicating. There's a Nazi Youth Party that puts the young boys in uniform and makes them part of the pack. Erwin's summer camp is Hitler Youth. Erwin thinks more of the Party than his parents, and will do exactly what they say. Any boy who behaves otherwise is ostracised or sent to the camp at Dachau where they threatened to send me and my family if I did not come to England. I was to listen. To pick up information for the German Secret Service... Harry, what does a man do when he loses his honour? If you mention any of this we are all dead."

"Has Cousin Henning a stammer?"

"As a matter of fact, he has. Go to Africa, Harry."

"Come with us."

"I can't. They'll kill Erwin. Anyway, they'll never let us all out of the country now they've made me work for the Party."

"Does Bergit know why you are here in England?"

"Of course not. It's the only piece of my pride I have left."

"And you are going to tell them about RAF Poling?"

"You knew on Friday why I came?"

"I work for the British Air Ministry, Klaus. It's why they sent you."

"What do we do?"

"Nothing. This conversation never happened and you forget that radar mast near Poling. And if you do manage to reach Rhodesia, where you will always be welcome, you will meet Sir Jacob Rosenzweig's estranged daughter, Rebecca. So yes, I have heard of Rosenzweigs. She's married to my farm manager, Ralph Madgwick. Why did Sir Jacob forgive your loan?"

"He's been getting Jews out of Germany to America. When I asked Uncle Werner point blank he said the transaction was quite fair. The cancellation of my mortgage in exchange for travel papers. The estate was worth one hundred and sixteen Jews to Sir Jacob Rosenzweig."

"They say he's quite a man. My bet is the write-off of your mortgage will look small against what he makes out of those Jews. Maybe Rosenzweig and your Uncle Werner are shrewder than you think."

"My God, do you think so, Harry? Somehow I'm going to pay back Rosenzweigs. After the war, if it happens. Growing up, Uncle Werner never struck me as anything but a gentleman from the old school."

"You think we're going to fight each other again?"

"I'm afraid we are."

"You are still a gentleman, Klaus. Whatever happens now I will never forget that. Let's go to the Running Horses. It may be the last time we can enjoy each other's company, old friend, before our two nations go again at each other's throats in a new frenzy of destruction."

"All that wasted energy."

For five more minutes they sat in silence on the old bench deep in their own thoughts, their minds roaming back over their lives, avoiding the present. Harry could hear a pigeon calling somewhere in the woods to be answered from far away, the birds calling to each other intermittently, neither flying to the other. Small white butterflies flitted in the blossoms of the wild flowers growing away from the shade of the big oak under which only the thick, green moss thrived.

"My mother came here when she brought her father back from Rhodesia to Hastings Court for burial: once she brought me with her. It was the strangest conversation I ever had with my mother."

Again they lapsed into a comfortable silence as his mother's words played again through Harry's mind.

"Don't you feel something special, Harry?"

"I feel at peace with the world."

"This is where it all began. The long journey of my life through Africa, something neither of us knew anything about at the time. I was sixteen, your father seventeen. We had loved each other in a different way most of our lives, only here knowing it was the love of a man for a woman, a woman for a man. So small a deed at the time. So beautiful. So vast in the consequence. Now father is back in his ancient home, beneath the same earth as his ancestors. That much I owed him for all the pain of exile."

"Grandfather loved Rhodesia!"

"He loved me, you and Madge and all your children. But this was his home and losing it was all the fault of me and your father loving each other too much; thinking only of ourselves, being selfish... Anyway, he's home and buried. I hope at peace. Your grandfather was a very lovely man. He built the windmills to bring water from the Mazoe River and give us all constant running water in the houses."

"He fulfilled his life on Elephant Walk."

"It was here he loved my mother. Here were his memories of love... Right here at this very spot were my first memories of love."

"What are you saying, Mother?"

"That under this old spreading oak your father and I declared our love for each other, my darling, and because of that our family odyssey began through Africa. Don't blush, Harry. You're too old to blush. You are a child of pure love. Be thankful. I always think it is why you have always been a good person."

"Mothers and sons don't talk about such things."

"Then they should."

WHEN THEY REACHED the Running Horses the Morgan was parked outside and Anthony was sitting on a bench with his back to the wall looking pleased with himself.

"The price I paid for the ride home. They're inside. Something about a new barmaid. What is it about barmaids, Dad?"

"I suppose it won't be long before you find out, Son. I hope that's lemonade in your glass. How was your flight?"

"Brilliant, Dad. And so much fun at Redhill."

"Indeed, I'm sure. How long have they been inside?"

"Ten minutes. Can I have a shandy?"

"You can have another glass of lemonade. How did you all fit in the car?"

"I sat on the back of the seat with my legs between Andre and Tinus, holding on for dear life."

"Don't let your mother hear about it, or Frank for that matter. He'll tell her just to get you into trouble."

"Did you two walk?"

"All the way. Your mother and Mrs von Lieberman are having a natter. You all right out here?"

"They won't let me inside until I'm eighteen."

"I should think not. Just don't fall off the back of the Morgan on the last leg of the journey home."

"Andre was hanging onto my left foot."

"He always was a practical soul."

BOTH ANDRE and Tinus were leaning over the bar to be as near to the barmaid as possible, or so it seemed to Harry; the girl was very young, her complexion in full bloom. As usual on a Sunday, in the bar were middle-aged men having a pint before going back for their Sunday lunch and an afternoon nap after eating too much of the roast at the family lunch table.

"She is pretty," whispered Klaus who had not broached the subject of his conscience again after getting up from the bench under the tree; both knew neither was going to talk about the subject again.

"Nothing ever changes in this bar," said Harry smiling. "Sunday tradition. The wives let them out for a couple of pints while they cook the Sunday lunch. We then all stuff ourselves and complain of overeating... As to be expected. Look at them. They're talking cricket and ogling the girl... What's her name, Tinus?"

"Uncle Harry! Didn't see the car when I looked to make sure Anthony was sitting on the bench."

"We walked. Order me two pints of bitter."

"Millicent," said Andre.

"That's a nice name. Millicent, give me two pints of bitter and whatever these lads are drinking and a lemonade for my son outside."

"On a week day I'd let him in the bar."

"Not until he's eighteen, Millicent, and that's a long time to go."

When the girl had gone to the middle of the bar to pull the new pints of beer, Harry leaned close to Tinus who was now standing with his back to the bar, one foot up on the brass rail as if he owned the place.

"Wasn't the first one's name Minnie?" asked Harry sweetly.

"You have too good a memory, Uncle Harry."

"What happened to Minnie, Tinus?"

"She married some chap. Like they all do. A chap who came down from Liverpool for the races."

"Lucky girl. Hope she's happy."

"Went back with him to Liverpool."

"Don't put your nose in the air about the foreigners up north. Fact is, we Brigandshaws came from Liverpool. Where the Pirate first learnt his trade. Inside of you is a small part of Liverpool... Drive slowly when you come back after the beers."

"How can I find out the cost of building a concrete dam?"

"I have the measurements of the gorge at home. The height and distance. There's a civil engineer in Birmingham and another in Coventry who can give you a rough estimate. I'll hand you all the correspondence I've had so far."

"I'm driving up to Oxford at first light tomorrow."

"Then we have plenty of time. Now you can turn round again and smile at Millicent, or has Andre got the edge this time?"

5

*T*heir conversation had gone on for an hour before either of them missed their husbands. It was easier for Tina to feel comfortable with a foreigner. Aristocratic wives who came to Hastings Court to enjoy the free hospitality always had their noses in the air when they talked to her, as if there was a small joke in the back of their heads as they condescended to talk to a woman, seemingly as an equal, whose mother and father were at the bottom rung of the working class living in a railway cottage, the father carrying suitcases for the rich. To Bergit von Lieberman she was Harry Brigandshaw's wife and that was good enough to let them become friends.

COMPLAINING to each other about the problems with servants had made the time fly and temporarily removed some of the worry from Bergit's mind. She had been the first to realise Klaus and Harry had gone missing. Now it felt again like the lull before the storm, that something bad was about to happen even before they returned home to Germany. Though she gave the impression her English was fluent she had to concentrate all the time, translating sentences from German into good English. The tension deep in her body was back on the surface, jangling her nerves.

"It's all so peaceful," she said. "There are terrible things about to happen in the world and here it is all so peaceful."

"Why shouldn't it be?" asked Tina, who never read the newspapers, saying they just made her worry about events she could do nothing about.

"You don't live in the new Germany under a Fuehrer," said Bergit bitterly. "Why don't you go and live in Africa? Far away from trouble."

"There's no trouble at Hastings Court. I prefer living surrounded by my own people. You forget Harry was a prisoner to a tribe of black savages. We nearly lost everything. Then I would have had to go and live in Africa. Now we have our money back from the government, I don't. I was going to be a poor widow living off the charity of my mother-in-law who is an aristocrat. Maybe I should have told you, my own family are working class. Here I am Lady of the Manor and that's how it's going to stay. Have you any idea what it's like to be poor? Some of them may look down their noses at me, but few of them have our money. Money is power, Bergit. I like it. It makes me feel safe. I have the children's future to think about. There's more to life than growing tobacco or running around the African bush with an elephant gun wearing a big hat. Tinus understands.

"He's getting himself a degree in economics. Going into business to make real money, not own an African farm. How long do you think those blacks are going to want us English running their country? A handful of Englishmen running a country the size of the British Isles. It's a fool's paradise where the sun shines too much and shrivels up the skin. Harry's family have been in these parts for nine hundred years. Harry wasn't even born in Africa, let alone his father; Harry was born right here at Hastings Court. They call themselves Rhodesians. They're Englishmen hiding under those big hats playing big white hunters. If our countries are going to war again for some obscene reason, so be it. We've done it all before, though usually we English fight beside you Germans against the French, if that makes any difference to war. You never know, maybe one day we Europeans will come to our senses and support each other instead of killing each other; and when we do, I want my children part of it, not part of some tin-pot country in Africa. Don't you miss your children, Bergit?"

"All the time."

They looked away from each other, both remembering what their lives were really all about.

"I hear a car," said Tina, breaking the momentary silence. "Sounds like the Morgan. I'll bet they've all been to the pub. If Anthony has been perched on the back of the car seat I'll skin him alive. Why do we never stop worrying about our children?"

"Because they are all we have to leave behind in the world. They are our immortality. The only way we survive, unless you believe in going to heaven. Klaus says heaven, if it exists, is a lonely place. That inside all of us is too much evil just waiting to get out."

"Don't you believe in the Bible? God's creation of man?"

"Darwin's theory of evolution knocked that into a cocked hat, if that is the right British expression. If God created the world six thousand years ago, how come the dinosaurs became extinct sixty-five million years earlier? I'm agnostic: I don't know. If there is a god in heaven he doesn't much care what we do to each other, quite often in his name. You only have to live through a war and its aftermath to have little faith. Look at the Russians after the war and their own civil war. Communism threw religion out the window. Maybe one day they'll believe again, when communism proves worse than what they had before. No one has found the perfect way to run society and no one ever will; too many conflicting interests."

"Come and have a cup of tea. I'll bet Harry thinks we've been talking trivia."

Avoiding his mother and the inevitable inquisition, Anthony went to see Mrs Craddock and find out how near it was to lunch; he was starving, having eaten his breakfast what seemed to him hours ago.

"In the conservatory today, Anthony. Among the plants and flowers. In my opinion it is going to rain at half past two when your lunch will be ready. And keep your paws off that trifle or I'll have more to say than words."

"What are you roasting in the oven?"

"Chicken."

"How many?"

"Two."

"Will that be enough? I'm starving."

"Out you go, Anthony. Now!"

"Smells absolutely delicious. Did I ever tell you, you are the best cook in the whole wide world."

"Every time when you are hungry."

. . .

HALF AN HOUR later Harry came across his wife as they all ran into the conservatory out of the rain. He and Klaus were laughing, having bolted the last fifty yards back from the Running Horses to keep from getting wet.

"You two have a good natter? Thought we'd leave you alone. Do you know, if they didn't close the pub at two o'clock none of those people would eat their Sunday lunch? Best law we ever made. The men get a good lunch, a good sleep and no hangover. The whole family sitting round the lunch table is the most important gathering in the world... So, what were you two talking about? Servants and children?"

"Actually religion and the terrible state of the world," said Tina. "Something you men would not understand further than what you were taught at school."

"Bishops was a very good school. Run by the church."

"That's exactly my point. Do you know Mrs Craddock laid lunch in here knowing it was going to rain? How does she always know?"

"What's for lunch?"

"Roast chicken, Dad," said Anthony, taking his place at the improvised lunch table, fork and knife in his hands on the table held vertical. "Only two of them. I hope there'll be enough for you."

"They are big birds, darling," said his mother. "Very big. Now put down the knife and fork and wait for lunch like the rest of us."

"I tried to have a look inside the oven."

"You didn't perch on the seat did you, Anthony?"

"Of course not, Mother. Andre's in love with the new barmaid. Her name's Millicent. Talked about her all the way home."

"Tinus did not drive fast?" Harry asked Anthony.

"Like a snail. Boring. I counted ten rabbits in the ten acres when we drove by."

"So you were perched on the back of the seat," said Tina.

"Mum, why do you always worry?... Tinus and Andre have gone with Frank to look at his rabbits."

THE NEXT MORNING Tinus Oosthuizen was the first to leave Hastings Court. His Uncle Harry was going to drive the Germans to Croydon Airport and their flight back to Germany later in the morning. Andre was staying, waiting for his rail pass up to London and what he told Tinus was going to be a brilliant career in the RAF, if he could stop himself hurling up before every flight. They agreed they were going to see lots of each other, which was reassuring for both of them.

"I think he's a spy," Andre had said when they shook hands to say goodbye the previous night in Andre's room. "He's asked me twice what I will be flying when I join the RAF. Your uncle gave him a queer look a couple of times before they went drinking in the Running Horses. Then they were quite chummy... Don't forget to get a hundred against Cambridge."

"Good to see you again, Andre."

"Me too."

The first blush of dawn was barely showing Tinus the shape of the trees outside his window as he buttoned up his shirt. His suitcase was packed for his return to Oxford. Twice in the night when he woke, Tinus had heard the owls hooting in the moonlight which shone over the end of his bed; when he had a journey to take the next day Tinus never slept properly, never sinking into deep sleep all night. There was something agitating about a journey whenever he was going.

As he pulled on his trousers and buttoned himself up he knew there was one last task for him to perform at Hastings Court.

The corridor outside his room was pitch-dark. No one ever left the electric lights on at night at the Court. Putting on the lights would throw a beam under the bedroom doors and wake people. Feeling his way carrying his suitcase, Tinus began walking down the old corridors, trying not to make the floorboards creak.

Downstairs he left through the front door. His feet crunched on the gravel where the new dawn showed him the green Morgan all on its own, waiting for him to get in and start the engine. Tinus opened the passenger door and put the suitcase on the near seat. Then he walked away with the birds singing their dawn chorus all around him from the bushes and the trees, most of the calls still foreign to him. On the farm in Rhodesia Tinus knew every bird and animal by its call, the variety far greater than he ever heard in England.

An animal barked from far away, one clear bark in the quiet early morning: to Tinus, the sound of a bush buck not a dog. A dog always repeated the bark many times, sometimes all night, something Tinus had understood as a child living on the farm in Rhodesia.

"Probably an old fox," he said to himself, walking down the last path through the yew trees to the ancient burial ground of the Mandervilles. Tinus wanted to say hello to his great-grandfather Manderville, who had been so important to him during his growing up years on Elephant Walk; especially after his father was shot dead.

"So much wisdom, Grandfather. So much you said to me still sounds in my head, saving me problems, giving me advice even though you are dead."

The new grave had been easy to find among his other ancestors, some sunk so low in the ground the gravestones were only inches above the grass and weeds. Some, Tinus suspected, had gone down forever below the surface. The very old graves of men and women long gone from this earth, without whom he knew he could never have found life.

It was strange and comforting to be among the graves of his ancestors, only knowing one of their lives, trying to imagine them love and laugh, play and call as children, grow old and grey and finally, exhausted, go to earth.

"What of those buried far away?" he said to himself. "Grandfather Sebastian killed by the Great Elephant, buried in Africa. All part of my tangled life, of what I am to give my children."

Head bowed in front of the new grave and headstone, Tinus paid his respects for a long time as the light of day found its way between the trees, searching out the graves of the Mandervilles.

Then Tinus went quickly, light of heart, feeling proud as he walked back up the path. At the car he opened the driver's door of the Morgan, got in and began the drive to Oxford, leaving the old house behind, still asleep, yet to wake to the new day and the parting of so many ways.

HARRY BRIGANDSHAW DROVE the car into Whitehall just before lunch. He had seen off the von Liebermans at Croydon Airport a few miles south. All of them wondered if they would ever see each other again, leaving Harry sad and silent as the twin-engine aircraft lifted into the air. Losing good friends, he told himself, was far easier than making them.

The receptionist at the Air Ministry gave him a look of inquiry as he passed the desk on the way to his small office down the far end of the corridor.

"You have a visitor, Colonel Brigandshaw. He's been waiting a long time."

"Had to go to the airport."

Most of the ranks used at the Air Ministry were the new titles adopted by the Royal Air Force after the war when it morphed from the

Royal Flying Corps; the RFC had used army ranks and worn Crown uniforms. Harry thought he was the only airman in the building they still called a colonel. In the new way he would have been a group captain, which to Harry did not seem quite right. Maybe, as he said to himself, the new generation of flyers like Andre and Tinus would be familiar with the new ranks; in the meantime he was Colonel Brigandshaw, Royal Flying Corps, Retired.

Seeing Timothy Kent in his office staring out the window over Horse Guards Parade came as no surprise. Harry had been expecting him, if not so quickly. When the man turned round and saw Harry he looked agitated. The door had been left open as if to hurry Harry up.

"Sorry to keep you waiting, Tim. Not that I knew you were coming. Had to drop von Lieberman and his wife at Croydon Airport."

"So they've gone?"

"Flew away up into the air. I waved to them."

"It's not the uncle we worry about. The cousin is an out and out Nazi."

"Cousin Henning has a stutter."

"How do you know, Harry?"

"Sit down, Tim. You're making me nervous. Nothing is ever quite what it looks to be. I gave him Poling so we shall see if and when hostilities break out. At the end of the visit Klaus gave me his word of honour he would not divulge the information, so we shall see. Luckily the mast is well away from the bunker with the radar screens and the airmen. That much I did not tell him."

"He had no idea you were testing him from the start?"

"At the start I did not even believe you, Tim. You chaps think there is an enemy agent behind every door. Hence the slogan you have hatched up in event of war: 'walls have ears'. Not very original."

"Is he an enemy agent?"

"Probably. Probably not. How the hell do I know? I'm a farmer from Africa where we don't find enemy agents behind doors, or behind bushes."

"Harry, it's serious. Information during wartime is the most important asset. If you know what the other bugger is up to you can do something about it. MI6 may not be glamorous but it can win or lose a war. I want to know everything he said."

"I gave him my word I would keep my mouth shut."

"I can make it an order."

"Then go to hell. They may call me colonel at the desk but I left the Royal Flying Corps at the end of 1918 and went home far away, which Klaus suggests is a good idea for me and my family right now. You know, Tim, if Rhodesia ever got into trouble and wanted help, do you think England would come to our aid like we did in 1914?"

"It's a colony for goodness sake. Anyway, you're English. You were born right here along with your family back into antiquity."

"We are a self-governing colony in control of our own police and military."

"Harry, don't let's argue. What did he say?"

"The one bit I will tell you. Uncle Werner saved the lives of one hundred and sixteen Jews. So make that one out. Now I have a favour to ask you. A friend of my nephew wants to join the RAF."

"Why?"

"Probably because he doesn't have anything better to do. I suggested it. He's South African, a Boer, Rhodes Scholar to Oxford. Scored a century against Cambridge last year. Top class rugby player. Can you get him into officer training school for me? An Air Ministry interview? A rail pass from Leatherhead to Waterloo? He's staying with us at Hastings Court."

"Can he fly?"

"Yes, he can. Rather well, according to my nephew. Just one problem. He hurls before every flight and doesn't like heights. I need the rail pass today."

"So you won't tell me anything?"

"Not a word."

"What's his name?"

"Andre Cloete. I'll write it down."

"We need as many pilots as we can get."

"I know you do. So now may I do some work? I'm late into the office as it is."

NOT FAR DOWN THE road in Fleet Street Bruno Kannberg was having his own problems with authority. In the morning when he went into the office and made some routine phone calls to government departments, looking for confirmation or denial on a story he was writing for the *Daily Mirror* on the number of air raid shelters in London (Bruno's research had not come up with one, other than the underground train network that was one large air raid shelter if they turned off the electric power to the rails), it was as if every door was slammed shut in his face. No one would talk to him.

By the time Harry Brigandshaw ate the sandwiches made for him by Mrs Craddock for his lunch, Bruno had phoned every publisher holding a copy of his book on the King Edward abdication that claimed the reason for the King stepping down in favour of his brother George had more to do with the former Prince of Wales's clique being inclined to fascism as a better alternative to communism, rather than his love for Mrs Simpson and his desire to be with the woman he loved. Suddenly no one wanted to touch Bruno's book or even talk to him.

By three o'clock in the afternoon he was standing in Arthur Bumley's office facing reality and the smirk on his editor's face.

"Farting against thunder, Kannberg. Go back to your office. Phone all those publishers you told me had yet to see your manuscript and by tomorrow lunchtime, everything will seem back to normal if you withdraw your book from publication. You have stirred the proverbial shit and likely stumbled on some truth that would gladden Adolf Hitler's heart. Some minor cover-ups through history have been for the greater good. Dear oh dear, can we believe all we are told? Whatever; the King abdicated and poor brother George has the job, luckily with a woman who makes by far a better queen than a now thrice-married American, however many laughs it might have given Roosevelt, the man of the people, the man with the New Deal. He's out, Bruno, not Roosevelt, the real or unreal threat eliminated from the body politic and everyone else gets on with the job. I also had a phone call from our own esteemed publisher. Dump your book, Kannberg, or the *Mirror* dumps you."

"Whatever happened to the freedom of the press?"

"You should know better than to believe in that bit of fiction. It's only a free press when those with real power want it to be. There are many ways to stop an unpleasant story. We are mere puppets, Kannberg. We do what we are told whether we like it or not. Be grateful for what you made out of the true and unabridged story of Genevieve. Don't be greedy. How are you enjoying marriage? I'll bet when it comes to your wife you do what you're told. Now off you go and make those phone calls. By the by, I still think it's a damn good book. It's all timing. Your timing was lousy. Even America hates fascists. I want that air raid shelter story by lunchtime tomorrow. That'll sell newspapers. Frighten the holy shit out of them when they find out there's nowhere to hide, which in turn will make Mr Chamberlain and his government pull out its collective finger. And that's called the power of the fourth estate, the power to rally the people. You can call it your revenge."

"I thought the government was doing a cover-up or ignoring the threat?"

"No, they want you to scratch their arse. Now bugger off."

"I get less now I'm married than before."

"Don't cry to me. I warned you of women's cunning. It's the only power they've got. Ask Mrs Simpson, though my guess is she said he wouldn't get it unless he married her. Throughout history the power of women has trumped many a king and once launched a thousand ships."

"Thank you, Mr Bumley."

"My pleasure to help. Just close the door behind you."

Back in his office Bruno Kannberg dropped the original manuscript of *The Abdication of King Edward* in the waste paper basket, went downstairs and hailed a growler taxi that passed down the street at exactly the right moment.

"Covent Garden," he told the driver.

For some reason beyond Bruno's logical comprehension, the pubs in the Covent Garden produce market were open for twenty-four hours of the day. Coupled with Gillian keeping him short now they were married and living in a two-room flat on the Edgware Road, and the dumping of his latest fortune in the waste basket, Bruno needed a drink. More than one drink. The book publishers could find out from someone else. By the end of the day everything would be back to normal without his help. Arthur Bumley would have seen to that. Like everyone else in the world they, whoever 'they' were, could make or break him; once again in his life the power was in someone else's hands.

By THE TIME Bruno submitted his scathing article on government ineptitude a day late, Andre Cloete was looking through the wide-open door into the Air Ministry interview room, his one small suitcase left behind the chair at reception. The three men behind the long desk were in blue uniforms, their peaked caps facing Andre on the table. The rail pass had paid for his railway ticket up to London for the interview, his last two and sixpence still safely in his pocket. To Andre it was clear Harry Brigandshaw knew the right people.

After ten minutes of inconsequential conversation, the man who

Andre later found out held the rank of air commodore, and was the President of the Selection Board, asked Andre when he would like to join the Air Force. It was clear they had made up their mind before he walked into the room.

"As soon as possible, sir."

"Well, of course you won't fly for the first three months. We're sending you to RAF Cranfield to an officer training course where you'll learn what it is to be a British officer. There's more to being an officer than flying an aeroplane, Cloete, especially if we give you a posting to one of our far-flung colonies. A chap has to know how to behave himself in the mess, you'll understand. After that we'll post you to flying training at RAF Boscombe Down near Middle Wallop. Boscombe Down is a bomber station but that's not the end of it. Your flying skills will be assessed there before the Air Force decide whether you go to Fighter Command, Bomber Command, Coastal Command, or heaven's sake, Transport Command. Your call-up papers will be sent to you at Hastings Court within the next few days. There is paperwork you must understand. You will not be the only recruit. Welcome to the Royal Air Force, Mr Cloete. And congratulations on your hundred against Cambridge last year. Fact is, the RAF have a jolly good cricket side. We play the army at the end of the season. You'll be a great asset to our batting. Good day to you, young man."

With his feet a few inches above the carpet, Andre left the interview room, his future decided for him. The same receptionist who, unbeknown to Andre had scowled at Harry Brigandshaw's lateness on the Monday, smiled sweetly at him as he retrieved his worldly possessions from behind the chair. Andre smiled back at her. Neither of them said a word. Even the girl at the desk had known he was in before he arrived, before any of them had had a chance to look at him.

'Just don't get a duck against the army,' he said to himself as he began the walk down Whitehall on his way to Waterloo Station, the two and sixpence still safely in his pocket. Thinking of phoning Tinus at Mrs Witherspoon's the moment he reached Hastings Court, Andre Cloete found himself whistling as he jangled the coins in his pocket.

PART 8

A MEANS TO AN END — DECEMBER 1937

1

---

*S*ix days before Christmas, Genevieve stood at the door of her father's Park Lane flat and rang the bell. She had slipped past the 'new' doorman Hughes, who had been in his post since 1922, even her father having forgotten the original doorman's name; she wanted to surprise Smithers. Outside in Hyde Park an inch of wet snow lay on the pathways as the day came to its close. After California, the cold and slush was miserable and her hands were cold despite tucking them inside her fur muff until the last moment. Pulling her right hand back inside the comparative warmth of the muff, she waited patiently for Smithers to answer the door.

The taxi from her mother's flat in Chelsea had been icy cold, something wrong with the heater which she only found out once the cab was on its way. Her mother, on a drunk, had been impossible; three days of trying to make sense of her mother's life had sent Genevieve, looking for shelter, to the flat her father kept up for his rare visits to London. After the audition, Genevieve was going down to Dorset by train to spend Christmas with her father and grandmother.

"Miss Genevieve! I'll be blowed. What a lovely beautiful surprise. Will you be staying with us? I haven't seen your father for months."

Inside the flat with the door closed it was warm. Smithers, like her mother, was drunk; the man pulled himself up straight and led the way into the lounge with its bay window looking across the road into the park, his back straight, his body leaning at a slight angle.

"Can I bring you a drink?"

"Why not bring your bottle in here and have another one with me?" she giggled.

"It's very lonely week after week on my own. Nothing to do. No one to look after. I don't really have any friends. Being a gentleman's gentleman doesn't bring me into contact with many people. I shall be most obliged to bring my whisky bottle, though in all honesty the bottle more rightly belongs to Lord St Clair. Drinking alone is a terrible habit, but what else can I do? I don't like the country and someone must look after the flat."

"The bottle, Smithers. It's cold outside. Can you make me up a room?"

When Smithers came back with the bottle of whisky on a silver tray with two glasses, she realised the advantage of having a barmaid for a mother that the whole world knew about. A bastard with a Lord for a father was suspended somewhere between the aristocracy and the working classes with none of the advantages or disadvantages of either.

"Your overnight case is in your usual room," said Smithers formally.

"Now sit down and tell me what's been happening in England."

Surprisingly, Smithers sat down comfortably in her father's armchair without a blink, pouring the drinks where he sat.

"Don't you know? We're preparing to go to war while kidding ourselves nothing bad is going to happen. Rather like Sir Francis Drake playing his game of bowls in sight of the sails of the Spanish Armada."

"I have a friend who is a journalist. I'd better give him a ring. First a drink to welcome me home. How is my father?"

"The strangest part of it all. Lord St Clair has grown fond of his late father's pigs. The cows, he tells me, talk to him. He is again riding a horse. Your father is now a man of the country as if London and this flat never existed. I'm too old to look after another man; every man has different habits a valet has to know by instinct to perform his job properly. Now, why are you in London, if I may ask without sounding impertinent?"

"It's Christmas. I have an audition for a London production and I'm tired of making films. *Keeper of the Legend* is finished, in the can as they say in America, making me an out of work actress. Films are made up of thousands upon thousands of bits the editors make into the film you see on the screen. Most of making a film is made up of waiting around. I want to go on the stage where from the opening curtain you stay in the part, not drink coffee and tea in the middle as yourself. A play is satisfying. You have an audience who reacts. You never know what people think of your film part until you read it in the paper. My Uncle Robert says it was like writing the book; he was never there to feel the reader's reaction, or hear him laugh. People on a film set do their jobs and rarely interact except to pretend they are having a wonderful time getting rich... Cheers, Smithers."

"Your very good health, Miss Genevieve. And welcome home. Do you have the phone number of your journalist friend or shall I look it up in the book?"

"He may not even be in England."

The contrast for Genevieve was overwhelming; from the chaos and noise of making a film, to the silent flat trying to cheer up an old and faithful servant her father had abandoned. She rarely drank anymore, neither liking the taste nor losing her control. Louis Casimir, who still called himself by his American name of Gerry Hollingsworth, drank through the day now he was living with his wife, his hands off the young girls prepared to do anything to get into films. Living in his house on the beach with so many people was like living on the film set all day long, not a moment to herself to be herself, to be normal. Always someone to impress. Always avoiding the looks of lechery.

No one wanted to know Genevieve, they just wanted to take her to bed. And this included some of the women in the industry, the women with power who were too old to attract a new husband or a handsome young boy they didn't have to buy, and had taken to relieving their frustration on pretty young girls flitting around the fringe of the limelight. There was a feeling of desperation among all of them, men and women, from stars like Gregory L'Amour, who in the end had given up trying his luck with her, to fat, bald-headed men like Mr Hollingsworth, who still gave her that look of longing, as if the only way he could satisfy his life was by making her his mistress; his star, whose father held one of the oldest titles in England, something Hollywood was only able to manufacture on screen.

The film industry had opened her eyes far too wide and what she saw she did not like. Everyone wanted something more. No one was satisfied with what they had; the wife, the car, the house, even the dress they were wearing. All those people milling around all day and night had made her grow up too fast. She'd tasted everything life had to give in a headlong rush and had ended up hollow, wondering what would give her satisfaction, the kind of satisfaction she knew people without such a high opinion of themselves found with each other in a family; a family that cherished each other instead of using each other for what they could get.

Looking at Smithers's watery eyes regarding her with so much genuine pleasure, she knew he was a better person than the rest of them put together; the man wanted her company to enjoy his drink, not her body, her fame or her new-found money.

"Do you know, Smithers, I don't drink very much but I think I'll have another one."

And there they were, she thought. A girl with a first name only. A man with a last name only. If she asked her father, Genevieve was sure he would have no idea of Smithers's first name. Maybe Smithers's mother had known long, long ago.

THE AUDITION the next day was a disaster. The play, *Private Lives*, was set in Paris in 1930, written by Noël Coward.

She was to play the part of Amanda, a divorcee who smoked cigarettes through a foot-long cigarette holder. Genevieve, trying to get into the part, had brought along the thin black holder for the audition. When her nerves made her hands shake, the lighted cigarette dropped from the end of the vibrating holder into her bag resting on her knees. Carrying on with the lines she had learnt on the aircraft that flew her to England from America, Genevieve had snapped shut the handbag and hoped for the best, the eyes of the character playing opposite bulging with dread, expecting the sight of smoke any moment from the bag. Her rendering of the part after that was appalling.

"You were just wonderful, Genevieve," the director gushed when it was over, Genevieve not daring to look inside the bag. "You will be wonderful at the Savoy Theatre."

Afterwards when she opened the bag the cigarette had gone out, starved for oxygen, her paper money quite safe. Convinced they wanted a big name, not a good actress, Genevieve took a taxi to Waterloo Station where she waited for her train to Dorset. Smithers had fussed over her so much she had not wanted to say goodbye a second time and had gone to the audition with her overnight case, the rest of her luggage still waiting for her at the left-luggage office.

When the train came in two hours later, she left the warmth of the coal fire in the waiting room and found her platform in the freezing cold. She had a first class ticket. Her compartment was warm. For the first time since leaving America she was able to relax, nothing to do now but listen to the rhythm of the train as it pulled out of the station and gathered speed.

Puffing through the countryside after leaving the built-up areas, everything was white: the fields, the trees, the farmhouses spilling smoke from their chimneys. Before she fell into a doze, lulled by the clack of the wheels on the rails, she thought of her mother and Smithers, hoping both would be all right in their own little worlds of four walls and a bottle of gin or whisky.

She had forgotten to phone William Smythe or Bruno Kannberg. To light up William's life was unfair. To tell Bruno her biography had stopped selling in America as quickly as it had begun was not what Bruno would want to hear after so much hard work. From Purbeck Manor she would put a phone call through to Tinus in Rhodesia and surprise him with 'Happy Christmas'; Uncle Robert had told her Tinus, like herself, had gone home for Christmas after Uncle Robert had spoken to Harry Brigandshaw on the transatlantic phone. Then she fell into a deep, exhausted sleep.

WHEN she finally reached Corfe Castle station it was pitch dark, one gas light burning in front of the small railway building. The old station master shuffled out wearing a thick uniform overcoat; the man, Genevieve knew, was Harry Brigandshaw's father-in-law and the grandfather of his children growing up at Hastings Court, something, Genevieve found, like her own life, strangely bizarre. Then her father came out under the gas light behind Old Pringle as Genevieve stepped down onto the platform. To Genevieve's surprise her usually formal father moved forward quickly, wrapped her in his arms and wouldn't let go. It seemed the pigs and cows had, as Smithers warned, changed her father's view of the world.

"How are you, my darling?"

"Wonderful, Father. That was quite a big hug."

Behind them the train began pulling out of the station on the last leg of its journey to Swanage.

"Goodnight, Pringle. Wish Mrs Pringle a Happy Christmas for me."

"Goodnight, my Lord."

"This is my daughter."

"I know, my Lord."

"Happy Christmas," called Genevieve over her shoulder as her father almost ran her to the car.

"It's freezing. Your grandmother is so looking forward to seeing you. She wants all the news of young Richard. She misses Robert and Freya now they've gone to America. Are they coming back?"

"I don't think so. Freya has her own family in America. She and Robert are back in the Denver cottage, Uncle Robert writing his book. Freya is trying her hand at a script for a movie. She's promised there's a part for me."

"Are you going back to America?"

"No. I'm appearing at the Savoy in a revival of Noël Coward's *Private Lives*. It's set in Paris, about a divorced couple who stay in a hotel with their new spouses. It is a comedy of manners."

"Is it any good?"

"It's very good. One of Mr Coward's best, in fact."

"How are you, Genevieve?"

"Better for seeing you."

"How's your mother?"

"Drunk. So was Smithers. He's lonely, Father."

"What can we do for him?"

"Maybe I can move into the Park Lane flat while I'm tramping the boards at the Savoy? Smithers is a dear."

"Yes, perhaps... Once the heater gives hot air, the car will be warm. There are fires in all the rooms we use at the Manor. Mrs Mason has had a fire burning to air your room for days."

On the way home they took the high road back to the Manor. The moon had come out from behind the dark clouds. Looking back, Genevieve could see the old ruin on top of its hill that had once been the home of her ancestors. The look of the brooding pile, pale and colourless in the moonlight, made her shiver as if someone had walked over her grave. The many stories she had heard of Corfe Castle flooded back to her mind.

"Is there really a priest's bolthole under the ruins? Did you really go down inside, Father? We had an American journalist on the set of *Keeper of the Legend*. He was hawking his own book, *American Patriot*, that he wants them to make into a film. Uncle Robert told me afterwards that

Hank Curley had once visited Purbeck Manor and left early one morning not telling anyone."

"Did he tell you why he ran away?"

"Not a word. Never even said he'd been to the Manor, despite knowing the story of my life."

"Old Warren dressed up as the family ghost and appeared at the poor man's bedroom window. Father had put the American in a downstairs bedroom on purpose so Old Warren didn't have to do any climbing. Curley wanted to see our family secrets under the priest's bolthole deep below the ruins of Corfe Castle and father couldn't have that."

"Are the now famous parchments genuine? Is the story of the *Holy Knight* historical fact? I heard from Mr Hollingsworth Curley had questioned Uncle Robert's veracity when the book was first published with Uncle Robert claiming his story was based on our family history."

"The parchments were written out in French and English by one of your ancestors who took the words off the tablets deep under the priest's bolthole. The tablets are genuine, Genevieve. No one but the immediate male descendants of the first Sir Henri Saint Claire have seen the original tablets. Which was why we dressed up Old Warren to frighten the wits out of Curley. He took off that morning from the Manor and went back to America without another word on whether Robert was lying about the parchments to help the sales of his book in America. Max Pearl, Robert's American publisher, who had been introduced to Robert by Glen Hamilton of the *Denver Telegraph*, wanted to see the family story to publicise the book; give it, as Robert once said, a hook for the newspapers to hang on to. And you know Freya was Glen's personal assistant at the *Denver Telegraph*."

"I am never sure when it comes to stories about the family," said Genevieve.

"In 1917, I was posted to Military HQ with Harry Brigandshaw where we met Glen, an American journalist in uniform. That much I can prove. Further back is more difficult. When a story is passed down the generations it takes on a nature of its own, becomes its own story with no one knowing the exact origin of how it began. Did everything happen exactly as it is said even in the Bible? I don't think so. Always in retelling a story we like to make it sound better, to enchant the listener. Whoever knows the truth about anything once it has happened and been passed by word of mouth and only then written down? Each of us sees a different truth to suit our own view of life."

"So you won't show me the tablets deep in the bowels of that hill behind us?" Her eyes were smiling at her father, not believing any more than Hank Curley, quite sure the men in her family were pulling her leg.

"One day Robert will have to show young Richard. That is part of both their heritages as next in line to the title."

"You're not going to marry and have a son?"

"I'm too old, Genevieve."

"Nonsense. You're never too old. Men in their seventies can father children. I rather like the idea of having a little brother. I'll get the truth out of him." Pulling her overcoat closed, Genevieve had a silent giggle to herself.

"So you don't believe what I've been saying?"

"Not a word, except the bit about Aunt Freya. I've just come from Hollywood. The parchment story makes for a great promotion. That much I understand. Max knows all the tricks. So does Mr Hollingsworth."

"So you think we invented everything to sell a book and a film? That the whole story of the book is a figment of your Uncle Robert's imagination?"

"Something like that. Anyway, it worked. Uncle Robert is a famous writer. By playing what the public are told is my own ancestor they have made me a famous actress as part of the publicity stunt."

"Would you question every story in the Old Testament in the same way?"

"Probably not."

"Maybe you should."

"My faith in my religion tells me what is true."

"So does my faith in my family. The good and the bad. When the parchments were written, your ancestor only copied down the stories from the tablets that left our family in a good light. He left out the rape and pillage. The murder of the infidels in the name of Christ. The stacked piles of silently screaming dead I have seen carved into those tablets deep in the bowels of your earth. That is why we don't want the rest of the world to see where we really come from. And that means all of us in this so-called civilised world. The rampaging knights of the Crusades belong to all of us. As God is meant to belong to all of us. No woman should ever see what I saw on the tablets in the cavern under the priest's bolthole. As Shakespeare said, 'the evil that men do is not interred with their bones but lives after them'."

"A mangled quote, Father. I think from *Julius Caesar*."

"Does that matter either?"

They fell silent in the car until they were almost at the Manor.

"When we get to the house I want to introduce you to Sally-Sue the Second," said her father.

"Who is Sally-Sue the Second?"

"My prize sow. She's just had seventeen piglets, all alive and well. Now that's something. What's more you can count them. A pity the moon's gone in or we would be able to see the old Manor from up here on the road, deep down there in the valley where we've always been... I hope you are hungry. Mrs Mason has been baking all day... And that's the truth."

WHILE GENEVIEVE WAS WALKING down the ice-cold corridor of the old mansion to find the fire in her bedroom out and the temperature inside as cold as the corridor, Old Pringle was putting his bicycle away in the garden shed, the hard pedalling all the way from the railway station having warmed up his body; only his nose was cold, pointing through the warmth of the balaclava helmet knitted for him in thick brown wool by Mrs Pringle. On his hands were homemade rabbit-skin gloves, the fur on the inside, made from rabbits he had shot with his shotgun to feed his family long ago when all the children were at home. As he put out a hand to open the backdoor that led into the kitchen, Old Pringle smiled to himself comfortably as he looked at the old gloves: like himself, the rabbit gloves were coming to the end of their lives.

Opening and closing the door as quickly as possible to keep out the cold, Old Pringle was engulfed by the warmth and the good smells of the food in the kitchen where the wood stove was always left burning, rain or snow, winter or summer as Mrs Pringle had the habit of saying. The sweet smell of baking bread pervaded the room. Next to the hot stove was his easy chair with the soft cushions for his old bones and beyond that, away from the side that housed the fire, hung sweet-smelling herbs that had come from the garden in the summer, now dry and fragrant when broken in his wife's plump hands before they went little by little into the cooking pots during the long months of winter. On the mantelpiece were photographs of their children, the living and the dead, to remind them both of the happy noise that had once rocked the rafters of the old railway house built at the turn of the previous century. The kettle was on the hob, boiling gently, ready to make his tea.

They smiled at each other as they had done over so many years without the need for saying a word. They were as comfortable with each other as they were with the house. With his dark blue uniform overcoat on the hook next to his balaclava helmet, the rabbit gloves stuffed one into each pocket, Old Pringle sank slowly into the comfort of his chair before taking off his boots and wiggling his toes in front of the stove close to where the burning wood was glowing hot through the grill. Then he sighed deeply and waited for the tea to draw in the old brown pot he watched his wife fill with water from the big kettle.

"The one they call Genevieve came off the train. Lord St Clair met her."

"Thought her in America."

"Back for Christmas, I should think. Now that's a queer one."

"No queerer than our Frank being Barnaby's bastard."

"You can't be sure."

"Just look at him. Like his father too. Right royal little brat if you ask me."

"The world's changed, Mrs P."

"Not for the better."

"Never does. Just the one train down and the one train up. What's for tea?"

"Kippers."

"My favourite. We're lucky, Mrs P."

"I know. Comes of a simple life. Not getting above ourselves. All you need is a warm fire, a cup of tea, and a pair of kippers with homemade bread and jam."

"Especially your plum jam, Mrs P."

Then Old Pringle smiled to himself for the second time in as many minutes; they were like two peas in a pod, perfectly content with their lot in life, never wanting more than they had.

When the kippers were put in front of him on a tray, he could see they were thick and juicy, the knobs of butter melting into the rich brown skin of the smoked herring; with newly baked bread hot from the oven and soaked with butter, it was as he always said, 'food sent from heaven'. Without looking up from the tray on his lap, Old Pringle tucked into his high tea with relish.

.   .   .

WHEN THE CALL came through from Genevieve to William Smythe the next day, it didn't help either; she had wanted to tell him about her part in the play, leaving a void in his soul. Earlier, Isaac, the old Jew who had forged his American passport and financed his trip with Horatio Wakefield to Berlin to report on the plight of the German Jews following the rise of Hitler, had phoned William's office in Fleet Street to say Fritz Wendel was dead, murdered and burned along with thousands of his fellow Jews. Fritz had been William's contact in Berlin, the man who had warned him in time to get out of Germany the day the Nazis arrested Horatio. The tears for Fritz were still wet when Genevieve had phoned.

"I just phoned Tinus in Rhodesia. Three minutes then the exchange cut us off. Person to person call, each second so precious. It's hot as hell on Elephant Walk. It was the best Christmas present I could ever have, hearing his voice."

"When are you coming up to London?"

"After Christmas. Probably after New Year. My grandmother is so pleased to see me you have no idea. Sally-Sue has seventeen piglets though they moved around too much to count properly. Father says there are seventeen. Except in what father calls his den this house is freezing. The old Manor needs people like the old days, according to my grandmother. Then there were a dozen servants, aunts and uncles, even the odd poor relation. With fires burning in every room the house was a lot warmer, but maybe they were just used to it. When I stand in front of the fire my face burns while my lovely little bottom stays frozen."

"Can we go out, Genevieve?"

"We can go out, William. I love going out with friends."

"Are we just friends?"

"I don't see how we can be any more."

"We were in New York."

"I was lonely. So homesick and glad for a friend from England."

"Was that all it was? And Genevieve, don't giggle. That really hurts."

"It was lovely. Lovely moments should be left alone to remain lovely moments for ever and ever. Not destroyed. When we are both old I am sure we will treasure our memory of New York."

"I want to treasure it now."

"I hear Dad in the driveway. He went to see a farmer in Mickleham. Have a lovely Christmas. I'm looking forward to seeing you, William."

"So am I," William had said miserably when he put down the phone after the line went dead.

The article he was writing in memory of Fritz Wendel became too difficult to concentrate on and William pushed away his portable typewriter. It was time anyway to tell Horatio Wakefield. The article would be better written without so much personal emotion. From the distance of hours, even days. Fritz had become a friend, a good friend, and good friends, William had found in his life, were hard to come by; too precious to lose for no other damn reason than having a religion someone else did not like.

Putting on his trilby felt hat along with his winter overcoat, William prepared to leave his small office and the warmth of his room.

"Going over to the *Daily Mail*, Betty. Look after the shop."

"How was Genevieve?"

"How did you know it was Genevieve?"

"I put her through, remember?"

"She's in love with Tinus Oosthuizen."

"Well that's good news."

"Not for me, Betty."

Had William turned round and looked at his secretary before going out the door on his way to visit Horatio Wakefield, he would have seen a whimsical smile on her pretty face, the look of a speculative idea that was just taking shape in her mind. Betty, like Genevieve, was twenty-three years old and said by many to be just as pretty. Some of her friends even said she was similar and wasting her time working in an office, even if the office was situated on Fleet Street with all the bustle and excitement of the international press.

"Maybe I'm not wasting my time," she said to the now closed door as she licked the tip of her index finger. "If war does break out he's too old to be called up into the army."

The idea of extracting her boss from his mooning over a film star had something to do with his appeal. Betty Townsend liked a challenge. Most men were too easy. The fact that William Smythe had never once given her the eye made Betty that much more determined; she hated being ignored, especially by men.

"Anyway, I'll bet he's never got her into bed," she said, before going back to her typewriter and her shorthand notebook with William's twenty pages of dictation for the day. "In an old kind of way, he's actually quite good-looking. I've never seduced a man over thirty before. Maybe he has some tricks even I don't know."

· · ·

"THE NAZIS HAVE MURDERED Fritz Wendel, Horatio. Isaac told me. If war breaks out I'm joining the bloody army."

"You're too old. Sit down, William."

"Genevieve is back in town and doesn't want to go out with me properly. I'll lie about my age. I don't look anywhere near thirty-five. People can't just go off murdering people over religion."

"They've been doing it down the centuries. When a man with power thinks he's right, he makes everyone agree with him. Poor Fritz. You told him to get out of Germany and go to America. It doesn't always pay in life to help other people. Being selfish is part of staying alive. Have you ever fired a gun?"

"I'll learn, Horatio."

"Isn't the pen meant to be mightier than the sword? I had a Christmas card from that chap Alfie Hanshaw I helped after Mosely's abortive march through the East End of London. Hanshaw must feel like you as he's joined the RNVR. Has a romantic idea to sail and fight on one of the ships he's helping to build... I was glad to get out of Germany. I have no wish to go back. Even on the turret of a tank with the flags flying. Before the flags fly there'll be millions of dead people. Little Bergit kept me awake all last night screaming. After the first time, Janet wouldn't wake up she was so tired. Being a mother of two kids and running her speech therapy practice is damn nigh impossible, despite Nurse Blanche. That poor girl really is ugly. Why does God make some people look unattractive? More important, why do we think one person is plain and another pretty? That one has never made sense to me. Blanche makes it up with a very sweet nature. Maybe she'll find another ugly person and have beautiful children. I mean not all of her family in the past could have been ugly or how did she get here?"

"What are you talking about, Horatio?"

"Anything but Fritz."

"I'm writing a requiem."

"I want to help. Thanks for coming to tell me. The whole thing gets more personal when friends get killed. Maybe I'll join the bloody army with you."

"Genevieve's got a part on the West End stage."

"She'd have been better staying in America."

"She'd phoned Tinus in Rhodesia for Christmas."

"I said sit down, William. You're making me nervous. Genevieve has never wanted to be your lover."

2

$\mathcal{W}$hile William Smythe was dreaming about a perfect monogamous life with Genevieve, Barnaby St Clair was going through his phonebook hoping to get a spark from one of the girls' names. Giving up a list he had foraged too many times in the past, Barnaby gazed out of the window from his Piccadilly town house at the desolation of winter in Green Park just across the road. In the street down below, cars and taxis were travelling up and down, along with a delivery van emblazoned with the name of Selfridges. There wasn't even a good-looking girl walking down the pavement.

Barnaby, sitting in the bay window on the second floor was racking his brain for something to do. During the morning he had amused himself talking to his stockbroker on the phone, giving CE Porter an order to buy shares in the British armament industry up to the amount of ten thousand pounds. The two of them had not spoken business other than to sell the market short before the stock market crash of 1929, when Barnaby had sold all his shares and put the cash with the banks in money instruments that earned interest without taking any risk.

Dabbling in the stock market again had been fun but the euphoria was quickly over once he put down the phone. Remembering how his brother Merlin had made a fortune during the war, buying shares in a company that made machine guns, had changed his mind. Barnaby was not like many of his optimistic friends, who believed in the diplomacy of

Prime Minister Neville Chamberlain. Chamberlain was certain war with Germany was imminent, according to an offhand remark of an acquaintance at a boring dinner party Barnaby had gone to in the hope of finding a girl or two he could woo and finally take to bed; even at forty-one years of age his need for new sexual partners was as rampant as ever.

Barnaby replayed the conversation in his mind: "The Prime Minister knows much more than we do. A friend of mine at the Ministry says all this appeasement talk from Chamberlain is to give us the time to re-arm. To build up modern equipment that can defeat the Nazis when war breaks out. The war that's coming is going to rely on sophisticated machines even more than the tanks which won the last, finally breaking the attrition of trench warfare. My friend says the next war will be won in the air."

"Poppycock, Marshbanks. The navy protects England and wins our wars by strangling the enemy's trade routes. Then the tanks go in. The English Channel can only be crossed by ships bringing an enemy in big enough numbers to worry us. It was the same whenever we invaded Europe. The navy, Marshbanks. Those fly boys may be glamorous but without the navy we'll be sunk."

Barnaby had ignored the terrible unintended pun of the old bore who liked the sound of his own opinions. Barnaby had smiled to himself. Marshbanks, whoever Marshbanks might be, was right. Despite the only unattached young girl at the dinner party having a face that resembled a horse, he found his evening had not been wasted after all. It was time to buy shares again. To buy shares in any company that was making or trying to make military aircraft. Even if some of the companies did not come up with the 'goods', as he put it to CE Porter the next morning, he would be on the right side of the averages.

Barnaby had always liked a calculated gamble based on inside information. In the old days after the Great War, he had first made his fortune buying and selling shares while borrowing as much money as he could lay his hands on from his bank against the security of his shares that went on up and up in the biggest bull run in history until, like all bull runs, it went bust.

When the phone rang in the hall downstairs, Edward answered the ring while Barnaby kept on hopefully looking for a pretty face walking along the pavement two storeys down below. Girl-watching from his bay window was perfect, as he could look down but the girls, or anyone else for that matter, Barnaby told himself, never looked up. It was the perfect spot for a voyeur with no chance of being caught; anyway, he reassured himself, there was no law to stop him looking out of his own window at what was walking up and down the pavement below.

"Mr Brigandshaw would like a word with you, sir," said Edward his valet after walking up the single flight of stairs.

"Oh would he?" said Barnaby, for some reason feeling a pang of guilt.

Putting down his small black book that had so far failed to spark in him enough interest to make him phone one of the girls, Barnaby left his bay window and walked down the stairs to the only telephone in the house, situated conveniently for everyone in the entrance hall of the townhouse next to the front door.

"Harry, this is a surprise. Where are you?"

"At the Air Ministry. I want a favour."

"Whatever for?"

"Because you owe me one. Meet me in the RAF club in half an hour. You can walk or, if you must, take a taxi."

"In the bar?"

"All right. In the downstairs bar. Tell the doorman you are meeting me if you get there first. You aren't doing anything are you?"

"Not really."

"I thought so."

When the line at the other end went dead Barnaby was smiling. It would take CE Porter days to pick up ten thousand pounds' worth of shares. If he questioned his brother-in-law without Harry knowing what it was all about he would find out the name of the companies with the best chance of making money when war broke out. Especially now Harry wanted a favour from him; Marshbanks had mentioned a friend at the Ministry but not which one.

"There's always a price to pay, Harry," he said to himself as he put on his thick overcoat before opening his front door to a cold blast from across the leafless trees in the Park.

With a round bowler hat on his head that Barnaby thought made him look professional, he walked down the steps onto the pavement and turned right in the direction of Park Lane. He felt like a walk now it was no longer raining. Swinging his rolled umbrella, he strode along on his way to the RAF club. Across in the park, somewhere from up a tree, a pigeon was calling. Being a club, the bar would be open even if the RAF club only let men into its precincts; no chance of finding a pretty face in a men's club.

"I wonder what he wants?" Despite them both knowing perfectly well his fatherhood of Frank Brigandshaw, the subject was never mentioned, so that wasn't it; for once in his life, the unwritten code of the English gentleman had worked in his favour, even if he had in a moment of mutual frenzy with Tina given Harry, first married to his sister, a pair of horns.

'Anyway, she was mine long before Harry got hold of her.' For a moment the picture in his mind of a young Tina gave him the spark he had looked for in his phone book.

"He's in the lounge, Mr St Clair. Colonel Brigandshaw said it was too early in the day to drink an alcoholic beverage."

Giving the doorman, whose name he could never remember, a pained smile Barnaby walked down the wide high-ceilinged corridor, with aeroplane photographs plastered up the walls on both sides, to the heavy oak door that led into the lounge and all the boring dark leather sofas and armchairs that reminded Barnaby of old men in their dotage, not dashing young pilots.

In the corner, beside the cheerful fire, Harry Brigandshaw happily waved to him without getting up. Apart from a waiter standing and holding an empty silver tray in the palm of his hand there was not another living soul in the wood-panelled room.

"You're a man-about-town, Barnaby, which is why we need your help. Sit down in front of the fire. You may remember me talking about my friend Klaus von Lieberman... That will be all, Kay. If I need anything I'll ring the bell. Go and have yourself a nice cup of tea with the chef in the kitchen... Very modern bell system in the club," Harry said as he watched the waiter go out and close the big oak door behind him. "That bell there is connected to a panel in the kitchen. Instead of making a noise, it drops a flag that has the word 'Lounge' written on the metal disc in red... Now we can talk in private. Waiters have very good ears; it alleviates their boredom on the job."

"What's all this about, Harry?"

"Take off your overcoat and put it with your brolly on the chair. I'm surprised the doorman didn't take them. Do you actually wear a bowler hat? I'd have thought a foxy hat with a green feather would be more your style for the ladies."

"You've never worried about the hat before."

"Maybe you should for the mission I have in mind for you; it stamps you as far too British. You do remember Fleur Brooks? The charming young girl who plays the fiddle in a band. When I first met the beautiful Fleur she was attending the Royal College of Music and playing Beethoven quartets."

"There's more money in a nightclub band. Unlike some of us, she won't inherit a fortune from her parents or her grandparents."

"Point taken, Barnaby. I was lucky. If you agree to my request, I will buy you a drink in the bar. It was so nice of you to come so quickly with so much on your plate these days."

Smiling sweetly at each other they both paused, the verbal duel at an end.

"A German aristocrat," went on Harry, having made and received a point, "is in London visiting a friend of mine who says she can cure the poor man's stutter, something I personally doubt though I have never stammered in my life, thank heaven. He is a Nazi. We even think the worst kind of Nazi who imagines Germany, and the Nazi Party in particular, dominating the world. One of the kind of men who crave power more than life, which makes them so dangerous. He is also, according to what we hear, very charming. Especially with the ladies, who find him equally attractive. We want you to make friends with Herr Henning von Lieberman, my old friend Klaus von Lieberman's cousin and son of General Werner von Lieberman, both members of Hitler's Nazi party. Our friend Henning made contact, if that is the polite way of putting it, with Fleur at the Mayfair after dining at the nightclub and dancing to her music. Fleur, who had been put up to the job by me in the first place, being a friend of my nephew Tinus and girlfriend of Andre Cloete, now a pilot in the Royal Air Force at my behest, initiated the contact with the German by flirting with him from the bandstand, something I understand she is very good at, which is where you come into the picture, my old friend Barnaby. Fleur is going to introduce you to Henning. You are going to introduce him to all the showgirls in London, most of whom I understand you are already familiar with."

"Why, Harry?"

"We want to know who he talks to. Seemingly casual meetings in clubs are common, especially where alcohol is served and strangers become familiar with each other. We want to know the people living in our island who are sympathetic to the German cause. We want to know the names of everyone he talks to, which is where your intimate knowledge of most people in the social swirl of London is so valuable."

"What's in it for me, Harry?"

"I'll give you the names of companies likely to receive further contracts from the Ministry of Supply. CE Porter phoned me after you phoned him this morning. CE, as usual, was looking for a favour. Now I want one. This is right up your street, Barnaby. Right up your street. What's more, you can mix business with pleasure to your heart's content."

"Is Fleur having an affair with this German?"

"That kind of question I never ask a lady."

"You've got your facts wrong, Harry. My friend is Celia, Fleur's flatmate."

"I don't think that matters, do you?"

"It does if Celia tries to put her claws into me again."

"Then ask her not to. Frankly, four of you out on the town makes a perfect cover. All the girls have to do is behave like flappers with you, Barnaby, playing yourself. I understand the girls only play the Mayfair at the weekend, but you probably know more about that than me. He's staying another month in London. Janet Wakefield, the speech therapist, has no idea we are having her patient followed."

"You want me to spy on him!"

"Keep a list of everyone he talks to. That is reporting not spying. The chaps in intelligence will check on your list. Where are you spending Christmas? Are you going down to Dorset?"

"Purbeck Manor in the winter is a morgue."

"Then party with the girls and the German. Andre Cloete unfortunately will not be having Christmas leave. Fleur wants to record some of her songs, I'm sure you know someone. Right up your street. How are you, Barnaby? Shall I ring the bell for tea?"

"I need a drink."

"Come on then, I'm finished for the day. So that's a yes? You can go round and make plans with the girls when we've talked of old times. I had a card from Robert in America. The film of *Keeper of the Legend* is a great success. Your brother is in the pound seats, though I suppose he'd now call it the dollar seats though somehow that doesn't sound right. And thank you for asking. My wife is very well."

"What are you all doing for Christmas?"

"The children will be running wild as usual. Tina has filled every spare bedroom with the usual hangers-on. Never mind. It amuses her. Living in the country can be boring so I'm happy with the freeloaders entertaining my wife while they drink my booze. I call it a small price for marital harmony. A busy woman is a happy woman. Not all of the guests are a pain in the arse. Fact is, this Christmas at Hastings Court should be quite fun. I invited an old sea captain from my days in shipping. Cyrus Craig is my age so he isn't really that old. When I phoned him to spend Christmas with us, to give me some protection from the rest of them, he said two of my other old friends were in England on leave from Africa. They both sailed home on Cyrus's boat. Bachelors in the Colonial Service, which means they don't have money to splash around in England. The perks that go with the job make them rich when they live in Africa. Back in England on leave or retirement the chaps from the Colonial or Indian Service have to be careful with their money."

"I met Captain Craig when you reappeared out of Africa, Harry. You were then a bit fuzzy in the head at the Hospital for Tropical Diseases so you probably don't remember."

"I met Vivian Makepeace and Thornton Holmes in Dar es Salaam after I escaped from the Tutsis. Cyrus was giving me my first proper meal since my seaplane went down in the Congo. In the hotel dining room, I think it was. Strange how something once so vivid can seem so far away. I lived in a round hut with a tribe of Tutsis for months and months on end and now it seems like someone else, not me, was living there tending to de Wet Cronjé before he finally died of malaria. Another life. I phoned Makepeace and Thornton and invited them for Christmas. They're staying at the East India Club. I want to find out what happened to my Tutsis. What happened to the British Resident in Mwanza who cashed me a cheque and countersigned the cheque I gave to the gun merchant who sold me the guns for the Tutsis as the price of my freedom. My body was so full of bugs by then I can't remember the chap's name."

For a moment it was on the tip of Harry Brigandshaw's tongue to ask Barnaby down to Hastings Court for Christmas until he remembered that his son Frank, who had just turned thirteen, was the spitting image of Barnaby St Clair and the other guests might notice. The three of them knowing was enough. Frank would hopefully never find out. Life, Harry thought, was strange; a bunch of bums, as he put it to himself, could screw up Frank's life.

"You were jolly good to me those first weeks after my ordeal in the Congolese bush, Barnaby. Thank you again. You were waiting at the docks when the ship's doctor and Cyrus Craig had me loaded into an ambulance. Even fuzzy I saw the goodness in you, Barnaby. I must ask

Cyrus what happened to the doctor. Shopped me to the press to make money. Can't blame him. Ship's doctors are paid peanuts."

"Always my pleasure, Harry."

"What are you going to have to drink?"

Feeling strange that Harry understood he truly cared for him, Barnaby followed Harry Brigandshaw out of the club's lounge. Outside the door, Kay was still waiting with his empty tray, making Barnaby wonder how the man failed to get cramp in his bent arm. Being appreciated by Harry had made Barnaby feel good about himself for the first time in a long while. Usually, he knew, he was plain selfish with only his personal needs in mind. Thinking of Frank, the sudden guilt made the good feeling quickly go away.

'You're a swine, Barnaby,' he said to himself. 'And one day you're going to get your comeuppance despite the odd patch of decent behaviour.' He told himself to think carefully before again upsetting Celia Larson; some girls used men as much as some men used girls. Celia Larson was not one of them. Barnaby had the suspicion that under the appearance of being a flapper was a serious girl who wanted a home and family of her own where she could play the violin to herself without having to impress an audience.

"You think we might have some dinner together tonight, Harry? Just the two of us?"

"I'd like that very much, Barnaby. We can talk about old times and Lucinda. I think about your dead sister every day of my life. Braithwaite wanted to kill me, not Lucinda. Likewise, Barend died and it should have been me. I've tried to be a father to Tinus but it isn't the same. He's assessing the viability of a major dam across the Mazoe River at the moment, home on Elephant Walk with his mother and sisters. If we go ahead I'm going to call the dam de Wet Cronjé, in honour of the civil engineer. That hippo coming up from the riverbed right in my flight path, is a nightmare I see in my mind's eye whenever I look back. Isn't it so often how small events like that hippopotamus coming up for air at that moment cause such horrendous repercussions for so many people? Tina was wonderful holding my family together while I was missing presumed dead. Why I don't mind how many guests she invites to Hastings Court for Christmas. I should never have tried the trip in the first place, putting so many people at risk."

"You can never foresee what is going to happen."

"I was selfish wanting to open up an air route down Africa. It was all about my ego."

"How about dining at the Café de Paris?"

"My favourite food. I'm only catching the train to Leatherhead at eleven-thirty from Waterloo tomorrow. Cyrus Craig, Vivian Makepeace and Thornton Holmes are meeting me at the station."

NOT FAR AWAY AT the East India Club, Colonel Vivian Makepeace, Controller to the Governor of British East Africa, was wondering why he ever bothered to come home on leave. He knew no one in England, other than the relatives who considered him odd for living his life in Africa. The weather in England was appalling and everything he did cost money from the meagre remains of his pittance of a salary. Were it not for the status earned in Dar es Salaam by saying how much he looked forward to going home every three years, he would have far preferred taking his six months' leave on the Spice Islands of Zanzibar, not far from Government House and a few miles up the Zanzibar Channel. The old Arab architecture and culture was far more soothing to his nerves than London, let alone the cost.

The invitation, out of the blue from Harry Brigandshaw to Hastings Court in Surrey, was a godsend, with neither himself nor District Commissioner Thornton Holmes daring to ask how long over Christmas they were allowed to stay. The idea of either of them wanting to spend Christmas with their relatives was appalling.

His Aunt Matilda, the matriarch of what was left of the Makepeace family and its fortune in England, always asked him the same question despite him now being close to retirement with a future of eking out a pension in some dilapidated residential hotel in Bournemouth: "When, Vivian, are you going to find a nice girl and settle down?" This time round neither of them had told their relatives they were in England.

To add to his feeling of doom, all the similar home leave sufferers from the Indian Civil Service talked of nothing but Gandhi and the British being kicked out of India while the chaps soaked themselves with gin-slings, their only route of escape as their lives and careers looked to be crashing round their ears.

The irony was not lost on Vivian Makepeace as he sat at a table not far from the bar, drinking the contents of a late-afternoon pot of tea. Here they all were where they did not want to be, knowing that what they had right now was likely to soon be beyond their means. None of them in the club had any training for anything other than running a crumbling empire where they were no longer wanted, a whole generation of men who had suffered the rigours of English boarding schools to train them to know how to behave like gentlemen and fairly administer an empire, with honour as their only reward.

"Like the Romans, Thornton, we're too damn honest. Most other people in history with authority squirrelled away fortunes in bribes while they had the power."

"What are you talking about, old chap? I need a drink. For a few days I won't have to pay London prices for my sundowners so I can afford a couple tonight. Even here inside the club it's bloody cold. So all that talk in '31 was true. The chap who looked like a tramp having lunch was the famous Harry Brigandshaw. Just as well, Vivian, you didn't get him thrown out by the hotel manager into the street."

"That was your idea, Thornton. It was you who said the chap was letting down the side, eating in a European dining room looking like a ruffian. I wonder what he looks like now? This Hastings Court is said to be quite the place to spend a free weekend. I can't understand why he wanted to invite us for Christmas."

"I'm going to the bar."

"Those Indian Civil chaps are a bore."

"They think us chaps in the Colonial Service are a bore. Are you going to tell Harry Brigandshaw his Tutsi friends annihilated their Hutu enemies with the guns he so kindly sent them?"

"Better not. We want to stay as long as possible. Someone said his wife was once a real looker. Do you think they'll ever kick us out of Tanganyika?"

"Probably. The colonies are too expensive, costing England money instead of making her rich."

"Just as well we're both close to retirement."

"I'm going to retire to Cape Town. They'll never kick out the Boers."

"The Boers won't have us."

"You sure about that?"

"No, I am not sure... There's a place at the bar, let's go and get a drink before we become morbid."

"If there's a war, do you think the Germans will invade Tanganyika? After all, it was German East Africa before the Great War. We only got Tanganyika in the Versailles Treaty."

"I have no idea. Do you really think there is going to be a war in Europe?"

"I have no idea. What happened to that chap in Mwanza who cashed a cheque for Brigandshaw? What was his name?"

"I don't remember his name but I did hear he was eaten by a crocodile. Went out alone with some ferry captain, got drunk and the two of them went for a swim, so it seems. When they found the ferry, if you can call it a ferry, there was no one on board."

"Not a bad way to go."

"I suppose not, we all have to go sometime."

"I hope they were very drunk."

"So do I. Pity we can't remember his name. Met him a couple of times. I rather think we both got ourselves a bit squiffy together. I'll remember his name if I don't think about it."

3

When Timothy Kent had approached Fleur Brooks with the strange request to befriend some middle-aged German, it was Timothy Kent who caught her eye and her interest; he had the most beautiful blue eyes that Fleur imagined would go with the blue uniform of the RAF with the white wings of a pilot on his breast... Timothy had come to the flat she shared with Celia in Paddington wearing civilian clothes. The knock on the door had come at a respectable eleven o'clock in the morning, by which time both girls had had their beauty sleep and opening the front door to a beautiful young man was a pleasure for Fleur, despite the cold draught of winter air that came with it. By luck, Fleur had bathed and dressed herself in a red pair of slacks that showed off her young body to the best advantage. Before the young man had opened his mouth he had looked at her from top to bottom and back again ending with a smile.

"My name is Flight Lieutenant Kent. Are you Miss Brooks or Miss Larson? Colonel Brigandshaw gave me your names and address. Colonel Brigandshaw has a request."

"I'm Fleur. Come in. Celia is still in the bath. We work late. Both of us are violin players in a band."

"At the Mayfair, Miss Brooks. For the last two nights we have watched the same man sitting at the same table close to the bandstand. He was on his own. How he managed the same table so close to the band we are not sure. Too many questions would have alerted the gentleman. He's a German. From what I could see, Miss Brooks, the gentleman is enamoured of you. When I mentioned the place and situation to Colonel Brigandshaw he surprised me. Apparently you know his nephew and Pilot Officer Cloete, the young South African who scored sixty-three runs against the army, enabling the RAF to beat them by two wickets last summer."

"Would you care for a cup of tea? Celia!" yelled Fleur. "Hurry up. We have a guest. I'm making tea."

"Who?" Celia, still soaking in the bath, had been quietly listening to every word, liking the sound of the young man's voice.

"You've heard every word," said Fleur still raising her voice. "Get your clothes on."

"Tea would be very nice."

"I buy the tea from Fortnum and Mason," Fleur said to Timothy Kent.

"Only the best... We would like you and Miss Larson to get to know Herr von Lieberman if he comes into the Mayfair again tonight."

"Oh, he will," said Fleur heading into the small kitchen and putting the kettle on the ring, lighting the gas with a two-pronged piece of metal on a spring that when pushed together sparked and lit the gas. "Just a couple of minutes. The water in the kettle is already warm... We have caught each other's eye on more than one occasion. I always smile over the bow of my violin at the customers to bring them back again. The more customers who listen to us three nights a week means we keep our job for longer. What's a smile when I'm sitting with the rest of the band? He's rather good-looking in a mature way... Celia? Did you smile at him? You know the man."

"Always smile at the customers, Fleur. It's the rule. Never break Martin's rules. What's Harry Brigandshaw got to do with this?"

"We work together, Miss Larson," Timothy Kent called through the still-closed door of the bathroom. "We work together in the Air Ministry, in intelligence."

"So you're not a pilot," said Fleur, disappointed.

"I'm a fighter pilot, actually, seconded for a one-year tour to the Air Ministry. There was quite a fight for the job. Colonel Brigandshaw was one of our best pilots in the war."

"What do you want us to do?" said Celia, opening the bathroom door to reveal herself fully clothed. "This is all intriguing me."

"My flatmate, Miss Celia Larson," said Fleur, annoyed with the way Celia was looking at Timothy Kent.

"If you are willing to help, could you possibly come over with me to the Air Ministry? Colonel Brigandshaw thought it would be easier for you to decline our request if he was not the one to ask in the first place."

"Is this for King and country?" said Celia, giving the young man a longer look of approval.

"I suppose you could call it that."

"Let's have tea first."

"Splendid... You have a very nice flat."

"You should visit us more often," said Fleur. "What's your first name, if that is not too forward?"

"We're always a bit forward in the Royal Air Force, or so we like to believe. Forward with the best aircraft, the best pilots and the best intelligence. My name is Timothy."

"Do you mind if I call you Tim?" said Fleur, letting her tongue slide slowly between her lips, just the tip showing.

"Not at all."

Going over to the small kitchen window that looked onto the back yard of the block of flats, Timothy Kent was smiling to himself, his back to the girls. Why was it, he asked himself, that girls in their early twenties had so much spark and life in them without all the baggage of wanting something material in return from a man?

WHAT HAD first caught Henning von Lieberman's attention on the first night he had taken himself to the Mayfair was not the girl's beautiful face but her beautiful playing. As an amateur cellist, Henning had recognised a classically trained violinist in a band playing a nightclub instead of the Albert Hall. The more he had listened, sitting on his own that first Thursday night, the more he became intrigued with the whole ensemble.

They were all classical musicians playing a blend of jazz and romantic music he had never heard in Berlin. There were even traces of Beethoven and Brahms woven into original music. Within the first three pieces he knew the music was their own, not composed by someone else for the all-girl band to perform, using their sex appeal and low-cut dresses to attract the nightclub customers; more importantly to Henning von Lieberman's love of music, the girls were enjoying themselves.

Watching the dancers on the small square of the dance floor next to his table under the bandstand, Henning could see the music was easy to dance to, not just pleasant to hear. The girls intrigued him, which brought him back the second and third nights having no idea he had attracted any attention, let alone the attention of the British Secret Service.

ON THE SATURDAY, when the evening was drawing to an end and the girl with the short dark hair had blatantly caught his eye, he asked the waiter to deliver the girl a note asking her to join him at his table for a drink. He was surprised when the girl brought the second violin player along as well.

With his speech impediment, Henning found talking to strangers an ordeal, even one at a time. Two became even more difficult. It was one of the reasons he had stayed unmarried after his wife and two children died in the flu epidemic that had swept Germany in 1919, as if the war had not been enough for everyone. After four years of fighting what had once been a country of friends, Henning had been mentally and physically exhausted, which had left him with a twitch in his right eye and an impediment in his speech that Mrs Wakefield had already spent two weeks trying to cure without very much success.

The loss of his family had left him devastated, bitter and vulnerable, a man who believed he had been abandoned not only by God but by the whole German nation and the whole human race. As bad went to worse, and the German economy collapsed under the weight of war reparations demanded by the victorious allies, any glimmer of light he could see at the end of the terrible dark tunnel was worth his attention.

Adolf Hitler, one of the most charismatic speakers Henning had ever heard, gave him the idea of hope, of restoring German pride, making his own life worth the living, making his daily drudgery worth the getting up for in the morning. Because there was nowhere else to look, Henning had joined the Party right at the start of the rise of German National Socialism, believing the alternative of complying with the Versailles Treaty was intolerable, the way for France to keep a jackboot on Germany for generations to come.

With his rise in the Nazi Party, helped by his army father's close involvement, it was imperative he be able to speak properly without the long embarrassing pauses caused by his stammer. On his return from a

Party mission to England visiting Harry Brigandshaw at his home, his cousin Klaus had promised him Mrs Wakefield would be able to cure his stammering, or at least bring it under control. It was by luck and Henning's father's help that Mrs Wakefield owed the von Liebermans a personal favour for saving her husband's life from the ferocity of the thugs the Party were forced to employ to keep the path clear for the new future of Germany that was going to once again make his nation great. Like Adolf Hitler, Henning von Lieberman, released from his misery caused by the war, believed the Third Reich could last a thousand years.

When the girls sat down at his small table, and as the rest of the guests began to get up and leave now the band had stopped playing, he had no reason to be on his guard. And when he spoke, remembering the instructions of Mrs Wakefield to use the tip of his tongue and not rush his speech, the words had come out with only the trace of a stutter, something that had not happened in Henning's life since 1917 and the last great German offensive.

When two days before Christmas Celia Larson introduced him to what she described as her beau, he was enjoying himself in London, relaxed for the first time in years. He was talking freely in the English he had perfected in his years at the London School of Economics soon after coming down from Heidelberg University, a young man without a worry in the world, with a young German wife and a hopeful career ahead with a Merchant Bank.

Sitting there so relaxed he was off-guard, his hatred for the Allies who had killed so many of his friends suspended by Mrs Wakefield and the lovely sounds of the girls' music playing in the Mayfair. In his mind sitting back in his chair smiling, he was young again. The girls were the same age his wife had been when he and Fidelia were married. Before he had heard of war. Before bitterness and hatred had tried to destroy his life. When they all went off for a late-night drink at Barnaby St Clair's flat, they were laughing together in the back of the taxi, two older men with two much younger girls all having fun.

HAVING DONE what he was told by the Intelligence Department of the RAF through their young spokesman, Timothy Kent, Harry Brigandshaw had gone down to Surrey by train with a clear conscience to spend Christmas at his mother's ancestral home at Hastings Court, his three friends silent in the first class carriage as the train ran through the stark winter countryside on its way from Waterloo Station to Leatherhead. What went on between Timothy Kent, Barnaby St Clair and the girls was out of his hands. If his friend Klaus von Lieberman's cousin was a spy, the British Intelligence Service would find out and he had done his piece, whatever came out later not something he would have on his conscience.

By the time Barnaby was entertaining in his Piccadilly flat late at night on what by then was Christmas Eve, as the time was well past midnight, Harry was fast asleep in the big double bed next to Tina, the fire still glowing in the grate some thirty feet from the foot of the bed. He was dreaming of Africa, as was his habit.

Tina, on the left side of the bed, was wide awake and miserable; she had finally realised her long-time hold over men was gone. Next year in November she was going to be forty. She was a middle-aged mother of five children. Not one of the men at her Christmas party had looked at her wanting to take her to bed. They were more inclined to look at her thirteen-year-old daughter Beth, a girl who looked like her mother when Tina was thirteen years old; when the St Clair and Pringle families had separated Barnaby and herself and the power of her sex appeal had first become apparent; when a shy, hooded smile could send a grown man's composure into lust and Tina's happiness soaring into the sky.

No one was interested in seeking her company now, never mind listening to her every word. Her life as she knew it was over, the years ahead a dark tunnel with nothing to find at the other end. Even Harry, poor old cuckolded Harry, hadn't touched her for a month. If it weren't for the others not looking at her, she would have put down Harry's lack of interest to his age and the almost twelve years that separated them. But it wasn't. Life was not fair.

There was Barnaby, by all accounts, running around with a twenty-two-year-old still having the time of his life while she, once considered the sexiest girl alive, was throwing weekend parties for people she barely knew in an attempt to still find something in life to live for. For all the fun she was having in England they might as well be in Rhodesia in the middle of the bush, drinking sundowners every night on their own and getting tight.

To add to her frustration, outside in the cold winter countryside, a pair of barn owls were hooting at each other like a pair of lovebirds with everything to live for still ahead of them. With the question of what old women did with themselves for the rest of their lives hammering away at her brain, Tina finally found solace in sleep, the warmth of her husband's body in the bed next to her comforting in her final moment of awareness. In the dream that came to her later in the night she was young again. Young again and happy. Pretty. In full control of her sex appeal.

WILLIAM SMYTHE WENT home that morning with the idea of spending Christmas alone. His only relative, Polly, his sister, lived in America and had not been seen or heard from since his mother's death. It was a lonely thought, especially after turning down Betty Townsend by not going down with her to Brighton for Christmas. A big mistake.

"We work together, Betty. Can't do it."

"Then I'll resign."

"Don't do it, Betty. I need you. There's just the two of us in the office. What would happen when I'm away on assignment? As a secretary you're a man's best friend."

"What's the matter with you men? Can't you see the mushroom on your doorstep?"

"Indeed I can, Betty, which is why I will not spend Christmas with you in some sleazy hotel in Brighton."

"It's a very nice hotel. Why spend Christmas alone?"

"Betty, it just wouldn't be right."

"Why ever not?"

"Because we are better off just as friends, and because I need you as my secretary... Don't you have a family to go to yourself?"

"Oh yes I do but you won't catch me dead going there."

"Why ever not?"

"You should have grown up with them."

Both of them had laughed with what, looking back an hour later, had sounded like hollow laughs. William had left the office to walk to the Tube at the Aldwych to head on home to his lonely Christmas.

BRUNO KANNBERG RECEIVED his call from Genevieve at lunchtime, the person to person call having taken all morning to go through, it being Christmas Eve. Gillian, his wife of less than a year, had answered the telephone in their two-roomed flat on the Edgware Road.

"I have a call for Mr Bruno Kannberg. Will he take it?" asked the operator.

From the small bathroom, Bruno heard his wife call out his name.

With only the money coming in from his salary at the *Daily Mirror*, Gillian had reduced his bank balance to just under five pounds, with bills outstanding that made his head spin. She had spent the advance for the *Abdication of King Edward* that never came, and told him their financial plight was all his fault. The only consolation at the time, as she spent the illusionary money, being sex for a few days as his young wife had worked off her spendthrift ways.

By the time the operator asked for him Bruno was back on short rations and had not had sex for a week, his whole body about to explode with frustration. To make it worse, Gillian had taken to walking around the cold flat without a bra under her thin blouse, her nipples sticking out like false promises, making him even more frantic, which seemed nigh impossible. His wife wanted to be taken to a smart restaurant for Christmas lunch which Bruno had pointed out they could not afford, his wife's hopeful mind still on the four pounds and shillings still left precariously in their bank account.

"Who is it?"

"The operator, darling. Long distance. Maybe it's your American publisher."

When Bruno heard the voice of Genevieve answer his tentative hello, he was surprised. He thought the book he had written on her life was out of print and out of mind. When he looked up from the phone his wife's face was expectant, an expression that he knew well could go one way or the other depending on the news.

"Where are you, Genevieve?"

"Happy Christmas. I'm in England, staying in Dorset with my father. How are you and Gillian?"

"We're fine, thank you."

"I have a nice Christmas present on the way to you from our publishers. With the success of *Keeper of the Legend* they did another print of our book in time for Christmas which I heard last night has sold out on both sides of the pond."

"How much, Genevieve?"

"Sorry to hear about the abdication book. When I spoke to William he said you had been made to withdraw the book. Something about the establishment not wanting their feathers ruffled. Sixteen thousand copies at full commission, half for you, half for me."

"Oh, that's wonderful. Just wonderful. Sixteen thousand half-crowns is two thousand pounds which at five per cent gives us one hundred pounds each. When will the cheque come?"

"They said it should arrive in today's post but you never know with Christmas."

"I've joined the Territorial Army, what with all the war flap. They're giving me a commission. They even pay us a little, which is another reason I joined."

"If you were that short you could have asked me. Give my love to Gillian and have a nice Christmas."

"We will now."

When Bruno turned round after putting down the phone his wife's nipples were again staring at him. When he looked up at Gillian's face she was smiling.

"Why don't we go into the bedroom, darling?"

"*Now?*"

"We can phone the restaurant for a reservation a little later if that will be convenient. It's much warmer in bed, don't you think? She's such a sweet girl. One hundred pounds! What fun. After Christmas we can go shopping without worrying about horrible money. Bruno, you are so clever."

His wife's small hand felt warm as she led him into the bedroom.

THEY HAD all arranged to meet for Christmas lunch at the Savoy Hotel where Henning von Lieberman was staying while he visited Janet Wakefield every morning for his therapy. From the hotel, the Chelsea house of the Wakefields, with the bottom floor kept aside for the practice, was just down the River Thames, a short ride in a London taxi. The room at the Savoy had been deliberately taken in the back of the hotel so as not to draw attention to his visitors, now masked by the visits of the girls and Barnaby St Clair as the four of them took in the sights of London. Someone had said to Henning during his year at the London School of Economics that to be bored with London was to be bored with life. Whichever way Henning looked at it, he was certainly not bored.

The meeting in his room with Rodney Hirst-Brown was arranged from a public telephone booth some distance from the hotel. Finding the man's telephone number had been a problem and it had taken Henning von Lieberman two weeks to track down, the man having left no trace of his whereabouts after he was fired from the Rosenzweig Bank in London, a branch of the bank that had been forced to cancel his Uncle Klaus's mortgage over the family estate in Bavaria in exchange for the lives of one hundred and sixteen Jews. The sweet irony of this made Henning smile as he awaited the three o'clock appointment in his hotel room on Christmas Eve, a time chosen, Henning had surmised, when people in London had other things on their mind than a German national trying to alleviate his stammer, diligently attending his therapy every morning excluding Sundays and Christmas.

There were eleven people living in England on Henning's list; all had similar gripes with the establishment.

"Hatred and greed, Henning," his father, General Werner von Lieberman, had told him before he left Berlin. "Hatred and greed. Often little men. Men who cannot get what they want from life by their own ability. Jealous, bitter little men who want their revenge on society for not having what they rightly consider to be theirs. Hating the success of others. These are the people we seek. These are the people who will sell out their own countrymen to get their revenge, assuage their jealousy, make themselves feel big and powerful. Make themselves hopefully rich. Such dogs of men are easy to train and let off the leash when the time comes for the Third Reich to take its place in history, when we can use such men to further our cause to defeat the enemy and restore the pride of the Fatherland. Given the right tools and incentive such men will be soft clay in our hands, my son. Even if you come back with a worse stammer it will not matter, provided you have put these men in place to do our bidding when the time is right."

As he sat waiting for the knock on the door he remembered his father's somewhat bombastic words, words that had grown more strident with the rise of Adolf Hitler and the importance of his father's career in the army and the Nazi Party. Some of the rhetoric aimed at the common man by Hitler had gone to his head.

'Never lose your perspective,' Henning thought to himself. 'Never lose the cold precision of a good mind. Don't let all the bloody excitement get into your head, Father. Not until we have won.'

When the knock came he got up like a cat, slowly, lithely, ready to do what was necessary to further the cause of raising Germany from the rubble of war to her rightful place among men.

"Come in, Mr Hirst-Brown," said Henning, shutting the door. "My name is Herr von Lieberman. It has come to my attention that we may be able to do business together. So kind of you to come."

"What kind of business?"

"I believe you hate the Jews. Like myself. How would you like to get back at Rosenzweigs for your wrongful dismissal? Banks can't employ a man for all those years and then just throw them out on the street. What about your family?"

"I don't have one."

"Come and sit down," purred Henning, who had enjoyed the flash of hatred he had seen in the man's eyes at the mention of the Rosenzweig Bank.

They sat down opposite each other in two comfortable armchairs.

"After we do business you will be rich and powerful, Mr Hirst-Brown. You will have the pick of the ladies. Women are attracted to power and money, don't you know."

"What's this all about?"

"A little early in the day, but have a drink with me. Let us first get to know each other. Tell me about yourself. What are you doing after your unfortunate dismissal from the bank? With some difficulty I found out where you live and the phone number of your landlady, a lady, I might mention, who was rather rude. She said you occupy the back room at the top of her house, information she only divulged after I mentioned you had come into a little money. The charming lady said you owed her three months' rent, something I have for you in my pocket so she won't throw you out in the street as she threatened at the start of our telephone conversation before she called you down to the phone."

"How do you speak such good English?" To Henning the man looked agitated, wondering why he had been invited to meet a perfect stranger in such a plush hotel.

"Partly because I went to university in England. I love England. I love the English. Your king, remember, is descended from Germans. We are cousins, Mr Hirst-Brown, with the same hopes for Europe in mind. You see, I also have a personal problem with Rosenzweigs which is what we have in common. That, and our mutual dislike of the Jews who, through their money, are trying to gain control of the world, don't you think?"

WHEN RODNEY HIRST-BROWN left the Savoy Hotel down the stairs, not in the lift as he was told, he had difficulty stopping himself from laughing. In his belly were three stiff whiskies and in his pocket three months' rent for the old bag who called herself his landlady. Out in the street Rodney looked around for a taxi then decided to walk to conserve his new-found wealth, received for doing absolutely nothing. He would give the old bag two months' rent and keep the rest to treat himself.

There was a pub he frequented near his room that opened at six. Finding a Tube station, he walked down underground. At Holland Park, when he came up again into the dark of Christmas Eve, it was almost six o'clock by the watch that had gone through the Palestine campaign with him so many years ago, a campaign still as vivid in his mind as yesterday. As vivid as the interview that got him fired from Rosenzweigs less than a year ago for borrowing one pound and twelve shillings from the petty cash to pay his bookmaker or have his bones broken by some cockney spiv who did not like being owed money for longer than a month.

Over the following three months he would have put the money back and no one would have been any the wiser. Now, every time he tried to get a job in the City, they found out from Rosenzweigs he had been fired for stealing. The German was right about one thing, he told himself as he pushed open the door to the Crown, feeling the warm air and smell of good beer wash over him. He hated that bastard Cohen for shopping him at Rosenzweigs, the bastard who had been after his job as chief clerk for years.

"Double whisky, Henry, and a Merry Christmas."

"You got the money, Rodney?"

"This time, yes. Take what is rightfully yours and put the rest of this ten shillings behind the bar for my future consumption. How does that sound?"

"You got a job?"

"Something like that. You know, there was a lord's son in our officers' mess in Cairo at the end of the war who stole fifty quid from mess funds and all they did was send him home early and demobbed him in England. Bugger soon got rich. I read it in the paper. I didn't even borrow a couple of quid and got the sack. The Honourable Barnaby St Clair. That was his bloody name. Nothing bloody honourable about him. There's no right in it, Henry. No bloody right in it."

"Glad you got a job, Rodney."

"Yes, well, we'll see how it goes. Chief clerk I was. Nearly got my head blown off twice in the desert by the Turks. Life's a bugger and then you die, Henry. From lieutenant to chief clerk to bugger all before I'm even fifty. Why don't women ever like men without money? I'm not bad-looking am I? Forty-three next birthday. No fat. Full head of hair."

"You're lucky you don't have a wife and three kids with a mortgage hanging over your head. I only get to lease this place from the brewery. Thanks for paying me back. Have the first one on me. Merry Christmas. Who paid back the fifty quid to keep it quiet?"

"Someone said it was his brother."

"Some people get all the luck. Steal a quid they lock you up. Steal fifty quid and they're more worried about getting their money back."

On his way home at closing time, with two months' rent still in his pocket to pay his landlady, Rodney Hirst-Brown asked himself the question that had been nagging in the back of his mind: how had Herr von Lieberman known he had been fired for stealing money from the bank, even if he had fully intended putting it back again rather than helping himself to more if no one had found out? Who had told the German?

When he staggered through the door the landlady was waiting, smiling at him, her right hand hovering just above the big pocket of her apron. Giving her the money without a word, Rodney climbed the flight of stairs to his room at the top of the house, wondering what he had got himself into. In his experience of life, no one ever gave him anything for nothing.

4
----

he Christmas tree at Hastings Court stood thirty feet high in front of the main stairs that rose from the heart of the old house. The children had spent all day up ladders decorating the tree with coloured glass baubles soon after the end of term and the start of their Christmas holidays. Frank had tied the Christmas fairy to the top of the tree by hanging over the banisters, causing his mother to claim in mock amazement that he'd given her a heart attack.

By late Christmas Eve all the children were in bed dreaming of their Christmas presents stacked high under the tree waiting to be opened on Christmas Day, with all the guests gathered to watch the ceremony after breakfast. At the bottom of each child's bed, tied to the railing, each of them had hung the largest sock they could find that during the night would be filled by Father Christmas coming down the chimney with his bag full of presents.

Just before midnight, both a little drunk from the wine that had gone with the five-course dinner in Mrs Craddock's best tradition, Harry and Tina crept as silently as possible into each of their children's rooms to fill the stockings with bags of sweets, oranges, bananas, toy trumpets for the younger boys and dolls for the girls. Anthony, turned fifteen in June, had not hung a Christmas stocking having for three years in a row watched his parents staggering around his bedroom trying not to giggle. Beth, in deference to tradition, had hung her stocking and fallen fast asleep thinking of William Stokes, Anthony's best friend from school who had come over for the day to kick a football with her brother and have some lunch before going home to his family to spend Christmas Day.

With everything Harry had to say to his wife, it was difficult to enjoy himself playing Father Christmas as much as usual. Every year, not including those spent with the Tutsi in the Congo, the ritual had been the same, with Harry hanging the stockings when his children were too young to do it for themselves. The coal fires in the children's bedrooms, like every other grate in the old house, were glowing warm in the dark with the curtains drawn and the cold of night outside the thick old window panes, small pieces of irregular-shaped glass held in place by leaden strips that had been put in place so long ago no one at Hastings Court knew when. Beth had not fully drawn the long curtain. Standing for a moment looking out, waiting to draw the curtains tight, Harry looked across through the tall trees, imagining the small yew trees that surrounded the ancient family burial ground where they had placed his grandfather Manderville after bringing him back from Rhodesia.

"Happy Christmas, Grandfather," he said quietly, holding his wife's hand as the moon came out to wash the stark winter countryside with a colourless light.

"Happy Christmas, Daddy."

"You're meant to be asleep."

"I know I am. Is it really Christmas Day?"

"Not quite, Beth. Go back to sleep. Tomorrow's a long day."

"Happy Christmas, Mummy."

Throughout the old house there was not another sound. When the moon went behind a cloud, Harry drew the curtain. When Tina closed the door behind them it never made a sound.

"She'll never remember being awake," said Tina. "Whatever you are going to tell me can wait till after Christmas. I don't want any of this spoilt."

"Do you think the children will be all right?" Both of them knew Harry was asking the larger question.

"Of course they will. Everyone goes through life. Some easier than others. Beth and Frank will have the hardest time because they want more than the others. Do you miss your grandfather?" Tina had known what he was thinking looking through the curtain.

"All the time. His wisdom. His smile that always spoke of hope when times went wrong. Even though I was twenty-one when my father was killed by the elephant, I thought of him as a father to me, not a grandfather."

"That's nice."

Far on the other side of the house, in the old clock tower, the chimes of midnight echoed through the house, the waves of resonant sound going out over the trees and countryside. They stood listening until the twelve chimes were complete.

"Happy Christmas, Harry."

"Happy Christmas, Tina."

Then they walked down the dark corridor, using the torch, to their bedroom where they undressed and got into bed, both of them falling asleep the moment their heads touched their pillows.

NEARER THE CLOCK TOWER, in a small bedroom that had once been part of the servants' quarters until Tina redecorated to accommodate her burgeoning list of weekend guests, Colonel Vivian Makepeace was wide awake, his heart racing, having been woken in a panic by the gong on metal. Not knowing where he was, he lay in the dark until his eyes grew accustomed and the dying glow of the coal fire in the grate brought back his sanity, yet he was still unable to stop the thumping of his heart.

Earlier at dinner he had drunk too much claret and too much port after stuffing himself with the best English food he had eaten since before Aunt Matilda ran out of the family money to live in genteel poverty in the crumbling home that had once been the pride of the Makepeace family. Once awake he knew from experience he would not go back to sleep, his body being somewhere between drunk and having a hangover.

Someone had kindly left a carafe of water and a glass on his bedside cabinet above where the servant had shown him the potty, the nearest bathroom being far down a dark corridor he would never have been able to find in the night. With the glow from the fire reflected in the glass, Vivian poured himself some water, feeling better once he'd drunk it in thirsty gulps.

Fortunately, he had no need for the potty and the embarrassment the next day of not knowing what to do with the slops. On mild reflection, Vivian concluded a tent on safari was more comfortable than an English country house, even if the food was not so prolific. Even then he was not sure if a slice of venison cut from the carcass of a kudu roasting over an open wood fire was not as good as Mrs Craddock's supper, when a man had walked all day and was hungry.

The damn clock had woken him striking midnight, waking the whole house with resonating bongs. The idea of finding a small place in Zanzibar to live out his retirement among the rich smell of cloves came back to him, the thought not unpleasant. What a man needed was often nearer than he thought, the conversation that morning with Harry Brigandshaw, the first they had really had on their own, coming back to him as he began to toss and turn, finally lying on his back to think.

"This is all right, Colonel Makepeace, but it just isn't Africa."

"Vivian please, Mr Brigandshaw." To Vivian Makepeace, a man had to have been a regular soldier to carry his rank into civilian life; fighting a war like Harry Brigandshaw, however brave, did not count, which was why he did not call Harry a colonel.

"Harry, please. You're an old friend and a guest in my house."

"Thank you, Harry. I'm having a ripping time."

"I'll bet you can't wait to get back to Dar es Salaam. Going on home leave without a purpose is a bore. Thornton confided he'd prefer to spend his leave in Africa, which brings me to my point. I'm also going home. Not quite home but near enough. An old school friend of mine has sold me his father's house in Cape Town where the son and I went to boarding school at Bishops. I spoke to the headmaster at his residence last week and found a place for Anthony. There's not a lot of difference in the education curriculum between England and South Africa. We can find the younger boys and Beth places in preparatory schools when we get there. There is going to be another war in Europe. I want my family out of the way. I'll be coming back and staying in London, working at the Air Ministry job they gave me. This war is going to be about aerial bombardment. The Germans will bomb London. The RAF will bomb Berlin. I don't want to be worrying about my wife and children when I should have more important things on my mind. My wife doesn't yet know I've bought the house in Bishop's Court."

"Why are you telling me this, Harry?"

"I want your opinion, Vivian. What's the situation in Africa? Are we going to hold on to the colonies in Africa or, after a war and England bleeding to death for the second time in a generation, will they, like India, demand their independence?"

"Probably. Whether they get it or not is another story. Don't quote me, civil servants are not allowed to talk politics. Officially that is. Unofficially Africa is a mess. We're putting in more money than we get out, if you exclude South Africa with their gold and diamonds, but that's in the hands of the Boers who've been there three hundred years. Roads, telephones, airports, extending harbours, medicine in the form of hospitals and clinics, education. Education is the big one and our Achilles heel. When a man is educated he wants to run his own country. Putting up schools and bringing in teachers costs a fortune, even helped by the missions of half a dozen churches."

"So you think I'm wrong to move back to Africa?"

"I'd get on the ship tomorrow if I did not lose face by not coming back for my home leave. My blood's gone thin, Harry."

"Mine never thickened. I was taken to Rhodesia as a very small boy, but I'm sure you've heard that story. My mother ran away from this house with my father and, apart from grandfather's burial, never came back again. She's still on Elephant Walk with my sister and my sister's three children for the moment. Tinus is due back at Oxford next month."

"Go with your heart, Harry. But everyone I spoke to at the Colonial Office said there won't be a war; that if Germany wants bits of Czechoslovakia and Poland, let them have those parts that speak German. No one can afford another war."

"Everyone affords a war when they have to afford it. Hitler wants Europe, not parts of Poland and Czechoslovakia. We'll be ready. We just need a little more time to re-equip ourselves with modern ships and aircraft."

"I'm hopeful our parts of Africa will be British for another twenty years. Until the generation being brainwashed by the missionaries come of age. Religion sometimes does more harm than good in its desire to spread a particular faith."

"That's all I wanted to hear. I hope you are enjoying yourself. The three of you can stay as long as you like. Cyrus will have to go next week as his ship sails. You and Thornton are welcome to stay out your leave at Hastings Court. I think you are wrong about religion. It teaches people the difference between right and wrong."

"Do you mean that, Harry? About Hastings Court?"

"Why? Don't you think the house is big enough?" They both laughed, uncomfortable talking religion. "Two days into the New Year the house will be empty. Make yourselves at home. Ride the horses, walk with the dogs in the woods. Anything's better than a London hotel. You see, I know what you chaps get paid. Terrible. My way of saying thank you for being got out of the Congo and back to my family. For doing the job you do."

Looking back on the conversation as the tower clock struck the quarter hour, Vivian hoped he had been right about twenty years. Already the Colonial Office was making plans to withdraw where the colonies were losing England boatloads of money, despite what it would do to British prestige in the rest of the world. In everything, he reflected, still wide awake, it all came down to money. Making money. Not losing it. Convinced that Harry Brigandshaw was wrong about another war, Vivian tried the old, stupid trick of counting sheep, falling asleep before he reached fifty to sleep right through the rest of the night to wake without a trace of a hangover and only the memory of gongs going off in the night.

IN THE SMALL room next door, Captain Cyrus Craig woke with a start quickly followed by the kick of fear in his stomach. Before traveling down to Surrey he had been told by the Admiralty that his days as a civilian were once again over. A phone call from a friend had told him he was about to be called up in the Royal Naval Volunteer Reserve, even before his ship sailed out of London on its outward voyage to Africa round the Cape.

"We didn't keep you on the Reserve for nothing, Cyrus."

"Surely I'm too old?"

"Don't you captain a ship at present? We've found you a corvette. Convoy duty to protect our wonderful Merchant Marine. My word, what would you do without the navy? You're to report to Plymouth on the third of January. Your call-up papers are being delivered to your hotel."

"How do you know which hotel?"

"We know everything, Cyrus."

"I'm going away for Christmas. Giving up my room in London in the meantime."

"Don't go too far away. Give me the new address."

"What do I tell the shipping line?"

"To find another captain. One without long-standing commitments to the Royal Navy. Actually they know. They gave us the name and phone number of your hotel."

The nightmare he had faced in the last war as a young lieutenant was coming back again. What they had said then about a war to end all wars was a lie. This time, getting out of bed to find his slippers, he knew he was going to get himself killed. The fire had gone out in the grate. Shivering, he pulled on his trousers. His slippers were under the bed where he had left them.

"Twice in one lifetime. What are the chances?"

The idea of the Atlantic in mid-winter was no warmer than the room. Outside in the corridor he could hear feet walking over the thin strip of carpet, creaking the old floorboards. There was a knock on a door further down followed by what sounded like a rattle of teacups. Cyrus held his breath, hoping. The sound of feet stopped outside his own door followed by a knock. Pulling on a vest, he got up from the side of the bed and, barefoot, walked to the door.

"Morning tea, sir. Mr Brigandshaw says to meet him downstairs when you've had your tea. It's a bit late."

"Are all the young girls in this house as pretty as you?" said Cyrus, grinning at the girl holding the tea tray, the large pot of tea covered by a red knitted cosy that had kept the tea hot all the way up from the kitchen.

"I'm from the village. Helping out. Times are not easy for my mum and dad. Herb's here too."

"Who's Herb?"

"My brother, Herbert."

"Tell Mr Brigandshaw I'll be right down. What's the time?"

"Half-past nine."

"I overslept."

"Happy Christmas. We open the presents at ten."

"I'd better hurry."

The young girl was still smiling as she put down the tray. Cyrus found a sixpence in his pocket and put it in the palm of her hand.

"Do you all get presents?" he asked.

"All the kids and all the servants, even us what come up from the village. The presents are under the big Christmas tree."

"Happy Christmas."

"Don't you have kids, you on your own? Sorry, sir, that's not minding my own business like I should be doing. I'm not a proper servant. If there's a war I'm going to work in one of them factories."

"My wife died having our son. What's your name?"

"Mary. Plain and simple, Mary."

For some reason the girl stood on tiptoe and gave Cyrus a kiss on the cheek before leaving the room and closing the door. Cyrus listened to her footsteps going away down the corridor.

Pouring himself a cup from the brown pot covered by the cosy except for the spout, Cyrus had not felt happier in months. The panic from his call-up had evaporated with the girl's peck on his weather-beaten cheek.

When he got downstairs properly dressed the big hallway in front of the main stairs was crowded with guests, servants and excited children. Somehow it all made it worthwhile having to go to war, even if war had not yet broken out.

"Christmas present, Cyrus. Chap just delivered it," said Harry Brigandshaw. "Keep those damn dogs out, Anthony!"

"On Christmas Day!"

"You've missed breakfast."

"All I could take was the tea and biscuits. Thank you, Harry."

"Thank you, Cyrus. Without you and Doctor Andrew Nash I'd likely have succumbed to my tropical diseases."

"Is that package what I fear it is?"

"I'm afraid it is, Cyrus... We really can't have dogs in here when we open the presents. There's enough chaos as it is. Do you know there's one of the cats fast asleep under the tree that will get spitting mad if the dogs find her?... Don't talk about it. Let's enjoy this Christmas. I've told Thornton and Vivian to stay here for the rest of their leave. When do you report?"

"On the third. Plymouth."

"Be my guest until then... My word, the children are making a lot of noise."

"They are what Christmas is all about, Harry. What life is all about. Keeping the home fires burning."

"What is it this time?"

"A corvette."

"Best of luck. All they let me do that's exciting is test fly the odd new aircraft."

What looked to Cyrus like an ornate oriental drum without a top cover, probably from Japan, was approached by Harry carrying a long-handled weapon with a round cloth ball at one end. All the children fell silent in anticipation. The drum was next to the tree at the foot of the wooden stairs. The guests and servants who were gathered with the children stopped talking to each other. The dogs were barking from somewhere outside the great hall when the clock in the tower began winding itself up noisily before striking the hour for ten consecutive, resonant bongs, followed by Harry hitting the oriental gong with his long stick a mighty swipe, sending the children into renewed frenzy, the younger ones jumping up and down in excitement.

Tina Brigandshaw picked up a present wrapped in Christmas paper from the pile spilling out from under the sparkling tree and called out a name. Harry Brigandshaw did the same with another present he found under the tree... One by one the presents were given out to the children and servants.

"Kim from Aunty Genevieve with love... Mrs Craddock from Mr and Mrs Brigandshaw with our sincere appreciation... Kim from Cousin Tinus... Mary Ross from the Brigandshaws..."

Cyrus, smiling at being part of their Christmas, listened happily to the litany while Mary's brother Herbert passed among the guests offering cups of steaming coffee, Cyrus having asked the young man his name.

The dogs got in somehow towards the end and found the cat without knocking over the Christmas tree in its precarious pot filled with earth, the big pot wrapped around in coloured paper, Frank's fairy at the top of the tree teetering for a moment. All around him the Brigandshaw children and their friends were tearing open their parcels to get at the presents inside, squealing with delight even if they didn't much like what they found.

In Frank's excitement at one big rip at the paper covering his box of trains, he hit his sister Beth round the face, making her look at her brother with a flash that contained nothing of the Christmas spirit. In a very long, thin box Cyrus watched Anthony find a four-ten shotgun of a Belgian make with a single long barrel that made the boy smile from ear to ear. His father placed a hand on his shoulder while his mother, watching from the corner of her eye, gave Kim, her youngest son, another present for the young boy to open.

When the underneath of the tree was finally bare of presents, with torn Christmas paper all over the parquet floor and most of the children nowhere to be seen, off with their presents, the guests were offered glasses of South African sherry by the same Herbert Ross who had brought them their coffee. Everyone was talking at once, the infectious excitement of the children having spilled over to the grown-ups as the spirit of Christmas ran riot through the old house, a joy to be seen, a joy for Cyrus to be part of, an image he was going to take with him on board the corvette when he took up his command in a week's time. A warm picture to take with him out into a cold Atlantic where his crew would train with him for the job, a job that Cyrus knew would soon turn from an exercise to a cold, bitter fight for survival.

When they went into the big dining room with its high vaulted ceiling and big fires burning half tree trunks at either end in the image of medieval England, Cyrus was convinced he could have eaten a horse he was so hungry. Everyone sat down at the long table, everyone smiling at everyone, no one being told where to sit.

By the time Cyrus reached his small room where the fire in the grate was again burning he was stuffed with food and a little drunk. Roast turkey served from silver trays with sage and onion stuffing washed down with a claret had been followed by a flaming Christmas pudding washed down with a thirty-year-old port that had screamed out to Cyrus to be sampled more than once.

With his clothes off and tucked up warmly in bed, he hopefully thought to himself, before he went to sleep, that he would be fit and able to do it all over again in the evening. His last thought was of corpulent Romans sticking feathers down their throats, something that to Cyrus was quite disgusting; it was better to put the fat on while the going was good.

JUST THREE OF them had sat down to Christmas lunch at Purbeck Manor, Genevieve giving the best solo performance of her career to keep the party going for her grandmother. It was her grandmother's first Christmas without her husband in more than fifty years. Genevieve was too tactful to ask how many years it was since the two of them had met back in a century with horses and carts and carriages, before the invention of the motorcar let alone the aeroplane; for Genevieve it was too far back to comprehend.

A small, cosy dining room had been created by her father soon after inheriting the title and coming to live at the Manor, to make it easier for Mrs Mason and Little Mavis, the maid. Both Mrs Mason and Little Mavis were coming to the end of their lives and missed the company of Old Warren, who had died soon after Genevieve's grandfather. The new cowman was Old Warren's son, the one who had stayed at home and carried on his family's tradition of working at the Manor. The man was married, his two unmarried daughters helping to milk the herd of Sussex cows Merlin had started by buying the first of the pedigree Sussex in 1917 with some of the money he had made by investing in Vickers, the makers of the machine gun that had been so successful in killing Germans on the Western Front.

The big banqueting hall, far from Mrs Mason's kitchen, was left to its memories of knights and their ladies, brooding alone with the fires cold at both ends of the long table, too big now the St Clairs were down to two living at the Manor. The chances of Robert and Freya coming back with young Richard and baby Chuck, born in October, were getting less by the day with war clouds gathering on the English horizon. The house, to Genevieve, needed children, lots of children.

The spaniel dogs had followed Mrs Mason in with the lunch and gone to sleep under the small table that Genevieve's father had found in one of the old storage rooms, a table so old no one knew its beginning. All three of them had put on paper hats. The wine had been poured into long-stemmed crystal glasses, the glasses to Genevieve as heavy as lead when she picked hers up.

"A toast, kind sir and lady. To my wonderful grandmother. To my fabulous father. To absent friends. To all the joy of life. I give you Christmas, everybody, the season of good cheer, the time to celebrate how lucky we are... There will always be an England! My friends, the King, God bless him."

Banging the table with the back of a spoon, Genevieve had made them stand and drink the Royal Toast, sitting down afterwards with a big grin on her face, looking from one to the other.

"I think I, as the Lord of the Manor, give that toast, my darling."

"In *Keeper of the Legend* the youngest knight proposed the toast. Consider me the youngest knight."

Soon she had them smiling, listening to her anecdotes of a country far away. Twice her grandmother had chuckled and asked, "Do they really do that in America?"

With consummate energy, Genevieve kept the party going until all three of them took to their beds for an afternoon nap to digest the turkey and Christmas pudding.

"That was hard work," said Genevieve getting into her bed to lie on her back and think of Tinus having Christmas out in the sun with maybe a lion or two roaring in the distance, black servants in red hats, white long shirts and short pants, padding round barefoot serving everyone long, cool drinks, the tall glasses clinking from the floating cubes of ice in the way he had described his home on Elephant Walk so many times to her in the past. "Next year, Tinus. Next year we'll Christmas together, wherever it is."

Then Genevieve fell asleep, dreaming of knights of old as the fire in the grate burned bright and light faded from the sky and outside it began to snow and the day was gone.

BY THE TIME Genevieve had fallen asleep dreaming of knights, William Smythe had spent his lonely Christmas Day eating a cold supper. Sitting in front of his fire, he poured himself another whisky from the nearly empty bottle, thinking miserably of his lost love.

The following morning, an idea came into his head. If Betty Townsend had not gone to Brighton on her own, which he doubted, she would be at home in the flat she shared with friends, friends that would likely welcome him into their home. Betty had said none of them had anywhere to go for Christmas.

Putting on his overcoat in the small hallway he let himself out of his flat, making his way to the Tube station. Finding a seat, he settled down for the short journey.

"What was the point of it all?" he said aloud to himself, trying to keep the picture of Genevieve out of his mind. "Whoever said 'it is better to have loved and lost' was a bloody idiot."

"You're wrong, young man," said the elderly woman sitting opposite. "It's always better to have loved, shows you have feelings."

"Did I just speak out loud?"

"You did. Merry Christmas."

He must have repeated himself he thought, as the train pulled out of the station. Maybe the old girl opposite was right. Maybe, just maybe he still had not lost.

"Hope springs eternal."

"Old, but true."

For the next fifteen minutes they journeyed in companionable silence, both of them keeping their thoughts to themselves.

HENNING VON LIEBERMAN'S suite at the Savoy, paid for by the Nazi Party, was the largest in the hotel; two big rooms and a large private bathroom. Before the successful lunch downstairs, Henning had made contact with three more on his list of eleven, interviewing them in the same way he had interviewed Rodney Hirst-Brown. No acknowledgment of what was in the future came into the discussions though all three discussed politics in Germany, where National Socialism stood between Russian communism and the rest of Europe.

Only Rodney had thought he was, in his own words, 'hard done by', the other three falling into the category of fanatics, people who considered a new world order better than the chaos of so-called democracy that had people voting for someone they knew little about.

The two men and one woman believed society had to be told how to run itself with strict rules that put people in their place. The idea of a pure uncontaminated race appealed to all three of them, much to Henning von Lieberman's hidden doubt. He was told in three different ways, order and discipline would stop the world fighting amongst itself. Everyone would be under control. Everyone would live according to his place. No one would be allowed to disrupt an ordered society; anyone who tried to disrupt and inflame would be brought to justice.

What all three of them wanted, while Henning encouraged them to rant on, was a well-ordered party comprised of dedicated men and women who would enforce the peace. It should allow the average citizen to go about his life without being disrupted, his life interfered with, or his property taken away on the whim of some idea like communism, that claimed everyone should be equal, everyone should have according to their needs while the communist hierarchy plundered what they wanted in order to live like feudal kings, as one of the three had pointed out triumphantly. Quietly, he had listened to their diatribes that to Henning, educated at Heidelberg and the London School of Economics, made very little sense. What the three fortunately failed to understand was that National Socialism, what others called fascism, was for the benefit of Germany alone. Fascism was a way of creating the most powerful empire that for Henning would dominate a peaceful world under German hegemony for centuries to come; fascism was merely the means to that end.

In between the interviews Henning entertained, making a palaver of the visits to his suite to cover over the more important visits of the eleven. After the formal Christmas luncheon in the Savoy ballroom, where in deference to Christmas the dining room had been silent of music, Henning invited his guests up to his rooms.

"I have a surprise for you, my dear Fleur. A surprise. Let us repair to my suite."

Only a controlled stutter was now impairing his speech, a worthwhile bonus from his trip.

BARNABY ST CLAIR was now bored stiff with the assignment given him by Harry Brigandshaw. He considered the German a man who liked young girls but was otherwise a bore, and certainly no threat to England. He was hoping he could leave Fleur with the German and take Celia back to his Piccadilly flat where they could do more than talk frivolous rubbish and eat too much food, the thought of not going home to his mother still at the back of his mind niggling away.

Upstairs at the man's suite, to be confronted by a large cello and two violins was as much as Barnaby wanted to take. Dance music was all right when a girl was in his arms, even pleasant, but classical music played on strings ground his teeth.

"You see, I also play an instrument," the German was saying, making Barnaby want to run for the door. "Borrowed from the orchestra. There is some lovely sheet music on the little stands for the three of us to play. Brahms, Beethoven, Bach. Wagner unfortunately never wrote music for strings. The maestros of Germany. The epitome of civilisation. Our music and our writers. The glory of Goethe."

To Barnaby, this man Harry said was a menace was definitely a crashing bore.

Plonking himself on a small sofa near the window where the curtains had already been drawn, he settled himself down to just about the worst that could happen to him at Christmas: listening to two violins and a cello, however well played. To add to his woes he was not even offered a drink. When the bows scraping on strings began, Barnaby had the notion to howl like a dog. "For this, Harry," he said under his breath trying not to wince, "everything I ever did to Tina is forgiven."

Then the music began in earnest. Folding his arms across his chest and shutting his ears, Barnaby St Clair wondered what else he was expected to do for King and country that could possibly be worse. Getting up and pulling back a piece of the curtain, Barnaby could see it was dark outside with the odd flake of snow drifting down outside.

With all the good food and wine he had consumed downstairs in the dining room, Barnaby, again comfortable on the couch, quickly fell asleep, the fluting sound of his snores washed over by the music of Johann Sebastian Bach. Not even the sound of bows scraping catgut penetrated his dreams.

PART 9

PEACE, FOR NOW — AUGUST 1938

1

For Tinus Oosthuizen, coming to the end of his last year at Oxford, the best part had been living among men and women who found thinking a pleasure in life. That and playing the most civilised game on earth, the game of cricket. So many people he met in the three years he found interesting, people searching for knowledge among the excitement of life.

Mr Bowden, his philosophy tutor, was so far the most important man he had met, the man who had led him into his reading and the first glimmer of an understanding about the reason for his life that had taken him further than his faith in religion. For Mr Bowden, Tinus understood, the great religious teachers in history were little different to the best philosophers, both trying to find in a short time on earth the meaning for life beyond animal pleasures in a hedonistic world always dominated by power and money.

Talking, discussing, reading what had been said during the centuries of civilised man had been the true worth of his years up at Oxford. The final examinations had been written to conclude his study of philosophy, politics and economics, Mr Bowden confident enough in Tinus to suggest he would receive a First in PPE.

"What are you going to do with your new knowledge, Tinus Oosthuizen?" Mr Bowden asked as the two of them strolled down the towpath next to the river, the summer day balmy, the air fragrant with the scents of flowers among the hum of insects, the sound that would always remind Tinus of England.

"Go home, I suppose. The idea of making myself a fortune in the corporate world has paled the longer I have been up at Oxford."

"Everyone has to earn a living. Choose something that keeps your mind alive. The body can be quickly satisfied. The mind takes much longer."

"I'd vegetate farming in Rhodesia with no one to talk to, or rather people to talk to who have something to say."

"Don't become arrogant. Everyone has something to say. You just have to listen."

"Some stories are better than others."

"There, I would have to agree. Be careful, Tinus. It's not all a nice world. Here, we wrap ourselves in our own conceit and the world's history of knowledge. It's a comfortable world that only requires the pursuit of knowledge... Good luck with the rest of your life. Don't forget to have fun. Never take yourself too seriously, but never forget that without fun life isn't worth the living. Now look at those two birds over there chasing each other through the trees. Now they're having fun."

"I think they're trying to have sex, Mr Bowden."

"Do you think so?"

"That's why the male is chasing the female while the female is playing hard to get. She wants the best flyer. The strongest male. Darwin, Mr Bowden. The survival of the fittest. That female bird wants the best for her children."

"I suppose you are right. But if we come down that far to the basics of life, I'll have to think all over again."

"It's not just sex and procreation surely? There has to be more than that."

"I hope so... Look, he's caught her. You were right. I'll be blowed. I thought they were flying around to have fun."

"They are now, Mr Bowden."

In comfortable silence they walked on half a mile before taking their separate paths, Mr Bowden to his wife and family, Tinus to his meeting with Andre Cloete who had come up to Oxford to see Tinus on a forty-eight hour pass from his squadron at RAF Uxbridge, not far from where the two birds had ended their dash around the trees.

They had arranged to meet under the same tree by the river where they had joined hands with Genevieve so long ago and gone out on the river. Sitting down on the grass bank out of the sun, Tinus had time to think on his own while he waited for his friend. He had a big surprise for Andre which made Tinus smile to himself with pleasure.

For some reason, Uncle Harry had shelved the plans for the big dam across the Mazoe River despite all Tinus's hard work during his trip home to Elephant Walk the previous Christmas, where the draw of Africa had again focused on his life making what he wanted to do with his future uncertain. To make the dam financially viable required an area of more than ten thousand acres to be put under irrigation, something that would have required his full attention for many years to come. It was one thing to plant thousands of orange trees, quite another to prepare the land and install the irrigation pipes for miles around the dam. A pump station was required to draw the waters of the Mazoe River and water the young trees at each of the thousands of round catchments to be dug around each sapling.

What his Uncle Harry was suggesting amounted to a complete industry for the Mazoe Valley: extraction factories for the juice and the oil from the skins, good houses for employees, electricity from the burgeoning national power grid, roads to take out the fruit to the plant, and management. Each time Tinus had done his sums the question of good management hung over the project.

People to pick the fruit was easy. People to work in the pulping factory was controllable. Finding the capital to invest was a simple matter for his Uncle Harry. Employing a scientist to come out from England to follow the fruit from the trees to the finished product was comparatively easy. What was difficult was finding an honest, dedicated man with a clear brain to watch over everything and find the flaws by thinking through all the problems before going ahead.

As they had taught him at Oxford, the vital link in the chain of business was management. Without good management all the workers in the world would be going round in circles with no one in the end making any money, the investment coming to nothing, everyone out of a job. And on his own, stuck in the bush with no mental stimulation other than miles of orange trees fragrant with blossom, he would go right out of his 'cotton picking' mind.

"Oxford's spoilt me."

"It spoilt me too, Tinus. How are you?"

"At least you're in civvies. Good to see you. You crept up behind me. Have you bought yourself another car?"

"No I haven't. I took the train. Flying officers don't get paid a fortune in the RAF. I can't afford another car at present."

"Bomber Command. My word, Andre. What happened to the fighter pilot?"

"It could have been worse. Let's the two of us find a boat and go out on the river."

"The three of us again, Andre. Why the meeting under the tree. Genevieve is going back to America to make a new film. She's coming up to say goodbye before she sails. She's joining us for the whole weekend. And she's late."

"All women are late. Wow, that is a surprise. Won't she be recognised?"

"No one takes any notice at Oxford. Come and sit on the grass while we wait. It's a beautiful day for a row on the river... It's going to be strange going out into the real world to practise all the theory... Are you getting enough cricket?"

"Weekends. Playing for Bomber Command and RAF Uxbridge. It's a good life in the Air Force provided you don't want to get rich. Now tell me everything while we're waiting for the famous Genevieve. What are you going to do with yourself when you come down from Oxford at the end of the month? Would you like a cigarette?"

"Thank you. Whenever I smoke, which is not very often, I wonder if the tobacco inside the cigarette came from Elephant Walk. All our tobacco comes to England to be processed."

"The price of tobacco will go up if war breaks out. You'll make a fortune."

"I suppose so. At the moment we are looking at oranges."

"Tobacco, Tinus. Plant more tobacco. In wartime people smoke like chimneys."

"Have you seen Fleur?"

"She has much bigger ideas. Your Uncle Barnaby started a company to record the girls' music and sell their records. Sold like hotcakes. Everyone is buying gramophones. Quite the thing. They want to listen to what they want, not just turn on the radio."

"Why did Uncle Barnaby do that?"

"I have no idea. Best he gets married to someone nearer his age and stops running after young girls."

"Young girls like his money."

"And his record contracts. They say half a dozen young girls are recording on his label. He even goes to the studio sometimes. When you have his money you can buy the best people to make the records. All you need is the right idea and money makes money."

"You're jealous, Andre."

"Probably. Anyway, I can't afford to do anything with anyone on a junior officer's pay. Even with my flying allowance. There's talk the squadron is being posted to Singapore."

"At least you're getting around. To answer your question, I have no idea what I'm going to do. One minute a chap's buried in the books. Then, wallop, he's looking for a job. Uncle Harry's allowance stops when I come down, so I'll be as poor as a church mouse."

"Join the club... How's Genevieve getting to Oxford?"

"Said something about a driver. She's rich. Going back to America to make more films. The play in the West End went all right but they don't make money in theatre, so I'm told. Chauffeur-driven car. That really is something... They must have paid her a fortune to go back to America."

Genevieve watched them talking together under the tree, holding back to take in the picture. They were still boys, innocent boys, having an animated conversation oblivious of their surroundings. They were clean-cut and pure of mind, something Genevieve knew she had lost a long time ago, probably never had. To be pure and innocent, she told herself as she watched enviously, you had to be protected by parents and money, confident of where you came from and where you were going, right at the beginning. Bastards, even aristocratic bastards, had to make their own protection, something she had done without help from her mother or father. She was rich, her investments making her richer with CE Porter handling her financial affairs. The thought of well-invested money gave her a good feeling of security.

"Darling Genevieve," Harry Brigandshaw had said to her when *Private Lives* came to an end and the new film contract had been signed with Gerry Hollingsworth. "The most difficult part of money is not making it, it's holding on to it. You have to invest wisely. Go and see CE Porter. He's a stockbroker friend of your Uncle Barnaby. I've done business with him. As investment men go, he's honest. More honest as he grew older. In the early days, Porter and Barnaby were up to all sorts of tricks. He'll give you a balanced portfolio spread across the financial world including America. Make you independent for life. Next time Hollingsworth wants something you'll be able to decide for yourself without needing his money. You'll be in control."

"I have him under my thumb."

"Later in your life the thumb might just slip. Money is the real power, Genevieve. Your power as a woman, on and off the screen and stage, will fade. It always does, no matter what we think when we are young. The power of money stays the same whatever our age. The first meeting with CE Porter we'll go together... When did you last see Tinus?"

"Not for a while with the play. I'm planning to go up to Oxford before I sail for America. I'm going by ship this time. Crossing the pond in an aeroplane is all over too soon. I like the change of moving from gentle England to rampaging America to be slow. On the boat I get used to the American lifestyle before I arrive. The shock is not so great."

"He's very fond of you, Genevieve. He's also a good man. You'd be safe with Tinus."

"Are you matchmaking, Harry Brigandshaw, sir?"

"Looking after friends, Genevieve. Getting married is life's big gamble as we all do it for the wrong reason. Physical attraction always transcends common sense. That, or it's purely a matter of money. You have to like the person you marry. You two like each other. Love is a lot more fickle. Liking someone can last a lifetime."

"He's still just a student."

"Tinus will do all right for himself, you can take my word for that. He's done a report for me which is quite brilliant. Were it not for the war clouds I'd build the dam and its complex tomorrow, putting Tinus in charge. I'd have to keep an eye on his inexperience, which would give me a chance to visit Elephant Walk. Now it's all on hold until Chamberlain faces Hitler and forces him to stop his games, or it's war. You once said you would like to live in Africa. If only my wife had the same wish. Bought a house in Cape Town to get my children out of harm's way but Tina won't have any of it. I even got Anthony a place at Bishops. Radley is a good school but too near the coming war. Porter will suggest most of your money going to buy shares in American companies. I've been buying myself. Nothing ever stays static. You have to think ahead. Give me a ring when you want to see Porter. And go and see Tinus."

"You frighten me, Uncle Harry."

"Not my intention. Just you can never be too careful in this life."

Bringing her mind back from the conversation with Harry Brigandshaw, she looked sideways at Gregory L'Amour standing beside her, taking in everything that was England. The man was enamoured with the Old World having come over to England at Gerry

Hollingsworth bequest to make her sign the contract for their new movie. They were sailing back to America together in three days' time. It had been Genevieve's idea to take Gregory with her to Oxford.

"I'm going to see old friends at Oxford, Greg. One's in the RAF. Both are pilots. Tinus is Harry Brigandshaw's nephew. He's just finishing his three years at Oxford. We call ourselves the three musketeers. I'm looking forward to the old feel of Oxford and the pleasure of good friends. If you like, come with."

"Would you mind? I've always wanted to fly."

"You fly, Gregory. Just not aeroplanes."

"Don't be rude. I'm serious. If there's a war and America keeps out, I've a good mind to join the RAF myself."

"Have you ever flown?"

"I want to learn. Your friends can maybe help me."

"You fancy yourself in the nice blue uniform. You are a romantic, Gregory. Never mind. Come with me. We can hire a car. Uncle Harry has some weird idea I should marry Tinus Oosthuizen. He's my best friend. No one ever marries their best friend. It would ruin everything. You have your affairs with people you know won't last too long. Not with friends."

"You're going to marry me, Genevieve. Every paper in America will run the photographs of our wedding. It will make us the most popular couple in Hollywood."

"I thought you were going to join the RAF?"

"Only if England goes to war with Germany."

"They both learnt their lessons last time. Why does everyone want to go to war?"

"No one ever learns their lesson if they don't want to. Not even you, Genevieve. When do we drive to Oxford?"

"Tomorrow. We can stay at the Mitre."

"You've done this before."

"I have."

HAVING the sense someone was staring at his back, a sense his Uncle Harry said he had honed in combat with the Royal Flying Corps in the war, Tinus turned round, the first to see Genevieve, and waved frantically. With a broad grin on her face, Genevieve waved back. Tinus and Andre got to their feet to welcome her. A young man was walking by her side.

"Don't I know the chap with her, Tinus? His face seems familiar."

"Should be, Andre, if you've watched Genevieve's movies. That's her co-star from *Keeper of the Legend*. Gregory L'Amour."

"Didn't the papers claim they were a couple?"

"Not according to Genevieve. The story sold papers and promoted the film. She said it was part of the job."

"Having an affair with the co-star!"

"No, idiot. Promoting what they call the Movie in America. What we call the Picture in England. Moving picture, get it? Here we go to the Pictures. There they go to the Movies."

"You're jealous of him."

"Why should I be?"

"He's rich, famous, and likely to have had an affair with Genevieve."

"Don't talk so loud or they'll hear you. Can we get four in the boat?"

"So long as he doesn't rock it. Can Americans row boats?"

They waited in silence for the newcomers to cross the lawn, Andre and Tinus having enjoyed their usual banter. Whatever Tinus might think in his private thoughts when the lights were out, in practical terms he was almost two years younger and out of what Andre would have called 'the running'. Somehow there was a different look about her, Tinus thought, as their eyes met with pleasure; the one eye of the mismatched pair was definitely darker, the iris going from dark brown to coal black like her father's. It had happened in the short time since they had last seen each other, Tinus having driven the Morgan down to London on a Saturday to see a performance of *Private Lives*. It made the brooding mystery in the girl, deep in her soul, more prominent, more dangerous.

"Gregory, that one's Tinus with the big grin. The lanky one is the pilot. His name's Andre. Hello! What a lovely day. May I introduce my chauffeur, Gregory L'Amour? He wanted to meet Andre and join the RAF when war breaks out."

"There's not going to be a war," said Andre, pleased at the idea someone so famous wanted to meet him. "Bomber Command, I'm afraid. I'm stationed just round the corner. Your first visit to England, L'Amour?"

"Yes it is. Call me Gregory. Fine country."

"Try it in the winter. Tinus says Genevieve plans staying the weekend at Oxford. I can run down to Uxbridge if you have a car. Take you up for a flip in one of our new bombers if the CO will give us permission. Should do. He also liked your film, Genevieve. Lovely to see you. Can you row, Gregory? Believe you Americans call everyone by their first names. I'm from South Africa. Tinus is from Rhodesia."

"Where's that?" asked Gregory L'Amour.

"To the north of us. An Englishman called Cecil Rhodes colonised the country in the time of Queen Victoria. I'm a Boer, if that means anything."

"Not really. But I sure as hell would like to visit with you at Uxbridge. You say it's a bomber station?"

"That's right."

"I can't yet fly a plane but I sure can row a boat. In Chicago you learn to row a boat before you ride a bicycle."

"Where's Chicago?"

"You're joking?"

"Matter of fact I'm not. I know nothing about America. We Boers have been nicely isolated from the world for three hundred years. Every time we tried to get away from the British they followed. Right up to the Old Transvaal."

"You can fill me in tomorrow in the car. I'm sure Genevieve will want to stay here with Tinus. If you Boers tried so hard to avoid the British, what are you doing here?"

"Flying aeroplanes. Only snag is, I throw up before every flight. Tightens the nerves. The boat's half a mile downriver. We're going for a row. Part of the tradition."

"I have an idea," said Tinus, who liked the idea better of being left alone with Genevieve. "Why don't I give Uncle Harry a ring? He knows everyone in the RAF. One of our most famous pilots in the war, Gregory. Twenty-three kills. If he doesn't know the commanding officer at RAF Uxbridge, the chances are the CO will have heard of my uncle. A bit of good publicity shouldn't hurt the RAF's recruitment. Uncle Harry says they are looking to train new pilots right now. If the press find out you want to be a pilot, Greg, every lad of eighteen will want to join up. You mind if I phone my uncle and suggest he lets the papers know where you will be? You'll have to wear the right gear to fly in one of our bombers. Make a sensational photograph."

"Can I say I'll join your air force if Germany starts a war?"

"Why not? Frighten the holy shit out of Hitler. Giving Hitler the Sudetenland without even asking the Czech leaders is a recipe for disaster, according to Mr Bowden. I think we're in for a fight and so does Mr Bowden"

"Who's Mr Bowden?" asked Gregory.

"My philosophy tutor. He says Hitler won't stop with the Sudetenland. He'll march in and take the whole of Czechoslovakia that isn't occupied by Hungary."

"He thinks it's that bad?"

"Said to me it's all a matter of time."

"You think my promise to join the RAF would turn the tide?" Gregory L'Amour was grinning at Tinus, quite sure his leg was being pulled.

"Definitely. Can't you imagine the threat of the hero of the Battle of Hastings, instead of wading ashore, flying a Hurricane over the Channel? Genevieve told me her film had been shown in Germany with subtitles. They'll shudder in their boots in Berlin, Mr L'Amour. The fact you are an American will send a message that won't hurt either. Later in life you can claim you were the man who singlehandedly stopped this German aggression, or whatever history will call the looming shindig. Mr Bowden says Hitler has his eye on Poland next. That Poland is the rub. We have a treaty with them that if either country is attacked, both countries are equally involved. That if Germany invades Poland, Mr Bowden says, we will be at war."

"You should be in Hollywood, Tinus. Have you ever tried to write a film script? You have a vivid imagination. You better go and phone your uncle. If I can stop people really killing each other, I'm in. After we filmed each battle scene in *Keeper of the Legend* the corpses got up and went for their lunch. That's how I like to experience war. The real thing would frighten the crap out of me, not this Adolf Hitler."

LIKE MANY THINGS in Tinus's life that started as a joke, even if underneath the image of Gregory L'Amour being more to Genevieve than a co-star evoked in him strong feelings of jealousy, as if someone was trying to steal his possessions, the idea took on its own momentum, swallowing up their idea for a row on the river. With Andre's urging, Tinus went back to his digs where he lived with Mrs Witherspoon and used her phone to call Hastings Court, no one being at the Air Ministry on a Saturday afternoon.

While Tinus talked on the phone, Andre talked to Mrs Witherspoon, who had been his landlady when he was up at Oxford on a Rhodes Scholarship, making the kindly woman beam all over her face. Having never been to a cinema, Mrs Witherspoon was unaware of the reason for students gathering outside her home, someone on their walk back from the river where they left the car to enjoy the sunshine having recognised Gregory L'Amour, who twice on the way had been asked to sign his autograph.

Anthony had answered the phone at Hastings Court and gone off to find his father. Ten minutes later it was all arranged, Uncle Harry promising Tinus the CO of Uxbridge would fall in with the plan to give the RAF's recruitment drive an unexpected boost.

"You should think of going into the publicity business, Tinus. This one has lots of potential. Does Genevieve want to go down to Uxbridge? She'd better. The two of them photographed together will make for an even bigger story. What a brilliant idea. I'll get hold of Horatio Wakefield. His wife thinks she owes me a favour for bringing her a patient. I'm sure William Smythe will love to see Genevieve. Bruno Kannberg of the *Daily Mirror* owes me a favour for letting him and his lady stay at Hastings Court where he wrote the book on Genevieve that has made them so much money. I'll think of some others. Timothy Kent will have some ideas. Pilots, Tinus, we need more pilots. The machinery is under control. What did you think of the PM's speech?"

"Mr Bowden thought it a load of rubbish."

"Only time will tell. Tomorrow at three in the afternoon at RAF Uxbridge."

"Uncle, you haven't even spoken to Andre's CO."

"I don't have to ask him, Tinus. Now be a good chap and look after your guests. Take them for a row on the river."

"Is the dam still on hold?"

"For the moment."

"So Chamberlain was talking rubbish?"

"In the sense of the words, yes. In the meaning, no."

"You're talking like a politician."

"Just get L'Amour to Uxbridge at three tomorrow afternoon. How are you, Tinus? I want to talk to you about your career. You'll be coming down here, I hope, when you've finished at Oxford. Then we can talk. Lovely day for a change. Give my love to Genevieve. How's the car going?"

"Like a dream. Andre hasn't bought himself another car."

"Some of the other pilots will have cars on the station."

· · ·

WHEN WILLIAM SMYTHE received his call he was not sure whether it would be better for his peace of mind to deny Harry Brigandshaw and so avoid seeing Genevieve.

"Are you still giving our American friends a run for their money, William? I'd suggest you be more kind to them. All businessmen are jealous if they can't break into someone else's market. Do you really think they are trying to chase us out of our colonies? I bought a house in Cape Town last year as a funk hole for my family as Tina hates the isolation of Elephant Walk. There isn't much of a market for America in Rhodesia and our tobacco isn't exactly competition for their farms in Virginia. Anyway, we have our plate full and shouldn't worry about the empire and American intentions. I rather think we are all part and parcel of the same big picture, so it wouldn't matter. Britain is still the largest foreign investor in America according to CE Porter. No one knows the exact figures but the idea sounds reliable. Everyone in business is chasing everyone's tail. Three o'clock at RAF Uxbridge. You're a good chap, William, so don't let me down. Don't you want to see Genevieve? I had the idea you were sweet on her. Do I have your word?"

"Of course, Mr Brigandshaw."

"It must be Harry by now. How long have we known each other?"

"Was it true Herr Henning von Lieberman, your old friend's cousin, was working for the Nazi Party when he was seeing Janet?"

"No idea what you are talking about."

"Didn't you suggest Janet could help cure his stutter?"

"I help a lot of people, William. Horatio should remember. I can't remember everything. Good heavens, I was fifty this year, or was it the year before? See what I mean?"

"My informants said you had him tailed the whole six weeks he was staying at the Savoy."

"Sorry, William. You've lost me. Will you phone Horatio and bring him down, or must I give him a ring? He'll need that chap Gordon Stark with him to take the photographs."

"Your memory for detail is remarkable, Harry."

"Do I detect a little cynicism, William? I suppose you'd have to be a little cynical as a newspaper reporter. Goes with the job. Old minds remember some things and not others. Usually the trivial."

"I'll bring Gordon with Horatio in my own car. Do we need a pass or something?"

"Just your press cards. They'll know you're coming at the guard room.

The SPs will have your names. In the RAF we call them Special Police. The army calls them Military Police."

"Your good memory again, Harry. How are the kids?"

"Like all children, they want their own way. Listened to you on the BBC Empire Service the other day. It gives me pleasure to see a man get on in this life. All you need now is a wife and children. Bachelors have too much fun. Not enough responsibility."

"Are you going to be at Uxbridge?"

"Whatever for? Anthony is playing for the Colts first eleven. Radley against Cranleigh, where my old friends Colonel Makepeace and District Commissioner Holmes went to school. They're back in Tanganyika. Spent some of their home leave with us. Such a small world isn't it, William? Anthony is not going to be as good as Tinus or Andre at cricket but playing the game is what really counts."

A moment later the phone went dead in William's hand, making him smile. Harry had a bad habit of not saying goodbye. It was, of course, he told himself, as he asked the operator at the exchange to get him Horatio Wakefield's number, the three of them all together; himself, Tinus Oosthuizen and Gregory L'Amour. Maybe Harry was right. He should repair his bridges with the Americans. Writing up Gregory L'Amour as a future hero would make some amends. So what if the empire went down the drain? All empires went down the drain in the end leaving most of the people pretty much the same, trying to scratch a living. With the advent of the aircraft the world was growing smaller. The Royal Navy would be unable to button up the new world. Evolution. The trick in William's mind was not to be left behind. Thinking of Glen Hamilton in America, who would syndicate the L'Amour story and scratch him more than a living, he remembered again how much he owed to Harry Brigandshaw for introducing him to the American.

Then he spoke to Horatio and made the rest of the arrangements. It would be good to see his old friend again, so that was something. Maybe Gordon Stark could be persuaded with Mr Glass's permission to sell him for a small sum the best of the photographs for the American newspapers. His life would go on with or without Genevieve, as he had found out with Betty Townsend, even if she was more serious than him. Seeing it was a weekend and Betty did not have to be in the office to answer his telephone, he would take her with them to see the aeroplanes. She would like that. Hopefully, Genevieve would not, something he rather doubted. When a woman did not care two little bits, trying to make her jealous with another woman was an act of futility, which just about summed up his whole relationship with Genevieve.

ONCE THEY WERE out on the river, no one took any notice. Genevieve had produced a hat that shaded her shoulders as well as her head. To the onlookers walking the river banks they were four students out on the water for a late afternoon row, laughing happily among themselves without a care in the world. In the middle of the river, steel craft, propelled by long, big-bladed oars, shot past them, the rowers in tight running vests taking no notice of anything other than their rowing. Tinus and Andre gave a running commentary on the colleges of the rowers out practising for the upcoming inter-college regatta at the end of the month.

"The Boat Race was in the spring," said Tinus. "We won, of course. If these chaps do well in the regatta they may get a place in next year's Oxford crew. To get a blue for rowing is the biggest accolade a man can get up at Oxford or Cambridge. Sort of lives with you for the rest of your life, Greg. You see old men wrapped in their rowing scarves all the way up and down the river from Putney when we have the Boat Race. It's a bit like the FA cup at football. There's only one of them in the world... You row very well. Never sculled myself, neither has Andre. In Africa we stay on the banks of the rivers. Too many crocodiles and hippos.

"My Uncle Harry hit a hippo once, landing a seaplane on a river in the Congo. They were trying to get away from a storm or something. Killed his best friend, Iggy Bowes-Lyon, who flew with him in the war. You may have read about it. Uncle Harry went missing for a couple of years. The only one to come out of the jungle alive.

"Now that saga would make a good film, Genevieve. Why don't you ask your Uncle Robert or his wife Freya to write Hollywood a good script?... Don't the weeping willow trees look beautiful at this time of evening, drooping their wands into the river? Just the right spot for a picnic. Let's take her ashore and see what Mrs Witherspoon put in the hamper. She's such a dear. Andre found her first. I tell her that, after my mother, she would have been my next choice."

"I told her the same, Tinus," said Andre, as the old rowing boat glided into shore. "This all brings back such good memories. The Thames on a summer night when it isn't raining has to be the most beautiful place on earth."

"I'll still take the Zambezi with the game coming down to the water to drink at dusk, the small ones keeping a good look out for the lions. England is pretty. Africa is majestic. Vast. So much of it. The bush goes on forever. It's a different feeling alone in the bush, part with the animals, just one of them, as much afraid of the lions as the rest of them. One day, Greg, if you give up being a film star you should come out and visit us in Rhodesia."

"Why do I have to wait? I'm finding a whole new world right here and it's wonderful. My father's never been out of Illinois. Thank you, Genevieve. This is the best day of my life."

"She looks so beautiful," whispered Tinus, as the late sun, caught in under the picture hat, set off Genevieve's eyes, making her cheeks glow with the colour of a rosebud.

All three men stopped rowing the boat towards the weeping willows to look at her, making Genevieve spread her hands and open fingers over her face.

"Stop staring. You make me think of Gerry Hollingsworth, the one-time Louis Casimir who always stared at me and never said a word."

"Why did he change his name?"

"He's a Jew, Greg. Trying to protect his family. Why he came over to America. It's not good being a Jew at the moment in Europe. Why do people hate like that? What's the point? He may stare at me but so are you, even if the stare is a little different. He's the same. Having to run away must be terrible. His grandfather came to England from Hungary to get away. Why don't people like the Jews? I don't understand. Someone said it's because they crucified Jesus which was wrong, surely. I thought it was the Romans. Two thousand years. How long can you go on hating someone? People who do that must be sick. Poor Mr Hollingsworth. Now you know why he changed his name, so no one in the future will persecute his family for being Jews. Poor man says he can't even go to shul anymore... Who put two bottles of wine in the hamper?"

"I did," said Gregory. "I had them stashed in the rental."

"Good thinking," said Andre. "Who's going to jump out first? In England at this time of the year it doesn't get dark until ten. The twilight. Wine in the twilight, that some like to call the gloaming. Gloaming sounds better. Someone told me it's very old English. Before Chaucer."

"Let's stay out until it's very dark," said Gregory. "There's always reflected light on a river to row by. Just remember where I parked the car. What's the weather going to be like tomorrow for flying, Andre?"

"Perfect."

"It's just so good to be alive," said Gregory L'Amour as he jumped off the boat, holding it steady for the rest of them to come ashore without getting their feet wet.

WHEN BRUNO KANNBERG put down the phone and told his wife, her whole face lit up.

"Can I come with you, darling? Gregory L'Amour! Could you get a photograph with me and Gregory L'Amour together?"

"Harry Brigandshaw's nephew will be there. You remember, we met him at that restaurant in Greek Street where they break all the plates. It's Sunday tomorrow so you don't have to work. You may have to stay in the car if the RAF don't allow you onto a bomber station without a press card."

"I'll smile at them. I'm your wife. Don't they allow journalists' wives? Genevieve will talk them into it, darling. I can't wait. Are you sure Arthur Bumley will lend you his car? Film stars are so exciting. It was so clever of you writing Genevieve's memoirs. Do you think we are going to get some more money from the book? I can ask Genevieve. There should be more by now. Maybe you can offer to write a book about Gregory L'Amour and we can go to America if he's sailing back next week. On the same boat, wouldn't that be lovely? Just as well I haven't fallen pregnant."

"What about your job with the solicitors?"

"Oh, they won't mind. Shorthand typists are ten a penny."

"And the boat fare?"

"He'd pay for that if he wants a book. Lucky you had your name on the back cover. They should know who you are in America. I just can't wait. Do we know which boat they are sailing on? I'll bet it's a big one. First class. We'll travel to America first class."

"The flat, Gillian?"

"Pay a few months' rent in advance. Max Pearl will publish a book on Gregory L'Amour, I'm sure. Jump at it. We can ask him to cable us an advance against the royalty. This time you can keep the whole ten per cent royalty. Gregory L'Amour won't want any. He's rich enough as it is."

"The army will have to forget me tomorrow."

"Of course they will. Like shorthand typists, second lieutenants in the Territorial Army are ten a penny. You won't have to play your war games tomorrow."

"We're not playing games, Gillian. We fire live ammunition I'll have you know."

"But you never kill anyone, silly. We won't need the money they pay you as a part-time soldier anymore."

"I don't think you get out of the army that easily. I mentioned the exercise tomorrow to Harry Brigandshaw. Said the air force would put in a word. I'm to phone in sick and the TA will understand."

"It's just a game, Bruno. What am I going to wear? You are so clever, Bruno, knowing all these famous people. I've always wanted to mix with the rich and famous. Makes me feel special, not just some dull typist married to a journalist."

"Is it as bad as all that?"

"Not anymore. If you are sweet to me like this for the rest of the day and promise to take me with you, we can have a little bit of fun tonight. First phone Mr Bumley for the car. Where is the place we're going?"

"Not far from Slough."

"It's going to be a lovely day, I just feel it... Gregory L'Amour, whoever would have thought it? Gillian West with Gregory L'Amour."

"You're Gillian Kannberg now."

"I know, darling. But I still think of myself as Gillian West. Do I look pretty, Bruno?"

"Good enough to eat."

"Not for you, silly. I was thinking of Gregory L'Amour tomorrow."

First Bruno telephoned the adjutant of his unit and told him the truth. Then he phoned Arthur Bumley to borrow the car. To be absolutely certain he was going to get sex that night, something his wife had kept from him for a week, he phoned the Greek restaurant where they had met Tinus Oosthuizen and made a reservation for two. Half toying with the idea of suggesting sex to his wife straight away in her excitement, he decided to play the game safe. The immediate approach would have made it obvious he knew that giving him sex when it suited her was the way his wife made him do what he was told.

Smiling to himself in anticipation, Bruno was a happy man. Waiting for anything good was worthwhile. He even thought the waiting made the sex, when it happened, even better. There was one thing for certain: he was never going to get bored having sex with his wife.

"We're going out to dinner," he called into the bedroom where Gillian was looking through her clothes for something to wear on the morrow.

"How lovely, darling. If the dress shops were open on a Saturday evening we could go shopping on the way to the restaurant."

Thanking his lucky stars for the government's fixed shopping hours, Bruno began mulling the idea of writing a book on Gregory L'Amour, liking the idea the more he looked at it in his mind. On the spur of the moment he decided to book a call to Max Pearl in America. Luckily, Bruno had his publisher's home number.

Better to have his publisher behind him before he asked L'Amour. With a good advance from his publisher, Bruno hoped he would once again be able to keep up with his wife's spendthrift ways.

"The more money, the more sex," he whispered to himself as he went about making his plans, more horny than he could remember ever being before.

2

———————

Taking his lead from Harry Brigandshaw, and to prevent confusion at the guard room and the wooden sentry box at the entrance to Royal Air Force Uxbridge, Group Captain Lowcock, the station commander of the three bomber squadrons, declared the Sunday afternoon an open day to the public; anything the RAF did not wish the press to see was hidden away in locked hangars, including the three new twin-engine Blenheims that were capable of flying to Berlin and back again.

Geoffrey Lowcock knew as well as Harry Brigandshaw that the RAF's Achilles heel in the event of a war, a war that neither of them believed could be avoided, was a lack of skilled pilots. A sea rescue plan had been put together by Coastal Command to 'fish' pilots from the 'drink' who bailed out of damaged aircraft into the English Channel and get them back to their squadrons within hours of being pulled out of the sea. Destroyed aircraft were replaceable. Skilled pilots were not.

"It's just as important to train pilots now, Geoffrey, as it is to build advanced aircraft the enemy knows nothing about. Make it an open day. Get a brass band. Fly anti-aircraft balloons; give the children miniature Union Jacks. Get the wives to lay on some grub. He's as big a Hollywood star as we'll ever get."

The brass band and the miniature Union Jacks suggested by Harry Brigandshaw had been a problem; the rest had fallen quickly into place.

By three o'clock on the Sunday afternoon RAF Uxbridge was ready for visitors, the SPs on duty at the entrance ready to wave in the people without any questions.

WILLIAM SMYTHE ARRIVED with Betty Townsend as a cushion to Genevieve and to stop himself feeling so miserable at the thought of seeing Genevieve with Tinus Oosthuizen and Gregory L'Amour. They were the first of the press to arrive, so it seemed.

"What's going on, Will? These chaps are far too friendly. Thought they'd frisk us at the least," said Horatio.

"Open day, sir," answered a tall man in a blue uniform with a red band round his blue peaked hat. Horatio Wakefield was sat in the back of William's car next to his cameraman, Gordon Stark. Janet had declined the invitation to join them, preferring to spend Sunday with the children.

"Has he arrived?" asked William.

"You are the first, sir. Please call at the guard room and someone will show you round. I've never met an American before. She's the one though." The SP was smiling with anticipation written all over his face, annoying the hell out of William.

"Talkative bugger," said William as he drove onto the station. "Most unlike any policeman I have known. Do you remember those buggers in Berlin, Horatio? They never said a word or gave the glimmer of a smile. I always thought they were enjoying themselves frightening the crap out of me. Sorry, Betty. The word just came out. What a lovely day. Isn't Harry Brigandshaw meant to be here? There's another car coming in behind us. Do you know what L'Amour looks like?"

"He'll be with Genevieve," said Horatio.

"There's another car behind the other car," said William, looking through the rear-view mirror. "This is going to be a circus. Get your camera ready, Gordon. I say, the place does look smart. All the stones on the side of the road are painted white. Some poor sod doing jankers, I think they call it."

"What's that?" asked Betty, craning her neck to see who was in the car behind.

"When you do something wrong they give you nasty jobs," said William.

"The man driving behind us is in uniform," said Betty. "The girl I recognise. That's Fleur Brooks from the Mayfair sitting next to the driver. Plays the violin. I can't quite see the girl behind but I think she's also in the band. There's an older man next to her who looks bored. The other car is being waved on. Yes, it's them all right. He's better looking in the flesh than he was at the pictures. Tingle, tingle. What wouldn't I do to get my hands on him."

"Is there a girl in the car?" asked William, keeping his eye on the road and avoiding his mirror.

"A girl and two boys. Where does she find them? The other two are quite dishy. One of the boys is waving at us."

"Tinus Oosthuizen," said Horatio. "Harry Brigandshaw's nephew. Someone's coming into land in a Tiger Moth. I'll take a bet that's Harry Brigandshaw. Drove to Redhill aerodrome and flew up with his friend John Woodall who teaches people how to fly. How did he get it all together so quickly? I suppose when you've run a shipping line this is a piece of cake. Nothing like experience."

"The girl has just blown you a kiss, William."

"You mean Genevieve," said William, keeping his head straight.

"Why don't you look at her? Oh dear, so it's like that? Real competition."

"Not competition, Betty."

"Thank you, sweetheart. A bloody film star blowing kisses at my boyfriend and that isn't competition," she said flatly.

"You're my secretary."

"Give me time, lover-boy."

"The last time I was at a military aerodrome was in Warsaw," said William to change the subject. "Couple of years ago. Even remember the lad's name who showed me around. Studying Law and flying part-time for the Polish air force. Count Janusz Kowalski. Harry told me to tell him to come to England if Germany overruns Poland. Spoke good English. Wonder what happened to him? You remember, Horatio? Fritz Wendel, God bless his soul, sent me to one of their air shows. Pilots were good but the planes antique in comparison to what we and the Germans have to fly. Must have finished his law degree by now. Father was a judge or something. Big estate in the country. Old aristocracy. Do you know the Polish army are still riding horses? Genuine cavalry. The Germans will make mincemeat out of them despite our treaty to defend the Poles. I mean how long would it take us to get an army to Poland? One of those treaties that isn't worth the paper it's written on, if you ask me. Just show to frighten Hitler, which it won't. I'm not sure we've got anything that could fly nonstop to Warsaw and back, so the RAF won't be any help to the poor bloody Poles."

"Why don't you ask them?" said Horatio. "Now's the time. Not that they'd tell you. If war breaks out, do foreign correspondents become war correspondents?"

"Depends what they do. Probably. What happened to that German Janet had as a patient? Did she cure his stutter?" asked William.

"Funnily enough she did. I liked him. Not all Germans are bad."

"He's a member of the Nazi Party, for God's sake," said William, parking the car next to what he took to be the guard room. Genevieve's car was right behind them.

"Knew a chap who was a member of Mosley's party," said Horatio, ignoring William's reference to Henning von Lieberman. "Now there's a dangerous bastard."

"Say that again. If war breaks out they say they're going to lock him up for the duration. What people do in pursuit of power!"

"Someone was saying in the office Gandhi is one day going to be prime minister of India when he's kicked out the British Raj."

"Never. The Muslims won't let him. Can you imagine the Hindus and Muslims living side by side without us British keeping the peace? America wants us out so they can move into the Indian market... You were right, Horatio. That was Harry Brigandshaw landing the Tiger Moth. Here he comes. You'd never think looking at him he nearly died in hospital. Must be seven years ago. Time flies. The group captain with him must be the CO. Come on. This is where we all do some work. Glen Hamilton said on the transatlantic phone this morning he'll sell anything I can get on L'Amour wanting to be a flyer. His last film was a howling success in the States, apparently. Film stars sell, Horatio. Come on. Betty, be a dear and keep lots of notes. Gordon, start flashing your flashbulb. Your editor, Mr Glass, will sell me the photographs but only for the American market... What's that bloody great balloon doing up there in the sky?"

"WILLIAM'S IGNORING ME," said Genevieve, waving back at Horatio Wakefield as he walked across to the guard room. "Why are we stopping? Look, it's Uncle Harry with an important-looking man with a peaked hat and two rows of ribbons on his chest."

"What have you done to William Smythe?" said Tinus innocently, turning to Gregory L'Amour. "He's a freelance journalist with big American connections. Uncle Harry said something about the press and RAF recruitment for pilots. Looks like more than just the four of us. Coming towards us, Gregory, is my Uncle Harry and John Woodall, who certified my competence to fly an aircraft, back in 1933 it must have been. Must be the CO with them. Quite a reception, Greg. What's the Honourable Barnaby St Clair doing here? Must be Uncle Harry again. Andre, it's Fleur and Celia and a chap in RAF uniform who looks like he knows what's going on. You'll get a flip by the look of it, Greg. There are more cars coming in. About half a dozen and everyone in civvies."

"Do you mind if I take a photograph, Mr L'Amour?"

"Aren't you Gordon Stark, Horatio's photographer?"

"Afternoon, Tinus. The RAF have made today an open day at Uxbridge. Bit of public relations after Chamberlain's talks with Hitler."

"Has it anything to do with Mr L'Amour and Genevieve?"

"Everything."

"Uncle Harry! How are you? Mr Woodall. How nice to see you again."

"My nephew, Geoffrey. Not a bad pilot. Group Captain Lowcock, Tinus. Mr L'Amour," said Harry putting out his hand. "Harry Brigandshaw. Welcome to the RAF. Genevieve! Where's my kiss? How's your grandmother and father?... Come over here, Barnaby, and get yourself introduced. Look at all those cars."

"What's the balloon for?" asked Betty, looking at the group captain.

"The steel wires anchored to the truck make it difficult for enemy aircraft to fly over the runway without clipping their wings. In time of war we have balloons like that all round the field. Group Captain Geoffrey Lowcock, Mr L'Amour. Glad you could help us. Our American cousins are greatly important to us. Met some of you Americans in the last war. Good pilots."

"Can I have a photograph with Gregory, Genevieve and the group captain?"

"After we've had a cup of tea. I'm going to take you up myself, Mr L'Amour."

"Call me Greg, Geoff."

"Well, I could I suppose."

"Do I get a uniform?"

"We can arrange that I suppose. Honorary RAF officer for the afternoon, how does that sound? Miss Genevieve, how nice of you to come. You are even more beautiful than in the pictures."

"He's an old flatterer."

"Not at all, Harry. It's only flattery when it isn't true. I believe you are leaving us again for America?"

"Next week," said Genevieve. "I never know if the coming week is this week or next week. Greg and I are sailing back together. My word, Uncle Harry, you really did work the phones; here comes my biographer, Greg. The man who helped me write my memoirs. Bruno! Come over and meet Gregory L'Amour. Gillian, how are you? I don't have to ask if Uncle Harry had a hand in your sudden appearance. Gregory, why don't you ask Bruno to write your story in a book?"

"Only a pleasure," grinned Bruno putting out his hand. "Great minds think alike, Genevieve. I phoned Max Pearl and he's quite interested. He said he's met you on the set of your movies, Mr L'Amour."

"Call me Greg."

"This is my wife, Gillian. We recently got married."

"Can we make a photograph of us all together, Mr L'Amour? I'm your greatest fan, I'm sure."

"Call me Greg, Gillian. With all the flashbulbs going off, come and stand next to me and give the cameras that big smile. You can join us, Bruno. I read Genevieve's book, of course. Very well written. Why don't we have a talk before I sail for America?"

"If you agree in principle, we can be on the boat and have four full days to go into the right detail of your life. We wrote most of Genevieve's book staying at Mr Brigandshaw's beautiful home outside Mickleham. You need quality time with the subject to write a good book. My wife is a top-class shorthand typist and helped us on the Genevieve book, so a lot of groundwork can be done on the boat."

"Sounds as if you already made plans. Why not? All publicity is good publicity. If you want to last in films you have to keep your name in front of the public. Do we get to share the author's royalty from the publisher? Genevieve tells me it's important to stash away some money for when we lose our bit of fame and no one wants to read about us in a book, let alone write one. Money is the lifeblood of the future. You can run out of fame but don't run out of money."

"Five per cent of retail, Greg," Bruno decided on reflection.

"Then we have a deal. We're travelling first class on the *Queen Mary*. Do you have your passports in order?"

"Always, Greg," said Gillian, posing next to him for the cameras. "I will phone the shipping company line first thing in the morning."

"Do we get a big advance?"

"Of course. My husband will phone Mr Pearl in the morning. Give us your word on the book and we'll have him deliver your bank a cheque in California."

"New York. Genevieve and I will be living in New York for our next movie."

"As man and wife?"

"Not at all. She won't marry me."

"Did you ask?"

"He doesn't have to, Gillian," said Genevieve. "We understand each other very well. Despite all the press to the contrary, we are not a couple... William! Come over here. Why are you ignoring me? Who's the lovely girl by your side?"

"Betty Townsend, meet Genevieve. How are you, Genevieve?"

"I was going to phone."

"I'm sure you were. I was coming backstage that night I came to *Private Lives*."

"Did you like it?"

"Of course. You were in the play."

"What a lovely day," said Gillian.

"It is, isn't it?" said Genevieve. "Andre, you'd better go over and say hello to Fleur and Celia. For some reason the world seems very small today. What do you say, Uncle Harry? Grandmother is so sad after Grandfather died. My father's fallen in love with the cows and the pigs, if you can believe it."

"I will drive down for a visit. Your grandmother is very special to me. We have a little reception for everyone in the officers' mess... Come along, everyone. This is going to be a party. One rule. No drinking before flying so we all drink tea. My word, what a beautiful day. Barnaby, why are you looking so grumpy in the company of such lovely girls? Fleur. Celia. You both look lovely. Barnaby tells me your records are selling like hot cakes. Timothy, thank you for driving down at such short notice."

"My pleasure, sir."

"By the grin on your face I rather think it is," said Harry, looking from Timothy Kent to Fleur and back again.

"How are you, Harry?" said Barnaby.

"Excellent. Quite excellent. We were going to have little flags to give to the children... Where's Janet, Horatio?"

"At home with the kids. Sunday's the only time she has any peace from her speech therapy."

"She won't have much from young children. Mine are in a permanent state of noise."

"Talking of *Private Lives*, Tinus," said Genevieve, sweetly, "Vera sends her love."

"Vera?" said Tinus abruptly turning round from his conversation with Andre, who was looking embarrassed as a junior officer with everyone else on equal terms with the group captain monopolised the conversation. "Do I know a Vera?"

Andre, having watched Tinus blush from the roots of his hair down his neck at the mention of Vera, controlled his laughter, knowing just as well as Tinus who Vera was.

"She said you shared a boat."

"Oh, that Vera," said Tinus offhandedly. "We travelled together on the *Corfe Castle* in '35. Where did you meet Vera?" He was going to add 'how does she remember me?' but thought better of it, his whole body in a panic as he recalled his first sexual encounter at the bottom of a lifeboat.

"She took over my part after I signed the film contract."

"Is she any good?"

"Better than me, don't you know. But I can always practise. Maybe we should practise together, Tinus?"

"I'm not an actor."

"I think you are doing very well at the moment. She even said you were going to introduce me to her as part of the bargain. You should always keep your end of a bargain. Vera said she kept hers, even if her part was somewhat brief. Tinus, I do believe you are blushing for the second time. It's rather sweet."

"I haven't seen Vera since the boat trip."

"That was her point."

"What was all that about?" asked William, who had been listening to every word coming out of Genevieve's mouth in the hope she would say something that would stop his longing, the interplay between her and Tinus only making it worse. William knew exactly what it was all about without having to be told.

"I have no idea," said Tinus, recovering himself. "Absolutely no idea... Did someone say something about a reception committee in the officers' mess?"

Tinus was looking around, taking in the feeling of an operational air force station that he knew someday soon would be his home, as Genevieve and Gregory L'Amour were swallowed up by the press.

"I'll show you," said Andre. "I think we've lost Genevieve again to the journalists. Poor Greg's being eaten up alive. I don't ever want to be famous. Just look at the poor fellow trying to be so polite to everyone at once. Who's the pilot with Fleur and Celia?"

"Flight Lieutenant Kent," said Tinus. "He somehow works with Uncle Harry. First time I saw him in uniform."

"What does your uncle do at the Air Ministry?"

"No idea. One minute he's test flying prototypes at Redhill, next minute he's looking for German spies. I prefer not to ask questions. There's talk his friend in Germany is a Nazi, so it's not so simple. Uncle Harry likes Klaus. Trusts him. That much I do know. After the war, Herr von Lieberman visited Elephant Walk on his honeymoon. One day trying to kill each other up in the air, next day best of friends on safari in the African bush. Wars and people in wars never did make sense. Like my grandfather being hung by the British, a Boer doing his job fighting for his own people while married to my grandmother who was English. Make sense out of that one. Now we're going to do it again against the Germans with the Boers on our side as they were in France in the trenches. Man never stops bickering. When he can't have his own way, he wants a fight. Sometimes the idea of living in Africa far from everybody is very attractive."

"I know what you mean," said Andre.

"Let's get that cup of tea they're talking about."

"She caught you on the wrong foot, didn't she?"

"Yes, she did. Didn't think women talked about such things," said Tinus.

"We do," replied Andre.

"Only to our best friends. Not to a stranger. What was Genevieve trying to get at?"

"Do you want my opinion?"

"Why I asked, Andre."

"She's jealous of Vera. Underneath all the banter of the three musketeers, friends just having fun, she's in love with you."

"I'm too young."

"That's never made any difference."

"She's famous. Next month I won't have an allowance and probably no job."

"Women don't see it that way. They see the potential. For themselves and their children. It's part of evolution. They think with their instinct that some call their heart. Basic, primal instincts all the way from the slime of evolution, according to Darwin and Freud."

"You've lost me."

"She wants her turn in the boat, Tinus."

"What about Greg?"

"He's been in the boat. So has William Smythe, the way he was looking at her. She wants you in the boat where she wants to keep you. She's in love and you're blind. I'll take you to the mess and then I must change into uniform. Once on the station we have to be dressed properly."

"She's going to America."

"She'll be back again."

"Why?"

"You're here, Tinus. First love makes a strong impression on all of us for the rest of our lives. What comes afterwards never seems quite the same."

"I'm far too young to settle down."

"Doesn't have to be tomorrow. Life takes its course. The mess is in that building over there. Go and join your Uncle Harry while I get changed."

"I like the feel of an RAF station."

"So do I. My guess is it won't be long before they'll be asking you to join up."

IT WAS the first time Barnaby St Clair had been allowed into an officers' mess since stealing the fifty pounds from the mess funds at the end of the war and been kicked out of the army. All the other officers, he remembered looking round the familiar surroundings, had private incomes from their parents; the St Clairs were too poor to send him a penny. In the mess, rounds of drinks, quite often for everyone in the crowded room, were added to each officer's card in turn by the mess steward, the bill payable once a month. Not to pay one's bills was beyond the pale.

In the euphoria of the Turks and Germans finally collapsing, Cairo had been a place of high celebration. The war had ground Barnaby's nerves to the point that even a distant gunshot made him jump. Getting drunk every night trying to forget the dead officers he had met and fought with was only part of the problem. What he was going to do with the rest of his life was more to the point.

In 1918 the only trade known to Barnaby was that of a soldier, which was coming to an end. The CO had put him in charge of the mess funds. For three months Barnaby had been able to keep his unpaid bar bill to himself, but when the CO found out and ordered him to pay, he had had to find some money.

Asking his father was hopeless. Merlin was still somewhere in France. Robert had enough problems of his own with his foot blown off. He had already borrowed as much as he could from wealthy fellow officers, who were giving him the bird once they saw they were not getting their money back. Just before Barnaby was due to leave Egypt and go back to England and likely be asked to leave the service as, unlike some of the others, he was not a regular officer, he had taken fifty pounds from the mess fund and paid all his debts, leaving himself just over five shillings to see him into civilian life when he reached England to join the ranks of the unemployed.

The adjutant must have been watching him. Instead of being cashiered they had sent him straight to England and ordered him to resign his commission. Maybe they had appreciated his efforts in the Arabian Desert fighting the Turks, something he cynically doubted. He was one of them. Out of the top drawer. The Honourable Barnaby St Clair, younger son of a baron of ancient lineage who just happened to have run out of money.

It was more a matter of saving their collective face, kicking him swiftly out of the army rather than putting him on trial. Afterwards, he heard his commanding officer had paid in the fifty pounds. One day when the opportunity arose he was going to pay back the CO his money. Paths usually crossed again. He owed the CO for his social position in England and from that, his subsequent fortune which had grown from his contacts. Otherwise his equals would have sent him to Coventry for the rest of his natural life, a dishonest Englishman in the service of his king, a fate worse than prison, some thought a fate worse than death. No one for the rest of his life would have talked to him let alone done business: the whole British Empire was based on trust and honesty which excluded even the whiff of bad behaviour or corruption, with ostracism for anyone breaking the code of a gentleman.

Looking around the familiar room with the long bar at one end, it made Barnaby physically shudder at the thought of what should have happened to him without the understanding intervention of Colonel Hugh Parson. Then Barnaby saw Harry Brigandshaw watching him and walked across the room to get away, he hoped, from his bad memories.

"Feel like old times, Barnaby?"

"Certainly brings back memories. Not all of them good. There were so many chaps we left behind. I was just remembering I owed a man a debt."

"Pay him back."

"If I could find him."

"Ah, Barnaby. Leave that one alone. There are some debts you can never repay. You have to live with them. Someday you'll have a chance to help a young man yourself."

"You know a lot more about me than you pretend."

"Lucinda was very fond of you, we all are. It's just sometimes you get out of control. Thank you for keeping an eye on von Lieberman. We have eleven names on our list to watch for if war breaks out. Forewarned is forearmed."

"I didn't think anything happened. The things I do for King and country."

"He was sliding them up to his suite in the Savoy in the middle of all your gallivanting, which made him careless. I've already thanked Fleur and Celia."

"Will they call me up again if there's a war, Harry?"

"Probably. You were a damn good soldier. Just a fool in those days when it came to money."

"I didn't have any. You don't even know what it's like not to have money."

"I did in the Congo, Barnaby. There I had nothing. Not even my freedom. Do you want to join up again?"

"I'm too old."

"You're experienced. That will count for a great deal in the beginning."

Across the room, standing on his own, Harry saw Timothy Kent who caught his eye.

"You'll have to excuse me, Barnaby. You'd better go and join Fleur and Celia."

"They're all right surrounded by young officers. I've told them to sell their records to the media and have their photographs taken as many times as possible. You have to push music to make the public pick your record from the rack. I asked William Smythe to say something about them on the BBC Empire Service. He laughed. Said young girls and the state of the world had nothing to do with each other. He's getting a bit pompous now he's famous. How can they only serve tea at a time like this? You'd better go, Tim's waiting for you. Just ask him from me when we can leave. It's my car but he was driving."

"They'll get a lift back to London if you want to go," said Harry.

"Think I will. Celia and I don't see much of each other anymore."

"Thank you for bringing them. They're having fun. Tim had to be here, seeing he organised this shindig."

"They would at their age. At my age I should have five children and a nagging wife."

"She doesn't nag me, Barnaby."

"I was not referring to Tina. How is she?"

"Unhappy. Unhappy with herself. She thinks the world has passed her by. I want her to take the children to Cape Town out of harm's way. She has her brother in Johannesburg but that hasn't persuaded her, however much Albert helped Tina to become who she is in society. It was Albert who employed Miss Pinforth to teach Tina to speak properly."

"Bert doesn't like me."

"I wonder why? Tina thinks she'll be a fish out of water in Bishop's Court."

"If the shit hits the fan she'll go. I'm getting out of here. Makes me nervous. Too many ghosts. Tell Kent I've gone. He'll tell the girls. You should get some recruits out of this shindig, as you put it so succinctly. There is nothing like involving the public. I've done my bit."

THROUGH THE CROWD, Timothy Kent watched Barnaby leave the room. Out of the window he saw him get into his car. The two girls surrounded by blue uniforms took no notice. Even Fleur was fickle. Tim waited for Harry Brigandshaw to cross the crowded room where people were standing drinking cups of tea.

"What's the matter, Tim? Barnaby's gone. He's bored. If you can't get a lift back you'll have to take the train. I'll ask Bruno Kannberg. Borrowed his editor's car and there's only two of them in the vehicle. His wife wanted herself photographed with a film star."

"We think the Gestapo have arrested your friend Klaus von Lieberman."

"Why?"

"It seems he's trying to extract his son from the Hitler Youth Movement where they indoctrinate all the youngsters. You can make anyone a fanatic if you catch them young enough. The churches have been doing it for centuries."

"What happened to his wife?"

"She's on the estate I suppose. All reports coming out of Germany are sketchy."

"Could it have anything to do with us rumbling his cousin?"

"I hope not. They shoot them in Germany for treason."

"They shoot traitors everywhere, Tim. Is there anything we can do to help?"

"Bugger all. You either follow in those political situations or get right out of the way."

"I told him to go to Rhodesia."

"Probably wishes he had, poor sod. My guess is he's in for a very bad nightmare. Maybe you should have left him in his burning aircraft after all. When the Gestapo want information you don't want to give, it's better to be dead."

"They'll have found out about our radar at Poling even though Klaus said he'd never repeat it."

"Casualty of war, maybe he can give them Poling to get off the hook."

"I hope so. What does a man do when his country is going haywire? Do you mind if I give his wife a ring?"

"Not at all. We're not yet at war. Just make it a normal social call and ask for her husband. Be careful you don't make it worse for them by letting the Germans know we found out. They'll have taps on his phone."

"Maybe I should go."

"*To Bavaria*? You work for the Air Ministry."

"Not officially. I'm just an old pilot helping out. I can fly myself across if someone will lend me an aeroplane."

"On your own, Harry?"

"The thought just occurred I could take my nephew. He's due down from Oxford any day. Nothing much to do then and we have a lot to talk about. He's a damn good pilot."

"You'll need more than that Tiger Moth of Woodall's."

"See what you can do for me, Tim... My word, this is becoming a circus. I think I'll need quite a big aeroplane and fly into Switzerland. The von Liebermans are not far from the Swiss border. If Hitler's prodigy doesn't want to leave his Youth Movement and is the cause of the trouble, at least I can get the rest of the family out of Germany. I owe that to Klaus if he is locked up. What a bloody state of affairs."

"What would you do with them?"

"They can go and live on my farm in Rhodesia. The biggest chaos in history has always had an end. Sanity, fortunately for mankind, always prevails or none of us would likely be here, Tim. The old process of evolution would have come to an end once and for all."

"You'd better hire a civilian aircraft at Croydon."

"Good idea. Come and have a cup of tea."

"I've had one."

"Then have another, Flight Lieutenant Kent. No, not Croydon. The Isle of Wight. I know a man with a prototype flying boat who might let me give it a test flight. Plenty of range to reach Lake Constance, or is it the Lake of Constance? When I found Klaus's estate many years ago I noticed a whole lot of water over the hill, so to speak."

"When did you last fly a flying boat?"

"The day I hit the hippo in the Congo."

BY THE TIME Harry Brigandshaw took off in the Tiger Moth with John Woodall to fly back to Redhill and pick up his car for the drive to Hastings Court, he was feeling pleased with himself. The day had proved a success.

"A dozen youngsters asked me questions," John Woodall had told Harry before they climbed up into their plane. "With the Gregory L'Amour story in every British newspaper, the RAF will be inundated with enquiries from young lads. Piece of genius, Harry."

"You just have to give the newspapers what they want. A good story that sells papers. America will have the story in a few days. William Smythe is well known in the States, even if some like to hate him for suggesting American concern for our colonised subjects is not completely altruistic but guided by big business. They've been slavering over our Indian market for textiles for years. Cotton comes from America on British boats to Liverpool and our cotton mills in Lancashire and the subsequent cloth goes to India to make saris. All the Indian women have to do is wrap the cheap, colourful cloth around themselves and look beautiful. America wants their cotton mills in the southern states to make the cloth and the American ships to take it to India. No one says that, of course. Gandhi wants Indians to boycott British textiles but the Indians don't yet have the machinery to go into the mills. Gandhi is political, America commercial, in William's opinion. Whenever there is change in the market, someone makes money and someone loses. I've told William to tone it down. When we get into another brawl with Germany we're going to need all the help we can get... So the big film hero wants to be a fighter pilot. Geoff let him take the controls for a couple of minutes dressed in his flying gear with Gordon Stark taking photographs beforehand. Should get the glamour of the RAF across to all the Gregory L'Amour fans. Young people like to copy their heroes. Tina has another dinner party tonight so we'd better get on with it, John. Thanks for your help. How many asked you for flying lessons?"

"Three."

"I told Bruno Kannberg and Horatio Wakefield to put your telephone number in their papers. That's the *Mail* and the *Mirror*. Don't know about the others. Just have your girl ready to take the calls."

"Harry, how do you think of it all?"

"One favour deserves another, John. It's how the world goes round."

3

———————

*W*hen Bergit von Lieberman took the call from Harry Brigandshaw the following Wednesday she was beside herself. Erwin had gone off in a huff having been rude to his mother and Klaus had still not come home. She was numb with fear with no idea of what was really going on. The two younger children were still staying with friends for their summer holiday; either the children went away or friends came to stay to give them something to do. On their own they were always complaining of being bored, of not having anything to do.

Except for the servants, Bergit was alone in the house having to now run the day to day workings of the von Lieberman family estate. Bergit was not sure which was worse: Erwin telling her the Fatherland was more important than his family, or Klaus being taken away in a stranger's car without a word to her before he left.

The row with Erwin had erupted two weeks earlier on his seventeenth birthday when Klaus told him it was time to come home from school in Berlin to learn how to run the estate, there being no money to send the boy to university or finish the last year of his schooling. They had been in her husband's study when the shouting match began. Without another word to his father, Erwin had run out of the house, Bergit following him to find out what the row was really about.

"What's the matter with you?" she had said in the driveway outside the old house. "How dare you be rude to your father?"

"He doesn't understand."

"What doesn't he understand that you at seventeen understand so much better, Erwin?"

"The Fatherland. The Party is our salvation. Germany will be glorious again. The Fuehrer will lead us to conquer the world. I don't want to work on the estate. I want to work for the glory of the Fatherland. On my eighteenth birthday I shall join the Luftwaffe. Germany needs pilots. Father should have known that. We want war to obliterate the memory of our defeat."

"Don't talk tripe."

"You are an ignorant woman in defiance of the Party. No one questions the Fuehrer."

"How dare you? I'm your mother. Go inside and apologise to your father. The servants heard every word."

"The servants will always do what they are told. So will you, Mother. We will all learn to do what we are told, according to Mr Hahn."

"Where are you going?"

"Back to Berlin. To work for the Party if I am no longer to go to school. The Party will now look after me. Mr Hahn understands the destiny of Germany."

"Who is this Mr Hahn?" said Bergit, now in a panic at the thought of her son in the air force, the memory of Klaus flooding back.

"Our teacher in the Hitler Youth Movement. Heil Hitler!"

The boy had given the sky a stiff-armed salute and walked down the drive on his long walk to the railway station to join the people who had stolen her son; Bergit had her hand to her mouth, her eyes pricking with tears.

A week later three men had come for Klaus and taken him away. She had heard the first part of the conversation when a servant called her husband to the front door, from where she was standing halfway up the stairs holding the banister and looking down.

"You are required to come to Berlin, Herr von Lieberman. Please come to the car. No, you will not require a suitcase. Now, Herr Lieberman. To the car. Your wife will be told by the servant you have left the estate."

"Where am I going?"

"Berlin. We have some questions to ask you, Herr Lieberman."

Bergit had run up the stairs to watch from a second floor window as they took him away in the long black car. Then she was alone in the house, left with the servants with no idea what to do next. The servant who had answered the door and found her in the room was surly, no longer the polite domestic of the past. Cold with fury, Bergit had reflected on their future. Erwin was probably right. The servant was a member of the Nazi Party. In the end, they would all learn to do what they were told or perish.

The same servant called her to the phone, telling her there was a call from England. When she picked up the receiver the man was standing near to the small ivory telephone. The rest of the servants had been frightened of him ever since the three men had taken her husband away in the black car. He was watching her as she said hello.

"Bergit. It's Harry Brigandshaw. How are you all? Thought I'd call and say hello to Klaus. After your visit to England I thought we would pay your beautiful home a visit and do some horse riding. May I speak to Klaus?"

"He's not here, Harry. Ran up to Berlin for a business visit. Finding buyers for the potatoes and the onions. We like to sell straight into the big shops and cut out the man in the middle."

"When's he coming back? I'll call again."

"Not for a while, Harry. He's staying with his Uncle Werner."

"So everything is all right?"

"Everything is wonderful, Harry. How are Tina and the children?"

"They are fine. How is Erwin getting on at school?"

"One year to go and then university," Bergit lied, the sweat coming out on the palms of her hands as she wondered if the servant understood English or whether someone else was listening on the line at the telephone exchange.

"If you ever need help, Bergit, you know where to find me."

"Why would I ever need help, Harry? Germany has recovered from the hyperinflation. Why don't I get Klaus to call you when he comes home?"

"How are Gabby and Melina?"

"Sailing with school friends on the lake."

"Lake Constance?"

"It's only twenty miles away. The pass through the Alps is easy to travel in the summer. Children like friends their own age. Us old fuddy-duddies, I think is your odd English expression, are boring to the children in the long summer holidays."

"Don't I know it? Your use of English always amazes me, Bergit. Just tell Klaus I called."

"It's a long way to come to ride a horse, Harry."

"I suppose it is. We were just thinking of you. So you are quite all right?"

"Never better, Harry."

"That kind of English is more American."

"Goodbye, Harry. Thank you for calling."

Smiling for the benefit of the servant, Bergit put down the phone and walked through the house into the garden that led into the woods where she walked and walked, playing through every word of Harry's conversation in her mind. It was not difficult for Bergit to understand Harry had phoned for a reason. Harry Brigandshaw knew something was wrong. The fact he knew made her even more frightened.

HARRY KEPT LOOKING at the phone in his hand, the call to Germany having come to an abrupt end. Then he put the receiver back on the hook in his office. Timothy Kent was sitting in a comfortable chair on the other side of the desk.

"What happened, sir?"

"I think she brushed me off. Said Klaus would call me, rather like don't call us, we'll call you. He's in Berlin on estate business and Erwin is still going to school, according to Bergit. Her voice was taut, as if someone else was listening to our conversation. She gave me the feeling she was frightened. Sometimes in life, Tim, you can do more harm than good. It's often better to mind one's own business. I think this may be one of them. My blundering over to Germany could create a disaster for whoever is left behind."

"Are you going to call the Shorts factory?"

"Set it up, maybe. Left it open for Mrs von Lieberman to come back to me. Yes, I'll phone Crookshank, though it's a bit of a cheek. Never met the man. Just heard on the grapevine they have developed a viable flying boat. I don't think we should do anything more direct for the von Liebermans at the moment. Tinus will be disappointed. He liked the idea of flying to Switzerland. Two of the von Lieberman children are in Switzerland. On a sailing holiday with school friends."

"Hope she has the sense to leave them there."

"So do I. Poor Bergit. Apart from the servants she's all on her own by the sound of it. When you go out, ask the girl to get Crookshank on the line for me. It's better to be prepared."

Harry went back to the work on his desk, trying to concentrate. When the call to the aircraft engineer at Short Brothers was put through to him half an hour later, he had temporarily forgotten the call.

"Harry Brigandshaw," he barked into the phone without thinking.

"Crookshank."

"Mr Crookshank. Sorry to get the girl to get you on the line. You don't know me and what I'm going to ask is highly impertinent. Would you like me to test fly your new flying boat?"

"You don't know me, Colonel Brigandshaw, but I certainly know you. Your epic flight down Africa that ended so tragically inspired us here at Shorts to try harder to build a viable flying boat. The first Short Empire flew a little while ago, as you probably heard. We're building them for Imperial Airways. They've ordered six of the big aircraft that can fly twelve passengers in the kind of comfort they would get on a ship. We think it will make a financially viable airline. But if you would fly the Short Sunderland for us, its military variant, with all the attendant publicity, I'm sure the company would be delighted. How did you know my name, Colonel Brigandshaw? That I designed the plane?"

"Iggy Bowes-Lyon knew you in the war."

"You never heard another word of him?"

"Just disappeared with Fred Dwyer, the civil engineer who was on his way to Rhodesia to help build a dam. We're going to call it the De Wet Cronjé Dam when it's finished."

"Where do you want to take our plane?"

"To Lake Constance in Switzerland."

"I suppose you have a reason?"

"It may not develop."

"Call me again, sir. This call is quite a privilege, I'm sure. The Short Sunderland would be perfect for Coastal Command."

"I'll pass that on."

"The girl said she was calling me from the Air Ministry so I presumed..."

"Let me fly the aircraft first. You'll be pleased to know there are no hippopotamuses on Lake Constance."

"So that's what happened?"

"Came up for air right in front of me as I came into land on the river. I hit the animal with the float and careered into the riverine trees, smashing the seaplane beyond our ability to repair. Cost three good men their lives. More, in fact. I bribed the Tutsis with a consignment of guns to get out when de Wet died of malaria. The crash had paralysed him. Now my guns have slaughtered the rival Hutu clan, a rivalry that goes back into Congo history. It never seems to stop, Mr Crookshank."

"Please call me Phillip. Phil, really. At least the Solent won't be used to kill people. Save people, maybe. Land on the sea if it isn't too rough and pick up downed pilots."

"Coastal Command." Harry was smiling. No one missed an opportunity to sell.

"That's right, Colonel. Anytime you want to fly her, give me a ring. He was a good friend of mine, Iggy Bowes-Lyon."

"He was my friend too. I miss him. All his friends miss him. Really good friends are hard to find."

"You can't blame yourself, sir."

"But I do. Oh, yes, I blame myself all right. My conceit wanted to fly the first airline down Africa."

WHILE HARRY WAS SITTING in his office alone, worrying about his friend in Germany caught in the spider's web of men's ambition, Gillian Kannberg, who still thought of herself as Gillian West, was having the time of her life. She had never travelled in anything first class before and it suited her well, a way of life to which she would dearly like to become more accustomed. Everyone on the *Queen Mary* knew Gregory L'Amour and Genevieve, even if some of the high society tried to ignore the two film stars in their midst. Genevieve had declined sitting at the Captain's table saying they were all too old and stuffy, though not to the Captain's face.

They had their own table, the four of them, giving Gillian the kind of prestige she had longed for all her life and never found as a shorthand typist with a father who was a grocer. She was in her element, having spent as much as she could of the book advance in the short time before they sailed for America, her onboard wardrobe competing with the best of the younger generation, all by the look of them from the British and American moneyed class.

After several days into the voyage, and soon to be entering New York

Harbour, she even thought lowering her sights to marry Bruno was not such a bad decision after all. Happy to be part of the writing process when it brought her close to Gregory L'Amour, she knew the writing of the book was going well, Bruno's journalistic instincts for getting to the facts that sold newspapers standing him in good stead. The book was going to work. The rise of young Joseph Pott from obscurity to world acclaim as the film hero that was Gregory L'Amour even brought tears to Gillian's eyes, the sure sign every shop girl in Britain and America would howl their eyes out with sentimental joy when they read her husband's book. Even if Gillian had little or no talent of her own, she knew now her husband had the chance of giving her what she wanted, the glamour and ability to brandish wealth in other people's faces.

"You're going to be the writer to the stars, Bruno."

"You think so?"

"Of course, darling. After *Genevieve* and *Boy Rising to the Stars*, every rich and famous person in America will be after you to write their story."

"I never thought of that. Just one book at a time, Gillian. That's me."

"You have to think big to get to the top, darling. Where your talent deserves to be. Oh, how I love you. This is all such a thrill. I had a little talk with Lady Murtherville and she was the one who started the conversation. She had seen all the films. Those are the kind of people with whom we'll be socialising with in the future. We'll be able to cock a snook at people like Art the Bumley."

Bruno, ecstatic that he had had sex every night for a week, had no wish to suggest to his gorgeous-looking wife that what she had just suggested would not be very nice. That putting one's nose in the air had the habit of bringing about a nasty fall. Hoping his luck would carry through their last night on board, he tried to kiss his wife on the lips, only to be offered the side of her cheek.

"Don't be silly, darling," she said, giving him the same look Bruno supposed she would give to a naughty boy. "People can see."

"We're husband and wife. This, for all intents and purposes, is our honeymoon."

"We must always keep up appearances when we are someone. Kissing in public, really!"

"Are we someone, Gillian?" asked Bruno.

"Of course we are. You are the writer to the stars. I promised to show Lady Murtherville the photographs taken by Gordon Stark of me and Gregory that appeared in all the English papers."

"Just one, Gillian. The *Daily Mirror*. After I twisted Horatio Wakefield's arm to let me have the photograph which I presented to Arthur Bumley as something of a prize, seeing I do not take good photographs."

"Never mind. She doesn't know how many papers. Sounds better to say all the papers rather than just one."

Bruno watched his wife go off down the sunlit deck in pursuit of her new-found friends with a feeling of misgiving. Then his mind went back to the time he had given Arthur Bumley the photograph just before they left to go to America.

"Is it a coincidence, Kannberg, your wife is in the photograph?"

"It's the only one I could get from the *Mail*."

"I see. And now you want to follow the man to America and expect me to give you leave?"

"That would be nice. I can write a piece or two about the looming war from an American perspective while I write his book in my spare time. We're travelling first class."

"Are we now? She really has got you by the balls."

"I'm afraid so. Ever since the book was agreed to I've had it every night."

"You poor fellow. Lovestruck by your own wife. When she turns it off again you'll really climb up the proverbial wall... It's a good photograph, of both of them. Would the front page make your wife amenable for a nice long time? An American perspective to the air force story of L'Amour will sell. Go, you poor fool. Go with my blessing. I just hope one day you will find you have had enough of her in bed and see the wood for the trees. Until then you are besotted and there's nothing to be done to help. The rumour I heard yesterday from a dear old friend is Hitler is still laughing up his sleeve at Chamberlain's 'Peace for our time' little speech. Pompous idiot, the Prime Minister. If there is a war they'd better give Churchill the job, even if he is an aristocrat. When he wins we can throw him out and vote in the Labour Party. I love people. They are so predictable... Not a bad-looking girl, your wife. Why don't we give her her maiden name in the photograph? The readers know the Kannberg name as yours. Can't have favouritism can we? Whatever next? Sometimes we call it the phoney war. This one's the phoney peace. If anyone wanted my opinion, which often they don't despite me trying to give it to them, I'd say all hell is about to let loose."

. . .

WHAT STRUCK Genevieve was their complacency. Everyone on board was so self-satisfied, seeing only what was right in front of their noses, from the old dowagers right down to the crew. No one saw even the sea beyond the rails, just their world on board without fear or thought. They seemed to Genevieve to have what they wanted and anything else beyond the present was superfluous, to be ignored. The contrast with the bomber squadrons lined up on the end of the field came back to her vividly.

Then all she could see in her mind's eye was Tinus looking at the aircraft with shining eyes.

"What are you thinking of so intensely, Genevieve?" asked Gregory next to her at the ship's rail, both of them staring out at the running sea.

"That none of this may matter after all."

"We land in New York tomorrow."

"Thank goodness. And please, Greg, whatever you do in the future, don't try and be a hero. I may not be around you at the time to tell you to stay at home."

Taking in Genevieve's faraway look, Gregory understood.

"You're thinking of Tinus, not me, aren't you, Gen?"

TREASON IF YOU LOSE (BOOK SIX)

CONTINUE YOUR JOURNEY WITH THE BRIGANDSHAWS

What the older generation of Brigandshaws feared has returned. The world is no longer on the brink of tears.

Having joined the Air Ministry, Harry Brigandshaw is itching to fly but deemed too old. He has no alternative but to stay in London, working to keep his fevered mind at rest and running for shelter as the chilling air-raid sirens sound. To keep his wife and children out of insanity's reach, Harry sends them to Cape Town. But from so far away, can he stop his boys from enlisting, whilst other younger men are fighting for their lives in the skies above London?

For the beautiful film star, Genevieve, she has no choice but to watch from afar. She's petrified she will lose her man even before their love has had a chance to flourish. Along with other indomitable pilots, will her darling survive the greatest fight of his life?

Through the eyes of the Brigandshaws and their friends, Peter Rimmer yet again brings to life their lives and loves during the harrowing times of World War Two in *Treason If You Lose*, the thrilling sixth instalment of this historical fiction series.

DEAR READER

Reviews are the most powerful tools in our kitty when it comes to getting attention for Peter's books. This is where you can come in, as by providing an honest review you will help bring them to the attention of other readers.

If you enjoyed reading *On the Brink of Tears,* and have five minutes to spare, we would really appreciate a review (it can be as short as you like). Your help in spreading the word and keeping Peter's work alive is gratefully received.

Please leave your review on the retailer site where you purchased this book.

Thank you so much.
Heather Stretch (Peter's daughter)

PS. We look forward to you joining Peter's growing band of avid readers.

PRINCIPAL CHARACTERS

~

The Brigandshaws
Harry — Central character of On the Brink of Tears
Tina — Harry's wife, formerly Tina Pringle
Anthony, Beth, Frank, Dorian and Kim — Harry and Tina's children
Sir Henry Manderville — Harry's maternal grandfather who lives on Elephant Walk
Emily — Harry's mother who lives on Elephant Walk

The Oosthuizens
Madge — Harry's younger sister and wife of Barend
Tinus — Madge and Barend's eldest son
Paula and Doris — Tinus's younger sisters
Barend (deceased) — Madge's husband

The St Clairs
Merlin — Eldest son of Lord and Lady St Clair
Robert — Second son of Lord and Lady St Clair
Barnaby — Youngest son of Lord and Lady St Clair and one-time lover of Tina Pringle
Freya — Robert's American wife

Lord St Clair — Seventeenth Barron of Purbeck
Lady St Clair — Mother to Merlin, Robert and Barnaby
Genevieve — Merlin's illegitimate daughter

The von Liebermans
Klaus — A WWI German pilot shot down by Harry Brigandshaw in 1917
Bergit — Klaus's wife
Erwin — Klaus and Bergit's eldest son
Gabby and Melina — Klaus and Bergit's daughters
General Werner — Klaus's uncle high up in the Nazi Party
Henning — Werner's son

Other Principal Characters
Alfie Hanshaw — A shipyard riveter
Andre Cloete — South African school friend of Tinus
Arthur Bumley — Editor of the *Daily Mirror*
Betty Townsend — William Smythe's secretary
Bruno Kannberg — Latvian journalist of the *Mirror*
Captain Cyrus Craig — Captain of the SS *Corfe Castle*
Carmel Casimir — Louis Casimir's wife
Celia Larson — Fleur Brooks's friend and student at the Royal College of Music
De Wet Cronjé — Harry Brigandshaw's ground engineer
Doctor Andrew Nash — SS *Corfe Castle*'s doctor
Edward — Barnaby St Clair's manservant
Fleur Brooks — Celia Larson's friend and student at the Royal College of Music
Fred Dwyer — Harry Brigandshaw's civil engineer
Fritz Wendel — A Jewish informant living in Germany
Gillian West — Bruno Kannberg's girlfriend
Glen Hamilton — Editor of the *Colorado Telegraph* and friend of Harry Brigandshaw and Robert St Clair
Gregory L'Amour — An American actor
Hillier — An old German man living in Berlin
Horatio Wakefield — Journalist at the *Daily Mail*
Iggy Bowes-Lyon — Harry Brigandshaw's friend and co-pilot
Janet Bray — Horatio Wakefield's girlfriend
John Woodall — Flying instructor at Redhill Aerodrome

Louis Casimir — Jewish film producer who changed his name to Gerry Hollingsworth

Max Pearl — Robert St Clair's American publisher

Mr Glass — Editor of the *Daily Mail*

Mrs Craddock — The cook at Hastings Court

Paul Dexter — Louis Casimir's chief of publicity

Pippa Tucker — Friend of Janet Bray

Sir Jacob Rosenzweig — A Jewish bank owner

Smithers — Merlin St Clair's manservant

Tembo Makoni — Boss boy on Elephant Walk and Harry's boyhood friend

Thornton Holmes — District Commissioner of the Tanganyika Territory

Timothy Kent — RAF Pilot seconded to the Air Ministry

Vivian Makepeace — Controller of British East Africa

William Smythe — Journalist and friend of Horatio Wakefield

ACKNOWLEDGMENTS

∼

With grateful thanks to our *VIP First Readers* for reading *On the Brink of Tears* prior to its official launch date. They have been fabulous in picking up errors and typos helping us to ensure that your own reading experience of *On the Brink of Tears* has been the best possible. Their time and commitment is particularly appreciated.

Alan McConnochie (South Africa)
Hilary Jenkins (South Africa)

Thank you.
Kamba Publishing

Printed in Great Britain
by Amazon

77328010R00305

Double Jeopardy

Double Jeopardy

Martin Stratford

ISBN 978-0-7090-8965-0

Robert Hale Limited
Clerkenwell House
Clerkenwell Green
London EC1R 0HT

www.halebooks.com

2 4 6 8 10 9 7 5 3 1

Typeset in 10.5/13.5pt Palatino
Printed in Great Britain by the MPG Books Group,
Bodmin and King's Lynn

For my wife Pat
Thank you for all your support, encouragement,
belief and proof-reading.
With all my love.

ONE

THE MAN WHO had engineered the two murders stood in the shadows fifteen feet back from the mouth of the alley. He wore an old raincoat with the collar turned up and a hat pulled down low over his eyes. This was partly to hide his face, but also to keep out the icy wind that blew between the buildings. He was holding a pair of night-vision binoculars to his eyes and stood patiently watching and waiting. In one pocket of his coat was a mobile phone, stolen that morning, and in the other a bottle of whisky. In the unlikely event of anyone using the alley at 10.30 on a Wednesday evening, he could swiftly swap the binoculars for the bottle and would slump down against the wall. The chances were that whoever came along would walk by quickly without giving him a second glance.

The alley opened out on to a small square in the entertainment section of the City of Havenchester, situated on the north-west coast of England. The square had a grassed over centre, a sprinkling of seats and five trees. It was crossed by three paths and was popular in the daytime with office and shop workers alike as a pleasant sun trap for eating lunch away from the noise and fumes of the traffic that flowed sluggishly through the city centre. In the centre of the grass was a statue of the Duke of Wellington – after whom the square was named – sitting stoically on his horse and no doubt wondering why God had invented pigeons. A mixture of offices and shops lined the square, with a small independent cinema lurking in one corner. The alley divided two blocks of Edwardian houses that had been converted into offices and were dark and unused at that time of night. Directly across the square from the alley was a restaurant that served good, unpretentious food and drink and had an accordingly discerning regular clientele. It was called Little Italy, a fact proclaimed by a modest illuminated sign over the front window.

From the watcher's position in the alley, it was possible to see in through the wide front window of the restaurant, unadorned apart from a single menu placed at eye level on the right-hand side by the door. With the binoculars, it was almost possible to lip read the two women who sat at the last table to the left of the window. He was not concerned about what they were saying; he only wanted to ensure that it would be the last conversation that they ever had. The elder of the two women beckoned to the waitress and the man tensed for a moment, but they were only ordering coffee and he relaxed again, leaning his shoulder against the damp dark wall.

In the restaurant, Julie Cooper took a sip of her unsweetened black coffee, swept her long black hair back over her shoulder and smiled with great affection at her companion.

'At least we'll be able to do this more often again, now that it's all over.'

'Yes, I've missed our dinners together, and our shopping expeditions.' Joyce Kemp, Julie's aunt and godmother, raised her coffee cup and chinked it against her niece's. 'Here's to more good meals.'

'And to more shopping.'

'Even better.' Joyce was Julie's mother's younger sister and when the elder sister had died shortly after giving birth to Julie, she had been both companion and surrogate mother to the child when Julie's father was away. They were now each other's only remaining close relatives. Joyce had smooth, pale-blonde hair cut in a page boy style, twinkling blue eyes and a heart-shaped face. She was small boned and looked fragile, but had an inner spirit and resilience that made her a capable and formidable businesswoman.

Julie reached one hand across the table and squeezed the other woman's hand.

'It's been so good to talk to you, Aunt Jo. I think that's what I've missed most over the past eighteen months, not having someone I could trust and confide in when I needed to.'

Joyce nodded. Her niece was a detective sergeant in the Metropolitan Police having been fast tracked into the CID from university and promoted after spending over a year undercover, infiltrating one of London's biggest drug distribution networks, and a further six months following a series of arrests working on the court cases. Operation Snowball, which indicated that someone in the Met had a sense of humour, had ended two days before at the Old Bailey with the conviction of Theodore Jarrow, the head of the organization. Joyce had not questioned Julie too closely about that time and could only imagine what an enormous strain on her twenty-five-year-old niece it must have been. Although Julie's name and picture had been kept out of the papers, Joyce had gleaned enough from the story and the things that Julie had said to gain some impression of the stress of living a fictitious existence on a daily basis, knowing that a wrong word or a single slip could mean exposure and probably a painful death. At least that was all behind her now.

Whilst growing up, Julie had often spent time at her aunt's flat, or on holiday with her, and the close bond that had been created had developed their relationship into that of close friends as well as relatives, particularly as Julie grew older. Even as an adult, Julie had still enjoyed visits to her aunt and one of the worst elements of her work undercover had been that she was unable to continue that contact, both in order to maintain her cover and to avoid bringing her aunt into danger. She now had a month's leave and was determined to make up for the past year and a half of stress and uncertainty.

'I need to spend a few days on business next week, apart from that I can have the rest of your leave off with you – if you want me to.'

'That will be great.' Julie smiled at the older woman. 'I just want to relax. Take the boat out, go diving, chill out.'

Both women were expert sailors and scuba divers and Joyce owned a motor boat that she kept moored at a marina a few miles up the coast. The coast immediately north of Havenchester was lined with coves and caves as well as a number of small islands that provided plenty of interest for skilled sailors and divers.

'It sounds wonderful.' Joyce returned her smile. 'It would have been even better later in the year, but we've dived at this time of year before.'

'Yes; I'm afraid I couldn't arrange for the legal system to organize its timetable in a way that was better suited for a holiday.'

'We could go abroad somewhere.'

'No.' Julie shook her head firmly. 'I've been living a lie for eighteen months; I want to spend the next four weeks as myself in a place that's familiar. I suppose I need to touch base with my real life again – if that doesn't sound odd.'

'Of course not, darling. We'll do exactly as you want.' Joyce squeezed her hand. 'But are you sure you want to spend your time with an old broad like me – haven't you got a nice hunk you can turn to for a romantic interlude?'

Julie grinned and squeezed back.

'Old broad be damned – your mental age is lower than mine sometimes. And as for romance, the sort of men I've been mixing with lately aren't the type I'd want a relationship with – most of them only want women for one thing.' For a moment her mind slipped back into the fictitious life she had been living and she shivered suddenly.

'Sometimes I think I'd rather have a normal straightforward job, like yours.'

'Even the antique business has its criminal side, you know. Stolen goods, faked masterpieces, there's plenty of opportunity for the enterprising crook.'

'OK, I accept your life is as eventful as mine.' Julie finished her coffee.

'I wouldn't go so far as to say that. Let's go back to the flat – we have a long day's shopping ahead of us tomorrow.' Joyce signalled to the waiter, not realizing that she was also signalling the start of something else.

In the alley, the man was speaking into the mobile phone.

'They are about to leave – get ready.' He watched the two women put on their coats and walk towards the door. For the first time he felt real tension as the time for action was approaching. He waited for Joyce to open the door. The sound of the bell echoed faintly across the square to the alley.

'Now.'

The motor bike came out of a side road that led into a narrow lane which ran by the side of the cinema. The two women had turned left out of the restaurant and were walking past the darkened shops next door. They walked side by side, continuing to map out their plans for the weeks ahead, heads slightly bowed against the wind, taking no notice of the motor bike coming towards them, gleaming black and gold in the street lights. The bike was not speeding, the two black-clad and black-helmeted figures riding on it not drawing attention to themselves.

As the bike approached closer to Julie and Joyce, the pillion rider unzipped the front of his jacket and pulled out a silenced pistol. Joyce was on the outside of the pavement, nearest to the road and Julie had turned towards her aunt, responding to something she had said. She heard the first shot as an anonymous plop. Joyce staggered and gave a low moan. There were two more shots that sent Joyce reeling backwards across the pavement as Julie looked at her, her own body frozen for a moment in horror and shock. Relief at the end of a long and dangerous operation had left Julie unprepared and had slowed her reflexes. Time seemed suspended for a moment as the bike drew level and the next bullet entered Julie's chest, spinning her round. The next plop merged with a blazing pain in her forehead and everything went black. Julie didn't hear the final shot that hit her again in the chest as she fell back limply and heavily against the grille covering a shop window, the back of her head smacking against the silvery metal. The pillion passenger was twisting round and had fired the last shot behind him. He faced forward again, replaced the gun inside his jacket and the bike moved on steadily, turned down into the road at the next corner of the square and was lost to sight.

In the alley, the man nodded in brief satisfaction to himself, noticing with mild surprise that his mouth felt dry from the tension. He turned and walked without haste back down the dark passageway away from the square. The alley doglegged and then it merged with another quiet street. He dumped the whisky bottle in a litter bin and walked on towards the car-park where he had left his Transit van. There were a few other pedestrians about, but nobody paid the slightest attention to him, just another person protecting their face against the chill wind and drizzling rain.

Back in the square, Julie and Joyce lay motionless on the pavement. Julie was slumped against the shop window, blood oozing through the front of her coat from the two holes in her chest and more blood trickling down her face from the wound in her forehead.

Joyce lay on her back, arms outstretched, eyes open and staring sightlessly up into the night sky.

The man from the alley collected his Transit van from the multi-storey car-park where it was just another anonymous vehicle amongst all the rest. As he drove down the ramp, he could hear sirens faintly in the distance and coming nearer. He wondered idly whether they were going to Wellington Square. He drove sedately through the city, careful not to attract attention. Traffic was busy enough to maintain the van's anonymity to the many CCTV cameras stationed strategically throughout the city but not enough to cause him any major delays. The city had recently mimicked London and introduced congestion charging, but that didn't apply in the evening so he hadn't left a record in that system. Not that it would have mattered; he had purchased the van legitimately the day before from another part of the country and using false documents that had been kept aside for some time, ready for any emergency should it arise. After twenty minutes, he was in the outskirts of the city, suburban housing mixed with local shops and some open countryside. Shortly afterwards he turned off on to a narrower, unlit road that delved deep into the wooded countryside that lay to the north. He was pleased to note in a strangely detached way that he felt perfectly calm now and was whistling softly to himself.

An hour after the shooting, he had left Havenchester well behind and was driving through the enveloping blackness of unlit country roads. Only an occasional headlight coming towards him from the opposite direction and providing brief moments of additional illumination broke the illusion that he was alone in the night. He was nearly at his destination and glanced briefly at his watch. He'd made good time and only hoped that the buggers were there ahead of him and hadn't got lost. He had everything planned out exactly, but you couldn't always rely on other people.

He turned off the road just ahead of the lights of a small village and, after a few minutes, arrived at the entrance to a disused airfield. His headlights illuminated a pair of broken wire-mesh gates which hung open, only half secured to posts that could have been templates for the tower at Pisa. His headlights carved the way through the dark, the van bumping up and down as he followed the old potholed road, now liberally spotted with grass and weeds and even the occasional bush, towards the main hangar. He drove inside and let out a small sigh of relief as the headlights revealed the motor bike and the two figures standing beside it. They had removed their helmets, which hung on the handle bars on each side of the bike like a pair of monstrous ear-rings. He pulled up and switched off the engine, leaving the headlights on so that they could see what they were doing. He wouldn't be there long enough to flatten the battery.

'Hi.' One of the bikers gave him a brief wave. 'Worked like a charm, didn't it?'

'It did indeed.' He got out of the van, bringing with him a brief-case from underneath the passenger seat. It had been a small, calculated risk to leave the case in the van in the car-park, but he hadn't wanted to carry it around with him whilst supervising the hit. At night a man with a briefcase was more memorable – and more likely to be a target for muggers – than one carrying nothing. He put the case on the bonnet of the van and the locks clicked sharply in the night air. In his peripheral vision he saw the two bikers moving towards him in anticipation. 'And you have earned yourselves a bonus.' His tone was conversational as he lifted the silenced gun that was the only thing in the case, turned swiftly and shot the nearest biker through the head. The second man reacted far too slowly. As his companion was toppling bonelessly to the ground, he tried to open his jacket to get at his gun, but was dead before his hand reached the zip.

The man from the alley walked over to the two bikers. There was no need to check their pulses, both had a neat red-rimmed hole in the middle of their forehead and both stared up at the gloom of the hangar roof with frozen shock in their open eyes. Allowing himself a moment's satisfaction, he returned to the van, put the gun back in the case, closed it and replaced it in the vehicle. Then he walked round to the back and opened the rear doors. There were two rolls of canvas and some rope inside. Each biker was carefully wrapped up and secured inside a shroud of canvas and the two parcels put inside the van. He then lowered a wide plank from the back of the van and rolled the bike up inside, securing it with two more lengths of rope. He satisfied himself that the bike wouldn't sway around, took the helmets off the handlebars and tossed them down beside the bodies of their owners. He then pushed the plank back into the van and closed and locked the doors. The man was sweating slightly, but he knew it was only through exertion, not worry. The whole of phase two had gone remarkably smoothly.

Only phase three remained. There was an old mine two miles away that he had reconnoitred that morning. The entrance to it had been secured with a rusty old padlock that he had already removed on his first visit and replaced with a new one that he had purchased himself from a superstore. Fifty yards in from the mine entrance was a short side passage full of rubble and other junk. An ideal place to dispose of his load and then he was finished for the night. All in all it had been a very satisfactory evening. You couldn't beat careful planning, and he felt particular satisfaction that he had been able to work out the plan and put it into operation in such a short time-scale.

Whistling softly, he got back into the van and drove away.

'How is she?'

Detective Chief Superintendent Leo Jason, a tall beefy man with a ruddy complexion and an unruly thatch of now thinning tawny hair that, coupled with his first name had given him the inevitable nickname of The Lion, did not like hospitals. His wife had died the previous year after a long battle with cancer and the smell and taste of the wards seemed to have filled his life for so long that he could hardly stand being in one. Even a private hospital that had many of the attributes of a hotel couldn't dispel the feeling. He was a man who liked to be in control and having to hand that control over to doctors and nurses – no matter how capable he knew them to be – added irritation to the dislike. The fact that he couldn't smoke didn't help, either.

The doctor, a calm, attractive woman in her mid-forties and a very capable clinician, didn't sense the extent of the superintendent's feelings, but she felt the unease that many had when they visited a hospital and she smiled comfortingly as she answered him.

'Physically, she is making a good recovery. Considering that it is less than a month since she was shot and considering the extent of her injuries and the shock to her body, her physical recovery is amazing. Of course, she was in excellent physical condition.' She paused and glanced at Jason, as if to make the point that the same could hardly be said for him. 'Mentally ...' She pursed her lips and shook her head. 'To be honest, I am far more worried about her mental state. She blames herself for her aunt's death and that will take her a long time to get over – if she ever can.'

'We'll be offering her counselling, of course. There are some excellent doctors who work regularly with police officers.'

The doctor nodded doubtfully.

'I'm not sure she will be particularly receptive, but we'll have to try.'

'May I see her?'

'Of course.' The doctor glanced at him. 'She has already been fully debriefed – she insisted upon it, even though I felt she was too weak at that time.'

Jason raised a reassuring hand.

'Don't worry; I know about that – I've read the report in detail. I'm not here to undertake anything official. I'm her boss; this is mainly a social visit to see how she is doing. Last time I saw her, she was unconscious with three bullet wounds.' He didn't add that it wasn't just pressure of work that had kept him away since then, although he had made sure of being kept apprised of Julie's progress all the time. He had been all too aware of the outcome the last time he had been to see someone in hospital and he needed to be sure that she would recover before making a visit. He reflected ruefully that perhaps Julie was not the only one who needed counselling.

The doctor smiled again.

'I'm sure she'll be pleased to see you.'

Jason wasn't, but he nodded his thanks and was shown into the neat single room, bright and light with windows overlooking a garden area. Julie Cooper sat up in bed, a bandage across her forehead. Her face was pale and her expression held little of the spark and animation that Jason, who had been in charge of Operation Snowball, knew should be there. She wore a baggy white T-shirt with a Rolling Stones tongue logo on it. A book lay open face down on the bed and she lay back on puffed-up pillows staring across the room at the blank screen of the TV that hung suspended from the ceiling like a geometric bat.

'Hello Julie.' He spoke gently, moving a chair closer to the bed and sitting down.

Julie moved her head and dipped it briefly in acknowledgement.

'Good morning, sir.' Her voice was stronger than he'd expected, but flat and empty of emotion. He thought briefly that he would rather she was hostile, blaming him for involving her in the operation that had had such a devastating aftershock for her, than showing nothing at all.

'Your doctor says you are recovering well.'

'Yes, I could be out of here by the end of next week.' She spoke like an automation, repeating what the doctors had told her. 'I took two bullets in the chest and both missed anything vital by a fraction. The first bullet saved my life: it spun me round so that the head shot went across my forehead rather than into it. They say I was very lucky.' She didn't sound as though she believed them.

'You were,' Jason decided to be brisk and businesslike to try to dent Julie's veneer of self-contempt. 'Although being young and fit helped as well.'

Julie didn't respond. She shifted slightly so that she could talk to Jason without moving her head too much and winced at the sudden sharp reminder of the broken ribs that had deflected one of the bullets.

'It doesn't change the fact that my job effectively killed my aunt.' The fingers of her right hand plucked at the edge of her sheet in a nervous gesture that was totally out of character. Jason felt the growing tentacles of despair – it looked as though the doctor was right and he was probably going to lose one of his best young officers.

'That's rubbish, and you know it. We didn't expect any retaliation once you'd given your evidence. Police officers have been attacked in the past to silence them before they can report or give evidence, but it is very rare for them to be attacked afterwards purely as revenge. There's no percentage in it and most professional crooks won't do anything unless it nets them a profit.' He glared at her, hoping to spark some sort of response.

Julie's mouth twisted into a humourless smile. She knew exactly what he was trying to do.

'No, it breaks all the rules, doesn't it? It's a shame it isn't really a game and we can't just line up all the characters again afterwards and start afresh.' She paused and for the first time showed a little real interest in the conversation. 'Has Jarrow admitted that he ordered the hit?'

'No.' Jason pulled a face. 'The bastard admits that he isn't sorry it happened, but claims he knew nothing about it.'

Julie nodded. No surprises there then. It certainly didn't mean that Jarrow wasn't behind the killing. Being in prison is not a deterrent to ordering a murder – or any other criminal action – if you have the right contacts and Jarrow was as well connected as anyone in his area of business, with plenty of money to grease any necessary wheels. Not to mention plenty of time to make the arrangements.

'And the shooters?'

'No trace, I'm afraid. They were tracked on CCTV whilst they were in the city centre, but after that they moved off the radar. There's still a dedicated team working on it in Havenchester, and the Yard is providing back up. We've been watching for any known villains who might have been involved trying to leave the country, but nothing's turned up yet. We've followed up a few sightings, but they were false alarms. If they'd any sense, they would have ditched the bike pretty quickly, and anything that's found abandoned that might be the one has been carefully checked out, but no joy so far. There's a lot of woodland and forest in that part of the world to search, not to mention several lakes.' He didn't mention needles and haystacks, but the thought was clearly there.

That didn't surprise her either. She nodded slowly.

'I'll need to continue my leave once I get out of hospital. I have to go back up to Havenchester for a while.'

Jason frowned.

'I hope you're not thinking of taking the law into your own hands?' He tried to sound disproving, although he privately felt that digging around up there might help Julie to get some of the hurt and self-recrimination out of her system. He made a mental note to speak to someone on the Havenchester force and get her a little unofficial support.

'My aunt is dead.' The minute trace of interest seemed to have died again. She took a deep breath. 'She had a flat and a business up there and I'm her next of kin. There's a lot I need to do.'

Jason nodded. If he had noticed that she hadn't answered his question, he didn't show it.

'Of course.' He nodded. 'We'll arrange some protection for you.'

'I wouldn't bother, sir – they won't try again.' Her eyes met his and reflected deep pools of pain. 'Jarrow has already sent me to hell. If he wants revenge he's got it. Why would he want to put me out of my misery?'

TWO

JULIE GOT OUT of the taxi that she had taken from the station and the driver opened the boot and removed her two suitcases and travelling bag. She paid the driver and added a generous tip – chivalry should be rewarded. For a moment, she stood on the pavement and looked up at the block of luxury flats overlooking the river where her aunt had lived. Tall and slightly curved, the main impression was one of a vast glass yacht, its sail enveloping the wind. The views were, indeed, spectacular, as she well knew. Julie tried to analyse how she felt, depressed at the thought that her aunt would no longer be there when she arrived, but with a underlying comfort at returning to a place of which she had so many good memories, both of childhood and adulthood. It was two o'clock in the afternoon, the sun shone fitfully from a grey, cloudy sky and an occasional spot of rain floated in on the chilly wind. Julie shivered slightly, turned up the collar of her coat, lifted her cases and walked across to the entrance to the flats. Automatic doors slid open smoothly, the warmth of the foyer a welcoming haven from the wind.

A uniformed commissionaire sat at a desk to the right of a row of lifts. The entrance way was clean and bright, a fitting tribute to the level of service charges paid by the residents. The commissionaire lowered the newspaper he had been reading, smiled and nodded to her.

'Good afternoon, miss, it's good to see you back.'

'Thank you, Norman.' The commissionaire was an ex-soldier who had stood – and sat – guard over the desk since Aunt Joyce had moved in to the luxury apartments ten years before. Normally, Julie would have stopped and chatted for a while unless she was in a hurry, but today she just wanted to get upstairs to the sanctuary of the flat. 'Mr Kingsley is due at three o'clock. Send him up as soon as he comes, please.'

'Certainly, miss.'

The lift arrived and took Julie and her luggage swiftly up to the ninth floor – two floors below the penthouse, but if not in the lap of luxury, at least well over its knees. Julie reached her aunt's door – hers now – took the key from her shoulder bag and let herself in. She knew that Simon Kingsley had arranged for the flat to be cleaned and the beds changed ready for her. The smell of fresh furniture polish hung in the air as testimony to the presence of the cleaner.

Julie walked through the square hall into the large open lounge with its wide picture window, balcony and spectacular views across the river. She went across to the windows and stood for a moment looking out across the north of the city. The sun chose that moment to find a small slit in the clouds and the river gleamed as she watched it, rippling gently, like a thick, silvery brown snake. A barge drifted past and rounded the bend in the river towards Nelson Bridge.

Julie stepped back from the window and took her cases through into her bedroom. It was the one that she usually used, the middle sized of the three bedrooms. She was not yet ready to use her aunt's room as her own. She lifted the cases on to the bed ready to unpack, took off her coat and hung it up in the long fitted wardrobe with the mirrored sliding doors that made the room seem larger and brighter. The furniture was modern and functional, matching Julie's own taste.

Julie decided not to unpack immediately and instead started walking slowly through the flat, looking about her as she entered each room, pausing in anticipation. She did not quite know why at first and then she realized that she was waiting for her aunt to appear with her warm smile of welcome and her soft friendly voice. Squeezing her eyes shut against the tears that suddenly welled up, Julie went through to the kitchen and started to get coffee ready for Simon Kingsley's arrival. Although the pain of her loss had not lessened, she found over time that she could hold it enclosed for a while until she let down her guard and a memory flashed into her mind to tear through the fabric of the flimsy protection she had built up and cause the pain and tears to flood out again as strongly as ever.

She found that busying herself with simple mundane tasks helped and she spent far longer than was necessary preparing cups and saucers and sorting through the larder – which Kingsley had also arranged to be stocked – for biscuits.

Kingsley was prompt, ringing the bell at three o'clock exactly. Julie took his coat and led him through into the lounge. The solicitor placed his scuffed brown briefcase down beside a deep red leather armchair and lowered himself into it. Julie fetched the drinks and biscuits on a tray from the kitchen.

'Ah, chocolate digestives, you remembered.' He beamed with pleasure as if her small feat of memory was the most remarkable thing that had happened to him all day.

'Aunt Jo always said she had to get a packet in specially for you.'

'Indeed.'

Kingsley was a tall, thin, very intelligent, if occasionally rather pedantic, man in his mid-fifties with a rumpled, kindly face, topped by an unruly thatch of still thick grey hair. He had on a well-worn dark-grey three-piece suit, pale-blue shirt and grey and blue striped tie. His black Oxford shoes gleamed. At first glance, some assumed that he was rather fuddy-duddy, but they soon realized the keen mind that lay behind the mild blue eyes.

Kingsley leant forward, selected a biscuit, took a bite and surveyed his client anxiously for a few moments through gold-rimmed spectacles. He had known Joyce Kemp for many years, as a family friend as well as her solicitor and had met Julie on several occasions. He thought she looked drawn and tired, which was hardly surprising, considering what she had been through. Sitting opposite him on the settee, she nursed her coffee cup on her lap, her legs together in an almost schoolgirl pose.

'How are you?' he asked.

Whether it was his position as her solicitor, or whether it was his links of friendship to her aunt, Julie felt she could be more open with him than she had been with the psychologist she had seen a few days earlier and who had tried in vain to get through her barrier of grief.

'Physically, I've amazed the doctors. Everything seems to have healed up pretty well. There's a scar on my forehead still, but that's starting to fade. People will soon stop thinking I'm Harry Potter's elder sister.' She pulled a face. 'Mentally, of course, as I'm responsible for killing Aunt Jo, it's a rather different matter.'

'You aren't responsible at all.' As a long time friend, Kingsley permitted himself the luxury of speaking rather sharply. 'The people who are responsible are the bastards who fired the shots and whoever paid them to do it.'

Julie sat silently for a moment. Then she gave a brief nod of acknowledgement.

'Not bad,' she said. 'In fact you're better at it than some of the doctors. Not any more convincing, I'm afraid, but better.' She paused and looked at him. Kingsley almost winced at the depth of torment in her eyes. 'I'm sorry, you are sweet to be concerned, but this is something I've got to try to deal with in my own way and in order to do that, I need to accept it in my own way, too. So let's just deal with business please.'

Even as she spoke, she knew that one small thing had changed. As she had been growing stronger and healing, she had found that there was another emotion as well as the grief building up inside her. It had begun in a small way, but had gradually grown to equal status – the rage (anger was too mild a word) that demanded retribution. But that was something she had no intention of sharing with her solicitor – not at the moment, anyway.

Kingsley deliberated on having another go, but decided (correctly) that it would be useless.

'Very well, you are, after all, the client.'

He lifted his case on to his knees and opened it, taking out a slim file.

'It's actually quite simple. Your aunt owned this flat and a number of very valuable investments. She also owned a half-share in the three antique shops that she ran with Laura Tilling. You inherit this flat, its contents, her car and the savings. Mrs Tilling inherits the half-share in the shops.'

'And how much are the savings?'

'They are considerable. The shops are very successful and have made her a lot of money. Even after death duties, you could live here quite comfortably without having to work again.'

Julie nodded slowly.

'Aren't I the lucky one?' she said in a detached, flat voice.

The River Haven bisected the city in a series of twisting curves, narrowing as it moved into the surrounding countryside before disappearing underground in a roughly north-easterly direction.

The main shopping area, including a vast new covered mall, was situated in the centre of the city on the north bank of the river. Citizens of Havenchester spoke of going north in the same sense as Londoners spoke of going up west. Apart from the new mall, most of the shops were in original Regency or Georgian buildings which were rightly protected by the city's planning laws and so an aerial view of the area showed tall buildings to the south and generally much shorter ones to the north, as if the city had been given a rather lopsided Mohican haircut. Spreading out from the central hub of shops lining the river itself, rather like the rays of a sun half dipping over the horizon, were a number of narrower streets, some merely cobbled, which had survived the centuries and housed many of the more exclusive shops and businesses.

JL Antiques was situated in one such small street in the centre of the city. The street consisted of several very exclusive shops that served the needs of the very rich and those who aspired to be. On one side was a gentleman's bespoke tailor whose family had been clothing the rich and famous since the late eighteenth century. On the other was a jeweller, the contents of whose windows sparkled under carefully positioned artificial light. On the day after Simon Kingsley's visit, Julie walked from her apartment block to the shop. It took nearly an hour, but she felt the need for the exercise after having been confined to her bed and hospital for a number of weeks. She wore jeans and a padded jacket and felt warm from the exercise despite the cold wind. There was a steady stream of pedestrians filing past the shop windows, although most seemed to be browsing rather than seriously considering a purchase. Having glanced at the prices in the jeweller's window, Julie couldn't say she blamed them.

There were bow windows on either side of the antique shop's doorway. One window contained five Victorian paintings displayed on easels that perched on steps of wine red velvet. Each

23

painting displayed portraits of various no doubt eminent persons of their age, apparently in various stages of dyspepsia. The other window contained two modest displays, one of delicately painted porcelain figures and the other of silverware.

A bell rang with an appropriately subdued toll in the depths of the shop as Julie opened the door and went inside. There were two well-dressed assistants, one male and one female, both dealing deferentially with clients – a shop like this wouldn't dare admit to having a customer. The shop appeared well stocked without being cluttered, with a series of smart display cases for the smaller items and larger pieces placed strategically around the floor. A number of paintings hung around the walls, all of them cleverly lit to show them to maximum advantage. An attractive woman with short-cut brown hair and wearing a simple black trouser suit and white blouse came forward quickly from the back of the shop as she saw Julie come in.

'Julie, how wonderful to see you.' She took Julie's hands in her own, kissed her on the cheek and stepped back. 'How are you?' Her good-natured, slightly plump face radiated an equal mixture of bonhomie and concern.

'Not too bad, thanks, Laura,' Julie smiled at her aunt's business partner and closest friend. 'How are you and Archie?'

'We're fine. He's here today.' Laura Tilling's husband was the senior partner in a firm of accountants that managed the books of the three JL Antique shops, amongst many others. 'Come through.'

Julie followed Laura through a curved archway to the rear of the shop where there was a large office with two side doors, both closed. Seated at a desk on the left-hand side and peering with close attention at a computer screen was a well-built man with short dark hair and an amiable, rather angular face. He looked up as the two women came in, smiling and rising from his chair as he saw Julie.

'Julie, it's good to see you again.'

'Hello, Archie. Still doing your sums, I see.'

'No rest for the wicked.' Tilling gave her a boyish grin and kissed her cheek. 'Sit down.' He offered her the swivel chair next to the second desk and Laura pulled another chair round from the corner of the room to use herself.

'I'm sorry we weren't able to stay long after the funeral,' Laura said, 'I felt we were rather abandoning you.'

Julie shook her head. Her aunt's funeral had been held the week before in a cemetery just outside the city. At Julie's own request only a few chosen close friends had come and she had returned to London herself immediately afterwards.

'I'm just grateful to you for coming; it was a bit of a last minute rush. I'd only been out of hospital a couple of days, so I wasn't feeling much like socializing. I just felt I needed to get that first bit of closure out of the way so I could move on. I'm sorry if some of her other friends and business associates would have liked to have been there, but I didn't feel able to cope with that. I suppose it was selfish of me.'

'Not at all. After what you had been through, everybody totally understood. I thought perhaps we could arrange a memorial service later in the year, when you're feeling up to it.'

Julie felt a rush of affection for the other woman.

'That would be good. Give me a chance to settle things a bit and we'll talk about it.'

'Of course, there's no hurry.' Laura leant forward in her chair. 'How are things really?' She looked at Julie with concern and in the presence of two friendly people, Julie felt her strength begin to crumble a little and the need for support start creeping through. She took a deep breath and pushed the feelings to the back of her mind.

'Going through the things at the flat is pretty stressful,' she admitted. 'I started yesterday evening and I've been at it all morning. I keep finding things that remind me of something Aunt Jo and I did together and I have to stop for a minute, so it's rather slow work. I needed a break from that and I wanted to come and see you and thank you properly for the flowers, so I walked over after lunch. I thought I could pick up any personal stuff from her office as well, if that's OK?'

'Of course. Come though and have a look now.'

Laura opened the left-hand door and ushered Julie through into her aunt's office.

The office was quite small but neatly appointed with a quality carpet and wallpaper and a Queen Anne desk. A computer stood on another table to one side of the desk and there were two comfortable chairs. Julie opened one of the desk drawers and looked across at Laura.

'You'd better go through it with me, if you have time. I don't want to take any stuff that you need for the business by mistake.'

Laura nodded.

'The main thing relating to the business is her address book and I've already taken that because I needed to refer to it and contact people. Let me know if you're likely to want any addresses from it. Joyce didn't do much in the shop itself, as you know. She spent most of her time travelling round to look for stock and talk to clients. She was so well liked and had such a wide range of contacts. And she had such a good eye – she seemed to know almost instinctively if a piece was genuine or a copy.' Laura shook her head sadly. 'She is such a loss, both as a friend and for her contribution to the business. She was so good with people as well as spotting a good piece.'

Julie nodded, trying to focus her mind and keep back the memories that were itching at her brain.

At the top in the first drawer was a red-covered diary. She lifted it out and it fell open at a page in early February. There was an entry in her aunt's neat writing: '7.30 dinner with J at Little Italy.' Julie felt the tears well up again and closed her eyes to hold them back. Laura came over and saw the entry. She gave her a hug.

'I know, why don't you come to dinner this evening? I bet you haven't seen anyone apart from Simon since you got here.'

Julie hesitated. She knew that what she needed more than anything else was company, although she felt very little like making conversation. For a moment she was going to refuse, giving in to the reluctance to make an effort. She looked at Laura's expectant face and suddenly found herself changing her mind.

'Thanks, I'd love to.'

'Good, that's settled. Let's say seven o'clock. We can have a drink first. You know where we are?'

'Yes.' Although she had never been to the Tillings' house herself, her aunt had told her about it. 'I've got the address, and I know the area.'

'That's fine. Look, let me leave you to go through the desk at your own speed and get out everything you want to take. Then I'll have a quick look through it before you go. As you're walking, if there's a lot to carry, I'll take it home and you can pick it up this evening.'

Laura and Archie Tilling lived in the Brambly Wood area of the city. Not quite as upmarket as Stansfield, where the millionaires gathered, the area nevertheless attracted the rich and prosperous and was considered one of the most fashionable places to live. Some of the houses backed on to a tributary of the river which left the main flow to meander for nearly half a mile in a loose crescent shape past houses and through Brambly Common before rejoining its parent again. The Tillings' house was a large, five-bedroom modern detached residence with a long garden that sloped down to the river. It had been extensively renovated about twenty years before and Laura and Archie had been living there for just over five years, having purchased it at a relatively bargain price from the previous owner who was emigrating and wanted a quick sale.

Julie reached the house promptly at seven. She drove up the sweeping gravel drive in her aunt's pride and joy – a dark maroon MG that she had often said matched her perfectly – mature and sporty, with a surprising turn of speed. Julie parked by the front door, got out and rang the bell. She stood for a moment admiring the front garden, which looked neat and well groomed in the lights from the street and the house.

Laura opened the door, wiping her hands on the apron she wore to protect a well-made burnt-orange dress, and gave Julie a big smile and a hug.

'I'm so glad you came, I was afraid you'd ring up and cancel.'

'To be honest, I nearly did.'

Laura took her inside and hung her coat on a hallstand that looked like a small tree next to the downstairs cloakroom. The hall was large and felt bright and spacious with a few items of tasteful furniture. The parquet floor gleamed and looked fit for a small dance. Doors led off from the hall on either side of a wide staircase.

Julie handed over the bottle of white wine she had brought with her. 'I know Archie is a connoisseur, but the man in the shop assured me it's good quality.'

'Thank you. Come through. That's the study,' – Laura indicated

27

the first door on the right leading to the front room – 'and that's the dining room on the other side. We'll give you a tour later, if you like.'

Laura led the way across the gleaming floor. Julie had decided to try to feel better by dressing up for the occasion and her three-inch heels felt liable to sink into the polish on the floor with every step. Laura took her through to the big living room at the rear of the house. It held a comfortable three piece white leather suite, an impressive home entertainment system, including a plasma TV that wouldn't have been out of place in a small screen cinema, an antique bureau and two display cabinets of porcelain figures. French windows looked out across a long, neat garden, the illumination of a three-quarter moon showing a wide, long lawn bordered by trees and bushes glowing silver in the moonlight.

Archie stood up from one of the armchairs, kissed Julie on the cheek in welcome, thanked her for the wine and offered her a drink. Laura excused herself for a moment to deal with a minor crisis in the kitchen. Julie knew from Joyce that Laura was an excellent cook and prepared the meals herself whenever she could.

'You have a lovely house,' Julie said, sinking into one of the armchairs, which seemed to mould itself to her body.

'Thank you. We were lucky to get it. The shops had just started really taking off and we decided we wanted to move more upmarket. We'd only been looking for a couple of weeks when this became available and we snapped it up straight away.'

'How did Joyce and Laura meet?' Julie asked. 'She never told me that much about the business.'

'They were both working as technical advisers for an auction house. Joyce worked there part time and also had a small antique shop in an arcade in the city. She sold mainly small pieces – porcelain, silverware, that sort of thing and made a reasonable living. Laura specialized in painting and they got talking at work and became friends. Laura and I were already an item – although I was on a very lowly rung of the accountancy ladder in those days. The girls talked about merging their skills and buying a bigger shop. I put together a business plan for them and we managed to sell it to the bank. After a couple of years, it was going so well that we opened the London shop, and two years ago one in New York.

There's always a market for European antiques in America and once you get a reputation for reliable supply and quality, you can't go far wrong.'

'Don't tell me he's boring you with our business history.' Laura heard the last few words as she came back from the kitchen.

'Julie asked me about it, I swear,' Archie protested.

'Perfectly true,' Julie admitted, relaxing into the comfortable atmosphere. It was good to talk about her aunt with those who really knew her well.

'Why don't you take Julie into the dining room? Dinner will be ready in a minute or two.'

The dining room was at the front of the house and was dominated by a magnificent mahogany dining table and chairs. Gleaming plates, lit by a chandelier, vied with each other to dazzle the beholder. Julie soaked in the atmosphere of the room as Archie poured wine and Laura wheeled in a heated trolley.

'We don't always dine in such splendour,' Archie assured their guest with a smile. 'This is purely in your honour.'

The meal was excellent. The three courses melted in the mouth and for a short time Julie felt able to set her grief to one side. After a perfect lemon soufflé, they had coffee back in the lounge. Conscious of the need to drive home, Julie refused more wine and the rest of the evening passed off very quickly. Stories about Joyce inevitably came into the conversation to remind her of her loss like worrying a painful tooth. Laura had a fund of tales of their time in the auction room – particularly occasions when clients considerably over-estimated the worth of their items until brought sharply down to earth.

For the first time since the shootings, Julie felt as though she could relax. The sense of empty ache was still there, but at least the food and good company dulled it a little. When she left and got into the MG to drive away though, the pain came back with a vengeance and she knew with even greater certainty that before long she needed to take action and take it quickly.

It was time to start fighting back.

At ten o'clock the following evening, Julie Cooper parked her car in a quiet residential area of the city, turned off the engine and sat for a moment. She had never visited the area before but knew it was famous, or infamous, for its night-time activities. Julie had no real professional knowledge about Havenchester and that was a gap in her education that she desperately needed to fill if she was going to do anything about her aunt's murder. She knew that a rich source of information about the criminal underbelly of any urban area was often the local prostitutes, particularly those who had been around the block (often literally) for a few years. Even if they had no direct contact with the local higher up criminal elements, they would hear things whilst going about their business and would know who to be particularly nice to and the places and people to avoid. She was going to try to tap into that source of information.

It wasn't perhaps the greatest plan of all time, in fact Baldrick would probably have rejected it, but she had to start somewhere and it was better than doing nothing. If the killing had been contracted to someone local they were almost certainly connected to organized crime in Havenchester and most such organization's leaders had a thumb – if not other parts of their anatomy – in the sex trade pie.

Julie had decided that if she was going to get one of the street girls to talk she needed to blend in and appear to be no more than another working girl. After her time undercover, she was very comfortable playing a role and felt no more than the usual stirring of anticipation as she locked her car and walked back to the end of the street.

She was wearing a short black skirt, a tight white blouse with a low neck made even more revealing by a number of undone buttons, and a pair of high-heeled shoes. A short mac barely reached to the bottom of her skirt and would provide little protec-tion against the chill night air.

The road that she came to was a little wider and busier than the one where she had parked. A couple of cars drifted past, the drivers trying to appear casual as they peered around, and she drew into the shadows of a convenient hedge. The last thing she wanted was to have to deal with an interested punter.

When the road was temporarily clear, Julie crossed over. She was in a street of terraced houses, wheelie bins standing outside like so many short grey sentries awaiting morning collection. It might have been any ordinary domestic street apart from the two or three girls strolling along the pavement on the other side of the road. Julie glanced across but they looked too young for her purpose.

She walked towards a junction some fifty yards away where she could see a woman in a short, tight dress and pink fur jacket standing on the corner. Beyond her, further night-time walkers were in evidence. It looked as though she would have plenty of choice.

Julie crossed the junction and approached the standing woman who was staring towards her, her narrow face pinched and pale. The woman appeared to be in her thirties, which could mean she was anything from early twenties upwards, but she certainly had the appearance of having been around long enough to fit Julie's criteria.

The pale blue eyes in the lean face narrowed as Julie approached.

'This is my spot, bugger off.'

Julie raised her hands placatingly.

'It's OK; I'm not trying to muscle in on your pitch.'

'What do you want then?'

The eyes narrowed even further as the woman studied Julie more carefully. Puzzlement slipped into her gaze and the thin lips tightened.

'You're not from round here.'

Julie shook her head and launched into her prepared story.

'I've just moved up from London. I need to earn some cash and I need to talk to someone, find out a bit about the local scene.' Julie dug her hands into the pockets of her coat and shivered. 'I'm actually after an inside job, I don't like the cold.' She tried a companionable 'I'm-just-another-working-girl-trying-to-earn-a-crust' smile. 'Can you give me the names of any clubs where I might find something?'

The other woman said nothing, her expression still suspicious.

'Could we go somewhere and talk?' Julie pressed her.

The woman shook her head.

'I can't afford to lose the time.'

'What if I pay for an hour of your time?' Julie suggested.

The woman's hostility thawed a little as the conversation became more familiar.

'Girl on girl is extra,' she said.

'Nothing like that, really,' Julie assured her. 'I just want to find out about the local scene, the places that are OK and the ones to avoid. Can we just get a cup of coffee somewhere?'

As the woman hesitated she looked over Julie's shoulder. Her eyes widened in fear and she moved back from Julie without speaking.

'What's going on here? I don't pay you to stand around chatting.'

Julie turned round. The speaker was a lean, balding man with a scarred olive complexion wearing a well-cut fawn suit. He eyed Julie up and down with a slow appraisal, an appreciative smile cutting across his face. Julie looked past the newcomer. He had stepped out from the passenger side of a car that had pulled up at the kerb nearby. And the driver's door was opening.

Julie cursed to herself. She was really off form. Normally when undercover she was totally aware of her immediate environment and any changes to it. Not being so could often lead to very unpleasant consequences.

'So what have we here?' A gold tooth gleamed briefly at the edge of his mouth.

Her plan was clearly going down the tubes at a record speed, but Julie tried to salvage the situation.

'I'm looking for work in a club. I was just asking for directions.'

The man shook his head in mock reproof.

'You don't want to be working indoors, darlin'. It's much healthier in the open air.'

The car driver had reached the pavement. Like his boss, he was also bald, but he was not smiling and he was built on a mountainous scale.

Great, Julie thought, I run into a pimp and his enforcer first crack out of the box.

'I'm not interested,' Julie started to turn away.

'Not an option.' The pimp's smile widened. 'Come with us and we'll give you some on the job training.' He nodded at the driver.

Julie hesitated. She knew that she could probably disable both men, but it would involve moves that few street girls would be able to use and the last thing she wanted was to draw attention to herself. At least, no more than she had already.

As mountain man reached out to grab her arm, Julie pulled from her coat pocket the bottle of cheap perfume she had used to add scent to her role. She squirted the enforcer full in the face. He bellowed and slapped his hands to his eyes.

Julie dodged a lunge from the pimp, dropping the bottle in the process, pushed past the hooker, who was gaping at her open-mouthed, and ran back the way she had come. She couldn't move as fast as she would have liked. High heels were not the most ideal footwear in a chase and twisting her ankle was not a desirable option. She had an idea that once the big man's eyes had stopped smarting he would be keen to get his own back.

It was vital that she got to her car with a sufficient head start to be able to drive away before the pimp caught up with her, and that was becoming increasingly unlikely. She could hear his pumping breath as he gained on her and risked a quick glance back over her shoulder. Panic nearly set in. Another few yards and he would have her.

Julie grabbed the handle of the nearest wheelie bin and turned in a half circle, pulling it round behind her. It was heavy and the effort felt like it was forcing her arms from her shoulders, but the bin swung round and toppled over into her pursuer's path.

The pimp tried desperately to jump over the sudden obstruction but the edge of the bin caught him on the shins and he hit the pavement with a thudding slap and a loud curse. Julie darted across the road and down the street where she had parked her car.

She pulled her keys from her shoulder bag, unlocked the door and pulled it open. She slid into the seat, jammed the key into the ignition, started the engine, put the car into gear and slammed and locked the door in one continual fluid motion. Fortunately she was parked far enough away from the car in front to pull out without manoeuvring and her last sight of the pimp was his glaring face in her rear-view mirror as she roared away.

Julie turned left at the first opportunity, then right and left again, pulling into the side of the road only when she was sure that not even the fastest sprinter could catch up with her. She sat clutching the steering wheel tightly, her breath coming in shuddering gasps as reaction set in and tears started to trickle down her cheeks.

What an abysmal cock up. She shook her head in frustration and self-anger. She was a mess. It had been a mad idea in the first place and she'd gone at it with no real preparation, driven by the need to do something, the need to overcome a feeling of being surrounded by high brick walls, isolated and powerless. All she had achieved was to make herself feel even worse. At least the pimp and his minder weren't likely to spread the story about being defeated by a woman – it wouldn't do a lot for their street cred.

Julie took some deep breaths and dabbed at her eyes. Had she subconsciously put herself into danger as some sort of self punish-ment for the deep responsibility that she felt for her aunt's death? She wasn't usually given to such psychological self-analysis. Maybe she was just uncaring about her own safety?

Getting herself beaten up, or worse, wasn't going to achieve anything. Julie put the car into gear again and moved off. She was as determined as ever to get to the bottom of the shooting, but that night's fiasco had made her equally determined about something else as well.

She couldn't do it alone. She needed help.

THREE

ALEC TANNER HAD no way of knowing on that bright, chilly Monday morning in March that his life was about to change forever. He sat at his desk, an expression of calm contemplation on his craggy face with its thoughtful, humorous brown eyes beneath a thatch of shaggy brown hair. He ran a pencil meditatively along the edge of his broken nose and shifted his slightly under six-foot body into a more comfortable position.

Tanner was the owner of a detective agency, the staffing compliment of which consisted of Ella Lang, who ran the office and did some office-based enquiry work when required, the extremely capable Ted Manning, who shared the main investigatory work with Tanner, and Danny Worenski, who claimed, accurately, that he knew more about computers than the people who made them and could hack into anything anywhere. Danny did a lot of the agency bread and butter work as he had an accounting background and undertook financial and other credit checks on both individuals and organizations. They made, Tanner reflected, a good team. A fourth member of the firm had left just after Christmas having got homesick for his London roots. For the moment, they were managing without taking on anyone else.

The agency was based in a converted Victorian terrace in West Coven Road on the edge of the financial district of Havenchester. All the three-storey former houses along the road had been converted into offices. His building held a secretarial agency on the ground floor, the detective agency on the first floor, a firm of architects above that and the top floor had been divided in two, housing an importing business and a photographer. It was an eclectic mix that seemed to work and none of the businesses interfered with or had much to do with each other.

Tanner had arrived in the office later than usual that morning following a late night that had concluded satisfactorily for a client who wanted proof that one of his employees was selling information to a rival company. Tanner had obtained the necessary photographic evidence, but had not got home until the small hours.

Ella Lang came into the office with a mug of coffee and the post. She had a round, pretty, cheerful face surrounded by a mass of curly chestnut hair. Big golden hooped ear-rings swung rhythmically as she moved. As usual, her tight skirt was more north than south and there was a three-inch gap between her belt and tight, curving top that displayed an interesting view of firm, light-coffee coloured flesh. She grinned at her boss.

'I've made an appointment for you at eleven – a Miss Julie Cooper. She rang about half an hour ago and asked to see you particularly. I told her Ted was a far better detective, but for some reason she insisted on seeing you.'

'Obviously she only wants to deal with the highest echelons of the firm,' Tanner told her, ignoring her rolling-eyed response. 'Show her in when she arrives.'

Having indulged in their usual amicable repartee, Ella went back out to continue running the office and Tanner decided it was time to tackle his post. He reached for his letter opener in the shape of a small oriental sword, musing idly that as an aficionado of detective stories he should have been worried that he'd be found one evening sprawled across his desk with the knife in his back.

Julie arrived punctually and was shown in by Ella. She shook hands with Tanner, her handshake cool and firm, and he motioned her to one of the two client chairs in front of his desk. She had gone for a confident business look, wearing a well-cut and slightly severe dark-blue suit with a knee-length skirt under an open black leather coat.

Tanner felt an immediate attraction. It was not just physical – although he imagined he could practically see the sparks crackling between them – but as their hands touched he had an almost tangible feeling of warmth towards her. For a moment something in her eyes seemed to echo his feelings and he knew that she had felt the same reaction. Then some sort of emotional shutter swung down and the moment passed, although its after effects seemed to hang in the air between them. Tanner sat back down behind his desk and with a little effort got his professional persona into gear.

Julie sat and smoothed her skirt as she looked round the office, noting the large partners desk and the leather swivel chair behind it, the three grey filing cabinets (partly for effect as Ella had most of their records computerized), the two comfortable client chairs and the low coffee table between them. She glanced at the tall yucca plant that loomed like a triffid next to the window with its view of the offices opposite and a brief glimpse of the river beyond. The visual tour of the office gave her time to get her feelings under control and, when she looked back at Tanner, her expression was calm and controlled, all emotion firmly locked away.

Ella came in with a cup of coffee that she placed on the table. For a moment her eyes met Tanner's and she raised one eyebrow with a questioning look of amusement before going back out again. Sometimes, Tanner thought, Ella knew him too well.

'How can I help you, Miss Cooper?'

'Do you recognize my name?' Her voice was smooth and silky with a slight huskiness thrown in for good measure. Tanner considered popping outside briefly for a cold shower.

His brow crinkled briefly.

'There was a shooting a few weeks ago …' he began.

She nodded. 'I was one of the victims.' She took a deep breath and described the events of that night.

'Jarrow claims he had nothing to do with it,' she said at the end. 'That is, of course, crap – but I can't do much about him. What I can do is track down the men who did the shooting and whoever instructed them.'

'Where do I come in?'

'Although Jarrow operated from London, he had contacts all over the country. Whoever did the shooting knew this city; I am convinced they were local. I spoke to the city police this morning – DCI Mariner, who is in charge of the investigation into the shooting. I told him I wanted to do a bit of investigating myself and, although he wasn't happy, he said he'd allow it provided I reported back to him immediately if I found out anything. He suggested I spoke to you when I said I wanted someone to help me. I also rang my aunt's solicitor, Simon Kingsley, after I'd spoken to Mariner and he said he used your firm regularly and would recommend you. That was good enough for me so here I am.'

Tanner nodded. Mariner's father and Tanner's uncle had been close friends in the force. Tanner and Mariner had always got on well and he took care not to tread on official toes too often and to bring Mariner into those cases where he felt it appropriate. This arrangement had proven to be mutually beneficial and Mariner tended to cut the agency some slack when he could.

'What exactly do you want me to do?'

'I don't know this city very well. I used to come and stay with my aunt, but I need someone who knows the underbelly, the dirty places and the nasty people.'

The recommendations had perhaps lost a little of their gloss, Tanner reflected ruefully. They seemed to suggest that he was the man with a detailed knowledge of the grimy side of life.

'DCI Mariner admitted to me that the police investigation has run out of steam,' she went on. 'The shooters have disappeared into thin air and no one is talking. I want to hire you to work with me. I want you to take me round to meet some people who might have been involved and stir them up a bit, see what happens.'

'On the basis that if you poke the wasps' nest enough, the queen will come out?'

He had a feeling that in earlier times she might have smiled.

'Something like that.'

'Of course, we're likely to be pretty severely stung before that happens.'

Any trace of amusement vanished.

'I'm happy to risk that, if you are.'

Tanner thought for a moment. He took a large scale map of the city centre from his desk drawer, went round to the other side of the desk and spread the map out on the coffee table. He sat down in the other client chair and indicated the map.

'Tell me exactly what happened and where, as much as you can remember it.'

Julie leaned forward to study the map, her hair swaying down in a gleaming black curtain, her teeth worrying her lower lip as she

focused on difficult memories. Finally, she extended a neatly manicured finger to indicate the side of Wellington Square where the
restaurant was situated.

'I don't remember much,' she said. 'We came out of the restaurant and started walking to our left. We walked side by side, Aunt
Jo nearest the road. We were talking, catching up because we hadn't
seen each other properly for eighteen months, not paying much
attention to what was going on around us. I don't remember
noticing anyone else walking in the square. The bike is a vague
memory, coming towards us, not speeding, with two black,
helmeted figures. I barely looked up at it until Aunt Jo groaned and
started to fall. My reactions were far too slow – not that I could have
done much. I just felt shock then immediately fear, a blow in my
chest, then pain and darkness.'

Tanner nodded.

'They didn't ride round the square to get to you?'

'I'm pretty sure they didn't – I didn't see them when we came out
of the restaurant. I think I'd have noticed them if they had ridden
round from the other side of the square.'

'So they probably came out of the road leading into the corner of
the square that you were walking towards.' As he leant further
forward to study the map, Tanner was aware of her subtle perfume
and had to resist the urge to reach out to her. Maybe a cold shower
would be a good idea.

'Yes. The police found no one who saw them hanging around at
the corner, though, nor in the road itself.'

Tanner focused back on what she had said and thought for a
moment.

'There could have been a third person spotting for them.' He put
his finger on the map. 'I think there's a narrow lane here behind the
cinema. If the bike was out of sight round there, they would have
been out of general view but they wouldn't have seen you come out
of the restaurant. Yet they moved into action as soon as you came
out. If a spotter was watching the restaurant, they could have seen
you about to leave and tipped off the bikers.'

Julie nodded.

'You could well be right – but I didn't see anyone.'

'What happened after the shooting?'

'I was out of it. According to the police report, a motor bike with two people on it was seen pulling into Target Road just after the shooting. That means they went down the first road at the other end of the square. The man who found us confirms that – he was coming from a road that led into the other side of the square and saw no bike. CCTV caught what was probably them for a short while, but couldn't trace where they went.'

'Was there anything else useful in the police report?'

'One bike fitting the description was stolen from a car-park the day before. That's one reason I think it was a local job.'

'Who was the owner?'

'He works for the council. The bike was stolen from the Town Hall car-park. The owner reported the bike missing the same evening. He was at a council meeting on the night of the shooting – plenty of witnesses. He's in the clear.'

'OK.' Tanner thought for a moment. 'Can I suggest something a little more subtle to start with than immediately poking the wasps' nest?'

Again, the humour showed in her eyes for the briefest flash before being snuffed out by the iron control imposed by the weight of her grief.

'If you like.'

'I'd like to consult with a colleague. Come with me, if you like.'

They went out into the reception area. Ella looked up from her computer screen.

'Is Ted free?' Tanner asked.

'Yes, he hasn't any appointments this morning.'

Tanner led Julie across to a door to the left of Ella's desk, knocked and they went in.

Theodore Ambrose Manning was sitting at his desk looking through a group of photographs spread out in front of him. As well as being street wise and very useful in a rough-house, he had a very keen brain for spotting something that was out of context. A little over six feet tall and broad shouldered, he favoured sharp suits and blindingly jazzy ties. That day's effort featured Donald Duck.

Manning was third generation British of West Indian origin and even supported the English cricket team – which Tanner felt showed a spirit of integration often above and beyond the call of duty. He was a loyal and committed friend and Tanner was always grateful that Manning was on his side.

He introduced Julie and Manning stood up and shook her hand, giving her a smile.

'What can I do for you?'

Tanner explained the situation.

'Two people, probably, but not definitely, male. They work together, aren't worried about killing a cop and they possibly went to ground for a while in early February. They may or may not have resurfaced yet.' Manning summarized. 'Somebody must have heard or seen them before in connection with something nasty going down. That sort of person doesn't just spring up from nowhere. They're bound to have some sort of previous incidents to their name, even if this was their first killing.'

He thought for a moment.

'They may not be local, of course, but that seems a reasonable assumption to start with.'

'So what will you do?' Julie asked.

He gave Julie his most charming grin; the one he boasted made women go weak in the knees – and elsewhere.

'I'll ask around.'

'The police have been asking for weeks,' Julie pointed out.

Ted Manning's smile broadened.

'People answer me,' he said.

How long will it take you?' Tanner asked.

Manning rubbed a finger over his chin.

'I can leave this for now.' His broad hand indicated the photographs on his desk. 'I'll do some telephoning this afternoon and fix up a few meetings for later. I'll need to do the rounds of certain clubs and bars and some of the people I need to talk to don't come out to play until the wee small hours. Give me until this time tomorrow.'

'So can we be doing anything else while we're waiting?' Julie asked, when they returned to Tanner's office.

It was a good question. Tanner realized that he did not want her to leave. Although they had only met for the first time an hour before, he knew he wanted to see as much of his new client as possible. Even though she would be back again the next day, he was eager to get to know her better straight away; twenty-four hours was far too long to wait. Tanner was sure that deep down she was feeling the same way. He hoped so, anyway.

'Is there anything you'd like me to tell you about how organized crime is structured in the city?' he asked. 'After all, you've hired me for my professional expertise in that area. We can't really plan our strategy in any detail until Ted gives us some names tomorrow.'

'You're pretty confident he'll come up with something.'

'I'm absolutely positive. If Ted says he'll do something by a certain time, you just have to set your watch and wait.'

'Sounds like a good man to have around.'

'He is.' Tanner glanced at his watch. 'Talking of setting your watch, would you like some lunch? I can send out for some sandwiches or, if you'd rather, there's a pub nearby that does a good line in snacks.' He paused, aware that he was starting to sound desperate. 'Or do you need to be somewhere else?'

'No, I don't have to rush away and a sandwich in the office sounds fine. Thank you.' She gave him a polite smile and again the hint of something warmer seemed to be lurking in her eyes.

When Tanner asked Ella to pop out and get some sandwiches she gave him a knowing grin and a raised eyebrow that he chose to ignore with dignity. Her grin got even wider.

Having organized lunch, Tanner returned to his office, sat down in the other client chair and decided to risk a personal question.

'Your aunt was your only relative?' Good old Tanner, he thought, subtle as a bulldozer.

Julie nodded.

'My mother died when I was born.' She stretched out her shapely legs and settled into her chair. Far from objecting to the question, she found herself content to talk about herself and her past. Perhaps because she felt comfortable with the pre-murder memories and perhaps she also felt oddly comfortable with Alec Tanner. 'My father was Kenton Cooper, the archaeologist. We had some great times together – half the time he acted like an older brother rather than a father.' The gentle smile returned. 'He used to take me with him on some of his trips abroad, except when I was at school. That was where he did act like my father – insisting that I got the best out of my education. Because he was abroad a lot, I boarded at school during the week and spent weekends either with my father or, if he was out of the country, with Aunt Joyce. During school holidays I would either go out to wherever he was, or stay with Aunt Joyce – there wasn't anyone else. When I got older, I learnt a lot of things at the archaeological digs that you don't learn from books or schools – particularly how to look after myself. We were in Thailand for a while and I used to go off exploring on my own. A monk, who was a friend of my father, taught me Ki Thi, which is their local form of self defence and builds up confidence. He became my friend, too and I've been back to see him a few times, even after my father died. That was in my second year at university. When I graduated, I joined the police. I had originally planned to follow in my father's footsteps and, if he had lived, I probably would have done, but after he died, I decided I needed to do something different. I didn't see myself as Lara Croft.'

Julie continued her story, almost as if Tanner wasn't there and she was simply rerunning the film of her life to herself.

'I had always been close to my aunt; we used to do a lot of sailing, swimming and diving together around the coast. My father's death brought us even closer. She was the fixed point in the universe that I could always come back to. Now she's gone, it's like I've been set adrift. I'm not sure what I want with my life any more, so trying to get to the bottom of the shooting is giving me some-thing to focus on.' She broke off abruptly. 'Sorry, I haven't been that open even with the tame psychiatrist they sent to see me. You are a good listener.'

She looked at him curiously for a moment and seemed about to say something else when a knock on the office door broke the thread.

Ella came in with the food and placed it on the table together with some fresh fruit and a couple of cartons of fruit juice. She had also brought in china plates and proper glasses for the juice. Treating a client to lunch was a special occasion and Ella liked to do things in style. Tanner thanked her and she gave him a most unsec-retarial wink before leaving.

Julie opened her pack of sandwiches, took a bite from one and put it on a plate.

'Now it's your turn. What twists and turns of life have brought you here?' She poured juice for both of them. Tanner felt strongly that she was genuinely interested, not just making conversation as they ate.

'I've always lived in this city. My parents died in a car crash when I was in my early teens and I was brought up after that by my uncle – who was in the police then. When he retired, he opened this agency. I tried my hand at teaching, but it didn't work out, so I packed in my red marker pen and joined him as his partner in the agency. When my uncle died two years ago, I took it over.' He put on a TV quiz contestant voice. 'My hobbies are swimming and scuba diving and I go to the gym, without making a religion out of it. I also read detective stories – it's much easier in books. I've also done a bit of sailing – so we have quite a bit in common.'

She didn't rise to that.

'Are you married?'

'For a couple of years. It didn't work out and hit the rocks with a about the same force – and similar result – as the *Titanic*. We parted by mutual and reasonably amicable consent. She's remarried and lives in Scotland. They've got a couple of kids now. One or two attempts at relationships since then have fizzled out without much effort on either side and I am currently unattached and uncommitted to anyone or anything apart from this agency.' He paused. 'How about you?' He tried to sound uninterested. Julie told him later that he'd failed miserably.

Julie shook her head. 'One fairly long term boyfriend and a few shorter interludes, but nothing that led to anything. The last couple of years in the undercover operation haven't been conducive to a stable relationship.'

Tanner nodded.

'So, what's your view on the hit?' Julie asked, taking them back to the business in hand.

'It was probably arranged through one of the main crime organizations in the city. It could have been an independent, but that's unlikely.'

'Why?' She leant forward and poured some more juice. Tanner got another waft of her perfume but kept himself calm. No howling and salivating, he thought proudly, very professional.

'Firstly, the city is sewn up pretty tightly by the established mobs – they'd want their cut. Jarrow would know that and he wouldn't want to rock the boat – particularly if he's a sitting duck in prison. And secondly the independents tend to work solo – it's not the sort of career where you want a partner who could let you down. Organizations are different – they give more security.'

'If it was an independent, it will be virtually impossible to trace them.'

Tanner nodded.

'So let's assume they work for one of the mobs in the city. There aren't that many with that sort of clout. If that doesn't pan out, we can try the impossible later.'

'So now all we need is for Mr Manning to come up with the names.'

She got up as she spoke and Tanner helped her on with her coat. He felt again the twisting feeling in the pit of his stomach – he didn't want to see her go. He felt like a schoolboy having his first crush. It was ridiculous, but he didn't care.

'Would you like to go out to dinner this evening?' Tanner managed not to blurt it out too abruptly.

She frowned for a moment and he could see the hesitation in her eyes. They were standing by the office door, Tanner's hand on the handle, not wanting to open it. He knew he was getting vibes from her that were more than just perfume.

Julie could feel a mix of emotions stirring within her. Since her aunt's death, she had channelled her anger and guilt into a single-minded purpose that created a barrier against all other emotions. Now she felt that barrier, if not collapsing, certainly shaking a little, which was unsettling and almost frightening.

'Sandwiches for lunch, then dinner, do you treat all your clients that well?' Her soft voice held a lilt of mockery, and of something deeper she was finding it difficult to control.

'You're lucky; we have a special offer this week. Two free meals for every ten hours of contracted work.'

Her eyes studied him quizzically.

'You think we're going to spend that much time together?'

'More, I hope.' He was staring into her deep hazel eyes, willing her to give him a positive response.

For a moment, he thought she was going to say yes, then the humour and interest seemed to drain away.

'No, I don't think so, thank you. Maybe another time.' She was almost formally polite.

Tanner found that the door was open and she was walking away past Ella's desk.

'I'll be here at noon tomorrow, thank you for your help.'

The outer office door snapped shut. Tanner stood leaning against his office door jamb for a moment. Ella caught his eye, seemed about to say something and changed her mind. Yes, Tanner reflected, she knows me too well. He stepped slowly back into his office and closed the door.

FOUR

JULIE ARRIVED AS arranged at twelve o'clock the next day. Tanner took her padded jacket and hung it up as she settled herself into the same client chair as before. She was less formally dressed, in tight blue jeans, matching jacket and a white T-shirt. Ella brought in coffee and sandwiches and, as she left, Ted Manning came in. He dropped into the vacant chair and picked up a sandwich. In contrast to Tanner's open-necked shirt and casual attire, Manning wore a well-tailored suit with a pale-green shirt and a tie with Homer Simpson on it eating a hamburger.

'Boy, am I good,' Manning beamed at them.

'I know you are, O Great One,' Tanner said drily. 'So what have you managed to find out?'

'Well, the expense account took a bit of a beating, but it was pretty productive.' He took a swig of juice and decided they had been kept in suspense long enough.

'To cut a long evening and late night very short, there seem to be three pairs of likely local candidates. Harry Jarvis and Sam Hesky, who specialize in beatings but could well have extended their repertoire; Angie and Findon Wilson, a brother and sister act; and Jethro Harper and Kevin Winston.'

'Any more details?' Tanner asked, knowing there would be.

Manning finished chewing his last bit of sandwich.

'Harry Jarvis and Sam Hesky are a couple of right charmers who would duff up their grannies for a couple of quid. They work for Vernon Bridger.'

'Who's Vernon Bridger?' Julie asked.

'A very nasty piece of low life,' Tanner told her. 'He has a number of unsavoury businesses that operate just on the fringes of the law but his main line of work involves selling sex and drugs – preferably both together. He's clever, though; the police have never been able to pin anything concrete on him. He runs a couple of girlie clubs and strip joints that get raided periodically, but he's been careful, or lucky, and nothing major has been found – even though there's undoubtedly prostitution and more going on at both of them. I had the pleasure of getting a thirteen-year-old girl out of one of the clubs on one occasion. I was able to get her out before anything nasty happened, but that meant Bridger could claim that he didn't know how old she was and, when he found out, he was going to send her home. He has a very capable pet solicitor.'

'The other reason he's mainly got away with things,' Ted Manning added, 'is because witnesses conveniently lose their memory or disappear.'

'Sounds a distinct possibility he's someone Jarrow would have had contact with,' Julie said.

Tanner nodded.

'If you want a nasty job done, Bridger is your man.' He looked across at his colleague. 'Do Jarvis and Hesky have a record?'

'Various juvenile arrests, car theft, robbery, that sort of thing, then they moved on to serious assault and robbery and any other nasty jobs Bridger wants doing. They have been with Bridger's crowd for quite a while. I also understand that they weren't seen in their usual haunts for a while last month, although they're back now. They were possibly lying low until the heat died down.'

'Or sitting somewhere sunny spending their bonus for a job well done.' Julie's voice throbbed with anger.

'Yes, they're definitely worth looking into.' Tanner looked at Manning again. 'What about the other candidates?'

'The Wilsons are more freelance than the other two pairs. They'll turn their hand to anything they're hired for. Protection racket heavies, debt collectors, witness silencing, you name it. She's more vicious than he is – he holds them down whilst she sticks the knife in – often literally. They don't just work this city, so again Jarrow could have had contact with them.'

'And the last two?'

48

'Jethro Harper and Kevin Winston work for Harry Milton. They've been with him for about nine months – probably on his work experience scheme. The shooting is the sort of thing he might give someone like that as a test. Milton is even nastier than Bridger. He's more upmarket and he mixes with legitimate business, but that doesn't mean he's not involved in the dirty stuff, just that he uses gold knuckle-dusters. He owns a number of upmarket clubs, gambling as well as some more unsavoury things. In some ways he's worse to tangle with than Bridger because he's got the money to buy people. You never know who he might have in his pocket.'

'What charming people you know,' Julie smiled to take the heat out of the words.

'It keeps life interesting.' Manning smiled back.

'Do we have any photos?' Tanner asked.

'I had a word with Mariner and he said that he'd assume DS Cooper was asking and send round some mug shots – they should be here soon.'

'Haven't any of these people been looked at as part of the main police investigation? Tanner asked. 'We need to check that with Mariner.'

'I mentioned that to him,' Manning replied. 'Mariner has been looking at local lads, but he had nothing that points specifically at any of these characters. Without any concrete evidence, he had no justification for any detailed police enquiries to focus on them. He has no objections to us doing so, though.'

'It does feel quite liberating to be free to follow our instincts,' Julie commented. 'I could get used to it.'

'I hope we're not teaching you bad habits,' Ted Manning remarked, as he reached for the final sandwich.

'Client's choice – who do you want to look into first?' Tanner asked.

'How about Bridger?' she suggested.

'Make sure you've got your bullet-proof underwear on,' Manning advised.

'I never travel without it.'

Alec Tanner knew that Vernon Bridger conducted most of his business from a pub called the Rocking Horse in the north-west side of the city, an area of run-down multi-storey flats where not all the rats lived in the sewers. The Rocking Horse was in one of the better parts of that area – people only urinated in the street after dark. Tanner left his car a few streets away and they walked from there. If they upset Bridger, he didn't want to come back to four flat tyres, or worse.

The mug shots had arrived before they left and they had studied them before setting out in case Jarvis and Hesky were lounging in the public bar waiting to be interviewed. Not surprisingly, they weren't.

The pub was gloomy inside with small mottled-glass windows and furnishings of well-scuffed dark wood. The atmosphere was stale from old smoke.

The mid-afternoon drinkers were being entertained by a selection from the battered juke box that stood in one corner. A singer Tanner couldn't identify was screeching some lyrics he couldn't understand. Behind the bar a man with arms like piston rods was serving and wiping glasses and the bar top with the same grubby cloth. There was a selection of bar food – either crisps or nuts, neither of which looked very appetizing.

Tanner knew that Bridger kept the pub deliberately dingy so as to discourage the casual punter and he thought that Julie looked as out of place as a diamond in a sewer. They crossed the dusty floor to the bar – at least they seemed to have cleaned up any blood – and Tanner caught the barman's attention.

'Mr Bridger in?'

'Who wants him?' He carried on wiping the bar. He wasn't exactly welcoming them with open arms, Tanner thought.

'Alec Tanner – tell him it's only a social visit.'

The barman emitted an unhygienic-sounding sniff and gave his new customers a good staring. They stood patiently waiting, staring back. Eventually he declared the staring competition a draw.

'Wait there.'

He lifted the hatch at the side of the bar, walked round to the left and knocked on a door at the rear. He went in; they continued to wait. A few minutes later the barman returned and indicated with a jerk of his head that they should follow him. Beyond the first door was a short passageway and then another door. Standing in the passage by the second door was the clone of the barman. Between them, Tanner thought, they probably had an IQ of around 6 on a good day, but that didn't mean that he was eager to challenge them to a fight. The second man frisked Tanner for hidden weapons, then turned to Julie. She opened her shoulder bag for him and then pulled her coat and jacket open. It was clear from her tight clothes that there was nothing concealed elsewhere. The bruiser thought about a body search, caught Julie's eye and decided it wasn't necessary. He nodded, opened the door and they passed on into the inner sanctum.

Vernon Bridger's office was a considerable improvement on the public face of the pub. It was well furnished, with a couple of paintings on the walls and a deep pile carpet. Bridger himself sat behind a wide desk. The immediate impression was of a square head with a short thick neck resting on a rectangular body. His face was red and imposing, with dark features, black curly hair and thick eyebrows. Julie thought that he looked a bit like a clean-shaven and plumper version of Groucho Marx except there was no cigar and very little humour. He wore a very expensive dark-blue suit that looked a size too small, with a white handkerchief peeking from the breast pocket of the jacket. His thick fingers flashed with heavy gold rings.

'What do you want?' he demanded, suggesting he had little chance of winning a Mr Charm contest.

'I wanted to pick up some more tips from you about providing customer satisfaction.'

On both previous occasions when Tanner had crossed metaphorical swords with Bridger he had got what he wanted and Bridger had stayed out of jail. Tanner considered that to be honours even, but he knew he was unlikely to be on Bridger's Christmas card list.

Bridger eyed his visitor with increasing distaste.

'Who's the broad?'

Tanner looked at Julie.

'There you are, I told you he's a smooth talker.' He turned back to Bridger. 'This lady is Detective Sergeant Julie Cooper.' He paused. Bridger didn't gasp in amazement, stagger back, or look sheepish. In fact his expression didn't change at all. Tanner knew that didn't mean a thing. If Bridger had arranged the shooting, he would have known who Julie was already and had plenty of time to practise his best poker face.

'I thought you said this isn't official.'

'I'm on holiday,' Julie told him, looking round the room with the expressionless face that all police officers can adopt on appropriate occasions, giving the impression that they take special classes to perfect the look.

'She's visited all sorts of exotic locations,' Tanner said, 'but I told her that she hasn't seen anything until she's seen inside this pub.'

'Just cut the crap and tell me what you want.'

Tanner thought of suggesting that Bridger had seen too many American gangster movies, but decided to let it slide. He didn't seem to be getting particularly irritated, just bored.

'Jarvis and Hesky,' Tanner said.

At least that got a response. Bridger narrowed his eyes at Tanner, at least, as far as his podgy face could narrow, his eyebrows meeting like copulating caterpillars.

'Who?'

Tanner sighed. Bridger needed to take better acting lessons.

'Harry Jarvis and Sam Hesky,' he said. 'They work for you and we strongly suspect that they are responsible for the attempted murder of this lady and the murder of her aunt.' "Strongly" was perhaps overdoing it a bit, but Tanner wanted Bridger to think that they knew more than they did – which, he reflected, wouldn't have been difficult.

Bridger blinked and sat back in his chair. Tanner got the impression that he did look a little surprised, but perhaps his acting lessons had been better than he thought.

'What's that got to do with me?'

'They are your employees,' Tanner pointed out.

Bridger flapped a dismissive hand.

'If someone hired them for a killing, they did it through you,' Tanner persisted.

'You're talking rubbish. Jarvis and Hesky do work for me from time to time, just running odd jobs, but I don't own them. They're big boys; they don't have to do what I tell them, and they don't work exclusively for me.'

'That's not what we heard. How can I get in touch with them?'

Bridger shrugged. 'How should I know? I'm not their mother. Maybe they've gone to London or to Glasgow. As I said, I'm not the only one who employs them.'

'I think you're lying,' Tanner said. 'I don't think they wipe their bums without permission from you.' Poke the wasps' nest, he thought, as per instructions.

'I don't give a monkey's arse what you think. Get out of here.' He was starting to get angry.

Yes, Tanner nodded to himself, definitely too many American gangster movies.

'By all means.' Tanner turned towards the door. 'We just wanted to let you know that we still think the hit was arranged through you, and we intend to prove it. We are very good at digging up skeletons. It'll save you a lot of aggravation if you tell us where Jarvis and Hesky are.'

'Piss off.' His face was getting even redder than usual. 'I'm not worried by threats from you two. And if you bother my employees, I won't be responsible for the consequences. They don't like people interfering in their affairs – and nor do I.'

'That's a shame, because that's exactly what we intend to do.'

As an exit line, it wasn't particularly snappy, but it added a further shade of red to Bridger's face, so Tanner was reasonably satisfied.

'And how do we think that went?' Julie asked, as they walked back to the car.

'We'll know if we get a reaction,' Tanner said. He paused. 'How about going for that meal this evening?' He saw her hesitate again and pushed on quickly, 'All in the line of business. We can discuss the next stage of our campaign. I know a very nice pub a few miles outside the city; it's got great views.'

She gave in and nodded.

'Strictly business,' she said firmly.

'Strictly business,' Tanner agreed.

'I'll need to go home and change.'

'I'll pick you up at seven.'

*

The pub was situated to the north of the city. It stood on the edge of a tributary of the Haven and the food and the view were all that Tanner had promised. The gardens were illuminated by clever but subdued lighting and they had a window table, looking out across the magical scene towards the river. It was a significant contrast to the premises they had visited that afternoon.

The food was simple and well cooked and they relaxed into each other's company. They talked about their past lives, compared boating and diving stories and Julie went into more detail about her experiences on the archaeological digs with her father. There were times when she dropped her guard and seemed almost happy, but then something she said would remind her of her aunt and the sadness returned. At the end of the evening, as Tanner helped her on with her coat, she thanked him gravely for the meal and he felt his own anger bubbling up towards the people who had taken away the carefree fun person he was sure lay behind her grief. He silently renewed his commitment to help her track them down.

They left the pub just after 10.30 and drove back to Julie's flat, stopping on the way at a twenty-four-hour superstore so that Julie could buy a jar of marmalade as she had run out that morning and forgotten to get any earlier in the day.

Tanner drove into the same public car-park opposite the apartment block that he had used earlier and found a vacant slot. There were a few empty spaces and a single light in the far corner. The night was cloudy with no visible moon and the steady drizzle that had been around all evening and had started to build itself up into something more substantial, had eased off for a while. There was no one about. Tanner assumed that the car-park was largely used overnight by local residents and most would be home indoors in the dry and warm by that time. They got out and had just walked round the car when the rear doors of a red Transit van parked six or seven spaces away swung open and four men got out. They were all large; they all carried baseball bats and they all wore rubber masks. Julie and Tanner were about to be attacked by four clones of President George W. Bush.

The attackers spread out into a semi-circle and moved towards them. Tanner glanced round. Behind them were cars and a solid wall; there was no obvious exit strategy. The car-park was hemmed in on three sides by windowless building walls and the presidents were between them and the only exit. Their options seemed severely limited.

Still, Tanner thought, there are two advantages to being outnumbered when you are being attacked. The first is that it makes your attackers cocky, and the second is that they can tend to get in each others' way. Both of these factors could work to his and Julie's benefit.

Tanner turned to face the man on the end nearest to him, making himself look scared which wasn't necessarily that difficult. Tanner backed away two steps and the president moved after him, his two nearest pals hanging back to give him space whilst the fourth went for Julie. Tanner hoped that Julie's Thai self-defence was as good as she had said – he couldn't do anything immediately to help her. Tanner suddenly changed direction, moving forward rather than back and got a vital split second of surprise and indecision from his attacker. Tanner ducked inside the man's swing and hit him hard in the solar plexus. He gave a funny sort of whistling grunt and fell away, leaving Tanner holding his bat. Tanner kicked him in the head as he went down – nobody said he had to play fair, and he was worried about Julie.

As he turned to face the other three men, Tanner found that he needn't have worried. He saw the one who had gone after Julie subside to the ground having been struck with commendable force on the side of the head by a marmalade jar swung at the end of a plastic carrier bag. Not quite as effective as a club Tanner mused, but certainly more original.

The two remaining presidents found themselves in the unsettling position of having both the numerical odds and also the weaponry odds evened. Julie looked at though she could wield her confiscated baseball bat at least as effectively as the jar of marmalade. Tanner took advantage of the momentary hesitation and started moving towards one of the attackers as Julie backed slowly away from the other. Tanner's target moved back himself, which meant that Tanner was able to switch direction again and clout Julie's president on the back of the skull with a satisfying thud. He went down and lay motionless in a puddle.

The last man, finding the odds suddenly two to one against, turned and ran. They let him go.

Tanner turned to look at Julie.

'You OK?'

She nodded.

'Fond of marmalade in Thailand, are they?' he asked.

Julie nearly managed a smile.

'I'm going to have to buy another new jar; I think I must have broken that one.'

'Some people have no consideration.' Tanner managed to refrain from commenting that the guy had come to a sticky end. He was very proud of his self-control.

'That was sneaky.' Julie nodded towards the motionless form of Tanner's second victim.

'It's not just the ungodly who can fight dirty.'

Tanner rang the police on his mobile, requesting their attendance as well as an ambulance. Julie went round and removed the facemasks. None of the attackers looked familiar, nor did they show much sign of wanting to wake up so they had a quiet five minutes before the first police car arrived, closely followed by the ambulance.

Two minutes later, two CID officers turned up, one of whom was a detective sergeant Tanner knew by sight. Fortunately, he recognized one of the attackers as a thug with a long record, which helped to rubbish any defence they might have put up as being four innocent bruisers on their way to participate in a fetish baseball match when they were suddenly set upon by an unarmed man and woman.

Julie and Tanner's statements were taken verbally whilst the attackers, who had all regained varying degrees of consciousness, were inspected by the ambulance crew. Two were declared fit to be transported to the police station whilst the other (Tanner's second victim) was taken to hospital with mild concussion. The detective sergeant – vastly amused by the idea of marmalade being used as a defensive weapon – sent his colleague off in the ambulance with the third prisoner and the other two were put in the police car and taken away. All three ex-presidents maintained a sullen silence throughout this process.

Tanner and Julie undertook to call in to the police station the following morning to sign written versions of their statements and were then allowed to go back up to Julie's flat. The detective sergeant insisted on going with them to see them safely into the flat, just in case anyone else was laying in wait. No further attackers materialized, but they were both rather glad of the extra support. Despite what might be inferred from the antics of fictional private eyes, being attacked by four armed men was not a normal part of Tanner's daily routine.

Once the detective sergeant had gone, Julie motioned Tanner through into the lounge. She walked stiffly and felt as if she was on auto-pilot as reaction to the evening's excitement began to set in. Tanner felt a little shaky himself and was poised to demonstrate his prefect house training by volunteering to make them some coffee whilst Julie sat down and tried to relax.

'I miss her so much.' Julie slipped off her coat and laid it across a chair. 'And then those bastards ...' Her voice caught and she started shaking. She cupped her hands over her eyes and turned away. 'I'm sorry, I ...'

'That's OK.' Tanner moved across, turned her gently towards him and held her in his arms, stroking her back and saying some of the meaningless things that tend to be spoken on such occasions. How, Tanner reflected bitterly, can it possibly be all right?

After the first moment, when she seemed about to pull away, Julie melted forward and clung on to Tanner, her body soft against his, her arms round him holding him tightly, her face buried in his shoulder. They stood like that for some time. At first, Tanner was just holding her, giving her the comfort of another human body to cling on to. Then she hugged him a little closer and he returned the hug.

They were never sure afterwards who started to take advantage of whom first. Suddenly they were kissing, a tentative brush of the lips first, then something more. The attraction they had been feeling towards each other since they first met, coupled with Julie's need for release and reaction to the attack built up to an explosion of emotion that they doubted if they could have controlled even if they'd wanted to. It made everything else irrelevant. They barely managed to get the clothes off each other without leaving them in shreds on the floor and they made love with such mutual ferocity and greed that it was almost as if Julie needed to beat her grief from her body.

Afterwards, they lay naked on the sofa in each other's arms in a dazed mutual ecstasy.

Julie moved slightly and lifted herself up on to one elbow to look into Tanner's face, her hair sweeping down across his cheek and bare chest.

'My God,' she said, 'I needed that.'

Tanner started to laugh.

Julie was suddenly grinning at him, her face lighting up in a way that he had always known that it could. She snuggled in even closer beside him. Some part of the twisted mass of grief and rage and hate that she had been carrying inside her for weeks had finally dissolved away.

'It is a well-known scientific fact that after being affected by a traumatic death people need to affirm life.' Tanner told her.

Julie considered that solemnly for a moment.

'And I thought I just needed a good shag.' Her eyes gleamed impishly. 'I didn't realize scientific experiments could be so much fun.'

'You do need exactly the right apparatus.'

She giggled.

'Of course, you realize this means that you are getting involved with a needy emotional cripple?' She was watching his face seriously.

Tanner moved his head and kissed her gently.

'I have fallen in love with a beautiful, clever, foxy lady and I have never felt happier in my life.'

'That sounds good to me.' She paused. 'Foxy?'

'It's a compliment,' he assured her. 'It may be a little sexist, but it's definitely a compliment.'

'That's all right then. It's the motive that counts.'

'Did I also mention the brilliant sex?'

'That could have been a one-off fluke,' she pointed out, the sparkle returning to her eyes.

Tanner grinned at her.

'There's only one way to find out.'

They decided after a period of prolonged scientific research that it had definitely not been a fluke.

FIVE

IT IS A curious fact that it was a combination of Reggie Gray's weak bladder and poor sense of direction that provided the key which unlocked a trail of fear and death.

Reggie Gray was not in himself a very prepossessing person. A small, rat-like figure with a narrow face, shifty eyes and a pointed nose, he had lived off crime all of his life. He was a bully and a coward, a nasty if not uncommon mixture that led to his having been employed by a number of more intelligent people as a combination of messenger and enforcer. He was particularly effective in passing on unpleasant messages to those who were less violently inclined than he was. His specialist weapons were the knuckle-duster and the razor, both of which he could use very effectively, particularly if the victim was caught off guard, from behind, or was being held down. His current employer was Harry Milton, who called himself a businessman but was called a great many other things by both the police and others who came into contact with him.

On this particular evening, at the same time that Tanner and Julie were dining together, Gray was driving back towards Havenchester from an errand in Birmingham that had concerned a deal involving the distribution of certain illegal substances in which his current employer had significant financial involvement. The person he had been sent to see had made the painful mistake of skimming rather more than his allotted percentage from the transactions in which he had been involved. Gray had left his victim regretting his greed with a face that was unlikely to be completely repaired.

The cold and heavy rain was a combination that aggravated Gray's difficulties. There had been an accident just north of Birmingham involving a heavy lorry that had caused a delay and two-mile tailback, which had eased neither Gray's temper nor his bladder. He had left the motorway a few junctions further south than usual in order to avoid the chaos and, although he was still travelling generally north, he had managed to get himself lost amongst some of the villages which are dotted about around the outskirts of Havenchester, much of which was still determinedly rural, despite the apparent wish of both local and central government to build houses wherever they could.

He found himself following a winding road with a perimeter of tall, looming trees and becoming increasingly more desperate for somewhere he could both relieve and refresh himself. The road curved to the right and, as he rounded the bend, he saw that there was a light ahead. He slowed down and peered through the rain-spattered windscreen. The light came from a small pub that stood back from the road. As if by a sign, the rain started to ease and it had stopped altogether as he drove down the side of the pub to the car-park at the rear. Out of force of habit, he drove to the unlit back of the car-park and switched off his engine. Wasting no time, he ran across the puddle-covered gravel surface and entered the warmth of the pub with relief.

The pub was not packed, although there was still a reasonable number of people and a loud hum of noise. Apart from a couple of disinterested glances from people by the door, no one had paid him any attention as he went in. Gray dealt with his most pressing concern first and then made his way to the bar to order a pint of beer. He placed his order with the barmaid, paid, took a welcome sip and, leaning his back against the bar, turned to survey the pub and its clientele as he absorbed its warmth and atmosphere. There were tables dotted around and a number of dark nooks in angles of the walls, although not all were occupied. A noisy darts match was underway on the opposite side of the bar and a young man nearby was pumping money into a slot machine with intense concentration. The machine was giving out a lot of bright lights but not much in the way of cash. Gray pulled a face. Despite having most of the vices, gambling was surprisingly not one of them and he rather despised those who he saw as pouring their money away. He carried on with his survey of the pub's occupants.

He almost missed seeing them. A couple were sitting at a small table in a dark corner away from the main bar area, their heads close together as they engaged in what was clearly an animated and intimate conversation. Gray's glance swept past them, then registered what he had seen and moved back again. He paused with his glass to his lips, staring in stupefied amazement. He had never seen the man before in his life, but the woman he knew very well indeed. She had long, honey-coloured hair, a pretty face and, even though he could see little of it from that angle, he knew that she had a curving, well-proportioned body. Her name was Beverly Wallace and the only man she should have been in intimate conversation with was Harry Milton. As Gray watched, the man reached out and took Beverly's hand, leaned over and kissed her on the lips. It was a long, self-absorbed kiss and dispelled any doubt that the relationship between them was passionate.

For a few moments, Gray was not sure what to do. Constructive thought – unless it involved razors or heavy, blunt instruments – was not his strong suit. Beverly Wallace and her companion did not seem to have spotted him and he realized that it would be best if they were kept in ignorance of his presence. He turned his back to them and moved further round the bar to where he was shielded from the direct view of the corner table by other customers. Gray took his mobile phone from his pocket and, under the guise of making a call, manoeuvred himself into a position from which he could take photographs of Beverly and her companion. That provided the evidence in case Milton didn't believe him. Gray finished his drink in three quick swallows, put his glass down on a convenient side table and made his way back to the door, careful not to look in Beverly Wallace's direction. Outside, he buttoned his short car coat and stepped out into the night. There was still some dampness in the air, but the worst of the rain seemed to be over for now.

Gray paused and looked round, searching for the familiar car. He saw it, parked to the left and in the shadow of a side wall. He checked the number plate just to make sure. Yes, it was definitely Beverly's car. What the hell was she playing at? Well, it was actually pretty obvious what she was playing at, Gray grinned wolfishly as he thought of that, but two-timing Harry Milton was a good way to find yourself in a ditch with a bullet in the head – if he was feeling generous. A cheating girlfriend would face something much more prolonged. She must be mad. Gray's smile broadened. If he was lucky, he might get a chance to participate in the punishment. He felt a stirring of anticipation as he thought of that.

Moving towards his car, Gray considered his options. He could follow Beverly's boyfriend and find out where he lived. Or, he could get back to Milton's house so that they would be waiting there to accuse her when she arrived home. He decided on the latter course. He had noticed a signpost at a T-junction just beyond the pub, so once he got his bearings he should easily be able to beat Beverly home; she had seemed in no hurry to leave. He would get back to Milton's house as quickly as possible. It would be fun to be there when she walked in unsuspectingly to face Milton's anger and he was sure she would soon tell them who the man was and where he could be found.

Gray got into his car and drove slowly out of the pub car-park. There was no sign of anyone else leaving. He should have plenty of time. He turned right on to the road and drove up towards the T-junction. Stansfield, an area of prosperous houses and even more prosperous owners situated on the outskirts of the city, was one of the places signposted to the right. With a nod of satisfaction, Gray turned that way.

The new road was unlit past the junction. Once again, tall trees bordered the road and soon the only light was from his headlights carving into the darkness. After a couple of miles, there was no sign of further habitation and no more signposts. There had been a couple of what appeared to be minor roads leading off from his road and Gray began to panic that he had missed his turning. The road was narrow and winding and had several deep puddles that threw water against the side of his car as he drove on, speeding up gradually as his anxiety built until he was travelling far too fast for the wet and muddy conditions.

Without warning, it started to rain heavily again. Gray cursed as his windshield became suddenly obscured and the road dipped steeply downhill. He switched on the wipers in time to see the black and white zigzag warning of a curve looming up in his lights. He panicked and braked sharply, sending the car into a spin. The car skidded off the road between two trees and careered down a grassy slope before smashing headfirst into an old oak that had withstood the ravages of the centuries and had no intention of giving way to a cheap motor car.

Gray was jerked forward with the impact, his head smacked against the edge of the windscreen with a nasty thud and he slumped back in his seat, unconscious, blood trickling down the side of his face. The car lights had gone out when the car hit the tree, the engine died and silence and darkness returned. When the next car went past on the road five minutes later, the few signs that there were of the accident were hidden by the darkness and the rain.

Beverly Wallace drove up to the tall, wrought-iron gates and stopped. After a few moments the camera set into the brickwork of the right-hand post recorded her identity and the gates swung open. Beverly drove up to the front of the large 1930s house in Stansfield and pressed a switch under the dashboard. The doors to the double garage swung up and she drove in. She got out of the car, walked back outside and took a small remote control from her shoulder bag to close it again. She glanced at her watch. Eleven o'clock. Not too bad. Her stomach tightened at the thought of what she had to do that night, but she pushed the spurt of fear to the back of her mind. She must not do anything to raise any suspicions.

She let herself into the house and was just unbuttoning her coat when Harry Milton came out of his study into the large square hall. He stopped and looked at her, a smile on his face.

'Hello, Beverly – have a good evening?' He was a tall, well-built man with a narrow face and broad, square shoulders. He kept himself in good physical condition and the solid body was well muscled. When you saw him for the first time, he seemed amiable, even jovial, but if you looked into his eyes, there was a cold, calculating indifference that was anything but reassuring. He wore an expensive three-piece dark-blue suit with a thin white stripe, a pale-blue shirt and matching tie. He was always immaculately and expensively dressed, nearly always in a suit and tie, even when the weather was hot. He walked across to her and ran one hand up inside her coat as he drew her towards him.

'Yes, thank you,' she smiled, and managed to return the passion in the kiss that he gave her, as his big hand caressed her breast, squeezing it a little too hard and causing her to breathe in sharply.

'How is your sister?'

Milton liked to keep control of his employees and to constantly remind them that he could manipulate their lives. He was also pleased if, like Beverly, they had some spirit and an inclination to defiance; it meant that he felt even more power when they obeyed him. He allowed Beverly the freedom to go out but he always wanted to know where she was. A few months before she had started going to dance classes twice a week. Milton liked to move in rich social circles and had the money to indulge himself. He attended a number of social functions with other businessmen, some more scrupulous than he was and a few others less so. Beverly usually attended such functions with him and it added a touch of class when she could dance well, in addition to looking stunning in the expensive dresses he brought for her.

Beverly was also allowed to visit her sister on a regular basis. Milton did not know that her evenings out often had little to do with learning new steps – not for dancing purposes, anyway – and that she had only seen her sister twice in the last three months.

'She's fine, thanks.' Beverly knew that Milton couldn't care less how her sister was. She gave a not wholly fictitious yawn. 'God, I'm bushed tonight; I think I'll turn in – unless you need me?'

Milton was obsessive about cleanliness, if he did want her she would have time to take the shower that would be needed to wash away more than just sweat and dirt.

'I may pop along later, but I've got some business to finish now.' He smiled, squeezed her breast again and turned back to the study.

The 'business' was probably waiting for Reggie Gray to report in. Beverly knew that he had gone out on an errand that after-noon. She hid a shiver and walked up the wide staircase to her first-floor bedroom. A number of Milton's employees and acquaintances frightened her, but Gray gave her the creeps as well. Comparing Gray to Milton was like being scared of a snake compared to being scared of a lion. At least the lion had some outward appearance of being soft and cuddly, even if you knew he wasn't really.

Beverly had been Milton's lover for over two years, since he had spotted her working as a hostess in one of his clubs. They had separate bedrooms because he often kept late hours and he made a pretence of not wanting to disturb her. The truth was that he liked to keep her on her toes and on occasion would come in after she was asleep and expect her full attention. He didn't single her out for that sort of treatment, he kept all of his staff alert and ready to respond to his needs, whether related to business or pleasure. She knew that he saw her as just another of his employees, there to serve his needs and respond to his demands and to be removed when she became ineffective or troublesome, or he grew bored with her. After more than two years, she was aware that her position had lasted longer than many before her. That made what she was about to do a lot easier, if not less nerve-racking.

She got to her room and closed and locked the door. The bedroom was dominated by the large double bed that stood to the right of the door below a mirrored ceiling.

Beverly draped her coat over the end of the bed, crossed to the windows and drew the curtains. She undressed, went into the ensuite bathroom and took a shower. The hot water relaxed her a little and she quickly washed and dried herself. Putting on her dressinggown, she walked back into the main bedroom. It irritated her that she had to behave as if there was something wrong about her secret affair, when she knew that it was her relationship with Milton that was grubby and demeaning. Still, after today there would be no more grabbing illicit pleasure in smelly hotel rooms and the back of a car, like cheating adulterers or fumbling teenagers. She hugged herself and felt a thrill of pleased anticipation coupled with the ache of fear at what Milton would do if he caught them afterwards – or caught her leaving.

Walking over to the wardrobe, she slid back one of the doors, took down two large suitcases from the top shelf, put them on the bed and unzipped the lids. Quickly and carefully, listening out for the sound of anyone coming upstairs, she packed the cases with clothes and other essentials and the few personal possessions that she valued. A loose floorboard at the back of the wardrobe was lifted and the money and jewellery she had accumulated over the past two years was added to the cases. After checking the wardrobes and the rest of the room to make sure that she hadn't forgotten anything, Beverly closed the bulging cases and put them back into the wardrobe. They were heavy, but she wouldn't have to carry them very far. She put them on the wardrobe floor, hidden as much as possible towards the back behind some long dresses and coats. Milton never looked in her wardrobe, so they should be safe enough there. She left on the top shelf a third case, not quite as large as the others and with a strap that meant she could carry it on her shoulder. That would not be needed until later.

Selecting jeans, a thick polo-neck jumper and some soft-soled trainers, Beverly put them to one side. That was all she could do for now. Her heart beating much faster than the recent activity warranted, she unlocked the door, turned off the light, removed her dressing-gown and got into bed. She lay dozing, the mixture of excitement and fear building inside her and making her toss and turn. She woke from a light doze just after midnight as voices came up the stairs and she felt herself tense as she prayed that Milton would not pay her a visit. He wasn't the most over-sensitive of men, but he was bound to sense the tension inside her if he came to her that night. She relaxed as the familiar voice passed her door and she heard him enter his bedroom. From what she could hear of the conversation, it sounded as though Gray had failed to show up and they couldn't raise him on his mobile. Milton was clearly not best pleased. After a few minutes, she drifted off to sleep again.

It was two o'clock when the soft alarm in her wristwatch awakened Beverly. She got out of bed quickly and dressed as quietly as possible, alert to any noise from the corridor outside. She crept to her door and eased it open. The house was silent and in darkness. Apart from herself and Milton, there were four other regular occupants of the house: Jack Pace, Milton's bodyguard and general enforcer, and Horace Soames, Milton's secretary and accountant, both slept on the same corridor as she did. There were two live-in domestic staff, Janice Gardner, the cook, and Jane Weston, a young woman who was loosely described as a maid but whose job description covered far more than hoovering and dusting and who had formed an attachment with Pace. Gardner and Weston slept in

another wing of the house except when Weston was being entertained by Pace, but the other three would be roused if there was any
unexpected noise.

Beverly had a small torch in her hand, but did not use it as she
moved softly across the landing and felt for the banister rail. A
window at the end of the corridor provided a little filtered light
from the street outside, enough for her to make her way to the head
of the stairs. She went carefully down the stairs, walking at the edge
so that they would not creak. At the bottom, she paused again and
listened carefully. There was no sound. She walked round to the
cupboard under the stairs. Opening the door, she used her torch for
the first time as she keyed in the password that switched off the
alarm system. The system beeped twice as it turned off and Beverly
froze, waiting to see if anyone had been woken by the brief noise. It
was a good five minutes before the continued silence gave her the
courage to continue.

If anything, it was even more of a strain to go back upstairs once
more to her room, knowing she was getting closer to Milton again.
There was no convincing explanation that she could think of if he
found her wandering around the house in the dark, fully dressed
and carrying a torch. Beverly took a few deep breaths at the top of
the stairs to steady herself. Once back in her room, she took the
cases from the cupboard, put on her coat and put the torch in her
shoulder bag. With the empty case slung across her back and
carrying the two suitcases, she left her room and carefully locked
the door behind her. The longer it took them in the morning to
realize that she had gone, the better. She made her way back down
the stairs, once again glad that she would not have to carry her
cases very far. It might have been more prudent to restrict herself to
one main case and the one across her back, but she was determined
to take away as much as possible from the last two years – at least
in a material sense.

Outside the door to Milton's study, she put down the cases and
took from her shoulder bag the duplicate key she had managed
to get cut a few weeks before. She had taken Milton's own spare
key from his desk and he had almost caught her when she
returned it. The thought of what he would have done to her had
he realized the truth gave her a moment of blind panic. Beverly

took some more deep breaths, eased the key into the lock and turned it carefully. Even the faint click as the lock turned sounded like a crack of thunder in the silent house. This time she did not wait, from now on she needed to move as quickly as was prudently possible. Beverly opened the door, picked up her cases and went inside. It was tiresome having to move the cases with her each time, but if someone did wake up and come downstairs, she would stand still less chance of escaping detection if the cases were standing in the hall.

Putting her cases down just inside the door, Beverly locked the study door from the inside before she switched on her torch again and crossed to the large desk that dominated one side of the room. The room was wood panelled and had heavy leather armchairs and book-lined walls. Some books had been bought for decoration, but Milton had a good collection of volumes on both art and military strategy that he often perused. A number of original oil paintings were hung around the walls. Thick curtains covered the windows, but Beverly did not dare switch on a light in case it shone into the hall from under the door. The room smelt of Milton's strong cigars and gave the impression that his spirit was still in the room, watching her. Although that was just a piece of fancy, Beverly could have done without it slipping into her subconscious at that point. The only sound was the ticking of the ornate Louis XIV-style clock that stood in the centre of the imposing mantelpiece.

On the floor to the left of the desk stood a low table containing a globe. Beverly placed the torch on the edge of the desk and used both hands to move the table to one side. Beneath where the table had stood, a cleverly cut piece of carpet hid a small trapdoor and the door of a safe. It had taken Beverly some time to discover the combination, and she felt her heart thumping as she used it now, crouched by the side of the desk and peering down at the steel door below her. She turned the handle and lifted the door. It swung up and back, without sounding any alarms. Feeling a little happier now that she was so near to getting away, Beverly reached down and began to pack the contents of the safe into her spare case. It was mainly wads of money in pounds, Euros and dollars but there was also some diamonds, some packets of drugs and a small wooden box. Everything went into the case. She zipped the case shut, closed the safe and got to her feet again. Her hands were damp with sweat and she was shaking. She nearly tipped the globe off the table when she replaced it, and that made her sweat even more.

It was even more of a physical effort with the full case across her back and the two suitcases, but she got from the relocked study door to the front door and undid the bolts and the chain that secured it. As she opened the door and felt the cold early morning air cooling her hot forehead, she half expected to hear the alarms go off, but nothing happened. In the distance a police siren could be heard, proving that crime never slept. The thought made her smile wryly to herself as she pulled the front door closed. The snick of the front door lock seemed like a signal, heralding the point from which there was no turning back; all she could do now was to move forward and hope that her plans would work out.

The front drive seemed to go on forever. Beverly wished that she could have used her car, but opening the garage would have been an extra risk. Even if the noise didn't wake anyone, the car's absence was bound to be spotted early in the morning. This way should gain them an extra few hours, and that could be vital. She was trying to walk softly so as not to make too much noise on the gravel, but that in itself was difficult with the weight she was carrying. At least it had stopped raining heavily and there was enough light from the street ahead for her to avoid any obstacles.

At the gate, she put down the cases and stretched her aching arms above her head. She used her key on the gate, opened it, took her cases through and locked it again. The hinges creaked slightly and somewhere a cat called out as if in response. Fortunately, the camera was linked to the alarm system at night so there would be no immediate photographic evidence. The long wide road was deserted, the spaced street lamps giving it a silvery gleam. Beverly crossed quickly to the tall dark skeletal trees that rose from the woodland of the common on the other side of the road. She started walking to the left along a narrow asphalt path, split and crumbling with weeds. About twenty yards along on the right was a narrow muddy lane between the trees and she took that, the soles of her trainers slipping slightly on the damp ground. Her breath was coming in short gasps and there was a stitch in her side, a combination of her tension and the weight she was carrying. She should definitely have packed fewer clothes! The path was now no more than a muddy track and the light from the main road grew dimmer as she walked along, peering ahead to avoid the deeper puddles. Her designer trainers would be getting filthy. Still, she had plenty of money to buy a new pair.

Fifty yards down the lane, backed in where there was a flat grassy space between the trees, a car stood waiting in darkness, its bonnet pointing back the way she had come. There was just enough light in the gloom to make out Beverly's shape and, as she drew near, the driver's door opened and a figure came out and took the cases. Light from the car spilled out across the lane.

They kissed quickly and the driver hugged her.

'You're late, I was getting worried.'

'I was slower than I thought, I didn't want to make a noise.' She helped him to load her cases into the boot of the car as she talked. Relief flooded though her. She didn't have to carry the cases any further and she had got away with it: she was clear of the house without raising the alarm. 'I'm glad I don't have to earn my living as a burglar.' She turned towards him and hugged and kissed him again, feeling the relief turning to desire.

Her companion laughed and pushed her away gently.

'We'd better leave that for later. We don't want to hang around.'

They got into the car and, as the engine started into life, the headlights brought the trees into sharp outline. They drove back up the lane and turned right towards the motorway, away from Milton's house and on the first leg of what they hoped was the road to freedom.

SIX

WHEN THE FRONT door-bell rang at 9.30 Julie and Tanner were sitting in the kitchen enjoying the warmth of the sun beaming through at them from a clear sky. They had just finished a leisurely breakfast, having first carried out a further check after waking up to make certain that what had happened the night before really hadn't been a fluke. They had both showered and Tanner thought that Julie looked delectable in a dark-blue silk kimono-style dressing-gown with a dramatic orange and red dragon pattern. Her hair was tied back loosely and her face looked fresh and very young without any make-up.

'Could you answer it, please, whilst I make myself more presentable?' She got up from the kitchen table, demonstrating that there was nothing but Julie under the kimono.

'My pleasure.' Tanner got up, kissed her, and walked through to the hallway as she went into her bedroom.

Tanner peered through the spy hole to make sure the visitors didn't intend a follow up to the violent activities of the previous evening. When he saw the rather crumpled face on the other side of the door, with its thatch of untidy, straw-coloured hair, he relaxed and opened the door.

'Good morning, Ancient.'

Detective Chief Inspector Richard Mariner grunted a greeting and walked past into the flat.

'Morning, Alec.' Mariner was wearing his usual creased blue suit and wrinkled raincoat and carried a battered briefcase.

'Come through to the lounge,' Tanner said. 'Julie will be out in a minute.'

'Right.' Mariner lowered his lanky form into a chair and placed his case at his feet. He affected a world weary and slightly bored expression that had often led people to assume – incorrectly and to their cost – that he was not particularly alert or clever. In fact, he was both, and was one of the most respected police officers in the Havenchester force.

'Making yourself at home, I see.' He raised an enquiring eyebrow.

'You know that we offer a full service.'

'I hope you aren't—' He broke off as Julie came in, wearing jeans and a white sweater.

'Good morning Julie.'

'Good morning, sir.'

He stared at her closely for a moment, looked across at Tanner and then back at her. 'You look a lot better than when you first came to see me.'

'I've started to live a bit again. Would you like some coffee?'

'Yes please.'

'Carry on talking – I can hear you in the kitchen.'

'I've come to get your signatures on your written statements, to save you a trip to the station. I've also come to ask you not to start a war on my patch.'

'War?' Tanner tried to look offended. 'We are intent on spreading sweetness and light.'

Mariner didn't look convinced.

'Those goons last night didn't look very sweet after you two had finished with them.'

'Did they say who sent them?'

'No.' The chief inspector shook his head disgustedly. 'They're just local cannon-fodder. They've all refused to make a statement on the advice of their lawyer. There is one interesting thing, though: the man who came to give them legal representation has amongst his other clients one Vincent Bridger.'

Julie came though from the kitchen with three mugs of coffee on a tray.

'I said poking the nest would help,' she remarked.

'How about the van they used?' Tanner asked.

Mariner shook his head. 'Stolen earlier in the evening – just a dead-end.'

'It would be much easier if they used their own registered vehicles, wouldn't it? Crooks have no consideration.'

'Hmm.' He glanced across to the far side of the room where there was a small desk with a computer and other equipment. 'Is that an all in one printer?' He asked.

'Yes.' Julie looked puzzled.

Mariner nodded.

'Very useful, being able to make photocopies.' He opened his case. 'Here are your statements, if you'd read and sign them.' He paused. 'Well I never,' he said in a dead-pan voice, 'I've put an office file in my case as well by mistake. It is confidential and for official use only, but I'm sure you wouldn't dream of looking in my case, would you?'

'Certainly not.' Julie put the tray down carefully.

'Could I use your bathroom?'

'Of course. The door to the left of the hall.'

'Thank you.'

Once Mariner had left the room, Tanner opened the case and took out the thin file. It contained biographies, addresses and contacts for the six potential shooters that Ted Manning had identified. Julie had already switched on the printer and by the time Mariner returned, making some unnecessary noise about it, the file and its papers were back in the case and Julie and Tanner were studiously reading through their statements.

'Well?' Mariner asked.

'It all seems to be in order,' Tanner said, signing. Julie had already signed hers.

'Thank you.' Mariner placed the statements in his case. 'Of course, there's no proof that Bridger instigated the attack on you last night, and I doubt if we'd ever be able to prove it.'

Tanner nodded. 'We wouldn't expect it.'

'So can I ask – unofficially of course – what you intend to do next?'

'The fact that Bridger didn't like the idea of us poking around and asking questions about Jarvis and Hesky suggests that they might be worth looking into,' Julie said. 'I believe I read somewhere that Hesky has an ex-wife. It might be an idea to have a chat with her and get some more background before we do anything else.'

Mariner nodded solemnly.

'I see that you are very well informed. The divorce wasn't exactly harmonious, and there is a son that Hesky tries to see from time to time, so you might get something useful from her.'

'Did you interview her?'

'Not about his possible involvement in the shooting. As I told you, we didn't focus much on locals. I have had dealings with her on other matters, though. She hates the police almost as much as she hates Hesky. After Hesky she took up with someone else and we nicked him for armed robbery earlier this year. She's not very good at choosing her men.'

He finished his coffee.

'Thanks for the drink. Take care of yourselves. You need to watch your backs where Bridger is concerned.'

'We'll be careful,' Julie promised. 'Thanks for your help.'

Mariner got to his feet and picked up his briefcase.

'My help? I don't know what you mean.'

After Mariner had gone, they sat and read through the information from the copied file. The home and work addresses for Hesky's ex-wife were listed. Hesky and Jarvis shared the same home address, a flat in the south of the city. They decided to leave visiting the prime suspects until they had talked to the ex-wife. If she disliked Hesky as much as Mariner suggested, they might get some useful information from her.

April Thornton, formerly Hesky, worked at City Taxis, a radio taxi company in Kings Road – not to be confused with the London thoroughfare of the same name. Kings Road, Havenchester was long and winding and felt perpetually grey. Even when the sun came out, the light seemed filtered through dirt. The road was lined with a variety of shops and shop front businesses. The brickwork was dirty, the paintwork generally peeling and most windows looked like they could do with occasional contact with clean water. The pavements were cracked and narrow, but there were permitted parking spaces in the road. Most of the cars parked around City Taxis were presumably plying their trade from the establishment, but Tanner managed to find a space fifty yards further along.

The décor inside the shop matched the outside, with drivers

sitting around on a padded bench inside the door and a partitioned area towards the back which led to the control centre. A woman's voice could be heard on the phone taking a pick-up instruction. An elderly man with a pronounced beer gut wearing an open-necked striped shirt sat behind the counter.

'Help you?' he asked in a rasping voice.

'We'd like to speak to April Thornton, please.'

He gave them both a curious look, but didn't object. He swivelled round to face the rear of the shop and the woman who sat at a desk with three telephones and some radio equipment.

'Hey, Api, couple 'ere want to talk to yer.'

Tanner wondered, not for the first time, why even the shortest of names often had to be shortened even further.

Mrs Thornton finished giving instructions on the pick-up into the radio, got to her feet and walked across to the counter.

'Yes?' She was tall with a round face, short, curly hair and sharp blue eyes. Her clothes hung a little loosely, as if she had recently lost some weight.

'My name's Alec Tanner and this is my colleague Julie Cooper.' In view of Mariner's comment on her opinion of the police, it didn't seem prudent to give Julie's official title. 'I'm a private investigator and I'd like to ask you a few questions about Sam Hesky.'

Her expression got even sharper as she looked them carefully up and down.

'In trouble is he?'

'Very possibly.'

She nodded.

'I'm due for a ciggy break. Come through and we'll talk in the yard. Take over the phone, will you, Kenny?'

The elderly man nodded, got laboriously out of his chair and moved to the rear of the shop to take over the phone desk. Mrs Thornton opened the door at the side of the partition and beckoned them through. She picked up her handbag from the desk and they followed her to the back of the shop, past a small alcove with a sink and a kettle and an open door that led to a toilet which, judging from the smell, should not have been used without protective clothing and a gas mask. Beyond the staff facilities was another door that she unlocked, taking them through into a small rectangular paved yard. The air quality improved fractionally until she took a packet of cigarettes and a lighter from her handbag, lit up and took in a deep drag on her cigarette, letting the smoke out slowly through her mouth with a sigh.

'Right then,' she said briskly, 'what's all this about?'

'Sam Hesky is your ex-husband?' Tanner asked. She nodded briefly. 'We are undertaking an investigation for a client. The details must remain confidential, but Hesky's name has come up in connection with some activities that have adversely affected our client and we need to look into him further. Do you have much contact with him?'

She shook her head.

'As little as possible.'

'Does he see your son?'

'No.' Mention of the son seemed to have touched a nerve. She took another deep drag at her cigarette. 'Look, why don't you tell me exactly what you want to know?'

Tanner decided that they wouldn't get very far unless he was a bit more informative.

'We are interested in Hesky's whereabouts on a particular day. The eighth February this year. Do you happen to remember that day?'

He didn't have much hope that her memory would be that specific after several weeks, but to his surprise, she gave a snorting sort of laugh and nodded.

'I'm not likely to forget it.' She lit a second cigarette from the stub of the first.

Tanner thought Mrs Thornton might be more open talking to another woman. He gave Julie a glance and she took over.

'Why, what happened?'

'My husband got himself arrested. My current husband, that is.' She shook her head. 'I can certainly pick 'em.' She paused for a moment, presumably to consider her marital track record. It didn't seem to give her much satisfaction. 'They arrested him for armed robbery. Only the idiot tried to make a run for it, jumped over a fence, tripped and broke his ankle. I spent the evening of eighth February in the hospital with him and the copper who was guarding him. Then, when I got home, I found my son had spent the evening with his bastard of a father. I was pretty pissed off, I can tell you.'

Tanner felt a spark of anticipation and sensed that Julie felt the same.

'Was Sam Hesky there?'

'Not likely – he knows better than to come into my house – I've got too many kitchen knives with his name on.' She shook her head. 'No, Jimmy – that's my son – told me. Not that he wanted to, but I caught him at the sink trying to wash blood out of his T-shirt, so he didn't have much option.'

Julie and Tanner exchanged a puzzled glance. If Hesky was one of the two on the motor bike, where had the blood come from? Neither of the bikers had stopped and got close to Julie or her aunt.

'Whose blood was it?'

'His father's. It's a pity the bugger didn't do us all a favour and bleed to death.'

'Did Jimmy tell you what had happened?'

She shrugged.

'Just that his father had rung him earlier in the evening and told him that he needed his help. Wanted Jimmy to pick him and that prick Jarvis up in his car because they'd been hurt and couldn't drive. I didn't ask any more. Jimmy swore he hadn't been involved in anything criminal himself, so I just told him never to help his father like that again. That's always been my fear – that Sam would drag Jimmy into his world, make a criminal out of him. Jimmy's nineteen now, he's got a decent job, a mechanic in a garage. Not brilliant money, but he's learning a trade. Trouble is, he's always had a soft spot for his dad, can't see through him. He thinks Sam really cares about him.' She thought for a moment. 'I suppose he does care a bit, in a way,' she conceded grudgingly, 'but if push came to shove, Sam would put himself first every time.'

'We'd like to talk to Jimmy,' Julie said gently, aware that they were starting to tread on very dodgy ground.

'No.' The woman shook her head firmly. 'I don't want him involved.'

'It could be very important,' Julie pressed her. 'Please reconsider. We won't involve him with the police, but if he can tell us more about where his father was that night, it could be vital.'

Mrs Thornton paused and looked at them with a calculating expression.

'If Sam's done what you think he has, would it put him away for a long time?'

'Yes it would; he wouldn't be able to interfere with Jimmy's life any more.'

She nodded slowly.

'I'll need to talk to him first.' She made up her mind. 'Do you know Panters Park – just round the corner from here?'

'I do,' Tanner said.

'Right then. If I can persuade him, we'll meet you there at one o'clock. There are some benches we can sit on.' She thought for a moment. 'I'll tell him that you need to know where his father was so as to clear him from your investigation – if he thinks you're looking to get his father put away, he won't talk.'

Tanner nodded.

'That's OK.'

She wasn't prepared to shop Hesky to the police directly, Tanner decided, but as he and Julie were seen as being one step removed, talking to them was somehow OK within her particular social code; it wasn't like proper grassing. That was one advantage he had over the official police and he certainly wasn't going to complain about it.

'See you later, then.'

She trod her cigarette into the paving stones, probably wishing it was her ex-husband, and led them back out through the shop.

Panters Park was a rectangular oasis of green in amongst an area of grubby shops and terraced housing. An asphalt path ran round the outside, and at one o'clock it was being used by a couple of joggers who gave the park an appropriate name. As the park was only a line of shops away from a busy main road, the air quality for such exertion was not first class. In fact, as Julie and Tanner sat on a bench looking across the park, they thought they could almost see the air. A few straggly trees reached bare branches up to the now cloudy sky like petrified athletes frozen in the middle of a series of stretching exercises. Some pigeons pecked busily between a set of metal goal posts. The crossbars were bent down in the middle – no doubt, Julie imagined, by some enterprising local youngster.

It was nearly ten past one before Jimmy and his mother arrived and Tanner had started to fear that she hadn't persuaded him to talk to them.

Jimmy Hesky was a lanky lad who seemed younger than his nineteen years. He wore torn jeans and a scruffy leather jacket over a T-shirt with some sort of rude message on it. His lean, sharp face was spotted with acne and framed by long, curly dark hair and there was a certain animosity coupled with reluctance in his eyes.

'Thank you for agreeing to see us,' Tanner said.

He grunted.

'Mum said it might help Dad.' His voice was a little throaty and, judging from his yellow-stained fingers, he followed his mother's lead in the matter of nicotine intake. As if to confirm Tanner's thoughts, they both lit up as they waited for him to continue.

'We need to talk to you about the eighth February, when your father rang you and asked for your help.'

Jimmy gave his mother a not very filial look.

'What about it? Just between me and my Dad, that is.'

'He's been accused of doing something towards the end of that evening and it sounds as though you know what he was doing.'

'That's rubbish – he couldn't have done anything, he was hurt.' Jimmy broke off and looked down at his hands on his lap, cupped around his cigarette.

'Then that will help him,' Julie put in. 'I think you'd better tell us what happened.'

Tanner thought they were getting quite expert at this good cop, bad cop, business.

'Dad rang me at about eight o'clock.' Jimmy looked out across the park as he spoke. 'Said he and Uncle Harry had been hurt. They couldn't drive, and he wanted me to go and pick them up.'

'Where from?'

'Castle Street. There's a shop there that sells sex stuff, you know?' He gave them a smutty grin. 'He said he'd be in the alley next to the shop. When I got there, I parked by the mouth of the alley and went to get them. They were lying on the ground, out of sight behind some wheelie bins. Harry was unconscious with blood running down the side of his face and Dad was propped up against the wall holding his side. I managed to get them into the car. Harry was still out cold so I dragged him across the pavement and got him in the back. Then I helped Dad into the passenger seat. That's when I got the blood on my T-shirt. I wanted to take them to hospital, but Dad insisted that we went to this doctor he knew. I drove them there, and left them in the car whilst I went and knocked on the door. The doctor didn't want to come at first, but when I told him my father's name, he came out and helped me get them into the house. Harry was coming around a bit by then, though he was still pretty groggy.'

'Did your father tell you what had happened?'

'Not really. He'd been stabbed in the side, that's why he was bleeding and why he couldn't drive himself. He said something about the bastard in the sex shop, but he didn't mention any names or anything.' Jimmy shook his head. 'We got to the doctor's house just after nine. I waited for the doctor to confirm Dad wasn't too seriously hurt and it was half past by the time I left. Dad had a long cut in his side, but it wasn't very deep, it just bled a lot and was very painful and the doctor was going to start stitching it. There's no way either my Dad or Harry was going to be in a fit state to do anything to anybody after that.'

He looked suddenly very vulnerable and pleading. Just a son wanting to protect his dad, even if it was a toe-rag like Hesky.

'That's all I know.'

'OK. Thanks for talking to us,' Tanner said.

'Does it help to clear him?'

Tanner nodded. It wasn't what his mother wanted to hear, but they couldn't please both of them.

'Yes, I think it does.' At least, he thought, it cleared him of the shooting of Julie and her aunt.

'So what do you make of that?'

They had returned to Tanner's car and sat for a moment before driving off.

'It seems to clear Hesky and Jarvis of the shooting,' Tanner said. 'But if so, that poses an interesting question.'

'If Hesky and Jarvis didn't carry out the shooting, why did Bridger send the heavies to attack us?'

'Exactly.'

'So we carry on digging?'

'You're the client, it's your call.'

'I think we need to answer that question, even if it has nothing to do with the shooting. If Bridger is after us, we need to know why.'

'It could be someone else who happens to use the same solicitor.'

'You don't sound very convinced.'

Tanner grinned at her. 'I'm not. Let's pay a visit to Castle Street.'

'You just want an excuse to visit a sex shop.'

Castle Street was a modest thoroughfare of reasonably prosperous shops situated more towards the centre of the city. There was only one shop selling sex aids, books, films and a variety of interesting costumes. It was situated next to an alley, which was a promising confirmation of Jimmy's story.

They went in. The merchandise inside was, as might be expected, far more diverse than that displayed in the window. Julie did a double take at one item hanging on the wall above a rack of DVDs.

'What do you think that's for?'

'Perhaps we should buy one and experiment.'

A young woman was standing behind a long counter reading a magazine and chewing gum. There were no other customers. She looked bored to tears.

'Is the manager around?' Tanner asked.

'He's in the back.' She gave them an uninterested look and gave her gum another chew.

'Could you get him please?'

They didn't seem to be penetrating her boredom. She nodded, turned her head towards an arch behind the counter and called out, 'Herbie, there's someone to see you.'

Herbie turned out to be a short, rotund man wearing tight black trousers, a red frilly shirt and black bow tie.

'Can I help you?' His weak, pale-blue eyes were hiding behind thick black-rimmed spectacles and he glanced from Julie to Tanner with a half smile hovering nervously round his rather pouting mouth. Tanner couldn't visualize him beating up two street-wise heavies like Hesky and Jarvis.

'We want to talk to you about Vernon Bridger.'

The manager blinked rapidly, came round from behind the

counter and shepherded them into a corner of the shop, licking his lips. His assistant didn't look up from her magazine.

'Look,' he hissed in a desperate whisper, 'I'm paying all I can. I can't afford …'

Tanner started to get a feel for what the panic was all about. They'd stumbled on to a protection racket. Herbie had misunderstood and thought they had been sent by Bridger. It seemed a good idea not to correct him straight away.

'He's still pretty pissed off by what happened in February,' Tanner told him. Which was probably true, he reflected.

The little man started sweating. Not a pretty sight. Tanner nearly felt ashamed of himself.

'Look, I made a mistake, but I thought that had been sorted out. The other guys said …' His voice rose an octave.

'Hesky and Jarvis?'

'They didn't leave their cards.' The attempt at mild bravado didn't have much heart in it.

'Who beat them up – it wasn't you?'

'Of course not.' He frowned. 'Don't you know what happened?'

'We aren't told everything.' Tanner hoped Herbie's nerves would keep him talking for a bit longer before his brain kicked into gear and he realized they hadn't been sent by Bridger.

'After they came for money the first time, I asked a friend of mine to come and stay with me,' Herbie said. 'He was a big guy; he worked out at the gym and could look after himself. When they came back the second time, my friend beat the shit out of them and threw them out.'

'How did Hesky get stabbed?'

'Hesky pulled the knife; my friend was just defending himself, he …' The pale eyes widened as he realized what he had been saying. 'Just a minute, who the hell are you?' He tried, very unsuccessfully to sound belligerent. It was like being growled at by a hedgehog.

'Private detectives.' Tanner decided the misunderstanding had got them as far as it could. 'We're looking at the two men for something else that happened that night.'

'My God.' His voice got even squeakier and he started shaking like one of his own products. 'You've conned me. Get out.'

'We know most of it now; you might as well tell us the rest.'

'Bridger will kill me.'

'He won't need to know you've spoken to us.'

Herbie shook his head stubbornly.

'Look,' Julie took over. 'Whatever you tell us, we won't be talking to Bridger. But what you know could help put him out of business, which can only help you. What happened to your friend?'

'I don't know,' he said eventually, shaking his head miserably. 'I really don't. Nothing happened for a couple of weeks and I thought maybe we'd put them off. Then one afternoon my friend went out for a walk and never came back. Those two men came back again that evening and said that I wouldn't see him again and if I didn't pay for protection, I'd disappear too. I was petrified. I agreed to start paying.'

'What was your friend's name?'

'Salvador Sanchez. He called himself Sally.'

'Didn't he have any friends or relatives who'd want to know what happened to him?'

'No. He never saw his family; they washed their hands of him when he came out. His friends here just think he's moved on to London. I was his only really close friend.'

'Didn't you want to avenge him?'

Herbie started shivering again and shook his head.

'We weren't *that* close.'

Back in the car again, they had another case conference.

'Well, that makes things a bit clearer.' Julie said. 'Bridger runs a protection racket as one of his many sidelines. He probably focuses on those shops whose trade wouldn't bear too much looking into, so the owners are less likely to go to the police. Hesky and Jarvis do the collecting.'

Tanner nodded.

'When we said we'd look into Hesky and Jarvis, Bridger was afraid we'd find out about what happened the same night as the shooting. He wasn't worried about us proving Hesky and Jarvis killed your aunt, he was afraid we'd find out about Sally. That's why he wanted us taken out of action.'

'So we can cross them off our list.'

'But not before we get them added to Mariner's. Even if Sanchez's body has never been found, we can tell Ancient who did it and when, so he might be able to find some sort of trail.'

SEVEN

OF ALL HARRY Milton's employees, it was, oddly enough, Horace Soames who was least afraid of him. Even Jack Pace was more concerned than Soames at ensuring that he did not antagonize his employer. This was not due to any physical prowess on Soames's part – he was a small, dapper man with a perpetually calculating expression and pale-blue eyes behind gold-rimmed spectacles. He was, however, the most irreplaceable of all the employees. Thugs and strong-arm men are easy enough to come by – although those with real intelligence like Jack Pace, perhaps less so – but Soames had brains and a financial acumen that enabled him to assess the potential profitability of any scheme, whether legal or illegal, with impressively constant accuracy. He also knew where Milton's financial skeletons were buried, having interred most of them himself. He was pedantic and fussy, with an abhorrence of both dirt and violence, or, at least, of coming into contact with them himself. Even so, Soames was careful not to upset Milton, whose temper was never the most stable of his attributes.

The morning after Beverly had run away, Soames was being extremely careful, running everything he was about to say silently through his mind before committing it to his mouth. Milton, when he realized what had happened, had gone beyond anger to a quiet but intense rage that threatened to erupt at any moment. One wrong word, gesture or facial expression would be enough. It would be like treading on a sleeping cobra or teasing a shark with tooth ache.

Jack Pace had been the first to realize that something was wrong. He was usually the first in the household to get up and had been in the habit of touring the house as soon as he was awake and dressed to make sure everything was still secure. He had raised the alarm when he had discovered that the alarm was not, as it were, on to be raised. After checking that Milton had not been harmed and that there was no sign of any obvious theft or damage, Pace had returned to the study where Milton, in dressing-gown and pyjamas, his temper already approaching boiling point, sat with Soames, who as always was immaculately dressed and externally calm.

At first, Milton had accused Pace of not setting the alarm, an accusation which Pace had immediately rejected, pointing out that Milton had been standing next to him when he had done so on their way upstairs after their abortive wait for Reggie Gray. It had then occurred to the three men that Beverly Wallace had not yet been roused and Pace was sent to her room to fetch her. He returned a few minutes later to report that the door had been locked and when he opened it with his master key, Beverly was not there.

'Could she have been abducted?' Soames asked.

Pace shook his head.

'I doubt it. There's no sign of a struggle and no note. It looks as though some clothes and suitcases are gone.' He spoke woodenly, careful to let no emotion show on his face or in his voice as he reported to Milton.

That was when Milton's anger began to spill over.

'It looks like the bitch has done a runner then.' He frowned. 'Why would she do that?' He was genuinely puzzled. A man who lived for material gain alone, he judged everyone one else by his own standards. 'She wasn't being mistreated and I give her anything she wants—' He broke off suddenly and swore.

Soames was only milliseconds behind Milton's reasoning and he looked on in horror as Milton rushed over to the desk, moved the table to one side, almost dislodging the globe in his haste, and knelt by the floor. He could barely control his fingers as they scrabbled at the carpet, but eventually the safe door was uncovered. When the safe was open, Milton sat back on his heels and started swearing in earnest. Soames walked across and stood behind him, looking down into the empty cavity.

'How much?' Milton asked hoarsely.

Soames couldn't speak for a moment and then his brain clicked into gear.

'Half a million in currency, as much again in diamonds, another million in drugs. And in the box ...'

He didn't need to complete the sentence.

Milton turned his head to look at Pace. His face was stiff and calm, but Pace had never seen such hatred in his boss's eyes.

'I want you to get her back, Jack. I don't care what you have to do, who you have to bribe or trample on to do it. Just get her back.' He looked at each of the two other men in turn. 'If word gets out that I've been shafted by that tart, I'll be a laughing stock and that will never do – it will affect business.' He focused on Pace and his voice got even colder. 'But it's more than that, Jack, this is personal. No one does something like this to me. You get my stuff back and you bring her to me.' He closed the safe and got slowly to his feet. 'And I want her alive. I don't care if you have to damage her a bit, but I want her alive so I can finish her off myself, slowly.'

'Right.' Pace nodded. 'I'll get the word round to keep an eye out for her. Then I'll go and see her sister. She works for Bridger, so I won't have any trouble if—'

He broke off as his mobile phone rang.

'Sorry, Harry.'

For a moment, Soames thought that might be the spark to set Milton off, but Milton just nodded and Pace took the call.

'Yes?' Pace frowned and then rolled his eyes. 'He's what?' He shook his head. 'Right. Which hospital? Yeah – I've got that, thanks for ringing.' He switched the phone off and looked across at Milton. 'That was Reggie's sister. He crashed his car on his way back here last night. They took him to the Royal Hospital. Nothing's broken, but he was unconscious and he's only just come round. He'll probably be in hospital for a couple of days.'

'Stupid pillock.' Milton was more worried about losing someone who could help in the hunt for Beverly Wallace than he was about Gray's health.

'At least if he was coming back into the city he should have finished his job,' Pace commented.

Milton grunted.

'There's only one job that's important now,' he said. 'Find Beverly Wallace and bring her in.'

At the moment when Harry Milton was expressing a wish to find her, Beverly rolled over in bed and opened her eyes. Sunlight was coming into the small bedroom through thin curtains, illuminating the low-beamed ceiling, the simple furnishings and the thin mat on the floor by the bed. There remained a faint musty smell from the cottage being locked up and unused, even though she had left the bedroom window ajar. She always slept with the curtains drawn and a window open and she suddenly realized that she had no idea whether Jeffrey did too. She could hear the soft sound of his breathing beside her and deeper sound of the sea beyond the window forming a background to the sharp, constant call of the gulls that she knew would be circling the cliff top, hunting their breakfast. The thought of breakfast made her feel suddenly hungry herself. She stretched and turned to look at the man lying beside her. He seemed very young, almost boyish lying asleep with a lock of dark straight hair falling across his face. She smiled at him, leant across and kissed him.

Jeffrey Jones, known generally as JJ, opened one eye and yawned.

'Good morning.' He spoke thickly as he rolled over to face her. 'What time is it?'

She looked at the silver watch that she always wore to bed, often with nothing else.

'Nine-thirty.'

Jones groaned and ran his hands over his face. He felt as though he hadn't had any sleep at all. Memories from the night before came flooding back. Waiting in the woods, tense and worried, for Beverly to arrive. Imagining all the things that could go wrong and what would happen if they did. The immense relief when she came, labouring under the weight of her cases. The two-hour drive to the cottage that he had only visited twice before and never in the dark. The constant glances at the rear mirror for signs of pursuit and near panic on the few occasions when headlights got too close. Relief when they finally arrived after twice losing their way. Eventually crawling into bed and tossing and turning for ages despite his exhaustion, reliving what they had just been through and suddenly aware of the import of what they had done and the danger they were in.

At first, the plan had seemed exciting and romantic, a fitting extension of their passionate love affair. He had first met Beverly when she had come to take individual lessons at the dance school where he worked and he had been her teacher. She was a natural mover, but needed to learn the steps and the discipline of the ball-room dances. The first two or three visits had been purely professional. There had been an immediate easiness between them and they talked and joked as they danced. The mutual attraction had developed quickly and, as he held her and took her through the dance steps, they had started whispering to each other, carefully testing to see if each felt the same, making sure that they weren't overheard by the other couples on the floor.

She told him she was living with a man she didn't love, didn't even respect, but whom she feared. She had plenty of material things, but he gave her nothing else and wanted only one thing from her. Eventually, he would tire even of that and she knew that then she would be cast off to end up only God knew where and doing only God knew what – although she could have a pretty good guess. You didn't put her current occupation on your CV – at least, not on most CVs.

Their whispers had led to the first of the phantom dance lessons, when she had told Milton that she needed extra tuition and had met Jones at an hotel where the feelings they had been developing were consummated. More meetings followed. She learnt her dance steps easily, so she just had to pretend to Milton that she was finding it more difficult than she really was and the extra lessons were justified. Jones found out more about her, more about the man Milton whom she feared so much. Visits to hotels were supplemented by uncomfortable manoeuvrings in the back of Jones's car parked down wooded lanes or behind abandoned factories. Eventually, the surreptitious meetings were not enough and they decided to run away. Jones resigned from the dance school, giving a month's notice and they decided that they would leave at the end of that time.

Jones had an Irish friend from his student days who owned a

boat and would be able to get them across to Ireland. The friend also had somewhat dubious contacts who would be able to produce forged passports and other documents. From Ireland, with new names, they would get to America and disappear. One of the reasons they had to lie low in the cottage for a few days rather than try to leave the country immediately by boat or plane was to give the friend a chance to get the documents ready. He and his contacts insisted on cash on delivery and wouldn't start preparing the documents until Beverly had escaped with Milton's money so that she had the cash to pay for them.

Milton himself had many contacts in the US, so it was imperative that they were able to create new identities and have the money to set themselves up with new lives. With the contacts Milton's organization could call upon, using conventional transport links in Beverly's own name would be suicide in either Britain or America. In these days of computerized information, you only needed to grease one or two key palms and the information could be easily accessed. Beverly knew Milton was bound to come after them anyway, so she might as well steal from him as well in order to fund their new lives. It was, she thought, a bit like a witness protection programme except that it would be funded by the person they needed to be protected against. She rather liked the poetic justice of that. At least Milton wouldn't call in the police, although if they had to be found out, better the police than Milton's people. Also, with luck, Milton wouldn't find out about JJ, at least for a while, and that would make it more difficult to track them.

Beverly had lived her whole life under the control of men she had not been able to choose – first her violent father, then a succession of low-life chancers who had only wanted her for her body, and finally Milton, who was the same but with money to spend. Now she had chosen her man herself and that gave her an immense feeling of freedom and release, almost as if she had been reborn, despite the enormous danger that she faced as a result of that choice.

Their refuge was a cottage owned by Jones's brother, who was a financial trader in London and who owned a cottage on the north-west coast that he could use when he wanted to get back to his northern roots – which he did about three times a year. He had been happy for JJ to use the cottage for a few days, without knowing exactly why he needed it, and they planned to stay there until Jones's friend arrived in his boat, which was scheduled for three days' time. Until then, all they could do was lie low and hope Milton wouldn't trace them.

The cottage was a simple wooden dwelling on the top of a cliff above a shallow bay. There were a few other cottages around, but none within sight. A number of trees and thick bushes covered the cliff top, providing natural seclusion for each dwelling. A steep path led down from their cottage to the crescent-shaped beach, which was shallow enough for Jones's friend to pick them up in a dinghy. Beyond the cove to the right could be seen a narrow spit of land with a disused lighthouse on it. The nearest village was nearly two miles away by road. A narrow track led from the cottage to an only slightly wider B-road bordered by thick hedges and woods. There was little chance of anyone stumbling on their hideout by accident.

Jones intended to drive to the village later that morning for provisions and if asked would simply say that he was a keen bird watcher and was staying alone in his brother's cottage for a few days' holiday.

All these events and plans crowded back into Jones's mind as Beverly kissed him again. Yes, it was all going to be worth it. He kissed her back, tiredness slipping away from him. She pulled away with a laugh.

'Down, Fido. Plenty of time for that later. Sorry to wake you, but I couldn't sleep. I'm too excited and too hungry. Do you want some breakfast?'

He smiled ruefully and sat up against the pillows.

'I'll need to go into the village for some stuff – milk and bread and things. There's some tinned food in the kitchen, but nothing perishable. I'll get enough for two or three days, I want to keep the trips to the village to a minimum, just in case. Maybe make one more trip at the most.'

He swung his legs out of bed and reached for where he had left his clothes, hanging over an old wooden chair.

'Don't worry.' Now that she had escaped Milton's house, Beverly was feeling much more relaxed. She put her arms round his shoulders, starting to regret that she had put satisfying her hunger ahead of satisfying other needs. 'We are quite safe now; there's no way Milton can find us here, and he has no idea that you exist.'

There were few similarities between Horace Soames and Chief Superintendent Leo Jason, but one was their mutual dislike of hospitals. Although Milton had been less than sympathetic about Reggie Gray's accident, Soames had felt that someone from the organization should go to see him, if only to make sure that there were no adverse implications arising from it for them. It also gave him an excuse to be out of the house and away from Milton's volatile temper.

The Royal was Havenchester's biggest hospital, recently rebuilt on a new site at considerable expense and public disquiet at the closure of two other hospitals with Accident and Emergency facilities. Its glass walls sprawled over a considerable area and contained a maze of corridors that seemed to stretch for miles. By the time Soames had found a space for his car in the massive (and expensive) car-park, located Gray's ward on the fifth floor of the east tower and found his way there, it was well past midday and he was beginning to feel that it would have been preferable to stay at home and risk annoying his employer.

Gray was sitting propped up in bed with a bandage round his head. Not particularly photogenic at the best of times, his pasty face and bloodshot eyes looked even worse than usual. He was never one of the sharpest knives in the drawer, but even so, he wasn't usually as close to the spoon family as he now appeared. His face held a slightly dazed and unfocused look and his voice sounded thick and slurred.

'How are you feeling?' Soames asked, trying to sound as though he cared. He found a green moulded plastic chair with springy metal legs that was presumably for the use of visitors and sat down gingerly. The legs squeaked on the linoleum floor.

'I've got a foul headache and some nasty bruises, otherwise not too bad.' Gray's answer took a while to come, as if his brain was labouring in first gear. He reached across to the cabinet at the side of the bed, lifted a glass of water in a shaky grasp and took a deep swallow. Soames reflected with sardonic amusement that it was probably the first time since his voice had broken that Gray had drunk his water neat.

'What happened?' Soames took the glass from Gray and replaced it on the cabinet, more through fear of his trousers getting drenched than from any desire to be helpful.

'I was trying to get back to the house quickly and got lost on a back road.' Gray considered the question carefully as if it he was being asked for a complex mathematical formula. 'It was dark and raining and I misjudged a turning and hit a tree. I don't remember all that much about it. The doctor reckons I was lucky not to have done more damage.' He leant back against his pillows and closed his eyes.

'What did the police say?' Soames didn't want him dozing off until he had made sure there wouldn't be any comeback to the organization as a result of the accident. Milton had enough on his plate without being involved in some piddling police enquiry as a result of Gray's carelessness.

Gray opened his eyes again and managed to focus on Soames's face.

'I wasn't over the limit and the car was only a couple of years old, so they accepted that it was just an accident in the bad weather. No one else was injured and there wasn't any property damage, so they're not going to take any further action.'

'Good.' Soames sat back in his chair, causing it to rock alarmingly on its springy legs. He leant forward again rapidly. 'Why were you in such a hurry anyway?'

Gray sat up a bit straighter in bed, wincing as the movement aggravated his headache, and leaned forward as if to keep what he had to say confidential. The patients in the beds on either side were asleep. No one was paying them any attention.

'I saw Beverly Wallace in a pub with a bloke. I thought Mr Milton should know as soon as possible.' The bloodshot eyes seemed animated for the first time. 'They looked like they were more than just friends, if you get my drift.'

Soames felt a flutter of excitement. So it had been worth coming after all.

'Did you recognize the bloke?'

Gray shook his head and immediately regretted it. He lay back on his pillows again for a moment with his eyes closed.

'It's all a bit hazy at the moment because of the accident. He was a young guy and I didn't know him, but I can't remember much else. Doctor says I might have a bit of memory loss for a while, but it should come back soon.'

'Make sure it does, it's important.' Soames spoke abruptly. 'Beverly Wallace has done a runner with some of Mr Milton's property and he wants both of them back sharpish.'

'Strewth, I bet he does.' Gray felt a brief surge of excitement at the sudden realization of his importance, followed immediately by concern that he wouldn't be very popular if he didn't regain his memory quickly.

'They're keeping me in today for observation, but I should be let out tomorrow. I'll try to remember the details by then.'

'See that you do.' Soames got up. 'I'll come and pick you up tomorrow morning. Give us a ring if you think of anything before then.'

'Will do.'

As Soames turned to walk back down the ward, Gray's eyes closed again. He was sure that there was something else he had to say, but he couldn't remember what it was and thinking too hard made his head ache even more than usual.

The Pussy Kat Klub was about as subtle as its name implied and as proper as the spelling. It was situated, along with a number of other similar establishments, towards the centre of the city. Although ostensibly a membership only club, it catered for anyone who paid the ten-pound fee on the door and appeared to the doorman not to be likely to cause trouble at either the price of the drinks or the antics of the performers. The club was owned by Vernon Bridger and it says something about his other activities that it represented one of his more upper-class establishments – provided you did not enquire too closely about the activities in the rooms on the upper floors. It was designed to maximize profits – to charge as much as the market would bear for whatever services its clientele wanted. If a customer was prepared to pay for a service, Bridger was happy for one of his employees to provide it, no questions asked. He was even prepared for others to trade on his premises – drugs and guns being the main commodities – provided he received his commission.

Jack Pace arrived at the club at 5.30. He was feeling touchy and irritable, having spent most of the day contacting people throughout Harry Milton's organization, giving them photographs of Beverly and putting them on the alert to find her. He had spent time not just with those directly employed by Milton, but also with the even bigger group of those with various other occupations who received monthly payouts to be available as sources of information and support when called upon. In between the telephone calls and personal visits, he had also been trying unsuccessfully to locate Beverly Wallace's sister. He knew her home address, but she had not been in when he called and her flatmate had no idea when she would return. Pace was intelligent enough not to unnecessarily antagonize someone who might actually go to the police if threatened, so he had just left messages for Sandi Wallace to contact him. There had been three such messages. He had obtained Sandi's mobile phone number from the flatmate, but the phone had been switched off and the message left there gone unreturned. He had been the target of some biting criticism from Harry Milton as a result and wondered if Beverly had taken her sister with her. The flatmate was expecting her back and Pace didn't think she was lying about that, but she could have been deceived as well.

Pace knew that Sandi Wallace performed at the Pussy Kat Klub most evenings and so, although his temper had been rising steadily with his frustration, unless she was in it with Beverly, he had in all probability only been delayed for a few hours from hopefully getting a lead on her sister.

The doorman at the club knew Pace, took one look at his face and made no effort to stop him from entering or to enter into conversation with him. The young woman at the counter just inside the door made no attempt to ask for the membership fee; she too recognized Pace. Harry Milton easily trumped Vernon Bridger in the gangland pecking order and they did not want any trouble. When Pace asked for Sandi Wallace's dressing-room, he was directed there without question. If Sandi was in trouble, she might get some mild sympathy, but nobody in the club would be helping her against Pace.

Sandi Wallace was sitting alone in front of the mirror in the dressing-room that she shared with three other dancers, putting the final touches to her make-up. She worked from 6 p.m. to 2 a.m., with some short breaks. It was physically tiring but she loved dancing and was content enough with her life. She had a good figure, danced well and was popular with the clients, which meant that she was also popular with Bridger and the other senior staff in the club. She always took care of her appearance so she studied her reflection carefully. Her costume required little attention since there was very little of it. It consisted of gold bikini briefs that looked as though they had shrunk in the wash, several times, and a pair of strappy gold sandals with very high heels.

When the door opened she expected to see one of her three fellow performers reflected in the mirror, or possibly the club manager, who had taken to visiting her for non-professional reasons. When she saw Jack Pace, her feeling of contentment vanished. One look at his face was enough to tell her that it wasn't a social call. She turned round in her chair and tried a not very convincing smile, her brain racing with a jumble of panic-stricken thoughts.

'Hi, Jack.' She had met him a couple of times with Harry Milton and Beverly and hoped briefly that she had got a wrong impression.

She knew that she hadn't when he stepped up in front of her and placed his powerful hands on her bare shoulders, squeezing painfully. She gasped and tried unsuccessfully to squirm away.

'What are you doing? That hurts.'

'Where's Beverly?' he asked softly.

A lump of fear formed in the pit of her stomach.

'Isn't she with Harry?' She tried to look puzzled.

Pace turned away from her for a moment without speaking. He locked the dressing-room door, then, in one motion, turned back and hit her. The crack of the slap echoed in the room and Sandi cried out, lifting her hand to her cheek.

'Don't piss me around, ducky, I'm not in the mood.' He stared at her with a flat lack of emotion that was almost more frightening than anger. It was the look of someone who didn't care how far he went. 'Where is she?'

'I don't know, really I don't.' She started to tremble.

Pace swung his arm again. Sandi raised her hands and cringed down in her chair, looking up fearfully into his stony face.

'Mr Bridger won't be very pleased if you hurt me or mark me so

I can't perform,' she said. Even as she spoke, she knew it would be no protection.

Pace snorted

'Bridger will just have to grin and bear it,' he said. 'He'll probably blame you for being a silly cow and not telling me what I want to know straight away.' He paused for a moment. 'Still, maybe I should try not to make a mark.'

He bent forward, one hand holding her shoulder, forcing her down into her chair, whilst the other suddenly gripped her again. Sandi screamed out, almost losing consciousness. For a brief moment, she imagined someone hearing her scream and coming to help her, then she realized that was stupid. They'd know Pace was in with her and no one would interfere.

Pace moved behind her and his big, strong hands started to move over her body, one moment almost caressing and the next causing acute pain.

'When did you last see her?' His mouth hovered by the side of her head as he breathed the question into her ear.

'Two weeks ago.' She screamed again, tailing off into a sob as she hung her head. 'I swear it's true.'

'Where has she gone? Is she with someone – is someone hiding her?'

The questions kept coming, alternating with a jagged pain that seemed to jab through her body. She kept denying that Beverly had told her of any plans to run away. Eventually, Pace stepped back and looked at Sandi, hunched over in her chair, breath rasping, tears rolling down her face. His face remained impassive, uncaring. He looked round the room and saw her handbag on the shelf under the mirror. He picked it up and emptied the contents on to the counter. Make-up, comb, mobile phone, her keys and her purse dropped out with a cascade of other items. He looked in the purse, there was only money. He picked up the keys.

'I'll assume for now that you're telling the truth,' he said, cupping her chin in one of his hands and forcing her face up to look into his. 'I'll go back to your flat now and search it. If I find anything to suggest you know where she is, I'll be back and then you'll wish you'd talked, understand?'

She dragged in a sobbing breath.

'I don't know where Beverly is, I swear I don't. She hasn't told me anything about going away.' She met his gaze, blinking through her tears.

Pace grunted and his fingers squeezed her face.

'If she contacts you, then you contact me – right?' He pushed her face away.

'Yes, I will.' She nodded her head like a crazy puppet. 'I'll tell you straight away.'

He nodded.

'Make sure you do. You'd better clean yourself up before you go on stage – you look a mess.'

He unlocked the door and it slammed behind him.

Sandi sat for a while trying to get back her composure. Eventually she looked up at her reflection in the mirror, staring at the pain in her face and her red, tear-filled eyes.

'Oh, Bev,' she said, in a low, shaky voice, 'I hope to God he's worth it.'

Whilst in the village shop that morning, Jones had mentioned that he was staying in his brother's cottage, the binoculars round his neck hopefully providing support to his twitching credentials. The shop also served as post office and he was confident that word of his arrival would circulate pretty rapidly. He hoped that would satisfy any curiosity if lights were spotted in the cottage. There had been one other customer in the shop and he nodded politely to two other people that he passed in the main village street, other than that he met no one on his travels.

Arriving back at the cottage, he had prepared a late breakfast which they ate in the kitchen. After that they had sat dozing and watching daytime TV for a while on his brother's small set in the living room that was the only other downstairs room. They had gone back to bed in the afternoon, revelling in the novelty of being able to make love in comfort and without the fear of being traced to a hotel room. Afterwards, Jones prepared an early evening meal. Beverly had not cooked since she had taken up with Milton and even before that she had never achieved much more than cheese on toast or warming up a TV dinner.

After the meal had been cleared away and the plates washed –

Jones insisted that they keep his brother's cottage clean – Beverly started pacing the living-room floor, stopping occasionally to peer out of the window across the darkening bay and trying unsuccessfully to relieve the feeling of restlessness. She hated being cooped up and although she accepted that she needed to avoid even the faint chance that someone associated with Milton might be around the village and recognize her, she knew that after two or three days in the cottage, she would be climbing the walls.

'Let's go out for a walk after dark.'

'I'm not sure that's a good idea,' Jones looked at her dubiously.

'Oh, come on, there's no risk. You said yourself that the people in the village would accept that you are just using your brother's cottage for a few days. No one is likely to come spying on us.'

'Supposing someone sees you? I'm supposed to be here on my own.'

'So you've brought a girl with you to while away the time – that's not a crime, is it?'

She sat down on his lap and put her arms round his neck.

'Come on, we can go down to the cove. We'll wait until it's completely dark. No one is going to be down there at night.' She grinned at him and kissed him. 'I've never done it on a beach before.' She paused. 'Well, not all the way, anyway.'

He laughed at her, momentarily forgetting the ball of fear that had lived inside him, getting steadily larger, ever since they had first worked out their plans. He gave in, as they both knew he would.

'All right then.' He paused. 'We'd better take a blanket.'

EIGHT

AS IF TO demonstrate that beatings and assassinations are equal opportunity professions, Angie and Findon Wilson were a brother and sister team who made themselves available for general hire. According to Mariner's file, they lived together in a large barge on the canal that ran through the north of the city for several miles and had originally formed the veins through which its life-trade had flowed, leading from the docks to the factories and warehouses that lined its banks.

The morning after Tanner and Julie had cleared Harry Jarvis and Sam Hesky of shooting Julie and her aunt (if not of various other criminal activities), Tanner contacted Mariner from his office and suggested that investigation into the disappearance of one Salvador Sanchez might prove rewarding. Mariner seemed happy enough with their progress, even if they were back where they started. They exchanged a few amicable insults about gifted amateurs and hung up.

Having done his civic duty and helped the police with their enquiries, Tanner went through the day's post whilst Julie spread the file notes on the Wilsons on the coffee table and started going through them. There was nothing requiring his immediate attention in the post and having enjoyed delegating various tasks to his staff, Tanner sat at the table and looked at the Wilsons' file as well. It made interesting, if not particularly helpful, reading. Neither of them had ever been arrested, let alone sent to prison. They worked freelance and had been employed by both Bridger and Milton in the past, as well as others with similar interests.

The Wilsons' bread and butter work seemed to be debt collecting for a number of less than scrupulous bookies and loan sharks. They were suspected of a long list of assaults of varying degrees of seriousness, including two that had resulted in the death of the victim. It was unclear whether or not it had been deliberate. They had occasionally been questioned about these events but had never been charged, allegedly because they were quite prepared to widen their activities to include the family of their victim, regardless of age or sex, if anyone made a complaint to the police. Listed at the bottom of the file were three disappearances that could be linked circumstantially to the Wilsons, although there was nothing remotely resembling evidence that you could take to court. Judging by the list of alleged activities, the hit on Julie and her aunt would fit perfectly logically within their CV.

Tanner sat back in his chair and took a swig of coffee.

'Any thoughts as to how we can find out what they were doing on the evening of eighth February?'

Julie collected the file pages together neatly and passed them across to Tanner to lock away again, retaining the two photographs of the brother and sister for reference on their travels. She shook her head.

'Nothing very precise. We could start off by taking a look at where they live and see if that gives us any ideas.'

Tanner nodded.

'According to the file they don't socialize much but their local is a pub called The Tow Path down by the canal. If the barge or the canal doesn't give us any inspiration, we could call in there and see if we can pick up any local gossip. Someone might have seen them on the night in question riding a motor bike down the tow path and waving a silenced handgun.'

'That would certainly constitute evidence.'

'If only circumstantial.'

'Don't you just love our legal system?'

Julie stood up and reached for her shoulder bag and her coat.

'Still, we might get a decent pub lunch out of it.'

Tanner knew the Havenchester canal well, having walked and fished along it quite often in his early years. It took them some time to negotiate the city traffic, which seemed to have developed a permanent rush hour from around eight in the morning to eight in the evening, not helped by a recurring cycle of road works. Tanner eventually got them to their destination and found, remarkably, a parking space in a nearby side street of neat terraced houses with small paved front gardens. There was no one about; even the kids bunking off from school appeared to have found somewhere else to go.

Tanner took Julie's hand, leading her across the neighbouring main road to where it formed a bridge over the canal. They descended the narrow stone steps by the side of the bridge on to the tow path. The council and local community groups had spent some time gradually clearing the less appetizing lengths of the canal and there was now a considerable strip of tow path that formed a pleasant walk alongside the water. High blank walls of factories and warehouses, some abandoned, some still in use, and others converted or being converted into much sought after apartments, lined the canal at intervals. In other places, there were areas of tangled bush and trees. Occasionally, a narrow, dank tributary led off to the side into a dim wilderness as yet untamed by the renovators.

The sun was shining and it would have been a pleasant, almost warm, walk if it were not for the long stretches of shade and the chill wind that blew along the path, rippling the grey-green water at its side and setting Julie's hair flowing in raven dark waves.

Tanner squeezed Julie's hand and smiled at her. They were hoping to be taken for lovers having a romantic stroll by the canal – a disguise that was at least partly accurate.

'The Wilsons' boat should be round the next bend,' Tanner murmured, after they had walked slowly for fifteen minutes or so along the asphalt path, 'and the pub is about a hundred yards further along.'

His memory of the geography of the canal proved accurate and they followed the path round to the left where the waterway widened out to allow about ten barges permanent berths. To the left of the path was an open, rectangular, grassy area and beyond that a narrow alleyway between two warehouses that led back into the noise and bustle of the city. Even though Tanner knew that city traffic flowed only a short distance away, he was still struck by the illusion that they were in the depths of the country, almost in another world of calm and serenity.

The Wilsons' barge was called the Fandangle, which suggested a moderate understanding of the art of anagrams on their part. It looked well tended, with gleaming brass and polished wood and an intricate painting of a horse drawing a barge on the side of the cabin area. They strolled on past it, trying to look like casual walkers admiring the painting and the barges. There was no sign of occupation, but that didn't mean very much as both brother and sister were creatures of the night.

Angie was two years older than her brother and the natural leader. From the descriptions in the file, they were both tall and solidly built and both spent time weight training at the gym. Both had shoulder-length blond hair, sported hoop ear-rings and had tattoos on their left arms between elbow and shoulder. Findon's was a panther and Angie's a grizzly bear – Tanner presumed that was to demonstrate her cuddly feminine side.

None of the Wilsons' neighbours was around, although shadows moved behind lace-curtained windows as they walked by, suggesting that the local equivalent of neighbourhood watch was alive and well. Once they had passed all the barges, they stopped and Tanner glanced at his watch.

'It's nearly twelve. Shall we risk the pub food and see if we can eavesdrop on any interesting gossip?'

'Sounds like a good idea.'

'Well, it's an idea, anyway.'

The Tow Path had a small garden area running back from the canal to its rear entrance with four wooden seats and tables for the more hardy clientele who liked al fresco in all weathers. They were all currently unoccupied. Tanner and Julie followed a paved path along the side of the building and arrived at the front entrance. There was parking for a few cars at the front of the pub and a few spaces were already occupied, suggesting either popularity or committed drinking. Boards leaning against the wall by the door advertised a variety of delights for the patrons – pub lunches, a live band on Tuesdays, Fridays and Sundays and big screen sport.

They found the inside a pleasant surprise. There was gleaming, light-wood panelling, a long bar at the rear and a number of tables and chairs set round at intervals. A small stage stood to the left of the door, presumably where the live music was performed. There were a couple of obligatory gaming machines flashing brightly. The atmosphere was generally welcoming and there was a pleasant smell of food cooking. Four or five of the tables were occupied and three people sat at the bar, but no one paid them any particular attention as they walked in. The customers wore a mixture of suits and casual dress and none of them resembled the Wilsons.

They walked up to the bar where a young woman in a T-shirt and jeans was chatting to a middle-aged man who sat nursing a beer. She turned towards them with a smile.

'What can I get you?'

Tanner looked enquiringly at Julie.

'Ploughman's lunch and half of bitter,' she said.

'Same for me please,' Tanner told the barmaid. Equality in all things, he thought.

The barmaid nodded and called the order through to the kitchen area behind the bar.

'Just be a few minutes,' she said, having poured their drinks and taken the money.

'I see you have live music,' Tanner said, more to keep the conversation going than through any great interest in their musical repertoire. With a bit of luck he could steer things round to a discussion about their regulars.

'Yes.' She nodded enthusiastically. 'This Sunday it's The Eternal Sinners, they're a heavy rock group. They're absolutely brilliant. They play here regularly. If you're free on Sunday, it would be well worth trying them out.'

'I hope we don't get a repeat of the trouble we had last time,' the man raised his head and made the observation to the barmaid. He had the complaining air of a regular who was not best pleased at his local being turned into a rock venue.

She gave him a sharp look.

'That wasn't their fault,' she protested. 'The guy was drunk.'

'What happened?' Julie asked.

'One of the customers accused Glen, that's the band's lead singer, of trying to get off with his girlfriend. Mind you, Glen is pretty dishy; I wouldn't mind spending some time with him myself.' Her face took on a wistful look. 'It was after their first set. The band was having a drink at the bar and this guy started on at Glen. Glen was just chatting to the girl, who had obviously enjoyed the session, and her boyfriend got nasty. He told Glen to leave her alone, even though she seemed to be making all the running. Glen told him to chill out and the guy broke his glass and swung at Glen with it. It could have been really nasty. Fortunately, a couple of our regulars stopped him. One caught his arm before he connected and the other one decked him.'

'A useful couple of guys to have around,' Julie commented.

The barmaid smiled.

'One of them is a woman – they're a brother and sister who live near here.'

Julie looked at her with interest. There couldn't be many brother and sister acts around where the sister could deal with a man wielding a broken glass.

'And she helped to sort out the troublemaker?'

The barmaid grinned.

'She's the one who decked him. Elbow in the side of the jaw: *pow*.' She imitated the action with her own elbow, causing the regular to rear back in his seat in alarm. 'He went down flat.' Fortunately, she didn't try to demonstrate that part of the performance. The ploughman's lunches arrived and she put them on the bar. 'They're big fans of the group, always come to see them when they're playing here.'

That sounded promising to Tanner. Maybe they should expand their musical education on the coming Sunday.

'We're fans of rock music, perhaps we will come on Sunday,' Julie said, echoing his thoughts. 'What time do they start to play?'

'About nine o'clock, but get here early, there's always a good crowd. They're good value; play two one-hour sets with a half-hour break.' She was clearly a fan herself – although possibly mainly of the lead singer.

Tanner had a sudden thought.

'You said the band play here regularly?'

'Yeah – at least once every couple of months, sometimes more.'

'What date was the last gig – can you remember?'

She frowned.

'I think I saw an old flyer round here yesterday.' She fumbled around under the bar. 'Here it is – eighth February.' She looked at him curiously. 'Why?'

Julie put her hand on Tanner's arm and smiled at him with enough syrupy sweetness to cause a diabetic coma.

'Why, darling, that was our anniversary – we could have come here instead of going to see that terrible film.'

Tanner just managed to keep a straight face.

'So we could,' he managed.

The romantic comment caused the barmaid to smile at them and nod, erasing any curiosity she might have had as to why Tanner had been particularly interested in the date.

They took their lunches to a quiet table in a corner well away from the other customers.

'If the band started playing at nine, the first set would have ended at ten. If the Wilsons were here breaking up a fight soon afterwards, it lets them off the hook for the shooting,' Tanner commented.

Julie picked up a piece of cheese, took a bite, added a grape and chewed them thoughtfully.

'Looks very much like it,' she agreed. 'So that just leaves us with Jethro Harper and Kevin Winston.'

'And their boss – Harry Milton,' Tanner added. 'He's got quite an organization behind him, and he makes Vernon Bridger look like a pussy cat.'

Julie spread some butter on her French bread.

'He sounds delightful.' She took a sip of beer. 'At least we won't have to tangle with Ms Muscle.'

'I was going to leave her to you to sort out.'

'Always the gentleman.'

They got back to the office just before two and settled down with the last part of Mariner's file. They were starting to run out of options, and Tanner was beginning to worry about the impact on Julie if they drew a blank with the last two possibilities. It had undoubtedly helped her mental balance to be actively doing something that might lead to her aunt's killer and he wasn't sure how much it would knock her back again if she didn't have that to focus on. He had blithely talked about trying another tack if Ted's choices didn't pan out, but if the killers were an outside professional contract, he wasn't sure where to start. In any event, that angle was already being covered by the police and they weren't likely to be more successful than the official investigators had been with all the resources at their disposal.

On the positive side, Tanner was certain that their relationship was helping her as well, but it was still in its infancy and although it felt pretty strong at the moment, whether it was powerful enough to pull Julie through such a set-back remained to be seen. Still, there was nothing to be gained by speculating at that point, so he hid his anxiety and concentrated on the job in hand.

Jethro Harper and Kevin Winston were much younger than the other pairings they had been looking into. They were both graduates of the youth justice system, having started with ASBOs and worked their way up – or down, depending on how you looked at it. They had spent time in the same young offenders' institution for violent muggings, had been released at the same time and had teamed up. After that they had got themselves a reputation for violent crime and general unpleasantness, none of which had led to any charges. They had been on Milton's payroll for less than a year.

Harper lived with his mother on a council estate not renowned for the pro-social behaviour of its residents. Winston occasionally stayed there too, but although it was not thought to be his permanent residence, there was no other address for him. The rest of his family, none of whom had been in trouble with the police, had moved out of the city when he was in his late teens and were now living in London. There was not thought to be much, if any, contact between them and Winston.

Julie and Tanner spent the afternoon trying to trace an alternative address for Winston, but without success. Tanner got Danny Worenski roaming the ether to try to find some trace, both officially and unofficially, but even he couldn't find anything. Knowing Danny's ability to track down the most elusive of prey, it suggested that Winston was not the registered owner or lessee of any property he might be occupying. He also didn't appear to have filled in any official forms recently, or to have had any contact with any agencies whose records Danny could access – which was most of them.

At five, when Worenski came in to report his lack of success, Julie yawned and sat back in her chair.

'Why don't we call it a day? Don't forget, we're going out for dinner tonight.'

Tanner nodded. They might get some fresh ideas in the morning and a break would do them both good.

Julie had received an invitation to dinner that evening from Archie and Laura Tilling. When she told them about Tanner, he was immediately included. Tanner suspected that was both to satisfy their curiosity and because they were genuinely concerned about Julie and were happy that she had someone to bring.

'I suppose I'll have to wear a suit?'

'And a shirt and a tie. You'll also have to wash behind the ears – I shall be making an inspection.'

Tanner dropped Julie off at her flat and drove back to his own to shower and change. Suitably suited and with shirt and tie (and polished shoes – he didn't do these things by halves), he drove back to Julie's apartment. Tanner gave her a long kiss that she responded to eagerly for a moment before pushing him away gently.

'Not now; I've spent too long on my make-up and we don't want to crease your suit – or my dress.'

'Later then.'

She kissed him again, quickly.

'Later you can crease as much as you like.'

Tanner helped Julie on with her coat and they took the lift down to the car-park beneath the apartments. Julie knew the way so it was easier for her drive them in her car.

Tanner was welcomed warmly by the Tillings and was taken for a tour of the house by Archie whilst Julie chatted to Laura in the kitchen. He genuinely admired the rooms and the views and was particularly impressed with the boat that could just be glimpsed in the evening gloom, rocking gently in the river from the jetty at the end of the long, tree-lined garden.

'You like boating and water sports?' Archie Tilling asked, his face brightening with the light of the true enthusiast given an excuse to talk about his favourite subject.

'I spend as much time as I can on the water – or under it.'

'We'll have to take you both out sometime. There are plenty of good spots for fishing along the river.'

Tanner admitted that he was more into swimming and diving.

'There's plenty of scope for that, as well.' Tilling beamed at him. 'Laura and I both swim, but we haven't tried diving yet.'

'You should,' Tanner grasped the opportunity to be enthusiastic about one of his favourite hobbies. 'It's incredible, being down there with the fish and exploring the sea bed. It's like a completely different world.'

'Perhaps you could teach us,' Tilling suggested, as they moved away from the window and back downstairs.

'Any time,' Tanner assured him. He knew that Julie shared his love of diving, so that promised to be an enjoyable excursion.

Dinner matched the expectations raised by the splendour of the house and grounds and conversation turned – not unexpectedly – to the progress they were making investigating the shootings. They told them about their abortive investigations into Bridger and his men and that they had crossed the Wilsons off the list.

'We've only got one more line of enquiry at the moment, if that doesn't pan out we'll have to rethink,' Julie said.

'Who's that?' Laura asked.

'I don't suppose it's anyone we know, darling,' Archie Tilling said with a smile.

'It's a couple of guys employed by a man named Harry Milton,' Tanner said. 'You might know him – he's supposed to be something of an art buff.'

'Doesn't mean anything to me,' Tilling said, but his wife nodded enthusiastically.

'Why, yes, I do know him, as a matter of fact. We've sold him two or three paintings. He likes nineteenth- and early twentieth-century artists. He's got quite good taste and a keen eye. He also collects nineteenth-century porcelain; we've sold him one or two pieces of that as well.'

Her eyes gleamed with excitement.

'Do you mean that he's a crook? How thrilling. You'd never know it to meet him. I thought he was just a successful businessman.'

'Sometimes there's not a lot of difference,' Tilling commented drily.

'Don't be so cynical, darling.' She turned back to Tanner. 'But this is fascinating, Alec. What sort of crimes does he commit?'

'He's into drugs, gambling, high-class prostitution and he funds major robberies as well as some more legitimate stuff.' Tanner took a sip of the excellent wine. 'Not that I could repeat that outside this room without risking being sued for slander.'

Laura smiled.

'I promise I won't mention it next time he comes into the shop. It seems incredible. To think that the things he's bought from us have been funded from crime. And, as I said, he's actually quite knowledgeable about art. You've never met him Archie?'

Tilling shook his head.

'Can't say I remember him, but next time he comes in to buy something, you must let me know.' He sat back in his chair and smiled fondly at his wife. 'An accountant's life is a very sheltered one – I'd like to meet a real live villain.'

'I'll make sure I tell you,' she promised. She thought for a moment. 'He's actually rather charming.' She looked faintly surprised.

Tanner grinned.

'I'm sure he can be if he wants to, but knowledge of and interest in art doesn't necessarily mean respectability. I can assure you that his real personality is something much less appealing.'

Laura shivered and got to her feet.

'Oh well, enough of this talk of crime, shall we have coffee in the lounge?'

Over coffee, whilst her husband was showing Julie a recent acquisition of which he was particularly proud, Laura took Alec Tanner to one side.

'I'm so pleased to see Julie looking so much better,' she said. 'You are obviously doing her the world of good. We were quite worried about her when she came earlier in the week.'

She paused for a moment and glanced across the room to make sure Julie was out of earshot.

'I hope you won't take this the wrong way, but she has very few people to turn to and I was her aunt's best friend, so I'll have to risk sounding impertinent.' She looked closely into Tanner's face, as if trying to read his fortune. 'You know that Julie is emotionally very fragile at the moment. I wouldn't want to see her hurt if things didn't work out.'

Tanner smiled at her.

'Don't worry; I have every intention of making it last for as long as Julie wants me.'

Laura looked relieved, both at his answer and his failure to take offence.

'I'm sure you'll be very good for each other.'

Tanner looked across at Julie, who caught his eye and smiled.

He hoped she was right.

NINE

IF JACK PACE had hoped that Harry Milton's temper would start to improve when Beverly Wallace had been gone for more than twenty-four hours, he would have been sorely disappointed. However, Pace knew Milton much better than that and when he was summoned into Milton's study he saw without surprise that his boss was clearly in, if anything, a worse frame of mind than the day before. Milton and Soames had gone out on a long-standing business engagement the evening before, involving the purchase of certain substances frowned upon by the authorities, and had left Pace to follow up the suggestion passed on by Gray that Beverly had run off with a lover. Since the trail had turned as cold as an Arctic blizzard, and shed about as much visibility on the matter, Pace had made sure that he had not been around for Milton to interview on his return. In the morning, he had snatched a quick breakfast in the kitchen rather than sit in the dining room with Milton. He disliked being the focus of a disagreeable atmosphere at meal times; it gave him indigestion, although he had no qualms about imposing such an atmosphere himself on others.

Pace sat in one of the comfortable armchairs facing the desk and waited for instructions.

'Where's Horace?' Milton asked gruffly.

Soames rarely had more than coffee and a slice of toast for breakfast and he, too, had joined Pace in the kitchen.

'He said he had some errands to run following your meeting last night. He needs to raise some funds to cover the initial outlay.' Pace considered adding that this action was necessary as a result of the lack of cash resources in the safe, but, sensibly, decided to omit reference to the obvious. 'Then he's going to pick up Gray from the hospital.'

Milton snorted. He reached across to the ivory office tidy at the rear of his desk top, picked up a silver paper knife and started stabbing at his blotting pad. Pace had little trouble imagining whose skin was represented in Milton's mind by the pristine blotting paper.

'What does he think we are, an ambulance taxi service?'

'Doesn't hurt to show a bit of support to the soldiers; it helps morale generally.'

'Morale?' Milton spat the word back at him. 'What about my morale?' He stabbed once more, sharply, as if it was the *coup de grâce*, before tossing the knife down in disgust.

'Horace is bringing Gray straight here,' Pace added. 'He might have remembered something else that will help lead us to the man Beverly was with, so we thought it would be a good idea to question him more thoroughly as quickly as possible.'

Milton grunted and leant back in his swivel chair. He stared sourly at Pace's square, boxer's face with the faint tracery of scars round his eyes and the broken nose which dated from his brief but interesting career in the ring. The man who had broken Pace's nose had been the victim of a vicious assault as he was walking home a couple of evenings later. The man's assailant had come at him from behind out of the darkness of an alleyway wielding the ubiquitous blunt instrument and had never been identified. Pace had given up his boxing career shortly afterwards and joined Milton's organization. His opponent had not boxed again either – it had taken him three months to walk properly again.

'What happened when you went to the pub where Gray saw them together?'

'I spoke to the landlord and the bar staff. No joy there. It was a busy night and nobody paid either of them any particular attention. One of the barmaids remembered them vaguely, but she didn't hear what they were saying to each other, or remember when they arrived, or when they left. She clearly thought they were lovers. I made out he was married and I was a private dick working for the wife, I thought she'd be more sympathetic if she thought a woman was being wronged.'

'And was she?'

Pace shrugged.

'I think so, but she didn't remember having seen them before and I don't think anyone in the pub had anything else much to tell us. I couldn't press the questions too much, or they might have got curious. The car-park's at the back of the pub, so no one saw what car they were driving. Like I said, they weren't thought to be regulars so no one remembered them from another night.'

Pace stared woodenly at his boss after giving this report. Hopefully, he would remember the old adage about not shooting the messenger.

'Sod it.' Milton got to his feet and walked over to the window, staring out across the front drive. 'We've got to find them, Jack; I'm not going to let her get away with this.'

Pace nodded, glad that he was not being blamed for finding nothing when there was nothing to find. Milton wasn't usually unreasonable, but this was not a usual situation. In a detached way, Pace rather admired Beverly for what she had done; he hadn't thought she'd got the balls, in a figurative sense, of course. Not that that would make any difference to his reaction when they caught her.

'I've put the word out with everyone I can think of: we should get a response soon.'

Milton turned back towards his desk.

'You're certain the sister doesn't know anything?'

'I don't think she's the sort to value loyalty above pain. I thought I'd let her stew for a while, then go back and see her this evening. If she does know something and she's relaxed thinking I've bought her story, a second visit should do the trick.'

Milton nodded. For all his raging, he trusted Pace's judgement, particularly when it came to making people talk. It galled him not to be taking action, but he accepted that there wasn't much else they could do. They'd spread the net, now they needed to wait for the fish to swim into it.

It was gone midday before Soames arrived with Gray. Milton and Pace were having sandwiches in the dining room when they heard the car pull up in the drive. They were joined by the other two men a few minutes later.

'What took you so long?' Milton was not a student of the bedside manner.

'Sorry, Harry.' Soames helped himself to a couple of sandwiches and sat down at the table with a sigh. 'We had to wait for a doctor to confirm Reggie could be discharged.'

Reggie nodded solemnly. He still had a pad of bandage taped to the right side of his head as if someone had lobbed a snowball at him and it had stuck.

'Said I was lucky not to have brain damage.' Gray tried his martyred look, but just looked self-important.

'Got a bruise on your arse as well then, have you?' Milton growled at him, singularly unimpressed. Soames smothered a grin and Gray had enough sense not to push his injury any further.

'Have you remembered anything else about the bastard?' Milton took a bite out of his sandwich as if he was tearing the head off a chicken, and glared at him.

Gray shook his head. He felt distinctly hard done by. After all, if it hadn't been for him, they wouldn't have known about Beverly Wallace's fancy man, or had any idea what he looked like.

'We need a more accurate description, what you've given us so far could fit half the population.'

That was, perhaps, a slight exaggeration, but Gray took the point.

'Well, I took his photo on my phone.' He looked round the table proudly.

This announcement wasn't quite greeted with the expressions of delight he had expected. Indeed, Pace and Milton looked singularly annoyed. Milton glared at him. For a moment he was speechless, but not for long.

'Why in buggery didn't you say so before?'

'I only just remembered. My head …'

Gray was lucky that he didn't sustain a matching injury on the left-hand side of his face. Milton took a deep breath and snapped his fingers.

'Well, don't just sit there, you stupid bastard, show it to us.'

Gray fumbled in the inside pocket of his coat and produced his phone. His palms were sweaty and his fingers kept slipping on the keys as he switched it on. Fortunately, the battery was still charged.

The other three men gathered round as he eventually called up the picture.

'I know him!' Pace exclaimed.

'What?' Milton swivelled to stare at him. If the bastard was actually in his own organization …

'Yes, it's her dancing instructor.' Pace nodded slowly. He found a good memory for faces invaluable in his job, particularly as he was often under instruction to rearrange the features. 'When Beverly's car was in for repair a few weeks ago, you got me to take her to the dance studio and pick her up again a couple of times. I had to wait for her to finish the lesson both times. That's the bloke who was teaching her – I'm positive.'

Pace met Milton's eyes.

'It makes sense. I was wondering how Beverly had met someone; I couldn't see anyone in the firm being stupid enough and I couldn't see how she could manage to spend any length of time with an outsider.'

Milton nodded and his eyes hardened.

'It makes sense all right. Now we're getting somewhere. Go over to that dance studio and see what you can find out. Take Gray with you. I don't suppose he'll be there, but you should be able to get a proper lead on him, and her.'

He looked across at Gray.

'Are you sure they didn't spot you?'

Gray nodded.

'I'm positive, boss. I was on the other side of the pub and they only had eyes for each other.'

'Good. That means they won't expect us to know about him, so he might not be so careful about covering his tracks. Find out where he is and you'll get both of them.'

For the first time in thirty-six hours, Milton allowed himself a small smile.

'Then you take him out and you bring her to me.'

Beverly Wallace was starting to feel like a prisoner, having swapped the mental restraints of living with Milton for the physical restraints of not being able to leave the cottage.

They had gone to bed soon after their walk to the beach the night before. As a result, they had woken early that morning, the gulls screaming their morning alarm call outside the bedroom window, and had breakfasted much earlier than they had the day before. This was a mistake, as it just made the morning seem longer. Daytime TV had not improved; indeed any novelty that there was had rapidly warn off. They were restricted to the four terrestrial channels, and two of them were intermittently fuzzy. Jones made a mental note to advise his brother to invest in a satellite dish. Still, to be fair, he didn't use the cottage in the same way. His brother and sister-in-law wanted the cottage as a base for walking and swimming and from which to drive out to explore the surrounding countryside. It was a place to sleep and to have morning and evening meals; it was not intended to be lived in for the whole day.

Beverly and Jones had an early lunch and spent an hour or so in bed, which, admittedly, did pass the time much more enjoyably, but now the rest of the afternoon and evening stretched before them interminably. They started a game of Monopoly, but playing those sorts of games was not Beverly's forte and she soon tired of it. Nor was she a great reader.

Indeed, she was just beginning to appreciate the reality of what she had done. Not that she had changed her mind and regretted leaving Milton, she still adored JJ and she wouldn't have returned to Milton even if she had been able to and keep breathing. However she was an outdoor person, she loved going out shopping, going to clubs and the cinema, or even just taking a car ride and she felt horribly boxed in. She had, she admitted to herself, not thought through in detail exactly what running away from Milton would entail. It had at first just been a wonderful plan with the promise of freedom at the end of it, something she had dreamed about for weeks, but the reality was proving to be far less romantic. Even the threat of Milton, forever in the background, could not overcome the boredom. She had pictured in her mind the two lovers running from the pursuing villain, but had not pictured sitting around doing nothing in a cottage that was barely equipped even for twentieth-century living.

And there were at least two more days of this. JJ had contacted his friend by mobile phone that morning and had been told that it would be at least forty-eight hours before the friend could arrive with their papers and there was a distinct possibility that it would take another day after that. She didn't think she could stand it.

Getting suddenly to her feet, she pulled on her waterproof jacket and tucked her jeans into a pair of short boots.

'What are you doing?' Jones, sprawled in an uncomfortable armchair trying to find something he had yet to read in the paper he had bought at the village shop the day before, looked across at her in concern.

'Let's go for a walk.' She put her hands in her jacket pockets and turned towards him with a determined expression.

Jones stayed where he was, dropping the paper by the side of his chair.

'It isn't safe, darling. What if—'

'Rubbish.' She over-rode his objections briskly. 'There is no way that anyone in Harry Milton's organization knows anything about you and it is absolutely impossible that they could find out about this cottage.'

'It's still risky.' He had no experience of serious crime or criminals and he had sometimes felt that Beverly exaggerated Milton's influence and activities, but her nervousness had nevertheless affected him as well, particularly since they had actually taken the irrevocable step of flight. He read the papers and saw the news and knew that such people did exist. 'You said that his organization is pretty efficient.'

'It's not that efficient. He doesn't have a crystal ball or magic powers. I'm not going to sit around here jumping at shadows and pulling my hair out. I'm going out – are you coming with me, or shall I go on my own?'

He got reluctantly to his feet and went to get his coat. As he put it on, Beverly gave him a bright smile and a deep kiss.

'Thanks, lover boy.'

He managed a smile in return and opened the front door. He had to admit that he was feeling quite claustrophobic himself, and Beverly was probably right, how could Milton trace them?

The air was sharp and clean and felt refreshing as they followed the narrow path from the small, scrubby cottage garden towards the cliff edge where it branched out, one arm leading to the steep but reasonably negotiable route down to the beach and the other curling round to the right and disappearing into the thick woodland.

'Let's stay up here and go through the trees.' Beverly slipped her hand through the crook of his arm and steered Jones along the right-hand path.

There was no one around and the trees and bushes formed a natural barrier from the wind that gusted along the cliff top. The sun was still quite high in the sky and some warmth penetrated between the branches of the trees. Some were still bare, but there were sufficient firs and other evergreens together with tall, tangled bushes to provide that feeling of cut off seclusion to be found in most scarcely populated woodland areas.

'Tell me more about Milton and why you got mixed up with him.' Jones put his arm around Beverly's waist and hugged her to him. Over the period of their affair, he had gathered a brief picture of her former lover and his organization, but it had come in fragments, short comments at different times, tagged on to another part of a conversation; she had never spoken of Milton at any length. Nor had she spoken much about her earlier life. He had met her only sister and liked her, knew that Beverly had run away from her abusive father, who was now dead and that she despised her mother for staying with her husband and taking his side against her daughters.

'You're better than he is in the sack, if that's what's worrying you.' She turned her head to grin at him and saw his serious expression. She decided to answer his question; after all he deserved that much at least after what he was risking for her.

'When I left home, my only real male role model was my father and he wasn't much good in that respect – or in any other.' She spoke softly and reflectively, returning his hug and holding it, drawing on the strength of contact with his body as she mused on the past. 'There was a series of men after that, none of them wanting as much from me as I wanted from them; none of them worthwhile. I suppose I was desperately looking for a man who would give me the affection I couldn't get from my father and I ended up having a string of men who just wanted to control and manipulate me as much as he did. They weren't all as violent as him, but that's about all you could say about them. None of them amounted to very much, or had any money. I'm not saying I've got a brilliant mind or anything, but I needed a man to want me for more than my body.' The relief of having someone who cared for her to talk to made her pour out her story in a fast-flowing stream of words.

'When Harry Milton came along I knew he'd want to manipulate me even more than the others and was far more dangerous, but at least he was rich and didn't mind spending money on me provided I did what he wanted. By then I'd given up on the idea of finding anyone who cared about me for myself. I figured that if I could only have men who wanted to use me for one thing, I might as well live in luxury while they were doing it. Harry wants to own things, he wants to make money and he always wants to win – he doesn't care what it costs or how he cheats to do it. I was just another possession that he owned and could do what he liked with. The only things he really loves are his paintings and antiques. He's got them all over the house, but the really precious ones he keeps locked away in a room on the second floor. No one but him is allowed in there, not even Jack Pace or Soames. He even cleans the room himself. When he's at home, he goes in there at least once a day, presumably just to sit and look at them. I asked to go in there with him one time to see them and he went really quiet like he does when he's angry and said that if I ever tried to go in there he'd kill me. And when Harry Milton says something like that, it's not just a figure of speech.'

She shivered.

'He gave me the creeps, and he knew it – and liked it. Then you came along and I realized I could have a real life with someone who loved me and cared about me and I had to get away from Harry at all costs.'

She snuggled closer to him.

'That's enough about Harry Milton; even talking about him gives me the willies.'

They walked on for a while in silence. Occasionally they saw another cottage, once they heard the sound of a car in the distance and once somebody calling to their dog in another part of the wood, but otherwise they could have had the world to themselves. They followed a series of barely defined paths through the trees and managed to loop round so as to arrive back at the path by their own cottage about an hour after they had set out. Beverly felt completely refreshed and cheerful, looking forward now to an evening in with the man she loved. She stopped them by the front door and kissed him happily.

'Thank you for coming on the walk, it was great. And, you see, there was nothing to worry about. Like I said, we're quite safe. Nobody can possibly find us here.'

Veronica Ambrose, owner and chief instructor of the Dance 'Til You Drop dance studios did not know what to make of Jack Pace. He certainly did not look like a representative of the Inland Revenue; despite what his identification card said. Jones was not the only one with friends who specialized in forged documents. Pace had used the identification before and as well as finding it amusing, he had also found that people were generally unwilling to antagonize someone they thought would be able to look into their tax affairs and would provide the information he wanted without questioning why he wanted it. She thought his companion looked more like the sort of person who would be involved in tax evasion rather than inspection. Or was it avoidance, she could never remember?

Still, Pace had a certain persuasive charm and she saw no reason to challenge his right to ask questions about her former employee. Indeed, she had a generally unsuspicious nature as well as a talkative one. She took Mr Pace and his companion, Mr Gray, into her small, cluttered office at the rear of the spacious dance floor and closed the door on the music and the four couples who were dancing to it with fierce concentration under the critical eye of a young male instructor.

'No, no, no, it's four basics and a *back* step ...'

Mrs Ambrose motioned her visitors into two rather rickety chairs and sat behind a desk littered with piles of assorted paperwork, two or three of the top sheets of which showed evidence of having been used as coasters. She was a tall, erect woman with short grey hair and an amicable expression. Before speaking, she inspected her visitors through a pair of large blue-rimmed spectacles which gave her a slightly owlish look.

'As I was saying, Mr Jones left last week. We were very sorry to see him go, he was an excellent instructor. He knew exactly how to get the best performance out of his students.'

Gray seemed to find this amusing, but Pace ignored him and kept the discussion on a professional level.

'He has applied to us for self-employed status and has sent the relevant form to our local office, but there appears to be an error in his address. When we wrote to him there, the letter was returned.' Pace took out notebook and pen from his jacket pocket. He hoped she wouldn't ask any technical questions. Horace Soames had briefed him on what to say, but if they went off script, he was going to have to play things by ear and might say the wrong thing. 'He put you down as his employer, so as we had to be in the area on another matter, we thought we'd call in and get his address from you. I assume you do have it?'

'I have his home address, but he said he was going to move out of the area, so he may not be there.' She opened the bottom drawer of a battered grey filing cabinet behind her desk, flipped through a few files and withdrew one. She opened it on the desk and inspected the papers inside. 'Here we are – it's 76 Tollpuddle Gardens, Havenchester West.'

'Thank you,' Pace consulted his notebook and pretended to check the information with the open page, which was, in fact, blank. 'We had it as Havenchester East, which may explain the problem. Do you have a telephone number for him?'

'I only have a mobile number. He told me once that he lived in rented rooms.' She gave him the number.

'Thank you. That is the number we have, but there was no reply when we tried it. Do you happen to know where he was going after he left you?'

She shook her head.

'I'm afraid I have no idea. I did not even know that he had applied for self-employed status – perhaps he is intending to set up as an instructor on his own. He was friendly and personable enough, but not very communicative about his private life. You might want to check with his landlady. He was a sensible young man, so I would imagine that he probably left a forwarding address with her.' Her tone suggested that she would not give such a testimonial for every young man that she knew.

'I'll do that.' He nodded, started to close his notebook, paused and added a final question. 'Do you happen to know if he has any relatives in the city?'

'He has a married brother in London whom he gave as next of

kin; he never mentioned anyone else. I believe that the brother
has done very well for himself; he works for a bank, as far as I
remember. I suppose Mr Jones might have gone to stay with him.
He might have felt that there were more opportunities in
London.'

'Do you have an address for the brother?'

Mrs Ambrose consulted her file again. Had she been of a more
suspicious nature, she might have wondered whether providing
that information was strictly necessary, but, like many people who
were faced with apparent officialdom, once she had accepted Pace's
story and started answering his questions, she continued to do so
automatically.

'Kenneth Jones, Apartment 7C, Kingsway Towers, Barbican. I
have a telephone number for him, as well.'

Pace duly wrote the information into his notebook, put it away
and got to his feet. The chair swayed a bit, but remained intact.

'Thank you for your help.' He smiled at her.

'My pleasure.' She smiled in return; he really was a very nice
man, even though his colleague was a bit odd. Still, he had clearly
suffered a head injury recently so perhaps that explained it. She saw
them out of the building and turned back to watch the class, the
visit disappearing into the depths of her memory as she concentrated on the steps being performed in front of her with varying
degrees of expertise.

76 Tollpuddle Gardens was part of a four-storey Victorian terrace
that had seen better days but still held a hint of former glory, like an
out-of-work former soap star opening a supermarket. It had been
divided up into separately rented rooms. There was no Jones on the
list of tenants inside the archway over the front door, and Pace rang
the bell marked 'A Kemp – Landlady'.

The door was opened by a short angular woman with a sharp
expression, wearing a pinafore apron and with her hair in curlers.
She could have stepped straight into the role of landlady in a black
and white British comedy of the fifties or sixties.

Pace didn't bother to use his tax inspector persona; he gave no
explanation, just said that he was looking for Jeffrey Jones and was
he in?

'Mr Jones? He moved out two days ago.' Her voice rasped from gossip and cigarettes.

'Did he leave a forwarding address?'

'No, he didn't. He paid his rent up to date and said he was going travelling and didn't know where he'd be. He asked me to keep any post for him and said he'd call back in a month or so to pick it up, although he wasn't expecting anything.'

'You've no idea where he went?' Pace was starting to get irritated by Jones and his disappearing act.

'No, he loaded his cases into his car and off he went.'

'What sort of car was it?' Pace seized on the new information eagerly.

'It's a Volvo, I don't know the exact make. A small one, silver colour, it was.'

'Registration?' he asked, without much hope.

'Starts with a Y.'

Pace sighed.

'Do you know if he has any relatives or close friends in the area?'

The landlady thought for a moment. She took a packet of cigarettes from her apron pocket and lit one, presumably as an aid to thought.

'He's got a brother who came to see him once. He works in London for one of those big accounting firms or something. Nice man.'

'Kenneth?' Pace thought that if the woman started having any doubts about answering his questions, the fact that he knew the brother's name might help to allay any suspicion.

She nodded, apparently happy to tell him all she knew.

'Kenneth. That was it, Kenneth Jones.'

'Did he stay here when he visited?'

'No, my Mr Jones went to stay with him. The brother owns a cottage somewhere up around here. It's not in the city; it's on the coast north of here. He said it was about an hour's drive or so away.'

'Where is it exactly?' That was more like it, a cottage hideaway sounded very promising.

'I don't know, he didn't tell me.' She seemed disappointed not to be able to help. 'He said it was a nice quiet spot, well away from the beaten track.'

This was sounding better and better.

'When did they go?'

She pondered for a moment.

'Sometime last summer – July, I think. It was about the time of my Alf's birthday.'

Pace didn't bother to find out more about Alf, whether he was husband, brother or son. He nodded his thanks and motioned to Gray that they were leaving.

'What do we do now?' Gray asked, as they walked back to where Pace had parked the car. Although impressed with Pace's interrogation techniques, he was starting to get bored. He preferred extracting information with the aid of a razor.

'We need to find out where that cottage is. If they didn't try to get right away immediately, they'll be lying low somewhere and that sounds just the place.'

'So how do we find it?'

Pace looked grim.

'I think it's time we paid another call on Beverly Wallace's sister. And this time, we'll make sure we get the truth out of her.'

Gray smirked. That sounded more promising. Maybe he'd get to use the razor after all.

TEN

WHEN JULIE AND Tanner arrived at the agency the following morning they found Ella was already there looking calm, neat and efficient as always and wearing her usual combination of skirt and top that were tight and short in all the right places. Tanner thought it amazing that she didn't have a permanent cold all through the winter. They smiled good mornings at each other and, as Tanner followed Julie into his office, he caught Ella's eye. She gave him a wink and a big grin that probably constituted insubordination. Tanner grinned back at her.

Ella brought in two strong coffees which Tanner hoped would get his brain cells working. He went through the post as he waited for inspiration, but the coffee didn't seem to be very effective. Julie sat at the side of his desk at his PC trawling through various internet sites to pick up details of any companies or businesses Harry Milton was involved in. She was also trying to see if she could find any trace of Harper and Winston. Her frown indicated that she wasn't having much success in either enterprise.

Tanner thought that it was beginning to look as though they were going to have to use the same tactics with Milton that they had with Vernon Bridger – go charging in and see what happened. The trouble was that Milton was both cleverer and more dangerous than Bridger. He might react, but just as likely he would deny everything, sit tight and wait for them to make another move. And Tanner wasn't sure that there was another move for them to make. He felt as though he was trying to plan an attack in chess with all his opponent's pieces out of sight on another board altogether.

After half an hour, Tanner had sorted the post and was deliberating whether to see if another coffee might be a help or a hindrance. He was just going to ask Julie for her opinion when there was a light tap on the door. Ella came in and closed the door behind her.

'There's a woman just come into the office. Her name's Sandi Wallace and she says she wants to see you and Miss Cooper.'

Julie looked up from the screen, rubbed her eyes and looked across at Ella with puzzled interest.

'She asked for both of us?'

Ella nodded.

'Yep. I thought that was interesting enough for you to be interrupted. I asked her what it was about, but she says she'll only talk to the two of you. She looks pretty het up about something.'

'You'd better bring her in then, please,' Tanner said.

In view of their lack of progress in the department of bright ideas Tanner thought it wouldn't do any harm to see Sandi Wallace. If she specifically wanted to see Julie as well, it might lead to something. Besides, he was supposed to be running a detective agency, so he couldn't just limit himself to one client, no matter how involved he was getting.

Ella opened the door again and stepped aside for Sandi Wallace to walk into the office. Tanner and Julie's first impression was of the barely controlled nervousness in her round, attractive face. She wore a high-necked dark-green jersey and knee-length black skirt with a brown suede coat and brown boots. Her eyes were covered by a pair of enormous sun glasses, even though it was a cloudy day. Tanner jumped to an immediate conclusion as to the reason for that – it wasn't likely to be because she thought she needed protection from his sunny disposition.

'Please sit down, Miss Wallace. I'm Alec Tanner and this is Julie Cooper.'

'Thank you.' She spoke without opening her mouth very far, as if afraid of spilling out too many words, and sat down with a stiffness and care that was not in keeping with either her age or her looks. Tanner's guess about the glasses was starting to look more and more probable.

'What can we do for you?' he asked.

Sandi Wallace sat without speaking for a moment, her small shapely hands gripping the shoulder bag that she had placed on her lap, the knuckles gleaming white. She looked to be one nervous shock away from breaking down completely. Tanner thought for a moment that she was reconsidering her decision to come, but she must have been gathering her thoughts because when she spoke her voice was low but firm and determined.

'I want you to help my sister Beverly; I think she's in terrible danger. I want you to find her and warn her; help her if possible.'

'Why did you specifically come to Miss Cooper and me to help?' Tanner asked gently.

'I work in the Pussy Kat Klub as a dancer. The club is owned by Vernon Bridger, so I know a bit about what goes on in the city, the people who run certain things. I heard people talking at the club. I heard them say that the two of you had threatened Mr Bridger and that when he sent a team out to teach you a lesson, you taught them one. That sounded as though you wouldn't be afraid to help me. And that you might be able to succeed.'

'Is it Bridger that your sister is in trouble with?' Tanner asked.

She shook her head.

'No, it's a man called Harry Milton. Do you know him?'

Julie and Tanner exchanged a startled glance. Perhaps this wouldn't turn out to be a separate case after all.

'I know him,' Tanner confirmed. 'I've met him a couple of times, although not, as it were, in a business sense – either his or mine.'

She looked blank for a moment, and then dipped her head in a brief nod, like a nervous bird spotting a fast worm.

'Why is Milton a danger to your sister?' Tanner asked.

Sandi Wallace gathered her thoughts again.

'Beverly has been Harry Milton's permanent live-in girlfriend for more than two years now. For the last few months she's also been seeing someone else – a man who was giving her dancing lessons. His name is Jeffrey Jones. Two days ago she ran away with him.' She paused.

'And Milton is jealous and wants her back?' Tanner completed.

She shrugged.

'It's partly that, perhaps, his ego doesn't like to be thwarted. But it's mainly because she emptied his safe before she went. I think there must have been a considerable sum in there and not just in money. Beverly told me some of her plans last time we met. I was part of her alibi. Some of the time she was seeing Jeffrey she was supposed to be seeing me, so I had to be in the know in case I met Milton or any one in his organization who might be able to report back. I warned her against antagonizing Milton, but she said she loved Jeffrey and she wanted a new life with him. I can't say I blamed her for that.

'Milton has a minder, a man called Jack Pace. Beverly ran away early Wednesday morning and that afternoon, Pace came to see me at the club just before I was due to go on stage. He tried to find out if I knew anything. I pretended that I didn't, even though he knocked me around a bit and threatened worse if I lied. But I knew what they'd do to Beverly if they caught her. They didn't know about Jeffrey at that stage, so I just played ignorant and he believed me. He took my key and went and searched my flat, but there wasn't anything there for him to find.'

She took a deep breath before continuing.

'Pace must have found out more after that. Yesterday afternoon he came again and he brought a low-life called Reggie Gray with him. They knew about Jeffrey and they think he and Beverly have gone into hiding in Jeffrey's brother's cottage. They thought I knew where it was and they tried to make me tell them. This was the result.' She took off her glasses and looked across the desk at them. There were two massive bruises round her eyes. The right eye was completely shut, the area round it black and swollen. The left was a little better, only partly closed although still so swollen it seemed that she must have had trouble seeing at all. 'There are similar marks all over my body,' she added. 'I won't be dancing for a while.'

'Did you tell them anything?' Julie's voice was soothing, but there was a clear edge to it. She was hoping Pace and Gray might get a dose of that medicine themselves.

'No.' Sandi shook her head. 'I'm not sure I could have held out from telling them, but I really don't know where the cottage is. Beverly wouldn't tell me – she said it was too dangerous for me and if I genuinely didn't know I'd be more convincing because they were bound to question me after she'd gone. I suppose it worked. I must have sounded genuine, because they threatened to break bones if I didn't talk, but in the end they held back from that.'

'Bully for them,' Tanner said in a dry voice.

'Gray wanted to cut me, as a lesson, but Pace stopped him. I doubt if it was for compassionate reasons, I suppose they didn't want to risk involving doctors and hospitals unless it was absolutely necessary.'

'What exactly do you want us to do?' Julie asked.

'Find out where the cottage is and get there before Pace and Gray. Warn Beverly and Jeffrey that Milton knows where they are and that they have to leave and find somewhere else to hide.'

'The police could find them more quickly,' Julie pointed out, omitting to mention that she was the police, albeit on extended leave.

Sandi looked really frightened for the first time.

'No, we can't involve the police. If Milton or Bridger found out I'd gone to the police, they'd kill me. If you do it, with any luck they need never know that I've come to you. Please help me.'

Tanner nodded.

'We'll do what we can. What can you tell us about Jeffrey Jones's brother?'

Sandi gave a sigh of relief and some of the anxiety seemed to fade from her face. Tanner thought that she had more faith in them than he did. If Milton's people had already found out about the cottage the day before, they could be there and gone before he and Julie had even located it.

'His name is Kenneth. He works for a finance company in London and travels abroad quite a lot. He's married and lives in the Barbican somewhere – I don't know exactly where.'

'What about the firm he works for?'

'They haven't mentioned it to me.'

Sandi twisted her slim fingers together on her lap.

'Thank you so much for agreeing to help. If Milton gets to Beverly he'll kill her. I've got to do all I can to help her.' Despair was starting to creep back into her voice.

'Do you know where Jones worked and his home address?' Tanner asked.

'Yes.' She took a notebook from her shoulder bag, wrote on it and tore off the page. 'That's the dance studio where he worked and the place where he rented rooms. I've never been to either of them, but Beverly mentioned the studio when she first went there for lessons, before the affair with Jeffrey started. She told me where he lived when I started covering for her. If Milton had ever contacted me when she and I were supposed to be together, I could have left a message there; not that I ever had to.'

Tanner nodded. Beverly seemed to have thought some things through quite thoroughly, even if her love life was pretty complicated – and dangerous.

'We'll do what we can.' He gave her his card. 'Ring the office if you need to contact us or if Pace comes back. If we aren't around, you can leave a message, you can completely trust everyone who works here.' He paused. An idea had been nagging away at the back of his mind as they were talking and the more he thought about it, the more likely – and unpleasant – it became. 'You said you aren't able to work for a while because of the beating you took, are you intending to stay at home for a few days?'

'I suppose so. I hadn't really thought about it,' she looked puzzled. 'Is it important?'

'It might be better if you stayed somewhere else.'

Alarm flared in her eyes.

'You think I might still be in danger?'

'It's possible. I don't want to frighten you unduly, but one of the reasons they didn't hurt you so much that you couldn't get around might be that they're following you in the hope that you'll lead them to Beverly. They could well have followed you here. When Pace had your key he could even have bugged your flat.'

Sandi started to shiver. Tanner wondered if he should have been so blunt, but it was more dangerous for her not to be aware of the potential risk.

Julie came round the desk, sat on the edge of the client chair and put her arm round Sandi's shoulders.

'Alec is just speculating,' she said gently. 'It may not be like that but he's right, you need to keep alert. Did you notice if you were followed here?'

Sandi swallowed and shook her head.

'I didn't really look. It didn't occur to me. My flatmate was out when Pace went round with the key, so I don't know what he did there, he just left the key at the club when he finished. He could even have copied it.' She looked forlorn and defeated. 'I'm not much good at this sort of thing. I always try to avoid trouble.'

'Is there anyone else you can stay with – a friend, perhaps?'

She shook her head.

'Most of my friends are connected with my work; they work for Bridger or someone like him. Some of them would probably turn me in, either for money or through fear, and those I can trust would be in danger because of me; I couldn't lay them open to that.'

Tanner thought for a moment.

'One of our former clients might be prepared to help,' he said. 'She's in the Territorial Army and a pretty formidable lady. She wouldn't take kindly to two men beating up a woman; you'd be safe with her. She owns a keep-fit studio and runs defence classes for women in the evening. She said I could call on her if I ever needed a favour. I'll need to speak to her first, of course.'

He gave Sandi Wallace a reassuring smile.

'I'll contact her and see what I can arrange. Someone can go home with you so you can pack a bag.'

'Thank you so much. What about your fees? I have some money.' She fumbled in her shoulder bag and brought out a small wad of notes. 'One hundred and fifty, is that enough? It's all I could get at short notice, but I have some savings I can draw on.'

Tanner nodded.

'That will be fine for the moment. Don't worry about paying more than that for now, this might tie in with something else we're working on. We'll let you know tomorrow when we've had a chance to look into it. If you'll wait in the outer office, I'll start making arrangements for you.'

Sandi got to her feet, wincing as she put her weight on her left leg. 'Gray's handiwork,' she said in answer to Julie's look. She put the glasses back on and Tanner opened the door for her. Julie watched the new client limp out. She hoped very much that they'd be able to have words with Mr Gray.

'If we can help Beverly Wallace, she might be able to give us a lead to Harper and Winston,' Julie commented as Tanner went back to his desk. 'If not, she could give us a useful insight into Milton's organization.'

'Yep, the same thought occurred to me. I think we need to consult the oracle again,' Tanner picked up his desk phone and asked Ted

Manning to come over. Manning arrived in a few seconds, full of boundless energy as always, and lowered himself into the spare chair.

'What's up, doc?'

Tanner gave him an outline of Sandi Wallace's story. Manning nodded thoughtfully.

'Could be exceedingly useful, that could.'

'What do you know about Pace and Gray?' Tanner asked. 'Could they have shot Julie and her aunt?'

Ted leant back in his chair, frowned for a moment and then shook his head.

'I don't think so. Pace is a hard man and he could easily be a killer, but he works directly for Milton who uses him for all the nasty personal chores, presumably on the basis that if all that is done by one man and that's someone he can trust, he can sleep easier. He might have used Pace if Julie had busted one of his own rackets, but he wouldn't risk him by hiring him out. Gray is an even nastier piece of work in many ways. For Pace, hurting people is just a job, Gray enjoys it. Gray tends to use a knife or a razor rather than a shooter; he does debt collecting, puts the frighteners on, that sort of thing. He and Pace don't generally work together; I don't see them as a hit team. I still think Harper and Winston are our best bet if Milton took the hit job.'

'You do know the nicest people,' Julie commented.

'It was worth a thought,' Tanner said, 'it could have simplified matters considerably.'

Manning grinned. 'You know your trouble, you want things too easy.'

'Yeah.' Tanner thought for a moment. 'We need to look after Sandi Wallace first. You remember Annie Thorpe?'

Manning's grin broadened.

'Intimately,' he said. Tanner raised his eyebrows. Knowing Ted Manning, he meant that literally.

'Do you think she would look after Sandi for a few days if you asked her nicely? Let her stay in her spare room? She said we could call on her for a favour if we needed to. She was very impressed with our service, as I recall.'

'Yes, indeed. And the after-service care as well.'

*

Tanner introduced Sandi Wallace to Ted Manning and left him to arrange matters with Annie Thorpe whilst he and Julie went to visit Jeffrey Jones's last known place of residence. Before they left, Tanner took a look out of the front office window to see whether he could spot someone watching the front of the building who might have followed Sandi. There were no obvious loitering pedestrians, but there were a couple of parked cars that could have fitted the bill. There was also a café diagonally opposite where a shadower could linger and watch the building entrance. A watcher wouldn't know that Sandi wasn't visiting one of the other occupants of the building, of course, but a glance at the sign by the front door would make the detective agency the first choice in the circumstances. Sandi wasn't likely to be interested in either a secretarial career, or having her picture taken. The more Tanner thought about it, the more convinced he became that, with little else to go on, Milton's people would aim to convince Sandi that they believed her story and then watch her to see where she led them. He doubted if Pace or Gray would actually do the watching – apart from anything else, she would recognize them – but they would certainly be within call.

As far as Tanner could make out, no one followed them on the way to Tollpuddle Gardens. Not that it's very easy to tell in the midst of city traffic, but none of the cars behind them when they left the agency were still there when they got to their destination. Of course, Tanner thought, that could just mean that they were better at tailing than he was at spotting.

When they reached the house, Tanner pushed the buzzer for flat 1A , which had a very faded card that he could just decipher as reading: 'A Kemp – Landlady'. After three pushes and no reply, he deduced that she was out (they didn't call him a master detective for nothing). He then tried 3B – T Gorringe. After a few moments a disembodied voice that was just about recognizable as female croaked out of the grille and asked his name and business.

'My name's Alec Tanner. I'm a private detective. I'm trying to locate Jeffrey Jones. I think he moved from the rooms next door to you and I wondered if I could a have word with you about him.'

There was a moment's silence and Tanner thought she had switched off on him. Then there was another crackle from the grille that he presumed translated as some variant of 'OK' and the door buzzed and clicked open.

They walked into a narrow, gloomy hall that smelt of dust and long dead meals, but fortunately nothing more objectionable. They went up the even narrower and gloomier stairs to the second floor where two doors stood facing each other on either side of a small landing with faded carpet and grubby window. A lace curtain that was more lace than curtain hung limply across the window. Both doors sported dark-brown paint that was starting to peel; the door to the right had 3A screwed on to it in gold letters. 3B was already open, with its owner standing waiting for them. Tanner introduced Julie as his colleague; it seemed easier than a more complicated explanation of her official ranking.

T Gorringe – they never did discover what the 'T' stood for – stood aside and invited them in.

The inside of the flat was a pleasant surprise. Although small, the living room was bright and cheerfully furnished with several paintings and ornaments spread around at intervals. There were two armchairs of slightly faded but not threadbare flowered material. Ms Gorringe had clearly stamped her own personality in the room. A TV stood on a table in a corner by the window with the sound turned down. A smiling host seemed to be discussing a burning issue with the studio audience. Tanner thought that the intellectual content was probably improved without the words.

Ms Gorringe's brown eyes stared at them curiously from behind pink-rimmed spectacles. Her nose was as red as her cheeks and that, together with the handkerchief clutched in her hand revealed why they had caught her at home on a workday morning.

'We're sorry to disturb you,' Tanner said, after they had accepted her invitation to sit down.

'That's all right,' she spoke thickly. 'I'm getting pretty bored up here on my own anyway.' She paused to dab at her nose. 'Don't worry, I'm not contagious any more.' She smiled reassuringly.

Tanner wondered if the germs knew that.

'We won't keep you long,' he assured her. 'We're trying to locate

Mr Jones rather urgently and, as he's moved, we wondered if you knew him very well and might know where he'd gone.'

'He moved out one evening a couple of days ago,' she said. 'We were quite friendly, living on the same floor here. We used to pop into each other's rooms from time to time for a chat and a cup of tea. He was a good neighbour; I was sorry when he left.'

'Do you know where he went to?' Julie asked.

'No, I'm sorry I don't. He said he was going abroad with his girl-friend, but things weren't fixed up yet and they were taking a short holiday first. He didn't say where.'

'It's to do with his girlfriend's sister that we need to contact him,' Julie said, which wasn't a complete lie. 'We understand that he might have gone to his brother's cottage – do you know where that is?'

She shook her head again.

'I know that he has one, Jeffrey went to stay there last year with him, but I don't know exactly where it is. I believe it's somewhere north of the city, on the coast, but he didn't say exactly where.'

'You wouldn't have his brother's address or phone number, I suppose?'

'No.' She thought for a moment. 'But I know the name of the firm he works for, would that be of any use?' She seemed delighted to be more positive. 'It's called Kenton Anderson, it's quite a big finance firm in London. Is that any help to you?'

Julie nodded, it was, at least some progress.

'That could be very helpful indeed.'

They left Ms Gorringe to nurse her germs and went back down-stairs. As they were already in the building, Tanner tried the landlady's door on the way out, but there was no response to his knocking. He supposed that was what was meant by an absentee landlord.

By the time they reached the top of the flight of narrow dark stairs that led to the Dance 'Til You Drop dance studio, Tanner was surprised some people had much breath left for dancing.

As they came through the swing doors that led into the studio, several couples were on the floor. A tall woman walked over to them, moving with the smooth grace of the professional dancer and smiling pleasantly. Tanner and Julie walked towards her, keeping to the side wall so as to avoid being trampled by the dancers, and they met halfway.

'Good afternoon. If you are interested in lessons, we have a beginner's class this evening, or more advanced tomorrow.'

'We haven't come for lessons, I'm afraid,' Julie told her. 'We'd like to talk to you about a former employee – Jeffrey Jones.'

She looked startled.

'Are you with the Tax Office as well?'

'No.' It was Julie's turn to look surprised. 'Why should you think that?'

'Well, two gentlemen from the Inland Revenue were here yesterday asking about Mr Jones.' She started to look concerned and glanced at the dancing couples as if suspecting one of them might be a spy. 'Perhaps you had better come into the office.'

They followed her into the rear room and sat down facing her as she moved behind her desk.

'My name is Veronica Ambrose, I am the owner of the dance studio,' she paused expectantly.

'I'm Alec Tanner, a private detective,' he gave her his card. 'This is ...'

'My name's Julie Cooper. I'm a police officer, but at the moment I'm on leave and I'm working with Mr Tanner.' Julie showed her warrant card. She thought giving Mrs Ambrose her official title would make her more receptive to their questions.

Mrs Ambrose blinked at them from behind her spectacles.

'Is Mr Jones in some sort of trouble?' She asked. 'First the tax inspectors and now detectives.' She shook her head. 'He seemed such a level-headed, respectable young man, but you can never tell these days.'

'I doubt whether the two men yesterday were real tax inspectors. He isn't so much in trouble as in danger,' Julie told her. 'We need to find him urgently to see that he gets protection.'

'Good heavens,' Mrs Ambrose eyed her visitors shrewdly. 'You mean the two men yesterday were the ones wanting to harm him?'

'It seems likely. What did you tell them?'

Mrs Ambrose shook her head in self-reproach.

'I thought there was something odd about them, but one of them, at least was very plausible.'

'What information did you give them?' Julie asked again.

'His home address and mobile phone number and his brother's address and home number.'

Julie and Tanner exchanged glances.

'You have Kenneth Jones's address and telephone number?'

'Yes.' She took out a file from a filing cabinet and gave them the details.

'I do hope I haven't helped them to find him.'

Julie nodded; so did she.

When Julie and Tanner got back to the office, Tanner immediately rang Kenneth Jones's home number. He got an answering machine and left a message for him to ring back urgently as they needed to contact his brother. Then he rang directory enquiries and got the number for Kenton Anderson. There were three numbers, one of which was the head office, so he tried that first.

A receptionist put Tanner through to Mr Jones's personal assistant. She told him in a cool, efficient voice that Mr Jones was meeting with a client in the client's office and couldn't be contacted, but he was expected back at their offices soon after five and she'd get him to ring Mr Tanner then. Tanner thanked her and told her to emphasize that it was very urgent. She agreed to do so. The temperature of her voice seemed unaffected by the urgency.

Tanner tried the home number again at fifteen minute intervals without getting past the answering machine, which didn't seem to appreciate the urgency either. Just after five, Ella put through a call from Kenneth Jones.

'Thank you for ringing back. As I told your PA, my name's Alec Tanner; I'm a private detective working in Havenchester.'

'You wanted to speak to me about my brother?' He had a strong, no-nonsense, voice with a distinct northern accent that suggested life in London hadn't affected his roots.

'Yes, I need to contact him urgently. I believe he is staying at your cottage up here and I was hoping you would give me the address.'

There was a moment's silence whilst this was digested.

'My brother specifically stated that he did not want to be disturbed.'

At least, Tanner thought, he wasn't denying that his brother was at the cottage.

'Do you know why your brother wanted to use the cottage?' Tanner asked.

'He wants a few days' holiday with a friend.' The tone was still cautious. 'And I still don't know why I should be discussing my brother's private affairs with a stranger.'

'Your brother is in serious danger, Mr Jones. He has run away with the girlfriend of a very dangerous man called Harry Milton, a man with serious criminal connections. I believe that they are intending to lie low in your cottage; they believe they are safe there because they don't think Milton knows about your brother. However, I have discovered that Milton does know about him, and that he is staying at the cottage, but he doesn't yet know exactly where it is either.' Tanner hoped that was still true. 'I have been hired by the girlfriend's sister to find them and warn them to change their hiding place.'

The pause this time was even longer.

'Supposing this remarkable story to be true, how do I know that you do not represent these people who are trying to harm my brother?'

Tanner closed his eyes and swore under his breath. Kenneth Jones was right, of course, but there was only one way to convince him, and that meant further delay.

'If you ring Detective Chief Inspector Richard Mariner at the Havenchester City Police serious crime squad, he'll vouch for me. Could you ring him straight away and then phone me back?'

'Very well.' The offer to involve the police seemed to impress him.

'I'll give you the number.'

'Don't worry – I'll get my PA to find it.'

Tanner sighed; there was so little trust these days. Still, Jones was right again, Tanner could have arranged for someone to answer the other number and call themselves the Havenchester City Police.

It seemed to take hours, but it was only just over ten minutes before Jones rang back. This time his voice was less restrained and more concerned about his brother.

'Chief Inspector Mariner has vouched for you,' he said, 'and confirmed what you say about this man Milton. My cottage is situated on the west coast near the village of Lower Winkley. It is not immediately on a main road and it is quite difficult to find, I'll give you precise directions.'

Tanner wrote them down.

'Thank you. Have you been contacted by anyone else?' he asked. 'I think Milton's people found out about the cottage yesterday and they were given your home number at the same time.'

'No one else has contacted me. My wife has been away for a few days and there were no messages last night on the answer phone at home. I have been with a client all day and have had no messages other than yours that were not work related.' He paused and the business-like tone crumbled a little. 'Please do all you can to help Jeffrey.'

'I will,' Tanner assured him. Whether they could do anything was another matter. 'We'll leave for the cottage now. I'll get him to call you later.'

That was assuming Jones would be in a fit state to ring his brother later, Tanner thought. The fact that Kenneth hadn't been contacted was worrying; it suggested that Milton might have other ways of locating the cottage and could be hours ahead of them. They could easily get there and find it empty.

ELEVEN

HARRY MILTON HAD cultivated many and varied contacts in many and varied walks of life and he owned every one of them in some way or other. Some he had let off gambling debts in return for present or future favours; some had asked him for help and had received it, not realizing that they had put themselves into a similar position to Dr Faustus, their devil being somewhat less immortal, but no less demanding. All were expected to repay their debt at some point and most of the things he required meant that once you had done them Harry Milton had a hold on you for life. Sometimes when he cultivated one of his contacts, he had no specific idea of the use he would be able to make of them; he just felt that it might be useful in the future to have access to whatever they might be in a position to provide.

One such contact was a man called Simon Joiner, an employee in the Havenchester City Council tax offices. Mr Joiner was too fond of risking his salary on the performance of horses that seemed incapable of finishing a race unless they had other horses ahead of them and, as a result, he had run up significant debts in one of Milton's businesses. It had occurred to Milton that someone working in the council's tax department would have access to the sort of personal information that could well prove helpful and he had accordingly cleared Joiner's debts from his books.

Now was the time for that debt to be called in.

At nine a.m., Harry Milton was on the phone to the council offices. There were occasions when he felt that the personal touch obtained maximum co-operation.

'I'd like to speak to Simon Joiner, please.'

'I'm sorry, Mr Joiner is not available this morning.' The female voice sounded genuinely disappointed for him. 'Can someone else help?'

Milton's voice grew slightly less pleasant.

'No, I need to speak to him personally. Can he be reached?' Milton usually had others making initial telephone contact for him, so that by the time he came on the line the person he wanted was already there and ready to speak to him. He was not used to being frustrated.

'He's at a seminar this morning at our training centre.' The voice told him brightly. 'We have some new performance indicators to meet and all the senior managers have to—'

'Yes, I see,' Milton cut in. The only performance indicator he was interested in at the moment was the length of time it would take to get his hands on Beverly Wallace. 'When do you expect him back?'

'There's a lunch laid on, so it will probably be after two. Can I ask him to ring you?'

'No, I'll phone back later.'

He slammed the phone down and scowled. His working life was being disrupted and that annoyed him. Worse than that, the longer things dragged on, the more time there was for word to get round that Harry Milton had been shafted by his own girlfriend. Such stories undermined his position in the sort of businesses he was mixed up in and that affected his influence, which could have a detrimental impact on both his profits and his control over his empire. He was very conscious that it could take just one young bright spark to think that Harry Milton was an easy target and things could get very messy indeed. He was completely confident of his ruthless ability to win through, but it was a waste of time and effort he could well do without. Things were nowhere near that stage yet, of course, but he needed to get the matter sorted quickly and that meant making an example of Beverly Wallace.

His mood was not improved an hour later when Jack Pace came in to report that the man he had watching Sandi Wallace's flat had followed her to an office building in the centre of the city.

'One of the occupants is Tanner's detective agency.'

Milton swore and added further stab marks to his blotter with his letter opener.

'That's not a coincidence.'

'Hardly,' Pace agreed. 'Do you want us to pick her up again when she leaves?' He too was feeling the pressure of them not having located Beverly Wallace yet. Any doubts about Milton's authority would inevitably reflect back on him, and that could be dangerous.

Milton thought for a moment. It was tempting, but he was aware that he needed to keep police interest out of his affairs and taking out his anger on Beverly's sister, although temporarily satisfying, would not achieve their main aim and it could lead to complications.

'No,' he decided reluctantly, 'just keep having her followed. This doesn't necessarily mean that she knows where her bitch of a sister is; she could have hired Tanner to locate the cottage for her so that she can warn her sister that we're on to her.'

'So do you want us to keep tabs on Tanner as well? In case he finds them before we do?'

Milton frowned. Important as this was, he didn't have unlimited manpower, certainly not of the calibre needed for smart on-the-spot decisions.

'We don't know he'll be looking into it personally.' He killed his blotter twice more. 'But if he is and he gets lucky he could lead us there.' With a final stab, he made up his mind. Being so indecisive irritated him. This thing had really got under his skin. 'Do we have someone who knows Tanner by sight?'

'Yeah, we can use Lenny Kelly. Tanner got his brother sent down for theft a couple of years ago.'

'Good.' Milton nodded. Kelly was someone who could use his initiative. 'Put him on to it. And tell Lenny not to let himself be seen.'

'Right.' Pace nodded, his face impassive. Giving unnecessary instructions like that showed just how rattled Milton was becoming.

After Pace had left, Milton tried to concentrate on the papers in front of him. Looking at details of the money coming in from his various enterprises and assessing the profit-making potential of new activities usually focused his mind totally, but today he couldn't concentrate. Images of Beverly kept coming into his mind, of how she must have duped him over the past months, laughing at him behind his back. For someone who got a lot of his pleasure out of controlling other people, to discover he had been manipulated himself was hard to bear.

Finally, he gave up. He needed to relax; there was too much going round inside his head. He took his key ring from his trouser pocket, selected a small key that had no duplicate and unlocked the top right-hand drawer of his desk. He removed another key from inside, closed the drawer and locked it again, pushed back his chair and got up. He left the study and walked upstairs to the door of the room on the top floor that was always kept locked. Using the key from his desk, he opened the door, went inside, switched on the carefully placed lighting and turned to lock the door again. Then he sat down in the comfortable leather swivel chair that stood in the centre of the room. He sat for a few moments, closing his eyes and breathing deeply to relieve his tension. Then he opened his eyes again and started studying the painting on the wall in front of him, one of several that hung at intervals around the room. Each painting was by a master, each lit by its own soft spotlight. The room's only window was covered by a thick blind that was never raised. Behind the blind was a secure grille. Beneath three of the paintings were small display cabinets, each holding a few exquisite pieces of porcelain. This was his sanctuary, the one place he could come to relax fully.

After a few moments, he felt the inner peace and almost sensual pleasure that always came to him when locked away with his treasures and a smile crossed his face. As always, it added an extra dimension to his pleasure to know that he could never bring another person into this room, because everything in it was stolen property.

Lenny Kelly had been lucky. He had reached the junction with the road in which the detective agency was situated and he was just about to turn right towards it when he saw Alec Tanner driving past, accompanied by an attractive brunette he assumed was Julie Cooper. Kelly changed his indicator from right to left and took advantage of a brief gap in the traffic two cars behind his quarry to pull out smoothly in pursuit. Tanner had been concentrating on the traffic ahead and had not seen him; the woman had glanced incuriously at his car as he reached the junction and then turned her attention elsewhere.

Kelly was a tall, thin man of mixed Irish and Afro-Caribbean parentage. He had curly dark hair, a complexion of milky coffee and an almost permanent expression of humour and goodwill in his green eyes. He found humour in nearly every situation, but could be cold, calculating and totally ruthless when he needed to be. He had worked for Milton for several years and although he could turn his hand to a number of activities when required, it was behind the wheel that he felt most at home. His driving skills were exceptional and his assessment of traffic, timing and space was the equal of most motor sport drivers. He had acted as getaway driver on several occasions in the past, but as Milton's activities started to assume a veneer of respectability, he was now employed more for general driving, as Milton's chauffeur when necessary and for following people.

The city-centre traffic was heavy with the usual congestion caused by road works, vans unloading and the sheer volume of cars and Kelly was able to keep three or four vehicles between him and his target car without fear of losing it. They moved through the business area of the city and then out to more residential areas. Traffic thinned a little and speeded up to over twenty miles an hour. He saw Tanner's car turn down Tollpuddle Gardens, and followed. There were no other cars between them now, which was a nuisance, but when Tanner pulled over and parked, Kelly drove on past and turned down the next side road on the left. He spotted a space on the opposite side of the road and quickly turned his car and parked facing back up towards Tollpuddle Gardens again.

Kelly left his car and moved cautiously to the end of the road. He saw Tanner and the woman standing by the entrance to a house twenty yards away on the other side of the road. When they went inside, he sauntered casually along the street and walked up to look at the door. None of the names meant anything to him. He made a mental note of the number and strolled back to his car. Unless Tanner did a U-turn in the road, which considering how narrow it was with cars parked on both sides seemed unlikely, he would have to drive past the mouth of the road Kelly was parked in. Kelly could then start up and resume his tail. It would be a bit of a risk, but he'd be certain to be spotted if he just loitered in the street and if he took refuge in a doorway, someone might get suspicious and ring the police.

He got out his mobile and reported back to Pace.

'They're at 76 Tollpuddle Gardens.'

'That's where Jones lived. Keep following them. Don't let them see you.'

Kelly grunted. He hardly needed telling that. He reached over to the back seat and picked up the official-looking clipboard that he kept there. The front sheet was a form he had picked up from his local council office. He pretended to be making notes on the form whilst keeping a watchful eye on the T-junction ahead. He had found that a single person sitting in a car might look suspicious, but someone sitting and filling in a form on a clipboard was always accepted without question as being on official business.

Half an hour later, Tanner drove past and Kelly started his engine and moved out after them. Again, he allowed a couple of cars to get between them as soon as possible.

Tanner's next stop was a public car-park. Fortunately, Kelly had already pulled further back and two other cars entered ahead of him. He drove in behind them without being spotted by Tanner and parked in the next row of spaces. He backed in so as to get a quick start if necessary.

Kelly followed Tanner to the pay and display machine and got a ticket for an hour. He knew Tanner by sight because he had seen him in court when he had given evidence against Kelly's brother. However, as far as Kelly was aware, Tanner did not know him, so there was little risk.

From where he was parked, Kelly could sit in the car and look across the street. He watched Tanner and Cooper cross the road and go through a doorway at the side of a shop. He peered across at the notice over the doorway and frowned. What on earth were they doing going to a dance studio?

He shrugged to himself mentally and got out his mobile again.

It was ten past two when Milton telephoned the council again. This time, he was successful and Joiner was available. Milton identified himself and could hear the alarm in the voice of the man at the other end of the line. Those moments gave him almost as much pleasure as his art collection.

'I need you to do me a favour.'

'What is it?' Joiner asked cautiously.

'A man called Kenneth Jones owns a cottage somewhere on the west coast north of the city. He's bound to be registered as the council tax payer and I want you to get me the address.'

Joiner paused. The phrase Data Protection Act sprang into his mind, but he didn't feel there was much point mentioning that to Milton. He briefly considered refusing, then recalled stories of what happened to punters who failed to pay gambling debts to people like Milton.

'I'll try,' he said eventually, 'but it sounds like it isn't in my council's area.'

'I'm sure you have contacts with colleagues in other authorities.' Milton's voice was silky smooth.

'Yes, but—'

'Here's my number,' Milton had no wish to mess about; they both knew Joiner was going to do what he wanted. 'I'll be waiting for your call.'

Milton hung up; he hoped the clown wouldn't take too long over it.

Pace knocked lightly and came into the study as Milton finished his call.

'Lenny's reported back a few times. He picked up Tanner and a woman – presumably Cooper – just as he got to the agency. He was lucky, he saw them driving past as he got there. He followed them to Jones's flat and to the dance studio. Now they've gone back to the agency.'

Milton grunted.

'What happened to the sister?'

'She was taken back to her flat by Ted Manning, the guy who works for Tanner. They came out with a suitcase and drove off.'

'Where to?'

Pace hesitated.

'We don't know, Manning spotted our tail and lost him.'

Milton snorted.

'Sometimes I think I'd do better employing a gang of monkeys.'

'I don't think it matters. Tanner wouldn't be going to Jones's flat and the dance studio if he knew where the cottage is, he'd have gone straight there. Sandi Wallace must have been telling the truth about that, even if she lied about knowing Jones himself.'

Milton considered that for a moment and then nodded.

'Yeah, you're probably right. Let's just hope my contact in the council comes up with that address.'

It was after four o'clock when Joiner rang back and Milton was starting to get edgy again.

'I've found the information you wanted. The cottage is in the West Linton council area. It took a while to track it down.' He paused, but didn't receive any acknowledgement of the difficulty of his task. 'The cottage is called White Cove View and it's near the village of Lower Winkley.'

Milton hung up with a grunt of thanks and called for Pace.

'I've found out where the cottage is.' He gave him the details. 'Get Gray and go over there. Contact Lenny Kelly and take him as well. We don't need to follow Tanner any more and with three of you there shouldn't be any slip ups. Bring Beverly and Jones to the garage.'

The garage was an old building situated on the edge of a decaying industrial estate, away from prying eyes and ears. It was well soundproofed and had often been used by Milton in the past when he wanted a quiet word with someone.

'Ring me when you're on your way back and I'll meet you there. Bring both of them there if you can, but if that's a problem, finish Jones on the spot and just bring her. She's the one I really want. And make sure you bring my property back as well.'

'Yes, boss.'

Pace was already on his way out.

Jeffrey Jones got the call that they had been waiting for on his mobile shortly after breakfast. Beverly, who was clearing away the cups and plates, could hear the relief in his voice and she was already smiling to herself in anticipation.

'That's great, Sean. Thanks for all you've done. Yes, I know exactly where you mean, we'll see you there at nine.' He turned to Beverly with a big grin, swung her around in his arms and kissed her.

'We're on our way at last. Sean has our new papers and he is going to pick us up from the jetty by the disused lighthouse at nine tonight. We'll have to walk there but that shouldn't be a problem. He says it will be easier for him to find us by the jetty than trying to pick us up from somewhere in the bay. He knows this stretch of the coast well and, as there's a full moon tonight, he says the old lighthouse should stand out clearly. In any case, he can take a bearing from the new one.'

The old lighthouse that stood beyond the right-hand point of the bay had been taken out of commission in the late eighties and replaced by a new, fully automated version further along the coast.

Beverly pulled him close and hugged him. She was starting to feel almost light-headed thinking that the nightmare might nearly be over.

'That's brilliant.'

She thought for a moment.

'Couldn't we drive the car over there?'

'I'd rather leave it here out of sight. I'll ask Kenneth to dispose of it once we've got away. If we leave it exposed by the lighthouse and someone reports it, it might alert Milton too quickly.'

Beverly nodded.

'I suppose you're right. I can't always have the easy option.'

Jones smiled at her.

'Once we're home and clear, I'll make sure you always have the soft option.'

Beverly looked at him seriously for a moment.

'Don't make promises you can't keep. I don't mind roughing it in a good cause. Is it deep enough by the lighthouse for him to be able to get his boat up to the jetty?'

Jones shook his head.

'No, he'll anchor his boat off the coast and pick us up in a motor dingy. Do you mind that? The sea might be a quite rough in a small boat.'

Beverly laughed.

'I think I can put up with a bit of sea sickness if it gets us out of the reach of Harry Milton.' She hugged him again. 'I can't believe that we're on our way.'

'Nor can I.' He looked at her. 'We need to think of a way to cele-brate.'

'What do you suggest?'

'Well, we can either watch television, or we can amuse ourselves upstairs.'

'Do you mean to take advantage of a poor helpless female?'

'Unless you can think of something better?'

She grinned and took his hand.

'The old ideas are usually the best.'

When they came down again, even the TV that they spent the rest of the morning watching didn't seem as tedious as before.

After lunch they went for what had become a regular walk through the woods. Beverly stood for a while at the edge of the cliff, arm in arm with her lover, and looked out across the bay. She was starting to feel quite attached to the view, although she would be glad to be away from it. The broad curve of the cliff followed the sweep of the bay below with the pale sand that gave the cottage its name. Looking along the cliff top to the right, the woodland came almost to the edge of the cliff and she could not see any of the three cottages she knew nestled like theirs a short distance back from the cliff edge. Beyond the cottages, the woodland thickened and spread backwards, forming a natural barrier between the village of Lower Winkley and the sea, before thinning out again as it reached the point of the cliff above the far side of the bay. Beyond that point, out of sight, the cliff fell away sharply to merge into a flat broad spit of land that jutted out like a natural pier into the sea. The old light-house, dirty white now from the weather and the spray, stood at the end of the spit of land like a long-forgotten sentry still doing its duty. The end of the spit and the lighthouse could be clearly seen from where they stood. On their side of the spit of land, poking out at the foot of the lighthouse towards their bay, was the old grey stone jetty from which they were due to be collected that evening. Beyond the lighthouse, five great jagged columns of rock called the Devil's Claw thrust up from the sea like the fingers of a massive hand lying cupped below the surface ready to drag down any unwary ships that drifted into its clutches. The new lighthouse was out of their sight, further along the coast.

Looking at the rocks, stark and hostile against the grey-green sea, white foam breaking at their bases, it was easy to see how they had got their name and to imagine an ageless, malevolent being lurking beneath the churning water.

Beverly shivered at the fancy and pulled Jones on along the cliff. Perhaps she wouldn't miss the view quite so much after all.

As usual, they saw no one on their walk and got back to the cottage cold but invigorated by the crisp country air.

When they got back indoors, Beverly rubbed her gloved hands together.

'We need to warm up.'

'And how do you suggest we do that?' Jones raised his eyebrows in mock enquiry.

Beverly grinned at him.

'You weren't short of ideas this morning.'

Laughing, arms around each other, they went upstairs.

When they came down again Jones went into the kitchen to start to prepare dinner.

'Blast, we need some more eggs, butter and milk.'

'Can't we make do?' Beverly, in jeans and a thick jumper came to the kitchen door.

'This will be our last meal here; I want it to be a good one.' He closed the door of the small refrigerator. 'I'll walk into the village; the shop should be open for a while yet. It won't take long if I cut through.'

'OK, darling, hurry back.'

He grinned.

'We're starting to sound like an old married couple already.'

He followed the short-cut through the wood to the village that came out just by the edge of the village green. He walked quickly, feeling really happy for the first time in days and he was at the shop in less than fifteen minutes.

The single village shop seemed to hold far more goods inside than the outside appearance indicated, rather like a commerce-related Tardis.

The shop's owner was a friendly widow who, as a result of her position as sole provider of sustenance apart from the pub, knew everyone in village. Although assisted by her son and his wife, she was almost always in the shop herself and she had remembered

Jones from when he had stayed at the cottage with his brother the year before. His visit to the shop earlier in the week had resulted in several minutes of conversation about his brother, the weather and village life in general. Although on this occasion he was eager to make his purchases and get back to Beverly, he liked the lady and when he saw that she was alone in the shop, he prepared himself for some necessary small talk.

Her opening words sent all thoughts of small talk, and of dinner, from his mind and a cold shaft of fear running through his body.

'Good evening Mr Jones.' She seemed surprised to see him. 'You've only just missed that friend of yours who's coming for dinner. He was in here not five minutes ago asking for directions to your brother's cottage.'

'I can see where Lower Winkley is, but how do we find the cottage?' Reggie Gray peered at the map book in front of him as if expecting the information to suddenly appear on the page.

Jack Pace spared a quick sideways glance to glare at him. They had picked up Lenny Kelly on the outskirts of the city, where he had left his car in a quiet side street, before taking the main A-road that roughly mirrored the line of the coast northwards. After forty minutes, they had left the dual carriageway and branched off on to a B-road, before turning again to follow the signpost to Lower Winkley. They were now driving along a narrow country lane bordered on both sides by a combination of woods and hedges. A number of narrow tracks led off on each side of the road, some had signs but others did not. None of the signs was for White Cove View Cottage.

'If we don't see anything,' Pace said, 'I'll drive into the village and ask for directions.'

Gray frowned.

'Is that wise? They'll be able to identify us.'

Pace's glare grew stronger. He did not like his ideas to be questioned, particularly by a goon he regarded as having the IQ of a retarded squirrel.

'If we do this properly, there won't be any evidence left that anything happened that we could be accused of. Besides – how else are we going to find the bloody place if it defeats even your map reading skills?' Even as he spoke, he knew Gray wouldn't respond to the sarcasm – he'd probably take it as a compliment.

Pace peered ahead through the windscreen. Although it had been a clear day, the sun was dipping to the horizon and the hedges and trees were throwing deep shadows across the road. 'Besides, if we don't get there soon, it'll be dark and if Beverly and her bloke try to make a run for it we could find it difficult to spot them. They know the area better than we do. Unless you've got a better idea?' Again, the sarcasm was completely wasted on Gray. Pace glanced in the mirror and saw Lenny Kelly grinning as he sprawled across the back seat. At least he had a bit more gumption.

They reached the village less than ten minutes later, having turned left on to a surprisingly broad road that twisted through a short avenue of trees before leading them past the inevitable church and pub. A number of picturesque cottages stood round the small village green. There were a few people about and the village shop was still open. Pace parked the car by the side of the green and walked across to the shop. An old man walking his dog across the grass stopped and stared at the car and its occupants with undisguised curiosity. The dog sat and looked bored. Pace turned and smiled at the man as he walked into the shop. No point in antagonizing the locals.

'Good evening, sir,' the shopkeeper stood alone behind the long, cluttered counter. 'What can I get for you?'

'I'd like some directions please.' Pace gave her his most charming smile. 'I'm an old friend of Jeffrey Jones. He's staying in White Cove View Cottage, his brother's place. He's asked me over for a meal this evening, but I've mislaid his directions and I seem to have lost my way. Do you know where it is?'

'Yes, sir. You've come a bit too far; the cottage isn't actually in the village itself.' The shop owner accepted his story without question.

'You go back up through the village to the T-junction and turn right. Then you take the fourth turning on the right. That leads straight to the cottage; there's no other property down there.'

He repeated the directions, thanked her and returned to the car.

Pace drove to the end of the green, turned the car round and went back the way they had come. The villager stopped again to watch them and even his dog seemed to be taking more of an interest.

Back on the narrow road, Pace counted the turnings on the right. The first three had signs with cottage names, the fourth did not. Pace grunted. That was promising; it suggested someone might have removed the sign to make the place more difficult to find.

The side road was little better than a track, a bumpy and narrow combination of stones, grass and mud. It sloped slightly downhill; Pace was able to keep a minimal touch on the accelerator and the evening was still light enough not to need headlights, so he could minimize any advertisement of their approach. After a short distance, they came to a flat grassy area on the left-hand side of the track. Pace pulled over on to it and turned off the engine.

'We don't want to warn them that we're coming. Come on.'

They went the rest of the way on foot, moving carefully and keeping to the side of the track, ready to dodge back out of sight when they came into view of the cottage, just in case they were spotted from a window. Pace didn't want any slip ups, he could imagine Milton's reaction if they let their quarry get past them. After twenty yards, the track turned sharply right and opened out on to the flat open area that held the cottage and ended at the edge of the cliff. The cottage stood unlit in front of them. There was a car parked at the left-hand side, which suggested both that the cottage was occupied and that they weren't expected.

Pace held them back out of sight for a moment by the turn of the track.

'Lenny, you wait here in case they try to make a break for it. You'll be able to cut them off if they run for the car. Reggie and I will go round to the other side. Reggie can watch the outside there while I go in. If I miss them, you two can get them when they come out. Remember, Harry wants the woman alive; the bloke can get the chop now if it's easier.'

'What if they overpower you?' Gray asked.

'A civilian and a woman?' Pace didn't bother to answer the question.

Leaving Kelly where he was, and keeping inside the edge of the tree and bush line, Pace and Gray moved carefully round to the other side of the cottage. There was no indication that they had been spotted by anyone inside the cottage. Leaving Gray crouched behind a bush, Pace ran quickly across the few yards of open ground to the edge of the cottage wall. There was still no response from inside. Keeping flat to the wall, and ducking under a window, he edged round to the front door, which had a glass panel at the top. He picked up a loose stone from the path and gave the window in the door a sharp tap. A piece of glass fell inside and he was able to lever out two more pieces. He had made very little noise and the cottage was still silent. He took out his gun, put his hand through the hole in the glass, turned the latch, opened the door and stepped quickly inside.

The door led straight into the living room. One glance told him it was deserted and there were no hiding places. He paused for a moment to listen and heard nothing. He glanced at the newspaper on the coffee table. It was only a couple of days old, so someone had been there recently. The living room ran the whole length of the house and there were two doors in the right-hand wall. He opened the nearest and stepped through into the kitchen. It was empty. Plates were laid on the table but there was no sign of food being prepared and the cooker was cold.

With a sudden feeling of concern twisting his stomach, he stepped back into the living room and went through the second door. That led to a small hallway and a narrow flight of stairs. He checked the cupboard under the stairs and found only dust, an old coat and a couple of pairs of muddy Wellingtons. With his concern rising, he rushed up the stairs. There were only two rooms, both leading off from a narrow landing. The bathroom door was open and it was immediately obvious that the room was empty, although the toiletries, toothbrushes and paste on the shelf over the sink were fresh. The final door was closed. He flung it open so that it banged back against the wall and stepped quickly inside. Unsurprisingly, it was the bedroom. The door of the single wardrobe hung open, a few clothes hanging inside. There was no one there. There were three suitcases, two on the floor and one on the bed. The case on the bed was open with clothes hanging out of it as if someone had been frantically searching for something at the bottom. Someone who had definitely left in a hurry.

Pace swore and went back out on to the landing. He paused and looked up at the ceiling. There was a small hatch and a ladder attached to the blank wall below it. It was just possible someone might be hiding up there. He went up the ladder and pushed open the trap, aware that his head would make a good target when he poked it through, but too annoyed to care. Before risking his head, he fumbled round with his hand and found a light switch. There was only three feet of space to the roof, so very little room for an attacker to manoeuvre. He thrust his head up through the hole, gun ready just in case. No one was laying in wait up there, just the water tank and another quantity of dust.

He went back down the ladder again and into the bedroom, his mind running through the options. Their quarry had obviously bolted. It was possible that they were coming back, but he doubted it. He checked the cases; there was no sign of the money. He was sure he had only just missed them; there was every sign of a hurried departure, otherwise they would have taken the cases and the car. Where the hell had they gone?

His professional pride was hurt and, more importantly, Milton would have his hide if they got away.

Jones stared at the shopkeeper, his brain momentarily numb with fear. Mumbling something, he turned and ran out of the shop, leaving the owner staring after him in amazement. These city folk, always in a hurry.

Once outside by the green, Jones got a grip on his panic and started to think. He took his mobile phone from his jacket pocket, fumbled for agonizing seconds to call up his directory and dialled Beverly's number. He had purchased new mobiles for them both a few days before they had run away and they had disposed of their old phones. Sean was the only outsider who had the numbers, so Beverly would know that any call was safe to answer. He had a frantic few moments before she responded.

'Hello?' Even knowing the phone was secure, her voice sounded nervous.

'It's me,' he spoke rapidly. 'Someone's just been asking directions for the cottage at the shop. It must be Milton's people. They're on their way now. You've got to get away. Don't hang around just leave. I'll meet you by the lighthouse. Keep in the cover of the woods as much as you can.'

'But how—'

'Just go, quickly.'

Beverly felt panic rising and crushed it down. She shrugged into her coat, slipped her phone into the pocket, then she ran upstairs. It was all very well saying go now, but there was one thing she wouldn't leave behind. She rushed into the bedroom, flung open the wardrobe door and pulled out the carry case that held the contents of Milton's safe. She glanced out of the window. It was starting to get dark and they'd have to hang around the lighthouse for a while. She picked up one of her cases, dumped it on the bed and pulled out some of the clothes. At the bottom was the powerful torch that she had bought the week before, anticipating that it might be useful. Then she ran downstairs again, grabbed her shoulder bag from the living-room coffee table, pulled open the front door and ran outside, pulling the door closed behind her.

There was no sign of anyone and she couldn't hear a car.

Although she didn't know it, Beverly reached the shelter of the trees and bushes just as Pace parked his car up the track and switched off the engine. She started to run through the trees, but after a minute her brain started reasoning again and she slowed down. If she tripped and fell it would be catastrophic – the last thing she needed was a twisted ankle, or worse. Also, if someone was looking for her she was likely to make more noise running and her movement would be more noticeable. She slowed down to a swift walk. She looked back once, but saw no sign of pursuit and that calmed her. As she walked, she tried to imagine what could have gone wrong. She could not believe that only that afternoon she had been standing looking across the bay, happy and anticipating her escape from Harry Milton's influence. Now she was literally fleeing for her life. She was grateful for the afternoon walks, which had given her a reasonable idea of the layout of the area.

The best way to the lighthouse on foot was to follow the line of the cliff top through the trees, past the three other cottages, before reaching the top of the cliff at the further edge of the bay. There was a path down the cliff on the far side, out of sight of the cottage. Beverly moved diagonally to her right so that she would pass across the tracks leading to the other cottages rather than passing them in the open. Once past the third track, she entered the thicker woodland that lay between the village and the cliff. There was no defined path, but there were enough gaps between the bushes to enable her to angle back to her left towards the cliff edge. She stumbled once across a rising root that was difficult to see in the gloom and she slowed a little more and trod more carefully. The strap of her case dug into her shoulder and seemed to weigh a ton, but she adjusted its position and moved on. There was no way she was leaving the money behind; it was their only hope for a decent future. She felt a little better now that she was in the final stretch of woodland. With any luck she'd come out by the edge of the wood close to the cliff edge on the other side of the point of the bay.

Beverly reached the edge of the tree-line without mishap and found herself only a few yards away from the narrow but negotiable path that ran down the side of the cliff on the far side. Even more aware of the danger – and appalling consequences – of falling, she scrambled down the path. It was a mixture of rock and scrubby grass, but the light was better outside the trees and she could see where she was going reasonably well.

The path ended at a gentle slope that led down to a patch of open land beside a rocky track that became the narrow spit of land leading to the lighthouse. This was the most dangerous part of her journey. Up until now she had been hidden from anyone looking from the cottage by the bulk of the cliff jutting out like the prow of a great ocean liner. About halfway along the spit of land, the cliff would cease to cover her and she would be in plain view of anyone standing by the cottage and looking that way. There was no cover at all and the distance seemed to grow further and more exposed the longer she looked at it.

As she stared across towards the lighthouse, Beverly saw a dark figure standing by the side of the tower that was hidden from the cottage. The figure beckoned to her. She felt a surge of relief and ran across the final thirty yards to fling herself into Jones's arms, clutching him tightly. Her heart was thumping and she felt breathless, but at least they were together again and away from immediate danger.

'Did you see anyone?' he asked anxiously.

She shook her head.

'No. Mind you, I didn't stop to look; I just grabbed the money and a torch and ran. What happened exactly?'

'The woman in the village shop said that someone had come in about five minutes before me asking directions to the cottage and saying I'd invited him to dinner. I didn't know whether she meant five minutes literally, or she just meant it was a little while before. I was scared I'd be too late and they were already there when I rang.'

Beverly shivered.

'Thank goodness they weren't. But how on earth did they find out about you?'

Jones shook his head.

'I don't know and hopefully it's not really important any more. We can lie low here until Sean comes to collect us.'

Beverly nodded.

'Do we have to stay out here though?' She shivered again and dug her hands into her coat pockets. 'That wind's icy cold.'

'We need to get inside out of sight,' Jones agreed. 'I checked the door just now, but it's securely locked. Besides, it's on the side facing the cottage. We'd be in plain view of anyone looking around from up there, so it wouldn't be a good idea to be spending time trying to force the door, even if I could manage it. There is a window about four feet from the ground on the seaward side of the lighthouse. That might be a way in.'

Jones led the way round to the window, which had six square panes of grubby glass. He took out his penknife and opened the blade. Reaching up, he tapped one of the lowest panes of glass hard with the end of his knife. The pane shattered, the noise lost in the whine of the wind. Beverly looked out to sea. There were a few ships, no more than dark smudges on the steadily darkening horizon, but nothing close enough to see what they were doing.

Jones tapped all the glass from the square, careful to leave no jagged edges he might cut his hand on. Then he reached inside and found the catch. It was stiff with misuse and awkward to turn from outside, but he eventually managed it and pulled the window open, despite the squeaky protest from the rusted hinges.

'Wait here a moment.'

He put his knife away, reached for the sill and pulled himself up. The years of dancing had given him good muscle power and he managed to lift himself on to the sill without too much difficulty. He paused, perched on the sill, and looked back at Beverly.

'Hand me the torch, please.'

She passed it up and he switched it on. There was nothing on the floor beneath the window, apart from twenty years of accumulated dust and grime, so he dropped down inside and swung the torch beam round. An old table and three chairs stood by the wall to his left and immediately opposite a flight of metal stairs led up to the next level. He crossed to the front door, but a moment's inspection told him there was no way he could force the lock from the inside. The window would have to be the way in.

Jones lifted the table across to the window and then went back to inspect the chairs. They all still looked remarkably sturdy, if very grubby. He took two over to the window, placing one by the side of the table before he climbed up and lowered the second chair out of the window to Beverly.

'Stand on that, it will be easier for you to climb through.'

The area of rock at the foot of the lighthouse was reasonably level. Beverly placed the chair against the wall and stepped on it. She handed her case to Jones and then took his hand as he helped her through on to the table.

'You're spoiling me.'

'You remembered the torch.'

He squeezed her hand. Despite the danger they were still in, just achieving the small success of breaking into the lighthouse to find shelter seemed to have rekindled the romance of their adventure. Beverly climbed down on to the second chair and then on to the floor whilst Jones lifted the outside chair back up through the window and pulled the window closed as far as he could. The rusty hinges would not completely close and the broken pane was apparent from close inspection, but at a quick glance it would not be very obvious that the window had been tampered with.

Despite the rather damp atmosphere, they were disturbing a lot of dust and Beverly started coughing.

'If we've got to be here a while, let's try to get to the top.' Jones put his arm round her and gave her a comforting squeeze. 'That will give us a better view and we should be able to see Sean coming, in case he's early.'

It would also give them a chance to see Milton's men if they approached the lighthouse, but he didn't put that depressing thought into words. He was very aware that although they were well placed to be picked up by the boat, they were also boxed into a trap with no other exits if they were cornered. Night had almost fully fallen, but the stars had already appeared in the clear sky and there was a bright full moon.

'Come on.'

He picked up the bag from the table and led the way over to the stairs. He used the torch sparingly. A little greyish light was coming in through the windows, giving some blurred shape to the rooms and their contents, but that also meant a light might be spotted from the outside. Still, it was better to risk that than to trip and fall down the stairs.

They made their way carefully up each of the flights of stairs. The lighthouse had been cleared of most items when it had been locked up and apart from a few pieces of furniture and some dusty rags and other discarded items of little use, the rooms were empty. After stopping briefly on the way to get their breath, they arrived on the floor immediately below the lamp station. Jones risked another quick circuit of the torch. There was an open (and empty) storeroom to their left and straight ahead a metal spiral staircase led up to a trap door and the platform above.

Jones went up the stairs and tried the catch. It moved more freely than the window catch and he lifted the hatch and laid it back on the floor above. The lamp level of the lighthouse consisted of the old lamp mechanism in the middle of the floor and curved glass windows all around. Beyond them, accessible through one of the windows, an open walkway followed the circumference of the building. The windows were grimy on the inside, but the outside had been kept cleaner by rain and sea spray. Jones found an old cloth and wiped an area on two or three of the windows so that they had a partial view of the spit leading to the lighthouse, the bay and the sea. He had thinned the dust to a smear rather than actually cleaned the glass, but at least they had some sort of a view.

As they stood looking down toward the land, the moon slid behind a block of cloud and night suddenly closed in. Jones looked up at the sky ruefully.

'Well, that was a good idea while it lasted.'

The cloud formed a thick wedge, but with clear sky beyond, the moon would be out again before long.

They sat on the floor, ignoring the hardness and the dirt, put their arms round each other for warmth, and settled down to wait. The wind howled round the top of the tower, but at least it was dry and the glass seemed to have kept some of its insulation. Although it was cold, they were under cover and protected from the most severe effect of the elements. It was, Jones reflected, by no means the worst position they could be in.

Fifteen minutes later, that complacency was shattered by the voice that spoke suddenly from six feet away.

'Hello, Beverly,' said Jack Pace. 'We thought we'd never find you. Harry is most anxious to see you again.'

Pace came out of the cottage, ignored Gray's puzzled enquiry, and ran to his car. He opened the glove compartment, grabbed the powerful binoculars he always kept there and raced back to the cliff top. Making sure that he kept away from the edge, so as not to be standing out against the skyline if anyone looked his way, he surveyed the woods and the bay below.

Nothing.

Fighting down the irritation that rose within him, he started again, traversing slowly along the edge of the woods, looking for a glimpse of colour or activity that shouldn't be there. As his inspection reached the far point of the cliff, there was a flash of movement just beyond that caught his eye. He focused on the old lighthouse just in time to see Beverly race across the end of the spit and disappear behind the far side. He stepped back quickly from view, lowered the binoculars and smiled thinly.

'Got you,' He muttered, under his breath.

He turned back to Gray and Kelly who were standing by the front of the cottage. Kelly had his usual half amused look and Gray was still frowning.

'Given us the slip, have they?' Kelly asked.

'Not for long.' Pace walked over to them. 'They must have heard us coming or something and made a run for it. They're in that old lighthouse over there.' He jerked his thumb over his shoulder and looked at Kelly. 'Go and get the map from the car.'

When Kelly returned with the map, they bent over it together and looked at the road layout around the village.

'We can get there easily by road.' Pace's finger stubbed out the route. 'We go back up the road towards the village, drive past the village turnoff and take that next road on the left. That takes us down to the track that leads across to the lighthouse. We can park back there off the track somewhere and go across after them.'

He looked up at the sky.

'It'll be fully dark soon and there's some cloud to cover the moon. We should be able to get near them without them spotting us.'

'Do you want us to sabotage their car in case they get past us again?' Gray asked, eager to start venting his violent feelings on something even if it was inanimate.

Pace thought for a moment.

'It's tempting, but no. If we get hold of them without too much trouble, we can bring them back here and collect their cases and stuff from the cottage. One of you can then drive their car back. If we dispose of them and their car and there's nothing at the cottage linked to them, there won't be any evidence pointing to us either.'

Gray nodded. He always admired those who could think and plan ahead better than him – which covered most of the people he came into contact with.

The three men walked back up the track to their car. Pace drove down to the cottage, turned round and went back up the track. The headlights swung across the trees and bushes, creating long shadows that swayed and danced as they passed. He retraced their route along the narrow B-road, drove past the road to the village and then took the next turning left down towards coast.

The side road was steep and twisting for a few hundred yards before levelling out. There was a clear, harsh silvery light from the moon and Pace risked switching off the headlights as he coasted round the next bend.

The old lighthouse lay before them at the end of the long spit of land. The track widened into a flat stony area and Pace pulled over on to that and parked. The only sounds were of the wind and the sea. To their right the new lighthouse sent a strong beam sweeping out across the water, giving it fluctuating silvery high-lights. There were lights further along the coast, but nothing close to them. The lights of two or three ships could be glimpsed on the horizon.

Pace nodded in satisfaction. Whatever was about to happen, there shouldn't be any witnesses – apart from those directly involved, of course. He glanced up at the sky. The area around the lighthouse was bathed in light; if anyone was watching for them they would be clearly seen. A bank of cloud was moving sedately across the night sky and would cover the moon in a few minutes. Pace decided to wait and move in under cover of the darkness that would bring. Their quarry was boxed in, but it would be better to catch them unawares and capture them without a struggle than to risk alerting them. There was nowhere for them to run, except into the sea, but there was no sense in making life unnecessarily difficult.

Once the cloud had drifted across the moon, Pace led the way along the track and on to the rocky trail that led to the lighthouse. Kelly and Gray followed without speaking. They paused by the curved wall of the tower and Pace walked to the front door. He had a small flashlight in his pocket and risked a quick inspection of the door. It showed no sign of being tampered with so they must have found another way in. He briefly considered that Beverly and Jones might have gone back inland again, but dismissed the idea. There was no point in coming all the way out there unless they were going to take shelter in the building.

His reasoning was confirmed when they reached the window and discovered the empty square. Pace got the window open without too much noise and lifted himself up over the sill. When he found the table against the window, he was certain he was right. He turned and beckoned the other two in. Kelly's tall and wiry frame easily made the journey, but they needed to help Gray, whose shoes scrabbled at the wall as he was hauled up.

Standing in the dark, they waited and listened. There was no sound other than the wind and the crash of the sea against the shore and the rocks. Pace used his torch again briefly to locate the stairs and they moved upwards carefully.

As they reached each floor, the three men checked it quickly before moving on. When they got to the floor below the lamp, a murmur of voices drifted down from above. The speech sounded soft and undisturbed; they hadn't been alerted by the raiding party from below.

Pace had already drawn his gun. He looked upwards and saw the square of paler grey in the ceiling above the spiral staircase. Slowly, careful not to make any noise on the metal steps, he walked up and through the hatchway with Kelly and Gray close behind him.

When Pace stepped out through the hatch, he saw Beverly and Jones sitting on the floor a few feet away, engrossed in each other and not looking his way. Pace stepped forward to allow the other two to come up behind him, switched on his torch to illuminate the two figures on the floor and spoke with great satisfaction.

'Hello Beverly. We thought we'd never find you. Harry is most anxious to see you again.'

While Beverly and Jones sat stiff with shock, Kelly moved quickly round the lamp to come up on the other side of them and cut off any movement they might have made in that direction. Sitting on the floor, they had no way of finding the momentum to take any action, even if they had not had two guns focused on them.

'Get up, very slowly,' Pace ordered. 'Don't try any heroics, we're quite happy to hurt you if necessary. Harry doesn't mind what condition you're in when he sees you.'

Pace and Kelly kept them covered whilst Gray carried out a body search – taking an unnecessarily long time over Beverly's. He pocketed Jones's penknife, picked up the case, Beverly's shoulder bag and the torch and moved back behind Pace.

'The money's in the case,' he reported after a moment.

'Good.' Pace nodded with satisfaction. It was all coming together nicely. Harry would be pleased. 'Right then.' He inspected the prisoners impassively. 'We're going back downstairs and out to our car. Reggie will shine the torch on you and Lenny and I will cover you with our guns. Walk nice and slowly.'

Jones gave Beverly's arm a squeeze to try to give her some comfort, although he was feeling none himself. They had been so near to getting away with it and now … If there was the ghost of a chance he'd sacrifice himself to give Beverly the opportunity to run, but at the moment, any action would just harm both of them. He felt Beverly stumble as she tried to move and put his arm round her briefly.

They walked back down the flights of stairs in the order of procession that Pace had dictated. Pace went first, walking backwards and keeping his gun trained on Beverly and Jones who followed him. Kelly came next, with his gun on their backs and Gray was at the rear, shining Beverly's powerful torch down on the whole line, but careful not to shine it in Pace's eyes.

When they reached the ground floor, Kelly went out of the window first, then the two prisoners. He kept them against the wall at gun point whilst Pace and Gray climbed out. Nobody bothered to shut the window after them.

Jones had considered making a dive for Kelly whilst the other two were still inside the lighthouse, but the gunman kept several feet away and would have had no trouble in shooting both of them before he could be reached. Whilst Jones was considering the idea, Pace dropped to the ground and even that faint opportunity had passed.

The moon was out from hiding again and the whole area was flooded in silvery light. Gray moved up to Beverly's side, put his arm round her and gripped her wrist. She tried to pull away from him in disgust and he showed her the wicked stiletto in his other hand, its silver gleam matching the moonlight.

'Just keep next to me, nice and cosy,' he smiled at her.

Jones swore and started to move towards them, but Kelly's gun dug into his side.

'Not advisable.' The pleasant Irish lilt was amused. 'You'd have a bullet in the gut before you got two feet.'

Jones stopped and glared at Kelly, which only made him smile wider.

'Off we go then,' Pace directed them with his gun. 'The car's just up the road.'

When they reached the car, Pace opened all the doors. Jones was put in the front passenger seat with Kelly behind him, his gun pressed to the back of Jones's neck. Beverly was pushed into the back next to Kelly with Gray beside her, still holding her wrist and with his knife pressed against her neck.

'Fasten your seat belt,' Kelly told Jones. 'You don't want to bump your nose if Jack has to stop suddenly do you?'

'Better not brake too sharp, then,' Gray said with a snigger. 'Don't want me to jab my knife in her accidentally, do we?'

Pace turned the car and drove up the track.

They were back at the cottage in little more than five minutes. This time, Pace drove right up and turned round, parking next to Jones's car. He took out his gun and covered Jones.

'Lenny, go in and pack the cases while we wait outside. Have a quick look round and bring out anything that looks like theirs.'

'OK, boss.' Kelly slid out of the car and disappeared round the side of the cottage. After a few moments a light came on in the living room and another upstairs.

Beverly made a little moaning noise.

'Shut up.' Pace growled.

Beverly rolled her head.

'I can't, I think I'm going to be sick.'

Pace swore.

'Not in my car, you're not.'

He opened his door and motioned Jones out. He still wasn't sure if Beverly was trying a con and, as Gray didn't have a gun, he wanted to be in a position to cover both of them if necessary.

'Take her round to the side of the path,' he told Gray. He looked at Beverly with distaste mixed with suspicion. 'And you keep it in until you get out of the car.'

Beverly, clutching her hand over her mouth, was pulled out of the car by Gray. She turned towards the bushes and Gray, understandably not wanting vomit over his trousers, stepped back and eased his grip on her wrist. That was the chance Beverly had been waiting for. She suddenly raised herself from her crouch and shoved Gray away. Off balance, he stumbled and she ran at Pace.

'Run, Jeff,' she screamed.

Pace swung his gun towards her and Jones lashed out with his hand, a lucky blow that knocked Pace's gun to the ground. In the brief moment of confusion, they ran.

They might have got away with it if they could have turned away from the cottage, but Pace and Gray were between them and the pathway, so they had to run towards the cliff. Gray recovered quickly and was running along the edge of the woodland, so they couldn't immediately go off to the right. As they rounded the edge of the cottage, Kelly was coming out, alerted by the noise. He reacted swiftly, moving to trip Beverly as she ran past. From the corner of his eye Jones saw Beverly fall and turned back to help her, walking straight into a roundhouse blow from the hand in which Kelly held his gun. The gun butt smacked into Jones's temple and he went down in a boneless heap and lay motionless. Beverly cried out and, as she scrambled to her feet, Gray grabbed her wrist again, twisting it painfully up behind her back.

'You crafty little bitch.' He was spitting the words with anger. 'I hope Harry gives you to me after he's done with you so I can finish you off. We'll have some real fun, you and I, and you won't be faking sickness.'

Pace raised his recovered gun, glaring at Beverly. She had nearly fooled him and if she'd got away Harry would have taken it out on him. Pace looked round. They were only a few feet from the edge of the cliff. Harry wanted her taken in alive but he hadn't said the same about the boyfriend. Pace looked down at Jones, then across at Beverly. He gave her a nasty smile.

'Change of plan,' he said. 'We'll just take her gear with us. We leave his stuff and the car here. It'll look like he was staying here on his own and had a nasty accident.'

He turned to Kelly.

'Throw him over the cliff.'

'No!' Beverly twisted helplessly in Gray's grasp as Kelly nodded and moved over towards Jones.

Gray chuckled, and with that laugh something seemed to snap inside Beverly's reason and create an almost insane animal ferocity. She swung up her free hand and scraped her long nails down Gray's cheek. Gray cried out at the sudden shock and pain, dropped his knife and lifted his hand to his face, relaxing his grip on her wrist. Beverly twisted towards him and, her eyes alight with hatred, drove her knee as hard as she could between his legs. Gray gave a strangled gasp, his hands dropping to clutch at the affected area. His legs wobbled as he twisted round and bent over, partly in agony and partly to avoid a second attack in the same place. Instead, he presented Beverly with another prime target. She kicked out, all her frustration, rage and hatred of Milton and all he stood for boiling over into the strike. Gray, his legs already like jelly, sprawled forward. His head clipped the side of a coffee-table-sized piece of rock by the cliff edge and he slumped to the ground unconscious.

Pace was reacting almost as wildly and instinctively as Beverly. He came up behind her and swung his gun hand viciously at her head, moderating the blow slightly at the last moment as he remembered that Milton wanted her alive. It still felt to her as if the side of her head had exploded and she fell sideways on to the rock-strewn grass. As Beverly lay barely conscious, she heard Pace's voice, hard edged with suppressed anger.

'Don't just stand there, Kelly, throw the bastard over.'

TWELVE

ALEC TANNER WAS feeling frustrated.

By the time Kenneth Jones had given them directions to his cottage and they had got down to the car, the cholesterol of the rush hour was severely clogging the transport arteries of the city. They found themselves in a line of solid traffic. It took five minutes to reach the end of the street. They could have walked it in less, he thought disgustedly. If he had been James Bond, he could have swung out of the line of cars and driven along the pavement, miraculously avoiding injuring any pedestrians, although demolishing at least two barrowloads of fruit and vegetables, before screaming down a narrow alley on two wheels and launching the car off the quayside into the river, flicking a switch to turn the car into an amphibious vehicle in mid air so that they could zoom off up river through uncongested waters. As it was, they just had to sit and wait it out, hoping that anyone sent by Milton would be stuck in the same traffic jam that they were.

Julie spent the time checking the map for their route. Tanner spent the time tapping the steering wheel in annoyance and muttering 'come on' under his breath. Julie, he accepted, was the more productive.

'We want the city ring road, then the A777 north, then there's a B-road. Lower Winkley should be signposted when we get near it, so we can start looking out for the turning to the cottage.'

Tanner nodded. The one thing in their favour was that Jones's cottage was not easy to find without detailed directions. With any luck anyone else looking for the cottage would get lost and waste time driving round. He had plenty of experience of the country lanes in the area north of the city and he knew how confusing they could be, particularly after dark. One narrow road bordered by tall hedges and woods looks much like any other.

After considerable cursing from Tanner and hooting from other drivers, they eventually got through the centre. Tanner felt they had inhaled enough carbon monoxide in thirty minutes to last a life-time. When they got to the roundabout that led on to the ring road, they found that three cars had had a minor accident. It didn't look as though there were any serious injuries, but the police and ambu-lance services were on the scene and there was the usual crawl of other traffic going past so that the drivers could absorb every detail of the scene.

Once on to the ring road, Tanner could speed up and the A777 was moderately clear. There was a commuter belt north of the city, but the A-road had been widened to three lanes a few years before and that helped things along. The sun had set and darkness closed in once they were away from the immediate sphere of the city's civilizing influence. As always, the planners seemed to have considered that most roads beyond residential areas do not require lighting, no matter how busy they are. Still, at least they were moving.

Julie was settled back in her seat. She had unzipped her jacket in the warmth of the car and had the map book perched on her knees. Tanner was jealous.

'This next bit should be plain sailing.' Julie was tracing her finger along the open page of the book.

'Wash your mouth out, young lady, haven't you ever heard of Sod's Law?'

She flashed him a grin in the darkness.

'I got my Girl Guide badge for map reading. I'll tell you when we're near the turn-off.'

For once, Sod's Law didn't apply and they reached the B-road without any more delay. There was little local traffic about and after ten minutes of steady driving, their headlights carving a steady glow through the darkness, the sign for Lower Winkley gleamed white in the lights.

Once on to the narrow meandering road that led towards the village, Tanner slowed down a little, partly so as not to lose their direction and partly in case they met anything coming the other way. If they did, someone was going to have to travel in reverse for some distance.

A sign on the right indicated that Upper Winkley lay in that direction.

'There we are,' said Julie, sitting forward, 'the cottage is down the next but one turning on the left.'

'OK.'

Tanner glanced to their right. They were passing an area of open woodland that ran level with the road, with trees and bushes dotted around randomly. He slowed right down and drove off the road into the woodland. The car bumped a little over the rough ground and Tanner stopped with a couple of trees between them and the road. He switched off the lights and the engine. Darkness drifted in around them, diffused by the glow from the moon. There was the faint sound of a car engine ahead of them, but it was impossible to tell the exact direction and distance.

'From what Kenneth Jones told us, the track to the cottage is pretty narrow. If Milton's men are around, we don't want to meet them head on. They've no doubt got guns, which would put us at considerable disadvantage. I suggest we walk from here.'

Julie nodded.

'Good job I also got my Girl Guide badge for woodcraft.'

They got out of the car and walked to the edge of the road. They were both wearing black jeans and jackets, so there was little chance of their being spotted from any distance. Tanner had a heavy torch and he knew that Julie had her shoulder bag, which no doubt contained one or two useful articles. Tanner didn't want to risk the torch except in an emergency in case Milton's people were about. Although, he thought, blending into the darkness as they did, until they reached the turn off to the cottage they were probably more at risk from a car being driven too fast down the narrow road.

Now that the car's headlights were off, their night vision improved, helped considerably by a reasonable amount of light from the full moon. They moved along by the trees until they reached a point where the road bent round to the left before straightening again. As anticipated, there was a narrow track leading off to the left just ahead of them.

'I hope you are impressed by my intrepid navigational skills,' Julie murmured.

'I'll buy you a new woggle when we get back.'

Tanner saw a brief glimpse of a smile before they moved forward and down the track, treading carefully and watchful of the area ahead in case they met any of the opposition coming the other way. The moonlight was still strong enough that he didn't need to use his torch to avoid their bumping into trees, although they needed to be wary that they didn't trip over any ground level hazards.

They reached a bend in the track and could see a light ahead standing out in the darkness, sharper than the moonlight. Moving forward they saw the cottage, framed against the sky. There were lights on upstairs and down. Two cars were parked outside, apparently both empty. Tanner touched Julie's arm and motioned to the right. They moved forward again slowly, keeping close to the fringe of trees and bushes on that side. There was no sign of anyone standing at either of the lighted windows, and the light would destroy their night vision anyway, but two cars suggested that Milton and/or his minions had located their quarry and there could be people lurking in the bushes.

Suddenly a shout echoed from the other side of the cottage and there was the sound of struggling and curses. Ignoring the cautious approach, Tanner and Julie ran forward and stopped by the side of the cottage, looking round it towards the edge of the cliff.

They were just in time to see Beverly Wallace launch her kick into Reggie Gray's backside, causing him to lose his head-butting contest with a nearby lump of rock, followed by Jack Pace knocking Beverly to the ground and turning to the lean man who stood a short distance away.

'Don't just stand there, Kelly, throw the bastard over.'

Tanner and Julie decided it was time for them to get involved.

'I'll take Kelly,' Julie muttered and moved forward.

There was no time to argue. Besides, Pace was armed and Kelly's hands seemed to be empty, so Tanner was happy to tackle the bigger man, particularly as Pace didn't know he was there yet.

The ignorance didn't last long. Tanner swung his torch down on the wrist of Pace's gun hand and he dropped the weapon with a cry of pain. From the corner of his eye, Tanner saw Kelly look up and then he had his own problems as Julie launched a flying kick at him. After that, Tanner had to concentrate on his own battle.

Pace recovered from the pain and shock remarkably fast. Tanner aimed a punch at the hinge of the big man's jaw that should have ended matters, but Pace managed to evade it and get in a punch of his own that, even though he turned away from it, hit Tanner in the chest with enough force to send him sprawling.

Tanner started up again quickly. There was no way he could afford to give Pace time to look round for his gun or weigh in with his feet whilst he was on the floor. Pace tried a follow up kick, but Tanner rolled clear and caught the raised foot in his hands, lifting and twisting as he came up off the ground.

It wasn't a particularly elegant effort, but Pace was very conscious of the edge of the cliff and tried to fall inland as much as possible. Tanner moved in to finish things off, but Pace managed to trip him up, and a moment later Tanner was on his back with Pace on top of him. As Pace was both stronger and heavier, that was not good news.

Fortunately, Tanner had learnt a lot of his fighting skills from his uncle, topped off by instruction from Ted Manning, and both his mentors were of the opinion that fighting dirty was far more acceptable than losing.

Risking a small earthquake around the Marquis of Queensbury's grave, Tanner twisted Pace's ears and, as he pulled back, Tanner was able to heave himself up a little and head butt his opponent. Tanner thought it probably hurt him as much as it did Pace, but it gave him the opportunity to roll out from under. As Pace got to his knees, half blinded, Tanner kidney punched him and that exposed the thick neck for the finishing strike.

Tanner considered kicking Pace while he was down, but it didn't seem necessary, so instead he looked round anxiously to see how Julie was doing.

Kelly was laid out on the ground unconscious and Julie stood over him looking as calm and poised as ever, in contrast to Tanner's gasping breaths.

She gave him a salute.

'Mine weighed more than yours,' Tanner said, when he'd got enough breath back.

Julie grinned and knelt down to take a look at the crumpled form next to Kelly.

Tanner turned to the woman he assumed was Beverly Wallace, who was kneeling up, still dazed, but looking at him with a mixture of hope and fear. He spotted Pace's gun a few feet away, picked it up and gave her what he hoped was a reassuring smile.

'Beverly Wallace?'

She nodded.

'I'm Alec Tanner and the attractive young Amazon over there is Julie Cooper. Your sister asked us to come and help you.'

'Sandi sent you?' The dazed look was starting to fade.

'Yes; she thought Milton had found out where you were hiding.' Tanner glanced around the battlefield. 'It looks like she was right.'

'How is Jeffrey?' Beverly had managed to get to her feet and walked unsteadily across to Julie.

'He'll be OK; he's starting to come round.'

Tanner looked down at Pace. He was still sleeping, but that desirable state might not last long.

'We need to get Pace and his mates tucked away somewhere before they wake up. Is there anywhere in the cottage we can put them?'

Beverly shook her head.

'I don't think so.'

'How about a strong, lockable cupboard?' Julie asked.

'There's the cupboard under the stairs, but I don't think it's got a lock on it.'

'That might do.'

Five minutes later they had transported Pace, Gray and Kelly, all still unconscious, into the house and dumped them in the cupboard under the stairs. A line of blood ran down the side of Gray's face, but his skull seemed intact and he was starting to mutter. There was just enough room in the cupboard for the three of them, provided they were good friends and didn't get cramp. Tanner and Julie brought the kitchen table through into the narrow hallway, turned it on its side and jammed one end against the cupboard door and the other against the opposite wall. The panel in the centre of the door was thinner than the outside, but the table edge was across the middle and they lodged two of the kitchen chairs in between the door, the table legs and wall so that they couldn't be shifted very easily. The three men certainly couldn't get out without making a lot of noise, providing plenty of reaction time. Tanner had emptied their prisoners' pockets and taken their guns and Gray's knife, so he thought the arrangement was good enough, at least in the short term.

By the time they finished incarcerating Milton's men, Jeffrey Jones had recovered consciousness. Beverly had helped him into the living room and she sat beside him on the settee, dabbing at the side of his head with a damp cloth she had found in the kitchen. They were both complaining of blinding headaches – which was not surprising, Tanner thought, considering they had both been hit on the head with the blunt end of a gun. Beverly had some aspirin in her shoulder bag. Tanner fetched some water for them to swallow two tablets each and Julie followed him out of the kitchen with mugs of strong tea.

Beverly took a sip of her tea and seemed to revive a little more. She looked at her watch, put her mug down on the coffee table and started to get up.

'We've got to get back to the old lighthouse; we're being picked up by boat in less than an hour.'

'You're not going anywhere for a moment,' Tanner said firmly. 'You need to finish your tea and give the aspirin a chance to work. And we need to have a talk.'

'But ...' Beverly subsided back on to the settee and looked at Jones in concern.

'We need some information from you,' Tanner said. 'I think you owe us that much at least.'

Beverly seemed disposed to argue, but Jones put his hand on her arm.

'He's right, darling. Let's just answer the questions, the sooner we do that, the sooner we can get going.'

He looked at Tanner for a nod of confirmation and Tanner gave it to him. In fact, he wasn't quite sure yet what they were going to do with the two runaways, but there was no sense telling them that before he got the information he wanted.

'Why is Milton so keen to get hold of you?' Tanner asked. 'Surely he hasn't sent his main man after you just in a fit of jealous rage?'

Beverly hesitated and looked at Jones again.

'We'd better tell them everything.' Jones told her. He looked across at Tanner, his eyes tired and his face drawn. Tanner got the impression he was still a little bewildered and close to giving up. He supposed that coming within seconds of being chucked over a cliff could do that to you. 'Beverly emptied Milton's safe as well,' he said.

'Yes,' Tanner nodded, 'that would do it.'

'It's our stake money,' Beverly put in quickly. 'I earned it, putting up with him for two years.'

'Where is it?' Tanner asked.

Beverly didn't reply, but Jones clearly wanted the questioning over and was too exhausted to play games. Tanner nearly felt guilty at taking advantage of his weakened state, not that it would stop him doing so.

'It's in a carry case in the boot of Pace's car.'

Tanner took Pace's keys from the side table where he'd put them, went out to the car and came back with the case. He unzipped the top and lifted the contents out on to the coffee table. Tanner studied the collection for a moment before returning the cash to the case and putting it on the sofa next to Beverly.

'I suppose you think that's a reasonable payment for saving us.' There was a thread of contempt in Beverly's voice as she viewed the items left on the table.

'That's not the payment,' Tanner told her. 'That lot is being handed over to the police. The figure and the diamonds could well be stolen property and there are enough drugs on the streets already without adding to them. No, our price for helping you is something different.'

He paused. There were bumping noises coming from outside the room.

'Sounds like our prisoners are getting restless,' Julie said.

Tanner got up and went out into the hallway.

'Shut up and keep quiet in there,' he said.

There was a pause and then a gruff voice snarled through the woodwork, 'Let us out, now.' It was not the tone of one used to being disobeyed. Tanner assumed it belonged to Jack Pace.

'No.'

There was another thump against the door.

'We can't breathe in here.' That was a different voice, less assured and more plaintive. Tanner guessed it meant that Gray had woken up completely now.

'If you want ventilation, I can always put a couple of bullet holes in the door,' Tanner told them. 'Of course there's no guarantee where the bullets will go.'

There was silence. He guessed they'd decided there was enough air after all.

Tanner went back into the other room. Julie's eyes crinkled at him.

'Way to go, tough guy.'

'I hope they do suffocate.' Beverly spoke with some force. She looked across at Tanner. 'So what is your price for helping us?' The fact that Tanner had threatened Pace and his colleagues seemed to make her more disposed to co-operate.

'Do the names Jethro Harper and Kevin Winston mean anything to you?' Tanner asked.

She looked surprised at the change of tack.

'Sure, they work for Harry – at least, they used to.'

'What do you know about them?'

'Not a lot. They joined the organization sometime last year, just a couple of gofers, I think. Jethro was a weirdo, but I liked Kevin, he was cute.'

From what they had heard about Harper and Winston, 'cute' was not a description that sprang immediately to Tanner's mind, but he supposed that was the feminine perspective.

'They came to Harry's house a few times and I used to talk to Kevin a bit. Sometimes I was just hanging around and it got boring, so I chatted to the help. Harry didn't mind so long as we didn't talk shop.'

'Have you seen them lately?'

She thought for a moment.

'Not for a few weeks. I heard that they'd moved on elsewhere. That was just a rumour, though; it doesn't pay to be curious about Harry Milton's business affairs.'

'Do you know how we could find them?' Julie asked her.

'I didn't really talk to Jethro. I think someone said that he lived with his mum. Kevin has a girlfriend.' She frowned in thought. 'Her name is Connie, Connie Preston and she lives on the Yarrow Estate – I don't know exactly where. Reading between the lines, I think she's a hooker and it sounded as though she likes a good time, but he used to talk about her as if he cared, you know? I suppose she might know where he is.'

'Thanks.'

It was a lead, at any rate, better than nothing.

'What's the significance of the figurine?' Tanner asked.

'Harry collects them, and paintings. There are a number round the house, but he has a special collection locked away in a room on the top floor. He's the only one with a key and no one else is allowed in there. The rumour is that the stuff in there is all stolen and he enjoys gloating over it. Maybe that was meant for the stolen collection.'

'So why was it in the safe?'

She shrugged.

'Perhaps he only got it that day and hadn't had time to put it in the room.'

Tanner nodded; it was a reasonable assumption. That could give them a hook into Milton's affairs, although he couldn't see immediately how it might work.

'There's nothing else you remember about Harper and Winston?' Julie asked. 'Nothing else he told you? It could be important.'

Beverly seemed genuinely anxious to help them now. There's nothing like threatening someone's enemies to get into their good books, Tanner thought. She looked quite disappointed as she shook her head.

'No, I'm sorry.' Her face was strained and she sounded near to collapse; she seemed very young and vulnerable as she sat on the settee holding Jones's hand.

Tanner looked across at Julie and raised his eyebrows. Julie shrugged her shoulders.

'You're the boss,' she said. 'It's your call.'

Tanner thought for a moment.

'I take it the other car out there is yours?'

Jones nodded.

'Yes, the Volvo.'

'And you know the way to the lighthouse by road?'

'Yes.' Hope glimmered in his voice and Beverly suddenly perked up.

'I have to tell you,' Tanner said in his most formal voice, 'that in my opinion it is your duty to stay and give the police the information they need in order to prosecute Pace and Milton.'

Tanner knew perfectly well there was no way they'd agree to that, but at least he wouldn't have to lie to Mariner – not too much, anyway.

Beverly looked at Tanner as if he'd suggested they all go outside and jump off the edge of the cliff. He thought she probably considered the end result would have been the same.

'No way,' she said. 'I'm not giving evidence against them. Besides, we'd never survive long enough to get into court. Harry's got contacts everywhere.'

'Police protection …'

She gave him a look.

Tanner nodded. 'OK, then. I've said my piece. We can't stop you leaving if that's want you want to do.'

They both got up with alacrity. The aspirin seemed to be working.

'As soon as you drive away, I shall be phoning the police and I'll tell them exactly what's happened,' Tanner said. 'I'm sure they'll want to interview you, so if your friend's late picking you up, the police will probably do it instead. If he's on time, I expect you'll be out at sea before they get here.'

Jones nodded.

'Thank you, for everything.'

They collected their cases and Julie and Tanner sat looking at each other without expression until they heard the car start up. Headlights swung past the window and the car bumped off up the track.

'You old romantic softy, you,' Julie smiled at him.

Tanner pulled a face as he took his mobile phone from his jacket pocket.

'Let's hope Ancient shares your opinion. I think it's time we roused him from his comfy armchair.'

THIRTEEN

MARINER WAS, PREDICTABLY, not best pleased. He arrived shortly after ten o'clock, having the advantage of a police siren to ease his way, and brought with him a police van and four officers. Julie had gone to collect Tanner's car while they were waiting and the front of the cottage was starting to resemble a car-park.

Pace, Gray and Kelly had been evicted from their cupboard and placed in the police van, where they were receiving rudimentary first aid. None of them seemed unduly damaged by their imprisonment and they said nothing when they were taken outside. The looks they gave Julie and Tanner made any verbal comments superfluous.

Mariner sat with Julie and Tanner in the living room. His sergeant sat to one side taking notes and Mariner was staring down at the items on the table. Julie and Tanner had taken Beverly and Jones's position on the settee.

'So you just let them walk away,' Mariner said for about the third time.

'Drive away actually,' Tanner corrected him. 'I didn't think we had any right to detain them. Besides, we'd run out of cell space. We didn't want to add to the prison overcrowding statistics.'

Mariner wasn't amused.

'That didn't stop you dealing with Jack Pace and his pals.'

'That was different,' Julie put in, looking wide eyed and innocent. 'We were frightened of them.'

Mariner snorted.

'It looks like it. With any luck, they'll sue you for assault and false imprisonment.' He seemed to relish the idea.

'I don't think that's very likely,' Tanner said. 'Apart from the fact that Milton won't want the publicity, we have Sandi Wallace and Kenneth Jones to call on in our defence. Besides, those weapons on the table will have their fingerprints on them.'

'Anyway,' Julie said,' we had no real grounds for holding Beverly and Jeffrey. Milton isn't likely to admit to being robbed, is he? So what evidence is there of any crime committed by them?'

Mariner grunted again.

'You mean apart from a small fortune in heroin, an assortment of deadly weapons and some possibly stolen property?'

Julie and Tanner looked at him in silence.

He sighed.

'You're quite right, of course. I don't suppose we'll even get very far with a case against Pace and co. With Beverly Wallace and Jeffrey Jones gone and not available to press charges of assault and kidnap we have very little evidence that would actually stand up in court. Milton's solicitor will have his soldiers back on the street in five minutes; in fact his pet poodle could probably do it in less than ten.' He sounded disgusted.

'Meanwhile, we have a clue,' Tanner pointed out.

'So it was all worthwhile, then?'

'Come off it, Ancient, we've undoubtedly saved two lives, you've got some drugs off the street and some stolen goods to return and Milton is, at the very least, severely embarrassed. You've also got the chance to give three of Milton's men a night in the cells before his brief springs them. Not a bad night's work. You might even make the firearms offences stick.'

'They'll probably suggest you planted their fingerprints on the weapons after you'd knocked them out.' Mariner grinned suddenly. 'Still, as you say, it's better than a couple of murders. And Milton losing face with the criminal fraternity won't be unhelpful.'

'Is Bridger likely to make things tough for Sandi Wallace?' Julie asked.

Mariner shook his head.

'That's one bit of good news. We got a statement from the owner of the sex shop and a neighbour has come forward who might have seen the abduction of his friend. Bridger's going to have enough to worry about without going after Sandi Wallace. Particularly as he knows if anything happens to her, we'll be breathing down his neck for it. The same goes for Milton. I shall make very sure Pace and his friends get that message before they're released.'

'You could let them know, in passing, that we got the details of the cottage from Jones's brother and not from Sandi, so she wasn't holding out on them in that respect,' Julie suggested.

Mariner nodded and looked across at his sergeant.

'Have you got enough to type out their statements, Bob?'

'Yes, sir.'

Mariner got to his feet.

'Let's call it a night, then.' He looked at Julie and Tanner. 'Come in sometime tomorrow and sign them.' A thought occurred to him. 'We'd better let Jones know his brother's safe.'

'I called him while we were waiting,' Tanner said. 'And Julie spoke to Sandi.'

'Good.'

They followed him out to the cars, leaving the cottage locked up as best they could. Kenneth Jones had told Tanner that he would drive up the next day to secure the cottage and pick up his brother's car.

As they watched the police van drive away Mariner paused and looked at Tanner and Julie across the roof of his car.

'You've annoyed some very nasty people,' he said. 'Watch out for yourselves.'

'Don't worry,' Tanner told him, 'we'll be very careful.'

They slept in late the next morning and it was nearly ten before Tanner and Julie were ready to leave her flat. Tanner had spoken to Danny Worenski at the office an hour earlier and he had rung back twenty minutes later with Connie Preston's full address. Tanner didn't ask how the information had been obtained. After all, he thought, sleeping with a policewoman carried some responsibilities.

The phone rang again shortly after Danny's message. Tanner thought it might be Worenski with some further information, so he answered the call. In fact, it was Mariner to tell them that Milton's solicitor had got Pace and the others released. Preliminary discussions with his superintendent also suggested that they would be unlikely to pursue charges against the three men unless further evidence or more eager witnesses came to light.

'I did get him to agree,' Mariner went on, 'that the position will be reviewed if Pace and co try to play silly buggers and claim assault against you and Julie.'

'I take it "silly buggers" is a technical legal expression?'

'Yes. Mind you, their solicitor indicated that if we did nothing, they wouldn't either, so it looks like they want to call it quits.'

'Forgive and forget?'

'I think that would be putting it too strongly,' Mariner said drily. 'You still need to watch your backs.'

'Yes. Thanks for letting us know.'

'In the light of this, there's no rush for you to sign your statements, though I'd like to have them on record, they might come in useful.'

Tanner promised they'd call in when they could and rang off.

He hadn't expected much else, but it would have been nice if they could have kept at least one of Milton's minions in a cell for a little longer.

Ten minutes later, they were ready to go. Julie had just picked up her shoulder bag and they had reached the front door when the telephone rang again. Julie pulled a 'what now' face and walked across to answer it.

'Oh, Hi Laura. Yes, we're making progress, we think we might have a lead on one of the shooters – a guy called Kevin Winston.' She paused. 'No, we haven't located him yet, but we've found out that he has a girlfriend and we're on our way to see her. You just caught us.' She listened for a moment. 'Thank you, I'll ask him.' She moved the phone away from her ear and looked across at Alec. 'It's Laura. She'd like us to go to dinner again this evening. I think they're rather enjoying getting first hand information about crime.'

Tanner nodded.

'That's fine by me.'

Julie spoke back into the phone.

'Yes, we'll both be there. Seven-thirty. See you.' She hung up. 'Let's see if we can make it through the door this time.'

*

The Yarrow Housing Estate was named after a Cromwellian Commander who had defeated the Royalists on that very spot in a significant and very bloody battle midway through the Civil War. According to some sources, bloody civil war was still raging on the site, with guns and knives superseding muskets and pikes and various illicit substances instead of the dream of republicanism. The estate consisted of five high-rise blocks that, as they arrived, soared against the grey, rain-swollen clouds; huge ugly grey dominoes crying out for someone to flick them over with a celestial finger. Connie Preston lived in the West block, the towers being named, rather unoriginally, after the points of the compass – the fifth block being called Central.

Tanner parked just beyond a small muddy rectangle of grass containing two upturned shopping trolleys and, he suspected, several needles that had never been near a ball of wool. A frame for swings – minus the swings themselves – and a forlorn seesaw stood at one end, enclosed by rusting railings with a gap where the gate should be. Tanner's ancient car fitted in nicely with the others parked there. He had decided long before that as he was never sure where he was going to be leaving it unattended, a tatty vehicle which looked as though it had only just scraped through its MOT was more likely to still be there without further damage when he returned.

Running alongside the parking area in front of the flats was a wide slip road and beyond that the Yarrow Road, a three-lane highway leading to the Yarrow Roundabout. Tanner assumed that the planners must have been running out of names when they reached the area. The roundabout was a junction on the ring road and one of the major transport routes into and out of the city.

Connie Preston lived on the fifth floor of her block. There were two lifts, but as neither seemed to be working, they took the stairs. By the time they reached their destination, Tanner, deciding that there was only so much of the aroma of stale urine that you can stand to inhale, was very glad they were going to the fifth and not the twenty-fifth floor. Flat 54 had a blue door that was accessed by way of a graffiti-covered concrete walkway that overlooked the Yarrow Road and was open to the elements from the waist up.

Julie rang the bell. According to Beverly, Connie was a lady of the night in both senses of the phrase, so whether she had been earning or partying the night before, she should at least be at home at eleven o'clock in the morning and hopefully not too comatose.

At the third ring, the door was opened and a young woman with tousled blonde hair around a heart-shaped face peered out at them as if her pale-blue eyes were having trouble focusing. She was wearing tight white trousers, a very tight sleeveless pink top with the motto 'two of a kind' and, rather incongruously, bunny slippers.

'Yeah?' Her voice was thick with sleep or alcohol, or, probably, both.

'Hi, I'm Julie Cooper and this is Alec Tanner. We're trying to find Kevin Winston and thought you might know where he is.' They had dressed for their visit in jeans, T-shirts and scruffy jackets and hoped they looked suitably like people who might want to offer Winston a job.

'Who sent you?'

'A guy called Jake Reaper; he's a friend of Jethro Harper.' They had decided that making up a fictitious friend of Harper's was less likely to be challenged than using a real person, or claiming friendship with Winston directly, which might have made her suspicious. As it turned out, it was a wasted strategy since she accepted them without question. 'We haven't seen Jethro lately, either,' Julie added.

'They've gone away.' Connie stood leaning her head against the edge of the open door, showing no inclination to invite them in, but equally none to slam the door in their faces.

'Do you know how we can get in touch with Kevin?'

She shook her head and winced slightly. Julie assumed that the fuzziness was hangover rather than sleep induced.

'No, Kevin just said that he might need to get away for a while and a couple of days later he blew. I haven't heard from him since.'

'When was this?'

'I dunno, about six weeks ago, maybe.' She paused and decided to trust them with her opinion. 'If you ask me, he isn't coming back.' She didn't appear exactly devastated by the prospect, Julie thought, it sounded like Winston was the caring half of the relationship.

'What makes you say that?'

'He was always talking about going down to London; he said it's where the big money is. I expect he's there now, shacked up with someone else. Bastard.' She spoke without heat. 'At least I can sell his stuff.'

'He left some things when he went?'

'A few clothes, stuff like that.'

'You didn't know he was going, then?'

'He had a job on and said he might have to lie low for a while afterwards. Maybe he had to nip off a bit sharpish.' She tapped her nose and nearly missed.

'Can you think of anyone else we could ask? We've got a bit of business to put his way; there should be some useful money in it.' Julie thought she had better reintroduce the criminal element before Connie wondered why they were so curious about Winston's previous activities.

She shrugged.

'Jethro's his only real friend. You know they both worked for Harry Milton?' They nodded. 'I suppose you could ask him, but Kevin says he isn't too keen on people asking questions, so I wouldn't recommend it. Sorry I can't help any more.'

She obviously considered the matter closed. With a brief dip of the head, she closed her door.

'We must have caught her on a good day,' Tanner remarked, as they walked back towards the stairs. 'Winston and Harper disappeared around the time of the shooting and they definitely worked for Milton. It'll be well worth following them up.'

'We still don't have any real lead on where they are now, though.'

'No.' Tanner scrunched his brow. 'We might have to transfer our attention to London, or at least ask Ancient to get his colleagues down there to make enquiries. Ted has some people there he can talk to as well.'

'I've got some good contacts in London too, don't forget,' Julie reminded him. 'I'd rather stay up here and concentrate on Milton, though. If he did take the job, we need to find a way of linking him with Jarrow.'

They came out through the double doors at the bottom of the flats. Tanner decided that going down the stairs was considerably easier than going up. Apart from anything else, they didn't need to breathe so deeply. The edges of the doors scraped on the chipped concrete path as they pushed them open and walked across the pavement towards their car. Tanner saw a movement out of the corner of his eye. A car was racing along the slip road towards them. He caught a glimpse of a pale face in the back seat, an open window and the shape of a gun barrel and reacted instinctively.

Tanner shoved Julie to the ground and sprawled on top of her as bullets struck the building, the path and the cars in front of them.

As the car raced past, heading for the main road, Tanner felt a blow on one leg and a sharp pain over his right eye. He put his hand up to his face and it came away sticky with blood. He rolled off Julie and looked down. There was blood seeping on to his jeans as well and pain stabbed through his leg.

Julie leaned over him, her eyes wide with horror.

'Oh, my God, no, not again.'

Tanner laid his head back against the concrete and watched the grey cloud swirl dizzily above him as the pain in his leg pulsed and grew. So much for being careful.

FOURTEEN

IT WAS MID afternoon when Julie reached the antique shop. She was obviously in distress as she asked to see Laura.

'I'm afraid she is out at the moment, but Archie is in, I'll tell him you're here.' The assistant, who recognized Julie from her previous visit, looked at her with curiosity. 'Please wait there a moment.'

Archie came out from the back office, his smile of welcome fading as he saw the look on Julie's face.

'Come through, Julie.'

He followed Julie into the office and closed the door. A spread-sheet glowed on the computer screen. Archie pulled a chair across for Julie and sat in his own chair by the screen, swivelling round to face his visitor.

'What on earth has happened?' He studied Julie's face with concern. 'Laura said you thought you had tracked down the girl-friend of one of the killers.'

'Yes. We were just leaving her flat when a car drove by and they opened fire on us.'

Julie took a deep shuddering breath and Archie noticed for the first time a patch of dried blood on the front of her jeans.

'My God. Are you hurt?'

Julie shook her head.

'I'm OK, but Alec was hit. He pushed me to the ground and shielded me. He got shot in the leg and a head wound. He's going to be all right, but it was a near thing. He had mild concussion and he'll be in hospital for a few days while they sort his leg out.' She shook her head, her face twisted with self contempt. 'Anyone who gets close to me seems to get hurt.'

'Don't be silly.' Archie reached across, took her hands in his and squeezed them. They felt icy cold.

'Did you get the car number?'

Julie shook her head.

'It happened too quickly. They sped off and out of sight in the traffic.'

Archie nodded.

'Yes. It would be difficult to trace them. They could get anywhere from the Yarrow Roundabout, north, or east or back into the city.'

'The police found a car of a similar make and colour abandoned a couple of miles away, nowhere near any CCTV cameras, of course.'

'You didn't see who it was in the car?'

'No, but it isn't difficult to guess. Someone connected to Harry Milton. I can think of three potential candidates straight away.' Her voice was bitter.

'Is there anything we can do?'

'I just came to tell you about it – I didn't want to do it over the phone. I need to get home and change and then I must get back to Alec at the hospital, so I won't be able to do dinner tonight, but I'd still like to come and see you later in the evening, if you don't mind. I want to ask you and Laura to help me.'

'Of course, if we can.' Despite his offer of help, he looked surprised. 'What can we do?'

'Like I said, we are pretty sure that the man behind all this is a gangster called Harry Milton. We told you when we came to dinner before that one of his hobbies is collecting paintings and other antiques. I've come up with an idea for getting at him through his hobby, but I need you and Laura to help.'

'What exactly do you want us to do?'

'I'll explain tonight when you're both there.' Julie managed a shaky smile. 'Thank you.'

Archie squeezed her hands again.

'You know we'll both help you however we can.' He paused. 'I'm sorry; I should have offered you coffee, or something stronger. The look on your face drove everything else out of my mind. What would you like?'

Julie got up.

'Don't worry, I'm fine. I just need a shower and a change of clothes and I'll feel better. At least Alec isn't too badly hurt. I'll be with you about nine o'clock this evening, will that be all right?'

'Yes, that's fine. You can have that drink then.'

Julie nodded, her smile more normal.

'Thanks, I'll look forward to it.'

When Julie arrived at nine, Archie opened the door and welcomed her in. She looked much fresher and more relaxed than she had at the shop that afternoon. She was wearing a short leather jacket over a black satin blouse, open at the neck to reveal a thick gold chain, and a tight-fitting knee-length grey skirt that was slit up one side and just reached the tops of her high-heeled black leather boots. He thought she looked superb and said so.

'You look much more like your old self.' He kissed her cheek.

'Thank you, I feel a lot better now. Sorry for the wobbly display earlier.'

'You had good cause, by the sound of it.'

He hung up her jacket in the hall and led the way to the back room where Laura was waiting.

'It's good to see you.' Laura kissed her and studied her face anxiously. 'I take it from the look on your face and from what you said to Archie that Alec is going to be all right?'

'Yes. They've patched up his leg. He was sleeping when I left.'

'That's good.' Laura poured Julie a glass of wine. 'Sit down, dear. Have you had dinner?'

'Yes, thanks, I grabbed a takeaway after I left the hospital. Not as good as your food, of course, but I didn't feel much like eating.' She sat in one of the deep armchairs and took a sip of her drink.

Laura and Archie sat on the sofa opposite her and Laura looked at her expectantly.

'Archie said that you wanted us to help you catch this man called Harry Milton?'

'Yes. You said before that he'd brought one or two things from the shop?'

Laura nodded.

'That's right.' She looked sideways at Archie. 'We're really thrilled at the idea of being detectives, aren't we darling? What do you want us to do?'

'Milton considers himself something of an art buff and has built up a collection of paintings and other items.' As she spoke, Julie reached into her shoulder bag and brought out the box that Beverly had taken from Milton's safe. She opened it, took out the delicate porcelain figurine that lay inside and leant forward to place it on the glass-topped coffee table.

'What do you make of that?'

Laura reached for the figure and studied it carefully.

'It's a Staffordshire shepherdess. It's very rare, one of a very small number produced with that particular shade of pink colouring.' She looked at the base. 'Yes, the marks are right.'

'Do you remember it from the stolen property list?'

Laura considered.

'Yes, I think I do.'

'In a about two or three days' time, I'd like you to contact Milton and tell him that someone has offered the piece to you and told you that Milton would be an interested buyer. Your story is that you are checking to see if he is interested.'

'Where has this come from, then?' Laura laid the shepherdess back on the table.

'It was taken from Milton's safe earlier this week. We think that he had it stolen for his collection. Milton will assume that the person who stole it from him sold it on and told the buyer that he would probably want to buy it back.'

'So how does that help you?' Laura still looked puzzled.

'Assuming Milton buys it from you, we'll know that he has stolen property in his possession and the police will be able to get a search warrant for his house. We know that there are a number of other stolen items kept in a room that only Milton has access to. Once the police have found that room, they can take action against Milton and, as a part of that investigation, they can access his other records, which should lead to other things.'

Laura frowned.

'We'll do as you ask, of course, but isn't it all rather tenuous? You're assuming Milton will buy the item from us, that a judge will issue a search warrant on the strength of it and that there will be other information brought to light in the search. If one of those doesn't happen, you won't be much further forward.'

'I agree it's tenuous, but even if we just pin a possession of stolen property charge on him, it will be something. It's the best I can come up with at the moment.' Julie paused and finished her wine. 'We need to be as sneaky as he is and catch him off balance. It's no good reacting afterwards; he'll just slip through our fingers. He always plans well ahead, like this morning.'

Archie nodded.

'Yes, like being able to drive straight on to the Yarrow Road and away.'

'That's right, they—' Julie broke off and looked at him with a puzzled expression. 'I didn't think of it when you said that this afternoon, Archie, but how did you know that Winston's girlfriend lived near the Yarrow Road?'

Archie frowned.

'You told Laura when she rang you this morning.'

Julie shook her head.

'No, I didn't. I just said we were going to see the girlfriend of a man who might have been one of the killers. I didn't say where she lived.' Julie stared at him. 'If you knew where we were going,' she said, slowly, 'that means you knew about the girlfriend and where she lived and that means you knew about Kevin Winston.' She stopped again, staring at him with growing horror. 'But that would mean that you set us up to be shot at today and that you were involved in arranging for Aunt Jo and me to be shot.'

Archie was staring at her in silence, his face impassive, his normally amiable expression wiped away as if he was waiting to see what happened next.

Julie shook her head. 'But I don't understand – why should you have wanted to have me shot? Why should you care that I had broken up a drugs ring in London?'

Laura was sitting forward on the settee, looking at Julie in apparent bewilderment. Julie remained focused on Archie, working through the logic of what she was saying.

'My God.' Julie stared at him in sudden realization. 'I wasn't the target, I was the decoy.'

'What do you mean?' Laura tried to keep her voice sounding normal, but couldn't hide the nervousness she was feeling.

'The connection isn't me, it's the shop. The shooting wasn't

Jarrow getting his revenge, it was you murdering Joyce. My being there just gave you the opportunity to lay a false trail. That's why I wasn't killed, they had been told to make sure of Joyce first, which meant they were less accurate with me.'

'Very clever,' Archie said. 'But rather too late.'

As he spoke, Tilling leant forward to open a drawer at the side of the coffee table. When he sat back, he was holding a silenced gun. He pointed the weapon steadily at Julie, showing no sign of nervousness. Laura got up and, careful not to get between Julie and her husband, crossed to the door and turned the key in the lock. Archie stood up and Laura went to his side, calmer now that they were back in control of the situation.

'You are, of course quite right,' Tilling said, dipping his head in acknowledgement to Julie, who still sat looking stunned. 'Joyce was the real target. For some years we have been using the antique shops to launder money for Milton as well as providing him with a selection of stolen pieces. We worked partly through fictitious sales and partly through fencing other stolen goods to and from our less scrupulous clients.

'Your aunt knew nothing of this, but she spotted a stolen piece in the shop storerooms before we could pass it on and she was going to report it to the police. Laura played for time and said we'd got it from a reliable source and she wanted to talk to them first to get their explanation. Joyce agreed to wait, but we knew it was only a matter of time before she went to the police. Any investigation would have been fatal for us, so we had to dispose of her. Your presence made it look like a revenge attack on you.' His mouth formed a thin-lipped smile. 'You were very useful to us and we were actually rather grateful, so you weren't in any danger afterwards provided you found nothing out yourself that was a danger to us. We needed to keep in regular touch with you, of course, to keep an eye on what you were doing – which you most obligingly told us.'

He paused and looked at her reflectively.

'Once you started digging around Harry Milton, we started to get worried. Not only might you find something to suggest a connection between us, but if Harry was in danger of going down, he could well have decided to take us with him. We needed to be mutually supportive, you might say. That's why Laura tipped him off about your trip to the Yarrow Estate this morning. The attack was just to show that someone was still after you. If you had been seriously injured, it would have been a bonus, but it didn't matter too much. Now you are on our home turf, so to speak, we can deal with you much more cleanly. We can't have you running around knowing the truth, can we?'

Julie just sat looking at him, her face frozen and expressionless.

'I'll take that as a yes.' Tilling seemed to be enjoying himself. 'I won't shoot you here, unless you give us any trouble. We don't want any blood on the carpet. We'll take you off somewhere – suitably restrained, of course – and dispose of you. It will appear that Jarrow's contract was still running and the killers caught up with you again. We'll tell the police that when you got here this evening you told us that someone had contacted you to give you information about the shooting of you and your aunt. They wanted to meet in an isolated spot and would give you proof of who Jarrow had hired. As you were coming to see us anyway you suggested the common at the end of our road. A meeting by the war memorial, perhaps, a suitably isolated spot and not well lit. You were due to meet him at ten when there won't be anyone about, even the most devoted dog walkers are back indoors by then at this time of year. We'll say that you left your car here as it is only a short walk to the common. We can't drive you anywhere in your car in case we leave any unexplained DNA behind. When you don't return by eleven, we'll get worried and call the police.'

'The police will still go after Milton for it.' Julie still seemed to be in shock. She spoke in a numbed way as if slowly working out the solution to a complex puzzle.

Archie shook his head.

'Milton and Jack Pace have arranged watertight alibis for the evening. They involve some members of the police force, I understand, so even your friend Mariner won't challenge them.'

Julie frowned.

'That makes it all sound pre-planned.'

Archie nodded.

'Yes, it is. With Alec temporarily out of the picture, it seemed a good opportunity to get rid of you. I was worried about my little slip this afternoon and, as you seemed to be getting rather too close to the truth for comfort, we thought it would be a safe precaution to dispose of you this evening, even if you hadn't worked things out just now. After you're gone, we'll keep in touch with Alec, of course, offer our condolences and be suitably supportive; make sure he's kept off the right track.'

'Killing someone yourself is a bit different to hiring someone to do it.' Julie seemed to have recovered some of her poise and looked at Archie steadily.

Archie smiled.

'Don't worry, I have previous experience. I have already disposed of your aunt's killers. They only survived her by an hour or two and are currently residing down a convenient mine shaft. We couldn't let them live knowing of our involvement in the murder. Not that you will be joining them. We will be quite happy for your body to be found; after all, Jarrow will get the blame again.'

Julie looked across at Laura.

'And you'll go along with this; you backed what he did to Joyce?'

'Of course.' Laura had shed her kindly, supportive image like a snake shedding its skin and looked at Julie as though she was stupid. 'It was better than losing our lifestyle here and going to jail. No contest at all, really.'

'And of course you inherited her half of the shops.' Julie's voice was peppered with distaste.

'That really wasn't the point; we only had her killed because she was a threat to us. I meant what I said: we'll miss Joyce's contribution to the business.' Laura seemed keener to defend herself against accusations of poor business sense than of murder. 'Joyce knew nothing about the criminal side of our activities, she wouldn't have stood that for a moment had she known, that's why we had her killed. She was boringly honest,' Laura's face took on a sneering expression that made Julie want to smack her. 'All her money came from the legitimate trade, so you needn't worry, your inheritance is clean.' The sneer broadened. 'Not that you'll get a chance to spend it now.'

'And you got the gunmen from Milton?' They seemed disposed to talk for a while and Julie had no reason to hurry them on to the next phase.

'Yes. You were quite right to suspect Harper and Winston,'

Archie told her. 'They were a couple of young lads working for Milton. He didn't want your aunt going to the police, either, and was quite happy to help by providing the cannon fodder. Harper and Winston were a bit too keen on thoughtless violence and that made them rather too unpredictable for his business activities, so he felt that they were expendable. As I said, I disposed of them soon after they had completed their task.'

'That was a bit of a balls up on your part, though, mentioning the Yarrow Road this afternoon, wasn't it?' Julie decided it was time to give his self-confidence a poke.

Archie's smile hardened.

'Not at all, it was a simple misunderstanding. You told Laura that you were going to see the girlfriend of one of the killers. Laura knew who that was and she said to me that you were going to the Yarrow Estate to see Connie Preston. I assumed that you had mentioned the name and the place. Milton told us about Connie Preston; he had been keeping an eye on her in case she raised a stink about Winston's disappearance, but she swallowed the story that he had gone away to look for work. We may need to deal with her eventually, but she seems to have taken up with someone else now, so that probably won't be necessary. No one else is likely to care much when a yob like Winston disappears. When we heard where you were going, we tipped Milton off and he set up the shooting. He was starting to become rather concerned about your activities.'

'As a matter of interest, who did the shooting this morning?'

'I believe Jack Pace had the gun and someone called Kelly was driving. Harry said that they had reason to dislike you both.'

Tilling was still looking calm and amused, perfectly in control of the situation. Julie longed to wipe the smile off his face, but with the gun pointing unwaveringly at her stomach, it was not the time to do it.

'It will make it all the more plausible when you are found lying in the bushes on the common with a bullet in the back of your head. It will be assumed that there was still a contract out on you over your work on the Jarrow case. You were tricked into a meeting, overpowered and then executed.'

'If you take me along the street at gun point, you risk being seen by one of your neighbours,' Julie pointed out.

'That is precisely why we don't intend to take you out the front way. In fact, I think it's about time to leave.'

Tilling motioned with the gun for Julie to stand up.

'You will be accompanying us on a little boat trip. Laura will get your jacket – you aren't likely to have gone out on a chilly night like this without it and we want our story to look as realistic as possible, don't we?'

Julie said nothing as Laura unlocked the door, went out and returned with her jacket.

'There's nothing in the pockets,' she told her husband.

'Put it on,' Tilling told Julie. 'And don't try anything stupid. If necessary, I'm prepared to shoot you now and clear up the mess afterwards. If you behave, you'll get a nice quick death, if not I'll make it very painful.'

Julie shrugged into her jacket. There was a chance she could have flicked it in Tilling's face and unsighted him enough to go for the gun, but it was risky and she didn't know how Laura would react. The odds weren't good; it was worth waiting for them to improve.

'Bring her shoulder bag,' Tilling told his wife. 'She'd have taken that with her and we can leave it by her body.'

Tilling motioned with the gun and they went out of the living room, Laura leading, Julie next and Tilling at the rear, keeping a safe distance so that Julie couldn't swing round and go for the gun.

They went across the hall and into the kitchen. As they reached the back door, Tilling halted the short procession.

'And now,' he said, 'we just need to make sure you aren't tempted to try something when we get outside.'

He nodded to Laura. She went into the utility room at the side of the kitchen and returned with a length of cord which she used to tie Julie's wrists together behind her back.

'Right, then, I think were ready.' Taking it in turns to cover Julie with the gun, the Tillings put on old coats that were hanging in the utility room. Laura then unlocked and unbolted the kitchen door. Cold air swept into the kitchen as she opened the door and stepped outside.

Tilling gripped Julie's right arm above the elbow, and pushed the barrel of the gun into her side.

'Don't try to call out. We're well away from any of our neighbours and, as soon as I hear a sound from you, I'll use the gun. We're going to take a leisurely walk down the garden to the river. We've got a dinghy moored there next to our boat that's just got room for the three of us. It's only a short distance upstream to where the river runs through the common, so it won't take us long to get there. Don't expect anyone to be messing about on the river at this time of night, either. There will be no witnesses, I assure you.'

Julie didn't bother to respond as he tugged on her elbow and she walked out by his side on to the deep paved patio that ran the length of the rear of the house. The sky was cloudier than it had been the night before and the moonlight much more fitful. The lights were still on in the living room and kitchen, shining through the drawn curtains to illuminate the patio in a soft shadow-filled glow. There was an open balustrade along the edge of the patio, with a gap to their right where a short flight of stone steps led down to the wide lawn. Two stone pots with short, perfectly manicured palm trees stood on either side of the steps. On the far side of the terrace, the statue of an unidentifiable Greek goddess watched placidly over the proceedings.

Laura closed and locked the back door and walked down on to the paved path that led from the patio steps round to the right of the lawn and then on down towards the river. Julie glanced back up over her shoulder. The top floor of the house next door was visible above the trees and bushes that lined the edge of the garden, but the windows were dark and there was no sign of anyone watching.

The moon slid out from behind a line of cloud and spread a strong silvery light across the middle of the lawn, contrasting with the deep shadow created by the trees and bushes on each side.

'I have to say, it's a pity from your point of view that you didn't twig all this before.' Tilling seemed to feel the need to provide a running commentary as they walked along the path. 'If you had been a good enough detective to spot earlier on what I said about the Yarrow Roundabout this afternoon, we could have been in serious trouble. I was also worried that Laura was the only non-official person who knew you were going to see Winston's girlfriend this morning, so you might have realized that only we had time to arrange the ambush.'

Julie turned her head to look at him and for a moment her eyes met his. Her expression did more than simply poke at his confidence.

'I did,' she said. 'End game.'

As she spoke, she raised her right leg and drove the stiletto heel of her boot down hard along Tilling's left shin and into the top of his foot.

Tilling screamed out with the sudden shock of the sharp pain, dropped his gun and bent over, clutching at his injured leg. Laura swung round, her mouth opening in alarm as they were suddenly bathed in bright light from both sides and the garden came alive with movement.

Julie looked down at Tilling, her eyes deep pools of contempt.

'You're nicked,' she said, with considerable satisfaction.

FIFTEEN

HALF AN HOUR before Julie arrived at the Tillings' house, a small police boat, its lights having been dowsed some hundred yards back downstream, drifted gently into the bank beside the jetty at the end of their garden. A large beech tree grew close to the edge and a convenient thick branch was used to temporarily moor the boat and allow the four armed police officers, two male and two female, plus Mariner and Tanner to step ashore. Mariner gave a brief signal and the boat was untied again and allowed to float back softly into the night. There was another landing stage on the opposite bank where the boat would moor out of sight, awaiting Mariner's further orders. The dark waters of the river rippled gently in the brief passage of moonlight, chuckling against the jetty as if at some long forgotten joke.

Because Julie and Tanner had seen the garden before, they knew the layout and the small landing party had already worked out its placements, allowing them to move up the garden in silence. They reached the main lawn and split into two groups, Mariner and Tanner and one policewoman on the right and the others on the left. The fitful moonlight enabled them to keep in deep shadow and out of sight of a casual glance from the house. Occasionally, a shadow would pass across the curtained windows as someone moved round a room, but there was no indication of any alarm being raised. Halfway up the lawn they drew back even further into the shelter of the surrounding bushes and settled down to wait.

Tanner was very unhappy about Julie's plan, but she had insisted that it was the best way to confirm their suspicions, unless he could come up with anything better? Tanner couldn't. Nothing new there, then, he thought. His thoughts drifted back to earlier in the day.

After the shooting, Julie had called for an ambulance and Mariner, in that order, and had accompanied Tanner to the hospital. The bullet had gone through his leg and missed the bone. The head wound had been caused by a piece of sharp flying plastic created by one of the bullets hitting the rear nearside light of the car in front of where they were lying. They had been lucky. As Tanner had pushed Julie to the ground and fallen on top of her, they had been below the initial trajectory of the bullets. By the time the gunman had adjusted his aim, he was nearly past them and was unsighted by the parked cars. Apart from Julie having a few scrapes and bruises from the pavement and Tanner's relatively mild wounds, they were uninjured. The parked cars had suffered more than they had, although, ironically, Tanner's was undamaged.

By the time Mariner arrived at the hospital, Tanner had been treated. There was a thick bandage round his lower right leg, but he could walk on it with care. They had loaned him a walking stick and a severe young doctor who seemed barely out of short trousers was warning him that he risked splitting the stitches if he used the leg too much.

'If I can find someone to lend me a parrot, I'll audition for pantomime.'

Julie hadn't responded to Tanner's smile. She was looking worried and pensive.

'When you're ready, I'll drive you back to pick up your car,' Mariner had offered.

'We need to talk first.' Julie's eyes were narrowed and puzzled, as if she was trying to work out a riddle and the obvious answer seemed wrong.

They went out to Mariner's car, Tanner sat on the back seat with his leg up. Julie got in the front with Mariner and they half turned in their seats to include the invalid in the conversation.

'I'm sorry, but I need to ask you this. Did you mention to anyone that we were going to see Connie Preston?'

Mariner shook his head.

'No, I had no reason to.' He looked at Julie curiously and without offence.

Julie had looked across at Tanner.

'Alec, do you think we were followed this morning?'

Tanner had suddenly realized where her thoughts were leading. He would have thought of it himself, if he hadn't been shot. At least, that was his excuse.

'I'm sure we weren't.' he said positively. Knowing that Pace and his merry men had been released, he'd been particularly conscious of the need to check the surrounding traffic regularly.

Julie nodded.

'That's what I was afraid you'd say.' She had looked away from Tanner and stared out of the side window, her face hurt and bewildered. 'There's only one person who knew where we'd be and who could have set us up to be shot – Laura Tilling.'

Tanner had frowned.

'Laura admitted that she does business with Milton, so there's a connection there. But you didn't mention Connie Preston by name, or where she lived. Why should—' He had broken off at the look on Julie's face.

'It's more than just a connection; it raises a whole load of questions. I know it sounds bizarre and I don't know all the answers yet, but there's one way to find them out.' Her voice was grim as she set out her plan.

'But …' Tanner began.

She knew what he was going to say and shook her head.

'If I'm on my own, I'm more likely to be able to prod them into revealing themselves. I'll seem less like a threat, something they can deal with straight away.' She smiled without humour.

'So what will you do if they do react?' Tanner was already starting to have a nasty gut feeling about what she was suggesting.

'I'll play it by ear, see what happens. They won't do anything to me in their own house if they can help it. Don't worry, I'll be careful.'

Tanner's gut feeling began to get a lot worse.

His thoughts returned to the present, loitering in the Tillings' garden in the freezing cold with five police officers, waiting for something to happen. Hoping that something would happen so that the preparations would not be wasted, but dreading it as well. They were not sure what reaction would be provoked when Julie tried to goad the Tillings into betraying themselves – assuming, of course, that there was something to betray. They had the back garden covered and there was a vanload of officers parked a little way down the street outside ready for a possible frontal exit. Other cars were in place to block the street if they tried to take Julie away in a car. Each group of police had torches, battering rams and pistols that fired tear gas and smoke bombs. If Julie seemed to be in danger inside the house, they'd all go in together like the US Cavalry. Hopefully, Tanner thought, not like General Custer. The police were very aware, of course, that if they weren't careful they could end up with a hostage situation.

As a plan, Tanner thought, it had more holes than St Andrews, but it was all they had. And Julie was one of the most resourceful and determined people that he knew. He kept repeating that to himself. It wasn't a great deal of comfort.

After Julie had gone into the house, the ache in Tanner's leg had got worse. The leg had protested about clambering around in the boat and standing around in the cold was not improving matters. He tried a few on the spot exercises to keep it mobile. He had found he was able to get around without the walking stick and had left it behind in case he couldn't resist the temptation to brain one of the Tillings with it.

After what seemed an eternity, they saw movement on the blind over the kitchen window. A short while later, the door opened and a wedge of yellow light spilled out on to the patio. They watched Laura, Julie and Archie come out. Tanner felt his heart leap with relief at the visual confirmation that Julie was unharmed. As Laura closed and locked the back door and led the way down on to the lawn towards them, Tanner could almost feel Mariner tense himself beside him.

They could hear Tilling taunting Julie as they came across the grass, his voice mocking and confident. They heard her respond briefly and then give the agreed code words at the same moment as she stamped down hard on Tilling's foot to distract him.

As the police moved in, Tanner could see from the look on Julie's face that she wanted to stamp even harder on some other part of Tilling's anatomy, but she restrained herself and let Mariner organize the arrests.

By the time Archie Tilling had recovered enough to realize what was going on, his gun had been scooped up and placed in an evidence bag. With a bit of luck, Tanner thought, Tilling only owned the one weapon and if they could locate the bodies of the hired killers, it would add an extra element to the case against him.

Tanner moved round behind Julie and cut her wrists free. Then he turned her round, put his arms round her and hugged her tightly. Her response suggested that, despite her undercover experience, she hadn't been nearly as calm inside as she had appeared to be.

The Tillings were handcuffed and cautioned. Neither had spoken a word. They had gone from complete control and domination of the situation to total defeat in a couple of seconds and were both staring at Julie in a state of starched-faced shock. Julie didn't bother to say anything to them. She simply pulled the bottom of her blouse out of her skirt and lifted it up to a point just below her breasts. It wasn't intended as an erotic gesture; it simply revealed the microphone and wires taped to her body. Mariner and Tanner both had ear-pieces and had been listening to every word spoken in the house and the van in the road outside had been recording it all for posterity and the courts. Julie turned her head to look at Mariner.

'Did you get it all?' she asked.

He nodded.

'Every word.'

Julie relaxed and smiled.

'At least I seem to have done something right.'

'More than just something.' There was considerable satisfaction in Mariner's voice.

The Tillings had switched to staring at Tanner.

'Reports of my injuries have been greatly exaggerated,' he told them. He glanced at Julie. 'Although I will require a great deal of TLC. I have been in agony loitering about in the undergrowth with my bad leg.'

Julie grinned, her eyes completely free from pain of guilt for the first time since Tanner had known her. She tucked her blouse back in.

'Don't worry. As a special treat, I'll let you remove the bug.'

SIXTEEN

HARRY MILTON WAS in his study feeling edgy and irritable. The three carefully selected guests with whom they had been playing poker for most of the evening had gone soon after 10.30. Jack Pace had just left the room having announced that he was going to check that the house was secure before going to bed. Milton had grunted, envying his employee the fact that he had Jane Weston to share his bed. Jane might not be the most beautiful woman in the world, or have the sharpest intellect, but she curved in all the right places and walked with a wiggle that could make you cross-eyed. He decided that he needed a woman. He would have to visit his clubs and do something about that as soon as possible.

Milton scowled to himself. Part of the trouble was that he couldn't even go upstairs and spend a soothing hour with his paintings and other art treasures. As soon as he heard that Beverly Wallace had spoken to Alec Tanner and Julie Cooper, he had moved his illegal possessions to a safer location as a precaution against a possible police search of his property. The items were not that far away, but he had kept them crated in case a second move was required.

The telephone cut across his gloomy thoughts and he barked out a sharp acknowledgement as he answered it. The voice at the other end spoke in subdued but urgent tones. The call did not take long, but when it was finished, Milton's mood was several degrees fouler than it had been before.

Jack Pace was halfway up the broad staircase when his boss came out of the study and called out his name.

'What is it, boss?'

'I've just had a call from Den Fletcher.'

Pace's forehead creased. Detective Sergeant Fletcher was one of their best moles in the Havenchester City Police. A call from him after eleven o'clock at night, coupled with the look in Milton's face, did not suggest good news.

'They've arrested Archie and Laura Tilling.' Milton spat the information out.

Pace swore.

'They must have made a balls-up of killing Cooper.'

'Yes.' Milton looked disgusted at such incompetence. 'Fletcher wasn't involved in the arrest and he doesn't have any details, but he says Mariner was looking particularly pleased with himself, so I expect the bitch is still alive.'

'Do you think Tilling will talk?'

Milton snorted.

'Of course he'll bloody talk. He'll do as much as he can to save his own skin. He'll be squawking like a parrot with verbal diarrhoea. The only question is how long it will take him to give the cops enough information on us for them to act.'

Milton clamped down on his anger as he worked out the best next move.

'Mariner will have to get them booked in and questioned and he'll need to get a warrant to raid us here. They're partial to dawn raids, so we should have until early morning.' He thought for a moment. 'Go and tell Horace to come down. There's stuff he needs to sort out before we can leave. Then get Jane to pack you a couple of cases and switch off the lights as if you're going to bed. The cops may not be moving in for a while, but if I know Mariner, he's got a watch on the front gates in case we try to leave, so we don't want to do anything to alarm them. We'll all meet in the kitchen at twelve-thirty.'

'We'll be leaving the same way as the paintings then?'

Milton nodded tersely, his brain already running over the things he needed to do.

'When you've spoken to Jane, ring Reggie at the other house and tell him to expect us.'

As Pace turned and ran up the stairs, Milton went back into his study, his face stiff with rage. He knew who to blame for all this. He might have to go on the run, but if he got a chance he'd deal with Tanner and Cooper first.

'They got away?' Superintendent Mornington was a plain-spoken Yorkshireman who didn't bother to hide either his astonishment or his displeasure. 'There was no one in the house at all?'

Mariner was not happy. Although he was sitting in the chair facing his chief's desk, he felt more as though he was standing to miserable attention in front of an old-style headmaster who was bending a cane in his hands. Not that he could blame Mornington – he felt like giving himself a thorough dressing-down as well.

'Just the cook, sir. She claimed to know nothing about Milton's business activities. That may or may not be true, but I doubt if she knows much that could help us or she wouldn't have been left behind.'

'How on earth did it happen? I thought you had the place under surveillance?'

'We did, sir. We were watching the front entrance. As far as we knew, there was no rear access. Milton would have needed a helicopter to get out any other way.'

'I take it your surveillance team didn't notice a helicopter landing?' Mornington raised his bushy eyebrows, showing a slightly surprising turn of sarcastic humour.

'No, sir.' Mariner's face was as wooden as a forest. 'He didn't need one. It turns out that there was a rear access that we didn't know anything about.' He paused. 'Nor, to be fair, did the council's planners.'

Mornington sighed.

'What exactly happened?'

'We got a warrant for Milton's arrest and to search his house based on Tilling's statement and an armed team raided the property at five-thirty this morning. When we broke in, there was no one there but the cook. She claims to have gone to bed at ten-thirty last night with everyone in the house as usual and knew nothing more until she was woken up by us. We made a thorough search of the house to make sure there were no hidden rooms or anything, but we found nothing. We located the room where the stolen pictures were supposed to be kept but that was bare too.'

Mariner took a disgusted breath.

'My first thought was that the surveillance team must have missed something, but they swore there hadn't been as much as a stray cat through the gates all night. I organized a thorough search of the grounds. There was evidence of fresh footprints which suggested some activity in the garden last night. We checked right round the perimeter and eventually found it.'

'Found what?' Mornington snapped. 'Don't keep me in suspense, Ancient; this isn't a bloody mystery story.'

Mariner nodded. At least he'd called him 'Ancient' rather than 'Chief Inspector'.

'Sorry, sir. There was a brick-built storage shed at the rear of the garden. It seemed to contain just the usual garden junk, but we spotted that it backed on to a similar shed in the back garden of the house beyond. In fact, they shared a common wall. A section of shelving at the back of the shed swung open and there was a door behind it that led to a similar section of shelving on the other side. They must have gone through there and into the other house, which is in a road two streets away from the one Milton's property is in.'

'I assume there was also no one in when you entered this second house.'

'No, sir. There was sign of recent occupancy, though. We checked with the neighbours. A couple on one side heard activity sometime after one o'clock this morning. They sleep at the front and were woken by engines starting up and headlights across their window. The husband looked out and saw a small van and a car leaving the house. He went back to bed. He didn't notice the make or colour of either vehicle except that the car was dark and the van was light.'

'No chance of a registration number then.' Mornington's eyebrows did another round of exercises.

Mariner assumed that was a rhetorical question and carried on.

'The neighbours know very little about the occupants of the house, which was last sold about three years ago. We checked the land registry and the supposed owner is no one we know. Either Milton used an alias, or he got a stooge to stand in for him. We're checking into that now.'

'Milton's a careful man if he's had this prepared for some years,' Mornington commented.

'Yes, sir.' Mariner's mouth twisted. 'I suspect the rest of his escape plan has been equally carefully prepared.'

The superintendent grunted.

'Who else is with him, do you think?'

'Jack Pace and Horace Soames without a doubt and probably Jane Weston – she's Pace's girlfriend. They all live in Milton's house. One of the neighbours did spot someone around the second house yesterday and gave us a description that sounds like Reggie Gray, so he could be part of the mix as well.'

'If they had a van, they were presumably moving quite a bit of stuff with them?'

'It was probably carrying the stolen paintings and other artefacts that Milton kept in his secret room. There may be some other stuff as well, although I'd think he'd want to travel reasonably light. He may be intending to stash some stuff somewhere and come back for it later.'

'Can't we get a line on him through his business activities?'

'That may take some time. Milton seems to have done quite a bit of shredding before he left. There were two computers. Both had been smashed, presumably in an attempt to destroy the hard drives, but our boffins are pretty good at reconstructing that sort of thing – they're having a go at that now. There were probably some laptops as well but they could have taken those with them.'

'And you've no idea where they might have gone?'

'No, sir. We're checking all Milton's holdings and his company properties as well as anything else in the name that was used to buy the bolt-hole, but no joy so far.'

Mornington's expression suggested that he thought joy was likely to be in short supply for a while.

'There's little doubt he'll be trying to leave the country,' Mariner went on, 'so we've alerted ports and airports, but there are ways and means of getting round that, of course.'

'Hmm.' The superintendent looked up sharply. 'What about DS Cooper and your friend Tanner? Milton could well be blaming them for all this. He might have another go at them before he leaves. You'd better warn them that he's in the wind and probably pretty volatile.'

'I've tried, sir.' Mariner's voice suddenly sounded very tired.

'There's no reply from either flat, they haven't arrived at the agency and their mobiles are switched off.'

The two men stared at each other for a moment. It was left to Mornington to articulate both their thoughts.

'Bugger.'

A few hours before Mariner's uncomfortable interview, Harry Milton had awoken from a brief sleep in the back of his car. He had a headache and a pain in his back. He got out and stretched, yawning. Pace was already up and leaning against the side of the van.

'Morning, Harry.'

'How long would it take you to reach the flats where Julie Cooper lives?' Milton asked, rubbing at the small of his back.

Pace frowned thoughtfully.

'At this time in the morning? Not much more than an hour. It'll take longer later when the traffic builds up, of course.'

Milton consulted his watch. It wasn't yet six o'clock.

'I won't be able to start making the arrangements for us to leave until after nine and we won't actually get away until midday.' He looked across at the other man with an expression as warm as penguin's flipper. 'Do you fancy another crack at Cooper and Tanner?'

Pace's face split in a wolfish grin.

'It would be a pleasure.'

'You and Reggie can drive my car to Cooper's flat. If Cooper and Tanner appear before ten, pick them up. Take the anaesthetic dart gun and try to get the drop on them and bring them back here alive. If you don't see them by ten o'clock, give it up. You should easily get back here by twelve. I'll ring you on your mobile if there's a change of plan.'

'What happens if we can't get Tanner and Copper to come quietly?'

'Kill them there and then if you have to.' Milton's mouth stretched humourlessly. 'I'd rather see them die myself though – if you bring them here alive we can make it last.' He looked at Pace with flat-faced consideration. 'I'm sure you'll manage. After all, you've already worked out a way to get into the apartment block's car-park.'

Pace nodded.

'Yes, I just didn't get a chance to use it.'

'Now's your opportunity.'

It had been, Alec Tanner reflected, grossly negligent to let themselves be captured and their chances of learning from their mistake seemed to be disappearing rapidly. The relief of solving the murder had made them relax their guard dangerously. With the Tillings in custody and Milton set to join them, there hadn't seemed to be any need for caution. They hadn't just taken their eyes off the ball, they had stopped playing the game completely.

They had been walking towards Julie's car in the underground car-park beneath her apartment block when he had felt a blow on his upper leg followed by a sharp sting. Looking down, he had seen a hypodermic dart jutting from his thigh. Even as he pulled the dart clear and started to move sideways, seeking the cover of the nearest car as he searched the surrounding area for the attacker, he heard Julie exclaim and clutch at her leg. Well before reaching cover, he had stumbled to his knees on the concrete floor, his vision failing as his strength washed away. He had a brief vision of Reggie Gray's grinning face before he slumped to the ground unconscious.

When he regained consciousness, Tanner could feel movement. He was sitting upright in a vehicle; his arms turned sideways and linked to someone else's. Julie's perfume drifted into his senses and he opened his eyes.

He was sitting in the back seat of a car with Julie by his side. His right arm was round Julie's left arm and each of them had their wrists handcuffed together in front. Joined together through the circles formed by their arms, they couldn't move apart. It was, he acknowledged, a very effective way of restricting their movement. Once out of the car they wouldn't be able to move very fast and they would need to co-ordinate their movements carefully to avoid pulling each other off balance. Their current position was further restricted by the fact that they were both wearing seatbelts.

Julie was already awake and she flashed him a brief grimace that reflected his own annoyance at how easily they had been caught.

'Are you OK?' he asked.

She nodded.

'Under different circumstances, this might be quite fun,' she said drily raising her cuffed wrists.

Jack Pace glanced into the rear-view mirror when he heard their voices.

'I can assure you that what you've got coming won't be fun for you,' he said.

Reggie Gray chuckled from the passenger seat.

'But it will be for us,' he added.

Both Pace and Gray were inclined – understandably, Tanner and Julie had to admit – to gloat a little. They wouldn't say where they were going, but when Tanner asked how they'd got through the car-park's security, Gray was happy to tell them.

'Security?' He looked disdainful. 'I wouldn't call it that. You need a key pad code to raise the metal grille to get in, but there's just a pressure pad to get out and the grille doesn't drop back straight away. I just waited round the corner by the entrance for one of your neighbours to drive out and nipped in under the grille before it finished going down. Then I jumped on the pressure pad to make it go up again so Jack could drive in. We parked in a vacant slot near the lift and waited for you to turn up. Over two hours we were hanging about.' He sounded aggrieved.

'If we'd known you were waiting, we'd have got ready sooner.' Julie's comment earned her a snort from Pace.

They had passed through the centre of the city whilst Julie and Tanner were unconscious and had now reached the outlying countryside. After a while they came to a narrow bumpy road leading to a pair of decrepit metal gates that were partially closed. Pace got out and pushed the gates open with a rusty creak. A further short drive over an even bumpier road brought them out into an old deserted airfield. There were a few small buildings in various stages of dilapidation and a large hangar.

Pace drove through the open doors of the hangar and parked next to a small white van. Horace Soames, Jane Weston and Harry Milton had been sitting in the front of the van and they got out as the car drew to a halt.

'Any problems?' Milton asked as Pace got out of the car.

'Nope, easy as anything.'

Gray opened the rear door and leant in to undo the two seatbelts.

There was no room for Julie or Tanner to try anything and Gray moved back quickly.

'Out you get.'

Julie and Tanner shuffled across the seat together and got out, standing up carefully. Although Tanner's legs were a little stiff, particularly the injured one, the effect of the dart seemed to have worn off and his head was clear. Glancing at Julie, he saw her surveying their surroundings carefully and his heart lifted. At least they were both alert and ready to take advantage of any chance. The problem would be finding a chance to take advantage of.

Gray jerked his thumb to indicate that they should walk to the rear of the hangar. Pace had produced a gun, which he pointed towards them to emphasize the instruction.

Julie and Tanner glanced at each other and obeyed. There was still no obvious opening that wouldn't result in them being shot. Gray walked round to the boot of the car, opened it and produced a double barrelled shotgun. He moved over to one side, keeping the shotgun pointed towards the floor but ready to raise it if necessary.

'You have already cost me a considerable amount of money and caused immense inconvenience.' Milton spoke like a judge passing sentence. 'Now, because of you, I have to leave the country and my organization and start afresh again. I owe you for that and I've decided to settle the debt before I go.'

He stared at them with satisfaction.

'I want you to die slowly and in as much agony as possible.' Milton tapped his watch. 'Our plane will be landing here just before twelve. That gives us plenty of time. Jack will shoot you both in the knees and the stomach and we will be able to enjoy watching you writhing around in agony until the plane arrives. Jack will put you out of your misery just before we leave – I want to make absolutely sure that you're dead before we go.'

Milton turned towards Pace and nodded.

Pace moved forwards, aiming his gun.

There was one slim chance of trying something and Tanner hoped Julie was on the same wavelength.

'Before you shoot us there's something you need to know.'

Tanner was looking at Milton as he spoke and took a step forward. He was relying on the psychological inclination to wait for someone to stop speaking before responding. As he took the step that brought him into range, Tanner kicked upwards with all the concentrated force of a rugby player trying to score a penalty from the halfway line. The toe of his shoe buried itself in Pace's crotch and a jolt of pain shot through Tanner's injured leg.

Pace screamed and dropped the gun, clutching at his groin as he buckled over. This was the point where the co-ordination was essential. Tanner needn't have worried, as he bent towards the fallen gun, he felt Julie move with him. They would have a millisecond of advantage before Gray reacted and aimed his shotgun.

Even as Tanner started to crouch down for the gun, he saw Pace fall on top of it and dismay washed over him. Precious moments would be lost in moving Pace to get at the weapon. The next moment, his concern over the hitch to their last chance was swept away by a new problem as, with a howl of rage, Jane Weston lunged towards them at speed, her hands clawing towards Tanner's face.

If she had reached him, Tanner would have been lucky not to be blinded, but as the outstretched arms grew close he felt Julie move smoothly up from her semi crouch, pulling his arms with her. Pressing her hands on his shoulder for support, she launched a fierce roundhouse kick.

The toe of Julie's boot, travelling from right to left, connected with Jane Weston's solar plexus moving in the opposite direction. Air exploded from the attacker's lungs and her eyes seemed to cross and glaze over at the same time as she collapsed across the legs of her lover, making the gun even more inaccessible.

'Kill them!' Milton screamed, his voice as livid as his face. 'Forget about anything fancy, just blast them.'

Tanner felt his tiny flicker of hope flutter and die. It would take far too long to retrieve Pace's gun and there was fifteen yards of clear space between them and Gray. He could try to get in front of Julie and protect her from the first shot, although some of the blast would probably go right through him and there was no way she could escape the second barrel with no cover.

For a frozen moment, Tanner was sharply aware of two things. The look of sadistic glee on Reggie Gray's face as he raised the shotgun, temporarily lowered when Jane Weston had got into his line of fire, was coupled with the awareness of Julie's presence at his side and the aching sadness that they were about to lose each other so soon after finding ...

The shots boomed round the hangar, making him wince, but there was no impact and no pain. Instead it was Gray who jerked like a puppet with ague, his shotgun swinging upwards and discharging harmlessly into the air as he toppled backwards on to the cracked floor, twitched once and lay still.

Slowly, Tanner's brain started to function again. The shouted warning that had preceded the shot filtered into his consciousness. He registered Julie's face, mirroring his own astonishment. Slowly he turned his head to see Milton staring at the entrance to the hangar in open-mouthed horror. His gaze moved on to Horace Soames, arms stretched upwards as if he was trying to grasp the sky, and then to the dark-blue uniformed figures, most of them armed, who were moving purposefully across the floor. Amongst them was a familiar lean figure, wearing a Kevlar vest somewhat incongruously over his old raincoat.

The anxiety around Mariner's eyes eased as he focused on Julie and Tanner, both still standing and both still breathing. He gave them a brief nod of acknowledgement before turning his attention elsewhere.

'Harry Milton, I am arresting you ...'

Tanner turned towards Julie. His mouth felt parched and his jaw ached. He must have had it clenched for some reason. He licked his dry lips and managed the ghost of a grin as he spoke in a croaky voice.

'If it was physically possible, I'd give you the biggest hug you've ever had in your life.'

'I feel the same way.' Julie looked down at their wrists. 'I hope they've brought a key that fits.'

'I've got the next best thing.'

A police officer appeared at their side holding a small but efficient-looking pair of bolt cutters and moments later they could move apart.

'There's a gun under there somewhere,' Julie pointed towards Pace and Weston.

'Leave it to me.' The policeman signalled to a colleague and they began to sort out the still moaning bodies with clinical efficiency.

It was clear that they were not required to help with the tidying up. Tanner gently took hold of Julie's shoulders and carried out his promise.

A quiet cough separated them a short while later. Mariner eyed them with amusement.

'I take it you're both OK?'

'Thanks to you,' Tanner acknowledged. 'You certainly picked your moment, Ancient, how on earth did you manage it?'

'It was actually quite simple,' Mariner admitted. 'I was in the middle of an interesting meeting with Superintendent Mornington discussing how I'd managed to let Milton slip through my fingers when I got a message to say that Archie Tilling had decided to come completely clean and was making a full statement about the murder. He admitted to meeting his hired killers at a deserted airfield after the murder where he'd killed them before disposing of their bodies a few miles away. When I asked how he'd picked the airfield he told me that Harry Milton had suggested it. I knew Milton would be trying to flee the country and a direct connection between Milton and an old airfield seemed like a clue. I thought it was worth a look, so I got an armed response team together, turned on the lights and the sirens, and here we are.'

He paused and looked at them with an oddly quizzical expression.

'What is it?' Julie asked.

'If Tilling hadn't talked when he did, we wouldn't have got here in time,' Mariner said. 'You could say that Archie Tilling saved your lives.'

Julie's face pulled into a tired smile.

'We must remember to thank him sometime.'

SEVENTEEN

THE EVENING AFTER their showdown with Milton, Julie and Tanner were seated at a table in the swankiest restaurant he could find – and afford. Tanner, whose normal restaurant of choice gave away toys with the food, thought the place was so posh that even the knives and forks looked like they should have a Michelin star.

Julie looked stunning in an ice-blue sleeveless satin dress that clung to her curves and rippled as she moved, the perfect compliment to her long black hair. Tanner was even wearing a suit. Dressing up was starting to become a habit, he thought – if it carried on he might need to buy another tie.

'If you treat all your clients this well, it's a wonder you make any money at all,' Julie remarked, sipping at a glass of wine that, judging from the price, must have been made from platinum grapes.

Tanner felt a lump in his throat. After they had been driven away from the airfield, he had gone to the agency whilst Julie had gone to police headquarters and spent the afternoon with Mariner. It had emphasized the difference in their position. He was the private eye and she was the official detective who had a right to be a party to the official investigation. Tanner had gone back to his flat from the agency to change and Julie had gone to hers straight from the police station. Apart from a brief phone call to set the time and place for the meal they hadn't spoken since the police car had dropped him off at the agency.

Tanner let his gaze wander slowly over his companion, the warm glow he always felt in her presence tinged now with unease. Julie was clearly fully fit, mentally as well as physically, the last couple of days had proved that. Now the uncertainty of the future was starting to loom ever closer, his insecurity heightened by the fact that they were coming to the meal from different locations, like friendly acquaintances rather than lovers.

'What's the news from the cop shop?' He tried to keep his tone light.

Julie gave him a satisfied smile.

'Laura and Archie have been charged with Aunt Joyce's murder. Winston and Harper's bodies have been found at the old mine location where Archie said they would be, so the murder charge will shortly be tripled. Milton's been charged with conspiracy to murder, receiving stolen goods and kidnapping. There'll be more to add to that list, too, but it's enough to be going on with. Pace has been charged with two counts of attempted murder and kidnapping. Mariner's still working on what alleged crimes to charge Soames and Jane Weston with.'

Tanner raised his eyebrows.

'Alleged?'

Julie mimicked a zipper across her mouth.

'Milton and his gang have all refused to say anything since their arrest,' she said.

'Don't tell me they've lawyered up?'

Julie gave him an amused glance.

'It sounds like you've been watching too many late night repeats of "NYPD Blue".'

'You can't watch too many repeats of "NYPD Blue".'

'True.' She nodded solemnly. 'Anyway, the police are going through the books of the antique shop now and they've got enough evidence to get access to Milton's business accounts. Mind you, if Soames is as good as Mariner suspects he is, a lot of the evidence is going to be very well hidden.'

'And Archie is an accountant too.'

'Yep. It's not about crime, it's about number crunching.' She took another sip of wine.

The waiter brought their first course – a species of large mushroom wrapped in something else and with an accompanying small piece of salad. They both thought it tasted delicious.

'Even if some of Milton's business activities can't be used against

him, he and Pace will go down for attempted murder and kidnapping and for helping Archie Tilling with his murder spree,' Julie
said, after swallowing her last piece of mushroom.

Tanner watched her face carefully.

'There's no doubt about the evidence against the Tillings,' he
said, 'so you've caught your aunt's killers. And you know now that
she wasn't killed because of you.'

Julie nodded, her eyes warm with relief.

'Yes, I feel I can live properly again now.'

'And go back to work?' Tanner eyed her tentatively.

He was sure that if Julie went back to London they could make
their relationship work long distance – others had done it successfully before them – but it wouldn't be the same. Seeing Julie every
day for the past week had been something really special.

Julie seemed to catch Tanner's mood. She reached across and
covered his hand with hers.

'I've been thinking about the future,' she said. 'I had a long talk
with Ancient this afternoon and not just about the case. I value his
judgement and advice. As a result, I have a proposal.'

'Indecent?' As always when nervous, Tanner tried to make light
of it.

'Practical.' She met his gaze with a gentle smile. 'I'm quite a
wealthy woman now, you know. I have the freedom to make some
new choices.'

'Such as?' Tanner struggled to control the eagerness and hope
that was straining to take over his voice.

'Well,' she said slowly, tapping the corner of her mouth with her
finger, 'I suppose I could resign from the police – providing, of
course, that some alternative job was offered. I wouldn't want to sit
around all day doing nothing.'

'What sort of job did you have in mind?'

Julie shrugged.

'Retired police officers often go into private security, or something like that, don't they? For example, if there was a vacancy in a
detective agency I might be interested.' She toyed idly with the
stem of her wine glass.

Tanner couldn't stop the wide grin threatening to dislocate his
jaw.

'It so happens, there's a vacancy in mine at the moment.'

'Really? Now there's a coincidence.' She gave him a deadpan look. 'What time's the interview?'

'You've just had it.'

'Did I get the job?'

'What do you think?'

She gave him a wicked little grin.

'In that case, about that indecent proposal ...'